Y0-CAT-098

THE RISING

Journeys in the Wake of Global Warming

A Novel by
Tom Pollock & Jack Seybold

This book is a work of fiction. Places, events, and situations in this story are purely fictional. Any resemblance to actual persons, living or dead, is coincidental.

© 2004 by Tom Pollock & Jack Seybold. All rights reserved.

No part of this book may be reproduced, stored in a retrieval system, or transmitted by any means, electronic, mechanical, photocopying, recording, or otherwise, without written permission from the author.

First published by AuthorHouse 04/14/04

ISBN: 1-4140-9141-9 (e-book)
ISBN: 1-4184-3741-7 (Paperback)

This book is printed on acid free paper.

Printed in the United States of America
Bloomington, IN

All haiku and poems copyright © 2003 Jack Seybold
Art on Front Cover copyright © 2004 Tim Holmes
Art on Book One, Book Two and Book Three title pages copyright © 2004 Tim Holmes
Illustrations on pages 193 & 194 credit United States Geological Survey
vent—http://pubs.usgs.gov/publications/text/hotspots.html;
convection—http://pubs.usgs.gov/publications/text/hotspots.html;   volcano map—http://
vulcan.wr.usgs.gov/Volcanoes/Antarctica/Maps/map_antarctica_volcanoes.html)
Text on page 215 beginning with the quotation "Mega Tsunami Threatens To
Devastate U.S. Coastline—August 31, 2001" credit University College London as
original source; http://www.sciencedaily.com/releases/2001/09/010903091755.htm
Copyright © 1995-2002 Science Daily Magazine
Text on final page credit Astronomy Picture of the Day (APOD), originated, written,
coordinated, and edited in 1995, 1996, 1997, 1998, 1999, 2000, 2001, 2002, and
2003 by Robert Nemiroff (MTU) & Jerry Bonnell (USRA). NASA Official: Jay
Norris (http://antwrp.gsfc.nasa.gov/apod/ap020527.html) Photographic image on
Back Cover "Antarctic Ice Shelf Vista," Credit & Copyright: Helmut Rott (Helmut.
Rott@uibk.ac.at) (U. Innsbruck: http://dude.uibk.ac.at/) 1stBooks – rev. 03/23/04

To our families.

TABLE OF CONTENTS

PRINCIPAL CHARACTERS

(Ages at opening of the story)

Eli Barnes, 39 - San Quentin Inmate

Darcy Wallace Malone, 30 - San Francisco Homemaker
Reinhold Malone, 33 - Darcy's Husband, Real Estate Deal-maker
Tierney Malone, 4 - Daughter of Darcy and Reinhold
Finn Malone, 11 months - Son of Darcy and Reinhold
Mariah Wallace, 55 - Mom to Darcy, Grandmother ("Babushka") to
    Tierney/Finn
Elmer Wallace, 62 - Mariah's Husband, Dad to Darcy, Grandfather to
    Tierney/Finn

Dr. Charles Royer, 57 - Retired Air Force Surgeon
Rose Royer, 55 - Charles' Wife, Air Force Nurse
Kim Royer, 32 - Daughter of Charles and Rose, Congressional Aide

Dr. Peter Addison, 57 - Professor of Earth Sciences (his wife, Celia,
    deceased, was Charles Royer's twin sister)
Catherine Addison, 19 - Daughter of Peter and Celia, College Gymnast
Jason Lowery, 20 - Catherine's Boyfriend

Dupree Ransom, San Quentin Inmate
Erik Perez, San Quentin Inmate
James Salas, San Quentin Volunteer (whose identity Eli uses after an
    escape)

Paisley Overcroft, 39 - Modoc County Herb Grower
Ray Overcroft, 40 - Paisley's Husband, Modoc County Farmer

Maurice Beckwith, 65 - Modoc County Retiree
Chet Ragland, 55 - Modoc County Feed Store Owner

Robb Maxwell, Deceased Prior Owner of Modoc County Homestead

Gertrude Whiting, 70 - Modoc County Storekeeper
Malcolm Whiting, 51 - Son of Gertrude Whiting

Jacob Manikksen, 27 - Survivor from Berkeley
Nelson Ichimura, 25 - Defector from U.S. Marines
Agnes Miniata, 36 - Modoc County Native American
Yeter Gursel (nicknamed "Shaz"), 40 - Turkish, Sufi - partner of Agnes

WEBSITE

Chapter Notes, Scientific References, Links and other features are available at the Authors' website: http://www.risingglobalwarming.com

BOOK ONE

CHAPTER 1

Friday, January 6

ELI BARNES was a saint or a fool, and Dupree Ransom needed him. San Quentin's erstwhile drug kingpin was up to something disquieting when he slipped his ice cream cup onto Eli's tray in the chow hall. "I don't like this kind, man. You can have it." Eli had no doubt of Ransom's disdain, had seen him cower and abuse unfortunate loners—he had left the kid in West Block with a black eye and fractured elbow, for little more, apparently, than satisfaction of his inflated ego. Eli was not a vulnerable loner, recognizing a measure of security in the companionship of his cellmate, Moses Porter, and brothers in the Retreat Movement. But safety is a fragile commodity in prison.

Ransom feared no one, owed no one in San Quentin. The Chicano and White gangs gave him a wide berth. Even the guards gave him slack. Scuttle- butt claimed he had leverage on several who had smuggled contraband and shared the profit. Ransom should have been a target, but no challenger stepped forward.

Ransom's cellmate, Erik Perez, was equal physically, which made some de- cide the guards had set up a gladiatorial contest, but Perez deferred enough to keep a concord between them. His arms were covered to the wrists with tat- toos, and one on his neck announced his name: Erik. He was four inches taller than his cellie, but none of his stature was mental. Although both men were of mixed race, Perez was considerably lighter, so his tattoos showed well. Ransom had no tattoos—he wanted his sculptured physique unmarred by further deco- ration.

Ransom turned heads when he appeared, looking humble and sincere with bowed head, at chapel services two weeks in a row. He shook hands with those around him, including Eli Barnes, during the greeting of peace. He had stepped up at altar call to receive a blessing. He played the humble and devout seeker— even made the Retreat, made a moving speech at the end of it declaring his discovery of a new life. Still, any gift or favor from Dupree Ransom was unset- tling.

It was too blatant—not that Ransom had ever been subtle. Eli recalled Ransom's first day on the main line four years ago. He flowed into the cell block like a panther, pulling off his shirt, his muscles bulging as if they had been layered on and shaped with a trowel. He searched for a return glance with a satisfied smile that announced he was boss. When a guard told him to put his shirt on, he complied, taking exacting care in fastening the buttons. He parted his knees and dropped his pants to tuck in his shirttail, then buttoned them with measured concentration.

It was vanilla. Two rare, sweet cold ounces that highlighted the day for some of the somber men in the dank prison. Eli watched Ransom recede to a distant table, then stared at the lidded paper cup.

"Man, that's weird," said Moses Porter. "You almost don't want to eat it, wondering what's the payback."

Eli stole a glance at Ransom and Perez in boisterous conversation half the hall away. Although they drew a crowd in the yard by performing feats of strength, like Ransom's handstand on Perez' doubled fists, clasped in front of him waist high, except for maintaining their physiques and polished egos, their demeanor was that of typical convicts resigned to live out long sentences. They even began to attend Bible study classes on Tuesday nights.

It was all for show, Eli decided. Moses concurred. And the ice cream drop had been public. Under the circumstances it placed a burden on Eli. He did not relish being Ransom's pal, with some undefined obligation. He knew he had a reputation as a "good con," and he was not at all sure he wanted to share it with Dupree Ransom.

A SCHOOL of Antarctic krill drifts near the dark zone. No sunlight penetrates the thousand-foot thick Ross Ice Shelf, but the thin adjacent sea ice allows enough light to support the tiny, swimming plankton. On this day the intermittent thunder-snaps cracking from the ice shelf above increase to a frequency not felt before. Unequipped by evolution to tolerate such vibrations, the half-mile long school of *euphausia superba* orients in unison and flows, leaderless, like a river, north toward the Falklands.

CHAPTER 2
Saturday, January 14

ELI BARNES sat on the edge of a high bed in San Quentin's AIDS ward in a green room fading to gray. The heavy door had a window he could span with the fingers of one hand outstretched. "Yeah, Johnny," he said, "this is prime real estate. How long do you suppose the Governor and developers will let this sorry old place go on being used as a lockup?" What he was saying was trivial, he realized. To speak, however, was essential.

4

The bed with its burden of a gaunt body draped with clean white sheets and gray blanket took up most of the room. Eli could kick out and touch the wall from where he sat. How ridiculous to equip this Spartan cell with a lock or even a heavy door. Of the six thousand convicts in San Quentin, Johnny Diaz was least likely to escape.

Johnny's sad sunken eyes rolled half-heartedly. He took a quick breath, like a hiccup, and stared at the bowl in Eli's hands. Eli dipped a plastic spoon into the oatmeal and scraped the underside of it on the bowl's edge, then arced it over to Johnny's waiting mouth. He waited to see if the grizzled old convict would swallow or cough.

Eli could believe the talk about San Quentin being sold. The State of California was short on money after the energy scandals of 2002 and the dot-com collapse, the country's expensive wars of "preemption" and the war on terrorism—and this dilapidated old structure would take millions to upgrade. It would be easier to build a new prison with a new Death Row out in the boonies somewhere, where all the slammers in the prison boom at the end of the Twentieth Century were built. A Republican Assemblyman had already proposed a bill to do just that.

"You know how beautiful it is out there." He nodded toward the wall as if he and Johnny could see the sunset glow beyond San Francisco Bay and the amber and green mass of Mount Tamalpais. "When the economy picks up, they're gonna picture stacks of condos right here." Among the ironies of life in San Quentin was the fact that the AIDS unit exercise yard faced, through several layers of cyclone fence and barbed wire, one of the best scenic views in the Bay Area, with Mount Tamalpais thrusting its bulk into the Pacific sky across an expanse of the North Bay. Standing in that exercise yard earlier in the afternoon, he had watched a beam of bright sunlight pierce between heavy clouds, as if God were reaching down with long golden fingers to enjoy the water that lapped the stubby peninsula on which the prison sat. He waved at passengers on the boats skimming into the nearby Larkspur Ferry dock. Taxpayers. Solid citizens whose heads were filled with family, picket fenced yards with golden retrievers, weekend golf, salmon and chardonnay. Eli tried to put it into a haiku poem:

Blessed are you O men
    sailing on golden waters
        loved ones on the shore.

Johnny Diaz exhaled a long hiss through his nose. "D'ya ever find out what Dupree Ransom wanted?" he croaked.

"No," answered Eli. "I haven't seen him around since last week."

"Stay away from him." Johnny's voice was hoarse yet firm. He inhaled as if he would continue. "Ransom can't do you any good." Another sucking in of air. "But he can bring you down."

"I know, Johnny."

Johnny's bony hand trembled over to nudge Eli's arm. "Stay out of his way." He closed his eyes and sank into his pillow.

Eli waited until Johnny opened his eyes, then continued to spoon porridge, occasionally lift the blotchy head for a sip of water from a plastic cup, until Johnny closed his eyes and relaxed the muscles of his brow. It would not be much longer until Johnny's sentence was fulfilled, thought Eli, and he would be paroled to a much more beautiful place, with no wall between him and the gleaming shore, with maybe even salmon and chardonnay.

FOR THE THIRD YEAR running, on the islands north of the frozen continent, mid-summer populations of albatross and snow petrels, and even the cantankerous scua, soar. Only the aged ones, whose eyesight is dim, continue to fly over the ice shelves. Only they can tolerate the dazzling sunlight reflecting off the myriad ponds and water slicks once again multiplying exponentially on the skin of the shelves. The others, young and strong, insurers of the species, sense when they must nest to the north or die of disorientation.

"A SNOW CAVE is not like a motel room, Kim." Catherine Addison's pronouncement was not one Kim Royer could argue with. Kim, Senior Aide to Congressman Thad Parker, could tell her young cousin about practical issues of modern life, about law and government, about finance and economy, about aikido and self-defense, even about relationships and men. But what Kim knew about survival in Nature would fit in a file folder thinner than the menu she was now ignoring. They were having lunch in advance of tonight's meet between Catherine's U.C. Davis gymnastics team and Sacramento State.

"It seems to me that it's very much like a motel room. It's small and private and away from your father, which is as similar as it needs to be."

"Oh, that's not it at all!" Catherine sat erect. She had a gymnast's body and earnest, alert eyes. "Jason says it's an adventure. It's more a test of your hardiness. That's what he says. It wouldn't be a..." She couldn't think of the word. "I told Jason Dad wouldn't approve of us going off together to sleep in a cave, even if we'd be bundled in our wool clothes and sleeping bags. Jason says snow camping is not very romantic. It's a lot of work and you're just into survival. You have two feet of packed snow just a few feet above you, and it's hard to move around once you get inside. All you want to do is get comfortable enough to sleep."

"Why do you want to do something so uncomfortable?" asked Kim.

"It's an adventure. What if you had to survive an airplane wreck? You have to be tough and have grit. You get a confidence in yourself and your ability to use your wits and your nerve. Take away your luxuries, and what do you have? Jason says you find out you have lots of good stuff. It's good to discover that."

"How does Jason know so much about it?"

"Kim, he's a world class skier. He was on the Olympic team in Nordic Combined. That's where you ski and shoot a rifle. Well, he was until he injured his knee playing soccer. Now he goes on ski treks with friends where they camp out. He told me snow camping saved his life."

Kim allowed her amusement at Catherine's warmth toward Jason to show in a faint smile. "How did that happen?"

"Jason volunteers with the Forest Service and the Sheriff's Department to go on search-and-rescue missions, looking for lost campers. Last winter he was deputized to hunt for a bank robber who had escaped in the Sierra. He got separated from the team in a snow storm and had to make a snow cave. He had to stay inside for a day and a half. Luckily he had some trail mix and water. Next day they found the robber nearly frozen to death, but Jason skied back to camp none the worse for wear."

"So you think your dad would give his blessing for you and Jason to hunker down in an igloo for a day and a half?"

"No, that sound's awful. But I told Jason I'm willing to try it. I said I'd ask if we can use your family's cabin as a base, instead of ours. You could be there to chaperone the cabin, or your mom and dad. As for the snow camping, it's intimate, but it's claustrophobic. It's not like going to a motel."

The waiter took their order. Kim folded her arms on the table and looked directly at Catherine. "Intimate but claustrophobic. What an interesting combination of words. Inviting and yet forbidding."

"What are you saying, Kim?" Catherine admired her cousin, a role model to brag about to classmates. Kim's father, Charles Royer, was the twin brother of Catherine's mother, who had died

"Men are like snow caves, aren't they? You want them to be close and warm, but not suffocating."

"Jason has never been demanding or possessive," said Catherine.

Kim's smile broadened. She understood Catherine's desires and her fears, her fierce independence and her devotion to a doting father who saw in her the vivid shadow of her mother. The day Celia Addison died, Kim had held Catherine in a comforting embrace—Catherine was still in junior high and Kim was pursuing a career in business. Kim had sensed Celia's spirit passing into Catherine, who first wept, then relaxed under Kim's soothing, then sighed and helped prepare her mother's body. Catherine herself handed the wedding ring to her father. There was no confidence Catherine would not entrust to her worldly-wise cousin.

"Is Morgan Clark like that?"

Kim blinked. How had Morgan Clark entered the scene? "What?" she squinted.

"Is he warm, or suffocating?"

"What do you know about Morgan Clark?" Kim asked, temporizing.

The waiter delivered their order, bowed, said "Enjoy," and retreated.

"Mom's been spreading news about me, I see," said Kim. She spread her napkin and gathered her thoughts, deciding not to evade Catherine. "I've been out with him three or four times, and I'd say if given the chance he's a suffocator." She saw that Catherine was disappointed.

"Yes, it's too bad. There are a lot of positives in him. But he is a man who gets what he wants, with an unerring sense of making the best of his opportunities. Last weekend he flew us in a private jet to San Diego for dinner. It was a beautiful, extravagant, exhilarating evening, which I don't suppose I'll ever have again."

"You mean the suffocating thing?"

"Exactly. I think what he likes about me is the challenge. I was supposed to be off balance. We went out for dinner again on Tuesday, here in town, and he started getting clumsy and demanding. I'm afraid I'm going to be busy when he calls."

The conversation lapsed into quiet eating for a minute. Kim felt she had discharged her role model function, and she had not exaggerated. There were too many red flags attached to Morgan.

"What is Jason like?"

"Oh, Kim, he's always polite and well-mannered. His family are country-club kind of people back East, in Maryland, kind of conservative. In fact, one of the things I like about him is that, even though he leans right politically, he respects other opinions. He says Thad Parker's a straight shooter, though he would never vote for him. We get into arguments all the time, but he's not doctrinaire about it. Well, he can get condescending sometimes, but I challenge him, and he makes me think too. I mean, he recognizes my independence and lets me be who I am."

"I'm looking forward to meeting him. But I think it's going to be at your cabin in McCloud. The older generation have their hearts set on it, I'm afraid."

"What about you? Wouldn't you rather go to your family's place in Modoc County?"

"Well," said Kim, "it's at least an hour or two farther. I do have fond memories of being there when I was a young girl. My brother and I could take our dog Rusty out into the forest and feel like we were all alone. And there was an old man there, Mr. Maxwell, who lived up the road. He had all kinds of gadgets at his place, and he let Tom and me play there, and help him with his projects. It was even more fun than spending summers on my grandparents' farm in Iowa."

"What happened to Mr. Maxwell?"

"He died a few years ago, sort of mysteriously. It's too bad you never met him. He was a very nice man."

CHAPTER 3
Sunday, January 15

THE NATIONAL TIMES

Scientists and Media Await Ice Collapse in Antarctica

By Quincy Ulrich, Science Reporter

Scientists in Antarctica are expecting the imminent collapse of two enormous zones of ice called the Ross Ice Shelf and the Ronne Ice Shelf. Each one is the size of France—as big as New England, New York, New Jersey, Pennsylvania and Ohio combined. Some think the aftermath could threaten civilization as we know it.

The public won't miss out this time. In March 2002, no one saw the historic disintegration of the "Larsen B Ice Shelf" the size of Rhode Island. The lone observer then was a satellite. It took only three days.

This year Networks have sent hardy cameramen and reporters to join blue ribbon teams of university scientists in hastily erected bases near each ice shelf. The government has dispatched its own scientists, along with engineers and emergency planners, some shifted from the permanent base at McMurdo Sound.

It could be a long wait. No one knows for certain whether this ice will collapse before the Antarctic winter sets in, or even this year. Some say it could be five years away. But comparing daily satellite photos with those taken before the Larsen B event, experts expect this natural disaster by Valentine's Day.

If either or both of these ice shelves collapse, the impact on the world is unpredictable. Three long-term effects are likely, however.

The first—a small rise in sea level. A Ross collapse would add about half an inch to sea level. The Ronne would add about four. Big as they are, ice shelves float. If they were on land, the effect would be far worse.

A second effect would be the cooling of sea water around the globe, intensifying El Nino and causing extreme climate fluctuations everywhere—storms and floods in some places, drought and famine in others.

The third effect is less obvious. The ice shelves now shade the sea floor from the warmth of sunlight. The ice reflects the sun's heat back into space. Without the shade, the nearby ocean would warm and could start melting the ice on Antarctica itself. Sea level would rise dramatically—on every island and coastline in the world.

Some claim these catastrophes result from humankind causing global warming. Others point to evidence of natural warming cycles. Outside this debate, however, one thing is uncontested—the seas are likely rising, and coastal populations ignore this at their peril.

Whatever the consequences turn out to be, Nature is expected to put on a spectacular show. And the networks are ready.

A MUSIC of heavy raindrops on a corrugated metal roof played above mumbling files of men shuffling between painted stripes on asphalt. The rectangular yard outside the chow hall was a wash of gray, with a half dozen drab seagulls waiting in the rafters for scraps to materialize. The blue denim pants and jackets of the convicts and their blue cotton work shirts appeared black and gray in the dreary late afternoon. A few wore bright yellow rain slickers, like daffodils in a slag heap. A few men used the latrine on one side of the yard, fenced off by shoulder-high corrugated tin sheets, before joining the line.

A queue of men in bright orange jumpsuits appeared, accompanied by a green-clad guard, and took their place parallel to the line Eli stood in. They were mostly younger guys, from the Reception Center, which made up the bulk of San Quentin's population. They would be processed and perhaps sent to other state prisons and wear blue like the rest. They slouched or moved with careless swagger, naiveté and danger in their eyes. Some made a show of avoiding standing under the seagulls.

Eli habitually looked for haiku in a moment. The traditional Japanese seventeen-syllable poems suggested by volunteers from the Zen Center "should be spontaneous. They help you stay in the present." Eli composed:

I was once like you
    stylin' in my punkin' suit—
        your daddy's callin'.

A half dozen men at a time crossed from the sheltered yard to the chow hall door. Inside each man took a plastic cup from a rack and a plastic spoon, then received a sectioned plastic tray of food shoved by an unseen convict food server through an opening in the wall separating kitchen from dining room. The prison went to significant lengths to ensure that no occasion for preferential treatment arose, such as a better portion of food or dessert being given to a favored convict. The day's meal was a fairly good one: mashed potatoes and gravy with chunks of chicken; green beans, coleslaw, a soft brown roll, a square of chocolate cake, with icing. Not much—maybe the beans and slaw—would be banged into the trash cans when the trays were piled up near the exit. Eli wondered if there was some occasion for the icing. Was it Martin Luther King's birthday already?

He felt a sharp blow on his back. He whirled away from the impact, steadying his tray in one hand, and turned to glare—into the scowling face of Dupree Ransom.

Ransom's face relaxed at a discernible pace, with utter control. "'Scuse me, man. I didn't see you standin' there." There was no trace of humility. The apology was a demand.

"It's OK, man," Eli mumbled. He turned away to end the encounter, chiding himself for his lack of awareness. A keen sense of his surroundings, which usually anticipated jeopardy, had failed him. He heard Johnny Diaz's words echo: "Stay out of his way."

A burly black guard approached. He wore a green jacket with a California Department of Corrections insignia on the shoulder and the name SCOTT stitched on the right side in white block letters. He indicated with a deliberate nod a section of the rows of square metal tables. A single pedestal supported each table, with four metal seats radiating from it. Eli straddled one of the seats, across from Jerry Reeves, a gangly blond with prominent ears. Eli noted Ransom's progress to another row of tables, and felt the heat of shame on his ears. He had backed down from Ransom, without forethought. What else might he have done? Stare for several seconds to avoid being the down dog? He didn't have the control for that. Ransom had made his point.

A bald black man of middle years took the seat to Eli's right. Moses Porter sat in the remaining place.

Younger convicts would not sit at a mixed-race table. Better not to have something to explain to one's partners, homies, carnales. You needed them to watch your back. In times of tension guards would enforce segregation for security reasons. But things had been calm lately. Eli could mix with just about anyone in the prison. His father had been half black, his mother had told him. She was part Mexican. Eli's hair was thick and curly, his nose straight. People thought he was Egyptian, Sicilian, Latino, Greek.

Moses leaned toward Eli. "Sorry, man. I didn't notice him coming either."

Eli nodded. He slowed his breathing, centered himself. What was the object of Ransom's hostile act? If he wanted to keep Eli Barnes off balance, it was working.

Moses changed the subject. "I'm about ready for some sunshine. This reminds me too much of Seattle."

Jerry Reeves spoke through teeth clenched on a chunk of chicken. "Yeah, we ain't seen sun for a week. I ain't used to this. Moses, you want my beans?"

"Thanks, man." The older man scraped the beans onto his tray. "Jerry, didn't your mama tell you to eat your vegetables?"

"What for? I'm gonna die in here anyway. Why do I want to live a long time?"

"We're all maybe gonna die pretty soon," said the bald man. "I saw on the news where all that ice at the South Pole's gonna crack up and make floods all over the world."

"No shit?" Jerry scooped a spoonful of potatoes.

"Yeah. And I heard some guys saying they're gonna move us to prisons inland, or put us in work gangs to fill sandbags and shit like that."

"Not Moses," said Eli. "He's going before the board next month. Maybe he'll get a date this time. They wouldn't move him if he got a date. They'd let him serve out his time here."

Even as he said it Eli realized the futility of predicting what the Board of Prison Terms would do. There were grim grins around the table. What seemed predictable was that any of them would be denied for one or two more years. And even if they got a date, the Governor would likely yank it. The legacy of Willie Horton was alive and well. Every governor since Dukakis' defeat in 1988 had to be "tough on crime." Of the last four governors, the first slowed the flow of paroles dramatically, the second made it a trickle, and the third nearly shut off the tap altogether. Even convicts eligible for "compassionate release," because of terminal illness, had been denied. So San Quentin swelled to over six thousand, nearly double its intended capacity. California's prison system had grown from eleven facilities in 1980 to over thirty by the end of the century.

"Hell," drawled Moses, "I ain't got the chance of a turd swirlin' in a good toilet. You know the Governor's done sold his soul to the corrections officers' union. They put a ton of money in his election campaign. Folks say they aim to build about a dozen more prisons in California, and how you gonna keep all them prisons full lettin' men out?"

Eli had attended three parole hearings in his twelve years in San Quentin. At the most recent, two prison chaplains had testified in his behalf, and his prison counselor pointed out that Eli had been an accessory, that he was not convicted of murder. He had an exemplary work record in Protestant chapel, volunteered in the AIDS ward, was successfully pursuing a college degree, and helped with the Squires program that hosted groups of at-risk youths visiting the prison. He was denied two years. "Man, if they deny you, what shot has any of the rest of us got?" Moses had said.

Sixteen years and counting, and half of it without a visitor or even a letter. His mother had visited four or five times a year until her heart attack. He had not been allowed to attend her funeral. Eli consoled himself with the fact that his mother had seen him at his best—clean and sober, and going to church.

He knew of two half brothers and a half sister, but he had never seen them. He had dropped out of school and was living on his own by seventeen, working occasionally as a garage mechanic in Bakersfield. Then he enlisted in the Army. When he returned four years later a girl-friend became pregnant, and her father told Eli to leave town. In Fresno he met friends of a kind he would see again and again in San Quentin, even a few like Dupree Ransom.

Then there were guys like Moses and Jerry. If he ever got out, Eli wanted to have buddies like them on the outside. They would watch football together. Their families would go to church together and Moses' rich voice would lead the choir. They might live next door to guys like Sergeant Scott and get along just fine. But maybe Jerry's right, thought Eli. Maybe we're all going to die in here.

Scott walked by. "You boys about finished? There's a line of guys who'll be needing those seats pretty soon." Eli admired the way Scott could issue an order in such a polite way, so you wanted to cooperate with him. Many of the corrections officers seemed bent on demeaning and dehumanizing the prisoners. They were the interface of society's antipathy, visiting scorn and hardship where the judge and jury had left off. The job requirements were a high school diploma or some equivalent, and the absence of a felony conviction. Scott was one of the better ones. You might joke with him, and he would play along with it. But you didn't cross him.

13

They banged their trays on the inner sides of the waste barrels and put their cups and spoons in dishwashing racks. "Say, you guys ever notice how much Ol' Scott looks like that Harriman dude over in North Block?" Jerry said. "They're built exactly the same, with those heavy necks and broad butts. Hell, they were probably twins separated at birth."

"Yeah, I've wondered about that," said Moses. "Ever see 'em in the same room together? Maybe Scott's changin' into blues now and then as a under-cover operator." They chuckled at his joke.

These are the kind of bar buddies I should have had, thought Eli, when I was coming up. Even if I didn't have a father, I could have stayed cool with guys like this.

A MOTHER humpback leaps from the lapis waves. The edge of the ice pack by which she plays has receded southward this year ahead of schedule. The forty foot whale is mimicked by her two-year-old calf. A tinge of hunger drives them into widening circles. The tons of seawater washing through the fibrous baleen between their toothless jaws is yielding insufficient plankton this day. The mother turns north, tracking the wake of the vanished krill, her larynx drumming a low-frequency melody for her baby to follow.

CHAPTER 4
Tuesday, January 17

A PRISON IS like a spider's web, a grid of gummy cordage for the fatal en-trapment of unwary beetles or flies. The casualties are held fast, cocooned and stowed, helpless, to be devoured at the spider's convenience. Whatever hope you muster adds to the spider's relish. She knows you belong to her. She grows fat on the species of sacrifice. She grows smug in her dominance, her righteous contribution to the order of Nature.

Even a lower-level prison like San Quentin has hellish features: noise, lack of privacy, and the company you must keep. Harassment and intimidation from predators.

And the system, indeterminate sentences, the toying with inmates' minds by the administration and parole board. Residents of Hell would place fire and brimstone lower on their list of tortures, Eli Barnes thought. After a few years one gets accustomed to the constant din of male voices, shrill or growly, to the chatter and laughing, the cursing and threats, the jangle of clashing musics, the slamming of heavy metal doors, the peremptory demands of correctional officers, the announcements over the raucous intercom. One sleeps when he can, when something like peace becomes unanimous and the need to call attention to oneself is exhausted throughout the cellblock.

One longs for the blessing of solitude. Everyone inside feels loneliness, but they are never alone. They live in four-by-ten cages, thirty in a row, five tiers high. Some higher cells have bay views if rain washes the grimy windows—narrow glimpses of blue water through which an occasional boat might pass. Guards stroll by on a narrow walkway when the cells are locked, peering in if they please. Your cellmate must hop onto his bed so you can use the shoulder-width passage between the beds and the wall if you want to get to the metal toilet at the end of the little room. You must maintain understanding and compromise with this man. You must not let him assume authority—a tall order if it's someone like Ransom or Perez. And you must at times start again with a new cellie, as men are moved to other prisons, or go to the Hole, or—rarely—get out on parole.

You learn to blend. You don't want to be a black beetle on a white bark tree and get gobbled up by the swiftest or toughest bird in the forest because you have made yourself visible as a plump morsel of prey. You find a routine that keeps you safe. You learn when to use nuances of deference, when to bluff, how to use humor, flattery, jive, compromise. You learn not to be a threat and not to be a victim. You survive.

Eli Barnes created his own way of doing time—he made San Quentin State Prison his monastery.

For some there was solace in the chapels. Catholics and Protestants had their own concrete block buildings, adjacent to each other across a large courtyard from the Adjustment Center and Death Row. Jews and Muslims and Native Americans had offices off the same courtyard, behind a decorative fountain pool designed and constructed by convicts, and Buddhist meditation was done in the room shared by Jews and Muslims.

Eli had sampled most of the spiritual disciplines in the prison, had studied the creeds and practices. He could sit silently in lotus position for up to forty minutes of Zen meditation, and he found comfort in the sweat lodge, which occasionally the Indians were allowed to engage in on the playing field where the iron pile had been before it was taken away.

Many convicts had become fearsome body builders, and the weights were seen by the guards as potential weapons. Ransom and Perez, with their thick chests and hard shoulders would make guards nervous. Without the iron pile they kept their sculpted torsos solid and massive with daily hundreds of sit-ups, pushups, pull-ups from the bars of their cells or from the upper bunk while holding their bodies bent at the hips in a rigid L shape. Ransom would attract a crowd out in the yard doing pinch-grip pull-ups from two-by-fours supporting the basketball hoops.

Eli's exercise routine was an adjunct to his spiritual practice. Discipline of the body, he reasoned, parallels discipline of the spirit. Thirty to sixty minutes a day were devoted to pushups, sit-ups, squat-jumps, stretching. He ran laps around the ball fields.

Eli saw to it that his name was on the movement sheet every Sunday morning, and on the 6:20 movement as often as there were chapel programs during the week that didn't interfere with his classes. San Quentin was about the only prison in the state where you could study toward a college degree. He stayed busy. It had been years since he had felt boredom. He read for pleasure, for academic advancement, for spiritual growth, and for solitude. He took immense interest in his History of Western Civilization and World History courses. On Sundays after Mass, he followed up his study of early Christianity with spirited discussions with Father Quinn, the Catholic chaplain. Seeing Eli's interest in monasticism, the priest had supplied him with several books by the Trappist monk, Thomas Merton. "You're a good lad, Eli," said the priest. "I pray that some day you'll spend time at a proper monastery." He mentioned Our Lady of Peace Monastery and the Trappist house at Los Molinos.

Volunteers from the San Francisco Zen Center came to the prison to meditate with perhaps a dozen inmates. They told Eli of even closer monasteries. "There's Green Gulch, less than thirty minutes from here," said Edward, a shaved-head engineer who wore a rakasu and Buddhist robe. "And down near Big Sur, a bit inland, there's a more isolated space called Tasajara. They're like the Buddhist monasteries in Japan, which can be every bit as austere and strict as medieval Christian ones." Eli looked up all the locations on maps in the library.

Over horizons
    floating like a shredded cloud—
        the chanting of monks

He worshipped with the Catholics as well as the Protestants. The Retreat program included men from both chapels. The hymns soothed or lifted him. And there were the soft voices of women chapel visitors on Sunday mornings. They were gentle and sincere when they spoke to a man. They gave him inspiration and fantasies. Eli would ask outside volunteers at chapel programs if they went on retreats. Eventually he found one familiar with Our Lady of Peace Monastery, a Berkeley school teacher, Pamela Lindsay.

16

CHAPTER 5
Tuesday, January 24

THREE DOLPHINS cavort around a solitary sperm whale. The trio's auditory nerves filter the increasing cacophony of ice quakes. Not so the giant bull. The ache in his eardrums diminishes only when he swims directly north. He steadies his course, seeking the quieter habitat already found by his vegetarian cousins, the humpbacks and the blues. The dolphins leap in joy, exuberance mounting with each mile added between them and the earsplitting noise.

THE NATIONAL TIMES

Ross Ice Shelf Collapses in Antarctica—Eyewitness Report

By Ulysses Doxiadis, Science Reporter, On Location

It's 2:00 a.m. Although the twenty-four-hour sunshine is ablaze outside, we are sound asleep in our blackened, cramped bunks. We all awake at the same time. A sound like a distant freight train is rumbling outside. Simultaneously, the "night" watch team bursts into our quarters. "Get your parkas on! It's happening!"

The long-expected collapse of the Ross Ice Shelf is underway. The front edge used to be about twenty miles from our station. On a normal, very clear day you could just glimpse a tiny blue line of the Antarctic Ocean past the edge of the ice shelf. Though today is clear, what appears to be a layer of mist has replaced the blue line. But it's no mist—the sound betrays a different story.

Billions of tons of ice, hundreds of feet thick, are shattering, grinding, falling into the ocean. The majestic floating glacier is falling in on itself, sending plumes of snow and ice crystals a thousand feet into the air. It releases sounds of atomic proportions.

Within an hour, the ice directly below us is in its death throes. What had seemed, just hours earlier, a rock solid ice-covered plain stretching out from the edge of our mountain like a frozen Sahara Desert, is now dissolving before our eyes. Not exactly dissolving. There's no sound when something dissolves. This cacophony is ear-splitting. We fear for our ear drums. Some of us don the sound mufflers we have kept in our parkas for just this moment.

No, this is no dissolving. Imagine a transparent regiment of invisible monsters all in a line with unseen jaws five hundred feet high, eating away the clean edge of the serene, pancake-flat ice vista, then spitting out the remains in a jumble of crushed ice undulating in a chaos of waves mirroring the fury of the ocean underneath.

17

This is the ocean on which the ice shelf has peacefully floated for millions of years. The line of advance, we judge, is moving about five miles an hour. It's about five hundred miles, or was, from the front edge of the Ross Ice Shelf to the true land's edge of Antarctica. At this rate, in four days the ice shelf will be gone.

CHAPTER 6

Wednesday, January 25

IT WAS DIFFICULT for Dr. Peter Addison to determine Penny McCardle's age. The reporter for the *Sacramento Bee*, with her large hoop earrings, blond-streaked hair and perfect complexion, seemed indistinguishable from his students at the University of California at Davis. For years, his undergraduate students had resembled high schoolers, stubbornly refusing, it seemed, to evince the traits of maturity that college students had attained in his day. His judgment was not aided by the fact that his daughter Catherine, his baby, had arrived at university age before he was ready to accept the idea she was an adult. He could not wholly dismiss the perception that Penny McCardle was a precocious juvenile pretending to be a news reporter.

"And would you call the collapse of the Ross Ice Shelf a calamity, Dr. Addison?" Her brown eyes stared expectantly through enormous round eyeglasses. Both hands rested on the stenographer's notebook on her lap.

"It's not a calamity by itself. No, I wouldn't say that." Peter's elbows rested on the arms of his swivel desk chair, his fingertips tapping together as if he were trying to contain a cantaloupe-sized balloon. "It might be part of a calamity, one might say, but it's too soon to make that sort of judgment."

Penny McCardle seemed disappointed with the response. She pursed her lips while scribbling a shorthand note. *What did she want me to say?* mused Peter. *It's the worst disaster since Vesuvius?*

"It's certainly a momentous event," he continued. "It could be the portent of disaster if it indeed represents a significant advance in the effects of global warming…" Her pencil raced across the page for a moment and her eyes widened within the circles of her glasses.

"But, Miss McCardle," he hastened to add, "this is not a time for any panic. We have to study and measure and understand what is happening. I don't want to be responsible for the perception that there's anything Apocalyptic going on."

In his mind Peter heard the echo of his words. He realized with chagrin that he had provided the sensationalism she sought. He was certain he would read an ambitious article in the morning paper that would include the words "disaster," "panic" and "Apocalyptic"—and would lose the sense of academic moderation he had intended. No matter his emphasis on how preliminary his comments were, or how much remained to be learned. He could not smother her page-one ambition with intellectual jargon or cautious backtracking.

"Let me just get a couple of photos before I go," she said. Dr. Addison did not doubt he would look suitably glum in tomorrow's *Sacramento Bee*.

THE NATIONAL TIMES

Ross Ice Shelf Collapse Worsens

By Ulysses Doxiadis, Science Reporter, On Location

The Ross Ice Shelf collapse continued today. Looking to the days ahead, scientists have a broader concern—the 'ice sheets' on the land behind the failing ice shelf. They fear that parts near the coastlines could be released into the ocean by the collapse of the floating ice shelves. Unlike the 'shelves,' a major slippage of ice 'sheets' would create unprecedented disasters for mankind. They would raise sea level not inches but feet!

A mountain range divides Antarctica in two. West Antarctica is the smaller part. From it a long, thin finger called the Antarctic Peninsula extends north toward South America. The giant Ross and Ronne Ice Shelves lie to either side with the West Antarctic Ice Sheet in between. If all three collapsed, sea level would rise by twenty feet. Even the edges of the big Ice Sheet would raise sea level several feet.

Since 1900, the seas have risen seven inches. This may seem small, but in response the Dutch have added up to ten feet to their famous dikes.

Studies of the 'worst-case' assume the West Antarctic ice sloughs off over one hundred years. With that lead time, disaster to civilization could be averted.

But those studies didn't consider this month's events. No one has analyzed what would happen if the landed ice on the continent by the Ross and Ronne Ice Sheets suddenly were to tumble into the sea."

CHAPTER 7

Thursday, February 2

FOR THIS RIDICULOUSLY expensive location shoot, Neil Smith decided on a bright blue parka, which would show well against the unrelenting white background and match his network's logo. He directed the cameraman to pan from the snowy peaks down across the level white plain extending to the horizon. "They need to see how utterly enormous this landscape is."

Crevasses and oil slicks passed swiftly under the helicopter until the camera zoomed in on a tent city clinging to a cliff above the ice shelf—the International Observation Station, with its array of national flags whipping straight out in the wind.

Smith could not contain a vast sense of awe, and kept his thumb on the pause button of his recorder microphone. Crevasses opened into chasms, new cracks and fault lines propagating like lightning spears into the ice shelf. Chunks of ice the size of hundred-story skyscrapers fell in graceful, horrifying slow motion into an iceberg-filled sea, enormous splash plumes rising where they plunged into the water, clouds of mist rising from the rending of glacial ice.

Finally Smith began his report. "Today the Ronne Ice Shelf followed its sister, the Ross, into the sea.

"This was not unexpected. For the last several days, instruments planted this summer by helicopters at remote sensing sites on the Ronne have radioed data describing the accelerating frequency of internal fragmentation. At about 4:00 p.m., local time, the northern-most instruments began signaling this catastrophic collapse—the third within five years, including Ross and Larsen B."

The cameraman captured battleship-sized blocks breaking apart and plummeting to the ocean, a deafening roar of ice fragments and snow dust exploding into the air. The fragmentation front marched with the resolute force of a Roman phalanx five miles an hour toward the continental land mass.

Back on firm landed ice, Smith stared into the camera. "As the front advanced, station after station of instrumentation ceased broadcasting as they plummeted with their host ice into the ocean. Cold metal and electronic components were the only participants out on The Ice, but we human witnesses were experiencing what seemed like the death of gods. Grizzled explorers and hardened reporters wept, myself included.

"We expect to remain here five more days, to see it out. The violence of this historic event leaves all of us forever in awe of the incomprehensible power of Nature. Although we will return to our normal lives and confront events of more mortal dimension, no one who has witnessed what we have seen here today will ever again underestimate the cataclysmic havoc lurking behind the simple forces of weather and physics.

"Neil Smith, reporting live from the International Observation Station, Antarctica."

CHAPTER 8
Friday, February 3

EURO/AMERICAN hybrid mice pursue each other across the supply room floor at McMurdo canteen—a flurry of motion, a squeaky scream of death, and a body is left inert for the janitor's scooper. Descendants of bygone stowaways. Never before have the tiny rodents raised their hair and bared their vicious teeth in lethal attacks on one another. At breakfast, the Chinese research assistant raises laughter, suggesting the rats of Hangzhow act this way the day before every major earthquake.

OFFICER QUINCY SCOTT nodded as Eli Barnes returned to the cell block. "What's the matter, Barnes? You don't look good."

Scott touched Eli's arm. "Just a minute, Barnes." And then he realized what had happened. It was the hour Eli usually spent in the AIDS ward.

"Come with me, Barnes," he commanded. He walked alongside Eli, leading him back along his route, down the corridor, out into the yard, down a flight of stairs, giving him passage through the guarded gates. They glanced into Johnny Diaz's silent cell, then passed out into the deserted AIDS unit exercise yard.

"You come in when you're ready, Barnes."

Earlier that morning Eli had gone in to feed Johnny Diaz, even though Johnny had eaten very little the last three days. Johnny's listless eyes were half open, staring. His cheeks puffed with each periodic exhalation. Eli put the dish of pudding aside.

He spoke Johnny's name, then a little louder. Johnny's eyes closed, then half-opened again. Eli took Johnny's hand in both of his and prayed. "Lord, give Johnny strength and courage for a final journey on this earth. Comfort him on the journey, and welcome him into your house..." He continued for a quarter of an hour, repeating The Lord's Prayer when his own words faltered.

Johnny's breathing became more rapid. Eli sang soft and gentle songs. Amazing Grace. A Closer Walk With Thee. Deep River. He tried to imitate Moses' soul-stirring style, yet whispered his singing. It was his own desperate attempt to survive the anguished moment as well as to comfort his friend. He realized he had thought it: *my friend.*

There was a brief shudder, and then Johnny lay quite still.

Eli closed Johnny's mouth and eyes, then used the nearby basin and wash-cloth to bathe the inert, splotchy face. He covered him with his sheet.

"Goodbye, Johnny. Save us a place, man." Eli paused to commend Johnny to the care of higher powers. Then leaning on the door frame, he shuffled out of the cell to tell the guard at the end of the corridor that Johnny was gone.

It was a bright midday as Eli left Sergeant Scott by the gate. Through salt-water eyes, Eli saw a blurred Mount Tamalpais shouldering into a blue western sky beyond the layers of rusty cyclone fence topped with barbed wire. He followed the flight of seagulls swooping down to skim along the bay waters. He felt the water edging up along the shore, encroaching, enclosing him. He suffered the oppression of the gray prison yard, the heaviness of his confinement, the wasted years of all the wasted lives pressing their weight on this barren site, lapped by dark waves.

He paced along the fence in walking meditation. He heard the words of a Baptist minister echo in his mind, words spoken about a black astronaut after the Columbia tragedy of 2003: "He's in a better place now." And he recalled a talk given by Bud August at his Retreat four years before. Bud quoted Antoine de St. Exupery in *The Little Prince*: "You become responsible for what you have tamed." Eli had been tamed by the Retreat volunteers, and of course by Big Daddy Sisson, his AA sponsor in Soledad State Prison, and by Johnny Diaz. There were thousands of wasted lives in San Quentin, yes, but Johnny's gave him occasion to care, made him grow.

It gives me comfort
    to know the river is swift
        when you are downstream.

CHAPTER 9
Saturday, February 4

MORGAN CLARK completed the long arc of his swing and watched his ball soar toward the fairway of the seventeenth hole at The Links at Spanish Bay. The wind was unusually calm for the moment, so he had not compensated for it. He glanced out at the blue Pacific Ocean.

"I can't tell if the sea level is any higher, can you?"

"Well," said movie producer Sherman Sullivan, striding toward their golf cart, "we were shooting a scene at the beach in Carmel early this morning, and the beach was narrower than usual. Other than that, you can't tell. We had to get it done today because the weatherman says a storm is coming in from Hawaii tomorrow. He says that's when we'll see waves coming in higher and farther than ever."

Intent on lining up their fairway shots, they failed to notice a worker pounding a stake into the sand next to the boardwalk path fifty yards west from their parked cart. On the stake he tacked a sign: DANGER: KEEP OFF. HIGH WAVES EXPECTED.

STANDING BEHIND the tripod of a video recorder, Jason Lowery pointed dramatically at his professor to begin the Saturday morning lecture for his U.C. Davis geology seminar.

"A decade of studies anticipated," said Dr. Peter Addison, "that if both the Ross and the Ronne ice shelves collapsed, sea level might rise twelve centimeters, or about five inches, according to the U.S. Geological Survey. So where did the one foot come from? The estimate was based on the effect of volume differentials between fresh water and saline water."

A dozen students normally attended Dr. Addison's Saturday morning seminar. Now every chair in the classroom was taken, and a ring of visitors pressed against the walls.

"Floating ice displaces its own weight of the fluid it is floating in, so normally you can't see any change in water level if it melts. But in fact fresh water fills slightly more volume than its weight of saltwater. This factor, applied to the enormous quantities of ice we're dealing with, accounts for the five inches. Don't forget, these two ice shelves would have covered all of France two thousand feet deep."

Murmured comments buzzed around the room. Pens scratched along notepads.

"If only the floating ice shelves were involved, the five inch estimate would have been accurate. But next to the floating ice were enormous sheets of ice resting on the ocean floor—over a thousand feet thick in places. The sudden collapse of the ice shelves destabilized that ice, and even some of the nearby ice on land above sea level. When all that ice came into the ocean, sea level rose the full one foot we are experiencing.

"This is a vivid demonstration of the unpredictability of the natural forces with which mankind is contending in the ongoing saga of global warming and the Antarctic melt down."

Forty minutes later the students' discussion of the topic was still spirited. Dr. Addison entertained questions from the visitors, and recognized one of the raised hands as that of the reporter Penny McCardle.

"Can we anticipate any consequences locally, more than fifty miles from the ocean?"

"Well," replied Dr. Addison. "Consider that the docks in Sacramento are at sea level. And imagine the calamity if sea water got into the Central Valley water supply."

IN FORT WALTON BEACH, Florida, just east of Pensacola on the Gulf of Mexico, Whitney and Darlene Brittington searched for some sign of the Tea Cup Tina III, their 1991 Sunseeker Martinique 38 Sport Cruiser. Whitney scanned the horizon with powerful binoculars while Darlene, in high rubber boots, surveyed the boat's dock, now submerged. She pressed her cell phone to her ear.

"Yes, sir. The dock's never been under water before. In the wave action the tie-up lines must have slipped off the posts they were looped over. I guess she just drifted away... Yes, sir... Thank you."

"What'd they say?"

"He said the Coast Guard has received dozens of calls like this today. They've already recovered several beached boats. They'll get back to us when they find her."

MILDRED SKOWRONSKI reported on the CBOX Morning Show:

"Summer storms off Tasmania have propelled the surf far inland at the Edwardian Sands resort on the spectacular Eaglehawk Neck northeast of Hobart. The sea has destroyed all the beach-view cabanas. Wherever weather satellites show storm activity, there are reports of port facilities, fishing villages, resorts—anything sensitive to maximum high tides—seriously damaged on every continent."

CHAPTER 10
Sunday, February 5

PAMELA LINDSAY pulled her coat tighter around her shoulders against the crisp February breeze as she peered into the inmate craft shop, across the street from the small U.S. Post Office just outside San Quentin's East Gate. She stood alongside her friend Ernestine Carter, awaiting admission to the prison grounds. Officer Mason Pringmore swung open the wrought iron gate to allow a car to exit. The driver popped his trunk lid. Pringmore peered inside, then banged the trunk closed to signal the driver to proceed.

"How are you this mornin', Mr. Pringmore?" asked Ms. Carter, her freckled African-American face alight with her usual smile. She pushed her California driver's license toward the corrections officer with a dainty motion, as if ringing a shoulder-high doorbell. Her girlish manner warmed the chilly morning and seemed to disguise her bulk by thirty pounds.

"I'm busy as can be, Miz Ernestine," answered the officer. "There's a partial lockdown, and we're a little short-handed, for some reason. There might be a light congregation today." He handed her a clipboard for signing in and held her license without glancing at it while she printed her name, the date and time, and "chapel" in the appropriate spaces. The broad-shouldered guard marked a check by her pre-printed name on another clipboard, and returned the license.

"Those boys spend enough time in those little cells. Why you got to keep lockin' 'em up when they ought to be goin' to church?"

Ernestine was as regular a volunteer as San Quentin had. She traversed the Richmond-San Rafael Bridge from Oakland every Sunday morning for the Protestant service, and every Tuesday evening for a Bible study class. Inmates knew her as Mother Ernestine, and indeed she filled the role of surrogate mother for many of them. Pamela Lindsay had known Ernestine for only half the year, since they worked together as cooks for a team that provided the Retreat experience for forty inmates. You didn't have to be a prisoner to feel the maternal energy of Ernestine Carter, and Pamela sensed their bond early on.

"You have a nice day, Miz Ernestine," said Officer Pringmore, and he took Pamela's license. He compared the photo on the license to the prim ash-blonde in a black winter coat

"Lindsay, Pamela," she announced. "I should be on the list."

"Yes, ma'am. Here you are. Please sign in."

Several other people were admitted, all wearing khaki, brown, bright green or red. All apparently were experienced volunteers who knew better than to wear anything blue. ("You want to be sure they'll let you out," was the familiar reminder.)

At length eight people stood in a knot inside the gate.

"Yo, Mr. Salas," Pringmore called out to another arrival. "Here is your brown card, Sir." He stepped into the small office just inside the gate and emerged with a laminated card which identified James Salas as one with special training and authorized him to escort volunteers into the prison. Salas wore a black baseball cap with the letters SQ embroidered in gold on the front. He thanked the officer by clicking his heels in salute and pocketed the card.

Pringmore addressed the group. "All right now, are any of you carrying cell phones or pagers, knives, tools of any kind, explosive devices, nuclear bombs or other weapons of mass destruction, or objects that may be assembled and used as a flotation device?"

Most of the volunteers were familiar with Pringmore's recitation and grinned indulgently.

"You understand," he continued, "that should you be taken hostage we will do all we can to help you, but will not negotiate with prisoners to exchange any favor for your release."

They knew he was fully in earnest on this one. There were nods.

"You can head on down to the next gate."

It was a three hundred-yard walk along the street leading to the sally port in the wall of San Quentin. A row of buildings along the right side of the street, including the Protestant chaplain's residence, had the appearance of a middle class suburban neighborhood. The visitor and employee parking lots were down an embankment on the left. Ahead, a twenty-foot cyclone fence crossed the street fifty yards from the sally port, which looked like the barbican gate of a medieval castle, complete with a lattice of iron straps inside, reminiscent of a portcullis. An octagonal tower as high as the prison wall stood like a beacon tower inside the cyclone fence, with windows hinged at the top so rifles might be fired down from them. A guard in the tower controlled a sliding gate for admitting vehicles. A pedestrian gate at the end of a covered passage leading the last fifty feet to the cyclone fence was manned by a guard, who supervised the volunteers as they passed expectantly through a metal detection frame. When a screech issued from the detector, the volunteer would drop keys and wristwatch into a tray, step back and through the portal again.

"Thank you, Mr. Trainor," sang Ernestine. "How are you this mornin'?"

"Chilly, but I'm gonna live."

"You're not usually here on Sunday mornings," she said.

"Lotta guys called in sick or askin' for leave. I'm on overtime."

Pamela Lindsay, Ernestine Carter and the rest proceeded to the sally port. Inside the tall wooden door another officer asked them to sign in again, this time on a book with pages twenty inches wide.

"How are you this mornin', Mr. Reynolds?" Ernestine repeated her earlier greeting, with the same charm. The officer snapped a quizzical glance at her. Then he smiled, feeling for the name embroidered on his uniform jacket.

Pamela had been through the process a few times, always tense. Some of the officers could be stern and by-the-book. But this one seemed pretty relaxed for a rookie. Sometimes the rookies might cause delays getting groups into the prison by their awkwardness with the process and its various tasks. He took Ernestine's driver's license and typed her name on a keyboard, examined the resulting screen on his monitor, then asked her to hold her arms out from her body. He waved a metal detection wand from her shoulder to her ankles, front and back and down the arms, then waved her through the gridiron door.

"You forgot to stamp my hand, Mr. Reynolds," sang Ernestine.

Reynolds rolled his eyes and grinned. Then he stamped the back of her left hand from an ink pad covered with a yellowish green fluid. He asked her to hold her hand under a glowing blue light. He was careful now to follow the procedure exactly, to fix it in his mind. Pamela followed Ernestine into a passage ten feet wide with walls of concrete blocks lined with benches under framed photos of the warden and other prison officials. Salas, with his brown card, was the last to be admitted. He flashed the card to an officer behind a thick window that looked into a continuation of the passage, but was bounded by gates of iron bars fifteen feet apart. A jolting ker-chunk echoed in the passage, and the nearer gate stood ajar. When the group shuffled inside the gate and the last one pulled it shut with a clang, enclosing the group between the two sets of bars, the farther gate ker-chunked, freeing them from brief confinement. Pamela felt again a vague claustrophobia, the final certainty of the implacable barrier behind her, as if she were a blood cell passing from one chamber of the heart to another through a valve of iron.

Two more paces brought them to a heavy iron door which led into a large courtyard decorated with several stands of rose bushes. To their left, beyond a memorial to corrections officers killed in the line of duty, stood the three-story Adjustment Center wing. They all filed right, however, across the courtyard toward the Protestant and Catholic chapels. Pamela knew the chapels from several visits to the prison, and had heard from inmates the contrast to the Adjustment Center, the "Hole," a place of harshness and frustration, the prison's Purgatory, where the rebellious or unruly were chastened. "You can't hear yourself talk in there," a convict had told her. "It's where anger gets as concrete as the floor."

A trio of men in blue jeans and blue cotton work shirts waved and called out to Ernestine.

"Hi, Lorenzo. Hi, Donny. Hi Gary. How are you this mornin'?"

Clusters of convicts stood outside the Protestant chapel entrance. A group of Latino prisoners waited near the Catholic chapel next door, where a tall triangular tree nearby extended high over the roof of the Captain's Porch, a wing of offices north of the sally port. The giant Norfolk pine, native to Australia, showed above the prison wall to knowing motorists on the San Rafael Bridge. Ernestine had sought the tree on their drive that morning and breathed a prayer for the "boys" who might be worshipping in the chapels beneath it.

In the chapel the thumps, beeps and twangs of musicians tuning and warming up pierced the buzz of conversation. Pamela stayed close to Ernestine, drawing on her black friend's geniality and experience in this still unfamiliar and hostile place. The men in blue constituted a portrait gallery of lower class American life: tattooed, braided, slick, sloppy, loud, needy, cocky, tidy, surly, humble. They were black, brown, white. She noticed a couple of familiar faces and smiled or waved to them, men who had attended the Retreat in October. Each one approached to offer a handshake and assurance of how good it was to see her there. She realized again how hungry they were for the outside, and for female attention—and she represented both. Each time she had to be reminded of the man's name.

"Eli Barnes. I was on the inside team last time." The Retreat movement offered inmates who had made the Retreat the opportunity to serve on subsequent Retreat weekends as "table servers" who provided snacks, cleanup, logistical and spiritual support. Eli's Retreat had been four years earlier, and he had been an inside server twice.

"Oh yes, I remember you," said Pamela. "You're the one who writes poetry, aren't you?" She felt a confidence in his presence, a safety, and kinship that was at least literary or academic.

"I wouldn't honor my writing by calling it poetry," he said. "But thank you for doing it." She responded to his smile with one of her own. And she felt on guard. The leaders of the Retreat movement had warned her that inmates might display a charm that was really self-serving or manipulative.

"Oh, I thought it was quite good," she said. "I loved the one I saw about the meditating man in the garden. You must be a meditator."

"It's one of the things that keeps me alive in here. Spiritually alive, I mean."

"Is it hard to meditate here?" She avoided saying "in prison." As they spoke she let her gaze flit around the room at the fascinating assemblage of prisoners gathering, returning to Eli's face to assure him of her attention.

"Sometimes it's pretty noisy. But once a week some Buddhist monks come in to meditate with us in a group. Are you into meditation too?"

"Yes. In fact, once a year for a retreat I go to a monastery where they do a lot of meditation."

"Father Quinn, the Catholic chaplain—do you know him? He mentioned a women's monastery up near the coast somewhere."

"Yes, that's where I go. It's Our Lady of Peace Monastery, near a little community called Whitethorn. It's west of Garberville."

"I'm afraid I don't know Northern California geography. I'm from the Valley. I've never been farther north than San Quentin." Pamela noticed that Eli too was looking past her from time to time, and now he shifted his position so that his back was to the wall and he faced the double doors at the end of the center aisle. She turned, using the motion to point past the altar. "You just go up 101, only a couple of miles from here, all the way to Garberville." And she saw what Eli also seemed to notice: two men were strolling into the chapel entrance, both of them imposing, thick-shouldered and rugged. The shorter and darker of the two grinned when he looked toward Eli and Pamela.

"I'd like to talk to you after the service," said Eli as the two men sidled down the length of an empty pew towards them. Pamela nodded, smiled and joined a huddle with Ernestine and three of her "boys."

"That your girlfriend, Barnes?" she heard one of them men say. She pretended she had not heard as she introduced herself to Ernestine's group.

"I don't really know her, I'm afraid," said Eli.

Pamela was caught up in the spirit of the Garden Chapel Choir filling the building with harmony, never erring on the side of softness. Moses Porter possessed a powerful voice that could be surprisingly sweet when he soloed. The sermon, she thought, could only be described as athletic, stronger on emotion and rhetoric than scholarship or insight, but conveying a power of conviction. The service rose and fell in intensity, swelling to crescendos of passion and ebbing to serene refrains of reflection. The congregation could hardly be deemed passive, so unlike the churchgoers she was used to in middle class Berkeley. They called out unreservedly, or echoed enthusiastically the phrases of the preacher. They sang full voice, under the amplified lead of the choir. Prayers were punctuated with "Amen," "That's right," "Mm-hmm." Finally Pamela found herself unable to analyze the experience—she could only surrender to it.

She watched the two bodybuilders who had discomfited Eli Barnes. They did not look like poets, she thought. They swayed with their heavy arms waving over their heads, they bowed humbly during prayers. They made themselves indistinguishable from the rest of the men in blue—and yet they were different. The remark about "your girlfriend" had given them somehow a sinister presence; it had not been jovial repartee among buddies.

After the service Eli stood with Pamela and Moses Porter, outside the chapel, watching convicts traverse the courtyard toward the fore-post, back toward the cell blocks. "Do men ever go to Our Lady of Peace Monastery? Father Quinn says he goes there for retreats. Are there only women there, and priests?"

"Ordinarily it's all women, except for the chaplain, Father Terrence," said Pamela. "Every month or so they have a week for outsiders to retreat there. Some of them might be men. And a couple of years ago a man lived on the grounds and did skilled labor around the monastery."

The group had begun to walk toward the iron door under a covered station where a rifle-toting guard sat on a stool. They were approaching the painted yellow line on the pavement, like the penalty area on a soccer field, with the door in the position of the goal. Along the line were stenciled the words: OUT OF BOUNDS.

"Ladies and gentlemen, we have to stop here," Eli said. "Thanks for coming."

"We'll be back Tuesday night for the Bible study group," Ernestine said.

"See you then," Salas said.

"See you Tuesday," Pamela said. She noticed a quick widening of Eli's eyes, the slightest lengthening of his neck. Looking back over her shoulder as she ducked into the iron doorway, she saw he was still facing the departing group, although Moses Porter was already two steps on his way.

BOTTOM-FEEDING octopi and squid choke in the billows of silt rising from the earthquake-fractured sea floor. Small crevices split the million-year-old mud, slam shut a moment later, sending plumes of sediment skyward, ahead of the rising oceanic plate itself. Safe from the whales and dolphins, the cephalopods surface in droves, into the gaps between ragged fragments of ice shelf debris.

KIM ROYER stood with her electronic notebook at the ready as Congressman Thad Parker looked suitably concerned, staring from the Port of Sacramento's Wharf 6 at the water below, water that was a foot higher than it would normally be. A stately container vessel, the *Belvedere*, formed the backdrop for the news cameramen and photographers as Parker stood alongside the Governor, the Director of the Port, and the Mayor of Sacramento. One by one each "newsmaker" answered the questions of the small knot of reporters.

"The rise in sea level experienced along the coast has also been noticed here, of course," the Port Director said, "but it would not in any way affect the operation of the port, as far as I can see."

The Mayor expected the City of Sacramento to continue to play a vital role in the commerce of the Central Valley.

The Governor urged all Californians to remain calm, to report to their jobs or places of business as usual, to retain their confidence in the state and federal governments' ability to "rise to this challenge." The reporters appreciated the governor's quotable pun with chuckles.

"Congressman Parker, from the Washington perspective, can you offer any reassurance?"

Thad Parker was ready with a response. "Well, of course, the President is in contact with the world's foremost scientists, who are compiling data each day which will lead to an appropriate and effective response to the current situation." He had said nothing of substance, although he had satisfied the reporter's request for reassurance. "I expect to be called to a Congressional briefing on the situation in the near future. My office has been inundated with calls, but I am afraid there's little I can offer at this time beyond what can be learned by calling the U.S. Geological Survey, the Coast Guard, and the National Weather Service."

Kim Royer had taken notes on the photo op. As it was winding down, she overheard a TV reporter intoning to viewers on the Six O'clock News. "I'm sure Congressman Parker would like to lighten the burden on his staff, but I can tell our viewers that from the agencies he mentioned callers are likely to learn through recorded messages only the observable facts of sea level measurements, estimates of tide consequences, storms, and so forth. They will also be cautioned against unwarranted speculation."

She and Thad walked briskly to their car. "Kim, get together a press release right away, just in case some of these members of the Fourth Estate spin this funny." She made notes on her Palm Pilot. "And I'll need a speech for tomorrow's Rotary luncheon." Parker had a keen appreciation for Kim's strong background in history from her years at Amherst. She kept his speeches rich in historical references, enhancing his reputation for perspective and vision. "I'll bet the Romans never had to face anything like this."

"Well, Thad, environmental factors have been proposed for the demise of the Roman Empire. The wealthy had lead pipes in their homes, so there was lead in their drinking water. That may have killed off some of the best and brightest in the Empire. And a fierce barbarian tribe crossed into Roman territory one unusually cold winter by simply walking across the frozen Rhine River."

Thad didn't like the comparison with the Roman Empire any more. After all, the Romans "fell." "People always use that phrase, 'the fall of the Roman Empire.' And the USA is history's greatest experiment in democracy. I can't bear to think of it falling."

"The Roman Empire didn't just disappear," said Kim. "It remains in much of the world's culture. American culture is world-wide, for good and for ill, and its effects will remain long after the USA recedes into history, or metamorphoses into whatever will come from it."

"Do you envision our collapse, Kim?"

She didn't want to. "No," she lied. "But who knows what's being forged from the pressure of today's events?"

CHAPTER 11
Monday, February 6

THE NATIONAL TIMES

Red Alert on Antarctica? Meltdown Feared?

By Quincy Ulrich, Science Reporter

On Antarctica, the command structure at research stations has tightened dramatically following the one-foot rise in sea level. The U.S. military has been placed in charge of all press. The structure is the familiar model used during full scale war activities, prototyped in the 2003 attack on Iraq. All official press information is now disseminated in "war room" briefing sessions.

Outside of official channels, however, The National Times has learned of disturbing developments. The source? Short wave ham radio operators. They say the many large earthquakes there, reported worldwide for the past forty-eight hours without official alarm, in fact are feared by scientists to be direct precursors of volcanic activity. The private radio operators also allege a massive cover-up is underway.

Some experts suspect that events reveal an accelerated timetable for land-based ice slippage previously thought to occur over decades or centuries. Earthquakes and volcanic activity under the ice could trigger the melting of large areas of ice with heat from the center of the earth.

The magnitude of the consequences and need for emergency planning for unexpected and unstudied disaster scenarios could explain the war-based model of news management. It would be consistent with the beltway penchant for naming every major governmental effort a war on something, be it drugs, AIDS, the Axis of Evil, or perhaps now the sea itself. Some might call the news management a cover-up. Labels aside, one ham radio operator claims to now be transmitting clandestinely because the equipment of a colleague was confiscated.

CHAPTER 12

Tuesday, February 7

ELI BIT his upper lip, standing at the chapel entrance, only peripherally engaged with Moses and Jerry's conversation. His attention was on the heavy iron door beneath the gun walkway guarded below by a coil of razor wire, where an officer behind a window sat nonchalantly on a stool, his rifle pointed skyward with its stock resting on his thigh. Pamela Lindsay and Ernestine "Mother" Carter would emerge soon with James Salas and Bud August, who would lead their Bible study session. Two other convicts were approaching from the fore-post to Eli's right, each clutching a Bible, the collars of their denim jackets turned up against a falling mist. There was no sign of Ransom or Perez yet, though Eli had placed their names on the 6:20 movement sheet, as Ransom had ordered on Sunday. Maybe the evening would be pleasant and rewarding after all.

Moses Porter waved a beefy hand toward the newcomers. "Here's Thomas and Burris, lookin' like they been readin' psalms all afternoon."

"Well, that's what I been doin," Jerry Reeves said. "Ain't that what we're discussin' tonight?"

A movement and a flash of color caught Eli's eye, as James Salas appeared in his hooded red parka from the doorway off to their left, followed by Ernestine Carter, Pamela Lindsay and another man.

Eli snapped his gaze right, toward the fore-post. And just as he feared, two figures in blue were making their way toward the chapel. Their swagger alone would have identified them, if not their broad shoulders. Both were wearing dark watch caps. Was Dupree Ransom limping?

The Catholic chapel was sparely decorated, yellow cinderblock walls with brown alcoves over small side altars in which statues of Jesus and the Virgin gazed downward with eternal calm. A crucifix was large and central behind the main altar. Facing it, over the entrance, a painting bearing a convict's signature depicted Saint Dismas, the "Good Thief"—crucified with Jesus, who promised: "This day you will be with me in Paradise." Eli glanced up at Dismas every time he left the chapel. He was not shown in the agony of execution. Rather he was presented as a strong, clear-eyed young man, dressed for travel, confident and vigorous in the radiance of forgiveness. The convict artist had expressed the unspoken desire of nearly all the men inside the walls—the treasured prospect of cleansing pardon. Eli explained the painting to Pamela Lindsay while they waited for late arrivals.

Bible study followed its routine, but Eli was painfully aware of each detail. The eleven participants prayed holding hands in a circle, and he noticed who flanked each of the women—Erik Perez and Jerry were on either side of Pamela. The group sat in the two front pews, before the statue of the serene Virgin Mary in a blue gown, looking down from a short pedestal in her alcove, her palms extended outward. Someone had draped rosary beads across the spread of her hands.

The group read together a passage, this one from the Book of Psalms, and listened to a reflection from James Salas on the reading. Erik Perez was the only one who had not brought his own Bible, and he seemed out of his element. Ransom appeared much more alert, however, and managed solemn nods at appropriate moments. Salas asked for responses from the group. Eli felt reticent, unable to focus his thoughts enough to offer any insight in Ransom's intimidating presence. His eyes roamed around the group. Pamela smiled at him. He glanced at Ransom, almost directly behind him, and saw a faint grin flash.

Eli felt uncomfortable sitting in the forward pew, so that he had to turn with the others to face those behind. Ransom sat at the end of the second row with his arms folded, stroking his chin. His jacket was buttoned up, stretched over the bulk of his chest and arms. Perez was a lump at the opposite end of the row, next to Pamela, looking impatient as a linebacker at pregame prayer.

"We'll have some time for fellowship now," said Salas. "But first, Moses, will you lead us in a closing prayer?"

All bowed their heads. But it was not Moses' voice they heard.

"Everybody just stay real calm. Nobody'll get hurt if you all just do what I say." Ransom had stood and ascended the step of the altar rail, approaching the statue of the Virgin. He leaped up on the dark marble altar before the statue, and appeared to be embracing the Virgin's feet. After a tearing sound, he turned to face the silent group, grinning at their shock as he sat on the stone table. In his hand were two pistols from which he was removing lengths of packing tape that had held them in place against the back of the statue.

"These have bullets in 'em, but I don't want to make any noise or hurt anybody. I just got to get out of here before I get crazy." He might have been giving the prayer, so solemn and calm was his tone. The chapel was silent as a graveyard except for Ransom's voice. All eyes were on the guns. Eli saw Pamela's look of terror and reached his hand toward her on the back of the pew.

"Don't nobody move unless I tell you to, and then you better move quick." Ransom was glaring at Eli. "Perez, here's yours."

Perez backed out of his end of the pew and received one of the guns from Ransom.

"Where'd you guys get those?" James Salas asked.

Ransom smiled. "Had 'em for a long time, just took a while to figure out a use for 'em."

Eli realized it must have taken months of preparation to arrive at this situation. A guard would have been compromised or corrupted, or some intricate scheme would have been instigated, in order to have smuggled in part by part two guns. They must have been hidden somewhere away from the cell blocks before being planted in the chapel—it would be too easy for them to be discovered in the cells. The library? The craft room? And there had been no scuttlebutt, no stir in the yard or whisper in the cellblock. Ransom might be the only one in San Quentin with the guile and resources to pull it off.

"We got this all planned out, how me and Erik's gonna get out. Do what we say and it'll all happen with no one getting hurt. You ladies, stand over there by Erik."

No one moved.

Perez grabbed Pamela by the arm and she flew out into the aisle like a rag doll. There was a murmur from the benches and Eli stood.

"She won't get hurt unless somebody gets stupid!" Ransom hissed. "Barnes, sit your ass down." Perez held Pamela. She was trembling. Eli sat. Ernestine rose and shuffled out into the aisle. She took her friend's hand.

"Now Mr. Salas and Mr. August," continued Ransom, "take off your clothes." It took a couple of seconds for this to be understood.

"Hurry up, move! We need your clothes. We don't got all fuckin' night!"

The two men removed their parkas, sweaters, shirts, shoes and trousers and tossed them toward Perez, as Ransom directed them. Eli guessed that Ransom and Perez would pose as volunteers, and walk out the gate on the strength of Salas' brown card. They would have Ernestine and Pamela as hostages. How far would they take them? Would they have accomplices waiting outside the gate? The two volunteers sat in their underwear, shivering from time to time. The other convicts stared at Ransom with taut faces.

Ransom's next command took Eli by surprise. "Barnes, take off your clothes."

When Eli was standing in his shorts, Ransom said, "Now put on Salas' clothes."

He gestured with the pistol. Eli was baffled, but did as he was told.

Ransom moved behind the two women. He pushed the barrel of his gun into Ernestine's ribs, causing her to straighten. "This is taking too long. Move it!"

Perez then sat on the floor in the aisle, setting his gun beside him. He pulled off his shoes and slipped into Bud August's clothes. When he stood again, the parka was stretched tight across his shoulders and the pants were unfashionably high at the cuff.

"Now everybody do exactly as I say. When we leave, just sit right here and pray for twenty goddam minutes. I don't want to hear a sound, and don't go running out into the yard. You'll get killed. I own people in here who will see to it if I'm gone. And these two ladies are depending on you."

As they left the chapel, Eli was mystified. Why had Ransom not changed clothes? What greater leverage would he have with Eli as a hostage? Perez kept his gun, in the pocket of Bud August's parka, pointed at Ernestine.

"Here's the drill," said Ransom. "Everybody go out casual, just like normal. Barnes, you flash the brown card to get everybody through the double gate. Erik, you write the time in the sign out book after the name Bud August. Keep your hoods on. And ladies, you better act natural, because if any shootin' starts, your man Eli here's gonna catch just as much of it as Erik."

It appeared Ransom was sending them off on an errand. How was he going to take part in the escape, Eli wondered.

Ransom shoved his pistol into his belt and took from his jacket pocket a small tin, like a chewing tobacco can. Opening it, he swiped his fingers into a black substance that looked like shoe polish. He brushed and patted his hands together, and seemed satisfied with their adhesive quality. He unbuttoned his jacket and unbuckled his belt, then pulled it off. But he kept pulling and the belt seemed to elongate, foot after foot, as if he were a magician performing a trick. The extra length had been stuffed down his pant leg.

"Get going."

Eli peered back as the group shouldered into a steady rain. Ransom was edging to his left along the front of the Catholic chapel, trying to stay in darkness behind the decorative trees that relieved the stark concrete block façade, and the huge Norfolk pine tree that stabbed into the rainy sky, the beacon to outside volunteers. Soon he would cross the space from the chapel to the Captain's Porch. Eli could not imagine how Ransom might escape that way. A coil of razor wire crossed the walls. It would block Ransom if he tried to climb the downspout up to the roof.

Eli looked up as they passed over the yellow line painted on the pavement, with the inscription OUT OF BOUNDS. In the rain he could not see whether the armed guard above took much notice from behind his window. Perez pulled the heavy metal door open for Ernestine and Pamela, and followed close behind them. Eli took one last look back toward the Captain's Porch, and was astounded to see, through the rain, a glimpse of the leather strap of Ransom's belt, looped around the trunk of the Norfolk pine. The loop grew taut, then slackened and leaped upward to grow taut again three feet higher up the trunk. On the other side of the trunk, Ransom would be creeping up, like a monkey ascending a palm. Eli recalled Ransom showing off in the yard, his muscles' cords bulging as he did pinch-grip pull-ups from a two-by-four. He would be up among the branches in less than a minute. He might, Eli saw, edge out one of the longer branches that extended over the roof above the Captain's Porch. His weight might pull the branch down to deposit him with a short drop onto the roof. He would be above the razor wire. He would still have to get over the roof, perhaps by means of the downspout against the wall, get down the other side of the building, and negotiate the perimeter fences.

If that was Ransom's plan of escape, then why the elaborate ritual of swapping clothes and sending Eli and Perez and the women out through the sally port? Why didn't he just leave the Bible Study group to use the restroom, and slip away shrouded in rain?

And then he knew. He and Perez were decoys, pigeons. They might be discovered crossing the yellow line, or at some other point along the way. The commotion could cover Ransom's escape, especially if Perez were stupid enough to try to shoot his way out, or use his hostages to force a way. Perhaps Ransom had determined that Eli's lighter skin would more likely fool a guard who had admitted a Latino and an Anglo. What had Ransom told Perez? That he would cover him if he were intercepted by the tower guards outside the sally port, or at the east gate? Perez was not the brightest coin in the till.

Then Eli was through the door, into the passage he had seen only a few times. Once when he entered the prison twelve years before, and twice when he had helped to carry in supplies for the Retreat program. He felt in James Salas' parka pocket for the brown card and held it up. The door opened with a cha-tunk, and soon the four were between the two gates. Eli closed the gate, and it clanged loudly. Perez shot him a killing look and moved even closer to Ernestine.

But the second gate clunked open and they passed through to the portcullis and the lone guard waiting there.

Ernestine and Pamela showed the guard their driver's licenses and held their wrists under the blue light, each one showing a yellow glow where they had been stamped. They passed on to the sign-in book and wrote the time after their names.

"Good night, ladies," the guard said.

"Good night, Mr. Reynolds," Ernestine said. Her voice was flat, as if she were tired. Perez held Bud August's driver's license in the palm of his hand. He did not look at Reynolds, but said, "You forgot to stamp me on the way in."

There was a momentary pause, as if they were suddenly in a freeze frame video. Eli did not want Perez to lose this bluff. The wrong people could be killed. He waved the brown card and stepped past Perez to the sign-out book. He searched for Salas' name, just under the place he had seen Pamela sign out.

"OK. Well, next time remind me," he heard Reynolds sigh. Eli jotted the time next to Salas' and August's names, and quickly passed out into the rain, Perez close behind.

"Don't look up at the tower," Perez whispered through clenched teeth, no doubt following Ransom's briefing. Images of the last few months flashed in Eli's mind, of Ransom chatting with volunteers at chapel programs, apparently pumping them for details of security procedures. "Everybody act real natural." Perez's voice was strained.

If anyone in the tower took notice of them, there was no way of knowing. They passed through the pedestrian gate and along the sidewalk between the employee parking lot down to their right and the row of buildings across the street.

Visibility was diminished in the rain, but Eli turned to peer over his left shoulder back toward the prison's front wall. He wouldn't have seen without expecting it, but there was Ransom, descending a downspout, companion to the one he had climbed inside. Eli guessed he would duck behind a row of prison vehicles parked inside the twenty-foot cyclone fence. Perhaps he would depart by the pedestrian gate, or find another way past the fence.

Perez forced Eli and Pamela to walk in front of him and Ernestine. Eli could feel Pamela's anxiety as she clutched his arm. They hunched along in the rain past a row of offices, and near the East Gate three stately houses. Through the rain, lights on the Richmond-San Rafael Bridge reflected on the dark waters of San Francisco Bay. The guard emerged from his office wearing a plastic covering on his uniform hat. Ernestine and Pamela already had their IDs held out at arm's length.

"Good evenin', Miz Ernestine."

"Good evening, Mr. Pringmore."

"Something wrong, Miz Ernestine?" Officer Mason Pringmore had noticed her flat affect, her absent smile. Pringmore squinted at the two hooded men.

The gate rattled behind him. Perez was on him in a second, cracking his pistol butt on the back of Pringmore's head. He was thrown forward by the force of the blow and crumpled to his knees.

Two men dressed in black clattered through the gate and bound Pringmore's hands, feet and mouth with duct tape. Dupree Ransom appeared in the gateway, panting. He must have sprinted behind the houses on the opposite side of the street from them.

"Just keep still." He pointed his pistol at Eli and the two women. "You don't want anybody to die."

Perez dragged Pringmore back into his office. The two men in black hustled the women outside the gate and bound their hands, and at Ransom's direction taped them together back-to-back, a single band of tape gagging them both, and another band around their ankles. They were against the window of the craft shop, just outside the gate.

"Stand real still and you won't choke each other," hissed Ransom.

"The car's waitin', Dupree," said one of the two in black. They rushed out the gate, followed by Perez. Eli expected Ransom to end his life, but he realized that a shot would ruin the escape.

"Come on, Barnes. There's no looking back." Ransom pulled Eli away, past the U.S. Post Office and down the main street of the village clustered outside the prison's East Gate. Eli considered trying to wrest the gun away from him, but knew it would be a futile and fatal attempt. Ransom had already demonstrated his might, and the ladies at least were safe. He wondered what further use Ransom would have for him. One of the men in black appeared and helped Ransom bustle Eli down the dark street.

Within a block they arrived at an idling sedan without lights, parked on the wrong side of the street, facing east.

"OK, Barnes, this is the end of the line for you. Here, take Erik's gun."

Eli heard a raucous laugh from Perez inside the car as a hand emerged to offer the pistol. Its weight told Eli it was a fake. "See what the pigs do with a good con who tries to escape." Ransom showed his teeth in something like a smile. "What you think, Barnes? You think the Man is gonna let this slide because of your goody-goody routine? Or is he gonna throw you in the Hole for the rest of your life? So long, sucker." Ransom ducked into the car and it slipped away into the rain.

Eli pocketed the gun and turned toward the gate, but froze in the darkness when he saw two guards untying Pamela and Ernestine. Others were running down the street from the tower. The headlights of two vehicles began speeding toward the gate. Acting on instinct, he turned and sprinted. At the corner he dashed to his left, off the main street.

The house on his right faced the main street. It was dark. Eli clambered over the fence facing the side street and huddled behind it until he heard vehicles drive past, heading toward the bridge or the freeway into San Rafael.

Probably they're looking for a car, Eli thought. Pamela and Ernestine heard them say there was a car. They would think he was still with Ransom.

He's probably right too. The administration would be embarrassed and angered by an escape and hold it against Eli, even if Ernestine and Pamela would tell exactly what happened. Their testimony could be discounted because they're pro-convict liberals. Might the women even think he was in on the whole thing?

So what do I do now? I can't just stay here.

Eli had only instinct to steer him. At the end of the fence against which he leaned was a garage. He rose and crept toward it. He tried the doorknob, and it yielded. He slipped inside. He had to chance turning on a light. He felt along the wall for a switch, found one and flipped it up. A single dim bulb was fixed in the center of the ceiling. There was no car in the garage, so Eli could scan the walls. He located items he thought would be useful to him. The first was a bicycle. On a crude work bench he found a pocket knife, a flashlight, a pair of wool mittens and a small green box with its top torn open. Inside were half a dozen granola bars. He stuffed these items and a worn blanket into the bag attached on a platform behind the bicycle seat.

He snapped off the light. He decided he could not throw himself on the mercy of the System, or could do so just as well later as now. Capture was inevitable if he stayed here. Capture was likely in any event, and would probably mean he would be locked up for life, as Ransom predicted. But he might well have been facing that prospect if he'd never met Ransom at all. *And I can do time.* He had discovered that about himself. Incarceration was something he could manage. He had Salas' clothes, including a wallet with ID and some cash. He had transportation. He had nothing much to lose.

He closed the garage door behind him and pedaled uphill along the side street, which bent left doubling back toward the prison. He passed over the hill behind the prison, in the rain.

EVEN WITH A ONE-FOOT increment in mean high tide, sea water inundation in Bangladesh extends miles inland. To nourish evacuees, food lost to the salt water incursion is replaced by boiled, water-snake stew. The usage makes no discernible dent in the reptilian invasion.

GRADY SUMNER was an undistinguished graduate of the high school in Flat River in California's northeast corner. But town residents often called on "Grady the Geek" to program their VCRs and troubleshoot their computer hardware and software. He operated a ham radio in a garret above Chet Ragland's feed and hardware store, where he had a part-time job.

"You're done early today. Any more news from Antarctica?" asked Chet.

"Not a damn thing." Grady relished his casual profanity. "Yesterday I was in on a thirty-minute patch with a tech on The Ice. But today I can't get through. None of my contacts have either."

Chet smiled. "Maybe no news is good news, eh?"

JASON LOWERY was a frequent dinner guest in the home of his geology professor, Dr. Peter Addison, through whom he had met the captain of the U.C. Davis gymnastics team, Dr. Addison's daughter Catherine.

"The news mentions rumors the President might be assembling an emergency planning team. Are you in on that?"

"I'm afraid I'm not welcome there," said Dr. Addison. "I've come down too hard on the Administration for ignoring global warming and climate change. The press loves to make it a personal confrontation. Me against the corporate bottom-line guys and campaign donors."

Catherine poured three cups of tea. "Don't they need to know what you have to say, Daddy?"

"By now the Administration probably knows all I might tell them. Another rise in sea level could occur within a few weeks or months, especially if the earthquakes cause the loss of landed ice."

"Has that ever happened before?" asked Catherine.

"Partially," said Jason. "It's been documented on Iceland for decades that when ice is suddenly melted by an eruption, the release of its enormous weight triggers earthquakes."

Peter Addison sipped his tea, and peered at them over the steaming cup. "And the collapse of Antarctic ice shelves has released more weight than ever seen in Iceland. In my opinion, that's what's causing the new quakes down there. Worse, what if those earthquakes portend volcanic activity?"

"CLEAR YOUR CALENDAR, Kim. It looks like we'll be working long hours for a while." Thad Parker's tie was loose around an unbuttoned collar. People were often startled at his diminutive stature when seen up close. His appearance on television was large and commanding.

"I've drafted a position paper on global warming and the Antarctic events," said Kim Royer. "The legal team is working on the legislation package. I'm trying to coordinate them with Spivey's people and I've sent feelers to some of the key Republicans. This is an issue we can expect a bipartisan effort on."

"Good work, Kim. Take a look at this speech I'm giving tonight at the Executive Roundtable. See if you can punch it up, okay? I expect heavy press, and I hope we can calm people down before things get out of hand." He turned toward his office, then looked back over his shoulder. "Say, is Morgan Clark still giving you the rush?"

Kim smiled. "I'm way too busy for him, you know that. And I've told him that the conflict of interest issues are huge."

"You're right about that," agreed Parker. "He's giving me heavy pressure on the water legislation. I expect he'll be there tonight."

"Do you need me there?" asked Kim. "If not, I'd just as soon read a good book."

"Go right ahead. In fact, you can start packing for a trip to Washington. I want you there for the Antarctica briefing on Friday."

"Things are heating up pretty fast," she said. "Oops, I guess that's not the best metaphor these days!"

CHAPTER 13

Wednesday, February 8

THE BARS DISAPPEARED. *The vertical bars were drawn up into the ceiling and floor like the teeth of a giant shark opening its mouth. The horizontal structures dissolved. The front of his cell was open. It was a dark night, but a source of light slanted from somewhere to the left, along the tier. Eli was alone in unnatural quiet. Perhaps Moses had died. He raised himself up on his elbows to see out into the space beyond the opening. His feet drifted up under him and he was kneeling on his bunk. The upper bunk hovered over his head. He became aware that the source of light was moving, approaching the cell, as if a candle bearer were floating along the tier, or a candle alone. Then the light appeared, much brighter than a candle. A woman in a shining cloak regarded him with serene attention. He felt he should know her. His mother? Ernestine Carter? He opened his mouth to ask something, but no sound issued from his lips. Then the woman beckoned him to draw near. She drifted back, holding her hands out in invitation, in welcome, like the statue of the Virgin in the Catholic chapel.*

Eli forced his eyes open to a narrow squint. A scraping sound had pierced his murky consciousness, the scratch of a leather shoe on concrete. He was lying on a worn blanket on a concrete slab. He sensed he was in a strip cell in the Adjustment Center. It had been ten years since his last visit to the A.C., after a fight in the yard. He had been attacked by a gang of Chicanos, in retaliation for the beating of a Mexican by Anglo inmates. A couple of white toughs jumped in. The guards had roughed him up too, when he insisted he knew nothing about the reason for the attack, that he was an innocent victim. He awoke bruised and aching. And now he was aching again. *Had he been recaptured?*

He heard again the sound of shoe leather on concrete, and now the jingling of keys. He struggled to focus his eyes and his mind in the dim blur. The previous night flashed in quick images.

He had remembered to close the garage door. Perhaps it would be a day, or a week, before the bicycle was discovered missing. He had crossed the first road he came to, avoiding the freeway off to his right. He'd passed under a street sign: Anderson Drive, sped down the hill into the deserted streets of Greenbrae, past warehouses and a shopping area.

He had passed under Highway 101. After the road curved, heading toward downtown San Rafael, he took the first left he could, onto First Street. The downtown area was deserted. The street merged with others and became Sir Francis Drake Boulevard, passing through a series of wealthy communities, then residential and rural areas. He encountered only a few cars on the road, but was sure each one would be a police car. One was, but it glided along in the opposite direction without interest in a suburban fool pedaling along in the rain.

He had biked in the night for hours. The rain let up, and started again. There had been a couple of mile-long uphill stretches. Eli was grateful for the quality of the bicycle he had stolen, a mountain bike with twenty-one speeds. Still, he walked it up the steeper slopes. He snaked through a dripping redwood forest and came to the end of Sir Francis Drake where it careened right onto Highway 1 at Olema. He nearly toppled making the turn, struggling to keep the bike upright. He had to rest. He found a church on the left side of the road. He lay near a potted tree under the protection of an overhanging roof. He had fallen asleep, in spite of the hardship of the concrete.

Now he was fully conscious, aware that he still lay huddled in the scant warmth of James Salas' hooded parka. The jingling of keys, the turning of a lock, came from very near, just around the brick pillar that formed a shallow alcove for Eli's sleeping area. He dragged himself stiffly to his feet. A firm ache gripped him from the base of his skull down the slopes of his shoulders. Stabs of pain in his thighs told him they were about to cramp. He would fall.

A face and shoulder appeared around the brick pillar, a sandy-haired man with wire-rimmed glasses. He seemed startled to see Eli, crouching.

"Are you here for Mass?" asked the man. Eli saw a stiff white collar around the man's neck.

"No." said Eli without thinking. But then he recovered, made an effort to stand straighter. "But I'd like to come in to pray for a minute, Father. What time is it, please?"

"About a quarter to eight. I'm Father Bachman. Mass is at eight o'clock."

Eli followed Father Bachman through nine-foot wooden doors with heavy iron rings into a small square church, with perhaps a dozen pews on each side of the aisle, a brick block front wall. A wooden ceiling gave the church a warm feel. There was red carpet down the center and side aisles, a wood canopy containing squares of stained glass over the altar of black stone. It was the most beautiful church Eli had ever seen, though his experience was limited.

The priest turned a thermostat dial on the wall. A heating unit clicked on, and the sound made Eli feel warmer. He slumped into the back pew, near a heater vent on the floor, while the priest disappeared into a vestibule.

Eli's eyes felt dry. He rubbed them with his fingertips, and felt a vibration pressing the surfaces of his body. He felt as if he were lying face down on a gigantic latex balloon that was expanding and contracting. He had slept for perhaps two hours. He looked around the little church, at the familiar Stations of the Cross, like those in the Catholic chapel at San Quentin. He closed his eyes and felt himself falling asleep. Swaying to one side, he jerked himself upright. He slipped out of the parka and stood up to stretch and yawn. He twisted his torso to loosen his muscles.

A woman in a honey colored car coat entered, her silver hair bound by a silk scarf. She looked in Eli's direction for a second, then faced front and strode to the first pew. No sooner had she crossed herself than the door opened again. An elderly Latino couple glanced at him before taking places near the front.

Eli sat once again, taking the parka in his lap. Through the fog in his mind penetrated the fact that the garment was reversible, black on the "inside." He let the significance dawn on him. The noise of turning it inside-out seemed to fill the small church and echo in the rafters. If police were looking for a man in a red parka, this would increase the chance that they might overlook him.

As if in response, a man in uniform entered. Eli froze. The man's military green pants were like those of the guards at San Quentin. His jacket sported an insignia on the sleeve. The bicycle leaning against the wall outside had drawn the law to him, Eli thought. But the man passed by, genuflected a few rows away, and knelt. Eli relaxed when he read the insignia as the man walked by: U.S. Forest Service. He slipped into the black parka, the noise sounding to him like blowing into a microphone. He left the church.

He mounted the bicycle and proceeded back out onto the road in a thin drizzle. Within a hundred yards he felt his exhaustion return. His legs were leaden. But his muscles warmed and the pain receded. He congratulated himself for having kept his exercise regimen.

He had gone no more than a quarter of an hour when he came to the town of Point Reyes Station. The town was awakening. A couple of cars were parked outside a café, and one in the gas station. Eli stopped at a newspaper vending machine and used two of James Salas' quarters for a *San Francisco Chronicle* early edition. He was curious to check the news, but stuffed the paper into his bike pack. The newspaper would provide extra warmth if he had to sleep outdoors again. At the gas station he found the restroom door unlocked. He undressed and bathed himself using cold water and paper towels.

The bracing alertness of the bathing faded with the warmth of the clothing and he felt the demand of sleep. He thrust a handful of paper towels into his pocket, trudged outside and unwrapped one of the granola bars he had appropriated from the garage in San Quentin Village. He gulped water at a fountain, and ate a second granola bar. In the station's front window he studied a map of Northern California. He had ridden about twenty-five miles, he judged, during his night as a fugitive. He studied what lay ahead, to the north. He knew that he had already arrived at a tacit decision where he would go, and he memorized the route to Whitethorn, the most direct way he could determine, and at the same time, if possible, what might be the least traveled route. If he were to be recaptured, he thought, it would be at a real monastery, if he could make it.

The morning sun broke through parting clouds. Eli felt his face and shoulders relax with the new warmth on his face. He remounted his bike, and in a minute had left Point Reyes Station and was admiring vistas along Tomales Bay. He pedaled fifteen miles before he saw a sign: Miller Park—Fishing Access. He pulled off the road, found a parking lot behind a hill of eucalyptus trees. He settled in a comfortable spot to nap.

The afternoon sun was shining when he awoke, but clouds like charcoal were enfolding it.

Well, thanks, God, he thought. *At least I got a few hours' sleep, and I'm still free.* He had no way of knowing whether he had been spotted, suspected, reported. Certainly he was right out in the open here, and available for capture. Maybe that was his cover, he mused; he was too out in the open to be a fleeing felon. He was, for all the world to see, a hardy bicycle adventurer. Or was he, due to his need, an addled, desperate, deluded fox panting just beyond the senses of pursuing hounds?

He took the newspaper from his bike pack. At the top of page one was not the prison escape as Eli expected but a *Washington Post* story about secret reports to the White House corroborating rumors about earthquakes and volcanic heat in Antarctica, potential disasters in Iceland, the potential for sea level rise. Eli remembered Baldy speculating about prisoners being pressed into sandbagging service. Another article carried the President's plea for people to stay at home and avoid clogging the highways.

At the bottom of the page was the article he expected. SAN QUENTIN CONS IN DARING ESCAPE. He was relieved to see there were no photographs.

Three prisoners carried out a daring escape from San Quentin Prison last night and are still at large. According to prison authorities, the men used female chapel volunteers as hostages and managed to evade security procedures. One corrections officer was injured in the incident. Sergeant Mason Pringmore, a thirteen-year veteran at San Quentin, suffered a concussion when he was attacked by one of the escapees. Warden Harmon Blakeley told reporters that the escape was aided by outsiders who sped away with the convicts in a car that has not been identified. Authorities are asking for witnesses to come forward.

The article continued on the back page, citing inadequate staffing at the prison due to absenteeism, identifying Pamela Lindsay and Ernestine Carter as the hostages, and noting the role played by Bud August and James Salas—and their clothes. The chapel volunteers were "shaken but not harmed." A brief profile was given of each convict. *"Elias Barnes, forty, also African-American, has been incarcerated for sixteen years, and had been considered a model prisoner, according to Blakeley."*

My half-black daddy makes me African-American, thought Eli. *Never mind my white and Mexican blood.* Considering further, he decided the description was in his favor, as his features and coloring would not match the likely picture readers would have of him. And he was thought to be with Ransom and Perez, so a lone bicyclist might go unnoticed. Eli wondered what impact the news of his escape must have on Ransom!

The article concluded with the warning that all three fugitives were thought to be armed and should be considered dangerous. Perez's fake pistol still gave its added weight to Eli's pack. He considered tossing it into the ocean, as if it alone were responsible for the burning in his thighs when he labored up long climbs. But he kept it.

Eli glided along Highway 1, glimpsing Tomales Bay to his left until the highway veered right, away from the coast. He forced his feet to continue circling, his thighs to keep pushing. He pictured himself as Noah, his bike as the Ark, skimming through waves of rain occasionally broken by sunshine.

From time to time he walked the bike up the steeper hills, his legs and sit-bones, even his hands and shoulders, grateful for the relief. He rested while there was still some light and ate the last of his granola bars. He stopped at a gas station in the town of Tomales, where he bought an apple, a bag of peanuts and a California map, using three dollars from James Salas' wallet. The station attendant was a plump middle aged blonde.

"Tough day for bikin'," she remarked.

"Yeah. Well, somebody's gotta do it." Eli enjoyed his first repartee with a free person outside of prison, delighted in her laugh, her casual acceptance of him as a fellow citizen.

"You're a rare breed today," she said. "Not much traffic on the coast. I guess everybody's spooked about this sea level thing."

"I imagine we'll get wetter from the rain," Eli said. She laughed again. He studied the map, checking his recollection of the way. There were alternate routes, not shortcuts, but roads off the highway, as far as Valley Ford.

He plunged ahead through dark and rain. He was grateful that James Salas' parka repelled the rain, but the pants became soaked, clung to his legs, chafed his knees as he pedaled. Like the weather, his mind sometimes cleared, sometimes stormed—with dizziness, giddiness, anxiety, exhaustion. His determination was borne by the desperation of nothing to lose, nothing to return to. He encountered few vehicles. The article on the front page of the *Chronicle* mentioned that the main inland routes had been clogged with people attempting to flee the coast.

He found a deserted campground at Salt Point State Park. No one was stationed at the entrance in the drizzly dark. He napped, using his newspaper and blanket for warmth and shelter.

A dream reenacted an Army mission in Latin America. His sharpshooter ability had led to a secret assignment in which he was to assassinate a Colombian army officer. He was not told why, and did not question. He had stalked the man through drizzly jungles in the highlands and was gasping for air as the opportunity materialized to pull the trigger. His success led to a reward posting to Germany, but the incident sometimes haunted his dreams. He awoke, panting, about to squeeze the trigger again.

He bathed again in the campground's restroom, then resumed his march along the Pacific Coast Highway. He had to work out the stiffness that gripped his body during his nap. He hadn't realized how much strain biking put on the abdominal muscles and the smaller muscles of the hips and groin. In the night Eli passed through the quiet towns of Sea Ranch, Gualala, Anchor Bay.

NEIL SMITH recognized the man next to the PR specialist for the International Observation Station. He was Walter Farrell of the Department of Defense, the same man he'd encountered while reporting from two war zones. He could guess the words he was about to hear: classified, national security matter, restraint. Farrell knew how to elicit cooperation, and how to dangle the threat of loss of access.

Smith nudged his cameraman. "Maybe you should stay for the footage, but I'm getting the next flight out. Might as well leave the reporting to the government."

CHAPTER 14
Thursday, February 9

THE RAINS DIMINISHED as dawn approached. Eli was completely alone on the Pacific Coast Highway. The black of night changed to gray, the rain to mist. Ten miles north of Gualala Eli welcomed a shaft of sunlight and its faint warmth. He stopped to admire a vista of white cliffs that reminded him of a song he heard on the radio in his youth. "There'll be bluebirds over the white cliffs of Dover, tomorrow, when the world is free!" He composed a haiku as a prayer of thanks for his own tenuous freedom.

Those white angel cliffs!
    Angry winds and sea billows
      do not defeat me.

Suddenly he sneezed three times in succession, and wondered if he were catching a cold. All the elements were in place for it. He hadn't had a good night's sleep in two days, he was out in the cold and rain, and hadn't eaten well. At least the exertion was keeping his muscles warm. He stopped to drink at every fountain he saw.

The town of Elk received the sun's full blessing, a charming town, only a couple of blocks, with quaint, toney shops and restaurants. Eli remembered a couple who drove each month from Elk to the Retreat reunions at San Quentin. Clarence and Beth Herndon must live in a farmhouse nearby, not in the town proper. They didn't seem like wealthy folks. They looked like the couple in that old painting of the Midwest farmers, him holding a pitchfork. Eli smiled in appreciation for their sacrifice. He was grateful for them, and for all the volunteers who maintained in San Quentin a loving presence from the outside. He considered looking for Clarence and Beth, but decided making inquiries would call attention to himself.

Ten miles later his legs felt like two kegs of nails. He had just labored up the hill after Highway 1 jutted in to cross Salmon Creek. A temporary yellow highway sign had been placed at the beginning of the curve: Beware of water on pavement at high tide. He had to rest. Hunger gnawed at him. In prison he had sometimes skipped meals to meditate in his cell as a means of penance for his sins, inuring himself to hardship so that he might confirm his own discipline, both physical and moral. Moses joked that he was only escaping San Quentin's cuisine.

He stopped in the town of Albion to rest, buy a snack, and check the map. A café promised a hot meal and soft seat, but he knew he couldn't risk using James Salas' credit cards and felt he must conserve his cash. Within ten minutes the snacks reenergized him and he pedaled on to Van Damme State Park, where another sign warned of high tide flooding. He took advantage of a period of sunshine to sleep.

If the fog had allowed a horizon it would have been sunset when he hurried through Fort Bragg, the largest town on his route. He was wary of towns and their traffic. But he stopped at a grocery store for a sandwich from the deli case. He was puzzled by the variety of bottled water. Sixteen years behind bars had made him ignorant of the product's widespread use. He bought another newspaper, checking the front page in vain for an article about the prison escape.

He ate at an intersection at the north end of the town, standing, his bike leaning against a tree. He felt new strength, and after mild stretching exercises, remounted and headed off into the misty night, his small handlebar lamp illuminating an oval of pavement.

Hearing a car approaching from behind him, he pulled over to give it plenty of room to pass. But the vehicle slowed, keeping Eli haloed in light. Then the light around him became red.

Eli braked and dismounted. He stood crestfallen and trembling, knowing his time of exhausted flight was over. He had gone so far, had siphoned hope from every hour on the road. But now the inevitability of failure settled its weight on him. At least he would have rest and warmth, he told himself, reaching for consolation, and he sighed heavily. He had kept this moment in the back of his mind, had told himself God would bless him with the means of escape, or would decide prison is the place he should be. It was all in God's hands.

The car door opened and Eli heard footsteps approaching. Into the glare of the headlights a figure emerged. Eli discerned the outline of a man in uniform, a Highway Patrol officer.

"Where are you headed?" It was a deep voice. The question seemed friendly though, not suspicious.

Eli cleared his throat. "Not much farther. I thought I'd stop at the state park up ahead."

The officer closed the distance between them. His hands were empty at his sides. He was a short, fair-skinned black man with very short hair. A handsome young man.

His eyes searched Eli's. "This is a strange time of year for camping." He showed a faint smile. He seemed to be taking in a great deal of information about Eli. Eli clicked into a survival mode he had learned in army combat and in the streets of Fresno.

His mind dashed through corridors of thought, in frantic search for the right door. If there was any hope, it might rest on his response. The *San Francisco Chronicle* appeared. The article about people fleeing the coast.

"It's hard to get gas these days, with the panic going on. I've got to get up to my folks in Garberville." He was able to keep a calm demeanor. It had, he judged, the right mix of humility and confidence, tinged with anxiety, as if his mission were a matter of consequence.

The young man nodded appreciatively. "Yeah, this is gettin' to be a scary time. But you won't make it tonight, so you'd better stop. Mackerricher State Park is only a mile or so up the road."

Eli permitted himself a grin.

"But you know," the officer continued, "you shouldn't be riding a bike at night without a rear reflector. Some drivers are careless enough even when they can see you."

"Yeah, I guess. But I haven't seen but a dozen cars on the highway today, and basically zero at night."

"You'd better stop," the officer repeated.

Eli nodded. The conversation had reached a satisfactory pause point. If it could remain at this vague understanding, it was of course beyond anything he could have hoped. He was willing to promise to spend the night in the nearest tree if it would give him another day of freedom.

"Tell you what," the officer said. "I'll give you a couple of strips of reflective tape to put on the back of your jacket. At least until you're off the road." He did not wait for a response, but returned to his patrol car. Half a minute later he pressed two newly cut strips of reflective tape on Eli's back.

"Thanks a lot, officer. I appreciate it."

"Be real careful, man."

Eli welcomed this parting remark with its hint of dialect, a suggestion of camaraderie. He smiled and nodded agreement.

He decided to take the patrolman's advice. It was not raining, so he might have an opportunity for sleep. Besides, the cop might check to see if he actually stopped at Mackerricher State Park.

It was a short sleep, but restful. A sense of protection comforted him. He saw the serene woman from his dream, beckoning him from his cell. The sound of raindrops plopping on his covering of newspaper awakened him. He refolded the paper and stuffed it and his blanket into his bike pack. He was on the road again in darkness and in pelting rain.

NEWS BULLETIN, NATIONAL PUBLIC RADIO

This morning the Washington Post ran a story of chilling proportions. Reliable White House sources now corroborate what, two days ago, were only rumors. The White House has been receiving secret reports, they say, since as early as last Sunday, depicting a disaster more gargantuan than anything the government has ever modeled. According to the Post, a series of volcanic caldera may have become suddenly active under what is called the West Antarctic Ice Sheet.

We put in a call to Orin Victor a vulcanologist from the University of Washington. Here's what he told us. "When volcanoes activate under glaciers, they melt enormous amounts of ice with their legendary heat. This has been studied in Iceland, the world's largest active volcanic island. In 1996 over four cubic kilometers of water broke through the ice north of the capital, Reykjavik. It destroyed all

houses, farms, power lines, bridges and highways in its flood path. There was a
warning—a 5.0 earthquake days before the flooding. In 1783 a glacial flood melted
by the largest eruption ever recorded there, killed half the people on the island and
three-fourths of all livestock.

"The ice is far thicker in Antarctica. If volcanoes erupt there, you're going to
have much more cataclysmic effects."

AN ORGY of reproductive frenzy rages, uncontrolled, on the main sea floor. Water warmed by the Earth herself is diffusing into the frigid bottom waters, maintained for a million years at zero-point by the now-destroyed glacial ice shelves. Bacteria and algae go forth and multiply at astronomical rates. Hardy shellfish, accustomed to feeding and colonizing with near-geologic slowness, are hard-pressed to keep up with the new abundance.

PETER ADDISON looked up from his computer once again, at the map on his bulletin board showing Earth's crustal plates with the continents and their political divisions superimposed. And again he shook his head. The map showed clusters of red dots indicating the epicenters of earthquakes with more than five-point magnitude over a ten-year period. Virtually every one was on or very near the boundaries of the crustal plates. A few dots showed on the edge of the Antarctic continent, but none inland.

He picked up the *Sacramento Bee* he had flipped onto his desk, ticking off his points of agreement and disagreement with the *Washington Post* article on page one. He tried to convince himself that the story was inaccurate, or alarmist. Yet the image persisted of Antarctic ice jiggling, heaving, roaring. When he had tried to call his friend at Scripps Institute in San Diego for comment, he got only a recorded message.

He returned his focus to the computer, tapped out a message for his university web page, sent it to his students with email, and printed a copy to tape on his office door:

> Due to personal reasons, classes will be held online until further notice. My apologies to students who may have limited access to the Internet—the Office of Technical Assistance at the Administration Building can help with temporary solutions. If it is necessary for you to withdraw, I will do all I can to facilitate your re-enrollment in the spring quarter.

For the next hour Peter researched on the Internet and composed a lecture and reading assignments on Antarctica, and on Alfred Wegener, the pioneer who had proposed the theory of plate tectonics and "continental drift."

Two double knocks on the door told him his daughter Catherine was about to appear. She usually entered with the same enthusiasm she used to spring onto the vaulting horse, so he was surprised that she shuffled in with the indifferent spirit of a dropout.

"Bummer, Dad. They cancelled the gymnastics meet at Stanford on Saturday." She turned around and flopped back against his desk, half sitting on the *Sacramento Bee*.

"That so? Well." He thought for a moment. "It's probably for the best. Catherine, there are rumors the university may consider suspending classes for the quarter. They came from Washington D.C.—the faculty coordinator of the 'Quarter in D.C.' Program. I think we'll go home and pack for an extended stay at the cabin in McCloud."

Catherine whirled around to face him. "When did you have in mind?"

"We'll go tomorrow."

"But, Dad, I have a date with Jason tomorrow."

Peter smiled. "That should work out. Tell Jason to join us. I'll call his parents in Maryland and tell them he'll be staying with us for a while."

CHAPTER 15
Friday, February 10

THIS IS RAMONA HIDALGO, *for KBAY Radio, San Francisco.*

White House news observers have reported cancellation of long-standing White House appointments and the arrival and departure of dozens of advisers from the U.S. Geological Survey, FEMA, the Pentagon, National Guard—all agencies that would be involved in emergency planning, should the feared disaster in Antarctica come to pass.

WHEN daylight slumbers
    the creeping foam's harsh whisper—
        Don't neglect the sea.

By dawn Eli had passed the town of Westport. He leaned the bike against a tree and walked in a circle, windmilling his arms and rolling his neck. He frowned at his map, noting that if he stayed on Highway 1 he would reach Leggett and U.S. 101 in an hour or two. He wanted to avoid that heavily traveled north-south route. The scare with the Highway Patrolman had occurred under a veil of protection, he thought. The next time—or was there something else? "Be real careful, man," the young man had said. It was a code, perhaps, a greeting from a brother. Had he deliberately overlooked his suspicions of Eli? Did he in fact recognize him as one of the escapees from San Quentin?

Eli retrieved the *San Francisco Chronicle* and searched each page. On page five he found the article updating the prison escape.

San Quentin Prison authorities report that escapees Dupree Ransom, Erik Perez and Elias Barnes are still at large today. Efforts to recapture the trio have been hampered by strain on law enforcement resources stretched by what San Quentin Warden Harlan Blakeley calls the "sea-level panic." Blakeley speculated that since all three men were from Southern California, they might be trying to make their way south. The prison continues in lockdown mode, with most of the inmates being allowed only an hour a day out of their cells, for an afternoon meal and brief exercise.

Eli said a prayer for Moses and Jerry, and the rest of his comrades in San Quentin, wishing for them a guardian like Aaron "Big Daddy" Sisson, his first AA sponsor, who had died in Soledad.

Big Daddy was the nearest thing Eli had to a father. Eli was not the only man-child the three-hundred pound convict had taken under his wing, "and not even close to the wildest," Sisson declared. "Barnes, you better watch me close now, 'cause you ain't got much fuckin' sense." He steered Eli around the mine field of prison gangs, and negotiated Eli's way out of situations his anger and impetuousness had led him into. Sisson at fifty was no longer physically intimidating, but he employed a moral force among the inmates. When Eli returned from a stretch in the Hole for fighting, Big Daddy comforted and chastised him at the same time. "Boy, you gotta walk tall, but don't get your damn chin out past your chest. I ain't gonna let you get your fuckin' stripes like I got mine." He showed dimpled scars on his neck and shoulders.

Big Daddy kept up the pressure, kept up his commitment to the headstrong youngster. Gradually Eli found there might be something stronger than his pride, his anger and his need, something he could rely on more than the drugs, a "higher power." At first, the higher power was the respect and affirmation of Big Daddy. Eventually Eli recognized it was something bigger than Big Daddy, but inside Big Daddy, and inside Eli too.

The newspaper's reference to looting homes made him reflect that he had been on the cutting edge when he appropriated his bicycle. Had the homeowner made an abrupt evacuation? If so, then the theft would not be reported, keeping some of his cover intact.

But he had to stay away from 101. On his map he found a thin gray line indicating a secondary road parallel to the coast, connecting to Briceland, near Whitethorn. He would have to try it, if he could find it.

The Pacific Coast Highway left the coast, crossing Hardy Creek. Eli found himself in a forest and laboring up a difficult winding ascent. Within a couple of miles the road evened out, then descended to a picnic area in a redwood grove past the tiny settlement of Rockport, where Eli stopped to rest and check his map once more. He judged that the secondary road must be on his left quite soon.

Two miles later he found a wide path cutting off to the left and climbing at a steep grade. At the roadside a small sign indicated Mendocino County Road 431. A second sign offered ominous advice: "Road not maintained during winter months. Use at your own risk."

"I've got plenty of risk whichever way I go," Eli told the sign. "Probably smaller here than taking 101." And he began an arduous final leg of his trek.

The narrow dirt road seemed to climb forever in twists and ruts. A quantity of mud had washed down the mountain, leaving much of the road firm, but dips and sags were mucky. Eli chose to walk the bike up steep inclines, especially where mud made traction chancy. What went up inevitably headed downward, but the road twisted so that he couldn't make much downhill speed for fear of a spill on the uncertain surface.

Usal Road offered a couple of spectacular vistas of the California coast, but was in places a dark tunnel with walls of thick vegetation. If two cars met head on, one would have to back up to a wide enough place for passing. After an hour of vigilant trekking Eli had seen no habitation. He began to wonder why there was a road at all. Probably a fire road, he thought. Then he realized that there would be marijuana growers in these forested coastal mountains, and he hoped he would not encounter them.

He passed rills and waterfalls. He had to carry the bike over two washouts. On the second, his feet slipped, and he lost hold of the bike. He tumbled down the hillside, the bike landing on top of him, the pedal banging his ribs, the handle bar glancing off his forehead. He lay twenty-five feet below the trail, under the bike, waiting for the pain to subside, deciding if he could continue. If the stab in his lower leg signaled a fractured bone, he might never regain the trail. No, he would crawl if he had to. But could he crawl ten miles? Would his injured ribs accommodate labored breathing? He pictured himself in time-lapse, starving, shriveling to leather and bone, disappearing at last into the moist earth like the inconspicuous remains of a fallen tree.

He lay a long time on his back studying his surroundings to determine how to disentangle himself. He pushed the bike away and turned over, the effort generating a sharp pinch in his side. He gathered a series of slow breaths, testing his bruised ribs, and his pain and tension subsided. He tried to stand on the steep hillside, but slid further down the slope, grappling for roots or rocks. The bike remained above him. He labored to find footing, grunting and slithering, contesting with the cumbersome bike. He paused several minutes at each success to rest and reassess his route. At last he stood on the road, panting and brown with mud, taking stock, gauging his miseries. This was the punishment of Sisyphus. He didn't even know if this was the right road.

At least he had no fear of being spotted. He smiled. It was a measure of his resilience that, hunched over, throbbing with pain at the points of impact, with lungs like a sprung bear trap, he could grant himself this ironic consolation. The thought that this was the last leg of his journey kept him going—along with the reality that there was nothing else to do. He didn't know which direction would get him off this miserable muddy track sooner. If Our Lady of Peace Monastery turned out not to be a place of sanctuary, he resigned himself to live the rest of his life as an expense of the State of California.

He faltered twice more, staying on the road each time, adding more mud to his clothing. It was a day-long labor, and wan sunlight filtered through the trees at a shallow angle when the road angled downward. Eli struggled to hold the bike stable, riding the brakes, desperate not to fall again.

It seemed a sudden arrival at the place where the dirt trail that was Usal Road spilled into Briceland Road. "I am blessed, I am blessed," Eli whispered as he felt the firm pavement under him. The blessing persisted, as the road continued downhill for three miles. There was little need for pedaling. Eli felt light and giddy. He passed through an arch of overhanging trees, a picturesque tunnel of branches. No, a cathedral, he decided.

A one-lane bridge crossed a stream. Eli stopped, laid down the bike and descended the bank. He removed his shoes and socks and waded into the cold gurgling water. He splashed it on his clothes to clear off dried mud. "I'm John baptizing myself in the Jordan," he said. When he stood dripping and shivering on the bank, he raised his arms skyward, and no one was near to hear him sing. "Deep river, my home is over Jordan. Deep river, I want to cross over into campground!"

The road continued easy, and Eli peered down each trail or driveway. Would there be a sign for Our Lady of Peace Monastery? Had he passed it? A large shabby shed lurked behind a dilapidated fence. Eli passed on. A driveway was blocked by a chain holding a sign: *Posted—No Trespassing.* "You know that can't be it," he told himself.

And then. Eli brought his bike to a stop. On his left, twenty yards from the road, three redwood trees, a simple wooden slab between two redwood four-by-fours. Modest golden lettering: *Abbey of Our Lady of Peace.* Eli dismounted and walked the bicycle past the sign. His legs felt rubbery, his chest hollow. The exhaustion of his three days of flight weighed on him like chain mail. Beyond, a wooden bridge with parallel planks for vehicle tires crossed a vigorous stream, the same stream Eli had bathed in. The path then curved into a large bright meadow. Eli felt an impulse to genuflect, but knew he would tumble to the gravel. *I've been through the Purgatory*, he thought. *I've been through the Purgatory, and now I have arrived!*

He took in breath as if to comprehend the air of the place. His exhale shuddered at the end, and the inclination to weep startled him. He took long, slow breaths. *If I were a samurai warrior*, he reflected, *I would take out my brush and paper and compose a haiku.*

> On that turning path
> past the stream and wooden bridge
> my heart leaps—and sobs.

Further reflection sobered him. *I'm an escaped con*, he told himself. Would there be any welcome in this place of his fantasies? He thought of the Prodigal Son, falling on his knees before his father and begging to be taken in and treated as a servant. The analogy failed, he realized, for he was not returning to a home place, but seeking asylum where he was a stranger. And yet, the act of showing up here was a continuation of the humble submission to the Father's will he had begun at San Quentin, and even earlier with his participation in AA in Soledad, a habit of seeking truth and forgiveness, and Providence.

He steered across the bridge and followed the gravel road, dark after the rain, through a wide expanse of meadow. A group of deer grazed in the deep grass on his right, on the edge of a forested slope. To his left sat two low buildings, each with a row of doors. Several hundred yards ahead several crows alighted in the trees into which the driveway curled. Eli guessed the low buildings were the guest houses Father Quinn had mentioned. As he passed them he saw another bicyclist advancing from the trees. He cut his speed but continued pedaling toward the man. Eli guessed he was about to meet Father Terrence, the chaplain. He had a Marine crew cut, a ruddy face, and he wore a wool jacket and rubber boots, like a farmer. The man braked and regarded Eli with one foot on the ground, his head angled like a questioner.

"Are you Father Terrence?"

The man's face relaxed some. "Yes," he said as if the word were a question.

"My name's Eli Barnes. I'm a friend of Father Dennis Quinn."

Father Terrence smiled. "How is Dennis? Have you seen him lately?"

"Only last week. He's just fine. He told me this is a wonderful place for the soul. Father, I need a place to stay. A shed would do, I'm a rugged guy. I'm willing to work," he added.

The priest seemed to weigh this. "Well, there's a shed or two here. But how would Dennis like it if I put a friend of his in a shed? I'll talk to the abbess."

In his exhaustion Eli felt giddy. But he wondered if the priest realized that he was an escaped convict. Did they read the paper or watch the news here? Who else would arrive by bicycle, road worn, unshaven, disheveled and sodden, and call himself a friend of a prison chaplain?

"Follow me, Eli."

In a minute they leaned their bicycles against the concrete block wall of one of the low buildings. Father Terrence unlocked the first door and led Eli into a small dormitory room with a bed, a desk and chair.

"I'll be going over to the evening praises soon. But first I'll get you a razor and a towel. You can go in there and wash up. I'll leave you some clean clothes on the bed here."

It's heaven, Eli told himself forty minutes later. He had shaved and taken a warm shower, and was now dressed in Father Terrence's clothes. They were a little roomy for him, but comfortable. He had prayed in the shower, asking forgiveness and praising the Providence that had brought him to this sanctuary. He had been able to close his eyes in the shower, for the first time in sixteen years. "It's enough," he decided. "If I'm taken tomorrow and thrown into the Hole for the rest of my days, this mercy will be solace for all the years to come." It was an exaggeration, but he repeated it in gratitude.

He parted the curtain at the back of the little room, and peered out into the dusk. The group of deer had made its way behind the building and was skirting a fenced garden plot. He fumbled in his mind for a haiku.

The deer, unafraid
    grazing near the garden fence
      seek no further grace.

He heard a bicycle squeak to a stop. Then a knock on the door. Opening it he saw not Father Terrence, but a stolid-looking gray-haired woman in a mackinaw, a long denim jumper and rubber boots.

"You are Eli," she announced in a husky monotone with a foreign accent. "I am Sister Berta. If you will follow me, I will take you to dinner. You will need this." She handed him a flashlight. Although formal and stern, her words nevertheless had a welcome in them. This was not a corrections officer ordering a cell block to line up for chow. Sister Berta's hair was like a neat cap fitted on her head. She might have been seventy, but a youthful spirit buoyed her. She had a short, straight nose and high red cheekbones. Eli felt accepted by her without judgment, as if he were no more out of place than a tree or boulder.

Eli slipped into a heavy wool jacket Father Terrence had left him and mounted his bike. Sister Berta set a brisk pace along a path curving in a long S through a pleasant grove of redwoods and leafing trees. Three great redwood trunks—each would have filled two or three cells in San Quentin—stood sentinel at the entrance of another meadow, across which, in the gloom, Eli made out four or five buildings. The one straight ahead had large windows through which candles sent out a warm glow. She veered right, stopped, and gestured toward a small brick building with sliding glass doors. Eli saw Father Terrence inside, sitting at a table.

"Welcome to Our Lady of Peace," intoned the nun. "We have meditation and morning praises at five-thirty, if you are interested."

"Thank you, Sister," said Eli. She nodded, with a small, sweet smile.

A salad was set out at a place across the table from Father Terrence. He told Eli to help himself to a casserole between them. A basket of warm cornbread in a napkin completed the meal, along with a small jar labeled Monastery Creamed Honey. The casserole had bread and cheese in it, and beans, potatoes, onions, peppers. The aromas filled Eli's nostrils, made him dizzy. He felt himself on the verge of tears again. He thought of sixteen years of prison food. His lunches had been served in a paper bag: slices of bread and a tube of peanut butter if he was lucky, or sealed-in-plastic nondescript meat that the inmates called moose lips; a packet of sunflower seeds or snack mix, a hard apple or pear. Perhaps a dry cookie. Evening meals were hot, but he had never imagined them prepared with love, as he did this casserole and cornbread he shared with a kindly priest. He leaned onto his fists, savoring his thanksgiving and ready to hide tears if they came.

"It's all blessed, Eli," Father Terrence said.

Eli kept his curtains open. He awoke and stared out into the night. Rain hissed like a radio dial between stations, washing the meadow's grass and the gravel road. Such nearness to rain at night from a warm, secure bed was a distant memory, from childhood. He tried to make a haiku, but words would not form. He felt the comfort of crisp sheets and wool blankets, he felt his solitude.

Father Terrence had not questioned him. He seemed satisfied to be entertaining a friend of his old friend. He shared stories of their acquaintance, mentioning only briefly Father Quinn's association with San Quentin. He gave Eli a brief history of the monastery. It had been founded in the Sixties by three Belgian nuns of the Cistercian order, on land given them by Trappist monks. Sister Berta and one other remained. The current abbess was Sister Arlene, who had entered the monastery as a novice twenty-five years ago. Instituting the bottling of creamed honey as a supporting industry was part of her reformation of the community.

Eli had spoken vaguely of his own past, mentioning the hot summers in Bakersfield, his mother's cooking, working as a mechanic in a garage and an oil refinery. Father Terrence had been content to carry the conversation.

Eli drifted back into a fitful sleep.

He heard gunshots, muffled as if his ears were stuffed with cotton. He sat in a Ford Pinto, squinting through a stream of cigarette smoke. Another muffled gunshot, and then running footsteps, growing louder. Chancy sprinted to the car. "We gotta split, man. Gun it!"

"What about Nando?"

"He's gone, man. Get goin', get goin'!"

Tires spun on loose gravel and the Ford fishtailed into the street. "Where do we go?" Eli shouted.

"I don't know, man. Down the darkest street you can find. We'll have to ditch the car and the goddamn gun."

A second time he awoke, to intense silence. He dressed and walked into a starry night. It overwhelmed him, the silence and peace, starlight illuminating the meadow. The air was still, the trees motionless. He looked up at the stars, the wash of the Milky Way, the massive sprinkle of heavenly bodies. Eli Barnes had never experienced anything like this. He felt himself led to it, as if by a museum guide or a teacher. A very wise and kindly teacher. He found it hard to breathe.

A flow of tears relieved his burning eyes, and he stared through them at the glowing sky. He felt surges of silent sobs and let them continue until they were exhausted. When the heat of his face faded to cold, he felt he was forgiven. He returned to his cell.

"I'VE HAD THE FBI do additional background checking on you, Kim. It's necessary for your security clearance." This was Thad Parker's greeting to Kim

Royer when she arrived in his Washington office. She had managed to sleep a couple of hours on the red-eye flight to Reagan International Airport.

"Didn't I already have a security screening?" she asked, hanging her coat in the closet.

"This'll clear you for the high level meetings we're going to have the next day or two. The President has cleared his calendar to deal with emergency planning. It'll be mostly Republicans, but a few of us good guys are invited. Me because California's always key and because I'm ranking member on the Armed Forces Committee."

"What do you expect California to get out of this?"

Parker smiled. "You just cut to the chase, don't you? You could do most of my job yourself, you know that?" He took a long, thoughtful breath. "California probably gets coastal construction projects along with beefed up security and reinforcements at the military bases. Local law enforcement already has their hands full. I hope we'll find out what's going on at the South Pole, but even if it's nothing, the fear that's buzzing around is likely to bring out the full moonies. People are already into near-panic mode on the coasts."

"Do you think there's any reason to be afraid?"

"People have been conditioned to fear, Kim. The government and the press aren't antagonists, they're partners. Always selling the society a bogey man. If people are nervous, they'll buy something. Or they'll vote."

"My Uncle Peter says there might be something to it. He advised my dad to stock up supplies at our cabin in Modoc County."

"Don't get too comfortable here," said Parker. "The briefing is at one o'clock."

"I FEEL LIKE we're on vacation, Charles."

"We are on vacation, Rose." Charles Royer stabbed at the telephone's keypad, then leaned back in his armchair, offering his wife a tight grin. He had taken a long weekend away from his schedule of supervising interns at U.C. Davis Medical Center in Sacramento to prepare their Modoc County cabin for occupancy, in case his brother-in-law's cautionary advice proved valid.

Rose Royer spread a tablecloth on the dining table and set places for their lunch, providing for herself the missing half of the telephone conversation. "Hello, Peter," she heard Charles say. "How are things in McCloud? Yes, we're in Modoc now. Traffic was sort of weekend heavy on I-5, but not bad through Susanville. Maybe you were right about stocking our cabins. The upside is, Rose and I are on a honeymoon here!"

There was a long pause, punctuated by, "That's good," "Oh," and "I see," from Charles. Finally he said, "All I can say is good luck. I'll ask Rose if she had any advice on it and let her get back to you. I just wanted you to know we're here, and ask you to stay in touch when you hear anything we can't get on the news... We'll keep our answering machine on in case we step out... Okay... 'Bye."

Rose raised an eyebrow. "When I said we're on a honeymoon, Peter said he's afraid Catherine and Jason have something like that in mind too. He said they've got a study hall going there, with both of them trying to keep up with their classes on the Internet. Jason's got his laptop, but according to Peter there are lots of times when Catherine is the laptop! They're out skiing now. Peter's feeling Celia's absence at times like these, wishing she were here to help him."

"I'm afraid he's going to have to let go of Catherine. We had to let go of Kim long ago and trust that she has her morals and priorities stacked up reasonably well." She sat on the arm of Charles' chair. "Peter might need a good woman as much as Catherine needs a mother. He won't find another Celia."

"He's never bothered to look," Charles said.

Rose soothed his thin white hair. "Let's go for a walk up around the old Maxwell property after lunch. I'd like to be satisfied it's still deserted. And if not, I'd like to know what kind of neighbors we have. When we get back we can pretend we're Jason and Catherine!"

CHAPTER 16
Saturday, February 11

THE BULLETIN BOARD at U.S. Geologic Survey headquarters in Washington, D.C., boasts a still-warm printout of Antarctic satellite data: "No Tremors—Mount Paget (South Georgia Island) 2,934 meters, 9,626 feet; No Tremors—Mount Nivea, (Coronation Island, South Orkney Islands) 1,265 meters, 4,150 feet; 9% increase in tremors—Mt. Jackson (Antarctic Peninsula, Mainland) 4,190 meters, 13,747 feet; normal micro-tremors—Mt. Erebus (Victoria Land, Ross Island) 3,794 meters, 12,444 feet; 6% increase in micro-tremors—Vinson Massif (Stewart Range, Mainland) 4,897 meters, 16,066 feet.

THIS IS RAMONA HIDALGO, *for KBAY Radio, San Francisco. The White House, and other officials, are reacting to a sensational broadcast by the Star News last night. The Star News claims to have exposed a massive cover-up of scientific reports that predict a catastrophic meltdown of the southern ice cap due to lava from the center of the earth. The President's press secretary held a news conference this morning passionately de-bunking the Star News report. She said, in the prepared press release:*

"Media profiteers of thinly substantiated sensationalism are again attempting to fabricate news of pending catastrophe where none exists. The idea of a gigantic volcanic hotspot boiling up from the center of the earth and causing a meltdown of the ice cap in Antarctica, and a government cover-up on top of it, is the stuff of horror films. It is neither sound science nor an accurate portrayal of this administration's behavior.

"To our knowledge, geologists at Harvard and the University of California have collaborated on a highly theoretical study of so-called magma convection currents throughout the lithosphere, a layer of the earth which lies under Antarctica as well as every other continent on our globe. The study of these convection currents has been ongoing for years. We reference the work of U.C. Davis' Dr. Peter Addison and his collaborators.

"We are appropriately concerned with recent changes in the ice fields of Antarctica, and sea level changes. Governments of the world may need to make preparations against contingencies arising from recent ice field changes and earthquake activity. Because of the seriousness of these undertakings, and the highly coordinated planning effort they require, media personnel on Antarctica have very responsibly cooperated with our representatives to ensure that only accurate, reliable information is reported.

"The kind of catastrophe that the Star News has pandered to the American public bears no resemblance to reality and is simply the kind of blatant attempt to profit from media-fabricated fear and confusion that undermines our cherished freedom of the press and demeans the very First Amendment itself".

The Press Secretary did not take questions.

IN THE GRAY of early morning Eli tiptoed into the chapel. To his left, the altar table stood on a raised step of the smooth concrete floor. Father Terrence sat on a zafu cushion, facing Eli from the far wall.

A woman in a white robe sat to the left of the priest. As Eli stepped forward, he saw a dozen women in white robes with overlong sleeves, setting up their zafus along the walls, behind a row of benches. Several appeared as young as college students. He removed his shoes and assumed the lotus position. The ting of a Tibetan bell elongated in the air, like a fragrance fading.

Eli maintained a soft gaze upon the gray floor before him, concentrating on the rudiments of meditation he had learned from the Buddhists in San Quentin. Straight back, relaxed; breathing in slow rhythm, his belly expanding with each inhalation. He forced himself to stay within himself, ignoring the silent forms around the dim room.

He played the observer of the parade of his thoughts and feelings. Foremost was gratitude for his deliverance, the solace of this place, the window of peace in the night. He held Father Quinn in light, asking blessings on him. He pictured Moses and Jerry, no doubt undergoing lockdown as a result of the escape and the prison's staffing shortage. The volunteers would be locked out, the Retreat and chapel programs cancelled. Eli pictured San Quentin as a pond becoming viscous and stagnant. The evils, anger and anxiety, would rule unchallenged.

He realized he was analyzing, and went back to focus on breathing, trying to empty his mind. A trickle of thoughts and feelings became a swirling torrent, and it seemed only a few minutes when a bell announced the end of the meditation period. It had been forty minutes.

Father Terrence and the nuns bowed toward the tabernacle with its glowing candle, then faced the center of the room and began to chant. Sister Berta handed Eli several sheets of paper. He was able to pick up the melody by the third or fourth verse of each psalm, and join, in a murmur.

> *God is our shelter, our strength,*
> *Ever ready to help in time of trouble,*
> *So we shall not be afraid when the earth gives way,*
> *When mountains tumble into the depths of the sea,*
> *And its waters roar and seethe,*
> *The mountains tottering as it heaves. ~ Psalm 46*

Everyone sat. A woman with a graceful and stately presence rose and read from a thick Bible. She seemed young to be in authority, but perhaps she was older than she looked, like Eli.

Again the group stood, bowed and chanted. After a final bowing, a series of knells drifted in from an outside bell. They all sat. One by one the nuns left the chapel. Morning had broken, and daylight was streaming in from the front wall of the room, wall-to-ceiling glass in eight panels, where most churches would have a crucifix. Just outside the wall were four large redwood trunks, converging into a single tree at their base. As Eli sat admiring the view, Father Terrence bent to whisper, "Breakfast will be in silence. Follow me."

The Community Room, Eli learned, was in an adjoining building which the nuns entered through a hallway from the chapel, but which he and Father Terrence entered from an exterior door next to the kitchen. It was larger than the chapel, but had a similar wall of glass, offering a view of redwood trees, a meadow and hill. Eli followed Father Terrence along a table set with fruit and breads, a kettle of oatmeal and a bowl of granola. Eli took a chair that faced the glass wall with his plate on his lap.

Outside, crows and jays flew among the trees, a deer posed and then picked a way around the corner of a building. Eli was surprised when a fox ambled across the grass, but no one else took notice.

Sweet classical music drifted from an unseen speaker. Eli savored the experience, recalling the hard echoes of the boisterous cavern at San Quentin's chow hall. The plain silverware and simple pottery dishes were elegant compared to plastic trays and spoons. He observed the unanimity and focus of the community, in contrast to the scattered, raucous insanity of prison.

Tangled echoes fade
　　like streaming moss forsaken
　　　in a dark forest

Eli found several of the nuns attractive, and berated himself for what seemed a sacrilegious desire. The attraction was shallow, he told himself, like that which he felt for Pamela Lindsay. He didn't know them, had never known a woman well. In his youth he had affairs with four or five girls—he had never referred to them as women. All of them had been superficial, physical relationships. Conversation had been repartee, interplay, on external or practical matters. And there had been one-nighters with almost no communication. He felt a desire to approach a oneness with a woman. Volunteers of San Quentin's Retreat Movement had shown him there were finer dimensions to relationship than he had experienced in his rock-music-TV-and-booze cosmos. He glanced around the room, at the clean-cut nuns in their jeans or denim jumpers and wool stockings, and wondered how he would have treated them if they had met sixteen years ago. The man he was then would have defiled them, or spurned them. What about the man he was now? But, he reminded himself, these women were out of bounds.

There was a great distance between him and the boy he had been before his life in prison. Then he would have schemed and seduced, with no thought of any deeper connection than sex and the pride of turning a girl on. In prison he had been chaste, not from choice but from a revulsion for homosexuality and lack of other opportunity. Most inmates were obsessed with sex. Over the years he had resigned himself to celibacy. The focus had helped him in his sometimes rigid asceticism, but union with a woman had remained a deep longing. His contacts with female chapel volunteers had been awkward, but he had developed the charm of sincerity and the determination to be honest, to be a man a woman could trust—if he ever had the opportunity.

After breakfast he learned the routine was to wash dishes in silence. He found a dish towel and sought the proper place for each item he dried.

He left the kitchen wondering what to do. It had been long since he had to make decisions about how to spend his time.

"Eli." It was Sister Berta's husky voice. "Sister Arlene will see you at ten o'clock in the room where you had dinner last night. We will have lunch after Mass at noon. You don't have to come to Mass, but you are welcome. Also evening praises are at seven-thirty. You will eat lunch and dinner in the guest dining room."

"Thank you, Sister. Is there something I can do to make myself useful?"

"Why don't you walk around the property? Over that way is nice." She pointed up the hill behind the guest dining room. "If you want to work, you can dig the garden beds out by the guest house."

He took Sister Berta's suggestion and explored the land. He found an apple orchard, stands of redwoods and manzanitas, a brook and meadows. He was delighted to be a tourist, and composed several haiku. When he returned to his room he found his—that is, James Salas'—clothes on the bed, cleaned, along with a blue jumpsuit and extra underwear and socks and a toothbrush.

He reported to the guest dining room promptly at ten. Sister Arlene arrived a minute later and introduced herself. She appeared calm and efficient, yet warm, even motherly. Eli guessed she was in her mid forties, but Father Terrence had said she had been in the order for more than twenty-five years.

She reached out to shake Eli's hand.

"Eli Barnes," he said simply.

"Father Terrence says you're a friend of Father Quinn, and that you need a place to stay. I just want you to know, Eli, that you are welcome to stay at our abbey. There is work here for you to do. Today a truck will arrive from Los Molinos with stones to be unloaded."

"That's the men's monastery in the valley," Eli said.

She nodded. "Please feel free to join us in our liturgical life. You'll find the daily schedule in the desk in your room." She paused and seemed to gather gravity for her next utterance. "There is great trouble in the world. We're not afraid of it, but we don't expect to be untouched by it. We're grateful God has sent you to us. It may be that you will do us a great service."

"Sister, I'm sure going to try. Thank you for this wonderful hospitality. This is the most serene place I've ever been."

She nodded. "God has blessed us."

She had not mentioned any limit to the length of Eli's stay.

Mass was familiar to Eli, except that the nuns prayed aloud at the Prayer of the Faithful. One of the ones Eli had found attractive mentioned the chaos in society and prayed for peace and reason, that people would develop a greater stewardship of the earth. Eli remained silent. Even though he felt a connection to Sister Berta and Sister Arlene, he did not feel part of the community, but a stranger. He accepted the consecrated bread when it was passed to him.

At evening praises there was a third man in the community. Like Father Terrence and the sisters he wore a white robe in chapel. He was Brother Timothy, the monk who had driven the truck from the Saint Mary's Monastery at Los Molinos. Eli had met him when he rolled the truck to a stop by the guest house as Eli was sharpening tools in the garden's greenhouse shed after lunch. He was a taciturn man who spoke little but seemed lighthearted. Eli learned, more from Father Terrence than from Timothy, that the stones being delivered were left over from a building project at Saint Mary's using refurbished stones from a Medieval monastery in Spain. Brother Timothy was a stone mason who would begin construction of an arch in the cemetery plot of Our Lady of Peace Monastery, where the only person laid to rest thus far was the founding abbess from Belgium.

Eli had helped to unload the stones into a shed behind the honey factory, devising a plank to wheel the stones down from the truck bed with a hand truck. He was determined to work harder than Brother Timothy, which proved to be a formidable task. When the truck was unloaded, Timothy asked Eli to drive it back to the guest house while he conferred with the abbess. The truck lurched in first gear as Eli struggled to regain the rudiments of driving.

CHAPTER 17

Sunday, February 12

ON SUNDAY Eli was surprised to find the chapel full. Fifteen or twenty new people had been added to the congregation—men, women and several teenagers. Eli avoided eye contact, tried to make himself inconspicuous. By the prayers of the faithful it was clear they were locals, regular attendees of the Sunday Mass.

A woman prayed for calm in the world, for deliverance from evil. "I'm prepared to deal with natural disasters," she said. "but I'm afraid of the fear gripping our society. People are hoarding gas, buying guns and ammunition, circling wagons and becoming territorial, wary of strangers." Eli cringed.

"Fear is driving out love," she said. "I pray that love will prevail."

"I live over in Shelter Cove," said a man with flowing gray hair but a broad, youthful face. He could have been cast as an Apache chief in a western movie. "The place is nearly deserted. Everybody who lives by the water has moved out, it seems. I'm glad the abbey is here to be a place of calm and peace, and I bless you sisters for your dedication to prayer and holding the world steady in God's hands. I also pray for guidance for our government and world leaders."

After Mass Eli stayed in the chapel to meditate until the extra visitors dispersed.

CHAPTER 18
Monday, February 13

FOUR HUNDRED MILES north of Fiji, twenty-foot high waves pound the concrete church on the main island of Tuvalu. The reinforced building is all that tops the waves. Every other square foot of the island is submerged by each crest as it passes. The eye of typhoon Haakaali lies five miles north and is heading east-south-east. Three islanders are missing. All others—that is, one hundred twenty citizens who rejected relocation to Australia, eleven tourists and seven British marine biologists—listen to the Category Four onslaught, hoping and in many cases praying that the pilings, driven to bedrock but a year ago, will hold.

ELI'S STAY at the Abbey of Our Lady of Peace lasted one week.

He and Brother Timothy had the cemetery arch project well under way, and he worked in the greenhouse garden each day. The nuns were aiming toward self-sufficiency, particularly in view of the resupply difficulties touted in news reports. With gasoline becoming scarce, grocery deliveries were unreliable, and citizens had begun hoarding, depleting store shelves.

Eli made a point of eating sparingly, aware of being a guest in a time of scarcity. The observant Sister Berta urged him to eat more. "You need nourishment to work so hard." Before Berta, only Ernestine Carter had approached his mother's unconditional acceptance.

The quiet grandeur of his life amazed him daily. Six times a day or more the quarter-mile walk from guest house to monastery compound, through a peaceful wood, renewed his comfort and sense of blessing. He learned the markings and habits of the deer which grazed in the meadow, listened for the sounds of ravens' wings, like the snapping of napkins shaken to clear them of crumbs. He grew accustomed to the nearly tame fox Sister Berta visited with leftovers after lunch.

Although the guest bed was no more comfortable than his San Quentin bunk, it was luxurious for its security. After three days he embraced the enormous quiet. He knew that his mind once had been as jangled and deceived as Dupree Ransom's had ever been.

What was the distinction between simplicity and luxury? These nuns had discovered true wealth. If there were enough monasteries for each convict to spend a month in retreat, there would be no recidivism in prisons. He was confident that if necessary he could bear a life of incarceration, better than he had ever done. The peace of this place would always be with him. It was in him.

He treasured chapel times. Morning meditation, praises, Mass, evening prayer. There was no hardship for him, rather there was joy, in early rising, sitting in meditation, laboring. Eli spent an hour each day writing poetry or reading from the monastery's books after lunch in the guest dining room, where he discussed the news, philosophy and monastic life with Brother Timothy.

"People are afraid," said Brother Timothy. "And I don't blame them. They have not enough peace in their lives, in their hearts, to face the trial."

"You're not afraid?"

Brother Timothy stared out the window, at the fox waiting for the appearance of Sister Berta. He was not going to give an unconsidered response, Eli knew. "I find I do have fear," he said at last. "Like most of those people, it's fear of myself. My vigor and my peace are not so strong. I have to wait upon the Lord for my strength. And the community too."

"Will you be safe in your monastery?"

"If the worst comes, we won't escape it. Like Medieval monasteries in time of conquest or plague, we'll share the fate of society at large. I suppose people will come to us for aid, and we'll be obliged to help them. We'll strive to maintain our life of contemplation as well."

Eli wondered if his own contribution justified his continuation at the monastery.

Every day he worked in the garden after lunch, helping Sister Sharon, the gardener. The work was not difficult for him, but concentrating on it was. Sister Sharon constituted for Eli a most pleasant distraction. Fresh complexion, regular features, effortless grace and innocence in her movement. She seemed naïve and unaware of her beauty, and its effect on Eli.

In the chapel or community room he avoided looking at her, beyond brief glances, for fear of it being noticed by the others, especially Sister Arlene. But he stared longingly as she moved about the garden, and watched her from afar as she approached along the wooded path from the main monastery buildings. He fantasized touching her hand, even holding her in his arms. At Mass each day there was a greeting of peace and the nuns gave him a brief ceremonial hug. He was acutely aware of her position during this ceremony, and hoped she would be near enough to include him in her embracing.

When she spoke to him to direct his work he answered briefly to avoid awakening in her a sense of insecurity. He wanted to be close enough to catch the scent of the rose without inhaling too deeply.

He wondered if "someone like her" could ever be interested in "someone like me." He fixated on her so that it seemed he had known her long, or that the relationship was more involved than it actually could be. Not knowing how she felt about him was misery. He dreamed about her, recalled a smile, enshrined a glance, memorized a comment and the lilt of her voice. He knew that he was being inept and juvenile, and found it amazing that he could be so awkward, in view of his history with women.

"It's so quiet here," he said to make conversation.

"Yes," she said. "We're blessed with serenity." She was replanting sprouted seeds in the small greenhouse. Eli envied the care she rendered to the plants.

"You have an idyllic life here."

"Don't say that," she admonished him, but her rebuke was intimate rather than harsh. "It's a structured life, not an idyllic one. Every life has challenges. Every person has to face his or her demons."

"Yes," he said, and was thoughtful.

"You're a lovely person." He had blurted it out. He heard the echo of his words in his mind, and was sure they rang sincere and spontaneous, and yet they hung like a dark cloud.

She accepted the compliment with a sweet smile. Afterward he regretted saying it, feeling clumsy, putting her in an awkward position. She put away her tools and returned to the abbey. As Eli watched her walk toward the woods, he imagined her off balance, struggling with her vocation, with her desire for a carnal relationship, a loving relationship with a man. At best, he might hope that she was attracted to him, might want to get to know him, might like him for his frail virtues. Could he indeed be a distraction for her? Above all he dreaded the thought of seeming predatory.

He did not want to be responsible for her pain. She was a fragile treasure, a fragrant flower easily spoiled or broken. And all of this is happening in my mind, Eli told himself. What could she see in him? These were the feelings he might have had as an awkward adolescent—more pleasant even in its awkwardness than all of his other attractions to women, except Pamela Lindsay, which was, if possible, even more structured than this.

He began to consider leaving the abbey.

Horses do not bend
    fragrant flowers' stalks to them—
        they trample or eat.

CBOX TV, Kathleen Owens, late afternoon Anchorperson

It appears many people are taking to heart alleged reports of a possibly disastrous new rise of sea level. They seem more inclined to believe the tabloids than the White House. The tabloids have been crying "Chicken Little" about volcanoes in the Antarctic, while the White House has downplayed the risks.

Be that as it may, state and federal highway officials are reporting large increases in traffic flowing away from coastal urban centers, and to a lesser extent around the Gulf of Mexico. Roads leading north out of southern Florida are seriously jammed, as are highways leading through mountain passes in the East and West, including the Appalachian and Blue Ridge Mountains in the South East and the Sierras in California, Oregon and Washington.

The picture may not be as bad as some report, however. Our staff has determined that the number of people and vehicles probably does not represent a significant percentage of the population. Local authorities likewise take the position that this is no more than an especially heavy traffic jam due to a seasonal combination of early Presidents Day Weekend travel and normal, if heavy, commuter flow.

However, there are reports from both California and New York of traffic so severe that many cars are running out of gas, stalling on the sides of roads. Motel rooms along some routes are sold out. People are sleeping in their cars. Rural gas stations are running out gas. The American Automobile Association reports that towing and rescue resources are stretched to capacity.

For its part, Congress has scheduled a rare joint session tomorrow at 5:00 p.m. Eastern Standard Time, to consider the situation. It will be carried live on this station.

71

CHAPTER 19
Tuesday, February 14

ON TUESDAY Eli voiced his doubt about continuing at the monastery to Sister Arlene after Mass, the second time he had spoken to her, for usually he saw her and the other nuns, except Sharon and Berta, only in chapel and at breakfast.

"We do not deserve our blessings," she said. "Otherwise they wouldn't be blessings." She left him turning this over in his mind.

Our Lady of Peace was far more than a blessing. It was a necessity. Dupree Ransom and Erik Perez were likely hidden among the population of a teeming city, unaware of the satisfying seclusion of Eli's humble sanctuary. Unlike them, he could be perfectly secure in those he trusted to maintain his invisibility. His was a place of rest and recovery. Theirs, he imagined, was a state of constant anxiety and fear of betrayal, in which they would ever seek some leverage or profit.

He strove to earn his place here. With his help, Brother Timothy's work on the cemetery arch was nearly completed. Sister Sharon's garden was ready for planting in the spring. He slept soundly each night in uncomplicated weariness, and awoke early for meditation in calm anticipation.

Sister Sharon. Each day was an opportunity to admire her anew. Yet his only anxiety was in being drawn to her. He composed poems to celebrate and quell his feelings.

> *Under Stars*
> *I wish to stand at night with you*
> *And tell what I know of stars*
> *Hear your star lore too and listen*
> *If the stars would sing*
> *In a hilltop silent blackness*
> *Sharing wonder.*

He felt he could not share or confess his conflict without endangering his welcome. He must contain it.

> Roses in rich soil—
> the closing garden gate now
> does not veil their scent.

This aspect of his freedom had become an exquisite anguish. What would it lead him to, or from? Would the outcast deliver the debris of his life into this refuge? His anxiety infected his sense of security. The outsiders at Mass on Sunday—would they begin questioning about him? Would their inquiries spread to authorities?

Oh, Eli, he told himself, pacing to evening meditation, there is no such thing as escape. In San Quentin you were free, and here you are bound. You take your prison or your freedom with you wherever you go.

DR. CHARLES ROYER could exercise patience in his rustic Modoc County cabin, where he was accustomed to slowing his pace. But expectation of fast and clear telephone service had established itself as a longer and deeper habit. Finally, around noon, a dial tone and a clear line.

"Christine, I can hear you clear as a bell. What happened?"

"Nothing I did, Dr. Royer. But we'd better talk fast while the talking's good!" Dr. Christine Mandell was the most conscientious surgery resident Charles had supervised in his twelve years at the U.C. Davis Medical School. She was all business, all day, every day.

"How are things going there at the hospital? Any news?"

"Todd McKenzie resigned his internship to return to his family in Louisiana. It feels a little tentative all over. All elective surgeries have been cancelled. And there's a message for you to call Dr. Elliot, Chief of Medicine at David Grant Medical Center."

"Ah," said Charles. "I was expecting that." He covered the phone's mouthpiece and met his wife's questioning glance. She leaned over the dining room table, sorting supplies in the cabin's first-aid kit. "It looks like I'm going to be called to active service, Rose. I'm supposed to call the Chief at the hospital at Travis Air Base."

Charles was eager to tie up his business with Dr. Mandell. He would have more calls to make, and hoped not to struggle with the demons on the line. It wasn't easy. It was mid-afternoon by the time he reached his daughter Kim in Washington.

"Kim, I just wanted you to know I'll be coming to Sacramento, probably tomorrow. Will you be there any time soon?"

"Yes," answered Kim. "I'll be flying back tomorrow. But I'll be really busy. You can't believe the whirlwind this Antarctic business is kicking up. The President is going to address a joint session of Congress tonight."

"I can believe it," he corrected her. "I've been called to active duty. Apparently there is a dramatic increase in trauma cases, and the military seems to be gearing up to step into an emergency situation."

The pause that followed was more than might be accounted for by electronic transmission delay or waiting to see if he would say more. Kim did not seem surprised and was weighing her words.

"I can't say too much now, Dad, but that sounds about right to me. Hopefully the situation won't get out of hand, but we've got to have something in place."

Charles nodded as if Kim could see him. "Can we meet for dinner tomorrow night? Your mother and I haven't seen you since the weekend at your Uncle Peter's."

"I'm afraid I'll be too busy. I'll have meetings all day and into the evening, and a ton of writing to do. Will Mom be coming with you?"

"No. I've persuaded her to stay at the cabin. If the phones get to working okay, she'll be the one in the family who's stable. And I'm sure she'll be safer up here than in our house in Vacaville. Here, she wants to talk to you." He handed the phone to Rose.

PETER ADDISON watched the President's speech along with Catherine and Jason in the McCloud cabin on the flank of Mt. Shasta. Rose Royer baked bread in a cabin a hundred miles due east of McCloud, while she and Charles kept a solemn ear to their radio.

Good evening. I am here to describe, in general terms, an action plan we have now developed in response to recent variations in ocean depths and related information received from our research stations in Antarctica. Our reliable American scientists and officials down there are doing yeoman service, and we can all feel a deep pride for their dedication and service.

But before I address the action plan, I want to comment on increasingly wild rumors circulated by certain elements of the media painting a picture of a gruesome disaster about to happen. I am here to assure our citizens, and the whole world, that although the situation does appear to warrant serious concern, the idea that we cannot adequately respond and prepare ourselves for any eventuality is simply wrong.

Several years ago our nation came under attack with the heinous destruction of the World Trade Center. We came together as a nation. We initiated a powerful war on terror. We survived and have flourished. We are stronger today. And we may now need all of our strength. This will be a new war, to protect our coastlines not from the irrationality of terrorists and the forces of evil but from the possible ravages of an unprecedented and unexpected combination of the forces of Nature herself.

Our preliminary conclusions are these: a cyclical, long-term climatic warming trend around the continent of Antarctica has caused certain offshore ice fields to granularize and migrate into the ocean, raising sea level ten to twelve inches. The release of weight from the continent's shores increased the incidence of earthquake activity on the edge of the continent. It would be normal, we know from decades of experience in Iceland and Greenland, for some volcanic activity to follow. There is a possibility that some ice on the continent may melt or move enough to cause a small but measurable further increase in sea level. Our scientists are, as I speak, calculating the odds of this actually occurring and will report to me the kinds of increases we might expect, if any.

The media has suggested sea level could rise by several more feet. I want to assure all Americans, and our friends around the world, that it would take hundreds of years, maybe even thousands of years, for this kind of a thing to happen. What we are talking about right now would be measured in inches, or fractions of inches. Not feet.

Having determined that catastrophe is not imminent, nevertheless the threat to our economy and our national well-being from events that have already occurred and from possible minor follow-on episodes that are reasonable to expect, is sufficiently probable, according to the best advice I can obtain, to justify extraordinary preventive measures, commencing immediately.

Our plan, which I will detail tomorrow to a joint meeting of the Cabinet and the leadership of Congress, will involve marshaling every conceivable resource at our disposal, at the highest speed possible, to construct barriers to protect all citizens and important facilities in the coastal areas of our nation. The National Guard will be fully deployed to participate in this historic undertaking. This will be a construction contingency never before seen on the face of the earth.

I have heard of people hoarding essential resources. I want all Americans to hear me well—these are needless and counterproductive activities. In all cases, in every case, your best interests will be served by remaining where you belong, going to work or, if you are able, answering the call of your Country on a volunteer basis to help with the construction mobilization. Commerce and the other workings of our economy must not be disrupted. If anything does fall into short supply, we in the government will guarantee your access to all your basic needs.

With the help of God, and all our well-meaning citizenry, we shall prevail, once again, and as soon as possible return to the normal and re-invigorated functioning of our great and sacred nation.

Following the speech, Catherine Addison surfed the channels for news beyond congratulatory analysis by familiar pundits. What she found belied the calm confidence the President had attempted to instill in the country. Reports

75

continued to cover increasing traffic jams on highways leading away from the sea coast, accelerating statistics of stalled and abandoned vehicles, motels packed to overflow capacity, diners and coffee shops closed, sold out, service stations increasingly depleted.

"We have stories like this, from every continent, from Asia to Africa, from Europe to Latin America. Domestic U.S. airports in the coastal states are now crowded beyond the worst Thanksgiving crush."

The picture cut to people sleeping in a waiting room. A reporter faced a brown-haired young woman in a red wool shirt, tight jeans and hiking boots, hardly more than a girl, holding twin three-year-olds by the hands. *"I'm hoping for a cancellation to Phoenix. My grandmother lives there. She said we could live with her. But there hasn't been a single cancellation in two days."*

The reporter turned to face the camera. *"Reports from major foreign airports are the same—Americans from all walks of life trying to return to the security of their homeland, and long distance international telephone lines jammed worldwide. However, the Internet, we're told, is alive and well."*

CHAPTER 20
Wednesday, February 15

ON WEDNESDAY Eli sought again an audience with Sister Arlene.

"I want to thank you for all you've done for me," he said. "It's been an entirely different life for me. I mean, I've never known anything like this life. These five days are like the first five days of my life."

"Are you saying that you're leaving?"

Eli sighed and looked at the floor. He did not know where he would go, of course, but he felt that, in spite of what she had told him the day before, the blessing was unbearable. Beyond that, he felt that his presence put her and the community in a vulnerable position, harboring an escaped felon. Our Lady of Peace was too important for that. Perhaps above all, he felt his instability, the difficulty of attraction to the unattainable Sister Sharon, but he would not mention this to Arlene.

"Can you accept that God might want you to be here?" she asked. "Apparently He didn't want you at San Quentin."

Eli's head snapped up. *She knew!*

"Yes, I know that you are Eli Barnes, an escaped criminal. You did not hide it when you came here. The first thing you said to me was your name. Father Terrance knew it immediately too." Her gray eyes held him steadily. "I don't know what you did to land in prison, Eli. But clearly you have turned your life around."

Eli wondered how she could make such a judgment. He wanted to make himself worthy of it.

"I earned my time in prison," he said, "just like every guy there. The truth is I earned more than sixteen years, if I'd been caught for everything I did. But sixteen hours here does more to make a man right than a lifetime in prison."

"What is it like?"

"In prison they do everything they can to demean and diminish you. It's a power game, and they never let you forget who has the power. They take every opportunity to add to the punishment society has decreed, either through malice or just plain incompetence. There's a man at San Quentin, one of the guards. His name is Scott. Sometimes it seems he's the only one who could tell you what to do—and they're always telling you what to do—without scorn, or a verbal poke in the eye. Scott should be out of there. He doesn't fit in."

"Maybe Scott is there to give someone hope," Sister Arlene suggested. "Father Quinn has us praying for the men there every day, both the guards and the prisoners. Shall we say that your spirit was here long before you arrived?"

Eli took a deep breath. "You might not believe this, but I didn't really escape from San Quentin. I got caught up in a break by two other guys. Maybe you know Pamela Lindsay? She was part of the incident too, a hostage."

"We don't get a newspaper here, but we do receive news. We did hear about Pamela. If you're a friend of hers as well as Dennis Quinn, you come well recommended."

Eli told her the story of the escape, and then his trek up the coast. "I cried when I got here," he said.

Her head bobbed solemnly. "Do you know what the crying was about?"

He knew what she meant. It was not merely from relief. The tears had started forming before he encountered Father Terrance. He related his first night, his sobbing encounter with the stars. "It was about forgiveness. Maybe redemption."

"Yes," she said. "Yes. God can speak from the stars."

If he were to cry now he would not be embarrassed. Instead, he told her that he felt his presence put the monastery in jeopardy. Her response surprised him.

"I respect your feelings, Eli. Of course it's up to you. But you need a destination. And the roads are restricted, according to the news. Apparently you must be authorized to travel now. I'll see if I can get some authorization for you to take the truck back to Los Molinos with Brother Timothy. The phone has been unreliable lately, but I will try to contact Father Thomas, the abbot. And don't worry about the abbey. The tradition of sanctuary is alive and well."

AT THE NORTH POLE the solitary GPS station, anchored to the ice last summer, quivers like a pussy willow in a Kansas summer thunderstorm. Its data arrives in Washington intermittently, missing up to thirty minutes at a swath. In recent summers at latitude zero degrees North, ice floes had fragmented and drifted, exposing open sea. The sudden rise of sea level has cracked even the winter cover this year. The data indicates the station's ice is now a drifting floe in the sunless Arctic.

KIM ROYER represented Thad Parker at a meeting of representatives of FEMA, the Army Corps of Engineers and large construction contractors. Parker was occupied at a meeting of his own involving police chiefs, the Highway Patrol, mayors, FBI and ATF people, and commanders of military installations.

Kim made eye contact with Morgan Clark only when he held the floor to make his proposal for an Operation Seawell project. He had left numerous messages for her which were far down on her priority list for returning. When the meeting adjourned, however, he approached, as she knew he would.

"Kim, let's have dinner. There's so much to talk about."

She offered a wan grin. "I'd love to, Morgan. I'd love to be able to relax. But I'm afraid it's really impossible now. I've got to brief Thad on this, and then, you know…" Her hands spread as if holding a globe. "These are the times that try men's souls. Women's too."

He clasped her hand warmly. "Isn't there any way we can spend some time together?" His eyes penetrated earnestly. Her silent return gaze was eloquent— not discouraging, perhaps wistful. He touched her cheek with his fingertips. "Kim, I think I know what you think of me. But I know I have a lot to offer. And I can change the inadequate parts of me. For you I would. Kim… I want to be someone important to you."

"It's a very awkward time, Morgan." She saw the lines bunch on his brow, saw that he was hurt. Had he ever been so vulnerable? "God, this is a time of enormous events. It's just not the time to be thinking in terms of relationship."

He brought his face close. He had dark blue eyes. "This is exactly the time to think of it," he said. "It fits with the times exactly. We might be shaken right out of everything we thought was normal. You are an enormous event in my life, Kim. I want to be part of that… part of you."

Kim glanced around the room. A few participants were still gathering their materials. Two were watching their scene from across the room. "Walk me to a cab, Morgan."

He rode with her to the Congressman's office. "Kim," he said, "please don't mention anything about me to Thad. My proposal to the government will stand on its own, you know. I don't want it to have the weight of anyone's influence. And I particularly don't want you conflicted about me. I really am changing…"

"My report to Thad will be objective. Of course I'll mention you. I'm sure your proposal is competitive…"

He interrupted. "You're talking about my construction proposal, aren't you?" He grinned. "I'm a lot more worried about the competition for you."

She tightened her lips in feigned exasperation. There was quicksand where he was treading. He tried to recover. "Well, let me add that I'm not out to gouge Uncle Sam. If there's anything to this sea-level thing, I'll do the whole project at cost. I don't need to make any more money."

Kim saw that he was trying to be noble. And nobility, she feared, was new to him.

CBOX TV, Kathleen Owens, Late Afternoon Anchorperson

Do-Not-Travel advisories continue to pour out of the Highway Patrol and other authorities nationwide. To give you the flavor, from Cincinnati, Ohio here is one airport's no-nonsense command:

> *Space on commercial airplanes may be reassigned for those who need to respond to the National Emergency. You may be asked for evidence of your need to travel and may be denied passage without it.*

Efforts to clear highways of abandoned vehicles are underway in coastal states. There is no clear pattern of where the owners are, but stories abound of people helping people. Strangers are sharing motel rooms. Some communities have opened their high school gymnasiums, and are struggling to provide emergency food for stranded travelers.

Meanwhile, on the coastlines and coastal rivers, plans to build emergency levees, barriers and other flood defenses are being developed, publicized, and in some cases already implemented. The press liaison for the Office of Emergency Preparedness issued a statement that people in critical services such as fire, police and medics, with a laudable sense of responsibility, are hard at work.

Massive increases in security have been observed at airports, railroad stations, power plants and other critical facilities, such as the National Weapons Laboratory in Livermore, California.

CHAPTER 21
Thursday, February 16

ELI HELPED Brother Timothy do the finishing work on the cemetery arch. Then he stayed to do cleanup chores while the monk plodded off to do his spiritual reading. They had spoken little beyond the communication necessary for their work, which Eli accepted as the habit of the monk's life. Eli had grown to admire Brother Timothy's skill and dedication, his humility and simplicity. His broad hands and powerful forearms did not appear to be those of an artist, yet the finished arch had the timeless look of Medieval cathedrals.

At dinner Brother Timothy spoke. "So we're taking a couple of cases of monastery honey to Los Molinos tomorrow."

Eli simply nodded. He would be the taciturn one now.

"Sister Arlene has briefed me on a few things. She didn't come out and say why, but she said you're to seem to be a monk."

Eli watched him steadily, his cup of tea suspended under his chin with a curl of steam rising.

"Eli, I told her I would not lie about it." Eli's expression did not change. "But, I told her that I won't volunteer your identity either."

The little room seemed to contract. There was a sound of ravens' wings flapping outside. Eli began to speak, but the monk raised a finger.

"Y'see, Eli, we just finished the work on our abbey chapter house. It was built with stones brought over from Spain that were part of a chapter house there, which we restored for our place." He stirred his own teacup, pausing to compose the rest of his thought.

"Now some of the stones were lost or damaged, see? So I had to cut new ones and fit 'em in with the originals. I know each one of 'em, I know where they are. Now, if anyone asked me if a particular stone were a new one, well, I would admit it. But I would be more pleased if people couldn't tell. And if they can't tell, I'm not going to point 'em out."

Eli smiled. In effect, he thought, Brother Timothy had joined Sister Arlene in forming an unofficial parole board! They had decided that he should be free.

"That's fine with me," Eli said. "I respect your integrity, and I'm willing to accept God's will in this." He sipped his tea. "In everything."

As he walked back through the woods to his room in the guesthouse, Eli considered there were large differences between his new parole board and that of the State of California. At a parole hearing details of his crime would be rehearsed, perhaps testimony from victims, arguments from a prosecutor. The board would also hear of his rehabilitation or service activities in prison, his participation in educational and spiritual growth programs, AA, Squires. There might be letters from Father Quinn, possibly from Retreat volunteers, attesting to his fitness for release. But Sister Arlene and Brother Timothy had heard no evidence to weigh on either side of the scale. They had only the evidence of associating with Eli for a few days, ascertaining his fitness from his behavior, his earnest labor, his honesty, his piety. The biggest difference was the willingness of the Our Lady of Peace Monastery parole board to give him a chance. The State of California's Board of Prison Terms had the opposite penchant, the impetus to keep him locked up, to punish, to protect itself and society, to err on the side of caution, to bow to political pressure.

He spent time in meditation alone in his room. Tomorrow, he would leave this shelter, with the chance that he might stumble in the harsher light beyond the bridge.

The moonlight seems warm
   this night of watchful walking—
     Step out of shadows.

JASON AND CATHERINE were out skiing, so Peter Addison had his cabin near McCloud, California to himself. A cup of tea sat cold on the table beside him as he focused on his laptop computer. He had been exchanging emails all morning with colleagues around the globe, and now composed a letter to the White House.

> *I urge the government to consider the threat of major tsunamis originating from the collapse of ice fields in the vicinity of recent volcanic activity in Antarctica, as suggested by several of my colleagues.*
>
> *Glaciers typically move only inches a year. On Antarctica (and Greenland as well), the dynamics are different. Within the broad expanses of slow-moving ice, there are "streams" which may move a mile or two a year. Theories have been modeled suggesting that these streams rest either on relatively slick rock or on a slurry-like layer of lubrication, a mixture of gravel and water that has been melted against the rock by the enormous pressure of the ice above.*
>
> *Volcanic heat might dramatically increase the "lubrication" under the ice sheets. Earthquakes accompanying the volcanic activity are then likely to cause an immediate collapse of major portions of the ice sheets along Antarctic coastlines. The combined effect would precipitate fantastically large bodies of ice crashing into the Antarctic Ocean. The volumes might*

range in the magnitude of multiple cubic miles of ice! This would not only cause serious increases in sea level, but under the right circumstances would generate tidal waves across the world's oceans. Depending upon the intensity of these tsunamis, coastal cities could be completely destroyed.

There is no research available on the effect of such a sudden release of landed ice. If it has happened before, it might not be preserved in the current geological record. In other words, the geological record neither supports nor precludes the kind of event under discussion.

The nearest analogy, however, is documented in scholarly articles that describe mega-tsunami from volcanic collapses expected, long-term, in the Hawaiian Islands as well as the Canary Islands.

I will attach a list of prominent scientists to corroborate or amplify this warning. I urge you to immediately initiate a plan for orderly evacuation of populations near our coastlines. I recognize that it will be a gargantuan endeavor, but we cannot afford to ignore this contingency.

Sincerely,

Dr. Peter Addison

University of California, Davis

CBOX TV, Terry Winslow, evening Anchorperson

A central part of our sea level panic story today is a continued deterioration in the workforce of America.

Schools are closed in many communities, parents are keeping their children home, and teacher absenteeism is epidemic.

Most companies simply shut their doors in the early afternoon as absentee rates passed the threshold of functionality.

Even some essential services are now impacted by absenteeism. Land-line telephone calls are becoming a rarity. As operators and maintenance personnel fail to report for afternoon and evening shifts, it is becoming increasingly difficult to reset overloaded circuit breakers and reboot the computer systems. Cell phones, however, which require a less intensive workforce, are operable, but waiting times for available circuits are increasing because of over usage.

Occasional electrical brownouts and blackouts are being reported, too, once again from lack of operating and maintenance personnel.

In some areas, survivalist supply stores are completely sold-out.

Gun and ammunition stores likewise report a run on all merchandise except the most expensive weaponry. The same is true at many grocery stores, drugstores and hardware stores.

CHAPTER 22
Friday, February 17

ELI WAS REPAIRING the fence around the garden, where deer had bent the wire mesh by straining for something tastier inside it. He thought of a Robert Frost poem that had been quoted in San Quentin by a Retreat volunteer, about two farmers rebuilding the wall between their properties. One of them wondered what he was "walling in or walling out." What barriers was he building between himself and others?

He heard the clatter of the garden gate closing and looked up to see Sister Sharon entering the little greenhouse. He closed his eyes and clamped his teeth on his lower lip. The confluence of these thoughts, this scene—it was a poem, but not one he wished to write. He, fifty yards from her and outside the fence, she separate and within, secured from him by the barrier of his reserve, his reluctance. Her young vocation like her sprouts perhaps not yet rooted in her calling, vulnerable, waiting for spring and planting.

I accept it, he told himself. Only Daddy Sisson shared the reason, and he had taken it to his grave. Sharon waved to him when she finished her work and returned to the abbey.

Eli listened to news on the truck radio before going to Mass. Essential services were threatened with closure, or working with minimal staff, the newscaster said. The president was appealing for calm, asking citizens to report to work as usual.

Eli wondered about San Quentin. How would the inmates fare in a disaster, should it occur? He envisioned a prison riot, comparable perhaps to the disturbances in cities. What if the worst case occurred, and San Quentin were threatened by disastrous rising of bay waters? Would the government be unable to relocate or care for its prisoners, yet abandon them locked in their cells for fear of releasing them to wreak havoc on an already desperate society? The thought brought a claustrophobic adrenaline surge to his chest and face. He visualized crazed convicts, in darkness digging and bashing their way out of would-be tombs, using contraband knives, bed frames, bare hands and brute strength.

At Mass, Eli asked for prayers for inmates at San Quentin. "I know you often pray for them, and I'm grateful for that." All of the nuns and the two men in the chapel were looking at Eli. "I…" His voice faltered, then recovered. "Until recently I was one of them."

He glanced at Sharon. Her face was serene, with the compassion of a Madonna.

Sister Arlene rose from her bench. "Eli and Brother Timothy will be leaving us tomorrow," she said. "Eli, know that our prayers are with you on your journey, and that you have enriched us with your presence. May God be always with you." She smiled. "We will remind Him."

LIKE MOST of her San Francisco neighbors, Darcy Malone kept her television on constantly, waiting for fresh stories to break into the repetitive cycle of reports. The sight of the President snapped her to attention.

He called for national unity, praised "Operation Seawell" coastal protection efforts, and insisted that the odds of a serious event were slight. He decried partisan politics paralyzing the Congress and the irresponsibility of the media raising the specter of disaster without offering sound scientific foundation.

Finally, he announced emergency executive orders that would keep essential industries operating, prohibit civilian use of firearms and unauthorized travel, and ensure production and distribution of food and essential commodities. All of these executive orders would be enforced by local authorities and the National Guard. He ordered international borders closed, except for repatriation of American citizens.

And he asked the nation to pray.

CHAPTER 23
Saturday, February 18

THE SKY threatened rain. Eli and Brother Timothy had been following three army trucks and a jeep for twelve miles from Longvale, single file because stranded vehicles occasionally blocked the right lane of Highway 101's two-lane sections. There were hitch-hikers along the road, in spite of the prohibition on travel, mostly headed north. Now, close to Willits, the monastery truck waited while the military vehicles passed through a checkpoint gate. Brother Timothy received a salute from a rifle-toting soldier, then pushed Sister Arlene's letter through the window.

"This is from Sister Arlene, the abbess at Our Lady of Peace Monastery at Whitethorn," he said. "She tried to call to get us permission to travel, but she couldn't get through on the phone."

"Where are you going?" asked the soldier, without looking at the envelope. He wore fatigues and a camouflage-patterned cap.

"Actually we're returning to Saint Mary's Monastery in Los Molinos. That's up by Corning."

The soldier continued to look at the two men in the truck as his hands fished in the envelope for the document inside. Eli and Timothy wore white robes with cowls resting on their shoulders. He read the letter, then looked up.

"Brother Timothy and Brother Elias," he said. He handed the envelope back to Brother Timothy, stepped back and saluted. Eli realized he had not been breathing. He exhaled softly as Brother Timothy eased through the checkpoint gate.

Whatever they're concerned about, Eli thought, they're probably not looking for escaped convicts here. He wondered if Ransom was still free. He also had the advantage of the world's preoccupation with Nature's precariousness and Society's volatility. There had been no mention of him in the government-managed news on the truck's radio. If there had been, Eli decided, it would be to announce his capture, to show that the government was being effective. They would not want to add to the public's alarm. No, Ransom was still free.

It was a surreal drive through Willits. The town should have been as busy and bustling as Willits gets on a Saturday, but the few businesses open—three groceries, a drug store and a hardware—had young soldiers chatting near the doorways, rifles slung over their shoulders. Occasional pedestrians stared at the passing monastery truck.

Willits was the first town of any size the highway passed through. After morning meditation, praises and breakfast, they had climbed into the truck and crossed the wooden bridge over the creek where Eli expected tears as he had experienced upon arriving there, but none came.

How unlike passing out the sally port at San Quentin, this departure, Eli thought.

Breezes drift backward
    Across the bridge, and I know
        Death is also sweet

He would have been content if he had never again crossed that bridge to the outside world. Except, he reminded himself, he would have struggled with his feelings about Sister Sharon. He was probably not meant to be a monk, he decided. He had watched her pouring tea at breakfast, wholesome and serene. He did not know where she was from, even her last name. He would likely never see her again. Just as it was unlikely he would ever see Pamela Lindsay, unless he were recaptured and returned to San Quentin. But the two women had awakened in him a desire to join with a woman, one he could share his spirit with. He glanced at Brother Timothy. *Did he also have such a desire?* If so he had renounced it and was using his artistry and dedication to contemplation as creative outlets to live a celibate life, apparently a full and purposeful life. Was there a struggle, a cost?

Two cases of monastery honey had been loaded on the truck, along with Eli's bicycle, a very small cargo. Sister Berta had biked out to the guest house to give the two men a sack with sandwiches and fruit, two bottles of water. *And cookies*, Eli noted with a smile. She assured Eli that he would remain in the community's prayers. "I hope we will see you again. This letter is from Sister Arlene to Father Thomas. It will introduce you to him." She handed him a sealed envelope.

Brother Timothy took the turn onto Highway 20, and within an hour they were passing Clear Lake. Campgrounds along the lake were full, but not for their usual recreational purpose. Military vehicles were parked in the campgrounds, soldiers keeping order, rations being distributed.

"Lord help those poor people," said Brother Timothy. "What's ever going to become of this world?"

The going was slow on Highway 20, in occasionally heavy rain. Tow trucks were removing vehicles from the road. Timothy mentioned his confidence that they had enough gas to reach Los Molinos. "There's certainly no getting it here," he said, motioning to a cluster of stranded cars.

They reached Interstate 5 and headed north, eventually reaching another checkpoint near Orland. A trooper held them there for two hours, saying he had to radio headquarters to OK their passage. To pass the time, Timothy gave a history of the Cistercian order and their Eighteenth Century reformed branch, the Trappists. Finally they were allowed to proceed, and arrived in Los Molinos in less than an hour.

A row of oleander trees reminded Eli of Bakersfield. They led to the entrance gate of the Abbey of Saint Mary on the edge of the small town of Los Molinos, California. They had driven eight miles east from I-5, past farms and orchards, rows of trees appearing from the passing truck like spokes of a wheel. Eli stepped down from the truck to open the gate, then reclosed it after Brother Timothy drove through. It was nearly dusk.

Off to the right, a man in Trappist robes watched their entry from a golf cart. He waved to them. He had just come from a gray stone building with glass doors, located forty yards inside the gate, as if it were a reception center.

It was, Eli learned, the office of the guest master, along with the visitor center and bookstore, where the honey was to be delivered.

"You're in time for Vespers," the man said to Timothy.

Eli was introduced to Father John, the guest master, who regarded him, in his cowled robe, quizzically. Timothy explained that Eli had been a guest at Our Lady of Peace, and would be staying with them for a while.

"I'll get you a room in the guest house just after supper," said Father John.

They unloaded the honey, along with Eli's bicycle, at the bookstore. Brother Timothy parked the truck, while Eli rode in Father John's golf cart down the central road of the monastery. The road divided the monastery grounds into an industrial sector and a farming area, brick buildings on the right facing rows of walnut trees and vineyards on the left. Father John stopped at a solid wooden gate next to an arch of a stone fence. A plaque on the gate read: Monastic Enclosure; Community Members Only.

"Just follow that walkway to the chapel," he directed, motioning to the left. "I'll meet you after Vespers." He scooted through the arch to the cloistered area of the monastery.

Eli followed the path under a gigantic oak tree to the guest entrance of the chapel. Half a dozen men and women watched Eli's entrance. He was the only one wearing a robe in the guest section, two rows of benches facing the altar from the side. He assumed they were locals, like those he had seen on Sunday in Our Lady of Peace Monastery, or people on retreat. Gathered in the apse were twenty monks in white robes, some with black hoods and scapulas. From his week in Whitethorn, Eli had become familiar with the chanting and prayers of Vespers, the observance of day's end and celebration of having faithfully fulfilled God's will. For him, this had been a day of tension, being out in the world again, closer to recapture. But now the serenity of the monastery was wrapping him in a mantle of peace once again. On the road Eli had felt vulnerable, on edge. Here he felt secure. He knew he could live out his life here, just as surely as he would have done at San Quentin, but in a far richer mode. None of his energy would be given to survival, all of it to service and communion.

After Vespers Eli rode in Father John's golf cart to the guest house, next to the visitor center. Father John explained that the Compline service would follow the evening meal and begin the Grand Silence. He took from a refrigerator in the guest dining room a large salad bowl and set it on a table that contained utensils, plates and napkins, loaves of bread and a toaster. A pot of soup was simmering on a nearby stove.

When Eli had served himself, the door opened, and in walked the people he had sat with in chapel. They nodded to him as Father John motioned them to the serving table before leaving the room. A man and woman and a teenage boy joined Eli, and the others sat at a nearby table.

"Hi, I'm Norm. This is my wife Barbara and our son Blaine," said the man, extending a calloused hand.

"Call me Brother Eli."

Assuming that Eli was a member of the monastic community and that he needed to justify his own presence, Norm explained that his family was en route by bicycle, because they were unable to obtain gasoline, to Westwood, on Highway 36, where his brother lived. They were fleeing the gathering chaos of the Bay Area, where they lived in Vallejo. There had been a riot at their local supermarket. Police had declared a curfew and were patrolling the streets, along with armed soldiers. Their neighborhood was full of outsiders. Some men had tried to break into their house.

"We couldn't go on living like that, so we locked up and left, at least until things get back to normal." Barbara's uncle had made a retreat at Los Molinos, so they thought they might ask for a night's lodging on the way. If not, they planned to camp. They would set out tomorrow morning for Westwood.

"Pray for us, Brother Eli."

"Has it been a difficult trip?"

"We stayed off the Interstate and only had to pass one roadblock. Stayed with friends in Davis the first night. The only really hard part was biking in the rain. But we have ponchos."

The two women and a man at the next table joined the conversation. The man, his wife and sister were driving to their home in Oregon but ran out of gas on Highway 99 near Los Molinos. They had walked from their car and found the monastery. Father John had given them a room for the night and assistance in contacting the local authorities for aid.

"I sure will pray for you," Eli assured them.

Eli's sleep was peaceful, until he awoke at three-thirty. He had dreamed again of the woman beckoning him out of his cell. He dressed in the dark and walked out on the grounds of the monastery, crossing an irrigation ditch to stalk along in moonlight on the edge of the walnut orchard.

I walk in moonlight
　　the humble trees are silent
　　　and the woman's voice.

Nearing the chapel, he heard the monks chanting Vigils, and considered joining them, but decided not to disturb them by opening the door. He circled the building listening to the lilt and undulation of the ancient music in the monks' full voices. He came to the chapter house—stone from Spain. He leaned against it and listened.

There was so much uncertainty in the world, he thought. But here there was less of it. Something welled up, a voice perhaps, that assured him he wouldn't be here long. He wondered whether he was feeling again that he didn't deserve this blessing. He insisted to himself that God loved him and provided for him. Prison was awful, but God provided him a life that was fulfilling, even there. He could be of service. He could take that with him wherever he went. He remembered Sister Arlene's words: We don't deserve blessings, else they wouldn't be blessings.

He placed his hands on the cold stones. These stones had been abandoned in political/religious upheaval in Spain, then reclaimed by William Randolph Hearst to build a mansion. When the Depression made Hearst give up the project, they were abandoned again and vandalized in San Francisco's Golden Gate Park. Finally they were reclaimed by the monks, who formed them into a beautiful edifice, a replica of the original Chapter House.

A man can be forsaken and then renewed too, thought Eli.

Quarried long ago
    re-formed by an artist's hand
       these are precious stones.

THE PATIENT was a Sacramento police officer, wounded in a West Sacramento supermarket break-in. He had been careless not to wear a flak jacket, like some of the soldiers in Vietnam who found them too uncomfortable. It was unsettling for Dr. Charles Royer to realize that flak jackets were now essential equipment for policemen, that the population of California was so tense that riots would break out at supermarkets causing eighteen deaths, at last count, and hundreds of injuries. The first one had occurred in Los Angeles, followed by others in San Diego, Ventura, Bakersfield, Fresno and the Bay Area cities. Society was spiraling out of control as shortages spread and rumors of shortages. Medical facilities were heavily strained by the demand for service, and civilian hospital personnel were increasingly unavailable.

"You can handle the rest, Cecil."

Dr. Royer had watched Cecil Ward, the young African-American intern, deftly place sutures to close the patient's wound. They had removed a bullet from his abdomen, examined and repaired the damaged intestine. Charles commended Cecil, and prepared to join Dr. Alan Rehling on a head trauma case. The patient had been thrown from the bed of a pickup which rear-ended another vehicle trying to cut out of traffic on the shoulder of a packed freeway.

In his Vietnam days, each time he had gone from one battlefield casualty to another in the hospital at Cam Ranh Bay, he slipped into a new pair of gloves, just as he was doing here in California, scrubbing, incising, suturing— submerging emotion, delving for reserves of endurance. Letters from his sister then were refreshment for his soul. Celia understood as no one else could. From her own intense experience in battlefield operating rooms, from their fond connection as twins, she found the words of empathy and consolation, of humorous distraction and profound wisdom. She provided strength for his journey, even though she was leading protest marches and speaking at rallies denouncing the presence of United States forces in Southeast Asia. Human beings needed his services, and she knew that he offered them selflessly to captured enemy soldiers, to civilians caught in war's mesh, as well as to American servicemen. She would be exasperated by the fruitless pollution of the violence he was now confronting.

Dr. Rehling was grateful for his old friend's assistance. He had flown in from Reno on the same plane that brought Charles to Sacramento the day before. Charles had spent most of a week before his callup with his wife at their Modoc County cabin, preparing it for a potentially lengthy stay. His brother-in-law, Peter Addison, had convinced him that Nature seemed poised to deliver a heavy blow that California was ill-equipped to handle, and that preparing for survival mode would be prudent.

At day's end Charles drove Alan Rehling to the Royer home in Vacaville, leaving the Air Force jeep in his driveway. In the city's streets, slick from a rain squall and dark under cloud masses, a quiet gloom reigned, with few house lights to illuminate the shaded lawns. The jeep in the driveway offered some suggestion of normalcy to the eerily noiseless street.

The two surgeons had showered and eaten at the hospital, had caught up on their lives and families since the last time they had worked together at the Military Services Medical School in Bethesda. They watched the early news, which showed the Safeway break-in that had provided Charles' first patient of the day. Then they retired, Alan in the guest room, Charles feeling Rose's absence in their king-sized bed. He uttered a brief prayer for her safety and felt she was doing the same for him. At least she would have Cappy, their golden retriever, to keep her company.

CHARLES LIFTED his head. A sound had awakened him, glass shattering. He held his head suspended above the pillow, listening. There were scraping noises, and voices. The liquid crystal display on the alarm clock read 2:10. He slid out of bed and lifted a single slat of the venetian blinds. By moonlight he could distinguish shadowy figures on the other side of the picket fence and shrubs that bordered the yard and separated his house from his neighbors'. Two men were boosting a third through a window. Charles felt on the chest of drawers for his cell phone and returned to his post at the venetian blinds. With his thumb he dialed 911. Busy signal.

The man inside the window was handing a small bundle out to his companions. Charles could not discern words from their hoarse whispers. He pressed the redial button. Busy signal again.

He waited for perhaps half a minute. Busy signal again. He decided to take action. He stalked to the living room and flipped the light switch. Light spilled out the window onto the lawn. An urgent commanding voice was unguarded: "Hurry! Gotta split!" Charles peered out from the side of the living room window, taking care not to expose himself. The two men were scampering toward a dark car with a rumpled fender. The third man bolted out the front door of the house and joined them. The car sped away without headlights. Charles could not identify the make of the car.

Alan emerged from the guest room. "What's going on?"

"Some guys breaking in next door. I tried to call the police, but I get a busy signal."

They peered out the window from time to time and continued to dial 911. On the fourth attempt Charles got through. The dispatcher told him that if he was not in immediate danger his call was a low priority but a squad car would come by as soon as possible. Weariness blotted their anxiety, and after an hour they returned to bed. They left lights on in the living room and kitchen and drifted into uneasy sleep that lasted until daylight. As far as they knew, no squad car had come by.

CHAPTER 24
Sunday, February 19

"ROGER, HOUSTON. We read." The assembled crew of the International Space Station is wide-eyed to a member. "Classified encryption... On. Civilian disorder is approaching Status Orange. You are to open, read and be prepared to activate Protocol EV-2, to mothball the Station if your evacuation is ordered."

AFTER BREAKFAST, Eli washed dishes in the guest dining room. The travelers had eaten breakfast while the monks and Eli were in chapel for Lauds, and had left the grounds. Eli closed his eyes and prayed for them, as he said he would.

The door opened, and a short, wiry man in Trappist robes entered. Eli recognized him as the abbot.

"Hello, I'm Father Thomas," he said. Light flashed off his round eyeglasses.

"I'm pleased to meet you. I understand you have a letter for me from Sister Arlene."

"Good to meet you." Father John had told Eli to expect the abbot's visit. He shook the priest's hand and handed him the sealed envelope.

Father Thomas scanned the letter, smiling. "Well, Eli, you're welcome to stay here at Saint Mary's. Sister Arlene says you're a good worker. Since it's Sunday, you can start tomorrow. Father John will direct you. Sunday Mass will be at ten-thirty. You're welcome to join us for all our chapel times. Father John will give you a schedule. Please feel free to call on me if I can help you in any way."

Again there was no mention of a limit to Eli's stay. He was simply accepted on Sister Arlene's recommendation. He wondered about the letter's contents. He felt a formality in the warmth of Father Thomas' welcome. Even a necessarily worldly man like the abbot had a monastic simplicity in his outlook. Eli was accustomed to and formed by life in prison, also a singular and distinct environment, and grasped the notion that unique sets of behaviors would develop in the two settings.

"Thank you, Father."

The priest smiled and left the room.

In the late afternoon Eli rode his bicycle around the orchard roads, finding the limits of the monastery property. He noticed a number of bicycles leaning against the garages and workshops, the brick winery building, built by Leland Stanford. Apparently Father John's golf cart was not the primary mode of transportation here. At 5:45 he parked his bike next to the chapel for Vespers.

When he took his place in the visitors' area, Eli saw that the monks were seated in their respective seats facing the center of the apse. Father Thomas was standing before them, waiting for a late arrival.

"My brothers," he said at last, "I have received grave news. The President of the United States has declared today that the country will be governed under martial law."

Eli perceived a stir among the monks. Several turned to look at one another, but they remained silent. The abbot continued, "We are entering a dark night. Let us pray for guidance, for deliverance from evil, for peace."

The chanting began then as usual. Eli was unsure of the significance of Father Thomas' announcement. What impact would it have on the monastery? On himself? Would there be a military presence anywhere near Los Molinos? There was little nearby for the military to protect, like the grocery stores in Willits.

Eli became aware of the Psalm that was being chanted, one he knew.

> *You need not fear the terrors of night,*
> *the arrow that flies in the daytime,*
> *the plague that stalks in the dark,*
> *the scourge that wreaks havoc in broad daylight.*
> *Though a thousand fall at your side,*
> *ten thousand at your right hand,*
> *you yourself will remain unscathed,*
> *with his faithfulness for shield and buckler. ~ Psalm 91*

THE MORNING AFTER the neighborhood burglary Charles created a sign on his computer and made six copies, which he posted on doors and prominent windows of his house: "MILITARY PERSONNEL EMERGENCY HOUSING, CONTAINS NO FOOD SUPPLIES, CLOTHING OR MATERIAL. DO NOT ENTER." Probably useless, he thought, but worth a try. He set lights on a timer switch to go on at seven p.m. and off at three a.m. Might work. He realized on the way to the David Grant Medical Center at Travis Air Force Base that the jeep parked in front of his house had probably been the best deterrent in the absence of their dog Cappy, who although he was friendly with nearly everyone, had a keen sense of character and was an effective watchdog. Charles had spent Saturday at the University Medical Center in Sacramento, where he was responsible for surgery interns, but today he and Alan would join the staff at the air base.

Sunday, but not a day of rest. A day of surgery. Charles and Alan, weary from a short night of shallow sleep, labored in the third floor surgery suite until they could slump against the elevator walls descending to the dining room for an evening meal. Gurneys and beds turned some corridors into makeshift wards. Virtually all the hospital personnel, Charles noticed, wore camouflage fatigues.

After dinner Charles drove his jeep to the base's Air Museum at the end of Hickham Street. A young sergeant with the name Carey stitched on the right pocket of his fatigue jacket opened the door at Charles' knock and saluted. Charles explained what he was looking for, and after ten minutes Carey produced two rolled lengths of oilcloth, which he opened for Charles' inspection. On white background, the two banners read, in large blue letters: TRAVIS AIR BASE and AIR FORCE COMMAND.

"Thanks, Sergeant Carey," Charles said. "I'm hopeful this will keep my neighborhood a little safer." He pictured the area over his garage door emblazoned with these two banners.

"I beg your pardon, Sir," said the sergeant. "It looks like a lot of us will be doing just that. Perhaps you haven't heard that the President declared martial law today. Hopefully that'll calm things down, Sir."

Martial law. It's come to that, thought Charles. The decision to leave Rose at the cabin was confirmed. And he was now part of the vast institution given the responsibility to set things right. The United States Government was now police, administration and succor for every citizen and locale. If Peter was right about the calamity to come, it would take all the resources the government could muster to deal effectively with the situation.

At home in Vacaville, Charles listened to a message on his answering machine. It was the pleasant voice of his daughter Kim, which had smoothed many ruffled feathers of dignitaries and VIPs. "Dad, I can't talk much now, but I want you to know that I'm just fine. I can't spill any beans, but it looks like I'll have to do some traveling. I'll keep in touch best I can, and I know to look for you and Mom at the cabin if I can't find you at home or the university or the air base. I hope all's well with you. Let's agree to not worry about each other, because, you know, that's not much good. See you soon, I hope. Bye."

Charles recalled that Kim's boss was a ranking member of the Military Appropriations Committee, and that he and his essential staff would be well looked after. His curiosity was piqued. Where would she be traveling? Obviously to Washington, but why would that constitute spilling beans? Congress itself seemed to have been rendered useless, but key members would no doubt be among the decision makers of the military government. Perhaps government would be centered away from the coastlines, where chaos was most intense, to where the Administration would feel most secure. Texas? Colorado? He and Alan hung the banners, watched rebroadcasts of the President's speech, and enjoyed a restful night's sleep.

How often in one's life is it necessary to leave a place without certainty of ever seeing the place again? How often does it happen without the question arising at all? Charles could be fairly certain he would never see Vietnam again, or Bali, where he and Rose had honeymooned. He had not returned to Portland since graduating from medical school. "You can never go home again," he recalled the aphorism. But now, its meaning incorporated the possibility for many that home might no longer exist at all. As he left for the air base on Monday morning, Charles examined his home—the banners over the garage, the curtains Rose had ordered from North Carolina, the brick path from the front porch—as if for the last time.

CATHERINE ADDISON offered her father and Jason the opinion that she dreaded the sight of the President on television. "Every time I see him, I cringe. It means things are worse than the last time."

"Usually by an order of magnitude," Jason added.

They all sat on the comfortable old sofa that had graced the McCloud cabin for five years, their attention riveted to the television across the room.

After a catalogue of complaints about civil unrest and journalistic sensationalism, and reassurance about the success of Operation Seawell, the President came to his point.

"I declare that a temporary, though extreme, state of national emergency exists, unprecedented in our history.

"The consequences of continued disorder in the streets endanger the very existence of our nation, which I am duty bound by my Oath of Office to preserve and protect. Our collective leadership has determined that the only prudent solution is to transfer all legal decision making and law-enforcement authority to the well-disciplined men and women of our armed services, under my personal command as Commander-in-Chief. It is clear to us that power will be restored to our normal government within a matter of weeks, once the civil crisis is brought under control and the success of Operation Seawell is a predictable certainty."

"What's going to happen," asked Peter wryly, "to make the emergency go away? Is he going to reverse global warming by Executive Order?"

"All companies and institutions that bear responsibility for essential services will be contacted by their local military units and given guidelines for coordinated operations to ensure the maximum success and the minimum duration of martial law. Among these essential services will be all public utilities and transportation systems, all television, radio and newspaper communication systems, all health-care systems, including hospitals and emergency services, and all essential industries already classified as Strategic Industries under the Disaster Relief and Emergency Assistance Act.

"This is a moment of the most profound personal sadness in my lifetime. I dedicate myself to every one of you—men, women and children—who constitute the responsible citizenry of our great nation, to ceaselessly work to restore our Consti-

tutional government on the earliest day humanly possible. So help me God. Thank you."

CHAPTER 25
Monday, February 20

THE SILENCE of the monastery shifted from tranquil to solemn. Eli worked from nine to noon under Brother John's direction, folding and stacking laundry in the guest house, ironing linens on a large machine. He thought of Blaine, the boy from Vallejo who might have been thinking of trying out for the baseball team, or asking a girl to the prom. And now he had left everything but his anxious parents, a few possessions and a bicycle.

Walking to noon prayers, known as Sext, Eli gazed out at the skeletal orchards and vineyards that would soon show flecks of green. In the chapel he studied the monks. The majority were white. One was black, several Latino, two Asian. But there are no Ransoms here, he thought. All of these men struggled within themselves, not with those around them as objects to be used. They had humility that Ransom would find exploitable, easy prey, a complete mystery.

Eli chided himself for bringing Ransom into this sacred place. And he recognized that he himself had been such a person—with less flair.

The courtyard fountain
   Mirror for humble seekers
      Soiled by bird droppings

MONDAY WAS another full day of work. A couple of Charles Royer's interns had abandoned their internships to return to relatives' homes in the East and Midwest. But the hospital remained fully staffed, with experienced medical personnel like Charles and Alan taking up slack.

After checking on the recovery of his weekend patients, Charles was back in surgery, removing bullets from a teenager who looked hardy, like a high school football player. He and a couple of his mates had been wounded in a foolhardy attempt fueled by machismo and beer to confront a squad of regular Army troops guarding a food distribution warehouse.

In his post-op rounds, Charles noted that his patients needed skills beyond those of the surgeon. Many of them no doubt needed counseling. It was a traumatic time, the collapse of civil order. He had a routine and a purpose, but even he felt the strain: separation from family, and the disappearance of... what? The country?

In the evening he telephoned Rose, managing to get through the first time. Martial law had been effective in returning phone line maintenance. He reported his activities, his discouragement about the chaos in society.

"You make it sound worse than on the news."

"Rose, remember, the news is managed by the government now and they put the most positive spin on it they can. But martial law might be restoring order. Today wasn't quite as hectic as yesterday."

Rose confessed to loneliness. "There's plenty to do, I'm not bored. But I'm all alone."

"I should be there with you. Do you have your pistol handy?" Suddenly Charles felt that Rose might be vulnerable. Yes, she had her pistol. And Cappy was keeping watch.

"I know I don't need to worry about you and Kim," said Charles. "You can both take care of yourselves. Hell, I bet Kim's got a marine guarding her door. But society's got such a loose grip I feel uneasy just being separated. I'm going to try to give Kim a call."

"Take care, dear," Rose said. "I love you."

When he hung up, her words echoed in his mind, and Charles reflected morbidly, pondering if that would be the last he would hear from her. Immediately he shook the thought away, but he was glad he had said it too, "I love you."

KIM ROYER fielded calls all afternoon in her Sacramento office, with one or more calls on hold much of the time. The secretary was a no-show and necessity fell to the Senior Aide. The government's dedicated tie-lines were well maintained. She wore a headset to keep her hands free for retrieving computer files, writing notes and memos. The President's declaration of martial law had required considerable coordination of federal, state and local offices. She had never before spoken to so many generals in one day, or people filled with their importance.

There was a lull of nearly a minute, during which she typed an email message. Her intercom buzzer punctured the calm. "Colonel Royer on line one."

Kim depressed line one. "This is Kim Royer."

"Hi, Kim. It's your dad."

"Dad! All I heard was the word 'colonel.' I've talked to a dozen colonels today."

"I figured using my rank was the only way I'd get through to you. I just spoke with your mom. She's fine up at the cabin, but pretty lonely. I wish I could be up there with her. You be sure to give her a call when you get a chance."

"I will, Dad." She thought she sounded like a ten-year-old. "How are you doing? You still have your knack?"

"Never better. I told Rose I'm feeling out of touch, though, sort of scattered apart. With all that's going on, you can't tell what's going to happen. You know, when Rose said 'I love you' a while ago I flashed on the possibility of it being the last words I would hear her say. I know that's morbid, but it's a scary time, that's all I'm saying. Do you have a handsome marine guarding your door?"

"Sometimes." She was touched by her father's gloomy sentimentality. His attachment to her mother was perhaps the most secure thing she knew. She thought of them as the couple who decided to go down together on the Titanic rather than be separated. "I'm afraid I don't have much time for social life now."

"What about that rich industrialist of yours, Morgan Clark? You still seeing him?"

"Dad, you have to be careful with your terminology these days. 'Seeing someone' can have more meaning than you think. But I don't have time to even think about it." She hesitated. "Would you ask Mom to marry you during all this chaos?"

"You know I would. I'd ask her to marry me if it were the end of the world, and we'd have Gabriel play the wedding march on his horn." They both chuckled.

"Well, Kim, I'm not going to give you any advice. I'm not surprised that he'd want to hold onto you. It's you who's got to decide if he's the right one. But now I insist you call your mother. She's sure to have an hour's discussion with you. Better you than me!"

By now three lines were lit on Kim's phone.

EVEN THE ICE FISH are migrating north. North to escape the murk of the bottom waters and the alkali hot springs seeping into the sea brine. Competing for prey, a killer whale has slashed a twelve-foot squid and is now enmeshed in its tentacles, whipping side to side to loose the hooks and suckers. Futility engulfs the whale and it sinks within sight of the folded-rock peaks on South Georgia Island.

CHAPTER 26
Tuesday, February 21

AFTER MORNING ROUNDS Charles struck up a conversation with a helicopter pilot who had been transporting wounded soldiers to Travis. He had seen tanks on Berkeley's Telegraph Avenue near the campus, and soldiers with assault rifles guarding stores. An unorganized gang of juveniles tutored by action movies found how formidable tanks are and learned a fatal lesson. The soldiers learned some lessons too, finding it was difficult to shoot at fellow citizens, even when their numbers and intensity were magnified by desperation.

In the evening when the jeep turned onto Vacaville's quiet Mayfair Street, its headlights illuminated rounded black scars on the garage door and across the front of the house. Fragments of the bay window were scattered on the brick entry walk. The fire had been extinguished, or had burned itself out. One military banner hung like a limp flag of truce. The other lay in the driveway, partially burned. Charles saw that his was the only house on the block that had been vandalized. He called base, asking for assistance in removing a few remaining belongings to storage.

The hospital's interns' quarters were full. It was far past midnight when Sergeant Carey showed the two physicians their bedrooms in the base housing area along Hickham Street. Far safer than home. Though he was exhausted, sleep came with difficulty, and the intermittent rumbling of trucks along Hickham Street did not help.

THIRTY NONESSENTIAL SCIENTISTS are drawing lots for twenty unassigned seats on the C-150. It will be the last flight out of McMurdo until the imminent blizzard clears, probably in a week. The lone bacteriologist is offering one hundred dollars apiece for peoples' pick rights. As many as he can get. His face is pale, his eyes panicky. His parakeet is listless—birdseed is running out. "It's not about Pepe, goddammit," he says. "I had a nightmare. My wife was telling her sister I'd missed the plane and she'd never see me again."

CHAPTER 27
Wednesday, February 22

"I'M HERE for my checkup, Doc." A broad smile followed a snappy salute. With square shoulders and graying temples, the man in captain's uniform waiting in the surgery suite locker room was recruiting-poster handsome. Charles Royer had not seen Garth Elkins for ten years, though Christmas cards were exchanged annually since he had saved the young draftee's life in 1969. Subdural hematoma. Bleeding between the brain and skull. Charles had drilled burr holes in the skull to relieve the pressure and let out clotted blood. A minute's delay would have been fatal.

Garth had kept up an enthusiastic correspondence and had taken Charles' suggestion to "look up my sister and her husband when you get back to California." Celia Royer Addison had fondly recalled the young man's winning personality, and his oft repeated assertion, quite justified she was certain, that Charles saved his life. "That boy will do anything for you, Charles," she wrote. He credited Charles as his inspiration for applying to the Air Force Academy.

"It's great to see you again, Charles."

"Well, Garth, what are you doing back in uniform, and how did you find me?" Charles, Rose and Celia all attended Garth's graduation from the Air Force Academy in 1975, and Celia's final written correspondence was to congratulate Garth on his retirement twenty years later.

"Like you, I guess. They need veterans with skills. I was running my flight training academy in Colorado Springs when I got the call-up. I've been flying VIPs around the country, and I ran into your daughter Kim. Flew her and the Congressman to Washington and Denver. She told me I'd find you here."

Over lunch they caught up on the events of their lives since Celia's death. Garth had just flown in from Denver and would leave in a few hours to take a contingent of officers and their families back there.

An hour later Charles walked Garth to his plane, on a tarmac laden with pallets of supplies.

Garth grinned. "You know the military's a mystery. Seems like shipments should be going the opposite direction. No worry about sea level rise in Denver!" He shrugged. "I imagine I'll be back in a couple of days. Let's try to have dinner."

Charles watched Garth disappear into the plane, then examined a couple of the pallets. Food, medical supplies. He wondered if Kim would know who was organizing relief of the civilian population. Back in the hospital he called her office and had to be content to leave a message: "Are you all right? Leave a message at the base hospital about when and where I can call you. Our house in Vacaville was vandalized and is not safe. I'd sure like to hear from you."

When he left the hospital that evening a young airman at the reception saluted. "Dr. Royer, Sir, a message for you." The transcribed phone message contained a filial chiding: "Dad, I'm fine, just dizzy from being busy. Not always sure what city I'm in. Instead of dealing with phone frustration, get modern and use email! It's not guaranteed to be free from frustration, but it's fairly reliable for now. Love you. Kim"

CHAPTER 28

Thursday, February 23

ELI FIT comfortably in a rhythmic cycle of prayer, work and reflection. He joined the monks for chapel and work times, submitting to any of them as teacher, director, superior. He tried to work harder than anyone. Father Thomas counseled that he was in the "honeymoon period" of monastic life, and should be careful not to burn himself out. Eli assured himself that Sister Arlene had not told Thomas about his prison background. He ate alone, listening to news on the radio in the guest dining room. He retired soon after dark and slept.

News reports of lawlessness focused on the success of law enforcement and military personnel in maintaining order in coastal areas. Eli tried to reconcile that with the testimony of the family from Vallejo. If such people were to hear the same broadcasts, would they not be even more fearful, realizing that the generals and colonels being interviewed by newscasters were out of touch with reality—or were lying? The country, except for the Gulf Coast states, was apparently stable between the Appalachians and the Sierra. There was little mention of other countries.

The news included stories of resurgent patriotism and community spirit. Families in some neighborhoods were cooking community meals. Teenagers were volunteering for various programs of "Operation Safeguard America."

Eli wondered if San Quentin's residents had been transferred to inland prisons, or were working on the seawalls, as Moses had predicted.

Society's chaos began to impinge on the monastery. More and more people were asking for shelter and food. By Thursday the guest dining room was full.

Eli organized the simple meals for the refugees: Mexican and Filipino migrant workers, middle class families, single drifters. The monks struggled with their role in serving society versus their calling to a life of contemplation and solitude. Their hours of work were devoted more and more to serving the homeless. They set up a bivouac area for the wayfarers. Meals became more Spartan than usual as the monastery's resources became strained. Brother Malachy organized guests who stayed more than a night into a work crew to dig garden beds. The monastery would need to grow most of its own food. As Eli was spading the earth with them in the afternoon, he saw a dull-green jeep with a white star on its side parked near Father John's office. In a few minutes Father John was riding with the officer and his driver toward the monastic enclosure.

Eli ambled pensively along the rows of walnut trees toward his room in the still darkness after Vigils. Studying the silent peaked rows of tents in the grass between the guest buildings, he realized that he had been the vanguard of a significant burden on the monastery, the first of many mouths to feed. And he wondered about the mission of the Army officer. Would there be a government presence even here? Were they looking for deserters? Commandeering equipment?

He turned and strode back to the chapel, circled it to the chapter house. Once again he placed his hands on the reclaimed stone building. "I have been made new too," he said aloud. "But, God, I don't know where my place is. I feel it's not here."

"Where is your place, Eli?" The nearby voice startled him. Eli saw two glass circles glinting in the darkness. Father Thomas' voice was calm and reassuring. "I'm sorry if I startled you. I was just doing some walking meditation after Vigils, when I heard you. I've told you, you're welcome here."

"My place is in prison." It surprised Eli to hear himself say it. The words hung in the air like a spider suspended from the ceiling. "Father, will you hear my confession?"

"Of course. Let's go to my office."

Father Thomas opened the side door of the chapel and led Eli through the transept and out the other side. They passed a fountain pool and entered the abbot's quarters. Eli had not seen this part of the monastery.

They sat in armchairs facing each other. The office had a large, neat desk, but few decorations. Father Thomas lit a candle on his desk. It added a little to the light of the desk lamp.

"Are you baptized, Eli?"

"Yes, when I was a kid." Eli closed his eyes, composing his mind. Father Thomas waited.

"You don't know much about me, and I'm very grateful for your hospitality. I feel safe here, but in many ways I don't belong. Do you read the papers? Do you know about the three men who escaped from San Quentin State Prison a couple of weeks ago?"

"Yes," said the priest. "One of them was named Elias, I believe. It occurred to me that your name was more than a coincidence."

"For sixteen years I've been D15078, also known as Elias Barnes. I'll tell you what got me into prison."

THE HENGE CLIPPER II is riding out the blizzard at anchorage off Signy Island in the South Orkneys. Its motors are idling to keep its one hundred-foot length aligned with the wind. Sir Oliver Denton, philanthropist, anthropologist and high-altitude botanist, expects to scale the summit of Mount Nivea on Coronation Island when the storm abates to collect late-season lichens in the lee of prevailing winds. Afterwards, it's on to mainland Antarctica, where he will take his private helicopter to the face of the Vinson Massif for further collecting before winter sets in.

ELI SEARCHED for a starting place for his story. "I was born in Texas, but my mom moved to Bakersfield when I was two. I dropped out of high school when I was seventeen and worked in a gas station until I was old enough to join the army. I'd been arrested a couple of times, for shoplifting, beating up gay guys, public drunkenness. On my eighteenth birthday I signed up. It was the first taste of discipline I'd had in my life, except when I was kicked off the football team for cussing at the coach."

"What did your parents think about your dropping out?"

"Mom cried a lot, but she couldn't stop me. I was the man of the house. My father abandoned us when I was a baby—actually before I was born."

Military service was also the first time Eli had a success in his life. At the end of advanced infantry training he had a solid body and a marksmanship medal, and had been named squad leader. He got drunk with his buddies to celebrate. His marksmanship skills led to several missions he was not supposed to tell anyone about, and after each one he was rewarded with a long assignment in a desirable post where he was given ample free time and extra pay.

"I've told this story lots of times in AA meetings, but not the whole story. I don't suppose you've ever been drunk, Father, so you might not know how it can get hold of you."

"You can't assume we were born in these robes." Father Thomas smiled. "It is amazing the various paths that have led men to this abbey."

"I've lost days, even weeks, of my life in a fog of alcohol. I've been so drunk I had to learn what I did from the prosecutor in a courtroom. I'd wake up sometimes in bed with a drunken woman, and no idea how I'd got there. It happened when I was in the service in Germany, and when she woke up I couldn't even communicate with her. She was surly and repulsive, and I know I was just as ugly. I felt so rotten I just wanted to get drunk again.

"But one time... I remember the whole thing pretty well. Trying to forget it was what kept me drunk for months. There were three of us—me and a guy named Travis and one called Dixie—on a leave in Heidelberg. We drank pitchers of beer and shots of schnapps all night and were looking for women to pick up. But we waited too long, and all of the places were closing up."

Eli bit his lip. He searched the priest's face for assistance. He saw only a relaxed mouth and the circles of glass, as if the priest knew it was not his job to make this easy. He had been impetuous to confess at all, and now it was only momentum that impelled him.

"We found a girl." Eli saw again the look of contempt in the girl's eyes.

She stepped out of a taxi as Eli and his buddies approached. Dixie lurched to close the cab door in pathetic gallantry. She hurried to the door of her apartment, her key already in her hand.

"Well ya don't hafta be so conceited," said Dixie. "I'm jus' tryin' to be friendly, see? I'm really a nice guy. We can be friends. Sprechen zie Inglische?"

The taxi driver leaned to see her safely into the building, and when the door closed behind her, he drove away.

Eli and Travis resumed their awkward stroll, but Dixie stood swaying. "Wait a minute, guys." He crossed the street where he could survey the building. "Let's just watch a minute." Several minutes later a light appeared in one of the windows. "That's the one," said Dixie. He hurried across the street and into an alley, Eli and Travis in his wake. He pointed up at the fire escape. "Gimme a boost."

"You're crazy, man." Eli felt a silly smile on his face, and thought they were talking too loud.

Once he was on the fire escape, Dixie released the metal ladder, and Eli and Travis clambered up, laughing like sophomores. They climbed to the third floor and opened the window leading to the hallway. Dixie counted doors down the passage.

He gestured gleefully. "This is the one." He raised his fist and rapped on the door. Several seconds of silence elapsed. Dixie knocked again, three taps with his knuckle.

"Wer gibt es?" came a woman's voice from within.

"Polizei," said Dixie, lowering his voice an octave. They heard the bolt slide, and the door opened a few inches. Over Dixie's shoulder Eli saw the eyes, pale blue in the light from the hallway.

Instantly Dixie's hand was in the doorway, reaching toward the girl's face. She pulled back instinctively, as Dixie pushed the door wider. The struggle was unequal, and soon Dixie was inside, his companions following.

The girl shouted something in German, but got only a couple of words out when Dixie had a hand over her mouth, his other hand behind her back, holding her close so that his eyes bored into hers. "Just keep quiet," he whispered. "I'm not going to hurt you." He spoke as if to a child frightened by a dog, guiding her to a couch. He forced her to sit next to him, keeping an arm around her shoulders. He gestured with a finger to his lips. "Wir sind freunde," he repeated several times. "We want to have a drink with you," he said in English. He raised his hand with an imaginary glass, miming drink.

"I'll look in the fridge," said Travis. There were two bottles of beer in the refrigerator. Travis fumbled in a drawer until he found an opener. Eli sat on the couch on the other side of the girl. She turned to him as if for help, saying something in German. Eli recognized only the words "raus"— get out—and "bitte." She turned back to Dixie. Her voice was urgent, but she was whispering. When she turned to Eli again, tears welled in her eyes. Travis handed a bottle to Dixie and took a long drink from the other one, which he then handed to Eli. Dixie drank and then held the bottle to the girl's mouth. She shook her head.

"C'mon, have a drink," said Travis, taking the bottle from Eli to illustrate. She pushed Dixie's bottle away, until Eli restrained her hand.

"Just a friendly drink," he said.

Dixie held the bottle to her lips and poured. The liquid dribbled down her chin, onto her white blouse. Dixie clasped a handful of her hair and pulled her head back, pouring the beer onto her face. She coughed and choked, and began to sputter in German, her voice rising. Dixie closed his hand on her mouth again. "Quiet!" he hissed. She stared at him with wide eyes, her mouth contorted in fear. A high canine squeal issued from her constricted throat. Almost casually, Dixie reached to touch her throat, and

*in one motion ripped her blouse off. She screamed. Dixie slapped her hard
on her face.*

"I said quiet!"

Now she only whimpered.

"Las' one in is a rotten egg." Dixie grinned at his companions.

Eli's face was now twisted as he looked pleadingly at Father Thomas. "I
held her down for him and we all had a turn. I was laughing like a drunken id-
iot. She kept crying in German, 'Mutter, hilft mir.' It means, 'Mama, help me.'
I'll never forget."

When Eli was able to speak again, he whispered, "And I kept telling her to
be quiet." No one spoke for long minutes. Eli searched in the blur for the
priest's face and found there a look of alarm and of compassion. He felt something like a lava rock in the back of his throat.

Father Thomas studied him, touching his temple with two fingers, as if to
engage his memory, his judgment. He seemed to be waiting, to allow Eli to
continue or to signal an end.

"I'm sorry to burden you with this story," said Eli. "It's ugly enough in my
own memory. I've told it to only one person before. I hate remembering it."

"You'll always remember it, I'm afraid. It's a burden you've put on yourself, and of course on the young woman. Do you believe you are forgiven?"

Eli took a long, deep breath. "I know I am, Father." He related his experience on his first night at Our Lady of Peace Monastery, his elation and sense of
peace. "I felt like God's finger reached down from those stars and touched me
right here on my chest."

Father Thomas nodded. "Well, Eli, let's formalize it now, shall we? I ab-
solve you of all your sins, in the name of the Father, and of the Son, and of the
Holy Spirit."

Eli closed his eyes and let the absolution wash over him in a silence that
prolonged for several minutes.

"Father, I don't know if you're familiar with the Twelve Steps of AA, but
the fifth step is to share with God, with ourselves and with another human
being the exact nature of our wrongs. The Twelve Steps kept me sober and
clean for thirteen years, maybe because I told my story once to a fellow convict. He was my AA sponsor, a man called Daddy Sisson. That was harder than
tonight, because in prison you don't dare make yourself vulnerable. It took a
tremendous amount of trust, in fact a leap of trust. And Daddy never betrayed
me."

"But this incident can't be what landed you in San Quentin."

"No. It landed me in the guardhouse for two years until I was dishonorably discharged. The girl reported it, of course, and it was pretty easy for the commander to determine who were the guilty soldiers. The San Quentin beef is another story. You want to hear it?"

"It's your confession."

CALM DESCENDED on Travis Air Base's Medical Center. Charles Royer continued working at the hospital, supervising interns, performing surgery. Many patients were MPs or soldiers hurt in skirmishes with rioting civilians. They began speaking of the Bay Area as "the front"—"I'll be going back to the front..."

There was no shortage of food in the dining room. Charles and Alan found an empty table and parked their trays. Soon they were joined by a couple in scrub clothes. They introduced themselves as Lou and Bette D'Angelo, from Berkeley. He was a physician, she a nurse, both affiliated with Berkeley's Alta Bates Hospital. Their family had been moved to Travis by the military.

"The gangs are taking over in Berkeley, Oakland, Richmond, The City, San Jose." Dr. D'Angelo was a prominent plastic surgeon, accustomed to limelight for his work with celebrity patients and high-profile pro bono work. He had not been prepared for a gun barrel poked into his ribs, for being forced to drive his car from the hospital parking lot to a home in the Berkeley hills. There he removed a bullet from the shoulder of a wealthy and vicious gang leader, assisted by an OR nurse kidnapped from Oakland's Highland Hospital. Three scowling men looked on, and ordered two teenage boys to boil water or fetch whatever the doctor needed.

Charles asked why they had kidnapped a plastic surgeon.

"I don't know," answered D'Angelo. "They probably would have preferred someone from ER. I asked them where they got the surgical supplies. They just said, 'Get to work.' One of them told me, 'If he look like he ain't gonna make it, you ain't gonna be feelin' too good yourself.'"

"Did they have everything you needed?" asked Alan.

"Yes," said Dr. D'Angelo. "Especially drugs," he added wryly. "They kept us there until the next morning. They asked if the patient might be moved. I said yes, and they just carried him out to a car and drove away. It wasn't their house, it had been commandeered for the occasion from a number of houses up there that had been recently vacated.

"The nurse and I walked down the hill. Neither of us had a cell phone, and the phone in the house didn't work. We finally came to a military roadblock on Ashby Avenue."

"That was quite an ordeal," said Charles.

"I was frantic when he didn't come home," Bette said. "I'd had a long day at the ER, and I expected Lou would be late too. Then I heard gunshots off in the distance. Even on our street there were cars going by and men running. I went to the neighbors and we stayed up all night calling for the police. You can hardly get through, and when I did they took the report and said they'd call when they knew anything. I was reaching for the valium when he came riding up in a jeep about noon the next day."

"When they found out we were medical people, they offered to get our family out of Berkeley, up here where we'd be safe."

"Sounds like it's chaos down there," Charles suggested.

"Absolutely. I hear it's settled down a little with the imposition of martial law. But even the army is going to find it difficult to keep a lid on things. Gangs are growing, and fighting each other over turf. And they're moving into the well-to-do neighborhoods too, so a lot of people got out if they could. I guess we'll go back if the army can assure us we'll be all right. I understand they're guarding the hospitals heavily now."

That evening Charles called Rose to tell her about his reunion with Garth Elkins. He downplayed his conversation with the D'Angelos, to avoid alarming her. "But," he had to add, "the fabric of society is thin and tearing. I hear gangs are keeping order in sections of the cities, but their discipline is really shaky."

Rose told him she had seen activity at the old Maxwell place. "It was two women and a man," she said when he asked if she was safe. "They were looking the place over."

ELI WATCHED the candle on Father Thomas' desk dribble wax into a gnarled lump at its base.

"This one's not a pretty story either. After the army I went back to Bakersfield and lived with my mother for a few months. I had a girlfriend who got pregnant. Her father took me aside and said, 'I don't want you to marry my daughter. She'll have a miserable life with you. She'll never know what's around the corner. And when you leave her to go to jail, she'll just be stuck with those wasted years. Get out of her life.'"

Eli bit his lip. "So I have a son or daughter I've never met. I wanted to argue with the guy, but I couldn't. I was still getting drunk, getting in fights, losing jobs. I moved to Fresno.

"I worked in construction for a while, and most nights I drank or did drugs with some of the guys I worked with. I was twenty-four years old, still a punk with no imagination, no horizon. Like the guys I ran with. Two of them were brothers, Monte and Jaron Harris."

On February 11, 1989, Eli and his buddies were hanging out at their usual spot, a place called The Rally Bar. The owner was a guy named Sonny Conlon, one of the biggest drug dealers in Fresno. He also had hookers working for him. There were five customers that night, drinking hard enough to forget something. Monte Harris kept saying he had to get to Frisco, till everyone told him to shut up. Even his brother Jaron said he was tired of hearing it. Then Monte got real moody. Pretty soon two of the guys left, and Eli and the Harris brothers were getting drugs to sell from Conlon. One of Conlon's girls, a sassy redhead named Sandra, came in and asked for a drink.

"Hey, Sandra, what you got for me?" She handed Conlon some bills. He counted the money right away, then slapped it down on the table.

"You're holdin' out on me, Sandra." He gave her a hard stare. She was in no shape to stare back, she couldn't even stand up straight.

"That's all there is, Sonny. It's been a slow night. I need a drink."

"Here's a drink, you little slut." Conlon grabbed her by her belt and pulled her toward him then shoved her away so she fell back onto the floor. She had a purse over her shoulder, and she kept a hold of it as she fell. She scrambled to her feet as Conlon stood and loomed over her. He was a jowly guy with a big gut. He yanked the purse away, so she screamed and grabbed for the strap, and they started a tug-o-war.

All this time Monte Harris was taking advantage of the commotion by slipping behind the bar and getting his fingers into the cash register. He was still intent on getting to Frisco.

Eli told Conlon to leave Sandra alone.

"Mind your own business," Conlon snarled.

Sandra yanked at her purse. "Gimme it, you fat son of a bitch."

Conlon hit her, a heavy-handed slap that staggered her. She collapsed onto the floor. He opened the purse and turned it upside down so that the contents spilled onto the floor, including a clip of bills.

Monte was easing into the till, but Conlon was so intent on Sandra he didn't notice. He picked her up and threw her onto the pool table, pinning her down with his forearm across her neck. "You need a lesson, Baby," he said. "Hey, you guys, help yourself here."

Eli's heart was pumping adrenaline through his alcohol haze, and he sprang to his feet. It made him dizzier. Sandra squirmed under Conlon's arm, her bare legs thrashing as he tore at her dress with his free hand. The sight galvanized Eli. For an instant he was in an apartment in Heidelberg, and Conlon was a young soldier holding down a helpless German secretary. Eli sprang toward the table and seized Conlon's collar, yanking back. A button flew off Conlon's shirt and a sound gurgled in his throat as he tumbled backward with Eli. He scrambled to his feet with surprising quickness. Jaron Harris helped Eli regain his feet. Conlon faced them with a malevolent sneer, lurched forward and pushed Eli in the chest. "You don't wanna mess with me," he hissed. Then he looked around, aware that there had been three of them, and saw Monte behind the bar, trying to look casual in this tumultuous scene.

The artifice was instantly plain to Conlon. He stepped over to block the open entrance to the bar, and advanced menacingly toward Monte.

Sandra had slid off the pool table, sobbing red-faced, and snatched her purse. She dashed for the door with clattering heels, and faded out into the night.

Eli and Jaron called to Conlon to calm down, but he was muttering curses and threats as he closed the distance to Monte.

Monte stopped him by pulling a switchblade from his pocket and snapping it open. The shiny blade narrowed to a sharp point, which Monte slashed toward the big man. "Keep away from me, Sonny." Monte's voice trembled, so that it sounded like a plea.

Conlon felt his advantage, and with grim calm wrapped his hand around a whiskey bottle, gripping it like a club. Monte lunged and slashed, then dodged back like a fencer. Conlon hadn't moved, but now he brandished the bottle and growled, "Drop the knife, y' little shit."

Eli yelled, "Sonny, calm down!"

Suddenly Monte slashed again and caught Conlon's left forearm with his blade. The bottle fell from Conlon's right hand and shattered at his feet as he jerked back and screeched, watching blood drip down off his elbow. Monte scrambled over the bar and stood between his brother and Eli.

Conlon was shouting curses. He tore open a drawer behind the bar.

Monte guessed first what Conlon was doing. He bolted for the door Sandra had disappeared through, as Conlon rumbled around the bar with a handgun. He fired at Monte's back, missed, and fired again as Monte banged through the door. Conlon charged after him. He was crouching in the doorway for a third shot when Jaron hurled himself on the big man's back. The pistol thundered as they tumbled out the doorway onto the ground.

Eli followed and pounced into the grunting pile, grabbing for Con-
lon's gun hand. The gun barked again, and Eli jerked Conlon's arm. They
snorted and rolled, Conlon's blood smearing all three of them. A hand
pushed Eli's face as he yanked and twisted Conlon's wrist. Conlon was
kicking, elbowing, growling. Two more shots fired, and then Conlon lay
still on the oily asphalt parking lot.

Eli heard his own coughing, heaving breath and Jaron's, then a brief
quiet, then sirens.

The squat candle on the priest's desk had diminished to a nub. A pale daylight was beginning to dispel the darkness outside the office window.

"I think it was Conlon's third shot that killed Monte," Eli said. "Sandra's
testimony was no help. The last she knew, Conlon and I had squared off. I got
a homicide rap and drug charges. The two guys who left before the rumbling
started testified that I was often their supplier. Jaron was a prosecution witness,
and he got a lighter sentence."

Father Thomas pushed his glasses up on his nose. "The way you tell it, Eli,
you were caught up in circumstances."

"I told it just the way it was, Father. I'm not trying to go easy on myself.
I've said lots of times that I deserved my time in prison. I wish I could go back
and do the last twenty years of my life again."

"Well, you can certainly do the next twenty years differently, can't you?"

"Well, Father, that remains to be seen. I have no idea what the next few
days will bring, let alone the next twenty years."

"Life here in Los Molinos usually stays pretty much the same—although
these are extraordinary times. Do you feel that you don't belong?"

"I feel very comfortable here. If it weren't for the upheaval in the world,
I'd love to stay. And if it weren't for that same chaos, I'd probably have been
recaptured by now." Eli stared at the priest. "I saw an army vehicle here today.
I had a notion, or a fantasy, that they were asking about escaped convicts."

Father Thomas returned Eli's gaze. "You're an honest man, Eli. You say
just what's on your mind. I'll be honest with you, too. The army officer did
ask—or should I say warn me?—about deserters and unsavory characters." He
paused to let his words gather effect. "I told him there were no bad guys here,
and he let it go at that."

"Father, I won't make you strain your conscience again. You and Sister Arlene. Your communities shouldn't be put in jeopardy by me."

"Where can you go, Eli?"

"I don't know. Some place you don't know about, so you won't have to
lie."

"Eli," said the priest, leaning forward, "I did not lie. As I said, these are extraordinary times. But of course, you can decide. I suggest you go north and east. There might be isolated farms up that way where you can make a place for yourself."

He rose and circled behind his desk, took a map from a drawer, and spread it open.

A COLD DRIZZLE mists the "Panhandle"—a narrow, eight-block-long eastern extension of San Francisco's Golden Gate Park. Under its towering eucalyptus trees has sprouted a forlorn and vulnerable assemblage of tents and lean-tos. Long-haired young men and women huddle in meager shelter, casting acquisitive glances at the Victorian residences along the Panhandle's darker Oak Street side. Every second or third house is boarded up, but windows on the upper floors might yield to a nimble shelter seeker.

"Those folks ain't coming back," says one of the campers. "Somebody might as well get some use out of that house."

"We should try it tonight," answers his partner. "I'm sick of looking over my shoulder all the time."

Two miles north, a trickle of foot traffic crosses the Golden Gate Bridge, headed north toward Marin County. Most of the pedestrians carry large packs or push shopping carts bundled with clothing and camping gear. With traffic snarled on the bridges, it is the surest way to leave the city going north or east. For most, it is the only way.

CHAPTER 29
Friday, February 24

ELI SLEPT until noon. When the sun was low, he loaded his bicycle on the monastery's truck. Father Thomas drove him toward Red Bluff and showed him where to pick up Highway 36. Eli embraced him. "Thank you, Father."

"Eli, I commission you to take the spirit of Our Lady of Peace and the Abbey of Saint Mary to places where it is needed. Here is a letter explaining that you are on monastery business, if you need it. Again, I did not lie."

Eli tucked the envelope into the pack full of provisions Father Thomas had furnished. The priest laid a hand on Eli's bowed head. Might it be the last touch of compassion he would know? He was on his own again.

The road lay smooth and rolling, gaining elevation. Eli pedaled past green fields dotted with pocked gray boulders. He imagined them flung there by explosions of volcanic Mt. Lassen, rising white now in the distance like the sightless one-eyed giant Polyphemus who had hurled stones in every direction in a blind attempt to punish the fleeing Odysseus. Off to his left was Mt. Shasta's snowy bulk. The field boulders brought to mind the Sacred Stones that had been reformed to build the chapter house at Saint Mary's. These rocks were in their crudest state, scattered by violent upheaval, unformed, dusted over with moss, an impediment to farming. They were Eli before prison, before the shaping work of his stonemasons, Daddy Sisson, Moses, James Salas and the Retreat volunteers, Sister Arlene and Father Thomas. Before he had been loved.

His shadow lengthened before him on the road, then disappeared as the light waned. He had seen few buildings in ten miles, scattered farmhouses far off the road. He arrived at a cluster of buildings at a tree-shaded crossroads, or rather, a fork in the road. Highway 36 continued on the right, and County Road A-6 bore off to the left. The most prominent building was set under a welcoming sign proclaiming the Dales Station Grill.

Eli halted, feeling decidedly unwelcome when he saw the only car in the tiny parking lot, a black-and-white with the insignia of the California Highway Patrol. Few vehicles had been traveling in either direction on his ten-mile ride. Eli had not made any effort to avoid being seen. If he was fated for capture, he thought, then God must have further work for him to do in prison. Father Thomas' commission to take the spirit of the abbey to where it was needed would include San Quentin, or even Pelican Bay if he were sent there.

He wouldn't have stopped for a meal, even though he still had James Salas' wallet, with about twenty dollars in cash. Father Thomas had stuffed Eli's backpack with sandwiches, crackers, carrots and apples, and he would conserve the cash if at all possible. He had considered leaving the wallet with Father Thomas, for eventual return to James Salas, but that would have marked the abbot as the harborer of a fugitive.

So a stop at the Dales Station Grill would be only for rest and possibly information. Eli imagined there would be only a couple of people inside, the owners who lived next door, who would be familiar with the area and might give some insight into the lay of the land, the state of society. And yet, passing on would relieve Eli of the need for explaining his own identity and purpose.

He decided to take the left fork, called Manton Road on a street sign. It would have less traffic than the highway, and likely no police presence. It was a good road, lonely and nearly deserted. Eli stopped to eat, sitting on a roadside boulder, and to study his map while he still had enough light. He was headed now toward the town of Manton. From there he might head north to Shingletown and pick up Highway 44, which skirted north of Lassen Volcanic National Park. He would be gaining elevation, might encounter snow. Father Thomas had given him extra clothing, including a warm wool sweater, and a waterproof camping mat. He did not linger over his meal.

An hour later dusk had fallen as Eli climbed a long rise around a bend to find a farmhouse and barn, quite close to the road. A pickup truck was parked outside the barn. Under its open hood a man in overalls was bent, working one-handed while holding a flashlight in his other hand. A black and white Australian shepherd rose from the ground at the man's feet, barked twice and trotted toward the road. The man straightened and peered toward Eli, then aimed the flashlight.

"Hello," Eli called.

The man whistled sharply twice. The dog stopped. At a second whistled signal the dog trotted to the man's side.

"Wow! That's one smart dog," Eli said. He walked his bike toward the man, who waited, patting the dog's head. Wisps of white hair curled up from under a black baseball cap with an orange SF logo. The man had a short white beard and a long nose under bushy brows.

"Hi, my name's James," said Eli, reaching across the bicycle to shake hands.

The man had a firm grip. "Arthur Peters."

"I can hold the light for you."

"Well, thanks," said Arthur Peters, "but I think this'll take more than a little light. Do you know anything about engines?"

"I used to work in a garage. I'd be glad to get in there and see what I can do. Do you think I might spend the night in your barn and have a look in the morning?"

Peters studied Eli. "You on the move?"

"I'm headed for Modoc County," said Eli without hesitation. "I'm on a mission for a priest down by Red Bluff."

It seemed to satisfy the farmer. It couldn't have sounded stranger than the events of the last month, and his question indicated he was accustomed to the idea of refugees being "on the move."

CHAPTER 30
Saturday, February 25

ELI SLEPT under a wool blanket and cotton quilt on a cot Arthur Peters set up in the barn. The dog, named Molly, curled up nearby. Eli understood that other family members were in the house, but he was not invited in to meet them.

> Dark eyed dog, you watch
> awaiting pats and biscuits—
> any sign of love.

A dull gray light suffused the barn. Eli was sitting on the cot after his meditation, petting Molly, whose tail thumped on the floor, when Peters entered carrying a tray draped with a white dish towel. "My wife sent out some breakfast," he explained. Eli enjoyed the scrambled eggs and warm buttered biscuits with a mug of coffee.

A steady drizzle was falling, so Peters pulled the pickup into the barn. Eli listened, tapped, adjusted, inspected, and listened again. "I think you could use some fresh spark plugs to start with," he said. "And I'll bet you have a clogged oil line. It shouldn't take too long to check it out and clear it."

It took nearly the whole day, as additional problems were discovered. Eli and Arthur Peters worked together, their labor punctuated by passages of conversation. Eli learned that most people had welcomed the President's declaration of martial law, taking from it a feeling of security. It had been only five days, but in this rural setting life had not lost normalcy. In the towns and cities Peters was familiar with, Redding and Red Bluff on Interstate 5, there had been looting, burglary, a number of violent incidents. Now things were calmer. Folks listened to the news a lot, waiting for reassurance about the Antarctic. Peters hadn't seen much military activity. Few people came by on Manton Road, other than residents. He'd been in Shingletown last week and seen a few refugees.

Although Eli was anxious about the news, he did not want to ask about it. Was there still concern about escaped convicts? News dies fast, especially when there is a bigger story seducing the public's focus. He changed the subject.

"I've noticed a lot of rocks in the fields all along the road." He and Peters were sitting in the cab of the pickup eating lunch. "I'd think they'd be a nuisance for farmers."

"You'd be wrong about that," said Peters. "Partly anyway. Matter of fact, those rocks are one of our crops, you might say. There's lots of rich folks down in the Bay Area who like those lava boulders around their swimming pools or out in the front yard. It's a lot of work, but you can get maybe a couple thousand dollars for one boulder."

It was another twist on Eli's rock theory. He had value even in his cruder state, if someone had only recognized it and made the effort to dig him out of the crust he was stuck in.

Late in the afternoon Arthur Peters and Eli washed their hands in an outdoor basin by the barn. Eli still had not been invited into the house. He felt good rapport with the older man, but he could sense a distance between them, unlike the welcome he had from Father Terrence at Our Lady of Peace Monastery. When Eli suggested he would resume his journey, Peters said, "Well, if you don't mind sleeping in the barn with Molly again, I'm going into Shingletown in the morning. I'll give you a lift that far."

Eli was grateful. The drizzle had intensified into rain, and a ride in the pickup would save him fifteen hundred feet of climbing in ten miles. Also, it would get him a good distance from Arthur Peters' farm. Maybe that was part of the farmer's motivation. Eli had earned his lodging, but the hospitality was limited.

FINALLY A MESSAGE from Kim. Charles was handed a note by the surgical suite receptionist, transcribed from a phone conversation:

"Daughter Kim fine, doing more working than sleeping. Says she'll know where to find you. Loves you."

A MOTHER and her two toddlers, raindrops drumming on their black umbrella, confront a half-dozen soldiers at a New Orleans Cemetery. "Sorry Ma'am," the squad leader says. "We have our orders. No entry." The street is channeling a three-inch-deep stream of Gulf water from overtaxed dikes into the burial grounds. The soldier looks the three-year-old boy in the eye and says, "Your daddy's in heaven. All they've got in there's his old body in a box. He himself ain't there, Son. Now take your mama home, and don't worry no more."

CHAPTER 31
Sunday, February 26

FROM SHINGLETOWN, Highway 44 was a straight avenue through coni-
fers, an easy ride, even in rain, to Viola. Then the road bent left and right, but it
rose so steadily that Eli was surprised when he passed the five thousand-foot
elevation marker, and again when he reached the summit, where a thin blanket
of snow lay on the road at nearly six thousand feet. There were more bicycles
on the road than trucks, and almost no cars, not enough traffic to maintain
black stripes of tire tracks in the dust of snow. Eli felt for his tires' contact with
the road, especially on the welcome downhill of what his map called the "scenic byway" in the Lassen National Forest.

When the rain stopped, he rode bare-headed down the sheltered track of
the mountain road. Under James Salas' parka he wore the wool sweater Father
Thomas had given him. He stopped to eat a sandwich provided by Arthur Peters' wife, and the last of his monastery apples—after a quarter-hour
meditation sitting on a fallen log.

At Old Station he studied his map. He was at the intersection of 44 and 89.
Should he go east on 44 toward Susanville, or north along Hat Creek on 89?
He decided on the latter. It seemed somewhat less mountainous and was a
more direct route to his vague destination, and he remembered that Susanville
was the location of High Desert State Prison. He would avoid prisons.

He rode only a few hundred yards when he came to a sign indicating a
"geological area" on the right. He checked his map by flashlight. He had arrived at Subway Cave. His curiosity and fatigue led him past a barrier, several
hundred yards to a parking lot closed for the winter. Patches of snow lay on
the ground. His flashlight helped him find the way to a stairway, down two
dozen steps to the yawning entrance of a lava tube. Dripping icicles extended
like fangs from cracks in the roof just inside the entrance. Eli lay his bicycle on
the floor of the cave and strode in several paces.

He could not touch the roof of the cave, and it was twenty feet wide. He
played the beam of his flashlight on walls the color of rhinoceros hide. Down
the tube the light was unable to penetrate. The floor was rough with rocks frozen for centuries into the ground. Eli searched for a smooth place and spread
Father Thomas' sleeping mat on the floor, covered himself with a wool blanket
and slept.

He awoke at intervals in utter darkness and snapped on his flashlight. Each time he was quite alone in silence. His surroundings, though macabre, had the advantages of isolation and security. When he had reassured himself by playing the light on the chamber walls as far as it could penetrate, he was able to doze again.

At last, pale daylight shone at the cave's entrance. The icicle teeth hanging in the circle of light brought to Eli's mind the view Jonah might have had as he was about to be deposited by the whale on the shore where God wanted him.

THE TELEPHONE LINE sounded like a sandstorm. After four attempts, this was the best Charles could do. Rose was telling him something about the women who had moved into the old Maxwell property. Friendly folks. Charles quoted his message from Kim. Rose had heard from Kim also, approximately the same message: she's okay, working hard, no social life. Charles briefly mentioned having dinner with Garth Elkins before ringing off, tired of shouting over the sandstorm. He was relieved to hear she felt quite safe and had more companionship than an affectionate dog.

CHAPTER 32
Monday, February 27

THE MORNING FOG turned successively lighter shades of gray, marking the sun's attempt to penetrate. Eli pedaled steadily, sometimes hearing Hat Creek when he couldn't see it. The fog layer lifted, revealing the scenic land-scape. He passed Black Angus Lane, and right on cue a herd of grazing cattle appeared in a bucolic meadow on the opposite side of the road. But the cattle were white. Just like prison, thought Eli, the whites segregated in their own place.

He had not eaten since the previous afternoon, and his hunger made him consider whether he might seek shelter at another farmhouse as he had with Arthur Peters. A gravel road off to the right led to a cluster of buildings about a half-mile off the highway. He followed it along a wire fence enclosing a field where a cluster of cattle munched clumps of grass. The top wire of the fence was barbed every foot or so, another reminder of prison. He felt a sense of unease creep over him, a premonition of danger. He slowed and wondered what besides the barbed wire might have induced this vague warning.

When he was within a hundred yards of the house, he stopped pedaling and called out, "Hello! Anybody home?" There was no response, no sound or movement. Two cows in the field did not even interrupt their grazing to look his way. He applied the brakes and repeated, "Hello?"

The feeling of unease intensified in him, it grew heavy. He measured the open space before him and resolutely pushed down on the pedal, as if pressing down a fear rising like a bubble.

A sharp crack startled him, and the gravel ahead of him exploded with a pinging sound. The shot had come from the house, or perhaps the barn. Eli jerked the brake lever as his left foot found the ground. He froze. The nearby cattle trotted a few steps, shifted their heads right and left, then resumed their munching. Eli saw that an upstairs and a downstairs window were open, but he could discern no movement within. Deliberately he picked up the bike he was straddling to turn it around. He lifted his hand in a gesture of surrender and farewell. The shot had been intended to scare him, he decided, or it had been fired by someone too tense to shoot straight. Either way, he had better be going.

A second bullet twanged on the ground behind him. Eli sprinted, pumping his legs with frenzy. The shooter was competent, he decided, and his message of unwelcome was definite. Eli was panting when he regained the highway, but he continued pedaling as fast as he could.

When his mind and his bike slowed a little, he thought of Eric Perez's pistol, still at the bottom of his pack. It would be dangerous ever to show it, especially if he faced someone armed with a loaded weapon. He pictured himself flinging it in a silver arc into the forest, where it might rust in a clump of moss. At last, however, he obeyed a faint prompting to retain it for future unknown service.

In such dark forests
    Even a bent weak sapling
        Might serve for a staff.

He arrived at the village of Hat Creek, where a gas station and general store offered the opportunity to buy a sandwich. Three older men were in the store, evidently locals. One wore a western hat, the other two baseball caps. With little deliberation, Eli chose a plastic-wrapped sandwich from a refrigerated cabinet, a bottle of cola and a bag of peanuts. He wanted to supply as little distraction as possible to their desultory conversation. He would appear to be a man in a hurry, with a definite destination. He even regretted having to wait for change, as the sound of the cash changing hands seemed to wrinkle the silence. He sensed he would supply the topic for the next hour's gossip.

119

Alone on the highway again, he found a secluded grove to eat his meal. Then he resumed his trek, feeling somber and alone, the fog descending once more in the gathering gloom.

Night had fallen when Eli arrived at the sign indicating "Flat River 87 miles" with an arrow pointing to the right. It was the intersection of Highway 299. For hours Eli had supported a burden of dread, a mysterious pall on his spirit that made his legs heavy and his progress slow. Again and again he saw images of San Quentin, and in every one loomed the dense and menacing presence of Dupree Ransom. He thought again of throwing Perez's gun into the woods, as if casting away any remnant of his contact with the malignant twosome. He did not do it, and the heavy images remained in his mind, pawing for attention like a hungry dog.

Eighty-seven miles, thought Eli, only a day or two to Flat River. He plodded on, as the fog thickened and dripped onto the pavement. He passed a sign for Cassel Road, and found the highway steeply descending. It was a long curvy stretch, and Eli felt pain across his tense shoulders, and in his hands as they clutched the brake levers.

The road bottomed out as he passed the sign indicating Hat Creek County Park. He had descended to the valley floor where Hat Creek flows into the Pit River. The fog had given way to heavy drizzle, and Eli wondered if he could find a picnic table under which he might lay out Father Thomas' camping mat to sleep for a couple of hours. He turned into the park entrance and peered into the darkness.

The dread that had weighed on him earlier pounced again. He sensed he was being followed, or was dragging a persistent burden.

He dismounted and walked his bike to a broadleaf tree. He leaned the bicycle against the trunk, and unfurled the camping mat, which he spread on the ground.

After a few minutes of stretching, he sat in half-lotus position to meditate. He would calm himself, or pursue the demon that was pressing him. He counted his breaths, from one to ten, beginning again when he lost track. His pulse and respiration slowed. Then the images came. Dupree Ransom's leering face. Erik Perez hulking behind him. James Salas kneeling in his underwear, Ransom pressing his foot to Salas' chest and pushing him back onto his elbows. Ransom embracing Pamela Lindsay like a gladiator, forcing her head back by pulling her hair behind her downward, pressing his face into her neck.

Eli's eyes flew open. He realized he had stopped breathing. He felt a weight of frustration, and gasped audibly.

He calmed himself again. *Where are these thoughts coming from? They're in me. I am giving life to evil.*

He gave his head a rough shake. *No! I asked forgiveness, and I am forgiven. But the evil is with me.* He would have to face it.

He stuffed the mat into his pack and remounted his bike. His eyes were brimming. He rode languidly, mechanically, preoccupied. His face was wet in the rain.

A chalky cliff loomed ahead, the road curving around it just beyond the place where Hat Creek flowed under the road. Eli forced himself to concentrate on steering among fist-size rocks left on the narrow shoulder by recent roadwork. A further awareness intruded: vehicle headlights were approaching from behind him.

Suddenly the handlebar twisted in his hands as the wheel struck a rock. His left hand lost its grip, and he jerked with his right. He overcorrected, struggling to regain control. The front wheel hit another rock and veered out into the road. Eli seized both brake levers and threw his right foot out for balance as he heard the liquid skidding of the vehicle. He caught a second's glimpse of headlights aiming left off the road. The side of an SUV was hurtling toward him. The rear bumper struck the front wheel of his bike, and Eli was thrown down. He landed on his right arm, clutched to his side to protect his ribs. His left forearm crossed his face, scraping the pavement.

Eli could not breathe. He rolled over onto his back, his right arm limp, his darkened left hand clawing up at the rain.

THE ROOKERY where Mt. Jackson's slope meets the sea is home to a hundred thousand chinstrap penguins. Twenty thousand are still hatching eggs. Another fifteen thousand are chicks. The stattaco trembling of the ground increases. Dislodged stones roll toward the water. As a wildfire might spread through tinder dry grass in a Santa Ana wind, first a few, then hundreds, then thousands of the penguins stampede for the ocean. Abandoned, unhatched eggs roll with the stones. Chicks, when they aren't trampled, scream and follow the nearest adult over the edge. Those who can, adults and chicks alike, propel themselves north to an assumed safety.

A RASPING SOUND grated inward as Eli's chest attempted breathing motions. But some valve was stuck closed, so he could neither inhale nor exhale. He continued feebly clawing at the sky, watching his helpless gesture with distended eyes.

121

Then a young woman was bending over him, straddling him. He tried to speak but made no sound. She clutched his belt and lifted his hips off the pavement. Eli felt his diaphragm relax and air rush into his lungs. He gasped and groaned, staring at the girl, nodding his head.

"Careful, Catherine. Don't move him," shouted a voice behind her. Eli could breathe now, and his whispered "Thanks" came out in a rush. She released his belt as a young man appeared and clutched her shoulders, staring down at Eli. He had a black eye and a cut and puffy lower lip.

"If he's hurt bad, you might make it worse by moving him," said the young man.

"I didn't think of that," she said. "I think he had his wind knocked out." Then she bent over Eli again. "Are you all right?"

Eli swallowed and closed his eyes, trying to locate the pain in his body. Raindrops pelted his face. "My arm hurts," he hissed.

"Can you stand up?" asked the young man.

"I think so," said Eli. He sat up, wincing with the pain in his right arm. He grabbed for it, and felt the scraping of the tender raw flesh of his left hand against his sleeve. He held his injured arm close at his side.

The young man labored at getting Eli to his feet. Eli felt a stab of pain in his right hip, but it subsided when he was able to balance himself on his feet.

The young woman trotted to their vehicle, parked slantwise on the highway, its headlights stabbing shafts of light into the rain, and returned with a plastic water bottle. She took Eli's bruised hand and poured a stream of water on it. He gasped, but held his hand steady. His right arm still hung limp, throbbing. He took tentative steps, and noticed a stab of hip pain each time his right foot bore his weight. He shuddered through an intake of air.

"Let's get you into the car," the girl said. They steadied him as he limped, and eased him into the back seat, which, Eli discovered, was already occupied by an anxious-looking older man. His head was wrapped in a cap of gauze bandages. Over his left shoulder a brown leather strap joined another that encircled the man's torso. A pistol and holster, Eli was sure, lay against the man's ribs.

"You okay?" the man asked.

"I'm n-not sure." Eli was still shivering. "My arm hurts."

He was aware of the young man and woman securing his bicycle with its bent front wheel to the luggage rack. Then she opened the back door of the vehicle and rummaged behind him as the young man set himself in the driver's seat and turned back toward him.

122

"I'm awfully sorry," he said. "It was hard to see you in the dark and the rain. I guess I was going too fast. I'm really sorry. We'll get you some help."

Eli couldn't decide what to say. He had no doubt that it was hard for the young man to see, with his swollen eye. He nodded and continued to tremble.

The girl closed the back and opened the rear passenger door, holding a wool blanket, which she draped over Eli and tucked in behind his shoulders. Eli felt warmth from the blanket and his shivering subsided. As the girl settled in the front seat, the young man continued his apologies.

"Let's go, Jason," the girl said.

The young man cranked the engine, and soon they were climbing the grade on the opposite side of the little canyon. Eli was comforted by the warmth of the car, but his arm continued to throb. They were all silent, carrying their curiosity in abeyance, staring ahead through the swishing windshield wipers. Occasionally one of them asked, "How you doing?" Each time Eli answered, "I'm okay." He lay his head against the window.

It finally occurred to the driver to ask, "Where were you headed, mister?"

Eli froze. He realized how strange it must appear to be traveling at night in the rain, on a lengthy journey. Even though bike trekking had recently become fairly common during the state of emergency, he must look somewhat desperate.

"I'm on a mission for a priest near Red Bluff." He repeated the excuse he had used with Farmer Peters, hoping its vagueness would suffice again.

"I think there's an emergency room open all night in McArthur," said Jason. "It's about ten miles ahead."

Eli's wrist throbbed. He tried to find a comfortable position for it. "I'd just as soon not see a doctor if I don't have to," he said. "I don't have any insurance or any money." *Or an adequate identity*, he added to himself.

After a strained silence the older man spoke up. "I'm Peter Addison," he said. "This is my daughter Catherine and her friend Jason. We're going to my brother-in-law's cabin south of Flat River. He's a doctor, and I'm sure he'll be glad to help you." Then he added absently, "We've just been through a difficult ordeal ourselves."

Eli was not surprised by the last revelation, and was burning with curiosity. "My name's James Salas," he said just loud enough to be heard over the sound of the engine. A name and a suggestion of ecclesiastical sanction might give him sufficient legitimacy. "What happened?"

"I have a home over by Mt. Shasta," said Addison. "Last night it was destroyed by men who attacked and tried to rob us."

The three of them recounted their ordeal for Eli. As they spoke he could see they had not completely processed it, that each was revealing or discovering new details or insights about the story and their reactions. Outrage and anxiety stirred them as they spoke. Eli imagined that Peter Addison took a sense of security from the weapon he was wearing.

Catherine heard a creak from the porch. Through the slats of venetian blinds she could see human forms in the darkness outside.

"Who's there?" she called. Peter and Jason looked up from the Scrabble game they were playing on the dining table by the light of a kerosene lantern. Votive lights and one long taper were lit on the coffee table across the room and another on Peter's desk under the stairwell. The cabin was heated by fire in a wood stove.

There was a shuffling on the porch, and then the door frame splintered as the heavy oak door crashed inward. Three dark men plunged in. Two were bulky in heavy jackets, the third was slight.

"Hey, get out of here!" yelled Peter.

"Shut up." The darkest of the bulky men sneered as he held out a pistol, showing it as if it was for sale. "We haven't eaten in the last two days, man, so we need some food and supplies, and the keys to your SUV out there. Just sit down and stay quiet and put the keys on the table."

Peter surveyed the scowling men, and produced the keys. The gunman watched them in a sullen silence while the other two rummaged through the house. The larger one ran upstairs, threw down blankets and pillows from a bedroom. The slight one had taken boxes and packages of food from the kitchen cupboards. Now he began stuffing them into the pillowcases. They worked quickly. The big man grabbed the car keys from the table and the two of them took their plunder out to load in the SUV. The gunman studied his prisoners with a faint smile, as if enjoying their forced docility. Peter glanced at his desk, where his pistol lay in the second drawer. When they left, he might get in a couple of shots.

But the gunman made no move to the door. He waited for his companions to return. They looked at him expectantly. He handed the gun to the larger one. "Keep 'em in their seats," he said. Then he strode directly toward Catherine.

"It's cold outside," he smirked. "Maybe we'll stay a while and warm up."

Jason stood next to her. "Leave her alone!"

The man backhanded Jason across the mouth, knocking him back into his chair. He grabbed Catherine's wrist and jerked her toward the stairs.

Catherine shrieked and kicked him in the leg.

"Bitch!" he shouted, and jerked her off her feet. He carried her kicking and grunting halfway up the stairs under his arm as if she were a bundle of laundry. He grinned back toward those below as if to elevate their terror or their amusement.

At the top of the stairs Catherine twisted out of his grasp, and he yanked her back to him. She brought up her knee toward his groin, but he twisted away. He slammed her against the wall, held her there with his powerful forearm across her chest and drew back his hand. "You ain't gonna be so pretty in a minute if you don't be nice."

Peter was sitting closest to the man with the gun, who was enjoying the show with slack-jawed attention. Peter lunged at him, knocking him off balance. He clutched the barrel of the gun and tried to twist it from the big man's hands. But he was much too strong, and hurled Peter across the room. His head thudded against his desk.

When Peter had made his first lunge, Jason followed, and now he was struggling for the gun, hampered by the slight man pulling at his shoulders.

Peter groped in the desk drawer for his own gun.

The big man crashed his left fist into Jason's face, staggering him. But the separation gave Peter an opportunity, and he fired. The big man howled as the bullet smacked into his right shoulder. His gun exploded and dropped to the floor. Jason crunched into him with a body block and dived for the gun.

The third man had staggered back with Jason, had seen Peter retrieving his gun. He rushed to Peter and grabbed the gun just after it fired. He wrested it away and pistol whipped Peter with it. He turned and fired just as Jason did. Jason's shot was truer. The man jerked back as the bullet slammed into his chest.

Jason spun back toward the larger man, slumped against the broken door, his face contorted with pain and the cords of his neck distended as he groaned at the ceiling. He staggered out the door.

At the first shot, the leader of the group had abandoned Catherine and started down the steps, but she jumped on his back and they tumbled together to the bottom. He sprang to his feet and yanked her up by her hair. He held her in front of him, shielding him from Jason's gun.

"Get out! Get out!" Jason was shouting. But his voice sounded far away to him. The gunfire had deafened everyone in the room. He saw Catherine's face red with anger and strain. The man embraced her firmly,

125

looking over her shoulder, inching with sidesteps toward the desk, where Peter lay unconscious and the third man dead, Peter's pistol resting on the lifeless fingers of his outstretched hand.

"Get out!" Jason shouted again. Catherine leaned to the side, but a savage jerk brought her upright with the man's forearm across her throat. Peter stirred. He raised himself on his elbow and looked around as if trying to understand the scene. He reached for his gun. The dark man was quick. He reached out with his left hand, grabbed the kerosene lantern from the dining table, and flung it at Peter. Glass shattered and there was an explosion of flame. A streak of fire sprang up along the floor where the kerosene spilled. It ignited the dead man, licked along Peter's arm, and leapt up the curtains beyond them. Peter rolled on the floor, trying to get away from the blaze and to suffocate the flame on his shirt.

The dark man sprang forward holding Catherine like a sack of groceries, shoved her at Jason and dodged toward the door. Jason and Catherine tumbled over the coffee table into a heap on the couch. When Jason regained his feet, he sprang to the doorway and fired once more. The intruder had bundled his wounded friend into a pickup truck parked on the road, blocking the driveway. The engine roared and they sped away.

Jason turned to help Catherine with her father, who had torn off his burning clothes. She tugged him to the kitchen to splash water on him.

Jason seized a throw rug from the floor and beat at the flames on the kerosene soaked floor and open-eyed corpse. But it was futile. They spread to the desk, where paper blazed up brightly, and were eating into the wooden wall behind it.

Peter urged the youngsters toward the door. He knew the air in a burning room was more dangerous than the fire. Catherine ignored him and dashed up the stairs while Jason continued to beat the flames. She ran back in a minute with an armful of clothing. Now Peter clutched her arm and pulled her to the door. Jason followed them out, with a last glance at the forsaken immolated robber, from whose hand he had lifted Peter's gun.

Catherine scooped handfuls of snow for the men to hold on their throbbing injuries. Peter dressed in the SUV. He insisted that Catherine hold one of the pistols, in case of the attackers' return. She flinched and dived behind the SUV when a volley of shots crackled inside the house. The fire had found Peter's ammunition box.

"Let's get the hell out of here!" shouted Catherine. She drove to the fire station as the two men each peered out a window with a weapon ready.

The fireman on duty made several radio calls and fired up the lone truck in McCloud. He told the Addison family to wait at the health care clinic on Minnesota Avenue for the doctor and sheriff's deputy he had summoned. They waited an hour, resuming their armed vigilance, before a doctor arrived. Peter cautioned that they couldn't relax, since one of the attackers might also seek medical attention.

The doctor could add only aspirin to Catherine's original treatment of Jason: ice packs for the swelling. He said he would like to have an x-ray to help diagnose Peter's head injury, likely a concussion. But x-rays were out of the question, since there was no power available, except perhaps in Mt. Shasta. Peter preferred not to go there. He had a headache, but decided his injury was not serious.

"My brother-in-law is a doctor and his wife's a nurse. They're near Flat River. We can be there in a few hours."

It wasn't so easy. The sheriff's deputy, after hearing their story, insisted they make a full report at the Mt. Shasta office. He would accompany them there. "I'll get you some breakfast too. You've been through a tough night."

Everything took longer than anticipated, and it would be nearly evening again before they were released. An x-ray was taken at the hospital. The investigator, when he arrived, pressed for many details, particularly descriptions of the perpetrators and their vehicle. "Sometimes details occur to you hours or days later. Be sure to let us know if you think of anything else."

They stopped to see the devastation at their property. It was completely destroyed. They could salvage nothing. Jason and Catherine alternated driving numbly eastward through snow and rain squalls.

"You were lucky," said Eli. "Sounds like those men would have killed you."

Ransom and Perez? Eli had pictured them as the attackers. Had he not felt their presence as he biked along? He had stopped to meditate in the dismal park at Hat Creek, to deal with the heavy cuff of evil enclosing him. He felt certain of it. The conviction settled in his mind—Ransom and Perez, and maybe one of the guys who helped in the escape. They might have heard news reports suggesting they would flee south and were trying to cross up the cops. And it was common for San Quentin's inmates to speculate on this isolated northeastern corner of California as an escape destination, or a route to Canada. But now they would be desperate and without support, as Eli had been before arriving at the monastery. What further havoc might they produce, taking advantage of the chaos in society and the diluted effectiveness of law enforcement? They had found an isolated cabin with the faint beacon of firelight and lantern glow, an opportunity to rob and terrorize. Eli admired this little family for standing up to the scummy brutes. They had been lucky. Perez was dumber than he was degenerate, and Ransom always had to add domination to his depravity.

But his conviction wavered when he considered the sheer unlikelihood of such a coincidence. And Ransom and Perez would need the infrastructure of a metropolitan area to survive—they thrived on action and had more useful skills, and more support, in an urban setting. Besides, there was apparently no shortage of desperate people these days.

The third man. They had described him as black, as Eli had been described by news reports. Perhaps he had been burned beyond recognition, and it might be assumed that Elias Barnes, the third escaped convict, had died in the McCloud incident. The thought quickened Eli's heartbeat. He felt lightheaded. He might be on the brink of a new life, stepping out of the past as through a door, with a blank record, a new birth. For even if the perpetrators were not Ransom and Perez, they might be thought to be.

"I guess you can say we were lucky," Peter Addison said. "But somehow I don't feel lucky."

"I'm sorry. I didn't mean to make light of a terrible experience."

"It's okay. I know what you meant, and you're right. It's sort of like saying that you were lucky because we're on our way to see my brother-in-law, who's a doctor. It's probably better if we just go straight there, instead of stopping in Bieber or Flat River."

"I think going straight to the cabin would save a lot of time," Catherine said.

Peter studied Eli. "What about it, James? Can you hold on for an hour or two?"

"No problem." Eli felt relieved. They all recognized that community services had been stretched thin by the crisis, and that strangers were unwelcome, as their own experience had shown was a reasonable posture.

In the silence that followed, Eli studied Catherine, who was now driving. She must be full of rage and disgust, having been violated by the actions and threats of her attacker, by his very presence. She has the fire of a warrior princess.

And Jason. He's exhausted and demoralized. He must be reviewing the attack again and again in his mind, re-experiencing his wrath as he feels his pulse pounding in his swollen eye. What might he have done to forestall those terrible events? Peter was likely to share those feelings, along with lamenting the loss of his property.

They were all in shock, Eli concluded. He sat up straight, focused on relaxing his shoulders and breathing. He was surprised how much the letting go of tension eased his pain, although his swollen wrist still throbbed. Peter Addison was right without realizing it. Eli was lucky. And more than lucky. He felt himself once again under the care of Providence. He gave thanks for the family's deliverance, and his own.

"If you don't mind," Eli broke the silence, "I'd like to say a prayer." He waited, but there was no comment. Then he began, in the manner he had learned through years of services, the Retreats, and Bible study classes in San Quentin's Garden Chapel.

"Heavenly Father, we know that you are with us. We are thankful, Father, for deliverance from evil. We are exhausted and frightened by the evil in the world, but we are refreshed, Father, by your grace and your providence. I ask that you continue to travel with us, to bless this man who has lost his home, and these young people who have undergone such hardship and terror, with the light of your guidance. Let them live in your love, and be strong for the path ahead. May we not be overcome by trials, for we know that you are mightier than any evil, and you bring good to the world, as you sent your Son to lead us in your way. Send your healing upon me and upon Peter and Catherine and Jason, for I feel that you have sent them as a blessing in my life. We ask this in the name of your Son, Jesus Christ."

They all murmured "Amen."

HAD IT BEEN less than two weeks? Weariness weighed on Charles like a heavy coat. Casualties had increased, and the workdays lengthened. He saw at least one C-130 cargo plane roar off each day. He had heard no more from Kim, and struggled once again through a grainy call to Rose, who also had no further contact with their daughter, but seemed pleased to have met the two women who had moved into the Maxwell property.

It seemed incomprehensible that all this chaos could result from something that was yet to happen. *A mere one-foot rise in the seas—the world is challenged, but adjusting. Now a new threat? So the media says. But scientists insist sea level will rise no further, now. And yet there were vacated neighborhoods, shortages of goods and manpower, strife in the cities, martial law. How credible is the threat?* he wondered. He tried to call his brother-in-law, Peter, to ask his updated opinion. There was no answer at Peter's home in Davis, or at his university office.

Charles left messages and tried the McCloud cabin.

"We're sorry," intoned a mechanical female voice. "That number has been disconnected, or is no longer in service."

CHAPTER 33

Tuesday, February 28

IT WAS HOURS PAST MIDNIGHT.

"There doesn't appear to be any bony displacement." Rose Royer supported the forearm of the man introduced as James with her own, tucking his elbow against her ribs and holding his hand in hers so the wrist was straight. She pressed inquiringly on the bones and got no reaction. "Hold your wrist firm now," she said. Gently she moved his hand up, then down, and each time the man winced and drew in breath.

"I'm pretty sure it's not broken," she said. "We'd need an x-ray to tell for sure, but a fracture of one of the middle bones might not show up for a couple of weeks. I think if we treat it as a sprain, give it rest and ice and keep it immobilized, we'll see if the pain subsides in a week or so. I hope Charles can be here by then. He's a surgeon."

It had been a surprise to Peter Addison that his brother-in-law was not there to welcome him upon arrival. The last he had heard, Charles and Rose were setting up their cabin for a long stay. Then telephone communication became sporadic and undependable. Rose explained that Charles was called by his Air Force Reserve commander to report to Travis two weeks ago. He had insisted Rose stay in their rural cabin, where she would be safer. "He was relieved when I told him I've met the two women who moved into the old Maxwell property up above. They're very nice."

Rose eased James' hand to his side. "Let's have a look at you, Peter."

"The doctor in Mt. Shasta has already taken care of me. He says I'll have a headache for a couple of days, but I'll be okay. What I think we could use is some sleep, those of us that can."

Comfort might be elusive for both James and Peter, Rose considered, on beds in the cabin's two bedrooms. Jason fell asleep on a cot in the loft. As the three men slept, Catherine drank tea with her aunt, filling in details of the story that had been quickly told. Rose did not press her for the more painful items. She asked about James.

"We really don't know much about him. He told us he's on a mission for a priest. He's pretty stoical, and religious. He seems like he's been around the block, though, someone who can take care of himself."

When Eli sat up in bed, pain and stiffness gnawed at him. He twisted into his clothes and found he could not assume the lotus position on the floor for meditation. He sat on a desk chair in the bedroom. He was aware of morning stirring in the house, murmured conversation, as if to avoid disturbing sleepers.

He found a comfortable position with his back straight and relaxed. Edward, the Zen meditator he had sat with in San Quentin, had described what he called "healing meditation." "Call to mind a happy moment that might bring a smile to your lips," Edward had told him. "Capture the energy of the smile in your imagination, and direct the energy to the parts of your body in need of healing."

Easier said than done when you're in prison. But at length Eli had remembered seeing a little boy in a park in Bakersfield, maybe two years old, running with great delight toward a ball in the grass. The toddler's arms were bent at acute angles rotating around his chubby torso, his stubby legs with dimpled knees kicking out in a jerky gait. He was free and unburdened, holding nothing back from his exertion. Eli waited until the vision reappeared, felt his own smile matching the boy's, held the feeling in his eyes, in his throat, then felt it migrate to his wrist, his hip, his left hand. He imagined the energy warming these sites, penetrating them with light.

Some minutes later thoughts intruded. He was not comfortable here, didn't know how he fit in or what he was to do. He had got smug about improvising, about the protection of Providence. He realized, however, that the sense of dread which was growing just before the traffic accident might have been a message that he didn't have much direction or plan, that he was lost after the security of the monasteries. He was grateful that at least now he had a concrete situation, however vague and undetermined, that did not threaten him.

The most pressing need was physical healing. He didn't know the condition of his bike, if he were well enough to travel on it. Maybe the best thing was to seek bed and board here for a few days like he did with Arthur Peters. These folks seemed to feel responsible for him, and maybe he could make himself useful to earn his keep.

Or could this be the destination he had sought? If they would accept him, perhaps there was nothing better to hope for.

Freed to roam the world—
     Whither? The path is gloomy
     And I am limping.

He prayed for his mates at San Quentin, blessed James Salas and the man whose bicycle he had stolen, and Arthur Peters. As his meditation trailed into dream-vision, he saw again the woman with the candle. She seemed to be both Sharon and Pamela now.

A knock on the door, and Peter Addison peered in. "James," he murmured, "breakfast will be ready soon if you'd like to join us. Are you feeling OK?"

"Thanks, yes, I'll be right out." The room swirled around Eli when he stood, and he steadied himself against the wall before going out to join the family.

Rose was on him right away, checking his injuries. "We'll soak that hand in Epsom salts and get your arm in a sling to make it more comfortable. But first, sit down and have some pancakes."

Eli resisted the attention, but Rose insisted on mothering him. He was delighted, but embarrassed. Eating left-handed was awkward.

Peter and Jason also were mothered. Rose changed the bandage on Peter's head, reducing it to the size of a credit card, so his injury seemed diminished, and Catherine massaged Jason's shoulders. The men were subdued, depressed, needing and taking comfort from the women. Peter wondered aloud what was to be done. News reports had cities increasingly unsafe and travel dangerous too, and they might have to stay at the Royer cabin until calm was restored.

A rap at the front door startled Eli. His head jerked toward the sound, and he realized the movement called attention to him. His eyes met Catherine's for a moment. Catherine opened the door, but Rose bustled past her to welcome visitors she apparently expected.

"Come in," she said to two women and a man. "It's good to see you again, Darcy," she said to the younger woman. "This is my brother-in-law Peter Addison, and his daughter Catherine and her boyfriend Jason Lowery."

"And this is James," Rose said of Eli. "The poor man was knocked off his bicycle last night, and Peter brought him here so we can take care of him." Eli grinned and nodded awkwardly.

Rose introduced Darcy Malone as "One of those nice people I told you about, from up at the old homestead." She asked about Darcy's mother, Mariah, and Darcy's children, then looked expectantly at the couple.

It was Darcy's turn. She said, "Paisley Overcroft and..."

The man shot his hand toward Rose and interrupted, "Hi, I'm Ray Over-croft." His craggy but youthful face was untutored by deception, Eli decided; it would not disguise the man's feelings. "We have a farm down by Likely." Eli did not offer his injured hand, nor did Peter or Jason, but they nodded and smiled at the newcomers.

The Overcrofts gave brief background details. They had been Peace Corps volunteers in India, after which Ray worked as a farm equipment salesman in Davis. When they inherited a small legacy, they bought their farm in Modoc County. "A few days ago we met Darcy and her mother," Ray said, "and brought them up here to their property."

Darcy explained, "My mother inherited it from an uncle recently. We'd never seen it." Eli sensed a deeper story, and wondered if he would ever get to hear it.

As Rose brewed a pot of tea, Peter gave a capsule version of the calamity in McCloud, interrupted by frequent questions, gasps of outrage.

Ray and Paisley worried that something like the Addisons' tragedy could happen at their place, just off the highway. Darcy offered to let them store some of their belongings in the homestead barn.

An uncomfortable silence ensued. Eli wondered if the barn might include a sleeping place for him, like he had had at the Peters farm. He would not take Rose's bed again.

Suddenly Eli became alert, returning to the flow of the conversation, just as Rose was saying, "...feeling better now, James, I suppose?" He looked at Jason as if expecting a response from him. Then his mind clicked: James—that's me! He pulled himself together and said, as calmly as he could, "Oh yes. That is, I'm still a little stiff in a couple of places. But I'll be good as new in a day or two." A quizzical expression from Catherine disappeared in a blink.

Eli gave only a sketch of his own background, saying he grew up in the San Joaquin Valley, was in the army, worked in oil fields, and recently spent time in a monastery. "I was on a confidential mission for the abbot when I ran into you folks." He told himself that he had preserved honesty, although not integrity. He had told no lies. It might bite me in the butt later, but it's all I can afford right now. He felt himself cower into the refuge of personal histories that filled the afternoon's space and time. His own story he knew could take its place among them, but he would lock it away in a strongbox of shame and fear, and be glad of the sufficiency of his cover. He was on a mission for the abbot of Saint Mary's Monastery. His reticence confirmed that it was confidential, and no one questioned him.

Discussion turned to their isolation that was at once a blessing and a burden, and the enormous changes occurring in the world. Eli understood that all of them left the bulk of their thoughts and feelings unarticulated. Himself most of all.

Darcy was without her husband, as was her mother, but they were hopeful of their men's survival. Rose was confident her own husband and daughter were safe and productively occupied, but she wished they would arrive soon.

When they learned of Dr. Addison's background, Darcy and the Overcrofts peppered him with questions about the seriousness of the natural disaster the world faced. Peter and Jason created for them a picture of the earth's structure and the natural forces at work. "I'm afraid our foot dragging on global warming for the last thirty years might have exacerbated some naturally occurring calamities," Peter said. "Our hope is that it's something we can deal with. For now, perhaps our stay here might be somewhat lengthy, until the government gets a grip on environmental defense and civil order."

Darcy made a sound that might have been a groan. "My mother had a dream last night. She believed it was saying we're likely to be here for an extended time." Eli sensed that Darcy was a commando, someone to be reckoned with, not soft and gentle like Pamela or Sharon, but a straight shooter. She seemed strangely upset by her mother's dream, though, not so commando-like when she spoke of her mother.

A discussion ensued of the resources of the Royer household. Rose claimed supplies enough for an indefinite stay, but speculated on the need to expand her garden.

"I have a little experience with gardening," offered Eli, acutely aware of his exaggeration. "And I'm willing to earn my keep."

"Now don't you worry about that," said Rose. "You wait until you're healed before you start thinking about work. You're welcome to stay with us as long as you need to. Or want to," she added.

Questions were left unasked, Eli thought. "Thanks." He suddenly wished he were alone. "But I insist on sleeping on the floor. I do okay on the floor. In the monastery you get used to a little hardship." His words seemed to hang in the air like exhausted butterflies. He felt Catherine examining them.

"James," said Rose, "I think a cot in the barn might be comfortable enough. We can use your strength and skills when you're recovered."

Darcy equaled the offer. "You could sleep at our place, too, James. The barn has some clean rooms I'm sure will be suitable. If you'd like, come up tomorrow and take a look. I agree with Rose, there's no need to sleep on the floor. We have lumber for bedframes."

Eli's heart jumped at the suggestion. Privacy and anonymity. A barn would be the right place for me right now, he thought.

CHAPTER 34
Wednesday, March 1

DURING Dr. Charles Royer's late afternoon rounds, there was a distinct increase in men with camouflage fatigues bustling in the hallways, packing and stacking. They dismantled computers, work stations. The hospital appeared to be in the midst of remodeling. Or moving. Charles spent several minutes at one bedside to watch the news with a soldier recovering from surgery. The report was bland and repetitive, noting the deployment of government troops to quell unrest in coastal states, quoting calm messages from various scientists, detailing the availability of relief supplies.

Something disquieting was making its way into Charles' mind, but it took some minutes for him to formulate the thought. There were almost no reports from other countries. It was as if the American populace had enough to worry about without the panic in the rest of the world. Surely this was typical of American insularity, but, Charles realized, in this case the absence of news was chilling.

A corporal waltzed a load of boxes down the hall on a hand truck. "Where are you guys taking all this stuff?" asked Charles.

"I'm just taking it to a truck in the parking lot, Sir."

Charles walked along with him for a few paces. "Well, where's it going?" The man did not know.

Charles stalked to the office of Dr. Elliot, the Chief of Medicine.

"What's going on, Carl?"

Dr. Elliot pulled off his wire-rimmed glasses and polished them with his handkerchief. He appeared to be composing his thoughts. "Charles, all I can tell you is that as of now we're not admitting anyone to this facility. Within a few days we will be transferred to Denver, following the implementation of a contingency plan, but it's top secret."

Charles tilted his head, as if to enter Dr. Elliot's field of vision. "What's the contingency?" he asked.

The Chief of Medicine fixed Charles in his sober stare. "Charles, a half-hour ago a tsunami from Antarctica struck the Falkland Islands. It's very large, and heading north."

135

Charles strove to comprehend, to picture what Dr. Elliot had told him. "Is there any way I can get in touch with my daughter?" he asked.

"Do you know her email address?"

KIM OPENED the email.

> From: carl_elliot@grantmedcenter.org
> To: kim_royer@parker.house.gov
> 5:55 p.m. pst Mar 1
> Kim,
> Carl Elliot is loaning me his email. I'm sure you know about the terrible news. I know your head must be spinning. If you get this message, write back to Carl's email and let me know your situation. It looks like I might have to move, can't tell you where yet. I'm worried sick about you. Let me hear from you.
> Love, Dad

She replied

> From : kim_royer@parker.house.gov
> To: carl_elliot@grantmedcenter.org
> 9:01 p.m. est Mar 1
> Dad,
> We're arranging transportation. No time to write more. I'll reach you from wherever we land.
> Love, Kim

Kim wanted to cry, wanted to throw her computer. Instead she steeled herself to her task, uploading files to a secure remote site. Part of her watched herself working robot-like, holding down the cover of her emotions. She had been operating on too little sleep, too much strain, as had Thad Parker and nearly everyone else in government. And now the blow had come.

The denials and downplaying had all been false. Those at the top had known for some time—a week, a month? The predicted disaster in Antarctica was inevitable. Only its extent was unknown. Contingency plans had been constructed and prioritized, modified each day as top secret information had been corroborated or invalidated. She had picked up hints, puzzle pieces.

Then in the late afternoon she had nearly collapsed from exhaustion. Her muscles twitched and cried out for sleep. In desperation she lay on the carpet behind her desk and closed her eyes. It would only be a few minutes, she thought. She felt her spine come to alignment on the floor, felt her neck relax.

"Energy grid… California…" Words penetrated Kim's consciousness. She blinked her eyes. The voices came nearer. They were at the door of Thad Parker's inner office. "There's no choice about this, Parker," a gravelly voice said.

"You're talking about millions of people, General Austin," Thad Parker's voice rasped.

"Tens of millions, maybe," said the gravelly voice. Kim was quite awake now. How long had she been out? She lay still. "It's a goddam shame," the voice continued, "but it might come to that. Just be ready to implement the plan. We'll help as many as we can, but there's no way to save the California Aqueduct. Without it we just can't feed the population inland and on the West Coast both. Diablo Canyon and all the other coastal power plants will be disabled for years, too. The resources don't exist, Thad, to float the whole ship. We'll probably be diverting power inland too, from Washington, Oregon and California, except for the south."

"You can't do that," Parker said. "Without power, they'll be without water—they'll die like flies. Of course the aqueduct provided most of California's drinking water anyway, so…"

"No use fighting it. The plan's done. Be ready. Now let's get going."

Kim felt the general's heavy footsteps vibrate the floor beneath her. He stalked past her desk, out the door. She scrambled to her feet and waited for her head to clear. Thad was staring at her from his doorway, his face a blend of surprise and dismay.

"I fell asleep, Thad. I'm really exhausted." Her voice croaked.

Parker closed his eyes and breathed a long sigh that trembled at the end. "Kim, there's a helicopter waiting to take us to Reagan Airport, or maybe Andrews Air Base. We have to leave this instant. Our lives may be at risk. That tidal wave is coming up the Atlantic and it may reach us here in D.C.—they don't know for sure. But you're with me on the evacuation list for top government. Thank God. We're going to Sacramento, get my wife and kids. Then we'll have to move to Denver."

"ARE YOU OKAY?"

"I was meditating."

"Oh, sorry."

Eli reassured Jason. The young man probably imagined him grieving, Eli thought, as he himself would have been doing in Eli's motionless posture. Eli still could not assume the lotus position, so he sat on an old steamer trunk in the small barn Jason and Catherine had swept and furnished with two army cots and sleeping bags. Cappy the golden retriever had made it a dormitory for three. Eli decided to accept Darcy's offer. He would walk up to the Maxwell place after breakfast to meet Darcy's mother and children.

"Is that a habit from the monastery?"

"We did it every day." Eli chided himself for skirting the truth. "Maybe you'd like to try it sometime. It's as easy as breathing, but as hard as knowing yourself."

KIM SURRENDERED to a swarming dizziness as soon as they were in the long queue of planes awaiting takeoff to California. Reagan International airport had been a pandemonium. MPs and squads of Army troops cordoned off entrances and manned boarding gate ramps. Lines of people stretched out onto the tarmac to board smaller planes. Every plane, both civilian and military, was full and overfull.

"I'm supposed to be on this plane!" a red-faced man had shouted, waving a fan of folded documents. "You can't let it leave without me."

"Sir," an MP said curtly, "the ramp is locked. We'll get you on the next flight. Please be patient, Sir." The MP held his baton in front of him at waist level.

People had abandoned their assigned lines to plead with MPs who appeared to be more flexible. Some were abandoning luggage in their effort to secure passage. Kim had seen a young boy crying, searching for his lost mother in the swarm of adults.

"Stay right with me, Kim." Thad Parker had guided her through the crowd until they found the barrel-shaped General Austin, whom Kim recognized by his voice. They had been escorted by their own MP down a set of stairs to a knot of thirty people waiting on the tarmac to board a twenty-four passenger jet. Security and safety regulations were surely compromised.

It had been a terrible hour and a half waiting for takeoff. From the air, Kim saw solid headlights on every street and highway, heading west. But nothing was moving. When clouds obliterated the nightmare on the ground, exhaustion closed in and she was lost to nightmares of her own.

PATAGONIAN TOOTHFISH circle the cable connecting the ocean floor to the clicking buoy, uncomprehending of its mission to beam tsunami warnings via satellite to the world. A quarter-mile east, the Henge Clipper II steams south. On the surface of the open sea, to all but a high-tech buoy, a tsunami is but an imperceptible swell, offering no danger to ship nor creature. Sir Oliver Denton's manse in Cornwall has been swept into history, but his winter ranch on the Australian north coast will yet serve him. He says to his first mate, "The world will recover. We will fulfill our goal at the Vinson Massif and proceed to Australia."

ASSUMING the Dulles Terminal Control Area was too busy to handle Visual Flight Rules traffic, Ricky Milyus cruised his DeHavilland Dash 8 at low altitude. At last he spotted the flashing green and white beacon of the Winchester Regional Airport, and tuned his radio to 122.7, Winchester's published frequency. He was ferrying employees of Skylark Aviation out of Manassas, Virginia—and their families, along with four boys from the high school who had volunteered to fly in the baggage hold—to higher ground in Winchester, about forty-five miles northwest.

Radio traffic indicated he was tenth in line in the landing pattern, after a Cessna, whose lights he picked up seven miles out. He fell in behind the Cessna and slowed to 80 knots. He was relieved when he saw the runway lights defining their destination. It all looked so normal, but every aircraft was involved in the same quite extraordinary emergency, and there were quickly five more aircraft behind him in the landing pattern.

On the ground the passengers were greeted by volunteers from the Winchester Baptist congregation and taken to an emergency shelter. Ricky taxied immediately to the queue awaiting takeoff from the lighted runway. Another group of those alerted to the impending ruin, discouraged by the stalled highways, would be huddled on the tarmac in Manassas.

In the night sky, twenty-five minutes later he gripped the controls tightly, gazing into an ominous blackness below, still fifteen miles short of Manassas. As if he had passed over the coastline, everything ahead of him was black under a horizon marked by stars. He set the radio to the Manassas frequency, and heard only silence. "Manassas Tower, this is DeHavilland 178 Romeo. Do you read me?" He repeated it half a dozen times.

"DeHavilland 178 Romeo, this is Barron 2368 Alpha," another aircraft cut in. The voice rolled like an empty barrel. "The lights winked off down there twenty minutes ago. The tower is down."

The sight hidden in darkness from Ricky Milyus nevertheless appeared stark and horrible in his mind: the control tower, which had been trucked in from Colorado and reassembled at Manassas Regional Airport in 1992, would be horizontal amid saturated debris and corpses. He groaned and rubbed violently the tears from his cheeks. He saw only moonlight glimmer reflected below as he banked grimly and headed west.

CHAPTER 35
Thursday, March 2

THE SURGERY SUITE had become as noisy as a construction site. Men were dismantling the operating rooms, crating the recovery room machinery. Bedding was stacked in the halls. Charles was ordered to prepare patients for med-evac flights. Ambulatory patients were wheel-chaired to buses to be transported to the airfield. Late in the afternoon, Charles rode in an ambulance tending two of his patients who had to be loaded into a plane on stretchers. The tarmac was cluttered with crates and pallets. Crews were loading two giant C-130s.

"Hey, Colonel Doctor!" Charles whirled to meet the familiar salute of Captain Garth Elkins. "What have you got for me, some delicate passengers?"

Charles prolonged their handshake to lead the pilot away from his plane, as if to seek a quieter place for conversation. "Garth, you know about this contingency plan, don't you?"

They stared at each other for a second, each divining the other's thoughts. Garth nodded.

"I'll be back for you tomorrow." Garth's voice rose over the engine noises vibrating the air. "Charles, it looks like the government has decided it can't save everyone and we've got to put our resources into saving as many as we can. Into surviving this thing somehow."

"Surviving what? The U.S. military has been policing impossible situations all over the world ever since we were in Vietnam. Korea, in fact. Why can't we concentrate our resources here, in our own country? I know the situation is difficult, but we can't just abandon people." He grasped the younger man's shoulder, as if holding him accountable for the enormity of the decision.

Garth clamped a hand on Charles' forearm. His stare was compassionate and questioning. "You haven't heard, have you? Charles, I flew your daughter and the Congressman to Sacramento this morning. They're moving their headquarters to Denver also." He glanced over his shoulder to see if anyone was nearby. "I asked Kim to level with me, and she told me that a tidal wave hit New York today. Millions of people are lost."

The blow reeled him. He dropped his hands and opened his mouth as if to speak.

"We're crippled, Charles. We're not even sure what resources we have. I know it's the worst thing we've ever had to deal with. Worse than the terrorism, worse than the sabotage, worse than the goddam wars."

"Garth, I..." Charles grimaced and shook his head as if to clear away the forming picture. "I can't be part of this. A lot of good people will just get swallowed up. What about Rose? What about..."

"Charles, I'm sure they'll send someone to get Rose. They'll probably send you to get her yourself. Just be ready tomorrow. We'll need all the good people we can get."

ELI FELT UNEASY the first morning after a night in the homestead barn. But Mariah Wallace had been a gracious host at breakfast and assured Eli of his welcome. Now he and Jason were staking out a garden plot in the field near the Royer cabin.

Catherine's shrill voice reached Eli, but her words were indistinct, muffled from inside the cabin. He frowned, straining to discern Catherine's shouting. She flung open the back door. "Jason, James, come quick. Something's happened."

Eli dropped his ball of twine. "Okay, I'm coming right now. I'm coming."

Catherine clutched the door, breathless. "The radio says a tsunami is flooding the East Coast. You know, a big tidal wave. It sounds terrible."

Jason stared at her, paralyzed. "The whole East Coast?" She reached toward him.

Eli read their tacit communication. "I'll go get Darcy and Mariah."

In minutes, he was back with them, and Darcy's children. In the Royers' living room, everyone was clustered around the radio table. A deep voice said there was no danger on the West Coast, that the levee projects were successful. Rose started to ask a question, but Peter held up his hand. "We'll bring you further details as soon as they become available," said the deep voice.

Peter twisted the volume knob. "They're talking about a volcanic eruption last night in Antarctica down at the south end of the Atlantic Ocean. Near as I can tell, it started a tidal wave that came all the way up the Atlantic and hit the East Coast. They say the President and much of the government were evacuated to Texas. Rose just turned the radio on a few minutes ago, so I don't really know..."

Peter was interrupted by urgent honking from the front drive. Jason and Peter stepped out to meet Ray and Paisley Overcroft. "My God," Ray sputtered, "you can't believe what's happening. I don't know where to start."

Paisley looked ashen. They all went inside. Catherine dragged two more chairs from the kitchen.

Paisley described a mob scene at the Hotel Niles in Flat River.

Ray interrupted. "People were standing around the street outside the hotel, because inside, the town muckety-mucks had some kind of radio gear they were getting police broadcasts on. Every now and again, one of them would appear at the second-story balcony with a battery megaphone and tell everybody what word was coming in.

"They all kept talking about Mt. Jackson this, Mt. Jackson that. Seems Mt. Jackson's a big volcano down on Antarctica. They said it blew up last night. They said half the mountain fell into the ocean and started a tidal wave."

"Oh shit," said Peter. "I've read studies about such possibilities on Hawaii or the Canary Islands. I sent a message to the White House warning about just such a possibility. It is unbelievable."

Ray continued, "The official government broadcasts, according to people in the crowd, didn't really say much about what was happening in the East. We listened on the truck radio too…"

"I know," said Peter. "What we heard's damn skimpy."

"In town, some said the government didn't really know," Ray went on, "because all the communications were down. Someone said the Internet went down. But there's a kid in town who works at Chet Ragland's store they call 'the geek' who has a short wave radio and heard reports from other short wave operators out East. And some County Sheriffs have cop pals in cities like Sacramento and Fresno who have special communications equipment and inside information. Some of it's even from the military, they were saying."

"People were sort of hysterical," Paisley cut in. "I couldn't tell if it was one wave or a lot of waves. They were talking about waves hundreds of feet high."

Peter looked solemn. "That's what the physics predicted from the Canaries—a cascade of waves, the first one four hundred fifty feet high on the eastern seaboard." He shook his head at the rug, paced toward the window as if to discern more clearly by looking outside.

Ray didn't break pace. "I heard they washed right over New York City, Miami, Atlantic City. Other people were pooh-poohing those stories. Some said a wave swamped Washington D.C. Some claimed the government knew ahead of time. People were getting ready to fight each other over that one. Whatever, the government seemed to get all the top dogs out of Washington and the military installations. They all went to Texas. That's where the official government broadcasts were from anyway. Of course, wouldn't you know. Texas. I'll bet they did know ahead of time."

"It was so confusing," Paisley said. "But the men who came out on the balcony seemed extremely serious and frightened."

"I thought things looked ugly," said Ray, "like maybe the crowd would get out of control. So I said to Paisley, 'Let's get out of here.' Before we left town, though, we went by Chet's and checked your email, Mariah." Ray handed Darcy a single sheet, then fixed his eyes on the rug.

"Reinhold," Darcy said. Looking at Eli she added, "My husband." She read the message. "He sent this from New York, apparently just before the wave hit." She handed the page to her mother. Mariah read it, closed her eyes for a moment, and murmured to Darcy, "He survived."

Was she refusing painful knowledge? Eli wondered. Her words held a note of certainty, not merely comfort.

Catherine and Rose sank into the couch on either side of a stoical Jason. Cappy the golden retriever laid his chin on Jason's knee, as if aware of his special ability to console. The women tried to reassure him about what might have happened to his family in Maryland. "We just don't know, do we?" he said. "All we have is hope."

Peter broke the ensuing silence. "It's going to take us a while to get the real story. I'm sure it's true the government can't assess the damage."

Everyone deferred to Peter's clarifications and probability assessments of the hundreds of speculations flying around the room. Occasional new facts spilled out of the government broadcasts. "Damage" was being reported from, or about, places like London, Rio de Janeiro, the Ivory Coast, Capetown. One report said everything on the Falkland Islands had been destroyed. There was a consistent chorus about how safe the West Coast would be because the tsunamis were all in the Atlantic. Peter translated "damage" as "probably total destruction they won't admit."

An hour later Mariah led her brood and Eli back to the homestead. The Overcrofts returned to their farm—to get another load of their materials, and to "fend off anyone stupid enough to act on their bad ideas," as Ray put it.

CHAPTER 36
Friday, March 3

ELI ROSE at first light, dressed, and wrapped himself in a blanket. Seated in lotus position, he faced the rising sun and maintained a rhythm of slow breaths for forty minutes.

Dawn's exultant wedge
steadily dispels the night
and wounds the stillness.

He followed his practice of healing meditation, focusing first on his own injuries, then on the wounds of his new family, as he was beginning to think of them. Theirs were wounds of the spirit, he thought. More than anxiety about distant loved ones—the loss of their futures, of confidence in a world that had made sense for them. He might be the strongest one of the group. For him, in Modoc County there was freedom, save only for his concern for significant people he had left behind.

"I CAN'T BE part of this, Thad. How could you stand by and let innocent people be blind-sided?" Kim kept her voice a low hiss so their driver, a young sergeant, would not hear over the sound of the radio. The newscaster had just repeated the familiar words of the Secretary of Homeland Security:

The government urges all Americans to remain calm, continue in their normal pursuits, for the good of the country's economic and social framework. The government is doing all it can to ensure the safety of all Americans.

"Be reasonable, Kim. I didn't stand by at all. I fought damn hard to release information about the ice breakup. But it wouldn't have helped anyway. The blow was going to hit whether people were panicked or not. And there wasn't anything we or anyone could have done."

They got out at the Federal Office Building in Sacramento. Thad told the driver to return for them in two hours.

"Thad, I'm just sick about this," said Kim as they entered the office. "Sick about living under a military dictatorship."

"Martial law, it's not the same thing."

"Generals like Austin deceiving the public and then blithely abandoning them to chaos and doom? And how easily we accepted it every step along the way. The military has been gradually assuming more and more control. Isn't that what the Kennedy assassinations were about? Ever since then there have been "enemies"—Communists, rebels, drug lords, Saddam Hussein, terrorists—always a reason to have the military in charge, or at least foremost among the powers of government. Always a reason to increase military spending, benefiting the corporations…"

Thad held up his hand. "I hear you, Kim. But the government has to weigh costs and benefits, has to court the devil at times, has to rein in the military when it can, defer when crises arise…"

"But they can *make* crises arise," she wailed. "And how can they be 'reined in' when they have all power under martial law? What's happening here certainly *is* military dictatorship, or oligarchy with the military as hammer. No one's ever going to rein them in. The oligarchs have always wanted a reason to grab and hold the power. Now they have it in spades."

"I guess that's the way it is for now," Thad said. "And for now we have work to do. We've got to coordinate the evacuation of my staff and their families."

It took them several hours to make all the arrangements. Kim worked efficiently, submerging her feelings, back on robot mode. But when the tasks were done, the robot became flesh and blood again.

"Thad, I can't go to Denver with you. I've got to join my folks. I've come to the end of my public servant career."

"Kim, I don't know if I can do it without you. You worked on my campaign. You believe in what I'm doing. There must be people like us to work inside the government to keep it honest. As honest as it can be."

She leveled a piercing gaze. "This time it's the enormity of the lying—it's a habit, you know—and the strangle hold the military has on power... You can't fight it. You'll be corrupted by it too. There must be something we can do besides this monstrous 'contingency plan.' We can't abandon millions of people. What about setting up refugee camps?"

"Damn. I really admire you," he said. "Of course there'll be refugee camps. I'll fight for every possible humane value I can wedge into this beast. Whatever I'm able to do, even if it's miniscule, will be ten times more than I'd be able to do powerless and cut off in California."

She could see he thought it was hopeless. "Please, Thad, could you help me get to my family?"

THE REMAINING PATIENTS were convoyed to the planes, save a few still too fragile to move. After watching the last plane of the day crawl toward the low clouds, Charles shared a beer with Dr. Elliot.

"It feels all wrong, Carl. How can we leave, knowing the need for medical services in this area?"

"Yeah," said Dr. Elliot, "it's a grim time, a grim decision. It might be the end of the world, for all we know. It's certainly the end of a lot of things. If there's any way of preserving stability and a force for good and decency in what's left of the world, we've got to try to be part of it. We don't have much of the picture. We've got to trust that the government does."

Charles wondered if he did trust the government. "Does the government stand for compassion?" he wondered aloud.

"The decision to implement the contingency plan has happened. As military men we've got to obey orders, not question them."

"I do question them," said Charles. "As physicians we have a higher standard to live up to."

"Charles, we don't have any choice. There's nothing we can do here except be swallowed up along with others who can't be saved."

"What's going to happen to people left behind?" Charles was wondering about Rose, about his brother-in-law and his family, about many others like them. The government couldn't be considering them. This was the same government that decided to abandon the principles the country was founded on, from the Iran-Contra Affair to the Patriot Acts of 2002. His niece Catherine and her boyfriend had argued with him about their confidence in the government at Peter's cabin in McCloud. Would it be any satisfaction to them to know he was beginning to agree with them?

"Carl, this looks a lot like the scene in Saigon when the U.S. pulled out and left a throng of our allies to face the Communists. We helicoptered off the roof of the embassy with people clawing to get in."

"The government has done all it can," Elliot insisted. "Our resources must be deployed where we can assure success. It's triage, Charles. We've apparently got to forsake the coast and hope for the best. We just can't evacuate everybody. A lot of them are going to survive somehow, but if we stay here, we'll just squander resources trying to save people who won't make it anyway. It's a terrible thing to have to decide, but it has been decided. There are tsunami pounding the East Coast that are deciding it."

PETER ADDISON dialed the telephone obsessively, only to hear at best a scratchy recorded voice saying all circuits were busy. More often there was not even a dial tone. He hovered near the radio to glean truth from the managed news reports. If it's worse than these reports indicate, he thought, the reason must be that a wild-eyed populace would be absolutely unmanageable, proof against any effort to contain their rage and despair. But suspicion that the truth was being withheld would likely produce the same frenzy. Peter was sure the men who had destroyed his cabin were criminals, but he now was imagining that ordinarily law-abiding people might leap to similar lawless, violent measures to provide for their needs.

When not occupied with the unsatisfying communication technology, Peter studied a few notes that he happened to have with him, and poured over the map of Antarctica in the cabin's world atlas. He labored to visualize the ice shelves: Larsen A, B and C, Ross and Ronne, pooling with water, fissuring, sinking, crashing and floating off in fragments like the ice chunks in a monstrous marguerita. He pictured the rivers of ice sliding down the slopes of the Antarctic Peninsula, no longer slowed by the barrier of the ice shelves.

He realized the inadequacy of imagination to recreate the immense reality of the glacier-covered continent. So few people had experienced it first hand, it was like the moon, or outer space, or the ocean floor. It was too distant and unknown to appear in the popular consciousness as a threat. There had been warnings, of course, but they had always seemed like the academic ramblings of bearded, sandaled, bespectacled stargazers in ivory towers with telescopes attached. He recalled his interview with the *Sacramento Bee* reporter. His understated academic reserve seemed appropriate at the time, but it may have served only to bolster the arguments of industrial and political interests that needed to downplay global warming.

And now he yearned to be there. To see first hand the awesome power of Nature, as he had once seen lava pouring down the slopes of Mount Kilauea to the Pacific Ocean, and witnessed the bubblings and surgings from depths of Earth in Yellowstone. But he had to be content—and he was not—to piece together some understanding of the geological event of the era from untrustworthy scraps of information. He was like an art scholar in the Louvre limited to a nocturnal visit during a power failure.

Rose Royer took her turn occasionally at the telephone and radio. Peter comforted her with the thought that Charles and Kim were secure in their work, allied with the strongest entities available, the government and military. She distracted herself with housework and baking, and with checking on her patients.

She was amazed by Eli's progress. Both his hand and his sprained wrist were healing rapidly. He was able to handle tools and work up a sweat in the garden. "If you feel pain, James, you should rest," she told him, suspicious that he would neither rest nor admit to feeling pain.

CATHERINE JOINED Jason and Eli for a day's labor, along with Ray and Paisley in brief advisory stints between trips to their farm.

Peter joined them for the hour before lunch. "This might be extremely important for us if worse comes to worse," he said solemnly.

"How much worse can it get, Daddy?" asked Catherine.

"There's a great deal of ice water out there. The oceans have been getting colder with melting of the Arctic ice cap. Even without this catastrophe in

Antarctica, the variation in temperature might be leading to a stoppage of a regular movement of ocean water called the North Atlantic Current. It regulates seasonal weather patterns in North America and in Europe. If that current stops, we might have earlier and colder winters than we've ever experienced. We might not be able to count on normal agricultural output."

"A garden might be a matter of survival then?" asked Eli.

"I think we'd better get it right."

The workers continued soberly. They recognized a purpose beyond diversion from their melancholy. The communal labor served to create bonds among them. They turned over the earth and mixed in manure and mulch, and the work and togetherness was a cultivation of their collective spirit.

In the late afternoon they called it a day. Eli gathered up tools to haul them to the barn, clean them and put them away. He watched Catherine and Jason walk hand in hand, with Cappy dancing along at their heels or sniffing nearby foliage until he sensed their distance, along a path toward the forest. He blessed the comforting they would offer each other in the face of monumental uncertainty.

The rainbows are sleeping—
You can hear them in the trees
whispering your name.

He began his evening meditation.

CHAPTER 37

Saturday, March 4

CHARLES HARDLY SLEPT. He took a long walk in the dead of night, down Hickham Street, guided by the platinum glow of floodlights on the tarmac, where C-130s swallowed the last of the hospital equipment. Garth Elkins would arrive shortly after dawn to fly him and a dozen others, officers and civilians, to Denver to join the Mountain West Command.

Carl Elliot had described what he understood of the forming government structure. State governments were to continue in the areas not cut off from the central government, now located in Dallas, but government officials would be dependent on their military "advisors." Groups of states in the heartland would form military command areas where the federal government could guarantee safety, stability, and the continuation of services. Critical locations, such as petroleum or agricultural lands, would be secured by government troops, with the exception of California's rich Central Valley, which would be rendered useless in a short time by salt water in the Aqueduct. Local governments outside the federally secured areas would stand or fall on their own. The fate of vast domains of life and society, and when they might return to what had been "normal," were simply unknown.

Charles shuffled back to his room to shave and shower. Then, in his full dress uniform he saluted himself in the mirror—and decided to go AWOL.

Two hours later he faced his old friend. "Garth, do you know where Kim is?"

"I'm sure she's safe. Probably not in Sacramento any more. She's needed for the Congressman's staff in Denver," said Garth. "He's high on the House Armed Services Committee, and is involved in putting together the new structure of government. Guys like me have been activated to fly essential personnel and their families to the Government Service Command Areas. I know they're well cared for."

"Maybe you don't appreciate what I'm going through. Your family's safe and together in Colorado. Mine's fragmented around California. Rose is the only one whose location I know. And I'll tell you this much, I'm not going anywhere without her."

He said it as a matter of fact. Garth nodded understanding. "What do you have in mind?" he asked.

"I've never said you owe me one," said Charles. "And I won't now. But I'm asking you to drop me off in Flat River."

"Can we pick her up there?" asked Garth.

"I haven't been able to contact her for about a week. Events have caught up with us, and to tell you the truth, I'm not sure I want to be part of this new order."

"You know, Charles, this duty we're called to is in many ways the most difficult we've ever had. I know you won't serve well without being committed to it. I don't know how you dedicated yourself to it in Vietnam, the way Celia was tugging in the opposite direction. Maybe she was right then, and maybe you're right now."

Garth walked several steps toward the aircraft and turned. Charles had not moved. "Come on, guy." He grinned conspiratorially. "I've always said so: I do owe you one."

Charles rode in the cockpit, in the co-pilot's seat. When they landed in Flat River, Garth announced to his passengers that they would stop there only long enough to deliver a mail pouch. He took off within five minutes of landing.

Charles found that his uniform conferred on him a high level of respect and deference. No doubt people perceived he was the advance man of a government team that would implement a local version of federal martial law. He scanned the small parking lot for a taxi to drive him to the cabin, found none, and was about to inquire of a knot of men lounging at a respectful distance, when they all craned their necks toward the drone of an approaching aircraft.

He watched with them as the plane swooped to a smooth touchdown, then taxied toward the airport office. It was a Gulfstream V, exactly like the one he had stepped out of fifteen minutes before. Did Garth simply circle and return, he wondered? Two passengers descended the short stairway, a man and a woman. The man spoke to her for several minutes, hugged her, and returned to the plane. More than the unfamiliar short hairdo, the improbability of meeting her there prevented his recognizing her immediately. It was Kim!

An hour later they were twenty miles south of Flat River, headed east from Likely on the Buckberry Valley Road. They had persuaded a local man with four-wheel drive on his well-worn pickup to taxi them to the cabin for thirty-five dollars. "I'd be glad to take you up there. Give me something constructive to do," said Maurice Beckwith, who looked to Charles like a pint-sized Lyndon Johnson with thin hair and prominent ears. "Spelled M-a-u-r-i-c-e," he confided, "but it's pronounced 'Morris,' like the Cat." He was a talkative man, so they learned a great deal about him and the area. "It's been pretty warm up here this winter," he said. "You probably figured on more snow. Warmest February since my wife died five years ago. Kids moved back to Missouri, and they're trying to get me to join 'em. Might do it too. Don't know what keeps me here anyway. You'd think in a small town folks'd know everybody, but since Tess died, I seem to have lost touch. You folks gonna be here long?"

They established for Mr. Beckwith that they were father and daughter, long-time property owners in the area about to join Rose for an extended stay. Through calculated vagueness Charles allowed Beckwith to infer that he was indeed a government advance man.

"Of course folks here aren't too worried about any floods" said Beckwith, "but they're leery of people moving in from over on the coast. And lately it's gotten testy with store shelves starting to empty and telephone lines so unreliable, y'know. Nothing like a little emergency to get even conservative folks looking for government support."

Along the straight ribbon of Highway 395 Kim beguiled Beckwith, who did not hear well even without the rumble of his truck's engine, by calling springboard questions, about his business before he retired and details of the community and countryside. He carried the conversation, which rambled but did not abate until well beyond Likely. He had been a representative for a farm equipment manufacturer, traveling constantly around Northern California, Nevada and Oregon. His wife died only a year after they had settled into retirement in Flat River.

Charles led the conversation toward a less sensitive topic. "Last year I was looking for a Lambert bar clamp and couldn't find one in Flat River."

"Did you say Lambert? Shouldn't be hard to find," said Beckwith. "It's the best one on the market. It's possible the ranch supply store on Highway 299 would have it in stock." He continued with a long explanation of supply problems in more remote areas. "And these days you can wait a long time for resupply. Stores are running out of staples. You can't buy a battery right now in Modoc County."

By the time they reached the final turn off the county road, Kim thought Beckwith had run out of discourse. She was wrong. "Did you say you're a doctor in the Air Force?" he asked Charles. When Charles confirmed he was a physician, Beckwith described for five minutes the ringing in his ears. "I'm afraid it might be a sign of a brain tumor or something."

Charles cautioned him to calmly check out more likely causes, such as a buildup of wax in the ears. "Try irrigating your ears with warm soapy water, repeated a couple of times. That just might solve the problem and allay your fear." Beckwith asked him to repeat his instructions.

Although Charles was aware of Rose charging out of the cabin and wrapping Kim in a raucous hug, he finished his prescription for Mr. Beckwith's ear problem, paid him, and stood watching the pickup, until Beckwith waved energetically and pulled away. Then he turned to receive his own welcome.

As the three walked to the cabin, where Peter, Catherine and Jason waited on the porch, Kim voiced a thought she had been holding for over an hour. "Dad, I'm dying to compare what each of us packed, knowing that what we left behind might be lost forever."

Rose cut her stride short. "Oh, Kim, is it as bad as that?"

ELI HAD JUST FINISHED a second day of work on the Royer garden with Catherine and Jason when they heard the chugging of Beckwith's pickup. By the time they put their tools away the truck was bouncing back down the road. Inside the house a boisterous reunion with warm hugs and tears took place between Catherine and her cousin and uncle.

Due to his tender wrist Eli shook hands gingerly with Charles and Kim, but held the eyes of each for earnest seconds. In the case of Kim it was an especially pleasurable experience, for her beauty captivated him, and Rose's description of her had not included it. But for both it was a searching for any sign of suspicion or misgiving. Rose's warm introduction had set him in favorable light, he thought, and he wondered if he might continue to maintain his vague and benign identity.

His society for sixteen years had been composed largely of dropouts on the lowest rungs of the national culture. Now his community consisted of a physician/military officer of high rank and a sophisticated government employee, in addition to a learned scientist, a nurse, two college students and the farm couple who were college graduates with international experience. Eli relished his measure of anonymity, for it covered his lowly station, but he knew it was fragile.

Charles told his story first, outlining his experience since the holiday weekend at the Addison cabin. Peter's story, interspersed with his, shocked him. Jason still carried the mark of their ordeal in a dark half-circle under his eye.

"For the last two weeks I've seen the results of dozens of incidents akin to yours," said Charles. "I can only imagine that it will become worse, but there will be fewer medical people—if any—to deal with it. They shut down the medical facility at Travis, and I gather from a physician I met from Oakland that it's too dangerous to man the hospitals in the Bay Area without military protection. I'm afraid we're pretty much on our own now. The government is pulling back from the coasts to establish areas it can manage."

Kim amplified her father's remarks, revealing government obfuscation, secrecy and lying, all for the good of the nation, supposedly. The news weighed heavily on them, particularly on Jason, who now saw his family in Maryland at best in a situation like theirs in the McCloud cabin. If they had survived at all. "My parents have a summer place near Cumberland. They would've gone there if they could."

"Why can't the government trust people with the truth?" Catherine asked no one in particular.

"With some reason, I suppose, in this case," said her father. "Just look at the chaos in society. There is a need for martial law, after all. Charles' experience makes that plain, as well as our own at the McCloud cabin. There are lawless elements that exacerbate any emergency, but now even neighbors can be enemies if there isn't a strong sense of community."

Charles looked at Rose. "What do you know about the folks up at the Maxwell place?"

"They're pretty solid, seems to me." She described the women and children and the Overcrofts. "It looks like it's going to be really important now to work with them."

"They need to hear what you've told us," said Catherine.

"First thing in the morning," suggested Rose, "we should join with them and decide how we're going to make this all work out. Right now, let's all work together and make some dinner."

BUZZARDS HAVE NO need to circle now. Although overstuffed, they continue to fly. A flash of reflected sunlight on the top of a crag interests one. She glides down, passes over the carcass of a horse pierced by a shattered telephone pole, and three disarranged human corpses, settles to a landing near the green-and-white object of attraction. Not edible. It is a metal sign, white letters on a lawn-green background. *Welcome To Philadelphia.*

IN PRISON, regular exercise had been a way of holding off boredom and meaninglessness, a tool for self-esteem, even a matter of survival. As darkness fell on this twenty-fifth night of Eli's new life, the fatigue he felt represented a result outside the limits of his body. His exertion had left a rectangle of turned and enriched earth, a patch of soil that represented a new beginning in creation. It was a shared fatigue, with meaning for a community. Like his efforts at two monasteries, it had purpose and dignity, and conferred these blessings on those who participated in it.

Eli had begun to feel that he would never again live in prison. He was an accepted part of a very small society, a family, people he respected and could dedicate himself to. He did not feel the unconditional acceptance of Our Lady of Peace Monastery and Los Molinos, but at least he was not rejected. In time, perhaps he would prove himself to this community, would receive the gift of their pardon. He pictured himself in the garb of Dismas in the painting in the San Quentin Catholic Chapel—dressed for travel, having received absolution.

His new family was suffering considerably. For them the time and place of their lives represented tragedy, loss and uncertainty—if not dread. For him there was little to grieve. He alone among them was free and contented, hopeful and determined in the face of whatever challenges lay ahead. In some respects, perhaps, he was their leader.

He recalled an afternoon standing in the exercise yard of the AIDS unit, when he saw a shaft of sunlight between clouds, reaching down like the finger of God stirring the bay water. The image transposed into the finger he described to Sister Arlene, of God reaching down to touch his chest in a tangible gesture of forgiveness. And God might do it again. He might stir him together with his companions—not companions in misfortune as much as companions in possibility. Eli might bestow on them his own optimism, his determination to make a success of his life, not only to survive but to thrive. He would climb the mountain and his shout of jubilee would echo through the valleys. He must do it for Moses and Jerry, for Johnny Diaz and Big Daddy Sisson, for all whose lives were confined in failure and defeat.

Places like the monasteries might also be centers of renewal, if they could escape the chaos and destruction of human elements in the brewing troubles. Perhaps many of the good might suffer along with the rotten—it was beyond his knowledge or control. There was no explanation for being Chosen. There was only opportunity and responsibility.

If the country had died... If the world had died... Like Noah's world, it would be renewed. Like Shem and Ham and Japheth, he might be among those to spread regeneration to a cleansed creation. They might enter the ark and prepare to be the new children of Noah.

BOOK TWO

CHAPTER 38
Friday, January 6

SURF RAGED against the rocks a hundred feet below the outlook where Mariah Wallace stood, gripping the warm arm of her daughter, Darcy Malone. A brush of cold air descended over their faces, then over the cliff and downward to the restless sea. The outlook, famed for its anomalous downdrafts, was a favorite spot for casting loved ones' ashes into the Pacific.

Mariah broke their silent contemplation, her grip tightening. "This is the last time, Darcy."

Darcy flinched—said nothing. *That would be a blessing*, she thought.

Nineteen years ago at this cliff they began the annual ritual remembrance of Darcy's little brother, Luke. On "Little Christmas" that year, Mariah and Darcy had dropped his meager remains over the outlook's edge.

From his surprise birth, Darcy had imagined Luke as her own baby in a ten-year-old's maternal fantasy. His death was at least as traumatic for her as for her mother.

Darcy had turned twelve. A month later, despite a dark foreboding, Mariah had taken her to a Girl Scout outing, leaving two-year-old Luke with his father. Elmer swore he wouldn't leave, but that afternoon he told the carpenter who was renovating the family room to watch the napping Luke while he drove to the sports bar for his habitual bourbon-on-ice and flirting with the waitress. When he returned, fire engines and police cars had cordoned off the smoldering house. Luke's body was recovered from the nursery. The carpenter was convicted of arson and second-degree murder.

For a year and a half afterwards, Mariah lived unspeaking, losing herself in painting hundreds of pictures of Luke. Elmer drank himself numb for months—until he was so sick he was dragged by a devoted friend to ninety AA meetings in ninety days. Darcy raised herself in the vacuum.

Despite therapy, Mariah blamed Elmer. And Darcy blamed them both. But they rebuilt the home and stayed together, the horror gradually receding through routine and the cycle of years.

"The ocean looks forbidding today," Mariah said. "Even as we drove here, I was hoping to let go at last. The ocean seems to demand it, don't you think?"

Darcy scanned the Pacific surface sparkling in the sunlight under a cloudless sky. "The ocean's beautiful. Those feelings are in *you*, Mom, not the ocean. But it doesn't matter. I'd love to quit this ritual, if you will."

Mariah grabbed the locket of Luke's baby hair suspended on a thin gold chain at her throat, and in one swift arc broke the chain and backhanded the memory over the cliff. Her neck stung with the thin bruise where the strand scraped before it broke.

The return drive took them past San Quentin and onto the San Rafael Bridge toward Oakland. High above the Bay, Darcy broached her new source of anxiety. "Mom, I've been offered a job in Santa Fe. I haven't told Reinhold yet. They're talking a lot of money. I'd be acquiring art for their museum. I need help with the decision. Advice."

Mariah's face darkened. "You mean you'd take the grandchildren to New Mexico—so far away?"

"We need the money. Reinhold's deals take so long it seems forever between checks."

"How much are they dangling—to make you leave us like that?"

"That's the problem. It's way over a hundred thousand dollars. It seems too much."

"A museum?"

"Well, I wouldn't really be working for the museum. I'd be with a nonprofit funded by donors."

Darcy drove on in the silence. Finally, she blurted, "It scares me, Mom. You know, because of what happened at my old gallery."

"Now look, Darcy. You know I never believed that."

"Mom. Mahmoud's people really did try to make me launder their art. I told you everything." Darcy hesitated. *Well, maybe not quite everything.* "Please. Try to believe me. I'm afraid they're trying again. This time I have a husband and two children, though. I feel so vulnerable."

Her mother stared hard from the passenger seat. "It didn't make sense then, and it still doesn't. You never went to the police. Or anyone—the FBI, Homeland Security, the CIA. Darcy, Sweetheart, listen to me. You need a professional to tell you whether you're delusional again, like in high school. Really, Baby."

Those frenzied, muddled years, the pills, the rebellion.

After receiving a degree in Fine Arts from Dominican University in Marin County, with a minor in filmmaking, Darcy had reverted to her desperate high school behavior. She left the country with an Iraqi graduate student who had been studying chemical engineering at Berkeley. She came home nine months later and immediately joined a San Francisco art gallery, where she rose quickly in their import group. Two years later her Iraqi lover was killed, his car out of control on a lonely highway near Santa Cruz. Within a year she had taken up martial arts, married Reinhold Malone and abruptly quit the gallery. She told most people it was so she could get pregnant. She told Reinhold and her mother Mahmoud's death was a murder meant as a warning to her, and Middle Eastern men were threatening her unless she ran contraband art through the gallery. Reinhold had believed her. Mariah hadn't.

"Would you just do a simple reading for me, Mom? It would help."

Mariah studied the boats dotting the Bay. The distant look in her eyes was the tip-off that she was "seeing things." Darcy could often pick up the ideas herself, but not this time.

"Oh, Sweetie, I would if… I mean, when my emotions are high, I'm afraid of filtering—you know, slanting the answers the way my ego wants. I feel queasy thinking of Tierney and Finn going so far away. This is one you'll have to figure out on your own, Baby. I'm sorry."

CHAPTER 39

Saturday, January 7

"HEY, DARCE," Reinhold's voice rang out from the kitchen. "While you were at the park I took a call for you."

"Wait, would you, Reinhold? Just let me get Finn in his crib. Tierney, Honey, why don't you put your *Finding Nemo* video on?"

In minutes, Darcy threw her coat on the spare kitchen chair, kissed her husband on the cheek and poured a cup of coffee. "Now. What's up?"

"I should ask you that. In fact, what's up with Santa Fe?"

Darcy raised an eyebrow.

Reinhold continued, "Right after you left, a couple of men from Houston called you on a conference call. I said you were my wife. They asked what I thought about moving to Santa Fe. I guess my articulate silence underwhelmed them." He sipped his coffee. "Anyway, they're on the Board of the Museum in Santa Fe. Said the Museum had contacted you about working there. They were calling to answer any questions you had."

He tilted his chair back and laid his arm on the table in a gesture that said, "Your turn."

"Jesus, it hasn't even been twenty-four hours. I got a call out of the blue yesterday, from the Museum director, just before I went to Oakland to get Mom." She described the job, and went on, "I've been trying to clear my thoughts before I brought it up. I asked Mom for her intuition, but she wouldn't tell what she saw."

Reinhold leaned forward. "They must really want you. They pushed pretty hard. Friendly, you know, but aggressive. And chummy at the same time, in that professional way. Of course, that's my strong suit too. We got into the small world thing. Turns out they both know Troy."

Troy Blake was Reinhold's most important client. He used Reinhold to acquire land in Russia for commercial office and residential complexes. Reinhold had earned an impressive reputation in boom-time Moscow after the Iron Curtain "thawed" and free world capitalists raced to fill the vacuum created by Communist policies. When the ruble collapsed in 1999, Reinhold had moved to San Francisco, where Blake found him.

Darcy asked, "Did you react?"

Her husband gave her a long, steady look in the eyes. "I said you could probably do the job from here, what with the Internet, fax machines, airplane tickets and all." He blew her a kiss. "You know how much I love you, Munchkin. We could work anything out. But San Francisco's a pretty sweet place. And we have good kin here, too." He smiled and shrugged.

Darcy finished her coffee in silence. *If he only knew how much I love him, too. And how scared I am. And why... Oh, God.* Then she ran an Internet search on the men's names.

"Reinhold, come here a minute."

"What'd you find?"

"For openers, they're oil men, both past Presidents of the American Sovereignty Foundation."

"The right-wing think tank in Florida? That calls the U.N. the evil octopus?"

"Yup. Their oil companies have interlocking directorates. And, get this, they're both on the President's Strategic Petroleum Advisory Council."

"Heavy hitters. Even so, they think you're hot stuff. They knew all about the gallery—called you a superstar, I think."

"I don't like it, Reinhold."

"The old contraband thing?"

"Yes."

"Not these guys."

"Still scares me. But the money's big."

"Like...?"

"$175,000 a year. Plus bonus"

"Holy shit."

CHAPTER 40
Sunday, January 15

SKIES WERE BLUE over Oakland as Darcy pulled her SUV into the driveway of the family home to drop the children off.

Tierney was smiles all over when she saw Mariah, whom she called her Babushka—Russian for "Grandmother." Tierney gave her a half-minute bear hug.

"My goodness you're a strong girl," Mariah laughed.

"Well, I am *four*, you know."

Finn squirmed in Darcy's grip with the frenzy of an eleven month-old, until finally his grandmother turned and said, "Clap hands, clap hands." He swiped his hands backwards and forwards in more of a flap than a clap, his little palms managing to make contact a few times. It was more than enough to draw exhilarated praise from Babushka.

Grandfather Elmer was a little harder to react to. He was sooo tall—six, six. His clothes just hung on him almost empty, like he was a very tall stick doll. When he stood up, he leaned against a wall or a chair or something. His feet flapped and his knees pointed out and his skeletal hands dangled out of his sleeves and wobbled around out of control like clappers in tin-foil bells. He couldn't pick you up—or pick anything up. Getting around, he mostly walked, but in airports and crowds he used a wheelchair.

It always took Tierney time to warm up when she hadn't seen her grandfather for a few days. Finn's first reaction was usually to cock his head and examine this unusual creature, as he would an unfamiliar cat. But after his Mommy gave her father a hug, and Tierney began chattering with him as if all was perfectly normal, Finn warmed up too and gurgled away at his grandfather full bore.

In the lull purchased with animal crackers, Mariah walked Darcy back to the car. "I wish you'd give up this flying job, Sweetheart. Where are you going today?"

"Oh, Mom. It's my one escape. I need it—it's in my blood. Today we have a widow and her brother. They want her husband's ashes scattered around Mt. Diablo. It couldn't be a better day. I'll be back in three hours."

After Darcy quit the gallery, she had joined a friend in a graphic design boutique. Her friend unexpectedly inherited a chain of mortuaries and took

Darcy with her to be office manager and back-up pilot for the company plane. Among other things in her wild years, Darcy had become a skilled pilot.

The sun was hovering between afternoon and evening when Darcy returned. Mariah said, "Stay a minute? The kids are napping and Elmer's watching C-SPAN."

Without waiting, Mariah poured her daughter a Coca-Cola without ice, and herself a glass of red table wine. "Any developments in Santa Fe?"

"*Oh*, yes. Thursday two men from the Museum Board rang me. The same ones who called Reinhold last Saturday. Just happened to be in town, they said. We met for two hours. They upped the ante—said the nonprofit would let me work part-time for a private gallery they knew—wealthy clients, interested only in major works and collections. They also said their 'group' was planning a new museum for Mid-East antiquities in Santa Fe—for comparative archeological purposes. I'd be traveling."

"Did you like them?"

"Cold fish. Suits, narrow lapels. White shirts, tight little triangle knots in their ties."

Mariah smiled.

"Tooled leather briefcases with alligator trim. Spanish or Brazilian, no doubt. Empty eyes." Her voice trailed off. "You know. No passion."

"Still scared, aren't you?"

"*I dreamed I was in a runaway train. It was on a narrow point that ran way out into the ocean. Ahead, the track split. The left spur ran to the edge of a cliff. The right one led to another cliff.*"

Mariah nodded, hesitated. "Reinhold?"

"God bless him. He gave me the answer. I told them I couldn't make a decision until he's back from Russia and our vacation trip's over. It could change everything. If he gets the deal done, we won't need the money from Santa Fe."

Mariah looked distant. Took some wine. Changed the topic. "I threw out all Luke's things. The old curtains, too. His room's all sunny, now. It's not his room any more. My new office. His baby clothes, I took to the thrift store. All I have left is his little photo in my wallet."

Darcy took her mother's hands. She pulled her up and squeezed her tightly in her arms.

As Reinhold stacked the last plate into the dishwasher, Darcy eased the kitchen door shut and sat back down by her unfinished wine. "The kids are down."

He kissed her on the mouth. She giggled, "Later."

Reinhold picked up the paper. "Okay, okay. Did you read this article about Antarctica?

"They're expecting two huge ice shelves down there to collapse. They're both the size of France. That's twice the size of New England. Each one, Darcy. Think of it. They say *'the aftermath could threaten civilization as we know it.'* In 2002, one collapsed the size of Rhode Island, but no one saw it. It was called the Larsen B Ice Shelf. They did get some time lapse photos from a satellite. It took only three days. This time, it says, the networks are ready— they've got the usual media teams down there with the university crowd at the McMurdo Sound Research Base. Oh, and *'The government has dispatched its own scientists, along with engineers and emergency planners.'* Now listen to this. *'No one knows for certain whether this ice will collapse before the Antarctic winter sets in, or even this year. Some say it could be five years away. But comparing daily satellite photos with those taken before the Larsen B event, experts expect this natural disaster by Valentine's Day.'*"

"We'll be in Ireland," Darcy said.

"Then it explains what might happen if they do collapse." Reinhold scanned the story. "Sea level might rise four and a half inches, and it might cool the oceans, *'intensifying El Nino and causing extreme climate fluctuations everywhere—storms and floods in some places, drought and famine in others.'* Strangely, however, it might warm up the water near Antarctica. It says, *'The ice shelves now shade the sea floor from the warmth of sunlight. The ice reflects the sun's heat back into space. Without the shade, the nearby ocean would warm and could start melting the ice on Antarctica itself. Sea level would rise dramatically— on every island and coastline in the world.'*"

Darcy quipped, "You geek. I'll stay tuned." She stretched. "Meet you in the bedroom."

CHAPTER 41

Tuesday, January 17

DARCY ANSWERED the jangling phone. Through a fog of years the unmistakable scratchy voice renewed its familiarity.

"Darcy. It's Sylvester. How's my old apprentice? Been a while, eh?"

"Hey. Uh… How are you?" *Yeah, a while. More than a five-year while.*

During her third college summer, Darcy had visited her father's old friend Sylvester Isham in New Mexico. A war correspondent, he had covered the Vietnam air war, learned to fly there, bought a 1944 Staggerwing bi-plane, and had been flying bush fields from Santa Fe to Central America ever since. He had flown Life Magazine photographers around secret airfields in Honduras and El Salvador during the U.S.-backed war "against communism" in the sixties. When he learned Darcy had experience in video, he said, "I'll teach you to fly the Staggerwing if you'll go with me to Mexico and be my camera man for a documentary I'm making." She learned mostly on the rocky, pocked air strips of remote northern Mexico, taxiing through weeds, always on alert for a cow wandering into the takeoff or landing path. But she logged enough hours to get her license that summer.

Sylvester had written to Darcy's father at the end of the final shoot: "Elmer, your girl's not only one of the most talented camera men I've ever worked with, but her intellectual, physical and intuitive grasp of piloting are more exquisite than her artistic abilities. I've never seen a more competent student, or a faster learning curve. I don't know what you did, but congratulations! Of course, honestly, I know you didn't have a goddam thing to do with it and it's really all Mariah's fault. But she's a great kid. I'm glad to know her."

Darcy had flown consistently ever since. On their honeymoon, she and Reinhold visited Sylvester's hacienda just north of Santa Fe, and she tuned up some of her languishing bush field skills in the old Staggerwing. When the mortuary opportunity came up, she easily qualified for the required commercial license.

Sylvester didn't waste time. "Bumped into an old pal. Said he saw you last week. Remington King."

One of the Museum Board. "Oh, yes, from Santa Fe. He was out here with…" She feigned forgetfulness. "Was it Mr. Starcher?"

Sylvester now hesitated. *He knows damn well I know.*

He played along. "Yes. Bucky Starcher. I used to fly Bucky and Remington around the petroleum fields between Texas and Panama, even out to Yucatan and around the Gulf. Man, that was great work. They're world-class fellas."

Darcy said nothing. Sylvester filled in the silence. "You're unusually talkative today, my Dear."

She replied, "How's the Staggerwing?"

Sylvester ignored her sidestep. "They're wild about you, Darcy. Don't you get it? Why don't you bring your Irish dancing boy and the ragamuffins on out. We could all have some great times."

"Things are different now, Sylvester. I'm raising a family. I love it."

"Don't worry, Kid," he parried. "They won't bring up your past."

Darcy's throat went dry. "What are you talking about?"

"When they did the background check on you, they saw you got your first license here. They asked me about you. I told them what a smart chick you were. And a great pilot. But I didn't let on I knew... well, you know, those things you told me down at Rosa's, back when you were just learning what a cockpit was. Somehow they knew anyway about your days in Saudi Arabia and Japan."

Darcy had forgotten about Rosa's Tequila Cup. *He's the only one I ever told about Japan. God, what a dope I was.* She decided to risk. "Level with me, Sylvester. Who are these guys?"

It was his turn to hesitate. "All I can say, Kid, is they're important. What they're doing is important. There's stuff going on that's going to triple this country's energy needs. It's all part of a bigger picture."

Energy needs? What's that got to do with it? He's in deep. Too deep. Maybe he did tell. She tried to cut her losses. "I'm thinking about it. My husband and I agreed to think it over for a month. I'll tell you what, though. I'll call you when we decide. And... well, if I have any questions."

When Reinhold got home, Darcy flew into his arms before his raincoat was even off. "Hold me. Just hold me."

She told him about Sylvester. Except the Japan part.

"They've got to be on our side," Reinhold said. "No chance, Baby, that they're working for those bearded bozos you hung out with in Arabia. Maybe Washington needs you because you know some of that system."

Arabia. Darcy's voice quivered. "Do you think it has something to do with oil?" Without waiting for an answer, she cut it off. "Our side, their side. I don't care, whoever they are. I don't want any side. All that's behind me. It's got to stay there. You've got to keep me out of this. We've got our two little angels to think of now. Please, Reinhold. Keep me safe. Okay?"

"Don't worry. Don't worry. We'll be fine. It'll blow over. You wait and see. Let's just bide our time. We'll just keep stretching them out. They'll get tired, give up, go away. It always works."

CHAPTER 42
Tuesday, January 24

REINHOLD SNAPPED his suitcase shut and attached the security clearance manifest required by anti-terror regulations. His carry-on and computer could wait until morning. He flopped on the couch and picked up the paper.

The National Times
Ross Ice Shelf Collapses in Antarctica—Eyewitness Report
By Ulysses Doxiadis, Science Reporter, On Location
The long-expected collapse of the Ross Ice Shelf is underway... Billions of tons of ice, hundreds of feet thick, are shattering, grinding, falling into the ocean. The majestic floating glacier is falling in on itself, sending plumes of snow and ice crystals a thousand feet into the air...

The line of advance, we judge, is moving about five miles an hour. It's about five hundred miles, or was, from the front edge of the Ross Ice Shelf to the true land's edge of Antarctica. At this rate, in four days the ice shelf will be gone...

Reinhold frowned, then folded the paper with the story on top. He laid it on the TV where Darcy couldn't miss it after she took him to the airport in the morning. *This ought to take her mind off the Santa Fe thing for a while.*

CHAPTER 43
Wednesday, January 25

"YOU KNOW, REINHOLD, saying goodbye to you at the airport is..." Darcy's eyes flashed. "Why don't you take the Shuttle, like everyone else we know?" Her heart was empty already, her domain defenseless, her brain twisting around the unsettling silence from Santa Fe since the call from Sylvester. But those topics were out of bounds for young ears.

"Hey, come on, Darce, I just like to hang out with you and the kids after international check-in. Besides," he said over his shoulder, "Tierney hasn't told me what she wants from Moscow. You'll tell me at lunch, won't you, Sweetie?"

"Sure, Daddy—and I'll tell you what Finn wants, too."

Reinhold turned to Darcy. "A happy sendoff's important to me today. I've got to bring this deal in."

"I know. I know you do." With those words, unanticipated knowledge lodged in her mind, sudden and irrefutable, like learning of a family death or birth, when the world changes forever. She knew she would never go to Santa Fe. *If he doesn't make this deal, our lives will be radically different, but I'm not going back to live in darkness. He'll have to get a job, and we'll...*

"I'm not really worried," Reinhold's voice loomed into her awareness. "I think it's in the bag. Bavermaan and his Siberian cronies are hot to dump their office rentals in Moscow and Troy's got the dough. Maybe I could even come home early and fly with you and the kids to Ireland instead of meeting you there."

Their vacation was to start the day before Valentine's Day. Darcy and the children were to meet Reinhold in his home town of Ennis. They planned three weeks of showing off baby Finn and re-connecting Tierney to the clan. The families on both sides of the Atlantic were full of anticipation.

Darcy drove in silence along the Bayshore below the old Candlestick Park. Her mind was tracking chains of thought in a half-dozen directions. The Bay was sapphire blue in the brilliant winter sun, studded with diadems of waves scattered here and there by the whim of the North Wind.

Reinhold looked out the window. "Look at that low tide. It's as low as I've ever seen it. I don't think the Antarctic breakup will change things as much as they say."

Reinhold always watched the tides. It carried him back to his last summer job in the merchant marine before he left Ireland for Russia in 1990. *He's hoping for a big enough profit to buy a sailboat*, Darcy thought.

At the airport curb she dropped Reinhold and his bags, parked, and made her way with the children to the restaurant wait-room where he would join them after check in. The Barbie-doll hostess took her sweet time. Tierney ran to the window to look at planes and baggage trucks until her mother collected her.

"What's that in your mouth?" Tierney pursed her lips tightly. Darcy held out her hand. "Spit it out." Tierney slid a melting ice cube out of her mouth.

"Where'd you get that, Tierney?"

"Over there." Tierney pointed to a drink machine by the window. A dozen more ice cubes lay on the carpet, among other spillage yet to be attended. A heavy set man looked on, apparently disgusted, then insisted that the hostess make the staff clean the mess. Darcy followed him with her eyes, straining for a hint of recognition, then chided herself for allowing suspicions of strangers to constantly hover.

"I'm too hot in this coat," Tierney whined. "And I'm thirsty. Can I have a Seven-Up?"

Darcy deposited the ice chip in the trash receptacle. "Just take your coat off and put it on the chair. Nicely. You can have a drink at lunch."

Reinhold appeared in twenty minutes and they filed into the Sky Lounge Restaurant.

"Do they make Legos in Moscow?" Tierney asked after they ordered. "That's what I'd like. Finn says he would, too. I hope you come back early, Daddy."

Reinhold ate with gusto, but Darcy's appetite quotient was as low as the tide and she just kept rearranging the tomatoes in her salad. *Oh, God, yes, come back early.* She needed the fortress of his black-and-white thinking, the opiate of his naiveté, the aphrodisiac of the leprechaun twinkle in his eyes.

At the security barrier Reinhold kissed the children and embraced Darcy with a tender, lingering warmth. "Don't forget how well we've loved, my Darling. I'll always be with you."

Darcy gulped out their special reply. "We both know how well we've loved. Godspeed."

The tide was lifting the tiny whitecaps as the remaining Malones drove home to San Francisco. Darcy hugged the solid white line on the right of the slow lane, inspecting every vehicle that came close for strange men or sudden swerves, as if the ghost of Mahmoud was riding on the roof pointing her out to agents from the past.

CHAPTER 44
Thursday, February 2

"HELLO. Is this Darcy?" Mariah frequently guessed a caller. She was most accurate when the caller was under a high emotional charge.

"Mom. Tierney's really sick. She's running a high fever, a hundred and four. She's losing her coordination, stumbling around, slurring her speech. Lethargic like I've never seen. Her face was flushed when she woke up and she said she was hot, but everything else happened in the last three hours. Her regular doctor's on vacation and his substitute's a... Well, I wouldn't take a sick dog to him. I can't reach Reinhold in Russia. Tierney needs a hospital. Oh, Mom..." Darcy took a deep breath, regained her composure. "Tierney doesn't need an ambulance, but I need to get her help fast."

"Let me call Dr. Green. I know he'll help." Dr. Green was head of pediatrics at Children's Hospital in Oakland.

In minutes, Mariah called back. "I'll meet you at the emergency room. I'll watch Finn so you can be with Tierney. Dr. Green will meet us there. Do you want me to call Bridey? Or anyone at the mortuary?"

"Yes. You'd better call Bridey. I'll take care of work on my cell from the bridge."

Bridey O'Brien, the new nanny from Ireland, agreed to be on standby, to help any way she could, even sleep at the Wallace's to help with Finn if Tierney required extended hospitalization.

It would take Darcy twenty-five minutes to reach Children's ER. Mariah was less than five minutes away. She hurried down the hall to Elmer's back office, heard him on the telephone with a client.

When he hung up she explained the situation, and added, "With Reinhold in Russia, I'm going to tell Darcy to stay here for a few nights, so she can be near the hospital. I've called Bridey, the nanny. She can have the family room couch if she has to overnight here."

Elmer's face clouded over. He said, "Must be pretty bad. Tierney's usually healthy as an ox. I'll be here by the phone, Love, if there's anything I can do."

"Tell me what's going on." Dr. Green examined Tierney's glassy eyes. He was lean and athletic, with iron-colored hair and earnest brown eyes. Darcy responded to his calm demeanor with a controlled account, as he listened to Tierney's heart and lungs with a stethoscope.

"We're going to have to do some tests," he said. "Her symptoms don't match any easy diagnosis. Could be spinal meningitis. I'll take a spinal tap right now. Hours count with meningitis. Could be something else. There's a lot of strange diseases these days, with all the immigration and everything. Even global warming is spawning new maladies, you know. Any idea where she might have picked this up in the last, say, two weeks?"

Darcy hesitated, glancing out the window. "Last week we were at the airport, and Tierney was sucking a chunk of ice. She picked it up off the floor in front of a vending machine."

Tierney didn't make a sound as the doctor slowly inserted the giant hypodermic needle between two lower vertebra to take a sample of her spinal fluid. She just looked up at her mother with sad glazed eyes.

"I'm putting her on i.v. in the intensive care unit. Her vital signs are weak. We'll do everything we can for her."

Darcy kissed her daughter's forehead as the nurse took the wilted child away.

In the waiting room, the TV was on, low but audible. Darcy would normally have read the paperback she always kept in her purse, but today she was too numb. And the topic brought Reinhold to mind.

On the screen a reporter in a bright blue parka stood before an array of national flags blowing straight out in a strong wind.

"Today the Ronne Ice Shelf followed its sister, the Ross, into the sea."

He continued in voiceover as arresting pictures played on the screen. Colossal slabs of ice ruptured and plunged into an ocean burdened with icebergs.

Darcy stared with an involuntary clamping of her teeth. Reinhold, Santa Fe, Tierney, the Ice, all compressed her under an immense weight. She felt herself trapped as within a glacier, inching with enormous gravity toward some vague ruin.

CHAPTER 45
Friday, February 3

DARCY'S ANXIETY intensified into raw fear as she approached the nursing station from the elevator and saw the duty nurse's demeanor whipsaw. Business-as-usual slid into a professional, restrained compassion that masked intense concern.

"Good morning, Mrs. Malone. We moved Tierney last night to Room 402. The doctor thought she'd breathe easier on the respirator. That's the room, right over there, closest to our station."

The night before, Darcy had finally left Tierney's bedside at two a.m. Her child's tossing had stopped and she seemed to be sleeping, although Darcy worried it was a coma. The night doctor assured her, "She's not on the extreme list. Go home and get some rest."

Now, by the hospital bed again, each hour felt like a day. Darcy studied the green stabs of a heart monitor, spikes like mountain peaks convulsing from a barren plain, as the thin hiss of a tube taped under Tierney's nose fed oxygen into her little nostrils.

Mariah joined them at midday to spell her daughter, but Darcy said, "Mom, I've got to talk to you. Let's get some fresh air in the garden."

In the hospital patio Darcy searched for a way to begin as they walked without speaking, elbows linked, through the labyrinth maze patterned with brown cobbles on the beige concrete. A Virgin Mary stood at the center, facing east. They paused on the white granite bench suspended in the hands of four tiny earth goddesses. Midwinter sun filtered through naked branches of a weeping willow as Mariah took her daughter's chilly hand between both of hers gently on her lap.

"Mom, in all these empty hours, wondering if she'll pull through, my mind keeps going over and over how this could have come to pass. At first, I thought Tierney just got random germs on a dirty ice cube she ate off the air-port carpet when we took Reinhold down there. I know you don't believe in random events, but to me it seemed like pure bad luck, or one of those things that just happen."

"You said 'at first.' What do you think now?"

"I suddenly remembered a detail I'd forgotten. The more I thought about it, the more vivid it got."

Mariah cocked her head.

"When Tierney showed me where she got the ice cube, a big, gnarly man was standing there. He had a scruffy, black beard, a big neck, and he wore a black silk turtleneck. Our eyes met for a moment, and then he went to the hostess and made a big stink about how they should clean up the mess by the drink machine. He spoke in a thick accent."

"So?"

"My brain kept repeating things like, 'Black leotards, commandos wear them; black jumpsuits, assassins wear them.' I started imagining he was one of the people Mahmoud worked for. The people who killed him. That they de-cided to use a biological agent on Tierney to scare me back into laundering their filthy stolen art through this Santa Fe job."

Darcy felt the pressure of her mother's hand. "Now relax, Darcy."

A sob caught in Darcy's chest. "I'm sorry, I just can't get it out of my head." She waited while a nurse walked by helping a teenager with new crutches, leg in a rainbow-graffitied cast.

"Darcy. Darcy..." Mariah soothed.

"No, Mom. I'm not making this up. I never told you the whole story. The night Mahmoud… died… he had gone to get Thai take-out… I gave him the money. When he didn't come back, I went to the phone. His wallet was there, and a little envelope that said, "If I'm not back by eleven, open this." I ripped it open. There was a letter, which said the Brothers had threatened to kill him to scare me, but if they got him my survival would depend on stonewalling them. I still have the note."

A cloud shadow darkened the cobbles. Mariah's eyes narrowed.

"They were only interested in making me manipulate the gallery's import license to cover border entry of their looted art. And 'exports.' He said they'd never believe he'd told me what was going on, and if I quit the gallery it would be too risky to kill me—the investigation would get too close to the whole scheme."

"Why didn't you tell the police?"

"I couldn't prove I wasn't involved. Mom…"

Mariah nodded encouragement, squeezed Darcy's trembling hands.

"I *was* involved. What I knew could have sent me to jail. Their ring was trafficking in stolen masterpieces. The really big ones. Rembrandts, van Goghs. Their clients are the biggest corporate moguls in the world. I was just a pawn. They don't sell the art. They trade it. Like baseball cards. And sometimes they trade it for favors."

"What do you mean?"

"Assassinations. Price concessions at OPEC meetings. Nuclear warheads. Money's nothing to these people. Power is everything. And status. Owning these paintings is how you rise in their club."

"You knew this?"

"In those days, I didn't care about anyone. I was cynical about everything, especially governments and corporations. That was before I met Reinhold."

The sun broke through again. Mariah took in a long breath as if she were gathering Darcy's story into a container.

"I didn't know names or details that could implicate people. I was really stuck. After Mahmoud's picture was in the paper, the morning they found his wrecked car, someone called with threats. I did what Mahmoud said. I screamed my lover's outrage, which was plenty real. I convinced them I knew nothing. They called twice more within a month, but then I quit the gallery, burned my bridges, and they stopped."

"This isn't so far from what you told us at the time, Sweetheart, although I never knew you had proof."

"I can show you the note—I never showed you before. But a couple of days ago something else happened. I didn't link it to Tierney until I sat there for hours by her bed."

Darcy studied the willow shadows dancing at their feet, undulating lines punctuated by dots of swelling winter buds awaiting spring.

"Remember in the paper last week, they found the bodies of two men from Iraq and published their pictures? The paper said they were terrorists. I didn't think anything of it, but two days ago in the park I bumped into the young woman who used to run the Thai restaurant where Mahmoud went that night."

Darcy stopped while a doctor in his stark white coat strode by their bench, avoiding the maze. "I didn't recognize her at first, when she tugged on my sleeve. But she said, 'Weren't you Mahmoud's girl?' and I knew instantly who she was. She said, 'Did you see those two dead Iraqi men in the paper? I thought of you. They were the two men I saw who forced Mahmoud into a car.'"

"Why are you telling me this now?" Mariah asked.

Darcy slumped over, elbows on her knees. Her gaze plunged into the web of sympathetic shadows. "I'm thinking of Luke. You always said we are responsible for all the consequences of our acts. I'm afraid, Mom. I'm afraid for Tierney and Finn because of what I did so long ago. If something happened, I'm afraid of the guilt. I couldn't face twenty years of grieving. I need the help now."

Mariah put both arms around her daughter and held her close. "Forgive me, Darcy. I beg you, forgive me for not being there. I preached, but that was it. I'm learning about responsibility only now. If I'd mothered you better, maybe... But it's not about guilt. It's true, we're destined to live the consequences of what we do. Or don't do. Think, or don't think. But responsibility means ability to respond. When consciousness comes, or expands, or strikes— the lesson is to respond. As best you can, hopefully wisely, but at least aware."

A puffed-up sparrow clung to a willow branch for a second—then flew on. Mariah wiped the tears from Darcy's cheeks and went on, "I believe you now, Baby. I think you're doing exactly the right thing. I'm glad you told me. Stay alert, think it through."

Darcy approached the final chink. *The Japanese part. She doesn't need to know. At least I'll protect her from that.*

Mariah's forehead wrinkled. "I don't know if the man at the airport was part of it. We'll probably never know, but I think at least your unconscious used his image as a trigger for bigger things. Like a dream. Like telling me the

173

whole story—bolstering your cautiousness about this strange Santa Fe business—honing your alertness while Reinhold's gone." She rubbed her brow. "We'll see this through together. Okay? I'm with you this time."

"Should I tell the doctors?"

Mariah got the distant look in her eyes. "No… No, it wouldn't add any insight, and the furor it would unleash would divert everyone's energy from Tierney. Especially yours. She needs you most of all. Stay focused."

Hand-in-hand, they returned to Tierney's room.

Mariah shut off the eleven o'clock news—the collapse of the Ronne Ice Shelf—when Darcy came home. They sat with Elmer at the kitchen table where Mariah poured three glasses of Oporto. Candlelight, and Mariah's usual incense, created a gentle ambience.

"I'm fighting despair, Mom. My brain keeps wanting to say, 'You're losing her. You're losing her.' But my heart just turns it off—won't listen. This afternoon, after you left, she went into hallucinations. She screamed about white fields and burning mountains, smoke and thunder. I don't know what it means. I just hang on, and I keep thinking, 'If I'm just hanging on, what's Tierney doing?'"

Darcy fell silent, staring into her goblet of blood-red Port.

Mariah looked at her in the flickering candlelight. She saw her not as a distraught, anguished mother with fatigue lines on her forehead, but as the Darcy-essence, at her best, as if silhouetted in happiness against the sunset, auburn hair blowing in the sea breeze, broad easy smile, hazel eyes that could look right through you or melt your heart, depending on her mood. Mariah's inner eye saw Darcy as a soul brimming with the most intense experience of a lifetime.

She slipped into the memory of Darcy's birth, and was engorged with the feeling of Darcy's whole lifetime, the ecstasies and torments, the tiny moments and the monumental ones, the galaxy still expanding. A stronger bond cannot be forged than the one between a mother and a child who nearly died together in childbirth. Despite the lost years. That's what she called them.

She looked out the dark window at the shadow of the leafless plum tree in the streetlight. Elmer's words shattered the feminine interlude like a stone tossed into a still pond. "Tierney's words… sound like something Nostradamus would say."

Mariah gave a start as her reverie evaporated, then intercepted his thought. "Tierney may have seen something profound. It may be a curse, or a blessing. Maybe both. I saw the pictures in my mind as you were speaking, Darcy. Not really pictures, just impressions, pre-impressions, like paints mixed on a palette before they reach the canvass. I think I'll draw a card for Tierney."

She reached behind to the bookshelf and produced her old Tarot deck. She shuffled it over and over, eyes shut, with practiced skill from years of usage. Then her hands were still. She fanned the sky-blue cards into a perfect semicircle, ran her fingertips over the smooth surface of the fan, back and forth. She withdrew three cards and laid them on the table in front of Darcy.

"Six of Wands—Trust. Ace of Cups—Ecstasy. And Eight of Worlds—Change."

Both women studied the symbols.

Mariah spoke. "Remember, they're not prophecies. They're just little windows into your own unconscious knowledge. I'd say you're supposed to trust Tierney. My intuition is, though, she'll be fine. The ace could be telling you to expect something ecstatic. Maybe it points to a sudden recovery, just like she came down with this so suddenly. Maybe you're supposed to let her be a little different for a while, a little changed, you know. I'm betting she'll be fine by the time you leave for Ireland."

"Do a card for her future—from now to Easter," Darcy said, ignoring her mother's comment about prophesy.

Mariah re-inserted the cards and shuffled again. She repeated the ritual and laid a single card on the table.

"The IX. Hermit! That's health. It connects to Virgo, ruled by Mercury. He's the messenger of the gods. Tierney has to walk her own path, Darcy. She has the strength, and the integrity. Make sure she has some quiet, alone time. Inner solitude allows her to anticipate her own future. The Hermit symbolizes the law of perfection, uniting material and spiritual realms—health and harvest. You two should have an epic six weeks."

Peacefulness settled over Darcy. She took her glass to her father's office to email Reinhold. She brought him up to date on Tierney, and went on:

> Today I remembered your story from the park that drizzly day over Christmas—how her little hand held your finger so tightly while you walked along not talking—and how she looked up and said, "Don't be nervous, Daddy. It's okay. Up there above the clouds, the sun is shining." Last night I prayed, Don't let her go up above the clouds. I want her here—with us, not the angels.
>
> At one point, Darling, I felt your presence and love so intensely I looked around for you. I wondered if you were dreaming of us just then.

I don't know why, but I expect to see her out of intensive care tomorrow morning. I'm feeling certain she'll be all right, Reinhold. Please don't worry. The crisis is past. She'll be strong enough for the vacation by Valentine's Day.

This emergency got me back to the important things. I'm trying to let the Santa Fe thing drift on its own. It's all made me realize just how much I love you. I'm happy you're there, doing what you're so fabulous at. I really miss you, Darling. It'll be so great to see you in Ireland. It seems like forever, but time will pass quickly.

Love you, love you.

Darcy

CHAPTER 46
Saturday, February 4

CBOX TV, The Morning Show with Mildred Skowronski

Now for the weather segment of our show, we take you to Phil Cox, reporting from the Monterey Bay Aquarium in Monterey, California. Phil?

"Thank you. The Antarctic ice disaster is playing out all over the world now, Mildred. I'm told sea level is a full foot higher than just a week ago. No one doubts that this is due to the incredible collapse of the Ross and the Ronne ice shelves in Antarctica.

At 6:36 this morning, it was high tide here in Monterey. You can see it's a beautiful day here. There were no ill effects at high tide. But, Mildred, the combination of a major storm and high winds along the coast could magnify that one-foot change. Waves could reach higher and farther than their historic extremes."

Phil, what do the experts predict next?

"The weather report is not comforting. The U.S. Weather Bureau says a powerful storm is moving from the Hawaiian Islands toward the West Coast. It's expected to hit landfall at Cape Mendocino late Monday or early Tuesday. Officials are planning to post warning signs along the beaches and piers here in the Monterey/Carmel area. We'll keep you posted."

Thank you Phil.

Next, we have a report from Christina Mathias in Fort Walton Beach, Florida, just east of Pensacola on the Gulf of Mexico.

"Mildred, I'm here with Whitney and Darlene Brittington in Fort Walton Beach, Florida. Whitney, tell us what happened to you this morning."

176

'Well, last year we bought ourselves a honey of a boat—a pre-owned 1991 Sunseeker Martinique 38 Sport Cruiser—twin Volvo two-hundred horsepower inboards—loaded. She was tied to our little dock out here. When we went out this morning to take a spin .... no boat. My family's owned this place for fifty years. My dad was a fisherman. He built that dock over there with his own hands. For the last ten years, the top planks have just been hovering above the high water line when the moon is dark and the tides are highest.

'This morning our little dock was underwater. The tie-up lines must have come loose in the wave action and our poor little Tea Cup Tina III just wandered away. We alerted the Coast Guard, and they'll find her. Probably beached somewhere.'

"Thank you, Whitney, and good luck to you.

"I checked with the Coast Guard, Mildred, and they have hundreds of calls like this. Older facilities just weren't built for this eventuality."

Thank you, Christina. Similar news is coming in from every coastline in the world. Summer storms off Tasmania have propelled the surf far inland at the Edwardian Sands resort on the spectacular Eaglehawk Neck northeast of Hobart. The sea has destroyed all the beach-view cabanas. Wherever weather satellites show storm activity, there are reports of port facilities, fishing villages, resorts—anything sensitive to maximum high tides—seriously damaged on every continent.

We've called the Office of Emergency Preparedness in Washington D.C., too, and we will report what they say when they get back to us.

Now for the sports wrap-up. In ice hockey...

Darcy's prediction came true. She found Tierney sitting in a ward with four other children, finishing breakfast. "The nurse said I have a fine appetite this morning, Mommy."

Darcy had three of Tierney's favorite books from her grandmother's house. Before the first two pages were turned, all the children in the wing were sitting in their bathrobes on one bed or another, listening to the dramas. When Darcy got on a roll, especially with an appreciative audience, she could render a story with the expressiveness of a professional script reader.

Out in the hallway later, the duty doctor told Darcy if Tierney's recovery continued at last night's pace, he was going to recommend discharge Monday morning. He seemed embarrassed that the hospital still had no diagnosis. "Probably tropical, clearly rare. Wouldn't surprise me to see a complete recovery after a week at home."

Tierney seemed perfectly happy playing with the hospital's toys and her new friends, so Darcy kissed her three times on the top of her head and said, "I need to go back to Babushka's house. I'll see you this afternoon."

After a quick feeding of chubby Finn Malone and a game of hide and fetch with pie tins and measuring spoons, Darcy put the toddler down for a nap and checked her email. Reinhold wrote,

I've booked contingency tickets back to San Francisco, if you and the children need me.

Darcy replied, "No need, thank the gods," and gave him an up-to-the-minute report. Then she drove down the hill into Berkeley.

Saturday afternoon was the weekly drop-in session at her martial arts school. She always kept one set of her nunchaku and manriki gusari under the front seat of her SUV. It was her favorite nunchaku, the red mahogany sticks polished to a velvet touch, the cast-iron links of the short connecting chain exuding strength in their jet black simplicity. She was less fond of the manriki gusari with its stainless steel, lead-weighted grips and long chrome-plated chain, but the art of its movement more than made up for its less genteel look.

Master Anh Thahn was of the Heiwa school. 'Heiwa' translated from the Japanese meant 'peace' and 'harmony' The device of the school was 'Learn to live, not to fight.' According to this principle, the teaching was slanted more to the 'art' than the 'martial' aspect. It was uncommon for a Vietnamese to have advanced so far in this Japanese tradition. But Berkeley had been a city of radical exceptions for a century, and these times were no different.

For his Saturday sessions, the Master rented a decommissioned, white-washed church. Darcy loved the street. Mariah and Elmer had lived two blocks up when she was born at Alta Bates hospital in 1974 during Elmer's law school years. Maybe there were a few more homeless now, too many chrome and stucco apartment units, and the annoying traffic barriers, but Berkeley stood eternal in her mind, a temple to the cutting edge of intellectual ferment and radical political vigor.

After the calming and centering exercises, Master Anh Thahn surprised the assembled students. "Today we will see how Darcy Malone is developing. Please stand here, Darcy." He gestured to the center of the exercise mat, his nunchaku swinging darkly in his left hand.

"Master, my life is in turmoil, my child's in the hospital, I haven't practiced for three days, and my concentration is way out of kilter. May I have permission to defer the test to a more suitable time?"

The Master inclined his head. "The skills I teach you are most highly needed at times like this. There is no better moment to reveal how you hold inside what I teach. Adversity furthers."

He stepped to the center and assumed the stance. Darcy surrendered, thought *I'll fight the Brothers for Tierney*. She centered and slowed her breathing. They faced each other motionless, muscles taut, eyelids relaxed, their interlocking gaze focused yet peripherally dispersed, like a summer cloud with lightning in its center.

As proficient practitioners, they sensed together the moment to begin. Their bodies rotated in graceful whorls, arms and legs darting out and retracting to the core in a rhythm punctuated by staccato thrusts that would dash a less skilled student to the ground. Their sticks whirled in a blur, whistling through the air in a drone reminiscent of distant thunder. Suddenly the Master made contact and Darcy was flat on her back.

Defeat was bitter for Darcy, frightening. The Master's face was a calm mask. "Let the energy recharge your center. Do not waste it on frivolous anger. No blame. Rise to a superior position."

They resumed. This time Darcy made contact. The Master retained balance. They were locked in combat. For a moment they froze in time. The Master disengaged effortlessly. He dropped his arms and stilled his weapon. The test was over.

"You have done well, my student. You learn well. May you prevail over all obstacles and keep your center in every maelstrom."

Darcy wanted to cry, both from the defeat and from the moral victory. But in the energy of the class and the Master, she directed the impulse inward and felt the electric tingle rocket through her spine, then expand in a sphere to encompass everything her sensory perceptions touched.

CHAPTER 47
Sunday, February 5

ON THE SIX O'CLOCK NEWS, Congressman Thad Parker stood alongside the Governor, the Director of the Port, and the Mayor of Sacramento, staring from the Port of Sacramento's Wharf 6 at the water below, a foot higher than it would normally be. One by one each "newsmaker" answered the questions of the small knot of reporters.

"The rise in sea level experienced along the coast has also been noticed here, of course," the Port Director said, "but it would not in any way affect the operation of the port, as far as I can see."

The Mayor expected the city of Sacramento to continue to play a vital role in the commerce of the Central Valley.

The Governor urged all Californians to remain calm, to report to their jobs or places of business as usual, to retain their confidence in the state and federal governments' ability to "rise to this challenge." The reporters appreciated the governor's quotable pun with chuckles.

Congressman Parker said nothing of substance, but his words suggested reassurance. "I expect to be called to a Congressional briefing on the situation in the near future. My office has been inundated with calls, but I am afraid there's little I can offer at this time beyond what can be learned by calling the U.S. Geological Survey, the Coast Guard, and the National Weather Service."

A brash young reporter got his face time on camera, commenting to viewers, "I'm sure Congressman Parker would like to lighten the burden on his staff, but I can tell our viewers that from the agencies he mentioned callers are likely to learn through recorded messages only the observable facts of sea level measurements, estimates of tide consequences, storms, and so forth. They will also be cautioned against unwarranted speculation."

CHAPTER 48

Monday, February 6

DR. GREEN was cheerful.

"The lab will continue running cultures for a week, to see if they can match the virus, but Tierney's underlying health is beautifully resilient and she's showing no more symptoms. Give her plenty of rest and fluids, and call me if you have any concerns. I'll let you know if we get a firm diagnosis."

As she left the hospital parking lot, Darcy caught herself again morbidly inspecting every nearby car and every strange pedestrian. *Get a grip, Darcy, get a grip,* she silently reprimanded herself. *You were never that important, even then. You can't possibly be, now.*

She poked on the radio's power button.

"*. . . We may not get heavy rains right here, but high wind is a certainty. Regardless of local variations, however, the sea winds and the storm center are pushing sea water directly toward the Golden Gate.*

"I'm in our news van just north of the toll booths here at the Bay Bridge Toll Plaza. Ten minutes ago, waves started sending water onto the tarmac. The Highway Patrol is watching closely.

"So far, traffic is moving slowly and steadily through the three- to five-inch deep pooling. But morning rush-hour traffic is backing up on both I-80 and I-580, so if you haven't already left home, we suggest you have another coffee and delay your transit for a couple of hours.

"I would be cautious about BART, too. Trains were running on schedule, but this flood tide is likely to send water over the walls along the Embarcadero in the city and it could penetrate BART stations and Muni platforms. They have personnel on alert.

"As for sea level, let's just say if all that ice in Antarctica were still frozen solid, it would take a major hurricane to have the effect we're seeing today. This is an all-time historic high. I'm afraid we can expect problems like this at least once a month, and they'll be worse every time a storm coincides with the new moon.

"This is Don Harrington for KBAY at the Bay Bridge Toll Plaza."

Darcy turned the radio off. Instead of using the on-ramp to I-580, she got in the I-80 commuter lane with the express flyover at Emeryville. "See, Tierney, we get to go through the fast lane because you and Finn and I make three. One, two, three." Tierney proudly repeated the numbers.

Even in the commuter lane, traffic faltered. By the time Darcy reached the top of the flyover, it was stop-and-go. Then, progress halted altogether. Between the trees lining the Toll Plaza, Darcy could see a blaze of flashing police lights. She felt her stomach tighten. *Easy, Kid, keep the grip.* She turned to the radio again.

The sports news faded into the 9:48 traffic update.

"At the Bay Bridge Toll Plaza, the Highway Patrol has stopped all westbound traffic due to the unprecedented flood tide. In the last twenty minutes wind-whipped waves riding the incoming tide have washed out the barriers around the radio towers here. Pooling in the vehicle plaza has now deepened to over one foot. Late rush-hour traffic is at a dead standstill, backed up on all approaches for at least three miles. These conditions are expected to last until 1:30 at the Bay Bridge and 2:00 at the San Mateo Bridge."

Four hours? Darcy was incredulous.

There was no way off the flyover. Drivers turned their motors off. Many got out of their cars, stood around in little groups.

By 10:45 Darcy had exhausted the SUV's entire reading supply.

By 11:30, the three Malones had sung every song they knew.

By 12:00, Finn had finished the one bottle. Tierney fidgeted. "Mommy, I'm tired of coloring. When are we going to go?"

The 12:00 o'clock national news headlined the flood tide story. Shoreline highways throughout California were experiencing closures. The perennial loss of cliffside houses in Aptos and Malibu were reported from storm, tide and the new sea level. One interview assured listeners there were no problems at the Diablo Canyon Nuclear Power Plant's cooling tower intake pumps.

There was a bit of action at 12:15: a med-evac helicopter from the Children's Hospital helipad zoomed close overhead and landed on the elevated portion of I-580. They could see tiny people in yellow rain gear running around, getting someone out of a vehicle and into the helicopter, which then took off to the east

At 12:30, Darcy noticed in her rear view mirror an enterprising individual wheeling a hotdog stand between lanes of parked cars. *No, it's not… Keep the grip.* She made the mistake of announcing the approaching treat to the children, only to see him reverse directions five cars short of her SUV, out of merchandise. Tierney's animated smile turned to a trembling upper lip, her eyes threatening to fill up like the toll plaza. Then Darcy remembered the emergency pack of animal crackers in the glove compartment, and loss of fortitude in the car was averted once again.

"Mommy, where's Daddy now?"

"In a big city called Moscow. That's in Russia, across the ocean."

"Can we find it on the map when we get home?"

"Sure, Sweetie. I know right where it is."

"Mommy, why do you and Daddy say that thing when you say goodbye?"

A new butterfly in Darcy's stomach flapped. She caught her breath. "Well, a long, long time ago a friend of mine named Dave drove his brother Michael to college. Near the end of the trip, Dave and Michael got into an argument over something stupid. They both got mad and stopped talking to each other. After Dave dropped his brother off at college, he left and neither one of them said 'I'm sorry.' Sadly, Michael died that night in his sleep. For some reason, he just needed to go back to heaven. At first, Dave felt bad that his brother might think he was still mad at him. He felt like he could never again tell Michael he loved him. But then Dave realized that he and his brother had loved each other well for their whole lives and up in heaven Michael would know he had always been dearly loved even if they had little fights or arguments and got angry with each other now and then. No one ever knows, really, when they'll need to go back to heaven. So when Daddy and I say goodbye to each other, like at the airport last week, it makes us feel good to remember that we've loved each other very well, and any little fights or arguments we might have don't change our love at all."

"Oh," Tierney said, "I see now."

At 1:30, Darcy saw vehicles at the toll plaza creep forward, right on time. The pulse of movement reached the Malone SUV in twenty minutes. Nearby cars fired up on cue as if an invisible official had announced Drivers, Start Your Engines.

They reached the toll plaza. Caltrans had suspended toll collection to facilitate traffic.

Darcy lowered her window for some fresh air. It smelled briny, putrid. The tarmac was littered with muddy debris, skeins of ice plant and moss, small chunks of driftwood, a smattering of styrofoam, waterlogged cardboard, plastic containers of every color and shape—the accumulation of months of trash that always blew eastward across the bay to lodge against the Oakland/Berkeley shore—now washed inexorably onto the Plaza.

"Pee yeeeww."

"That's not such polite talk, Tierney." Darcy rolled up her window.

They passed the tollbooths and crept across the Bridge, arriving home by 3:00.

Bridey had come in by BART and was a welcome new face-of-the-day to Tierney. Finn was zonked—plopped into the crib. Darcy turned to her email, finding a report from Reinhold:

> My Dearest,
> Negotiations are slower than I'd hoped. We've been backed into an extended political massage session. My team and the government boys who have to approve this thing are going up to a dacha to work some things out. It's called Zavidova, right on the Volga, 120 kilometers north of Moscow via Solnichnigorsk on the main road to St. Petersburg. They have winter skeet shooting, snowmobiles, caviar—you know the drill. Our best guess is we'll be there a week, given the supplies of vodka I heard them order. They'll have email there, but surveillance is severe and paranoia running high, so I won't write until I get back to Moscow.
> I saw the Bay Bridge on the news over here at breakfast an hour ago. From the helicopter footage, the toll plaza looked weird all inundated like that. I guess everyone will have to get used to it on bad days until they get better barriers. Over here, news of sea level has people worried about Russia's ports in the North Sea and Vladi-

vostok. And their favorite holiday beaches washing away in Thailand.

I'm ecstatic about Tierney's good health. Way to hang in there, Darcy. Give the kids fuzzy bear hugs for me.

You have all my love.

Reinhold

Darcy clicked reply and narrated their harrowing commute, gratis the newly-muscled sea.

She lay exhausted but unsleeping for two hours on her side of the bed, running and re-running loops of tape in her mind about goodbyes and heaven, shotguns and vodka, storm tides and lowlands in Denmark and Bangladesh, keeping images of art and Arabs, Mahmoud and car wrecks at bay, until she was finally lulled to sleep by the wind-driven rain that had blown in by dinner-time.

MARIAH had gone to bed. Elmer emerged from a drowsy lull to catch what was now called the "Evening Icecap Report."

On Antarctica, the command structure at research stations has tightened dramatically following the one-foot rise in sea level. The U.S. military has been placed in charge of all press. The structure is the familiar model used during full scale war activities, prototyped in the 2003 attack on Iraq. All official press information is now disseminated in "war room" briefing sessions...

The private radio operators also allege a massive cover-up is underway.

... Labels aside, one ham radio operator claims to now be transmitting clandestinely because the equipment of a colleague was confiscated.

Elmer turned the TV off, retrieved his journal from the nightstand, and wrote, "Have to be careful now what news to believe about sea level."

CHAPTER 49

Tuesday, February 7

THE NATIONAL TIMES

More Volcanic Meltdown Rumors from Antarctica

By Quincy Ulrich, Science Reporter

A thousand miles south of Rio, disquieting events are increasingly rumored. Yesterday, short wave enthusiasts in the U.S. were receiving messages from their counterparts in Antarctica. Today, no transmissions are being received. All efforts to contact the ham radio community in Antarctica have failed.

News teams on the scene are being given limited and obviously managed news briefings. Seismic monitoring stations in other places have, however, for three days now reported swarms of major earthquakes in the Antarctic reaching as high as 7.0 on the Richter scale.

Rapidly spreading rumors hold that another rise in sea level, double or triple the one-foot already seen, is all but certain within a few weeks or months. Encrypted messages to this effect are said to be streaming into the White House and the Pentagon. Conjectures abound that the White House is assembling an emergency action team.

In spite of the silence from Antarctica, scientists elsewhere have been willing to answer our questions. Some have pin-pointed earthquakes directly under the West Antarctic Ice Sheet near the old Ross and Ronne Ice Shelves. They say that when the floating ice "shelves" collapsed and pulled the "grounded" ice into the sea, the release of its enormous weight triggered the earthquakes. This phenomenon has been documented on Iceland for decades. The fear is that even more land-ice will collapse in the earthquakes. If so, sea level would rise everywhere. Add volcanic meltdowns on the land and you understand the extreme nature of the alleged encrypted reports.

CHAPTER 50
Wednesday, February 8

DARCY SPOTTED a rare on-street parking space just outside the Safeway plaza. She was treating Finn and Tierney to dessert at Starbucks after what the fully recovered Tierney now called "luncheon."

They were approaching the entrance when a man appeared, clad in a mud-smeared, camouflage raincoat and crumbling green galoshes. Under a rain-soaked newspaper hat his dark brown face and bloodshot eyes were framed by a mat of black hair and beard. Darcy suddenly felt the softness and warmth of her daughter's hand.

The man nodded, and with a practiced sweep of his arm pulled a cardboard sign from under his coat flap, tin cup dangling from a corner. The abrupt move startled Darcy. Tierney clutched her hand more tightly. Darcy read the placard:

THE WORLD IS ENDING!
THE ICE COMETH, MAN.
HELP ME WITH A MEAL.
IT MAY BE MY LAST.

Darcy smiled, stopped, let go her right hand. "Just a minute, Honey." She dug in her pocket, dropped two quarters in the cup, then took Tierney's hand again and walked on toward Starbucks.

Tierney asked, "Why did you do that, Mommy?"

"That man is very clever, Sweetheart. He just doesn't know how to get a job."

The aromatic air in Starbucks warmed Darcy inside and out. For the third consecutive day, flood tides had stopped traffic at the Bay Bridge Toll Plaza and, predictably, the weather was the conversation du jour.

The coffee girl had purple hair. "Nonfat latte and a carrot cake?"

Darcy smiled. "As always. Can you believe this rain?"

"God, no. MUNI was a total nightmare this morning," the girl said. "It took me twice as long to get to work today. They said the downtown tracks couldn't drain fast enough and the trains were all backed up at the turnabout."

Darcy grimaced. "Ugh. I hope Bridey—you know, our babysitter?— doesn't have trouble getting in on BART. The kids are going stir crazy cooped up in the house. I swear, I'm going to have to trade in the SUV for an ark if this keeps up."

The counter girl laughed obligingly, but Darcy winced at her dumb joke as she herded her brood toward the nearest vacant table.

She picked up an abandoned San Francisco Chronicle and skimmed the front page to the only story she hadn't heard earlier.

San Quentin Cons In Daring Escape.

Three prisoners carried out a daring escape from San Quentin Prison last night and are still at large.

According to prison authorities, the men used female chapel volunteers as hostages and managed to evade security procedures. One corrections officer was injured in the incident. Sergeant Mason Pringmore, a thirteen-year veteran at San Quentin, suffered a concussion when he was attacked by one of the escapees. Warden Harmon Blakeley told reporters that the escape was aided by outsiders who sped away with the convicts in a car that has not been identified. Authorities are asking for witnesses to come forward.

The article continued on the back page. Darcy skipped to the bottom "Elias Barnes, forty, also African-American, has been incarcerated for sixteen years, and had been considered a model prisoner, according to Blakeley." The article concluded with the warning that all three fugitives were thought to be armed and should be considered dangerous.

From the next table over a male voice said, "All that environmental news bores me too. I couldn't help notice you skipped it, like I did."

Darcy looked up. The man said, "I've seen you around the neighborhood before. Your kids sure are well behaved."

Darcy said, "Thank you." Then smiled and turned back to the paper, thinking *I know I've never seen you before.* As a child, before her rebel years, and again when the effects of her drug tripping wore off, Darcy had had an uncanny visual memory for faces. She had even taken a class on "reading" faces at a personal development workshop in Berkeley.

The man caught Tierney's eye and said, "What's your name?"

Before Darcy could intervene, Tierney said her name and asked, "What's that around your neck?" The man's navy blue velvet sweatshirt looked like a jeweler's display for his gold chain and pendant.

The man said, "Dr. Seuss would call it a medagallion, but grown-ups say medallion. Would you like one of my cookies? I have an extra." He reached across to Darcy's table with his offering.

Darcy's heart skipped a beat and she felt adrenaline surge through her whole body. This stranger had either stumbled upon or intentionally dropped a Brotherhood codeword she had learned from Mahmoud. Praying it was a coincidence, and that the cookie wasn't a biological agent, she quickly took the man's gift and said, "Why, thank you very much. I'm afraid we'll have to go now, though. I'm expecting a call at home."

As she hurried the children back to the car, she threw the cookie in the trash can. She turned to Tierney, "Never, never eat anything strangers give you, Honey. Never."

CHAPTER 51
Thursday, February 9

REINHOLD MALONE fired and missed again. The clay pigeon clattered unharmed onto the ice-solid Volga River. Approximately two out of every three of his clay pigeons were escaping this afternoon, giving him the worst score on the American team, which was losing badly to the Russians. He insisted it was last night's vodka, but the truth was he had never cracked the knack of skeet shooting.

Reinhold and Wyatt Gibson had their own snowmobile. After the others headed in for the banquet, they stayed on the riverbank and practiced shooting frosted pussy willows. An unlucky snow goose flew near—Wyatt's unerring blast transformed it into a bloody carcass skidding across the river ice. "Nice shot, but a bit of a waste, don't you think?" Reinhold commented. He and Wyatt had developed enough rapport to withstand occasional manly critiques.

Wyatt Gibson was an ex-employee of Troy Blake, now working for Chev-Al, the transnational oil consortium developing Russia's most challenging reserves. The consortium was to be the anchor tenant in the office complex Reinhold was trying to win for Blake, making Wyatt and Reinhold practically partners.

Reinhold had grown to like and respect the man during the negotiations. But Reinhold tended to like most people. He was more curious than cautious about stories of Wyatt's pre-corporate background. Rumor had it "Captain" Gibson had gone into the U.S. Army Special Forces after a Phi Beta Kappa career at Stanford and later was in the legendary intelligence corps that served Israeli commandos throughout the Middle East.

Reinhold's hand was on the ignition key to the snowmobile when Wyatt stopped him. "While we're alone, I wanted to talk to you." His eyes were wide and steely. Reinhold leaned back, tried to stay casual.

"What's up, Pal?"

"I've got a message for you. It's from high up in the U.S. government. I can't give you details of the source."

Reinhold's heart accelerated. He breathed the frigid air deeply, taking time to let his new perception of this man sink in.

"Okay..."

"Next spring the government thinks melting water from Greenland and the Arctic icecap could stop the Gulf Stream in the North Atlantic. Woods Hole scientists started predicting this in 2002. Looks like they were right."

"What's that have to do with me?"

"The energy needs of the U.S. are estimated to triple, because when the Gulf Stream stops, temperatures in North America will drop 10 degrees or more. That's why we secured the oilfields in Iraq, tapped the North Slope, got so cozy with Mexico and Venezuela. But we're having problems with Saudi Arabia and some of the oil nations in the West Pacific. And Nigeria."

"I don't get it."

"Your wife, Reinhold."

Reinhold steadied himself with the steering gear. "What the fuck are you talking about?"

"I thought you knew," Wyatt blurted. "Our people have been trying to get Darcy to help through our center in Santa Fe, New Mexico."

"Your people? What... I mean, what could she do?"

"Oh God. Well, I've started down the road, so I have to go to the end." His words became a torrent. "Your wife was part of a ring of Middle Eastern art thieves, Reinhold, who stole and traded masterpieces for their collector clients, the great sheiks who compete with each other to fill their secret galleries with the world's rarest items. She has knowledge of their system, and their people, which can help us gain leverage on the men who control the great Mid-East oil reserves."

Reinhold whispered, "I'm stunned, Wyatt. I really am. In fact, I'm not sure I believe you."

"You'd best believe me, Buddy. And when you get home, you'd best get ready to move to New Mexico. Santa Fe's a great place, you know. Besides, Reinhold, this whole deal with Blake and Chev-Al? It's part of the master plan for our control of petroleum in the coming crisis."

Reinhold asked naively, "Is this part of the Antarctic problem I heard about?"

Wyatt's face relaxed a touch. "Good. You're beginning to absorb. But, naaah, that Antarctic scare's got nothing to do with the North Atlantic current thing. The current's stopping because of the *Arctic* melt off. That's north, Reinhold. Not south. Although there's a little possibility that if too much melts in the south, that cold water too could impact ocean currents. But that's really not behind what we're working on."

Wyatt tucked his hands into his coat and chuckled, "We better go back. Someone might wonder why we're staying out in the cold."

IT TOOK all Darcy's strength to keep the car from being blown into the next lane by the wind blasting through the naked steel cables on the Bay Bridge. Even the weight of the SUV wasn't much ballast in the face of this energy. The twenty-four hour news station reported, *"Gusts on Mt. Tam are approaching one hundred ten miles an hour, and the Golden Gate is temporarily closed."*

Darcy and her partner, Winifred Klein, were headed for a 2:00 meeting in Alameda. Winifred hardly noticed the navigational issues—Darcy's upper body strength and mental concentration masked the effort it took to stay in her lane.

As they emerged from the tunnel on Treasure Island, Darcy turned the radio up. They fell silent. The report was from New York:

This morning the Washington Post ran a story of chilling proportions. Reliable White House sources now corroborate what, two days ago, were only rumors. The

White House has been receiving secret reports, they say, since as early as last Sun-
day, depicting a disaster more gargantuan than anything the government has ever
modeled. According to the Post, a series of volcanic caldera may have become sud-
denly active under what is called the West Antarctic Ice Sheet.

We put in a call to Orin Victor a vulcanologist from the University of Washing-
ton. Here's what he told us. "When volcanoes activate under glaciers, they melt
enormous amounts of ice with their legendary heat. This has been studied in Ice-
land, the world's largest active volcanic island. In 1996 over four cubic kilometers
of water broke through the ice north of the capital, Reykjavik. It destroyed all
houses, farms, power lines, bridges and highways in its flood path. There was a
warning—a 5.0 earthquake days before the flooding. In 1783 a glacial flood melted
by the largest eruption ever recorded there, killed half the people on the island and
three-fourths of all livestock.

"The ice is far thicker in Antarctica. If volcanoes erupt there, you're going to
have much more cataclysmic effects."

Darcy eased off the incline section of the bridge onto the level toll plaza.
"High tide was an hour ago, Winifred. Look at those white caps. The storm
pressure must be letting up despite this wind. No toll plaza flood today."

Several lanes were closed in the toll plaza. Flashing light barriers warned of
potholes worried open by the standing saltwater of the flood tides.

Winifred shook her head, as if to sort her thoughts. "I'm kinda freaked out
about this sea level thing, Darcy. But I've always been afraid of the ocean. The
pounding surf seemed so monster-like when I was little. As a teenager, I'd
stand on the cliff at the headlands and see the sun setting over the edge of the
ocean, and it just looked so impossibly big. It scared me, like the night sky
when you're far away from the city. Too big. You know what I mean?"

"You're a city kid, Winifred. This is just nature. And don't forget, the media always hypes the most sensational story of the week, whatever it is. This
volcano stuff, now. I think they're dabbling in Hollywood's waters, so to speak.
Besides, don't you think the government can protect the sea coasts from a
measly one-foot change in the water level? It'll just take a little time."

"Well, maybe. But I'm having nightmares about it."

Darcy ignored the comment. "I don't trust the government for everything,
but I think they're up to this one. See, look over there. That didn't take them
long, did it?"

She pointed to the side of the toll plaza. It was occupied by an armada of
yellow and orange construction equipment and a parallel line of concrete traffic
barriers with dirt and rock mounded in between. "Obviously to minimize traffic delays while the highway authority comes up with something better."

Dusk was approaching when Winfred got out at her flat on Dolores Street. Three minutes, and Darcy was at her apartment building's garage entrance. As she waited for the automatic door to open, she scanned the sidewalks a bit more carefully than usual. At the end of the block, a figure stepped quickly out of view. *The cookie guy?* She drove into the dimly lit garage, assuring herself, *I couldn't really see him clearly. Get a grip, Girl.*

CHAPTER 52
Friday, February 10

8:00 P.M. ON A FRIDAY in San Francisco is 7:00 a.m. Saturday morning in Moscow. With the children in bed, Darcy checked her email, hoping Reinhold would be back in Moscow now from the country estate. There it was, from late in the Russian night.

> My Dearest,
>
> Got your emails, God bless you. That flood tide sounded horrific. I'll update you when I can. Got back from the dacha at 8 tonight. Had to go right out for dinner and drinks. Too much vodka, etc.
>
> It makes all the difference in the world to know that the kids and you are well and happy. And safe.
>
> Love,
>
> Reinhold

Pretty cryptic, Darcy worried. *Safe?* But she resolved to wait another hour to call Reinhold, so he could wake up with coffee and maybe his favorite Russian breakfast: brown bread, Black Sea sausage, and what she called "that stinky cheese." In Russian it was called Tvorg.

She turned on the TV for some fluff, to the "entertainment news channel," the National Enquirer of the airwaves.

STAR NEWS T.V.'s Coffee Klatch anchor, Xavier Navarro, was interviewing earth sciences expert and activist, Naomi Rosenberg.

"There's a phenomenon in the science of geology known as 'Crustal Hotspots.' This is different from regular volcanoes.

"All volcanoes eject lava from beneath the crust onto the earth's surface. Lava is rock which is melted deep inside the earth by the pressure of billions of tons of rock above. Most lava is melted about sixty miles below the surface and finds its way through fissures and soft spots to the surface where it erupts as volcanoes.

"Here I have some charts to illustrate.

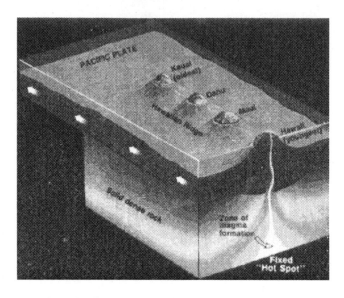

(http://pubs.usgs.gov/publications/text/hotspots.html)

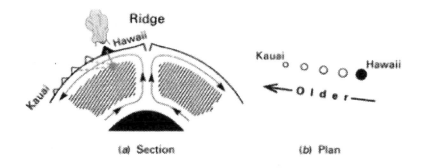

http://pubs.usgs.gov/publications/text/hotspots.html

"Sometimes, Xavier, lava comes not from sixty miles down, but from the astronomically hot inner core of earth itself, from approximately seventeen hundred miles below. This kind is often called magma. Where this happens is called a Crustal Hotspot.

"The most dramatic Crustal Hotspot existed long ago under Siberia. About two hundred million years ago, deep vents burst through and poured enough magma onto the surface to create a dome thousands of miles wide and several miles thick. Spread evenly over the entire Earth, it would have been ten feet deep."

Mind boggling, Naomi. Simply mind boggling.

"Okay. Now, there are smaller Crustal Hotspots several places on earth today, including Yellowstone Park, Iceland, Hawaii. But until now, Antarctica hasn't been studied enough to assess whether Crustal Hotspots exist there.

"However, you only have to look at a map of active volcanoes in West Antarctica to notice an ominous pattern. A CIA-based map, I might add."

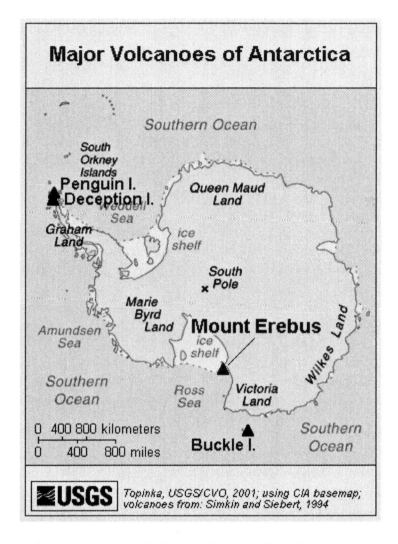

(http://vulcan.wr.usgs.gov/Volcanoes/Antarctica/Maps/map_antarctica_volcan oes.html)

"There are active, modern-day volcanoes in three locations: (1) here, on the Buckle Islands off of Victoria Land; (2) here, Mount Erebus, on the edge of the old

193

Ross Ice Shelf; and (3) here, on Penguin and Deception Islands, about three thousand miles further along the same line at the end of the Antarctic Peninsula. Is this line-up evidence of a string of Crustal Hotspots at the South Pole? At the Center, we say Yes. And others agree with us."

What do you draw from this, Naomi?

"Okay. The bad news? There's an obvious gap in the sequence. It suggests a fourth, missing Crustal Hotspot, evenly spaced with the other three. This places it directly under the West Antarctic Ice Sheet that borders the now-collapsed Ronne Ice Shelf.

"The very bad news, Xavier? This past November and December, scientists from two major universities conducted a study of gravitational mass variations in the earth's deep core beneath Antarctica. The results were to be published in the March issue of Science. These results supply the missing proof—proof not only of the missing fourth Crustal Hotspot but proof of magma surging up very recently toward the Antarctic ice. Magma roughly equivalent to the entire Himalaya mountain range."

Sounds terrible, Naomi.

"I'm not through, yet, Xavier. Six days ago, on February 4, swarms of 7.0 earthquakes under Western Antarctica were reported by seismic research stations around the world. Mysteriously, news was all but blacked out from Antarctica itself, under strict military management. Why?"

I suppose the military is suppressing the news until the government can assess its significance. A deep freeze cover-up, shall we say? What does it all mean? Can you put the possibilities in perspective, Naomi?

"Okay. Our researchers compared the current situation with the Lakagigar eruption in 1783 on the section of Iceland's Crustal Hotspot known as the Laki fissure. A chain of volcanic craters nearly twenty miles long formed along the Laki fissure.

"Set against what may be happening under Antarctica, the Lakagigar eruption was like striking a match across the street from a burning house. If the ice melted by Lakagigar was an ice cube, the ice about to be melted in Antarctica would fill an Olympic swimming pool.

"According to anonymous sources in the government—friends of mine, Xavier—not even rough estimates have been made of the number of miles of fissures that could be developing if the current storm of earthquakes is, indeed, a precursor of the Antarctic Hotspot breaking through."

Thank you Naomi. We'll stay in touch.

"Yes, we will."

Darcy snapped the TV off. She thought about seeing the toll plaza under-water, and the white caps clawing the edge of the emergency barriers on her way to Alameda. Somehow, notwithstanding the reputation of the Star News for abject sensationalism, the hotspot story had a frightening ring of authenticity. Her heart felt like a tom-tom.

She didn't wait. She dialed Reinhold's hotel. Got right through. Reinhold didn't even give her a chance to roll out the traditional lover's greeting he had grown so accustomed to hearing.

"People are in a frenzy over here, Darcy, from the latest rumors about Antarctica," he blurted out. "You've heard about the lava upsurge theories?"

"Yes. It's on the news here, too."

"Last night at dinner, the people from the Embassy couldn't talk about anything else. I got so nervous, I couldn't sleep. I finally went down to break-fast at six. The TV was on in the coffee shop. From the buzz of the crowd you'd think another World Trade Center had happened. What are they report-ing over there?" Without waiting for an answer, he lowered his voice. "I'm scared, Darcy."

Darcy contained her own disquietude. She started casually, "Oh, I don't know, Reinhold. The one foot sea level rise—it was scary on the toll plaza, I have to admit, but personally I think the government can handle it. At least the White House is getting everyone together to plan."

She hesitated. "They're throwing around a lot of pretty soft science, you know. Especially on tonight's news. I don't think anyone knows enough. That Siberian hotspot? Two hundred million years ago. Come on. It just couldn't happen as fast as they say, could it? Another thing—the oceans are pretty big. I mean, just incredibly enormous. I can't believe a sudden event could make them rise like they're talking. I mean, maybe another inch or two, but three feet! In a few days, or a week?"

Silence on the phone line unnerved Darcy. "What're you thinking?"

"I'm not thinking. I'm just scared. And there's more..." He stopped.

"What do you want to do? Head for Ireland early?" By instinct she held back her bigger question, *More?*

"How about we postpone the trip home, I mean to Ireland. Maybe I'll just come back to the U.S. I miss the children, and you. We need to talk. And now all this weird news. You know, people in Russia panic pretty easily. Much faster than in the U.S. Or even Ireland. Are the kids okay? Anything more about Santa Fe?"

He said it again. More. Darcy swallowed hard. *Need to talk? Is he trying to signal me?*

Again Reinhold didn't wait for her answer. "This feels just like 1999 when the ruble collapsed. Remember? Before you could blink an eye, the Russian army took over the streets and the highway to the airport was lined with tanks. I was lucky to have emergency dollars in my money belt. It feels like it's all going to happen again. I think I ought to get out of here and just come home."

Darcy's voice inched higher. "You mean I should scrap Ireland? Reinhold, I really want to get out of here. I'm scared too, but not about the ocean." She decided to marshal her arguments. They came like automatic rifle fire. "Besides, we're practically ready to go. Bridey did most of the packing today. How are your folks going to react? And everyone else? And how about your meetings? You have partners. And money at stake. You know how much this means to us. Why don't you see what your American friends are thinking this morning?" Darcy decided on-the-fly not to tell Reinhold about the man at Starbucks. He couldn't do anything for her anyway, and he sounded too worried to add more.

"Maybe I am over-reacting, Darling. Maybe it's just the old trauma bubbling up from ninety-nine." He hesitated. "Maybe you're right. Maybe we all would be better off in Ennis for a while. I'll see what happens this morning. Can I wake you up if…?"

"I'll leave my cell phone on all night, Sweetheart. By the way, the kids are great."

"Tell them I love them. Blow a little prayer into their room for me when you go to bed. I love you too, Darcy. Don't forget it, now."

"I love you too, Reinhold. Talk to you soon."

Darcy couldn't sleep.

CHAPTER 53
Saturday, February 11

"KNOW WHAT I just heard on the radio?" Mariah put a bag of groceries on the kitchen counter and took off her coat. She did not wait for Elmer's speculation. "The White House Press Secretary is debunking the Star News story about those volcanic eruptions in Antarctica."

Elmer laughed. "There's a case of not knowing who to root for if I ever heard one. The Spinmeister versus Buzz-buzzards."

"She says the government is appropriately concerned, but the media's only trying to profit from the fear they've created, 'fabricating news of impending catastrophe where none exists,' as she put it."

"Yeah," Elmer sighed, "as if the Administration hasn't used the media to spread fear for years every time it wants to raise military appropriations or change environmental laws. The government's not above sensationalism."

"She's complaining that the media are irresponsible and trashing the Constitutional right to a free press."

"I feel a letter to the editor coming on, or a speech at the next protest rally. Why don't they realize the best way to handle sensationalism is to ignore it? When you argue with it, you give it an air of legitimacy."

"You and I might think so, but I suspect the majority of Americans tend to accept the Government's version of things."

Elmer pursed his lips. "I'll bet the majority is skeptical. The government has poisoned the well too many times."

DARCY HAD finally slept around 5:00 a.m. Just in time, it seemed, for the children to wake up and need breakfast. She had arranged for Bridey to make a rare Saturday appearance to help her with the final details for the flight to Ireland.

Darcy's activities were punctuated by a constant checking of her watch and conversions to Moscow time. Her preoccupations gnawed at her normally effortless play with the children. She couldn't even manage the simple crossword puzzle in the *Chronicle*. Bridey sensed Darcy's inner chaos and spirited the children away for lunch at McDonald's.

Shortly past 1:00, Darcy's cell phone rang—just after midnight in Moscow. Caller ID identified Reinhold.

"Hello, Love. We managed to keep the deal on track. Tough sledding. Not the terms, I mean—the deal's spectacular. But nobody could concentrate. People are really frightened here. There are all kinds of rumors about Antarctica. The worst part is, everyone at the U.S. Embassy seems to be panic stricken."

"Like, how?"

"Remember Peter? The chief information officer at the Embassy. When you were here with me in 2001, we spent that crazy night drinking beer and schnapps to the wee hours with Peter and Julia, at the Red Velvet Cistern down by Red Square."

"Sure, I remember."

"He was always one of my best allies, and he could always book me a flight when everything else failed. About five this afternoon I went over to the Embassy. Peter couldn't even see me for forty-five minutes. When he finally did, he looked like a ghost. I said, 'What's wrong?' He looked at me like I was crazy. 'What are you doing here? I mean in Moscow? You should get the hell home. Don't you know what's about to happen?' I was speechless. He said, 'Antarctica. You know, the ice. This is gonna be bad, Reinhold. Really bad. I can't talk about it. It's classified—top secret stuff.' I said, 'I can't get a ticket to San Francisco, Peter. Can you help me?' He said, 'Oh my god! I'll do what I can. Come back tomorrow, around lunchtime.'

"Oh," Darcy almost whispered.

"So I called the airport to confirm my flight to Ireland, just in case. They were kind of squeamish, wouldn't confirm my ticket. I told them I knew the president of the airline in Dublin. They didn't care. They said to call again tomorrow."

"What should I do?"

"Darcy! DO NOT go to Ireland with the children. Do you hear me? Cancel the trip. I think things are going to get crazy everywhere. There's a guy named Wyatt here—Blake's client—he pooh-poohed it, but he's scared now too. I'll get back to San Francisco, and I want you there when I do. You know I have plenty of resources. Don't worry about me. Just take care of the children. We can go to Ireland in the spring, when the weather's better. Okay? Tomorrow morning, I'll wrap up with the real estate people and work on getting out of here. I'll probably have a Monday morning flight."

"You sure you want to do this? I mean, cancel the Ireland thing?"

"Yes. I'm begging you, Darcy. This is a full-blown emergency—whether you know it or not—whether they know it in America or not. What if the news is right? We just don't know. Listen to me for God's sake, will you?"

Reinhold never used language like that. Darcy felt queasy. *At least he's not scaring me about Santa Fe, today*, she comforted herself.

"Okay, okay. I'm okay. You're right, it'll work out. I'll cancel the tickets. We'll re-group just fine."

"I can take care myself. I got out of Moscow before. I can do it again. And if I can't call you, keep checking your email. I'll find a way to get an email off."

There was a little silence. "You're safe there, Darcy, in San Francisco. Give Tierney and Finn a hundred big hugs from me. Tell them Daddy said we'll have more fun in Ireland in the spring time. And Daddy'll be home soon. Okay?"

"Okay, Darling. Good luck tomorrow. I mean, you know, on the ticket home and the deal, both. I love you very much. So do the kids. Talk to you later. See you soon. Love you."

If Bridey hadn't swept in with the children just then, Darcy knew she would have burst into tears. As it was, she had to admire the bright, plastic giveaway trucks they brought back from McDonald's. She decided not to unpack until nighttime, after the children were asleep. Tierney began entertaining Finn with the new trucks, so Darcy took Bridey aside to explain about the Ireland cancellation.

"Oh." She looked at Darcy with a blank expression for a moment. "You know I have plans of my own."

"I know, Bridey."

"As soon as you were gone on Monday, I was leaving with my friends for that road trip through the Southwest. Are you asking me to cancel?"

"No, Bridey. No, you should leave as planned. We can make do."

While Bridey was saying goodbye to the children, Darcy quickly called Virgin Airways to change the tickets to April.

Then, to fill the time, and her mind, Darcy jacketed the kids and autopiloted her way to Starbucks. In spite of the phantom cookie man, whom she hadn't sighted again.

Her strategy for stress reduction was not entirely successful. The normal benign Saturday afternoon crowd had doubled—and it was a new group. They looked like people who usually worked Saturdays, unfamiliar with Starbucks rituals, congregating for the comfort of the crowd more than the coffee. More than one of the new breed looked askance at Darcy and the children as if to say, No mother in her right mind would bring children in here. The line was the longest Darcy had ever seen, and the wait seemed interminable.

The usual gentle buzz of discussion seemed more like the roar of a crowd at the Indianapolis 500. It was too loud for Darcy to overhear any consistent conversation, but she caught a phrase here and there. "…fucking government" — "…ought to get my disabled mother inland" — "…can't believe anything you hear, if you hear anything at all" — "…that nuclear power plant" — "…just leave everything and get the hell away from the ocean" — "…gonna have to stockpile …"

Darcy took the children's hands. "Let's get out of here. I know a better place that's more fun anyway." They walked two blocks up Market Street to a tiny Chinese storefront. There was no wait. Darcy bought three fortune cookies, three almond sugar cookies, two Seven-Ups with straws, and a steaming black tea in a paper cup with a plastic lid.

The storekeeper spoke little English, but with a smile as wide as his face gave each child a paper bag with a handle to carry their own cookies. Feeling newly important, they all walked briskly to the park near home, where they consumed their treats before playing on the swings and slide. Darcy's fortune said, "Be alert. Things are not what they seem." Tierney's said, "You surround yourself with people of wisdom." Finn lost his fortune in the wind. No one cared, and they returned home with a whole new outlook on matters at hand. Darcy's outlook was more unsettled, but the kids were delighted with the outing.

Darcy divided her time for the rest of the afternoon between the new red and green trucks and business calls. A lot of people didn't answer. By itself this would not have been unusual, but many failed to respond to her emails as well.

She called her parents in Oakland. They were surprised at the trip cancellation. But no one had ever been faster on the return volley than Mariah, who ended the short call with, "So, how would you like to bring Tierney and Finn over for lunch tomorrow?" Darcy accepted.

She didn't listen to any more news coverage. Today.

CHAPTER 54
Sunday, February 12

DARCY'S CELL phone rang. It was 11:00 Sunday night in Moscow. Reinhold was calm, "I've checked out of the hotel. I'll spend tonight with Stephanovich." Grigor Stephanovich, known to Darcy as Stephan, was Reinhold's best friend in Russia. "Peter couldn't come up with a ticket by this evening. I'm still pulling strings. But I'm going to the airport in the morning anyway. If I don't have a reservation, I'll negotiate with the agents there."

Darcy felt optimistic. "I can hardly wait to see you, Sweetie." Bolstered by his confidence, she blurted, "By the way, I haven't heard anything about Santa Fe lately."

He was silent. Way too long. "Darcy... Don't worry about Santa Fe. Judging from the embassy here, our government's way too preoccupied to... I mean... I still think it'll blow over. But if anyone contacts you... Just say you're still waiting for me."

She reeled as if from a blow. "Do you know something new? Did something happen over there?"

"No, Darling..." Reinhold's voice was flat, trailed off. "Just sit tight. Okay? Darcy? Okay?"

"Okay. No problem, Darling." Her throat was too dry to swallow. She understood that he was withholding something, that she was not supposed to pursue it.

Tierney was demanding the phone, so Darcy said, "I know you'll be fine, Reinhold. So will we. See you soon. Love you," and handed the phone over.

Tierney reported about the trip to the park. "My fortune cookie said you and Mommy are very wise people. I think so too, Daddy."

Darcy flashed to the park. *Be alert. Things are not what they seem.*

After a short listen, Tierney said, "Okay, Daddy, I love you too." Then quietly, almost as an afterthought, "I love you very well." She clicked the "Power Off" button and handed the silent phone to her mother.

Reinhold had always been a magician at talking airport people into letting him onto airplanes. Darcy's anxiety level dropped—at least about her husband's trip home. The shadow of Santa Fe, however, had darkened significantly.

"Time to go to Babushka's house," she chimed. *When in doubt, use de Nile*, she joked to herself. She pulled a bottle of cabernet out of the wine rack, and the children raced her to the elevator.

The garage itself smelled like swamp mold over the odor of industrial cleanser. It had never smelled any other way. It was the only part of their building Darcy hated. It was under-lit, and always felt dank and threatening. Darcy thought there must be a leak, but she could never find it. So she assumed there was an underground stream that percolated invisible moisture directly into the air, making it unbearably heavy and humid. Darcy liked her water where she could see it.

Tierney held her hand tight. She had once confided to her mother that the garage was a place of adventure, that to her it looked and smelled like maybe there was a secret door down here that would take you to Where The Wild Things Are. Her eyes had revealed, however, that it would be too scary without Mommy.

They made good time across the Bay Bridge. As always, there was the slowdown at the tunnel on Yerba Buena Island. But there was no flood tide today, no Sunday ball game, and all five lanes moved consistently past the toll plaza. The tarmac had been cleaned and the temporary tide barriers were being enhanced. Darcy noted the low tide. "Low" didn't look so low any more.

After lunch, Elmer was sipping coffee through a straw at the kitchen table. He commented, "A lawyer friend of mine has a vacation house in Shelter Cove. He called me today. He went up for the weekend, came back last night, said everyone had pulled out. It's a ghost town. This sea level thing really has people scared in some places. People he talked to are hoarding gas, buying guns and ammunition, circling the wagons and becoming territorial, wary of strangers."

Darcy was silent for moment. "Reinhold says the Americans in Russia are pretty panicky about it. Especially his friends in the Embassy, on the inside track. He's known this one man, Peter, for a long time. I think the U.S. government is mighty worried. I suspect other governments are too. But I think they're feeding on each other. I also don't know how many weird, secret axes are being ground in all this, but I'm suspicious, and I think they're all going a bit overboard. I just don't think the science is really there. On the other hand, even a few more inches of sea level might be enough to send governments into bunker mentality."

When Elmer disagreed with you, his first response was usually silence.

"You know, Dad, whether the science is right or wrong doesn't matter if the White House decides to put the nation on some kind of emergency footing. They talked about it around the World Trade Center, and they put more emergency laws into place after Detroit was nearly taken out last summer. Things could get whacked out of line pretty bad if Washington doesn't keep a steady hand on the tiller."

Elmer took a meditative breath, but the cords in his neck tightened. "Our civil liberties hang by a thread, you're right. But don't blame Washington, Hon'. Blame the folks who don't vote." He had been an anti-war activist in the Vietnam era and the radical viewpoint was never a long stretch for him. "The tragic truth is, the majority of those who actually vote embed their narrow values, and then when a seminal event comes down the pike, like this, we're all stuck with their goddam myopia."

When neither Darcy nor Mariah followed that thread he changed the topic. "I talked with Bob Stevenson today. He made his wife leave San Francisco with their three kids and drive to Salt Lake City today. They're Mormons, you know. Said he wasn't taking any chances. Of course, their church tells them they have to be ready for seven years of disaster at all times. Or something like that."

"One year," injected Mariah.

"You're right, Sweetheart. Only one year. I think every good Mormon family's supposed to have a one-year supply of beans and powdered milk and flour, or some list of food. And seeds and stuff. Guns and ammo too, I'll bet."

Mariah added, "The seven years was the famine Moses predicted. That's where the idea came from. He saw it in his dreams. He was right, you know."

Elmer listened, but wasn't deflected. "I'll tell you what bothers me. Bob has two brothers. One's a General, and the other works for FEMA in D.C. Bob said the military's on high alert, all leaves canceled. FEMA canceled all vacations too, even called people back from vacation. Bob said there's going to be a bigger mobilization than after Pearl Harbor. Only this one's for sea coast construction. Everything will be disrupted, he said. Factories, farms, public utilities, Wall Street, everything. How long is anyone's guess. His brothers and their friends, even the non-Mormons, are stockpiling supplies. In Washington as well as Utah. Some people he knows even think the catastrophe is so likely they're sending their families to relatives inland. Well, actually that's what Bob himself did."

Mariah sounded distant. "I dreamed of millions of people running from giant tidal waves. Saturday night, a week ago, it was. *And the waves swallow up my father's construction company, and all its cranes and trucks and bulldozers. I don't know how that happened, because he retired in the Sixties. And it wasn't even* California. Dreams warp time and space both, you know.

"*And all the farms turn brown in the dream. Somehow, I can see them from the air. Even though I'm in the water at the same time. I wake up when I'm swimming toward a merry-go-round floating on the ocean, trying to save Darcy, trying to get her onto the lion that's going up and down on the merry-go-round.*"

Darcy had the highest regard for her mother's dreams, visions and symbolic insight. Her premonition of Luke's death had cemented that part of their relationship. *As long as she doesn't tell me how to mother my children.*

Darcy turned back to her father, tapped her fingers rhythmically on the table. Her silences signaled a different process than her father's. Unlike the lawyer, the pilot was always at the ready to debate if she disagreed. She used silence only to buy time when information seemed threatening.

Elmer interrupted her process. "You know what a one-meter rise in sea level would do to the California Aqueduct?"

She shook her head.

"It would destroy it. The aqueduct funnels water out of Northern California through the Sacramento River Delta. From there they pump it into the big canals that take it to the farms and Southern California. That water's the drinking water for twenty-five million people, and it irrigates farmland that supplies a huge percentage of the whole nation's food. The key part of the Delta, where they pump the water, is below sea level, protected by a thousand miles of levees and dikes. The Dutch have nothing on us. This twelve-inch rise is one thing. But if sea level rises more, like they're talking, it would overrun those dikes and all that water would be useless from the salty sea water—useless for drinking and useless for farming. I'm telling you, the government scientists better be wrong about Antarctica. That's all I can say."

Darcy looked steadily out the window at the beautifully manicured garden. Particularly the rhododendron, her Mother's proud centerpiece of exquisite landscaping.

"Well, there's nothing we can do about it. These are the 'big changes.' You just have to wait and react, and then do your best. You always said, 'Things happen the way they're supposed to.' I'm beginning to believe you, Dad. When Reinhold travels, I never know if his plane will go down, or his hotel will catch on fire. When he goes to the store, I never know if a drug dealer in a high-speed chase will run him down in an intersection. So I just go on. I plan my best. I execute my plans, the best I can. And I try to stop every day and make sure I'm not counting too heavily on all those plans. And it all seems to work out. The way you said."

As an afterthought, looking at her mother, she added, "And I pray for the kids' safety, and I hope there's a God." She thought, *I bet I sound a hell of a lot braver than I am.*

Mariah stood and cleared the dishes.

Just before sundown, Darcy packed up the children and headed back to The City. Tide was rising as the family crossed the toll plaza.

At 8:30, she tried to call Reinhold at Stephanovich's. Stephan answered.

"Reinhold left for the airport fifteen minutes ago, Darcy. He's probably got his cell phone off to save the batteries. You can't always recharge out there, you know."

"What do you think his chances are, Stephan? How do you think he'll get home?"

"I think he can probably get to Europe, maybe even Ireland. I'm not so sure about getting across to the U.S. Even my people are finding it impossible the last two days."

"Is there anything you can do, Stephan?"

"I'd do anything for my friend. You know that, Darcy. I gave him a letter of introduction to the shipping company I do the most business with. I have six containers of generators going to Brazil from Murmansk within the week. The cargo line brings me back coffee in trade. They always stop in Antwerp after leaving Murmansk, and this trip I heard they have to drop some containers of Russian folk craft in New York for the Russian Trade Center there. I told Reinhold if worse came to worst he should get to Antwerp and show my letter to the captain of the ship. If he can't fly out of Europe, maybe he can still get to New York that way."

"I love you, Stephan. Thank you. How're you doing, yourself? These times seem more treacherous than ever."

"Just fine, just fine, Darcy. I'll be okay here. I have friends high up in the government, you know. And Army as well. You take care too, Darcy. We'll get together next year and laugh about how it all worked out despite our worries. Ciao."

Darcy went to bed early. She slept, in spite of restless gnawing on the day's images.

CHAPTER 55
Monday, February 13

"MONDAY MORNING," Darcy thought. "Fresh start." She spent the morning setting up pre-need mortuary meetings for the week—or trying to. At noon, she flipped on the streaming radio news channel on her computer.

You are listening to WINT Radio, New York, New York, your premier Internet Radio Home.

Concern continues to mount about the potential threat from Antarctica. Personnel departments show absenteeism ten percent above normal at large companies nationwide. The government response seems slow, but there will be a joint session of Congress tomorrow at 5:00 p.m. Eastern time to address what is now a crisis of undefined dimensions. The session will be carried live on all major news channels.

A short while later Darcy's computer flashed the red icon announcing email. It was from Reinhold, sent at 11:55 p.m., just before midnight, Moscow time.

> A kind ticket agent is letting me use her computer here at the airport. Have to be brief. Still don't have a seat home. I'm trying connections through Europe. Maybe through Shannon and see Mother and Father. I love you, you precious Valentine. I'll either email you or see you soon. Love to the children.
> Love,
> Reinhold

She worked hard all afternoon. Her focus, however, was only half on work. The other half was on the self-discipline of avoiding further news. By 5:00 she couldn't sustain the discipline. She turned on the evening news. The commentator lamented that many people seemed more inclined to believe the tabloid press than the government. Highways in coastal states were seriously jammed.

After dinner, and bedtime stories for the children, Darcy posted an email to Reinhold:

> Children are fine. Happy Valentine Day. Can hardly wait to see you, Darling.
>
> Love, Darcy

It was 6:00 a.m., Moscow time, but by now Reinhold could be in a much earlier time zone, or much later—heading east across Siberia and the Pacific, or west to Europe, Ireland and hopefully the Atlantic. Darcy had not a clue. She read sci-fi until the 11:00 p.m. news.

CBOX TV, Terry Winslow, Evening Anchorperson.

Our in-depth report tonight is also our lead story—the deepening national crisis fueled by rumors and confusing information about events in Antarctica.

News crews in international airports say Americans everywhere are desperately trying to come home. All international carriers into the U.S. are overbooked and no reservations are available.

At home, on mountain highways leading out of coastal cities, traffic is so severe many cars are running out of gas, stalling on the sides of roads. Motel rooms are sold out. People are sleeping in their cars. Restaurants are out of food. Rural gas stations are running out of gas, or at least claim to be, in a perhaps veiled attempt to stretch their supplies. The American Automobile Association reports that towing and rescue resources are stretched to the breaking point.

Sleep was difficult, once again, for Darcy. Irresistible thought overrode fatigue. She thought about her continued failure to reach many of the gravediggers. She thought back to her father's friends, Mormons and non-Mormons alike, with their stockpiled provisions and plans to send the women, children and old folks inland "just in case." She thought about Reinhold's friend, Peter, in the Embassy in Moscow, saying, "This is gonna be bad, Reinhold. Really bad. I can't talk about it." She thought about the Oakland toll plaza, awash with brackish waters of the wetlands on the edge of the Bay. She remembered her mother's dream. Despite Reinhold's ambiguity about Santa Fe, her unquiet past and its recent echoes seemed to be sinking into the quicksand of bigger events. Her fitful nightmares maintained the theme.

CHAPTER 56
Tuesday, February 14

THE EMAIL was from Stephanovich:

> Darcy:
>
> Reinhold called from the train station. The airport was impossible. It cost him a wad of American 20s to even get out there by taxi. He said he's taking a train to Germany. Munich or Frankfurt. Frankfurt's airport is much larger. Please let me know when you hear from him. Pray everything will be all right.
>
> Stephanovich

The day was a disaster for Darcy. One by one, people she had appointments with canceled. At 11:00 a.m. Eastern time, the White House had announced the President would personally address tonight's joint session of Congress. She turned to the Internet radio again.

You are listening to WINT Radio, New York, New York, your premier Internet Radio Home.

Across the country, again today increasing numbers of people did not show up for work. As word of the President's speech spread, people began leaving work early. On the West Coast, many just stayed home all day. More are reported leaving precipitously for non-coastal places they consider safe. Federal, state and local governments have all issued advisories telling people not to travel.

As if advisories would help, retorted Darcy in her mind. She turned to organizational work, but lack of sleep and worry about Reinhold and the Ice fragmented her concentration. She tried writing. Nothing came. She tried to nap when Finn went down, but after ten minutes she had to sit up. Later she rain proofed the children and headed out into the cold rain. Maybe Starbucks would be friendlier on a weekday.

Wrong. The crowd was scowling, almost threatening. The gothic counter-girl had quit, replaced by a crew-cut Marine type with large tattooed biceps and a neck that sloped to his shoulders. Back to the black tea and almond cookies. At home, Darcy felt much better, playing with the kids, reading to them, simply enjoying their presence.

Finally, the President's face appeared on the TV screen, framed by the Oval Office Presidential Seal. Darcy was impatient with what she felt was his patronizing scolding of the media, his implication that imminent calamity was nowhere but on TV news. He catalogued instances of the nation's strength prevailing against a variety of enemies, proposing—Darcy winced—a "new war" on the forces of Nature!

She relaxed when he appeared to give a straightforward account of the problem. Then she realized that he blamed the sea level rise on "*a cyclical, long-term climatic warming trend*," avoiding any human involvement. *Can't make any waves with the polluting industries*, Darcy commented.

He minimized the scope of the problem. "*I want to assure all Americans, and our friends around the world, that it would take hundreds of years, maybe thousands of years*," for a sea level rise measured in feet to occur. It would only be a few more inches.

Still, he said, the government would initiate preventive or defensive measures on the nation's coastlines. *How are we supposed to sort out these mixed messages?* Darcy wondered. *He promises a war on nature, but there's no big problem, but we're going to undertake a huge set of construction projects…*

The President then scolded panicky citizens for clogging roadways and hoarding resources, and reassured the public that the government would "guarantee access" to basic needs. He concluded with his usual pious invocation.

Darcy drummed her fingers on the coffee table. *Well, damn.* She fed the children on auto pilot, her mind thousands of miles away. The kitchen done, she thought *I've got to get out. I've got to compose myself without distraction.* She called Anna Malone, the wife of Reinhold's brother Rudolph, and arranged for them to watch the children.

She called Winifred. "Want to meet at the Blarney Stone for some beer?" Winifred lived just off Castro Street five blocks away from Darcy and Reinhold.

"Hey. I'd love to suck a Guinness with ya, Darce. Meet you there in twenty."

Darcy was essentially apolitical. Just not very interested, usually. She always picked up a lot of information, and wasn't without her own opinions—she always voted—but she had no passion to defend her ground or browbeat others into her own way of thinking. Winifred was of similar ilk. Maybe that's why they made such great business partners.

But tonight, Darcy and Winifred couldn't escape the Ice topic. They found two stools at the end of the bar. Darcy pantomimed a mug of beer, and held up two fingers.

"Schlauncha, Winifred." Darcy pirated the Celtic equivalent of Here's mud in your eye. They blew back the froth and quaffed the traditional first-quarter mug, listening to the chatter surrounding them.

The buzz centered not on whether there was a crisis, but how bad or how not bad it might be. Those with scientific knowledge, and those with sharp political insights, and those with regular uninformed opinion, all joined forces.

On the TV above the bar, the usual sports programming had been bumped for coverage of reaction to the President's speech. Highly unusual it was, for Irish national hurling or soccer to be submerged in the pub by American politics. The volume, extra loud for the live feed to be heard above the din of the crowd, added fuel to the inflammatory rhetoric among the pub's patrons.

"If the arrogant Yanks had only signed the Kyoto Accords...," sputtered one red-faced customer in a shamrock speckled, bright green sweatshirt.

"Oh, go to hell," came back his American friend in a black turtleneck. "You know goddam well it's all those raw Chinese, East German and Third World factories and power plants spewing unscrubbed CO_2. That's the problem."

A black haired, green eyed wannabe studio model sitting between them piped up. "I don't care whether it's global warming or not, whether the Americans did it or anyone else, I think we ought to get to high ground. Maybe Colorado. Who'll drive me?"

As if in response, the TV news blared out,

In every coastal state, and beyond, mayors and governors are urging people not to move around. They all make much of their personal coordination with the White House and the Pentagon...

"See," the Irishman nodded to the TV screen. "The men on high are tellin' you to stay fuckin' put. I think it's all bullshit. I'm stayin' here and keepin' my job. My boss says he's got a contract to help build these seawalls."

The TV switched to a man-on-the-street interview.

Here's what one artichoke farmer on the coast south of Watsonville has to say.

The picture cut to a grizzled Hispanic man in Oshkosh overalls and a battered straw hat, surf in the distance just past the neat furrows of his field.

"We all know these politicians. They say whatever they think will scare people into voting for 'em. I listen to my wife. She says no matter what the President says, the opposite's probably true. So I says to her, Jesus, Mary and Joseph, woman, then take the kids up to your mama in Reno. Tonight."

And how about yourself, Mr. Martinez?

"Me? I gotta stay here to make a living. I'll take care of myself."

The news itself dispelled the calm confidence the President had attempted to instill in the country.

Domestic U.S. airports in the coastal states are now crowded beyond the worst Thanksgiving crush. Reports from foreign airports are the same—Americans struggling to return to the security of their homeland, long distance international phone lines jammed worldwide. However, the Internet, we're told, is alive and well.

Darcy and Winifred communicated with eyebrows, eyes rolling, shoulders shrugging, grimaces. The spoken word was nearly impossible, even for this assertive pair, over the proliferating arguments among the Celts, the high-decibel TV, and the wailing Irish soprano belting out tragic ballads from the competing stereo on the opposite wall. After two refills and clearing the tab, they reentered the cool night air, faces sober as judges, brains racing against the uncertainty of the Ice.

When Darcy got home, she carried the groggy children to their beds and turned to her computer. Again, no email from Reinhold. She didn't expect any. He should be in the middle of the long train ride from Moscow to Munich—or Frankfurt—or wherever he could get a ticket.

As she sat numbly on the side of the bed, one phrase pounded through her mind, over and over: *What are the odds? What are the odds?* She reviewed the President's speech in her mind. This didn't sound like the speech of a government leveling with its people. Within Darcy's own recall, the government had lied to its people over and over again—the assassination of Allende, support of right-wing death squads in Central America, CIA drug dealing to raise illegal funds for illegal covert action in Iran, irrefutable evidence finally uncovered in 2005 proving the CIA and FBI were directly involved in the Kennedy assassination, denials of U.S. involvement in gas warfare by Iraq against Iran in the eighties when the U.S. was afraid the Iranian revolution would hurt America's big oil suppliers in Kuwait and Saudi Arabia. And the whole stream of blatant fabrications that surrounded the invasion of Iraq.

Darcy didn't want to, but she began to believe something very dangerous was happening in Antarctica.

CHAPTER 57

Wednesday, February 15

DARCY MADE some half hearted attempts at business calls. Few answered. About every fourth attempt to dial was met with a dead trunk line or the rapid beep of "No available circuits." Again, her backup emails went ominously unanswered. Regular mail delivery failed to materialize. Radio reports told of ever higher absenteeism—and questionable gasoline supplies even in urban areas now.

Darcy loaded the children into the SUV and drove to her favorite gas station. It was the last Chevron outlet in San Francisco where they pumped the gas for customers. The owner filled her tank. She showed him her two five gallon camping containers. He folded his arms, looked her in the eye and said, "I'm sorry ma'am. I know you're a regular, but we ain't dispensing stockpile gas. Just for moving vehicles. Sorry." He walked to the next car. Darcy was refused at three other places.

She drove to her branch bank. The ATM was out of money and lines to the teller windows were fifteen people deep. The kids' patience was holding, but she knew it was thin. Finally... the teller only gave her five hundred dollars. The branch V.P. authorized five hundred more, because he knew her well. He confided in a quiet voice, "I think we're going to have to close early. Headquarters hasn't called yet, but I think the situation qualifies as a genuine 'run' on the bank. I expect the call any minute."

Darcy knew of two other nearby branches. She collected one hundred dollars from the first. The next was closed, the doors not only locked, but chained and padlocked. There were about fifty people crushed around the entrance. Two policemen stood guard. They looked young and scared. One, with a battery powered hand-held megaphone, shouted, "Please disperse. Please disperse. Please return to your homes. The bank has informed me the vaults inside are locked and no money is available. Please return at opening time tomorrow. The situation should be normalized tomorrow."

Mid-afternoon, Anna called. "Rudolph took his construction crews down to the Presidio today, to FEMA and military command centers coordinating emergency construction. You know, sea walls, sand bags, pumping stations. He said they're really concerned about fresh water supplies, and the sewage system. Underground gas and electricity, telephone and TV cables, subways—that sort of thing. Rudolph was all fired up, 'in the national interest.' And he said, 'The government's willing to pay top price for experienced workers.'" Anna added, "I might even go myself, tomorrow."

Darcy imagined going with Anna.

By the time the children went to bed, it was Thursday morning in Europe. Reinhold's train, if he was on one, should be getting to its destination soon. She didn't expect a phone call, but she hoped for an email. No such luck.

She climbed into the empty bed, to re-charge with a good night's sleep. It seemed strange, but with gas in the car, a stash of twenty- and one hundred-dollar bills, and the prospect of doing physical labor as a service to the community tomorrow, she felt optimistic for the first time in days.

CHAPTER 58

Thursday, February 16

ON THE SNOW CHOKED STREETS of Frankfurt, Reinhold Malone had changed a twenty dollar bill at a tobacco shop for half the Euros the official rate would yield. The usual nighttime bustle was missing. The dives and night-spots were closing, and it was only 10:30.

He fumbled through the directory in the phone booth, found the number before the cold forced his mittens back on. The coins clanged and he heard the connection ring.

He recognized Wolfgang's voice. In gruff, official Russian, Reinhold barked, "Hello. Hello. Are you informed of the whereabouts of the American, Reinhold Malone? We know you are friends."

Wolfgang Schmidt stammered, then said, "Reinhold, you sonnovabitch. Where are you?"

Reinhold laughed, "Times are weird, Wolfgang, mind if I spend the night?"

IN THE CLEAR LIGHT of day, Darcy decided she was too uneasy to join the volunteers for "Operation Seawell." She chose playing with the children, cleaning the house, routines of detail, until she could make sense of events. She kept the radio and TV off. Her emotions were simply overloaded. She checked for email at least every half-hour. Nothing.

Mid-morning, she opted for action, poked her head into the children's playroom and said, "Let's go for a walk." Tierney became a whirlwind of excitement. As usual, Finn lit up, following his sister's lead.

They drove across town to the Marina Green. The parking lot was half empty. Free from her seat belt, Tierney skipped ahead of Darcy in her yellow boots and raincoat, frog umbrella bouncing above her head. Finn rode in his all-weather chariot-disguised-as-a-common-stroller.

The sun had been out for three days. The Bermuda grass was dry enough to walk on. Even with its seasonal chill, the steady wind had evaporated most dampness in its path.

The Marina Green earned its name today, Darcy thought. *I couldn't see a brighter green in Ireland.* Across the blue choppy water, past Alcatraz, the Marin Hills likewise dazzled the eye, green as emeralds.

The perennial kite fliers were out, even the experts, costumed in their turbans and balloon pants as if they really were from India or Pakistan. The usual scatter of Marina singles animated the expanses of lawn, jogging, energizing in Tai Chi Tuan or Chi Gong forms, shaping their beautiful bodies through the stations of the par course. San Francisco's best lives of young affluence were progressing normally.

Suddenly, Tierney exclaimed, "Mommy, it's the man from Starbucks. Remember? The stranger with the cookie." She pointed to the parking lot.

Darcy turned to see a man locking a white van. Two thoughts of confirmation raced through her mind. First, Tierney seemed to have inherited her mother's facial recognition talent. Second, a suppressed suspicion exploded— she had seen that white van in her rearview mirror all the way from the neighborhood and repeatedly convinced herself it was a normal coincidence.

Darcy kept her voice calm. "If he comes over here, just keep playing ball with Finn and don't come unless I call you. Okay?"

The stranger walked casually but directly to Darcy, hands in his unbuttoned navy blue raincoat, sash trailing lazily behind.

"Morning," he nodded.

Darcy nodded.

"Look, Mrs. Malone," he said, "I'll be direct with you. I work for the government. A special task force. I was assigned to stay in touch with you. But now they've recalled me to Washington. They told me to make contact."

Darcy's body was taut, her jaw set, but she stayed cool. "Go on."

"Your dossier details your whole involvement with the Brotherhood, the art thefts, the way they operated. We have the highest national need for help in getting to these people. It's about oil reserves for the next decade. Nothing to do with the current crisis. This is something that threatens the whole nation. You're very important to us. We need you in Santa Fe. I'll be back in March. This isn't negotiable. And don't try to run. We'll be watching, and we'll find you."

He turned to leave, then added, "We're tracking your husband, too. He's fine. He got to Frankfurt."

He sauntered back to the van, and drove off.

Tierney ran over. "What did he want?"

"Nothing, Baby. Nothing he can have. Go back and play."

The sun still shone, but it now seemed overcast to Darcy Malone. Through blurry eyes she watched the activity by the waterside. There were dump trucks, backhoes, bulldozers. Interspersed among them were swarms of people with shovels, jackhammers, picks and crowbars. Some had official yellow government gear on, but mostly they were in jeans, khakis, overalls, sweat suits.

Volunteers were filling burlap bags from piles of sand. A steady stream of trucks dumped loads of sand, gravel, railroad ties and boulders. A levee was rising along the edge of the water, four feet high and wide enough for vehicle traffic.

She looked across the inlet to the San Francisco Yacht Club. The official levee cut straight across the neck of land that supported the driveway into the clubhouse. The government had decided to abandon the famous Yacht Club. The members, however, apparently had mobilized, because intermittently a pickup crawled over the public works levee on a makeshift ramp, supplying a small workforce on the Club property with materials of their own. She couldn't tell whether the workers were members or hired labor. *Probably the members' gardeners*, Darcy decided.

The children's attention was captivated by the kites, and the dogs accompanying their owners, some with leashes. Darcy didn't point out the seawall work to the children. *If things get worse, they have plenty of time for anxiety. If not, they'll read about it all when they're old enough, and brag, "I was there, were you?"*

Back home, after snacks, Finn napped and Tierney settled in with a video game, "edutainment" variety. Darcy prayed to the God she only hoped for, *Get Reinhold home. I beg you. I need help.* Once again, she quelled her terror by blanketing it with her new mantra, "There's nothing we can do about it. You just have to wait and react, and then do your best."

FROM THE PICTURE WINDOW of Mariah's new office, she and Elmer surveyed the skyline of San Francisco and the emerald hills of Marin. A cone of frangipani incense burned to its final ash. Mariah used it, she said, to clear the energy of Luke which she had harbored here for so many years.

Elmer turned to her desk where her new computer sat humming, and said, "Ready for your next lesson, my little techie dove?"

He showed her how to set her news preferences. She clicked the new icon. On her Home Page, square in the line of the strongest optical attention, the one-word headline hit her like a bucket of ice water: "TSUNAMIS?" Her intuitive mind reeled, answering in a nanosecond with images of frightening proportions. Her dream loomed large—the tidal wave. But her linear mind had to read on, hoping against corroboration. Elmer peered over her shoulder.

Internet—Internews—International

The tabloid press this evening has broken another sensational disaster story, arising of course from, Where else? Antarctica. The Star News, again quoting anonymous but "generally reliable" sources, claims the government is now concerned about the threat of tidal waves from the collapse of ice fields in the vicinity of recent volcanic activity in Antarctica.

Volcanic heat is expected to dramatically increase "lubrication" under the ice sheets. Earthquakes accompanying the volcanic activity are then likely to cause an immediate collapse of major portions of the ice sheets along Antarctic coastlines. The combined effect would precipitate fantastically large bodies of ice crashing into the Antarctic Ocean, perhaps cubic miles of ice. This would not only cause serious increases in sea level, but under the right circumstances would generate tidal waves, called tsunamis, ricocheting around the oceans of the world. Depending upon the intensity of the tsunamis, entire cities along some coastlines could be destroyed.

Elmer took over the mouse. Instinctively he searched for sources appearing at the conclusion of the article. With the help of his favorite search engine he found what he sought. He excerpted the first article to forward to Darcy and Reinhold, and the rest of his email list:

"University College London (http://www.ucl.ac.uk/)—Date: Posted 9/3/2001— Mega Tsunami Threatens To Devastate U.S. Coastline—August 31, 2001 A tsunami wave higher than any in recorded history threatens to ravage the US coastline in the aftermath of a volcanic eruption in the Canary Islands. . . . The new research... reveals the extent and size of the mega tsunami, the consequence of a giant landslide that may be triggered by a future eruption of the Cumbre Vieja volcano. . . . A block of rock approximately twice the volume of the Isle of Man would break off, traveling into the sea at a speed of up to 350 kilometres per hour. . . . the landslide would create an exceptionally large tsunami with the capability to travel great distances and reaching speeds of up to 800 kilometres per hour. Immediately after Cumbre Vieja's collapse a dome of water 900 metres high and tens of kilometres wide will form only to collapse and rebound. As the landslide continues to move underwater a series of wave crests and troughs are produced which soon develop into a tsunami 'wave train' which fuels the waves [sic] progress . . . . Florida and the Caribbean... will have to brace themselves for receiving 50 metre high waves, higher than Nelson's column in London, some 8 to 9 hours after the landslide. . . ."

He went on to read Mariah pieces of a March 2004 *Scientific American* article suggesting warnings might be measured in days or hours, and a March 5,

2002 *New York Times* report of possible hundred foot high waves hitting California from Hawaii based on a November 8, 2000 silent earthquake under Mt. Kilauea. Mariah didn't wait. She called her daughter.

"Darcy? Your Dad and I just read that the media's now talking about tidal waves. You know, like I dreamed. Do you know where Reinhold is?"

"I think he's in Frankfurt, Mom. How could they be talking about tidal waves?"

"Your Dad just emailed it to you. What do you mean you *think* Reinhold's in Frankfurt?"

Darcy was breathing hard. "Oh, Mom, I've only been home a couple of minutes. The kids and I were at the Marina Green. When I was there, that strange man from Starbucks—the one I told you about, who dropped that codeword?—he came up and threatened me if I didn't take the job in Santa Fe. He said he was with the government, that it wasn't negotiable, and I have to get back involved in that Middle Eastern business. I'm just praying Reinhold gets here soon."

"You didn't say Yes, did you?"

"I didn't say anything. He said he'd be back in March. And then he said they were tracking Reinhold and that he had reached Frankfort. Mom, I'm so afraid. But I'm trying not to let it affect the kids."

Mariah's mind was blank. She looked for insight, but no pictures came. "Hmmm. What's your sense about it, Darcy. I mean, on your own, Reinhold notwithstanding. Is your own mind clear?"

"You're right, Mom. My mind's set. I won't do it. But the kids…"

Now Mariah's mind's eye saw four graceful loons gliding over a mirror-still lake under a full moon. She said, "Good, Baby. Good. I think things will work out. Stay close in touch, okay?"

Darcy hung up. She closed her mental closet door on the Santa Fe business, comforted by her mother's words. She ran to read the email from her father. Its effect was galvanizing.

All the tidbits, innuendoes, hard-core news and in-depth analysis of events in Antarctica congealed instantly on the screen of her mind with a logic she could not block. Could she escape tidal waves? What were the odds? Their building was on high ground. Was this even relevant? What supplies would she need for survival? She raced through her mind for checklists. She searched for a good survivalist website, clicked through to their recommendations and began sorting out the impractical, the inapposite and the simply outlandish. *Guns*

& ammo? No. Traps & snares? No. Bottled water, beans, rice, powdered milk. I'll make up my own food musts, thank you. Water purification tablets. Yes.

By the time Finn woke up, Darcy had decided she knew enough and had her own list for the moment. She bundled the children and headed for the neighborhood grocery first. The streets were strangely quiet. The car radio was reporting:

Highways leading to the Sierra, leading across the mountain passes to the presumed safety of Arizona, Nevada, Utah, Colorado, Idaho, Montana and Wyoming, the leeward side of Oregon and Washington, are impassable from thousands of stalled vehicles taken there against all advisories.

But the city streets were not impacted. People seemed to be hunkered down in their homes, as if they were bunkers or bomb shelters. Or arks.

The store shelves were sparse. Not empty, but half of Darcy's desired items were sold out. She stopped at the hardware store next. Then the thrift store for some old-fashioned cloth diapers and a quick browse through castoffs from a less technological era that might be handy in a temporary shutdown— non-electric can opener, hand cranked egg beater, clothespins.

She felt better as she schlepped the shopping bags into the condo. A little foolish too. *Did I really need to do this? I'm glad I didn't see anyone I knew.* Inadequate? *It'd take a week to really do this right. I'm better at running a mortuary than this survivalist stuff. I should have a Mormon housekeeper. Oh well, it was cathartic. Better a start than nothing. The good news is,* she laughed inside, *maybe that creep with the navy blue wardrobe will get stuck in Washington forever.*

She checked her email.

Midnight, Frankfurt, Germany.
Arrived safely. City's mildly chaotic. Am working on flights to the US. Staying with Wolfgang Schmidt and his wife. You remember them. He was part of the development team for the Chevron building in Moscow in 1994. He says seats to the U.S. are booked solid for weeks. I'll try my usual routine out at the airport in the morning.
I'm doing fine, but I miss you and Tierney and Finn terribly. Kisses and hugs to everyone.
Love, Love, Love,
Reinhold

After supper and book time, their mother's songs carried Finn and Tierney to the Land of Nod. She was exhausted, her self-discipline in tatters, her self-deception riding high. She felt confident she could judge the truth of information herself, regardless of the source. She turned on both the radio and the TV.

217

Everyone was carrying the tsunami story. Its effect on people was hardly surprising. As the news commentator said, between the tabloids and the White House, it wasn't even a contest. Schools were closing, absentee rates were shutting down companies, phone service was slipping, electricity blackouts were being reported, gun and ammunition stores, grocery stores, drugstores and others were seeing runs on their stocks.

Darcy looked in vain for news of what might be occurring in Germany.

CHAPTER 59

Friday, February 17

THE 1:00 P.M. NEWS streamed in on Darcy's computer, radio and TV simultaneously, reporting a collapse of bipartisanship in Congress.

Old fault lines open up again, she mused, as if she were the reporter herself, *over civil liberties, military authorizations, budgets, etc., etc., etc., ad nauseam, ad infinitum, ad terrorem. Cracks in the facade of unity have become gulfs. The extremists are gaining momentum on both sides.*

The rest of the news mirrored the deteriorating social order. Cell phone service was now iffy. Power outages were increasing. Emergency calls were going out for additional workers at fire departments, hospitals and airports. Banks were ordered closed by the Federal Reserve. The country was shutting down.

Advisories continued to flow from the centers of government. People were urged to remain calm. Tsunami stories were dutifully debunked. No one seemed to be listening. Darcy included.

She called her mother, tried to sound optimistic. Mariah was less sanguine.

"Your dad's worried, though he's almost too busy to worry. He's got a rash of clients all wanting to get their wills revised. I'm pretty worried, too, Darcy. I keep having that same nightmare. I really don't know what to do, if there is anything to do."

"Oh." Darcy was quiet. "Mom," she continued, "things look pretty bad to me, too. I'm actually worried about the stability of the government. In fact... well, that's why I called. The mortuary airplane's just down at the Oakland airport. I talked to Winifred and she said I could use it. If things get any worse, I think I'd like to get you and Dad, and Finn and Tierney out of the Bay Area. To Flagstaff, I'd say. It would take two trips. I'd fly you and the kids first, and come back and bring Dad... and Reinhold as soon as he gets home.

"I think if things get unstable, they'd sort out with a little time, but it might be better to be in a small town like Flagstaff, where you have family and old friends to take care of you. It's not really the ice or sea level I'm worried about. Just the temporary chaos and panic."

Mariah's and Elmer's ancestral turf was Flagstaff, Arizona. Mariah had at least six cousins there, counting both sides of her family. There was the Scottish side, descended from the lumberjacking brothers of her father, Robb Roy McMann—and the even earthier, sheep ranching line descended from the Basque family of her mother, Esperanza Romero. Most importantly, however, Elmer's sister, Delphine Wallace, lived in Flagstaff. Twice married, once divorced and once widowed, fierce in retaining her born name, she was as close as a sister to Mariah. Flagstaff was far inland, too. And seven thousand feet above sea level.

"I don't think your dad would leave. But you're right, Flagstaff would be about the best place to be."

"If I bring Finn and Tierney over, would you take care of them for a day or two? Just in case? I mean, you know, if I had to leave here in a hurry, I'd rather have them already in Oakland."

"Of course, Darcy. Just let me know."

"Then I think I'll bring them over now. Okay, Mom?"

"Woah! Now? Well, sure."

"See you in an hour."

It took Darcy two hours. Panic had crept into the city streets. People were no longer glued to their media. They were trying to get out of town. This was not commute traffic. Cars were packed with kids. Pets. Duffel bags. Suitcases. Camping gear.

The longest it had ever taken Darcy to drive to her old home was an hour and twenty minutes. But she finally made it. She just dropped the children off and turned around. Babushka understood.

In her karate slippers, men's red silk pajamas and a white terrycloth bathrobe, Darcy pondered her options. She had listened earlier to the President's declaration of executive orders, but only two points clung to her mind—the prohibition of unauthorized travel inside the country, and the closure of the borders to all but diplomats and military. Could she get her children out of harm's way? Could her amiable husband get back? She cursed the government for pretending normalcy would return after a simple long weekend. Her anger boiled over and she yelled at her erstwhile Maybe God, "Have you really ordained America above all other peoples? No? Well, maybe you better tell the President and his cabal." *The bastards.*

CHAPTER 60
Saturday, February 18

BY NOON, the national news seemed strangely sanitized—great progress on the sea walls, patriotic pandering, weirdly rosy holiday weekend fillers. Darcy thought, *I guess government news management's beyond the Antarctic and they've got the networks censoring themselves. I wonder if they have men with guns in the newsrooms.* The thought was cynical, but she really did wonder.

The local news, however, still seemed on the up and up. A news crew had their truck in a Safeway parking lot, telephoto lenses trained on the locked front door. Inside, a man in a white uniform—probably the store manager—stood, hands on his hips. A mob, Darcy judged about a hundred people, milled around, two-thirds men, mostly youths. Then, right in front of the news crews, a great hulk of a man swung a sledge hammer at the front door. It shattered in a shower of glass. The giant stepped forward and swung the sledge hammer at the head of the man in white. The man toppled. The camera couldn't shoot what happened to his head. The mob poured into the store, like ants over honey.

Most of the mob. Some in the crowd stalked toward the news truck. The reporter's voice lost its objective manner. "*It looks like we better get out of here. No law-enforcement personnel are anywhere on the scene, and this mob is looking ugly.*"

The scene on the TV screen became smaller, jerking with the lurching of the news truck over potholes and curbs.

Darcy felt nauseous. But she numbly kept watching.

Back in the studio, co-anchors chattered about freeway congestion and abandoned vehicles even on arteries within the cities. Interviews featured frightened drivers stuck in traffic jams, some without plans or destinations—they just wanted to leave the area.

There was weather news, too. The cold, high clouds Darcy could see out her window were expected to give way to light drizzle within an hour or two and turn into a major storm by nightfall. The storm was expected to last only a couple of days, but two more fronts were right behind on the satellite picture. The commentary suggested it was the same pattern as 1995, when the Russian

River and the Napa set all-time record highs and Darcy's mother lost her get-away house in Monte Rio as the Russian River crested fifty-six feet above normal. The "Pineapple Express" they had called it, the jet stream that rail-roaded cluster after cluster of storms from the tropics to California's coast.

"That's it." Darcy pounded the arm of the sofa. "I've got to get my family away from here. Right now."

At the 1995 Russian River flood, Mariah had been all alone in her house. By the time Darcy had arrived, she had already carried all the furniture, artwork and valuables upstairs, with a nice supply of canned sardines and white wine, and she said, "I'm not leaving here. I'll be fine. I love this place and I'll go down with the ship." It had taken all the courage a young daughter could muster to insist her mother leave with her.

This time her own children were at stake and she wasn't about to spend any time on an argument. She knew she couldn't drive the SUV across the Bay Bridge. She had seen on live TV traffic was stopped cold, bumper to bumper, people standing beside their cars. At the toll plaza, scattered groups walked toward the Oakland hills. Abandoned pets were running loose.

Maybe she could take Rudolph's motorcycle, she thought. She had a spare key and a casual but clear deal with Rudolph. She often took the Honda out for a spin when he wasn't using it, and he could use the SUV when it wasn't busy.

Darcy had a momentary twinge, wondering whether Rudolph would need the motorcycle later, what with all the abandoned vehicles. But Rudolph and Anna were resourceful, and the Irish community in San Francisco was large and tight enough to take care of them.

She thought about Winifred too—probably already over in Walnut Creek with her mother. She hadn't seen her friend for more than a day. And Winifred was capable.

Earlier that morning, Darcy had assembled the necessary flying charts for the route from Oakland to Flagstaff, folded them for flight usage, and carefully tucked them into the deep, inside pocket of her flight jacket. They fit nicely around the "travel nunchaku" she always kept there. She sequestered the money belt with her cash hoard in a zippered pocket.

She threw on the flight jacket and rushed down to the garage. The Honda was still there, a big Honda 1200 touring bike that Darcy secretly disdained as a 'yuppie-mobile' compared to the Harley she would own if Reinhold allowed. But it looked like a golden chariot of the gods today. She didn't hesitate.

She checked the gas gauge. *Damn! On reserve! Not even enough gas to get halfway to Oakland.* She rushed back upstairs. Grabbed the siphon hose they used to drain the tropical fish tank. And the big claw-hammer. As she dashed by a mirror, she reconsidered her clothing. She threw on her flying outfit: silk underwear for warmth, a pair of good, thick jeans, a plaid wool shirt, flight boots.

She grabbed the small black Harley Davidson backpack that matched her flight jacket. She stuffed it with whatever came across her line of vision: flashlight, batteries, a small toolkit she had assembled during her pilot lesson days, duct tape, a ball of string and a hank of nylon rope, ziplock bags. Quick to the bathroom cabinet—tooth stuff, band-aids, a lipstick, tampons. She grabbed some candy bars on her way through the kitchen. Then back to the elevator and down to the moldy garage.

In the dank, dim cavern she always hated, Darcy simply pried a car's gas cap off with the hammer and siphoned the Honda full. No ethical compunctions. She dried the hose on her Levis, stuck it in a plastic bag, then in the backpack. She glanced at the gas cap on the concrete floor where it had fallen.

Darcy was a consummate motorcyclist. Her pilot's training made it a cake walk to navigate a two-wheeled machine around abandoned vehicles, avoiding aimless people in the streets.

It took her twice as long as it might have, but she stayed in the neighborhoods of affluence all the way to the Bay Bridge onramp. Even in those neighborhoods she noticed small, moody crowds, in spite of the wind and cold drizzle that would prove the weather man accurate. Ominous groups, but not quite hostile.

On the bridge, there were still continuous, open lanes between stalled cars, where scooters and motorcycles were steadily easing through. Darcy sensed that with a touch more desperation, people might try to pull drivers off and use the cycles themselves for their own getaway. It wouldn't have made any sense, because there would immediately be a cascade of stopped scooters and cycles in the narrow lanes that still existed, and no one could get out. But no one had ever accused a desperate crowd of being rational. Every hundred feet that Darcy sputtered through, she offered a sort of informal prayer of thanksgiving to the god of escapees. A god she did believe in.

The virtual parking lot extended as far past the Bay Bridge as Darcy stayed with it. As she crossed the toll plaza, she wondered whether tide was high or low. But she dared not look. It took all her attention to balance the lumbering Honda upright in the slow parade of scooters and motorcycles still teasing their way through the chaos. She was tempted to blast someone with the truck-sized air horn Rudolph had installed on his macho-cycle, but she refrained. *Might start a riot.*

She stayed on the freeway. Her strategy again was to ride only the affluent streets once she left the orderly freeway culture, so she had to get past the poor neighborhoods of lower Berkeley and Oakland. She could hear sirens—fire trucks at least were getting around, unlike in large areas of gridlocked San Francisco. She could see, too, about a dozen plumes of smoke coming from the mixed residential and commercial areas of the "flatlands."

At last she rolled off the Piedmont exit and found the tree-lined streets leading into the pleasant coastal uplands that had been occupied following the 1906 earthquake by those of professional calling and those of old money. *A hundred years later*, she thought, *and another migration from San Francisco. Once again, escaping the forces of nature—and the forces of human nature.*

By the time she arrived at the old home, her parents looked as serious as an English couple at an Irish funeral. They had seen the Safeway newscast. They were aware no one could drive anywhere. The radio reported that downtown Oakland's streets, even as far up into the hills as Grand Avenue, were impossible with traffic.

"We thought you might be on your way," Darcy's mother said. "We kept trying your phone number. We finally got your neighbors. They said you didn't answer your door."

Darcy didn't stand on ceremony. "Now listen to me, Mom and Dad. We talked about this a couple of days ago. I'm going to fly Tierney and Finn, and you, Mom, to Flagstaff, in case things get worse. I know we don't think they will be worse, but it's hard to be sure. We know you can fend for yourself, Dad, here in the house until I can come back and get you. It should only be two days. You'll be okay. By then I feel sure Reinhold will be back, and I can fly him and you on over to Flagstaff, too. If we need to."

"I've already packed a suitcase for myself, and one for the kids," Mariah said.

"We can't take suitcases, Mom. We're going to have to ride the motorcycle down to the airport. Cars can't get through. You have to ride on the back and hold on to me. Finn's going to ride in his leather baby pouch on my front even though he's a little big for it now. Tierney'll have to be in between you and me. You'll have to brace her in with your arms. You can wear a backpack, if you think you can manage it. Rudolph's bike is a big touring bike and it can carry the weight, but balance is going to be tricky, especially coming down off the hills in this drizzle. It's going to turn to rain any time now, and with the rain comes strong wind. I've got to get us off the ground before that happens, so every minute counts. We've got to go right now."

Mariah grabbed her bright pink, waterproof daypack, tore open the suit-cases, and stuffed in as many of the children's clothes as the backpack would take. She added three disposable diapers for Finn, took two changes of under-wear for herself. She tucked in her toothbrush and a lipstick. As she was about to zip it shut, she saw the little packs of seeds she wanted to share with Elmer's sister Delphine and threw them in too. Zip. She was ready.

Tierney had her own little backpack. She kissed her little teddy bear's nose, and zipped him in.

The travelers put their winter coats on, their rain gear over that. Everyone hugged Elmer, several times. Eyes cried, but jaws held the sobs in.

For Tierney it was a thrilling adventure. But like walking through the mys-terious garage in their building, it would be just too scary without Mommy.

Darcy roared out of the driveway, Elmer leaning on the doorjamb in the shelter of the front porch. The clouds were heavy, and as dark as ever a winter afternoon had been in the Oakland hills.

There was no way to get to the Oakland airport without going through East Oakland. At first Darcy and her unwieldy passengers wound through the streets as high on the hillsides as she could stay. These were the high priced areas and everyone was still inside, their cars mostly in garages. Except for a three-quarter mile stretch where the power was out, everyone had living room lights on. It almost seemed cozy.

When she reached Edwards Avenue, Darcy had to turn west and descend into the flatlands. As the elevation decreased, the number of cars parked on the sides of the streets increased. In spite of the cold drizzle, there was the usual crowd outside the bar on the corner of Edwards and MacArthur. All eyes were on Darcy and the Honda. She didn't even slow down for the red light. Auto-mobile traffic was light and as luck would have it, no one was coming in either direction. No police, either.

At the intersection of International, they weren't so lucky. Cars were stopped in both lanes ahead of them, and there was thick, if temporary, traffic in both directions on International. The corner liquor store had its usual crowd, too, and as Darcy balanced the standing cycle, praying for the green light, three youths with wool ski caps signifying their gang affiliation recog-nized opportunity when they saw it. As they left the sidewalk, their casual saunter failed miserably as a disguise for their sinister purpose.

Darcy managed to turn the Honda clear of the fender in front of her be-fore the first of the trio reached them. The second and third youths had knives out. She could see them glint as cross-traffic headlights swept by. She felt Mariah's grip tighten like a cinch on a horse's belly. Darcy screamed "Hang on," as she revved Rudolph's well tuned 1200 ccs to an ear-piercing roar and simultaneously let go the air horn. The violence of the sudden sound caught the leader by surprise and his stride faltered. It was enough to give Darcy an opening to land a ferocious karate kick with her heavy flight boot square on the youth's left kneecap. Darcy had aimed at his groin, but it didn't matter. She felt the boy's knee bones crunch under the blow, and he dropped with a howl of pain and anger.

Darcy jammed the motorcycle into gear. It shot forward with a squeal of its rear tire, the young man's companions screaming obscenities in its wake. It fishtailed almost out of control, but Darcy steered it with the precision of a Blue Angel and the balance of a tight rope walker, and drove it up the wheel-chair slope of the corner curb, off the other side and along the gutter in the miraculously free bus lane for a hundred feet. There was a break in the traffic. She executed a deft U-turn, from which she careened back through the inter-section and on down Edwards Avenue. It took all her self control not to accelerate to a speed that would have meant certain death on the slick asphalt of the thoroughfare, but they were out of danger and within earshot of the airport.

At the airport entrance, Darcy took a right turn and a quick left into the private aircraft sector where she could see the Cessna waiting. She drove straight to it, a thousand feet from the airport administration building. Airport protocol required every pilot to check into the office, file a flight plan, receive approval and go through the routine checkout before takeoff. But Darcy sensed something would go terribly wrong if she followed the usual routine.

She left the motorcycle just behind the left wing, yanked open the door and shouted to Mariah, "Get in. I'll hand the kids up." Mariah scrambled up the foot brace and into the passenger seat of the cabin. Darcy threw the children in after her, and yelled, "Get 'em in the back and get everyone fastened in." Mariah did as she was told. With ballet-like movements, Darcy unlocked the chains anchoring the plane to the tarmac and tore the canvas cover off the propeller cowling. She vaulted into the cockpit and glanced toward the admin building.

A small squad of uniformed men burst out of the building on a run. In the dark afternoon drizzle, it looked like they were all carrying guns. Darcy recognized the National Guard uniforms. She could hear one of them shouting something through a power megaphone. Two of them fired rifles into the air. She checked the instruments by instinct, turned the ignition. The propeller whirled. She released the landing gear brake and taxied for the runway.

Mariah yelled over the roar of the engine, "They're shooting at us. Oh God, Darcy, they're shooting at us."

"Shut up, Mom. I need to fly this thing." Finn was screaming too, and Tierney was sitting frozen like a stoic, eyes wide, taking in every nuance of this moment of grown-up frenzy.

Darcy reached the runway, scanning as she approached it for any takeoffs or landings in progress. She turned west into the wind and jammed the throttle to "Takeoff maximum." The powerful little craft leapt forward like a bucking bronco out of the chute. Out of range of the National Guard rifles.

The Oakland airport was history.

Darcy turned on the aircraft radio. A calm voice from the Tower demanded she stop takeoff, identify herself, and return to the administration building. As her landing wheels left the runway, their tone changed. By now they had her aircraft ID number. "PCQ1070, PCQ1070. We warn you. We are under federal Executive Orders to identify any unauthorized airborne craft to the U.S. Air Force. They are under orders to force unauthorized airborne craft to the ground, and they have permission to shoot on sight at their discretion. If you do not reverse direction and commence returning to the airport within thirty seconds, we will identify you as an unauthorized airborne craft."

Darcy never flagged. She had taken off into the wind, blowing from the west, and was now over the bay. She banked south, keeping low, under the radar, crossed over the I-880 freeway and picked up I-580 heading east out of Hayward into the Dublin pass. The freeways were parking lots. She was on high alert for traffic helicopters. And police helicopters. None came into view, but she guessed their presence would confuse any radar close enough to the ground to pick her up. She knew the Air Force wouldn't touch her in such a populated area even if they could find her. It was all but nighttime anyway, which gave her extra cover.

Piloting was now simpler. When she had checked her instruments, she hadn't let her face reflect it, but in her racing mind she had thought, *Oh dammit, dammit! Only half a tank. What is it about gas today, for Chrissake!* She guessed Zooty hadn't topped the tank after his last funeral run. Zooty was the mortuary's main pilot. *He's always been in too big a hurry.*

That morning Darcy had made the calculations: Flagstaff was twelve-hundred forty miles on a straight shot down the San Joaquin Valley to the Tehachapi pass and then over the high desert through western Arizona. The fuel tank on the Cessna could probably get her all the way there without refueling, if people and baggage were under five hundred pounds and she had a decent tail wind. She would burn thirty percent more fuel flying at near ground level to avoid radar. Given the weather, however, she would probably have to do that anyway, because she most likely couldn't achieve adequate altitude to fly above the storm. And it was going to take a lot of fuel to climb up over the Sierras, following the freeway below radar.

She now knew, without even doing the math, that her gas would run out far short of Flagstaff. Probably right about the Tehachapi pass, in fact.

"Mom, I have some bad news."

"I know—the gas."

Darcy shot her mother a quizzical glance. Mariah was holding a grease-stained envelope with a scrawled message on the back. "This note fell off the instrument panel when I got in. Zooty says they're rationing gas and wouldn't let him refuel after his last ash drop. They told him he wouldn't be flying for a long time anyway."

They fell silent.

"How far can we get?" Mariah asked.

Darcy ran through some calculations out loud and ended, "About three hundred miles. Maybe three-fifty. Can't make Flagstaff."

"We can't even get over the mountains, can we?"

"Nope."

"Can you use car gas?"

"Only aviation fuel for this baby, I'm afraid. Never thought it'd be an emergency craft. But that's what we've got."

"Look," Mariah said. "What we're trying to do is get to the safest place we can find, where we can wait out the public panic. But it's got to be where you can buy more fuel to go back and get Elmer and Reinhold. I say let's head north to Modoc County. Remember a couple of months ago, my uncle Caesar died and left me that homestead up there in his will. I talked to his lawyers and they said it was livable but very remote. The town was Flat River. Do you have a map of California?"

The only flying charts Darcy had were to Bakersfield, Tehachapi and Arizona. She said, "Look in the snapped pouch on the door. I think Zooty has a California roadmap."

As Mariah studied it, she said, "There's an airport in Flat River. It might be kind of a redneck town where they hate the government and they'll ignore that Executive Order stuff and sell you the gas."

Darcy followed the freeway through the Altamont Pass, then swerved north.

The cockpit was not warm, but it was dry, and in their layers of coats and gear everyone felt cozy. With the steady drone of the engine and the gentle sway of the craft, Finn had stopped crying and fallen asleep. Mariah quelled her own inner turbulence, turned around, unsnapped Tierney's safety straps and invited her into her lap in the front seat so she could see outside. Everything looked like toys from the air—the little houses, the cars and trucks, the BART train parked in its cute, lit-up station, water towers, shopping malls. Everything Tierney had seen from car windows was there, but she shrieked with delight to see it so tiny and perfect and clean in the lingering twilight. She turned around in Mariah's lap and kneeled up, put her warm face right next to her Babushka's ear, and confided just loudly enough to prevail over the engine, "This must be what angels feel like."

Because the storm was blowing in from the south and moving slowly, after they turned north the plane could keep pace with the light, front edge of the weather front. Maybe they could even outrun it. This meant they could keep visual contact with the ground. Mariah's job became to track their progress on the roadmap and guide Darcy highway by highway toward their destination. As the night wore on, headlights became few and far between. There were times they couldn't tell whether they were following a car or aiming at the stationary lights of a farmhouse. Occasionally they passed over a small town where they could see street lights, stores and a service station or two.

The fuel gauge crept lower, imperceptible as a candle melting, but steadily downward.

They had flown far enough to have angled out of the storm, and in spite of the waning moon, the night sky was a blaze of stars, the Big Dipper dead ahead, Orion high and to the right with the Gemini twins not far behind but well above the eastern horizon. Tierney had returned to her own seat now, and both children were sleeping happily because for the first time in their lives they had dined on candy bars alone. Dessert first! And only dessert!

"We're on the reserve gas tank, now, Mom. I think we have about forty-five minutes to an hour of flight left. I'm going to have to set down in the next town we see."

Mariah answered, "The turns in the highway and the town's we've passed have all been in the right places. I think we're on track and Flat River's not too far ahead."

Five minutes seemed like ten, the next five like twenty, as they strained their eyes and attitudes forward, searching for a sight of civilization. An occasional car still marked the highway below, and every few miles there was another house, but no town.

"We're really on the edge of safety, now, Mom. I'm going to take it down near the highway, in case I have to make an emergency landing."

Darcy concentrated on keeping the airplane fifteen feet above the pavement. When she saw a car coming, she pulled up. At least no one swerved before they flew over.

Suddenly, the plane made little jerks, forward and back, and up and down as the engine coughed its last spoonfuls of gas. "Here we go Mom, we're going to set her down."

As gently as Darcy could wish, the plane glided onto the pavement and decelerated for a few hundred feet. Before it lost all momentum, Darcy eased it over to the shoulder. The right wheel went too far, passing over the right edge of the gravel roadbed, and the Cessna came to rest with its wings tilted twenty degrees from the level.

All was quiet now. Tierney and Finn still slept.

CHAPTER 61

Sunday, February 19

REINHOLD CLASPED his friend Wolfgang in a bear hug in the dawn's early light on the sidewalk outside the Schmidts' tiny apartment. "Thank you a million times over, Wolfie, and thank Elsa when she's awake. Your couch was great. I'll pay you back as soon as you can get to San Francisco."

Wolfgang laughed, then hugged Willie McLeish. "Good to see you, Pal, even if it was too short and at such an ungodly hour."

Willie McLeish had completed an inseparable triumvirate with Reinhold and Wolfgang during their two-year overlap in Moscow. Now, Willie was stationed in Berlin with a Middle East logistical support unit of the U.S. Army. He was in Frankfurt on leave, which had just been canceled because of the "Ice Crisis" and stopped by Wolfgang's to say a quick goodbye. It was deemed good luck by all. After two fruitless days at the airport, Reinhold knew a commercial flight was impossible. The three had quickly decided Reinhold's best chance was for Willie to give him a ride to Berlin and try to talk him onto a military flight back to the U.S.

As they drove off, leaving Wolfgang in a lingering cloud of freezing exhaust, Willie said, "You won't mind if I pick up another friend I promised a ride to, would you? His name's Hans Danzig. He's a helluva good man, even though he's a radical green-freak."

Reinhold nodded his assent. His veneer of joviality gradually turned inward as he looked out the window, pondering the uncertainties of his obsession to get back to Darcy and the children as soon as humanly possible.

Willie broke his reverie with a deadly serious tone. "Reinhold, you know you're one of my best friends ever. I don't know what's going on, and Wolfgang's not in on it, but I was ordered to bring you to Berlin."

Reinhold's heart raced.

Willie went on, "My commanding officer said they would put you on the first flight to the U.S. He said it was critical to get you and your wife relocated with some kind of a special task force. Do you know what I'm talking about?"

Reinhold hesitated, his mind racing for answers. "How the hell do they know I'm in Frankfurt?"

"I've got to believe there's a GPS bug somewhere in your clothes or your stuff. Reinhold, you've got to believe me, our friendship supersedes anything. If you need help, tell me while we're alone, before we pick up Hans."

Reinhold said, "I've got to think a minute. Maybe you shouldn't know more, if you really don't know what's happening." He weighed the benefits of easily getting to America but being in the hands of the government, against his ability to get back to Darcy on his own using Stephan's ship captain and maybe even negotiating for some help from Troy Blake in New York using the Moscow deal as leverage.

If anything, Reinhold could be decisive. "Do you think I could get to Amsterdam on my own, if I left you somewhere?" Reinhold knew Antwerp was a stone's throw south of Amsterdam. Answering part of his own thoughts, he continued, "Of course, they'd probably court-martial you if you let me go voluntarily."

"Let's see if there isn't some way for you to 'escape' on our drive—if we tell Hans you're an American environmentalist, I think he was planning to go somewhere near Amsterdam after Berlin and I'll bet he'd help you. It's not too far from the truth, anyway. After all, you are from California."

After picking up Hans, Willie managed to parlay his American military papers into passage through half a dozen police checkpoints. Germany, like the U.S., had instituted travel restrictions to stem a mass exodus from the coastlines that started with the tsunami news broadcasts. The three men bonded over discussions of the environmental catastrophe, establishing Reinhold's faux credentials with Hans in the process, and his need to reach Amsterdam. In between checkpoints they traveled at the reckless high speeds traditional on the autobahn, even though most vehicles were military or at least official in the crisis atmosphere of the day.

"Hang on. Hang on," Willie shouted. Their forward view had been obstructed for about half a mile by a wall of military transports, and suddenly the highway ahead was a blaze of taillights, smoking brake pads, and vehicles careening into each other in mass chaos. Their Volvo smashed sideways into an overturned Army semi. Willie had slowed enough that their seat belts prevented injuries.

"Get out and get over the bank," Willie screamed. "That truck's an ammunition carrier!"

The three men sprinted to the guardrail and leapt over, half-slid, half-fell down the embankment, then ran under the autobahn overpass just as the thunderous concussions of exploding ordinance began above their heads.

Willie grabbed Reinhold by the lapels of his jacket and pulled him close. "This is your chance. Our car will be unrecognizable. There'll be a lot of bodies, probably some unidentifiable. Here, change boots with me. I'll dump yours, because that's probably where they planted your bug. Give me your duffel, too—it could be in there." Reinhold saved only his Moscow deal portfolio, which he buttoned inside his shirt, his letter to the ship captain and his wallet, which Willie checked for electronics. Hans agreed to get Reinhold to Amsterdam. With that, Reinhold embraced Willie, and he and Hans wended their way through the vehicles jammed on the underpass street until they could beg a ride to the west.

THE STARS DIMMED. The children were still sleeping, so Darcy and Mariah stayed quiet, dozing until the sun rose. Tierney and Finn, once awake, got another candy bar for breakfast. Then they all climbed down from the uphill door of the plane into the frosty, high country morning air.

They walked north on the two-lane highway. Darcy again carried Finn in the backpack. Tierney was wide awake and sugar high, so she got to walk unattached, as long as she stayed near Mariah. The road stretched ahead bare and deserted. Hardly surprising, early Sunday morning, no telling how far from any town.

They approached a turnoff on the right, a dirt road leading to a yellow farmhouse, like a comfortable widow in a quiet church. Beyond the right-of-way fence lay a stubbled field striped with snow on the north slope of each furrow. The opposite side of the highway was bounded by a thirsty looking scrub forest of junipers, pinon pines and leafless, olive green mesquite bushes.

Darcy caught a movement in the trees. Three dogs picked their way just inside the tree boundary, drifting like schoolyard toughs. Two were German shepherds. The other was larger, and coal black. A Doberman pinscher.

Mariah made her voice conversational. "Back in Arizona, ranchers never let their dogs run free. If they banded together, you know, they became a pack, and no matter how tame as pets or work dogs, they reverted to their primitive hunter instincts. Once their ancestral blood rebounded, they were never the same. We used to shoot the packs, and if a dog broke free and came home, you had to put him down eventually."

Darcy slipped the backpack with Finn off her shoulders and positioned it on her mother's back.

Tierney was ten paces ahead. "Come back, Tierney, and walk with Babushka for a while, would you?" Darcy kept her voice calm.

"Oh, Mom. Why?"

"I think her hand's cold." After a moment, Darcy added, "Do what I ask, Tierney. Please." Her daughter understood and complied.

A zephyr stirred the dead winter grass, blowing toward the dogs. The pack angled for the highway heading into the breeze, slipped under fence rails into the clear right-of-way and approached the far edge of the asphalt. They were panting, tongues out, gazes fixed on the foursome.

"Mom, carry Tierney." Darcy reached into her flight jacket and slipped out her nunchaku.

In two strides the dogs became a snarling vortex, slashing across the highway like a dust devil. Without a sound, Mariah turned to blunt the attack. Darcy made a quick, ninety-degree turn and took a single, fluid step toward the dogs. She converted the torque energy of her simple body movement into the startup whorl of the nunchaku.

The lead German shepherd leapt at Mariah, growling from deep within his gut. Darcy's years of practice had become reflex. The outer stick cracked on the skull of the first German shepherd. He died in midair. The stick came full circle. The Doberman, too late to change direction, soundlessly mirrored the shepherd's leap, teeth bared, eyes wide and red as molten lava. The tip of the stick smashed his backbone just above his shoulder blade and deflected his trajectory from Mariah's throat. She caught the force of the dog on her arm. The teeth failed to pierce her coat sleeve, but she staggered. The dog fell, gurgling and twitching on the gravel.

Darcy threw her torso against the momentum of the stick's direction, and its third revolution shifted to horizontal, low to the ground where the other shepherd was hurtling for Mariah's ankle. The stick caught him below his chest, high on his front leg, which snapped like kindling under the blow of an ax. He yelped as he scraped the ground, regained his balance, and dragged his destroyed limb under his belly, bobbing with spiking yowls of agony, back across the road.

"Get the kids out of here," Darcy shouted. "And hide their faces." As Mariah ran north, the Doberman was still whimpering, coughing blood between spasms on the side of the road. Darcy waited until Mariah was fifty feet away, so the children couldn't see up close if she failed to block their view. Then she swung her nunchaku with all her weight onto the skullcap of the wounded animal, ending, at least for this lifetime, his pain and his brief career as leader of a hunting pack.

The growl of a motor pierced Darcy's sheath of emotion. A light brown pickup truck was approaching from the north. Darcy swallowed hard. She wiped the blood and flesh from her nunchaku onto the sleek fur of the motionless pinscher and ran to catch up with Mariah. The pickup slowed. Two figures sat in the cab.

The truck was covered with mud spatters and only the driver's side windshield wiper had cleared a patch for visibility, through which Darcy could see the driver was a man in a cowboy hat, about forty years old, face hardened in the sun. A rifle in a rack was silhouetted against the rear window.

The pickup turned left in front of them and stopped on the turnoff to the dirt road, blocking their way. The passenger side door opened and a second cowboy hat emerged.

Darcy put her right hand out to keep Mariah and the children behind her. She gripped the nunchaku handle. Her body still tingled and her chest heaved from the struggle just ended. She suppressed her impulse to vomit. She tightened the back of her neck and breathed into her belly. In a second she felt a measure of composure.

"Well, well, what's a little group like this doin' way out here on a nice Sunday morning?" It was a woman's voice. Darcy tried to relax.

Mariah eased her own shortness of breath. "We're in a fix."

"We were flying north from the Bay Area in my Cessna last night." Darcy gestured with her thumb back toward the south. "She ran out gas so I had to set her down on the highway a couple of miles back. Thought we'd walk north to find a town, because we hadn't passed any down that way for quite a while."

The woman's companion joined her. "We saw you take care of that dog pack, young lady. Mighty impressive. I don't think there's anyone in the whole county who can do Bruce Lee stuff like that. Saved your lives, I'd say. That

233

wounded one I saw running up the access—he'll probably die pretty quick in this winter weather."

Darcy kicked some gravel. "Where are we exactly anyway?"

"Well, it's about three miles back to the crossroads," the woman said. That would be our little hamlet of Likely—all of seven buildings and a dozen folks. Another eighteen miles and you're in Flat River. But let's not gab. You look like you could stand some breakfast before you figure out your next step. Just climb in the back. You can see the house."

In the farmhouse kitchen, Paisley Overcroft set out hot coffee for the grown-ups, cocoa for Tierney, and a plastic cup of warm milk for Mariah to hold for Finn. The radio was on.

We're about to switch to the White house, where the President is expected to announce a declaration of martial law. Marilyn, do you have any comments while we wait?"

"Yes, Will. Yesterday's broadcast of that horrific scene at the Safeway in California seems to be on its way into the archive of vivid, visual images that mark historic turning points. I think it will go down in history with the terrorist nuclear bomb that destroyed New Delhi, the World Trade Center, the 1968 Democratic National Convention in Chicago and the Kennedy assassination. Images that forever changed the psyche of the free world."

"I think you're absolutely right, Marilyn. Although we don't have footage, incidents like the Safeway riot began to spread in coastal areas of the nation last night, where many people are truly panicked. We're told this is the basis of the martial law announcement we're about to hear. I'd like to add, however, that in those same areas there has been a tremendous upwelling of public support for the national sea coast protection effort, Operation Seawell. On top of that—"

"I'm sorry to interrupt, Will, but The President is ready."

Darcy studied the faces of Ray and Paisley Overcroft, trying to discern any reaction to the news. All remained silent, and Darcy touched her lips with her index finger to signal Tierney.

"Good morning. This is a sad and historic moment in the history of our free nation. In the last two days, many parts of our fine country have been overwhelmed by lawless anarchy in the streets. Whatever the reasons, law and order have been overrun by a panicked populace. Civil society has come unglued. Governors and mayors all over the country have asked for federal help.

"Certain elements within our population have refused to trust the sound information coming from your government and other reliable sources, and have chosen

instead to believe the vicious sensationalism pandered to them by a profit-crazed, commercialized portion of our public media.

"Two days ago I issued Executive Orders designed to address both the increasing disorder and the sea coast emergency. As we all know, a massive, civil works effort, Operation Seawell, is under way to address certain risks arising from events in Antarctica. Many wonderful, patriotic citizens have risen to the occasion and are working day and night. We are succeeding as I speak.

"It is tragic, sinfully tragic, that large numbers of other persons within our society have chosen to undermine the very fabric required to support this historic effort at national preservation. However, we must play the cards we are dealt. I have met all night with my cabinet and top members of Congress. We have collectively decided that, to insure the success of Operation Seawell and possibly the survival of our country, in my capacity as President of the United States I must make the following declaration.

"I declare that a temporary, though extreme, state of national emergency exists, unprecedented in our history."

Military officers would be in charge in every city of ten thousand or more, he explained. Darcy guessed that they were quite far from such a place. Ray's face was fixed in a frown, and his head bobbed enigmatically.

"The use, carrying, display and acquisition of firearms and firearms supplies continues to be prohibited as spelled out under the Executive Orders. Travel restrictions and controls under the Executive Orders will remain or be amplified.

"Every citizen should locate the radio or television channel established to carry local emergency broadcasts in times of flood, earthquake, hurricane, or tornado. This will henceforth be the single, authoritative source of information for the direction of all civic activities, be they commercial or governmental in nature. Those channels, in turn, will identify which newspapers have been authorized to disseminate authoritative information of the same kind. Because malfunctioning of our media is at the root of this crisis of civil disorder, no media other than those just mentioned will be allowed to function until martial law can be lifted and the country can return to normal.

"This is a moment of the most profound personal sadness in my lifetime. I dedicate myself to every one of you—men, women and children—who constitute the responsible citizenry of our great nation, to ceaselessly work to restore our Constitutional government on the earliest day humanly possible. So help me God. Thank you."

Ray Overcroft snapped off the radio and the kitchen was silent, except for the happy babbling of Finn Malone. Babushka was helping him with the cream of wheat Paisley had stirred up for him. Tierney sensed, once again, that this was an adult moment which she should leave strictly to the grown-ups.

Ray was the first to speak. "Damn! I was afraid of that. But, you know, truth is, it might not make much difference here in Modoc County. I mean, Flat River doesn't even have three thousand people any more, and the county's under ten thousand, so no military unit's going to take over up here. Nothing much happens here anyway. Sierra Army Depot's over fifty miles south."

Paisley warmed everyone's coffee. Her ready smile softened her sharp features and summoned the attractiveness scattered in the recesses of her placid bearing.

"Thank you, Sugar." Ray smiled at her. "I'll tell you what does worry me, though. I told you before, Paisley, inventories in town have been dropping the last couple of weeks. Chet at the feed store told me most everybody's trucks around California have been diverted to that emergency sea coast construction. He said orders just aren't being delivered. I think this is going to get way worse before it gets better."

Paisley sat and sipped her coffee. "Well, we've got our supplies laid in. I'm just wondering what'll happen to all the poor people where the Army runs everything. I feel sorry for them. And all those young boys and girls in the service. You can bet they're not prepared to do this kind of thing. I feel sorry for them, too."

For Darcy's whole life, even through the bitterness of her mother's catatonic years, she and her mother had shared an uncanny pattern of parallel thought patterns. They only had to look at each other in moments of deep intensity, like this, and they knew what the other was thinking. Now their eyes were locked, eyelids limp, facial muscles relaxed—they could have been deep in prayer in a quiet church. Their minds flowed as one.

Escaped the chaos, the soldiers, the dogs ... Now it's martial law? Flying back to the Bay Area suddenly was a futile dream, for now. What about Elmer? How would they get back to get him? And Reinhold? Would he even get back to the U.S.? And their homes. Both women considered their family nests to be of highest personal value.

In a struggle to stabilize for survival, walling off the loss of remaining innocence, they narrowed their thoughts to action plans—action that could tie to the long-range movement forward of the basic themes of their lives. It was not about loss but about the interruption and restoration of continuity. Neither of them trusted the President or his right-wing party. But speculation on the consequences of the military "takeover" were displaced by more immediate questions. Could they get fuel to fly to Flagstaff? Could they find the homestead? If not, how would they get along for the next few days? Or weeks?

Ray Overcroft seemed tuned in as well. "I've got a fifty gallon drum in the back of my pickup, and a gas pump with a long hose I use to fill up tractors on the farm. Every farm around here has bulk gas for the equipment. I've got about five hundred gallons myself. Be happy to fill your plane, if it's not too thirsty, if you catch my drift."

"Thanks, but I can only fly on aviation fuel…" Darcy stopped mid-way. Ray's eye contact lingered a touch too long, cut short by Paisley's voice.

"Tomorrow's Presidents Day and no one'll be open in town, so we'll have to fill the time. Mill Creek Falls should be gorgeous just now—maybe I'll take you up there. Tuesday, Ray can take you ladies to the airport in town. You can buy gas for your airplane and be on your way. You'll have to stay a couple of nights, so let me show you where you'll sleep."

Darcy scanned her mother's face and decided to leave the homestead information for Mariah to disclose in her own time. Darcy simply replied, "Great."

The rest of Sunday filled without much effort on anyone's part. They drove to the airplane, taped a big yellow notebook page on the pilot's window saying, "OUT OF GAS." Ray had to fix a fence at the southeast corner of the farm and was gone most of the afternoon. Mariah used the Overcrofts' telephone to try to call Elmer, but all she got were busy circuit signals.

While the children took a nap, Paisley showed Mariah and Darcy around. The first stop was her prized herb operation, complete with greenhouse and raised-bed intensive French garden boxes for spring and summer. Conversation warmed as Mariah compared notes on her own herb garden and her childhood memories of the family sheep ranches in Arizona. The Overcrofts had a barn, a chicken house, an equipment shed, a windmill that pumped water into a large storage tank, and a padlocked storage shed. Inside, shelves and stalls held abundant provisions, stacked and labeled.

Darcy wondered if they were Mormons.

CHAPTER 62
Monday, February 20

MARIAH AGAIN tried to call Elmer, and again got solid busy circuits. Ray said he hadn't finished fixing the southeast corner post and trudged off, buckling his tool belt.

Paisley drove to the promised picnic at Mill Creek Falls. The scrub forest gave way to sagebrush and valley grassland, interrupted by two modest farms before they reached the intersection that proudly called itself the town of Likely. There was a general store, a saloon, a fire station and five clapboard homes, all in need of paint. A sign pointed right: Buckberry Valley Road.

They drove along a rocky creek, brimming with a vigorous run of snowmelt. Paisley played tour guide. "That's the South Fork of the Pit River. It drains the Buckberry Valley. Up at the north end of the valley is Mill Creek Falls, which brings most of the water out of the Warner Mountains."

Darcy sat by the passenger window. "Look at the ice shelves along the edges where the water's more quiet." Winter had not released its nightly grip.

The sloping hillsides narrowed into a steep canyon, barren boulder-packed sides at a forty-five degree angle leading up to a base of hundred-foot high, vertical dikes of black lava. "Late Cenozoic," Paisley commented, "easily sixty million years old. Read that in the Maillard Report, written in the 1930s."

They ascended into terrain populated with mature pines and graceful white firs. The narrow forest highway broke into an open vista over a pale green valley rimmed on the eastern side by stately snow covered mountain ridges.

"The Forty-Niners entered California through this valley. Those who came west on the Oregon Trail, anyway.

"And beyond," she nodded straight ahead, "that's the Warner Mountains. Most of it, from here north, is preserved. The South Warner Wilderness. Ray and I hike in there as much as we can, every summer. It's beautiful. Almost no one goes in there. No crowds, like around Yosemite, you know. That pinnacle—Eagle Peak, over nine thousand feet high."

They drove north along the edge of the valley, passing stretches of sagebrush, patches of wet marshland, and half a dozen sparse farms. Then east again into the fir, up the one-mile entrance road to Mill Creek Falls.

"Nice country," Mariah said, halfway through her sandwich. "Kind of reminds me of places I knew as a child in Flagstaff."

"Is that where you're from?" Paisley asked.

Mariah gave a thumbnail sketch of her Arizona background, then explained their situation, why they had left the Bay Area.

"How about your husband?"

"There wasn't room in the plane. The plan was for Darcy to go back and get him once we got to Flagstaff. With fuel being rationed, though, we'll have to make Plan B. We have a little piece of property up here, Paisley. We're going to try to find it. My uncle owned it, but he died last year and left it to me. I believe we could spend a couple of weeks there until things sort out. She caught her breath, felt a twinge from her intuition. Inside her mind there flashed a picture.

A dusty brown album snapshot of herself as a white haired, frail woman standing by Sather Gate on the U.C. Berkeley campus. It was overgrown with ivy. In the photo's lower right corner was penciled, in Darcy's unmistakable scrawl, "Mom's 95th, August 13, 2045."

Mariah stopped, knowing tears were next. "So, Paisley, tell me about you. Were you born around here?"

"Oh no. Actually, I'm from the East Coast. So's Ray. Well, sort of. He's from Johnstown, Pennsylvania. I'm from a little town south of Atlantic City, New Jersey."

She filled in details. They had been Peace Corps volunteers in India, then finished college at U.C. Davis. With a degree in sustainable agriculture she worked as a waitress in the economically stressed early nineties while Ray worked for a John Deere dealer. From Ray's parents they inherited enough to buy an inexpensive farm. Inexpensive translated to Modoc County.

"You have a pretty nice little operation down there," Mariah said.

"I'm happy. I think Ray'll always be restless. Johnstown was no metropolis, but Modoc County's pretty far from anywhere. Ray would really like to find peace in his heart. But he doesn't know how to look. I love my herbs, and the wilderness.

"Turned out, I never got pregnant. I could tell Ray was desperate for a family, but he wouldn't adopt. I really didn't want to either, to be honest with you. He never says anything, but I know he feels hollow about it, still." Paisley's eyes were moist.

She was saved by Tierney. "Mommy, I think Finn needs changing." She wrinkled her nose.

The sun was behind the western ridge when they returned to the farm, where Ray had prepared a hearty, pepper pot stew.

Darcy returned to the dinner table for coffee once the children got to sleep in their still unfamiliar surroundings. Her mind drifted to Frankfurt, wondering where her nomad husband was now.

Ray cleared his throat. "Darcy. I drove down to check your plane this afternoon. I'm sorry to have to tell you this, but it looks like someone tried to tow it off. I'm just guessing about this, but it looks like they might have broke the landing gear and when they couldn't steal it, they torched it. It was barely recognizable."

Mother and daughter exchanged glances. Paisley put her hand on Darcy's arm in sympathy. Darcy managed a show of courage. "I'll have to let the insurance people know as soon as I can." She didn't want to go into the connection with the mortuary.

Paisley said, "What will you do about your husbands?"

Darcy's lips were a thin line. Mariah fielded the question. "Well, first we'll do our best not to worry. They're resourceful boys, and we can stay in touch by email. Second, we'd have to wait for the government to lighten up anyway. When the time's right, we'll all be back together again." She glanced at Darcy, and everyone sipped their coffee.

In a barely audible voice, Ray tossed out, "We don't have email out here, but we can fix you up in town tomorrow."

Inside her eggshell veneer of bravery, Darcy's mind raced far beyond Ray's comment. Probably be reported to the FAA by the sheriff. Maybe they'll think we crashed. I wonder if the navy blue guy'll come looking for me up here. Or my body.

CHAPTER 63
Tuesday, February 21

THROUGHOUT MODOC COUNTY, radio programs reported tanks on Berkeley's Telegraph Avenue, soldiers with assault rifles guarding stores, juvenile gangs mowed down by automatic weapons, soldiers in trauma over shooting fellow citizens. Distant though it was, the world beyond Modoc County was staggering.

TUESDAY BREAKFAST featured Paisley volunteering to feed Finn. Mariah stepped outside at her daughter's request. She sensed both urgency and anxiety.

"Mom, I'll stay here while you go into town. I'd rather stay out of sight." She handed her mother some of the money from her flight jacket and a list of what might have been in suitcases, had they been so lucky—pajamas, underwear, toiletry, diapers—and some basics to help the Overcrofts with the unexpected visitation.

"Sure, Baby. I think it would be best too. I'll be as discrete as I can." After Darcy's reports about the man on the Marina Green, Mariah's instincts told her the danger was more serious than even her daughter feared. "No one needs to know that Darcy Malone's in Modoc County with her children. I'm not quite sure how I'll handle Ray, but I'll probably make up a story about Reinhold and Moscow. That sounds good, doesn't it? You know, like we don't really know why, but there are certain... umm..."

Darcy helped out, "Say, elements, who could use me and the kids against him while he's..."

Mariah picked up, "On foreign soil. That sounds scary."

Darcy nodded. "Yeah. So if the... authorities think we were killed in a crash, so much the better. Right?"

"We'll go with it. Now, today with the kids..."

"Wait, Mom. Let's not go back to you telling me how to be a good mother. Okay?"

Mariah felt the old sadness, but she knew the drill and yielded. Whenever Darcy was under high stress, the brittle scars of early adolescence with a mother submerged in grief and a father struggling through the haze of drink cracked open and Darcy became defensive over child-rearing advice.

"Okay. You're going to have a fine day out here."

It wasn't long before Paisley led Tierney and Finn, with their mother in tow, off to the "baby tour"—tiny chicks in the chicken yard, kittens in the barn, baby goats out in the holding pasture, and the warm little indoor places where they all slept through the freezing winter nights.

Ray backed the pickup over to the front door with a spray of gravel. "Darcy's not coming?" He was clearly disappointed, but recovered quickly with a grin that seemed tutored by Elvis. Mariah was shapely for a grandmother, and Ray lacked subtlety in his visual assessment. "Y'know, you and Darcy could be sisters."

Mariah ignored the remark. She settled into the cab and off they sped.

"Yesterday Paisley said you were both in India?"

"Yup. Got out of Davis in eighty-nine. Paize was class of eighty-eight, but she stayed around for me. Waited tables for a year at Gepetto's. The Muni Court Judge married us the day after I graduated."

"In Davis? What about your families?"

"They never met. Both our families are blue-collar folks, Republicans. Not at all pleased with their California rebel children. We didn't invite 'em."

"When did you go to India?"

"Spring 1990 we joined the Peace Corps. They assigned us to a village in Gujarat Province."

"Did you like it there?"

"I managed to help a few Hindu farmers add some new food plants to their 'cash' crops." He popped his eyebrows up twice to frame the euphemism. "Paisley worked, undercover so to speak, with the women on basic health issues, even though her only training was high school Home Ec. It was enough. She's damn smart, you know, creative, adaptable, rolls with the punches. I'm a lucky man."

Mariah silently agreed, and continued her conversational technique of interviewing. "Paisley said moving up here was a great thing."

"Yeah. She likes it a lot. Does great with her herbs and all. Me? Well, it's what I do." Ray looked into the distance. "We need some spirited women up here in Modoc. Like you guys. Paisley's too much alone."

Mariah gave a thoughtful nod. *He's the one who's lonely. Life's not such a great school if you don't listen.* She changed the subject. "Where do you do email, Ray?"

"Over at Chets's Feed Store. There's a kid there who's online all the time and helps some of us computer morons with email and stuff."

"Before we go there, could you take me by Lago and Swift ? You know them?"

"The lawyers? Sure. Ol' R. L. Lago is County Farm Commissioner. How do you know them?"

"I mentioned this to Paisley yesterday. When Darcy realized she was short on gas out of Oakland and we knew we couldn't make it to Arizona, I thought we should try to get up here because my uncle left me a piece of property near Flat River. When he died last fall, I talked with Sy Swift, and he said they had keys. He said there was a furnished house there, ready for occupation when Uncle Caesar bought it out of probate. I guess they were the lawyers for the previous owner, but Uncle Caesar died before he ever moved in. Anyway, if the house is okay, I thought we could buy some supplies and stay there a few days or weeks until things calm down."

Ray nodded. "Need any help with the legal beagles?"

Mariah eased into the topic of keeping Darcy's and the children's where-abouts low profile. Rather, no profile. "So I'd like to do this on my own. Keep it low-key, you know."

"Well, if you need help, I'll come back with you later. Meanwhile, I've got some business over at the Farm Co-op. They buy my crops every year. I'll buy you lunch at that little spot I showed you back there, the Black Bear Diner. Meet you there at noon."

At the front desk, the receptionist said Mr. Swift was out, but the paralegal who handled the Maxwell probate could take care of her. She punched the intercom, "LuEllen, there's a woman here to see you about that Maxwell property."

In moments, LuEllen Jones appeared in the hallway and introduced her-self. She stood solid in her light blue and white checked dress, a matching fabric belt around her well-packed middle.

Mariah presented her ID and enough knowledge about her Uncle Caesar to satisfy the paralegal, who then ushered her into a conference room. "Give me a minute. I'll bring the keys and a map. By the way, the place is called Max-well Acres."

When she returned, Mariah asked what she knew about the place.

LuEllen narrowed her eyes. She spun a mysterious tale. The owner, Mr. Maxwell, had been found dead on the property three summers back when he hadn't come to town for provisions for ten days. There had been a heat wave and his body was so badly decomposed the coroner waived an autopsy. Mr. Maxwell was about eighty at the time. He came to Flat River from Norfolk, Virginia, in 1992. They said before that he lived his whole life in an enormous mansion on the beach where they could see the Atlantic surf. His wife died in childbirth, the story went, just the one daughter. He bought the property and rebuilt—the original buildings had rotted and collapsed decades before.

The paralegal began to lose her edge, became downright talkative.

"Mr. Maxwell nearly always had a handyman on the payroll out there, at least in the early years. Picked them up at the local AA meeting. None of them ever stayed with him long, and none ever stayed in town after they left him. Mr. Maxwell never came to town himself. He always sent the handyman in for lumber and supplies.

"Gossip was Mr. Maxwell never received mail and never had visitors. But he took long trips somewhere. Sometimes he was gone three or four weeks straight. UPS drivers delivered quite a few packages over the years, from just about everywhere, they say. Delivered them to the lumber store for the handyman to take out. But no mail. There's no delivery out at the property, and he never got anything at General Delivery. Everyone's clear about that.

"I heard Mrs. Whiting befriended Mr. Maxwell. She's the storekeeper at Elmo's General Store down Highway 299 at the Adin crossroads. Her story, at least as it came out at the end of the gossip tunnel, was he belonged to some Scottish cult in Virginia and when he wouldn't turn his fortune over to them, he had to run for his life. How he chose Flat River, no one quite knows, except Modoc County's about as remote as you can get."

When Mr. Maxwell died, LuEllen's firm did the probate. They finally tracked down the mansion in the East where the only heirs, two unmarried granddaughters, were still living. Maxwell's daughter, their mother, died young.

"They were wealthy in their own right, allegedly," said LuEllen. "They refused to come out to California to help after the body was found. Told Sy just to send his jewelry, wallet and personal papers, give his clothes away, spread his ashes on the land, and sell the furniture and stuff with the property, as is. They just didn't even care about the probate. Sy wouldn't compromise on the price, but finally your Uncle came along. I remember him well. Part of the Basque community up here. Luigi—that's what we call R.L.—knew him at the Elks Lodge. He didn't seem too healthy, but he was excited about living way out there in the mountains. I guess you knew he had no children. When he bought the property, he had Sy rewrite his will. The rest you know."

Mariah studied the map, noting that Maxwell Acres was not far from the valley they drove through with Paisley. LuEllen commented, "It's pretty remote. There is one other cabin out there, though."

Mariah tried to call Elmer at several different pay telephones. None worked. She bought two newspapers from vending machines—yesterday's *San Francisco Chronicle*, and last Thursday's weekly copy of *The Modoc County Record*.

At lunch in the Black Bear Diner, she felt the scrutiny of the waitress, the hostess and a man at the counter. Their interest was not just that Ray was there with a woman, a stranger. Mariah saw Ray was a stranger too.

Conversation got easier with the food. From the way Ray talked about people he knew, she grew to understand just how conservative Flat River and Modoc County were. Somewhere between moderate Republican and the far right wing. She also came to know that Ray and Paisley were fundamentally outsiders here, even after eight years. "They never stopped calling us hippies," Ray chuckled. Mariah understood that by appearing there with Ray she was set up to remain an outsider.

They didn't linger. Ray paid the check.

At the feed store, the kid with the computers was away, but Chet took Ray and Mariah to his loft. Mariah nearly burst with pride when she accessed her email account, and Darcy's too, for her first time ever at a remote computer. She checked Darcy's first—reams of business and personal correspondence, but Mariah looked for only one message—from Reinhold. There was none.

She found two notes from Elmer in her queue, characteristically brief. The first assured her, "all's well here at the house. I'm eating just fine." On the second one, she caught her breath.

Nathan and Miriam came up. Federal troops have surrounded the communications building at the campus. We've resurrected the phone tree from the Vietnam days. We're protesting in Sproul Plaza day after tomorrow. Won't be the same in a wheelchair. Maybe better, who knows? Love, Elmer.

Mariah clicked "Reply," and spent ten minutes on a nutshell version of the low gas forcing them north to Flat River, Ray and Paisley's kindness, and locating Maxwell Acres. She didn't tell him about the airplane.

Driving back to the farm, already weighed down by Reinhold's silence and Elmer's propelling himself into the path of danger, Mariah's heart became heavier as Ray recounted what his friend, Chet, had distilled from his customers. "Full-scale activation of military and security personnel nationwide," he said. "Reserves, retirees, Boy Scouts, gun toting Christians. Other people, young and uneducated, doing jobs they're unqualified for. Untrained people in power demanding bribes and payoffs. Corruption magnifying incompetence. The military's forcing people to work in the projects to build ocean barriers around utilities, airports, power plants, port facilities, trying to maintain commerce, food supplies, basic services. They've thrown up road blocks to discourage migration.

"Even with the roadblocks, seems a lot of pretty strange people have blown into town the last couple of days. The motels are full, and the people don't even know what they're doing here. The sheriff's been running them out of the campgrounds every night. We're not used to this. We never have traffic like this in the winter.

"Flat River's tightening up," he continued. "The city fathers feel, with state and federal governments focused on the sea coast, Modoc County's going to be on its own for a while. They've empowered an Executive Committee to deal with the emergency. You know, like rationing food, medicine and other critical stuff if truck and railroad shipping doesn't start up again soon. The phones are mostly down. Everyone's pretty nervous about what's happening."

"Me too, Ray." Mariah's mind kept calling up the photo album image of her return to Berkeley at the age of ninety-five.

CHAPTER 64
Wednesday, February 22

"LET'S JUST TAKE Ray's pickup, Mom, and go alone. He's okay with that. We can find it on the map ourselves."

Mariah wasn't in discussion mode. "Look, we've got to trust Ray and Paisley. They know who we are, they know about the plane, about the property, they know you need to keep a low-profile for some vague reason. The best way to keep their trust is to keep trusting them. Besides, you can just look at Ray and tell. He may be a womanizer, but in everything else, he's a straight shooter."

Darcy didn't take to her mother's parenting advice, but when it came to judging people, no one had more clarity. Darcy herself had the talent, and she felt the truth of her mother's words.

Ray drove. North from the farm, east at Likely, double back along smaller and smaller roads, climb into the foothills approaching the wilderness area. About four miles past the Modoc National Forest boundary, they turned left on a two-tracked dirt road, bumped up a few more curves skirting a steep, tree-covered hill, then took a left around an ancient oak tree so old and big its lower branches rested heavy and tired on the uphill slope. By the oak, a sizable arroyo sliced into the edge of the hill, then took a sharp turn east, necessitating a two-culvert concrete bridge for the road crossing. From the bridge they saw two buildings about a half mile up a pretty valley, which changed from meadow to pines and aspens just beyond the structures. This little valley was home to Maxwell Acres.

The first building they passed was a small, friendly looking log cabin with a green shingle roof situated toward the front of a small parcel outlined by an old split-rail fence. A mud-rutted driveway ended in a circle in front of the cabin porch.

"This isn't part of our property," Mariah said. "The paralegal told me that before Maxwell owned it, the owner split the south ten acres from the eighty acres of the original homestead. Later, the owner of the ten acres sold two to a couple named Royer from Sacramento. The paralegal didn't know who owns the eight acres now."

Ray noted, "There's no electricity up here, you know. See that exhaust pipe on the barn behind the house? They must have a small generator in there. It's expensive to make your own electricity, but it helps when you want to wash the clothes."

Mariah thought she saw someone through a window as they passed. She kept it to herself, thinking, *No tracks in the driveway, and no vehicles in sight.*

They continued about a third of a mile toward a promontory that formed the north end of the valley. The buildings at Maxwell Acres looked dilapidated and makeshift to the eye, but closer inspection revealed they were rock solid and weather tight. They were all faced with unpainted redwood clapboards, weathered to a driftwood gray. A two-story main house, two guest houses and a huge barn formed a rectangle around a fenced yard.

Further up against the hillside sat a fifth building, probably a storage shed—it had a pitched roof with a hop-kiln ventilation chimney in its middle, and on the east end a small, second story addition that looked more like a watchtower than a room.

Other than a recent accumulation of dust and cobwebs, the main house was remarkably clean inside. "The lawyers sent a cleaning service out every few months for basic maintenance," Mariah explained.

The kitchen was fully equipped. The stove was a large, French wood burner that looked more like a converted locomotive than a cooking apparatus. They noticed a few electric lights. "Maxwell had an electric generator in the barn. The cleaning ladies used it when they came. Wastewater's handled by a septic system."

"Boy, Mom, you picked up a lot of information," Darcy said. "Nothing wrong with your memory either."

Mariah was happily surprised at the flush toilets and the running water. The kitchen faucet ran rusty water at first, but after a few minutes, while they opened drawers and cupboards, it cleared and was sweet when Darcy tasted it.

They saw the two guest houses and moved on to the storage shed. One of Mariah's keys turned the lock, but no one could get the doors to open. They were hinged to open inwards, but they wouldn't budge. "Sometimes dirt builds up inside these kinds of old buildings and blocks the doors," Ray said.

They explored the barn. Darcy was impressed. "All that equipment. Mr. Maxwell was sure ready to farm, wasn't he?"

Ray agreed. "Impressive."

Mariah produced a crude drawing the lawyers had sketched, pointed up the hill where the diagram said Spring. "Lets walk up there and see."

Memorandum from the Law Offices of Lago & Swift
148 Andalou Avenue, Flat River CA 96101

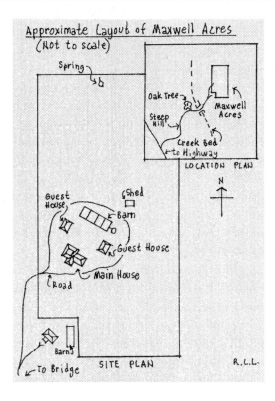

Ray said, "Pick me up on your way back. I want to look this equipment over better."

Ten minutes from the house, at the upper end of the property, they came to a natural cul-de-sac on the side of a brush-filled gully. Its steep bank supported foliage considerably more lush than the rest of the nearby terrain and was embedded with boulders of all sizes, many of them moss-covered. They saw a rivulet emerge from a limestone formation in the bank and run down seven or eight feet between two boulders, then disappear back into the ground through a bed of pebbles and fist-sized rocks. Darcy climbed down to the spring, cupped her left hand and scooped some water into her mouth. "Mmm. Sweet, just like in the house. Not too cold either. That's a nice spring and a good volume. You could pipe that water down to the compound easily. I'll bet

Mr. Maxwell did pipe some of this water down to that storage tank and that's why the kitchen water tasted so good. But where would the rest of the water wind up after it goes back underground?"

They sauntered down the trail in silence, in no hurry to leave the secluded beauty. Darcy broke the tranquility. "What do you think, Mom? Do you think Dad'll like it here?"

"Sure. Sure." Mariah felt a lump in her throat the size of a mandarin orange. The curled-edge Sather gate snapshot flashed into her mind yet again. *Could be a long time before Elmer gets here.*

Back at the Overcroft home, in the parlor by the fire when the children were in bed, the creeping impact of Reinhold's silence hit Darcy full force. Ray shifted back and forth in his chair, uncomfortable with crying women. He poked the dwindling logs in the fireplace and stared into the flames. Paisley laid her hand on Darcy's. "My only brother was lost on an expedition up the Amazon for three years. But he came back when I was twenty-six. Whether Reinhold returns soon, or a long time from now, I understand what you're feeling. Never stop hoping."

CHAPTER 65
Thursday, February 23

A HUNDRED METERS from the giant sign heralding PORT OF ANTWERPEN, Reinhold found the cargo dispatch office for Stephanovich's shipping line. He handed the embossed envelope to the bureaucrat in charge and said, "This is from one of your best customers in Moscow. It's for the Captain of the *Svetlana*. Get it to him immediately. I will wait here."

Less than ten minutes later a steward in a white uniform appeared, shook Reinhold's hand, cleared him through the makeshift police checkpoint and took him aboard. Within the hour they were underway and by early afternoon were entering the open waters of the Atlantic.

Reinhold was squeezed into one of five passenger cabins. The crew lashed a cot under the porthole. His two paying cabinmates spoke only Portuguese, but seemed affable enough. *I hope there's some reading material aboard, or this voyage could get tedious*, Reinhold teased himself. With gestures and grins, the two Brazilians took their new friend to the passenger lounge. Their faces reflected astonishment when the Captain came in, embraced Reinhold and invited him to the quarterdeck to observe operations.

Capitalizing on the initial graciousness of the Captain, Reinhold obtained permission to send an email under the vessel's URL. He reasoned that if the U.S. Army were interested enough to bug him, they probably had a monitor on his email account too. He hoped their surveillance was not sophisticated enough to catch his name passing through the general Internet. He sent his missive to Mariah, believing they would be watching Darcy's account as well.

> 4:00 p.m.
>
> Dearest Darcy,
>
> I'm emailing from the communications room on the quarterdeck of the Svetlana. I managed to sneak, bribe, beg and bully my way from Frankfurt to Antwerp. I'll tell you all about it when I get home. It's a tremendous favor for them to let me use their email. The captain okayed your using the ship's email address for a reply. Do not use yours or mine. Use Mariah's, or Elmer's.
>
> We should dock in New York late afternoon next Tuesday. I've emailed Troy Blake. I'll email you again from there.
>
> The minute I know how I'm going to get out of New York, I can start counting the days or hours until I see you and the children again. When I'm safe again in your arms in California, that'll be the happiest day of my life. Until then, God bless.
>
> All my love,
>
> Reinhold

MARIAH DROVE SOLO to Flat River. Her objectives: email, and supplies for the move to Maxwell Acres.

She combed through the depleted inventories of every store likely to have the necessaries to make Maxwell Acres habitable. She bought Levi's and denims, more old-fashioned cloth diapers, cleaning supplies, kitchen and household gadgets she thought Mr. Maxwell might not have considered. Whatever canned and dry food she could garner. In the military surplus store, as if by a miracle, she even found raincoats and work boots in the right sizes.

She returned to Chet's Feed Store, signed online and scanned the accumulated emails, mostly spam that was getting through because she was not on her own computer. Even with the social order in extremis, the spam kept flying. Suddenly, her eye caught Reinhold's screen name. Instantly, she realized why he was communicating through her. She read the message through incipient tears, printed it to take to her anxious daughter, and replied in judiciously inscrutable phrases, giving directions to the homestead where "she" would be, but little other identifying data.

Scrolling on through the junk mail, she was rewarded by Elmer. He was relieved to know where they had landed. And he was enthusiastic about Maxwell Acres. He went on,

> There were nine hundred of us at Sproul today. I'd say a third were our age, a third Darcy's generation, and thank God a third students. Nathan wheeled me to the microphone and we got the crowd red hot with the impact we had in the sixties. Nothing's changed, Mariah. Someone started a scuffle, it spread and the troops attacked. They arrested Nathan. Miriam got me in the van and we got out through Strawberry Canyon, but I had to abandon the wheelchair. As she sped out, I heard gunfire. Naturally, there's nothing reliable on the radio. The puppets talked about a "disturbance" and "calm was restored." Makes me want to vomit. We're trying to figure out our next step.
>
> I miss you terribly. It'll be great to see you as soon as the Fates permit. I love you more than you can ever know, Mariah, my darling.
> Forever,
> Elmer

Mariah swallowed her emotion and sent Elmer a new report. She signed off,

> We're moving from the Overcroft's farm out to the property tomorrow 'til we can get back to Oakland. Won't email for a few days—no way to get to town. Can hardly wait to see you, too. As soon as things quiet down, somehow we'll come get you.
>
> I'd be even happier if the whole world calmed down enough that we could come home instead, and then you and I could come back up here later this spring when it's warmer and the wild flowers bloom.
> Please, Love, be careful.
> I love you, too, my Darling.
> Mariah

"Back so soon, Mom?" Darcy jousted. It was shortly before noon. "I thought you'd shop most of the day."

Mariah didn't take the bait. She resolved to stay serious and compassionate. "I've got an email from Reinhold for you, Baby."

Darcy devoured the cryptic message. "Tuesday?" She sounded exultant and sarcastic simultaneously. She started to laugh, but it changed to sobs in a blink of the eye.

Her mother put her arm around Darcy's shoulders and said, "I know, he's made a huge step closer, but it still feels like it'll be forever. We just have to hang in there, take a day at a time."

After lunch, Mariah's eyes took on a faraway look. She said, "The paralegal in town told me the only one who really knew Mr. Maxwell was a woman down at the Adin crossroads. I think I should meet her."

Ray didn't need the pickup. He gave Mariah a roadmap, circled her destination, and she headed down the road for a second time that day.

No one was in Elmo's General Store when Mariah pushed open the screen door, jangling a harness bell set to alert the storekeeper. Her eyes adjusted to the shadowy light as she walked up to the worn counter by the cash register. She waited a moment, then cleared her voice, then waited some more, her heart in her throat. What was she doing here? She studied the faded blue and gold curtain hanging in the doorway just behind the counter.

After half a minute, a delicate, ghostly hand gripped the edge of the curtain and drew it aside. Mrs. Whiting materialized, diminutive, clad in a simple white smock with beaded moccasins on her feet and a shawl flung around her shoulders in a splash of blues and reds and yellows. Her snowy hair was compacted under an old-fashioned hair net. Her face was as wrinkled as a Pennsylvania dried-apple doll, but the lines were all kindly, laughter lines. There was something other-worldly about her gaze. At first, Mariah thought it was her brilliant, sapphire eyes, but realized that, although her hair had turned white, Mrs. Whiting's eyebrows were still rusty-brown, as they must always have been.

"I know who you are, dear. You're Mariah Wallace. A good Scottish name. Chet's a friend of mine, too. He dropped in yesterday, told me you'd inherited Maxwell Acres. I had a feeling you'd be by."

Mariah's voice was hushed. "Is there a place we could sit and talk? There are some things I need to know."

Mrs. Whiting tottered around the counter and grasped Mariah's right elbow. It was more for her own support, it seemed, but she also steered Mariah to the back of the store and through another doorway into a small den.

There were white curtains over the windows. Mariah had the impression that more light came through those curtains than there was outside. Opposite the door was a hardwood framed fireplace with a white marble mantelpiece cluttered with figurines, stones, crystal balls, small Russian icon paintings and

252

other esoterica. Among the brick-a-brack were four photographs in miniature silver frames chronicling the growth of a beautiful boy into a handsome young man. A small fire burned orange and yellow in the fireplace. Two overstuffed, black wing-backed leather chairs faced each other on either side of a small table directly in front of the fireplace.

Mrs. Whiting took Mariah firmly to a chair near the fire, released her hand and settled like dust into another chair. "What was it you wanted to know, Mariah?"

Profound sadness and happiness together were radiating from every corner of the room. Mrs. Whiting seemed to Mariah not to be made of flesh and blood, but of particles of light glued together by the gravity of happiness and sadness, wisdom and knowledge, compassion and distance.

"What do I need to know? Tell me what I need to know. About Maxwell Acres. About Mr. Maxwell. Why am I here? What am I supposed to be doing?"

Mrs. Whiting got up without a word and went out the door behind Mariah, who sat listening to the fire. Her mind was working at a level beyond her immediate consciousness. Her thoughts formed not in words, but pictures, pictures of things she knew nothing about—not what they were, nor where they were, nor who the people were, nor what kinds of creatures were there. Even the colors had no names. And there was music in her head—pervasive, mesmerizing music. She couldn't track the time. Mrs. Whiting returned, rattling two bone china tea cups in her hands, but not spilling a drop.

She sat down and began.

"Robb Maxwell was my friend. I think I was his only friend in these parts."

The lovely mystic of Adin laid out a mosaic of stories about Robb Maxwell, his homestead, vignettes from his parents and grandparents about clan Maxwell near Glasgow and the early days in Virginia, the nearby and faraway places to which he claimed he traveled, the worldly treasures he accumulated and the wisdom that came with them, and the many books on esoterica and spirituality she herself had gifted to him over the years. She salted the anthology with words of advice to Mariah about what time-future might hold for her at Maxwell Acres, words of warning, or coded parables and riddles. Mariah couldn't process them all, but they lodged deep within her heart, to be drawn up like cool well water when the need arose.

Mrs. Whiting had never visited Maxwell Acres. Rob Maxwell was an incurable recluse, she said. He had no visitors except the contractors and handymen, and the children of the neighbors. But Robb, or "Max" as she called him, described building his space up there, and the ideas behind it all, in endless detail when he would stop by for tea in the bone china tea cups on his way to or

253

from some unknown destination. Stories of these places wove into his enchanting conversations without precise reference as to year of visit.

"I never pried behind what he wished to tell. Max had a need for secrecy I never understood. To protect him, I let slip a fantasy about him running away from a Scottish cult in Virginia—told a couple of librarians and hairdressers in Flat River. I figured that would sound so scary, folks around would leave him alone to his heart's desire.

"Over the years, I've had many a dream about Maxwell Acres—and Robb. I miss him something terrible, you know. I just ache inside for him. I knew he was gone the day he died. I could feel the change. Didn't dream about that one. But I knew. In my mind I saw him just lay down one morning, and that was it. He didn't have a handyman that month. So they didn't find him for quite a while. But I was sure. I knew, but I didn't tell."

Mariah sensed part of the story was a smoke screen. "Do you have any incense?" Mrs. Whiting reached over to the bookshelf, picked up a stick lying there, and handed it to Mariah, who thrust it into the fire's edge for ignition. As she set it in a holder on the mantle, a streamer of smoke curled around both ladies. Mrs. Whiting understood.

"I can see your heart's a chalice, my dear, in which any revelation is transmuted into essence for the good. So let me show you the flame inside the lantern."

Gertrude Whiting's family had raised her in Virginia Beach, three doors down from the Maxwell mansion on the Atlantic Coast. When she was a teenager, Robb Maxwell and she fell passionately in love. He was older by a decade. A child resulted, but both families refused to harbor the scandal. Robb gave in to family pressure. He chose. Gertrude chose too. She fled to California. After he married and buried a wife acceptable to his family, and reared their two daughters to adulthood, Max fled too. He finally tracked Gertrude down to the Adin Crossroads. He bought the homestead and for a while tried to woo her again. But her broken heart could not heal. Robb could be a friend, but husband or lover she would not brook. The son he had fathered was beautiful, but a social misfit. Robb vowed if Gertrude wouldn't grace the homestead, no one else would ever be close to him there. Only twice did their son ever set foot on the homestead. His father never found the way to heal his son's bitterness. And no one ever knew Mr. Maxwell was his father.

Mrs. Whiting was quiet. Mariah stared into the dregs of her long-cold tea. She knew there was more to the tale, but this was all the muses called forth now, and it sufficed. It was the truth.

Mrs. Whiting started, as if from sleep. "I dreamed about you too, Mariah. I knew when Chet showed up here, that it was you I've been dreaming about for, oh, maybe two years. Never knew quite when you'd come. But I knew you would. I had to wait. To tell you all these things, I mean. Now you make sure you listen to your own dreams, Dear. I know you do, but in the time ahead you're going to need them more than you ever imagined. And let Maxie's place speak to you too. In any way it wants. It will, you know. Pay attention. Pay heed to everything."

Be alert. Things are not what they seem.

Dusk was approaching. They had reached the end. "Only tell the others when your dreams tell you to." Mariah wasn't sure who "the others" were, but she also knew not to ask.

"You've got to go now. Don't say 'Goodbye.' Just let me give you a hug and a little kiss. And take these gifts." She handed Mariah three objects.

The first was a multicolored leaded glass window-screen depicting a snow capped mountain floating in a sea of bluebells under a sky dotted with strange, inked symbols. To Mariah it seemed as skillfully rendered as a Cezanne.

The second was an exquisitely wrought silver box, a perfect cube five inches to a side, every space crowded with a tangle of carved mythological creatures, landscapes, ships, carriages, ladies and courtiers in fabulous costumes. In the center of the lid was embedded a smooth dome of amber the size of a half dollar.

Last, Mariah recognized a ragged-edged, blue cardboard box Mrs. Whiting held out. It held a well worn Tarot deck. It was the same deck Mariah had left behind in Oakland. The 'Voyager,' it was called. She had used her own for over twenty years. Now she had one to keep at Maxwell Acres.

Mrs. Whiting smiled. "The mysteries are for you to discover. They are not beyond your abilities. Love them, and they will love you back."

Mariah drove to the Overcroft farm in a state wherein she could mark the passage of neither time nor distance, a state beyond the veil of the world's normal four dimensions, a state which mystics say partakes of the Eternal, when reality is fluid, shaped by thought alone, and consciousness flows in all directions and none.

When she got back, no one was in the house. She went upstairs, lay down on her bed and stared at the ceiling, neither thinking nor registering any residue of thought or feeling. She was not sleeping. It was as if her soul was unfolding before her, like the petals of a fractal lotus in a private universe.

She heard the voices of the children entering below, followed by Darcy and Paisley. All lively and animated. Mariah returned to waking consciousness and joined the assemblage in the kitchen for dinner.

CHAPTER 66
Friday, February 24

THE MORNING was sunny and bright, though the still-wintry air would redden the nose in the shadows. Paisley provided boxes for the supplies Mariah had acquired in Flat River. It was only when Ray loaded it all in the pickup and Tierney saw the empty rooms that she realized they were leaving their new home. Five nights in the same bed, her new friendship with Aunt Paisley, and her comfortable familiarity with the house and farm, all added up to a strong sense of belonging and security that was now about to fragment in another exodus.

Tierney hid her face in her hands and cried. It was not a tantrum, but a quiet, interior cry that welled up from her soul. Paisley took her by the hand and led her outside. Tierney held tightly, sniffling as they walked to the barn without speaking.

When they returned, the tear tracks on Tierney's cheeks were all but dry, and she grinned up at her mother. In her hand was a frayed old rope, on the other end of which was a snow white, soft baby goat. Paisley said, "Tierney, I want you to think a long time, now, about the perfect name for your baby. When I come to visit at your new place in a few days, you can tell me then."

She scooped up Tierney and the kid goat and climbed into the back of the pickup. Between the boxes, they sat side by side on a gunnysack of oats. The others climbed in the front seat, and they made their way to Maxwell Acres.

Ray and Paisley helped unload. Ray checked the heating system. "Your heat comes from the kitchen stove, living room fireplace, and small, potbellied stoves in some of the bedrooms. Out the back door, there's a lean-to with a cord of wood sheltered from the rain and snow." He brought in a couple of armloads of wood and checked the flues and inside the stove. He gave Mariah and Darcy a short course on how to fire it up, regulate the heat and cook on it. They all went upstairs, Ray carrying enough firewood for the evening warmth, and repeated the instructions for the potbellied stoves. "I'll go start the generator in the barn."

After Ray left, Mariah felt out of herself, aimless, meandering here and there. She came to rest in front of an undersized window, off center to the north on the east kitchen wall, left of the big window over the sink. Spirit returned to her movements.

She opened the box containing her gifts from Mrs. Whiting, took out the leaded crystal window hanging and raised it to the little window. A pair of inch-long brass chains was soldered to the top of the hanging, each ending with a miniature Ankh. Mariah had spotted two tiny suspension hooks screwed into the lintel of the asymmetric window. They were spaced identically to the Ankhs, and when she raised the crystal pane to the window the Ankhs slipped onto the hooks. It fit exquisitely, with but an inch of daylight on each of the four sides.

The effect was magical and instantaneous. Prisms engineered inconspicuously but with ingenious precision in the design of the art caught the morning sunlight and projected tiny rainbows onto random spots on the floor, walls and ceiling, mostly in the kitchen but some all the way through the foyer. Mariah had noticed a twin window equally offset to the north in the livingroom wall. She allowed herself a thought. *Maybe somewhere in this sad, chaotic world there's a sister pane for that window, too.*

Ray returned from the barn. "Can't start the generator. Needs a new injection timer. I'll try to find one in town, if I can. Sorry. Candlelight tonight, I guess."

As the children explored, the adults swept and dusted. The entire front of the first floor was open, punctuated by a grand staircase leading upstairs. To the right was the large kitchen, with short, alcove walls and a rustic eating table. There were three dining chairs, although room for ten. To the left of the staircase was the living room, with built-in benches under the windows and several wooden tables, rocking chairs and rustic redwood easy chairs. In the center of the back wall was a large fireplace with an elegant mantelpiece.

The two hippie farmers from Likely finished their work. Darcy suggested they investigate the guest houses for anything immediately useful. The east guest house, like the main house bedrooms, had adequate, utilitarian furniture and little else. The west one was more curious. It was filled with a jumble of stored furniture, an eclectic collection of antique machines and unopened boxes with their original shipping labels curling at the edges. Paisley found some extra table chairs. Ray brought them to the kitchen. "Just in case you invite us to dinner someday."

Their usefulness dwindling, he and Paisley soon took their leave. As she exited the front door, Paisley motioned toward the mantle. A small silver box had appeared there. Ray looked back at her blankly. Paisley barely sounded the words for him. "Mariah belongs here."

For the rest of the day, Darcy and Mariah took turns at the two primary tasks of arrival: on the one hand, managing Finn and introducing Tierney to new pastimes, both in the main house and out in the yard with her pet goat, and on the other hand, cleaning, cleaning, cleaning, storing supplies, rearranging kitchen utensils and dishes, making the beds, making the house habitable for its first night of human residence in years.

Before sundown they managed to kindle a fire in the French 'locomotive' to cook up a good single-pot soup. Darcy bedded down with the children with a reassuring story in the center bedroom upstairs, directly over the front steps. Mariah took the bedroom on the southeast corner. She would be greeted by the first ray of sunlight over the Sierra in the morning.

CHAPTER 67
Saturday, February 25

THE POPULATION of Modoc County had welcomed the president's declaration of martial law. It gave them a feeling of security. It had been only five days, but in this rural setting life had not lost much of its normalcy. In towns and cities like Redding and Red Bluff on Interstate 5, there had been looting, burglary, a number of violent incidents. Now things were calmer. Folks listened to the news a lot, waiting for reassurance about the Antarctic. They hadn't seen much military activity.

MAXWELL ACRES AWOKE before the sun should have risen. A snow-spitting cloud cover masked the hour. Darcy resisted the temptation to mirror the gloom, rolling instead with her children's excitement for their new adventure.

At breakfast, Mariah thumbed through the weekly *Modoc County Record* she had picked up. She skipped the usual palaver about the success of Operation Seawell. She read aloud small, sobering items—gas rationing all over California, prisons locked down, hospitals canceling elective surgeries. She capsulized for her daughter a smattering of stories vilifying people who had "fled" to the inland, "shirking their responsibilities to society," often arrested for vagrancy in faraway places or forced back to their home towns and disassembled lives. She ended by summarizing a blunt and aggressive anti-newcomer editorial—"people aren't welcome—go home—do your jobs."

"Until we can leave," she concluded, "I think we ought to keep a pretty low profile. I don't think we'll go to town much. We don't want to use up Ray's gas, anyway, with the rationing and all. Until we know more, we're just going to have to make the best of it right here. It feels to me like it could be weeks. Maybe even months."

Darcy's face became flushed. She couldn't read her mother's thoughts, and exploded under the pressure with an accusation, "Mom. Suddenly you seem too comfortable here. You don't even want to go home, do you? The Bay Area sounds calmer than when we left. What? You want me to send Dad up here and you two can coast your years away in a mountain hideout?"

She watched for her words' effect. Mariah kept her face soft, if serious. "Things aren't what they seem, Darling. Blind restlessness could be fatal. Try to trust. Try to trust me."

Mariah marshaled all the power of her compassionate heart to cast an iron shell around the turmoil swirling behind the mask of her demeanor, for in the wake of Darcy's emotional salvo, into Mariah's private mind had surged what she could not yet tell her struggling daughter—the dream that only hours before had brought her bolt upright in the dark of the night.

The Wallace house in Oakland is in flames. Men in military uniforms carry Elmer's body out to the driveway, toss it into the trunk of their car—not a military truck or combat vehicle but a sedan only high-level officials use. One of the men says to the others, "So much for the organized resistance."

Although Darcy's outburst was still ringing in her ears, Mariah could not hold her ground against the push of the dream and succumbed for an instant to the bottomless panic of her imagination—*never again to see the beloved home where my child spanned the arc from infancy to maturity, never again to sleep under my cozy duvet, to don my beautiful clothes, the magentas and the Irish greens, the woolens and the silks, the elegant dresses and silly pajamas, never again to adorn my hair with the Spanish comb, my neck with the golden collar Grandmother brought from Egypt, my ears with the filigree from the Czechoslovakian Gypsies, my fingers and wrists with the jade, the coral, the turquoise, never again to grace my eyes across my first-prize painting from college, the Aiken masterpiece of Monument Valley, the Kachinas and sand paintings from Flagstaff and Santa Fe, never again to walk the streets of those towns of my childhood...* For an instant she fell weightless into a pit beneath her heart and cried within for the illusionary permanence of Incarnation's accumulations. And just as suddenly, out of that instant she broke through, back into the kitchen of Maxwell Acres' big house, and gently mustered a smile of sympathy toward her daughter's agony.

"I think the first thing we need to do is get a garden going. I wish I knew what we can plant outside that'll grow in this cold weather. Maybe Paisley can tell us when we see them again. Maybe we could rig up some seedling trays in the barn where the morning sunshine would warm them—you know, rig up a greenhouse, sort of. Then when spring really breaks, we could get them planted."

Without resistance from her mother to thrash against, Darcy swam with the current once again. "We'll have to figure out an irrigation system. I think I could do that." Then she got a faraway look in her eyes that Mariah knew signaled suppressed despair over Reinhold. "Tierney, help Babushka with the dishes, okay? Or play 'kitchen' with Finn. Mom, I'm going to take a little walk. Maybe I'll go up by the spring." She donned her green camouflage raincoat and work boots, and rattled down the back steps.

Mariah wondered whether Darcy had picked up the sense of the dream without being told.

As Darcy walked the trail to the spring, the trees sparkled with tiny needles of ice, and a light blanket of crystalized mist overlay the meadow like powdered sugar. About halfway up, a second meadow lay in a direct line between the barn and the spring. Darcy noticed a swatch of the meadow that had no frosting, about fifteen inches wide and straight as an arrow. She walked over and sighted along it. The north end pointed exactly to the spring, and the south end aimed at the center of the water tank by the barn.

She returned to the trail and kept going, searching in a third meadow for the same line. It was there. She thought, *I was right. Maxwell laid a line from the spring to the tank. The water temperature is above freezing. But even if it's only, say fifty degrees, it would warm the ground enough to melt a surface frost like this.* When she got to the spring, she couldn't tell how Maxwell had engineered the capture of the spring's water, but she was certain of her conclusion.

She ran back down to the compound of buildings, stopped at the water tank and listened. She could hear a steady stream of water gurgling into the tank from an inch-and-a-half pipe that came out of the ground from the direction of the spring and ran up the side of the tank. *Plenty of irrigation water.* She rushed to the house to tell her mother.

Mariah gave her daughter a cup of chamomile tea as they discussed the bits and pieces they believed they knew about agriculture of larger scope than a city garden. They recalled greenhouses they had seen in movies, and on a Girl Scout outing long ago to Watsonville. Soon, however, Mariah said, "I need to keep organizing and cleaning the house here. Why don't you take Tierney to explore the barn? And give that makeshift greenhouse idea a good assessment, while you're about it."

The light snow had turned to drizzle, the frosty soil to a muddy slick. Tierney and her mother held each other's hands tightly—wet and muddy clothing was simply not an option at the moment. Tierney's kid goat, however, developed instant socks of mud halfway to the knee.

In the barn, the crisp smell of clean rain ameliorated, in a friendly sort of way, the odor of old hay and the dust of years. The gentle drumming of raindrops, and moan of the wind around the outside corners and windows, added depth to the strange coziness of the enormous structure.

Tierney led her goat into a low-sided stall, designed apparently for weaning small animals, and began to feed it with scraps Mariah had given her from dinner and breakfast. To Tierney's delight, it had an insatiable appetite. It appeared that, for a long time to come, Tierney's primary activity would be hand feeding her kid with fistfuls of grass, hay, vegetable peelings, just about anything edible. To a goat, of course, practically everything is edible.

Along the north wall of the main bay, Darcy noticed great coils of plastic irrigation piping and hosing suspended from sturdy angle irons and giant meat hooks resting on inch-thick dowels set in the wall's timbers. She proceeded into the tackroom. There she found an old, short handled broom. She began working methodically through the clutter. She brushed off the accumulated dust and cobwebs with the broom.

She was thinking about the chaos they left behind in San Francisco and Oakland, the dark days of heavy-handed government that seemed to be closing in. She was grieving in a quiet way for their condo home, the collection of sentimental mementos she and Reinhold had assembled on vacations.

Her mind wandered to Russia, and Germany—and Ireland. Then other places around the nation and the world where she had friends, places where nostalgic memories were anchored from her childhood, teenage years, college and graduate school. Her eyes, and a corner of her intellectual brain, were registering the scope of the equipment collection, but her heart was a light year away.

When Darcy came full circle around the tackroom, she took a wide push broom and swept the plank floor clean. The vigorous activity brought her full attention back to the barn and her new "estate." She was conscious of trying to make it as clean as she imagined old man Maxwell kept it in his time. It was almost as if he were watching.

Her daughter kept up a constant stream of conversation with her goat, so Darcy could stay alert to her even when out of sight. Darcy climbed the steep, narrow stairs in the back of the tackroom. She was surprised to find the loft had been built out with solidly constructed walls.

In the center was a square opening to provide access to the ground floor. Above the center of the square hung an enormous block-and-tackle pulley system. The lifting end of the three-quarter inch rope had a three-inch steel hook with its own pulley. It was drawn back and held to the north wall with a peg, while the working end of the rope was anchored next to the peg on a twelve-inch ship's cleat. The excess rope was coiled in a perfect circle on the floor.

A dozen wooden shipping crates, unopened, lined the north wall. Darcy noticed some of the shipping tags revealed "Irrigation Valves," and "Three-Horsepower Water-Pump." She would have to make an inventory of this place eventually.

Along the south side of the barn, ten feet beyond the open square, was a storeroom. The double door was firmly locked and unyielding.

There were four rooms along the west side of the loft, and four more along the east side. Each had its own solid, well-hinged door with a brass doorknob, all unlocked. Inside, each room had a secure, double-paned, weather-insulated window. All were completely clean. The construction was so sound that little dust had penetrated into these rooms over their years of nonuse. It was almost as if Mr. Maxwell had expected people to come and live here.

Seven of the rooms were empty. The eighth had a collection of machines. It reminded her of a display in the Museum of Industrial Science in Edinburg exhibiting early Industrial Revolution inventions encrusted with gears, levers, rods and pistons, many powered by child-sized foot pedals. Two large oak roll-top desks sat against the left and right walls as Darcy entered, each paired with a matching captain's chair. The desk to the right was empty. In the center drawer of the left desk, Darcy found an old Bible, printed in 1851. All other drawers, save one, were empty. The one was filled with files which appeared to contain diagrams and instructions for machinery, along with invoices and shipping papers.

Although Darcy had one ear tuned to the sound of Tierney's voice below, her investigational awareness had never been more acute. Even before her mind noticed, her eyes told her the file drawer was shorter than the desk was deep. She took out the files, stacked them to one side of the desk, then pulled the drawer all the way out, taking care not to drop it on the floor. She put her face up to the shadowy blackness inside and let her eyes adjust. The panel at

the back of the cavity was split by a barely discernible vertical crack. On instinct, she pushed gently on the left panel. It held solid. Then she pushed on
the right panel. A mechanical trip-lock on the other side released with an audible click and both panels swung open.

The secret space behind was about four inches deep. Its only contents
were a two-inch crystal ball on a small brass stand, and a chamois bag the size
of a softball, held shut with a half-inch, red satin ribbon tied in a double looped
bow. Darcy didn't touch them.

She closed the panel, returned the drawer to its space, left the files stacked
on the floor and hurried down the stairs. Tierney said, "Mommy, I think my
baby needs to go back to the house for a nap." The baby goat was lying in
Tierney's lap, its eyelids at half mast.

Mariah had prepared a simple lunch. The warm soup made both Tierney
and Finn drowsy. As soon as they were out, Darcy grabbed her mother's hand.
"You've got to see what I found at the barn." Darcy grinned and giggled all the
way. Mariah smiled—this place has the power of peace even over my lion-
hearted daughter.

At the barn, Mariah wanted to stop and savor the beauty of her daughter's
rejuvenation of the equipment store, but Darcy dragged her up to the loft two
steps at a time. She commanded her mother through the exact process she herself had gone through. "Push on the right half of the boards in the back."

Mariah couldn't have handled the Crown Jewels of England more carefully
as she placed the bag and the ball side-by-side in the center of the desktop.
"We'll play with the crystal ball later. I'll put it on the mantle by the silver box.
See what's in the bag."

They could tell from the feel that the bag contained not a single object but
a trove of small articles. As Darcy prepared to untie the red bow she noticed a
brown marking darker than the shade of the light brown chamois itself. "Its
meaning will come to us, in time, Darcy, trust me." Darcy removed the ribbon,
opened two drawstrings that had been tucked inside the bag, and poured the
contents onto the oak surface.

There were six keys, each with a numbered ivory tag attached by a glitter-
ing keychain. There was a collection of coins that looked gold and silver in
composition, four nondescript stones the size of walnuts, a gold charm brace-
let, a pair of wedding rings, three other rings with gems in ornate settings, and
a small envelope sealed with forest green sealing wax. A slight aroma of Asian
spices reached the nostrils of the women—not unlike sandalwood or aromatic
cedar.

Darcy spoke first. "You know, Mom, everything on the property belongs to us. It's okay if we break the seal and open the envelope."

Mariah tried to keep the quaver out of her voice. Words in the sweet, quiet voice of Mrs. Whiting were crisscrossing chaotically through her mind. *It's like a dream where you can't hold on to what everyone is saying.* In almost a whisper, Mariah said, "Yes, I know, Sweetheart. I think everything here is meant for us."

In the envelope was a single sheet of white bonded stationery embossed with a vivid indigo border of scroll-and-leaf motif. In exquisite India ink calligraphy was a numbered list. Each numbered item was a cryptic rhyme or citation. Three of the citations were obviously Biblical chapters and verses, but to what the others referred was not obvious. Mariah said, "Maybe those numbers on the keys correspond to numbers on this list."

"Give me the Bible," Darcy said. Her eyes were drawn to the sixth reference: Acts 1:13. While Darcy thumbed through the old Bible, Mariah found the key with tag No. 6. Darcy had barely started reading,

"And when they reached the city they went to the upper room where they were staying..."

Mariah interrupted, "This has to be the key to the locked storeroom. The upstairs rooms in the main house aren't locked, so this is the only "upper room" on the property that has a lock."

Mariah was right. The storeroom lock opened easily, as if it had been oiled yesterday. Inside were neat stacks of gunnysacks, eight deep. Darcy said, "He must have hoisted these up with the block-and-tackle." They examined the shipper's tags on the gunnysacks. Oats. Barley. Corn. Pinto beans. White rice. Cracked wheat. Brown rice. Quinoa. Millet. Hops.

Mariah threw her arms around Darcy and began to weep. "Darcy, I have dreamed we are going to be here a long time. I think this upper room is a confirmation of a prophecy. I'm sorry." They held each other in silence.

They returned to the main house hand in hand in silent communion, pondering the profound questions raised by Mariah's prophecy.

Late in the afternoon, Tierney was on the back rain porch feeding "Billy the Kid," as Mariah had now, over her granddaughter's voluble objection, dubbed the family pet. Finn was smacking tin cups, spoons and pie tins around his corner of the kitchen. Four sharp raps on the front door shattered the moment.

No one had heard steps on the deck. They stood together as Mariah opened the door. A woman about her age stood smiling. She carried a steaming Dutch oven filled with a substantial-looking stew.

"My name's Rose Royer. I walked up from that cabin down there." She nodded in the direction of the green-roofed log cabin. "My husband and I have owned it for twenty years. I saw you folks arrive yesterday and thought, since we're neighbors, I'd introduce myself with an evening meal."

Mariah swept the newcomer inside with a gesture. "I think this is just about the nicest thing that's happened since we left home."

Mariah and Darcy had made enough progress for their first day, so the three ladies warmed the dining room chairs for the rest of the afternoon and well into the evening. They exchanged backgrounds and particulars, and how they all happened to take up shelter in a cold, remote mountain valley in the most remote corner of California without any men in sight.

The candles dwindled. Mariah and Rose stepped outside and decided that the stars provided ample light in the moonless night. Mariah accompanied her neighbor back to the cabin, returning through the nocturnal wonderland enthralled with its wild beauty, alone with her thoughts but for the voices and spirits that without fail surrounded her at times like this.

CHAPTER 68
Sunday, February 26

A SEAMLESS GRAY curtain of overcast differed from the endless Atlantic wavescape in texture only, defining a nearly invisible horizon in all directions. Reinhold was the only English-speaking passenger on the *Svetlana*. The captain, by nature, was courteous but withdrawn, and for the first time in his life Reinhold was compelled by circumstances to a contemplative existence. Over the course of his three-day sojourn, he had alternated between a feeling of overpowering insignificance when he dwelt on the enormity of the ocean's size and the inexorability of Nature's processes, and a feeling of soaring elation when he recognized himself as the carrier of the most complex system in the universe, a human being. Then back again, as one of six billion of them, and then back along the spectrum to his own individuality.

His hands rested lightly on the railing at the stern of the container ship, the frothing wake churning up from the propellers far beneath the surface. The serenity was shattered by a siren alarm. The vessel shuddered slightly, and Reinhold saw half the propulsion wake dwindle to nothing in a hundred yards. Their course began to swerve. The crew scrambled below decks to the engine room.

Reinhold joined the other anxious passengers in the austere lounge, await-ing news of what had happened. Communicating with passengers was a low priority for both Captain and crew. Only at dinner did they learn that the port-side driveshaft had "experienced a catastrophic failure." In other words, had broken down. They would be lucky to lose only one day on the scheduled crossing.

DESPITE THE PULL of mystery, Mariah and Darcy had agreed that break-ing the full code of the chamois sack should be savored bit by bit. By mid-afternoon, however, they couldn't resist one more.

The fourth reference was the Exodus story about storing grain for the seven-year famine. They decided the fourth key might gain them access to the storage shed. So during a break in the rain they loaded Finn in his new back-pack and trundled up the hill. Tierney and the goat brought up the rear at their own pace.

From the outside, the storage shed looked the least maintained of all the buildings. It was covered with weather-beaten planks on the walls and the roof. Its one, small window looked like it had never been washed, and was so dark there seemed little likelihood of seeing through it. The two doors, hinged in-ward, were of a different kind of wood and looked even older than the rest of the building. Each door had planks nailed irregularly as if they alone were keep-ing the door from collapse.

Darcy turned the double lock with a substantial "thunk, thunk," using the key given to Mariah by the lawyers. As before, however, the doors simply didn't give. The key from the chamois sack was for an entirely different kind of lock. They both tried to look through the little window without success. Not only was it covered with dust, inside and out, but the view was blocked from the inside by some object, maybe a plank, or a blackout curtain.

Darcy gave up. "I guess the cache for the seven-year famine must be somewhere else. Maybe Ray has an extension ladder and we could get access through that structure up on the roof. If we can't climb down through it, maybe at least we could see from there what's blocking the door inside. But that'll have to wait for a bigger work party."

As they walked back to the main house, the conversation centered on where to plant the gardens, what to plant, how to water, even how much water different crops might use. It was fast dawning on both women that they were not exactly educated to be self-sufficient farmers.

When Finn was down for a nap they heard Ray and Paisley's pickup.

"Aunt Paisley. Aunt Paisley!" Tierney ran down the steps and leaped into Paisley's arms.

"Well, young lady. Do you have a name for your little white friend?"

Tierney looked at her mother with fake petulance, then back to Paisley. "If I had my way it would be "Angel," but I got outvoted and I guess it'll be Billy the Kid. Aunt Paisley, how do you know if it's a girl or boy?"

"You're a farm girl now, Tierney. Let's go out to the back yard and we'll find out." They walked around to the back of the house. Darcy's eyes were wide. Mariah laughed and shook her head.

"Come on in, Ray. I think the stove's got a few hot coals left from this morning. We could heat you up some tea, if you like." Mariah looked questioningly at the holster and six shooter hanging from his belt.

Ray shrugged his shoulders, "Everyone's packing out there, now. I don't exactly like it, but I don't feel safe without it."

Changing the subject, Mariah described the storage shed dilemma. Ray offered to bring an extension ladder on his next trip to look through the ventilation shaft.

Mariah didn't hold back in sharing her insecurity about operating the generator, dealing with farm equipment and irrigation systems, and her questionable ability to grow sustainable amounts of food. Ray undertook to help. It was easy for him—it would be a month before his full attention was required for springtime preparation of his own acreage.

Mariah waited for Paisley and Tierney to finish gendering the hapless billy-goat while Darcy took Ray up to the barn to inspect the "dry goods," as the oats, beans and such were called in farm country.

In a moment, Tierney burst in with the news. "It's a little girl, Babushka." Then, hesitantly, "Is it okay to call a girl 'Billy?'"

Mariah smiled, "Why, sure it's okay. I know plenty of girls named 'Billy.'"

Ray described an increasingly police-oriented atmosphere building up in Flat River. The Executive Committee was turning more conservative than he had imagined. Many of the town's men had been deputized. Every household, of course, had its own collection of firearms. So arming the new ranks was not a problem. Official Sheriff's Office badges were, however, in short supply, and they had conscripted Harry, the blacksmith, into making temporary badges out of sheet metal.

The flow of strangers from the southern highways and the coast was increasing, and the newly deputized officers were visibly guarding all government property. Ray quit counting at thirty. They were on the street corners, at the entrance to the hospital, the Hotel Niles, the airport, and similar strategic locations. He said the "Masonic boys," members of the Grange, the Rodeo Posse, and the Junior Chamber of Commerce, had all been taken into the policing system. "No women cops," he added. "There's plenty of order, but I worry about 'em making up their own law."

The mood of the day had turned sober. "I guess we'd better go. I'll be back tomorrow with some tools, and some spare equipment I didn't see up in your barn."

When the growl of Ray's pickup faded in the distance, the Maxwell residents wrapped up their afternoon by experimenting with the tub, washboard and clothes ringer, stringing a clothesline so the afternoon sun might start drying the clothes before nightfall. Their third day at Maxwell Acres drifted into evening candlelight and a warm supper by the stove, belying an increasingly treacherous outside world.

ELMER WALLACE awoke with a start. It wasn't the low, diesel engine. The occasional moving van on their street, or a telephone maintenance vehicle at night, wouldn't have alarmed him. It was the crackling of walkie-talkies. Not a police radio either, evoking confident authority, even bravado. These people were speaking low, indistinct fragments.

Elmer louvered the shutter slats horizontal, looked out from his darkened room. A black shadow slid by, toward the front door. He listened. He heard more footsteps out the guestroom window across the hallway. He lumbered to that window. Two men with rifles, black jumpsuits head to toe, ski masks covering their faces, were standing on the lawn. From the front door, he heard glass break, clatter to the slate floor in the foyer. The door creaked open. Swift footsteps—at least two people—kitchen, pantry, living room, now the hallway. Elmer slipped behind the elegant guestroom drapes—Mariah's proud touch for the family gathering last Christmas.

A man stopped inside the doorway, shouted back to his companions, "I've got him. Hiding by the window."

Elmer knew he was the victim of military night goggles. He moved the drapes aside to surrender to his captors. All he saw was a blinding flash.

At that instant, Mariah shot upright in her bed at Maxwell Acres, scattering the blankets with an explosive arm. In her left temple she had seen Elmer in a coffin. It was vivid. Unambiguous. Final.

Her rational mind refused the knowledge. But her heart knew the truth. She steeled herself to contain the certainty. Until what? Corroboration? That was hard to imagine. Until they found a way to drive or fly there again? Harder to imagine.

Mariah slept no more. Her eyes were rivers—her pulse, war drums—her body, frozen aloneness.

CHAPTER 69

Monday, February 27

BY MIDMORNING, Ray and Paisley's puttering pickup chugged up the driveway again. Ray dropped Paisley off at the house. Darcy met her. "I don't know what's happened with my Mother, but last night she had a dream she won't tell me about. She's been crying all morning."

Paisley said, "Maybe she'd talk to me."

Darcy's intuition was to preserve Mariah's solitude. She knew her mother had an inner resilience of the highest order.

Ray continued around the outside of the compound to the back of the barn, where he unloaded his contribution to Maxwell Acres' collection of agricultural implements.

True to his promise, he brought an extension ladder, so in spite of the off-and-on light fog and drizzle, an expedition ventured up the hill to the still-unexplored storage shed. Mariah alone stayed behind.

The north side of the building had been cut into the hillside, reducing the elevation to the roof by five feet. But the roof itself was too steep to climb without a rope or ladder, especially when wet. Ray secured the extension ladder against two small boulders and extended the top section to just below the cupola.

The ladder was at a forty-five degree angle, so he looked like a bear walking up the rungs on all fours. When he reached the top, they saw him unlatch two fasteners and lift the free edge of the pointed cap of the cupola. The other edge was hinged, and when fully opened the pointed cap rested against two wooden blocks attached to the roof.

Ray yelled down to the fascinated bystanders. "This is really weird. There are a bunch of mirrors inside this thing, on all four sides, but the bottom's filled in with a solid wood plank, so it doesn't look like you can climb down inside from here. The mirrors look a little delicate. They've got gears and levers between the frames and the cupola. I don't know what to make of it, but I don't think we should mess with it until we know more."

Ray left the cupola open and climbed down. Darcy climbed up and agreed.

The group's disappointment was moderated by their intense curiosity and speculation about the building. They headed back to the compound, leaving the ladder in the barn.

Ray used the afternoon to open the crate of irrigation valves and set up a secondary line off the main pipeline at the top of the nearest field. Everyone chipped in advice about how to organize further tributary irrigation pipes and hoses, but Ray pointed out that nighttime freezing wouldn't be gone for another six weeks months and there was plenty of time to set up the final irrigation system when the time came.

Evening conversation was light, Mariah noticeably preoccupied. Consumption of the spicy stew, chili beans and baked potatoes with their olive oil herbal dressing, provided the primary focus. Dinner was followed by an assembly line dishwashing that took only a few minutes. The candles were still burning on the dining room table when the dishes were done.

Darcy invited the Overcrofts to spend the night at Maxwell Acres. Ray declined. "Thank you, but I've got to milk the goats and feed the chickens. But Paisley, you could. I'll just come back in the morning to put in another day getting that garden ready."

CHAPTER 70
Tuesday, February 28

"I SEE SOMEONE ELSE is down at the log cabin." Ray poured himself a cup of coffee on arrival.

Mariah's eyes were wide above dark circles, as if it took an effort to keep them open after two nights of little sleep. She filled him in. "They came in the middle of the night. I heard the dog bark—he's usually pretty quiet. The lights of a car came into their driveway. I cracked my window and could hear voices. It sounded like they knew each other. The dog stopped barking right away, so I assumed everything was okay."

"Do you think someone should check on your neighbor?" Paisley said.

"I'll bet it's Rose's husband or daughter," Darcy said. "I hope, anyway. She seems a little exposed, all alone down there. I'd vote for checking if we don't see her walking around by eleven."

Ray agreed. "I'll go with you. Better two than one, if there's a problem. Meanwhile, I brought the spare parts for the generator. I'll be in the barn. Keep me posted."

Midmorning, accompanied by both Ray and Paisley, Darcy approached the Royer Cabin cautiously, no one having yet emerged. She relaxed when Rose herself answered the door, took her arm and introduced the nighttime travelers: "My brother-in-law Peter Addison, and his daughter Catherine and her boyfriend Jason Lowery."

The fourth visitor looked out of place. Ill-fitting clothes, darker skin, weathered face, though young. His bandaged arm, however, fit the emergency room look of the other two men.

"And this is James," Rose said. "The poor man was knocked off his bicycle last night, and Peter brought him here so we can take care of him." James grinned and nodded awkwardly.

Rose introduced Darcy as "One of those nice people I told you about, from up at the old homestead." She asked about Mariah and the children, then looked expectantly at the Overcrofts. It was Darcy's turn for introductions.

As Rose brewed a pot of tea, Peter Addison related the ordeal that brought them and James to the Royer cabin. His own property in McCloud had been destroyed by brutal thugs, whom they had driven off. "One of them was killed." Darcy understood that the pistol Peter wore in a shoulder holster had seen recent duty.

She studied the new faces around her, absorbing the complex of relationships. Each face bore its own signs of anguish from the attack, distress at the chaos in the world, fear of the uncertainty that might lie ahead. Peter Addison, she decided, had an iron grip on his emotions and a high opinion of his place in the world of science. Darcy identified a tender part of herself in Catherine, motherless since adolescence, without a family ear to help her sort through the trauma at her father's cabin. Jason seemed to overplay both gratitude and deference, appropriate to his tenuous connection as boyfriend of his professor's daughter. James was like a Gordian knot, revealing little but unintentionally telegraphing mystery, overreacting to sudden sounds, and like Darcy studying every face in the room.

She noticed Paisley's demeanor darken as discussion of society's meanness swept through the group. Ray, too, turned somber. "It could happen at our

271

farm just as easily." He was uncharacteristically receptive when Paisley spoke an aside, "Maybe we should store some of our valuables up at the homestead, if they'd allow it."

Darcy touched her hand and said, "Of course, Paisley. Don't even hesitate. There's a ton of space in the barn."

Conversation seemed coded, more in cautious questions than staking ground to stand on. Talk of absent loved ones mingled with abstractions about global warming and civil liberties, isolation as both blessing and burden, and what the "long run" might entail.

Darcy found herself saying, "My mother had a dream last night.

"The floor of our house is covered by a nice, green lawn, like a living carpet. It grows and has to be mowed, and grows again. It's pretty and orderly and comfortable.

"My mother believes it was saying we're likely to be here for an extended time."

Darcy felt her chest constrict, and nearly choked. She held herself outwardly calm. "I'm not sure I agree, but…" Inside she felt a dawning of some awareness creeping unwanted into her mind.

Comments turned to the practical. Rose claimed supplies enough for an indefinite stay, but speculated on the need to expand her garden.

"I have a little experience with gardening," offered James. "And I'm willing to earn my keep." Rose assured him of an open welcome. He continued, "But I insist on sleeping on the floor. I do okay on the floor. In the monastery you get used to a little hardship."

"James," said Rose, "I think a cot in the barn might be comfortable enough. We can use your strength and skills when you're recovered."

He stared at the floor, and Darcy gave in to an impulse without assessing whether it was compassion or opportunity. "James, you could sleep at our place, too. The barn has some clean rooms I'm sure will be suitable. If you'd like, come up tomorrow and take a look. I agree with Rose, there's no need to sleep on the floor. We have lumber for bedframes."

Dusk was turning to twilight. While they were eating dinner, Darcy had recounted the visit to the cabin, including her offer to the man called James to sleep in their barn. Now she was upstairs telling the children bedtime stories, and Mariah dried the last plates and looked out the window. Rose was walking up from her cabin, alone.

"Can I talk to you, Mariah?"

They stepped into the living room. Mariah remained silent, eyes fixed on Rose's, which were questioning and compassionate. Rose cleared her throat. "I hope and pray this is just a bad coincidence, your last name being Wallace, but… Well, I was listening to the government broadcast after we ate. The radio said there had been riots in Berkeley. One of the leaders was named Elmer Wallace. Killed by gangs, they said."

Mariah's gaze was steady. Too steady, she knew. What would Rose understand from this reaction to such news? She took Rose's hand and all but whispered, "My husband's name is Elmer. It's possible it's a coincidence. It may be a long time before we can know. Until then, it's just speculation, Rose. Darcy and the children need their strength." She looked toward the stairs, heard Darcy's soothing murmur. "Let's keep this between us two. Okay?"

"Okay."

"Pray for him, will you? And us?"

Rose nodded.

From her open bedroom window, Mariah drew tranquility from the gentle shower that veiled but did not obscure her lovely view of the valley's eastern ridge. Although she had not doubted her dream of Elmer's death, Rose's confirmation added a solidity she found somehow comforting. Memories of Luke, the funerals of her parents, her abandonment of Darcy, and other wounds of the past, wafted over her with the cold, moist air of the night. She could now name the anniversary ritual at the Pacific overlook an obsession. Intuitively, she knew the narcissistic luxury of such grieving could not fit into her new future, as uncertain as it was, and she set an iron resolve to honor, but not to linger over, the lifetime of her relationship with Elmer that had now reached finality.

CHAPTER 71
Wednesday, March 1

THE DAY WAS IN ITS INFANCY when Ray and Paisley drove up the driveway and around to the east guest house with a load of "contingency stores." Mariah and Darcy helped unload. "I need to go on to town," Ray said. "I'll stop by Rose's and see if they need anything."

Mariah said, "I was guessing you'd go to town, Ray. Why don't you take Rose with you? Ask her to check my email, and Darcy's, would you? Here's a letter she wrote to Reinhold." She took Ray's hesitation as questioning whether

273

she also had a letter for Elmer, and she added, "There's nothing new that Elmer needs to know."

Darcy answered a gentle knock on the door. "Good morning, James."

"Morning, Darcy. Yesterday you said I could bunk in your barn. I'd like to try it. All I've got's in this pack. Except I left my bicycle down at the Royer's. It's a little banged up. Probably not much use here anyway, since I'm not planning to go anywhere very soon. I mean, if I can make myself useful enough around here. Do you think you could show me where I can sleep? At least for now. After I get settled, maybe you could show me something I could do to help you with the place."

"Oh, Ray," said Mariah, "could you get us three or four blankets, too?" She gave him cash.

Ray headed down the road, Paisley went to unpack and arrange things in the guest house, and Darcy walked with James to the barn. On the way she suggested he see the guest house, but he said he'd actually prefer the barn. He liked being somewhat isolated, he said, because of his meditation practice.

"The barn's clean," said Darcy, "but... Are you sure?" She showed him the loft. He settled in the southwest room. His backpack looked tiny and forlorn in the corner with his jacket on top.

Darcy took him downstairs and showed him the lumber, the tools, and the rest of the paraphernalia, much of which she couldn't name. "If you don't mind," James said, "I'll just build myself a bed frame. Maybe I can find something to serve as a mattress, too."

The afternoon found Darcy in the barn assembling another seedling box, and James nailing the cross beam on the footboard of his new bed. He worked awkwardly, occasionally wincing with pain in his wrist.

Catherine and Jason dropped in, fresh from exploring the western ridgeline, which had decent evergreen cover from the intermittent drizzle. The conversation evolved into a verbal tour of Maxwell Acres by Darcy. She regaled them with the upper room riddle and the failure of Key No. 4 to unlock the storage shed, and tantalized them with the mystifying system of mirrors in the shed's cupola.

"Mr. Maxwell was up to something," Jason said. "Must've been, to leave so many enigmas behind. Maybe there's a secret door in the shed. Like those perfectly balanced stone walls in medieval castle mystery films, that pivot when you bump a secret lever."

Inspired by their imaginations, James and Jason decided to tackle the storage shed if the weather gave them a break. Soon the sun broke through and their chance came. Catherine accompanied them to add feminine intuition. Darcy stayed behind with her seedling box, because by now Tierney and Billy the Kid were playing "farm" with Finn in the tackroom.

James and Jason started from the faux entrance, methodically tapping with hammers along the outside wall listening for empty spaces or a change in the density of construction that might provide a clue. They soon found a promising change—the "tap, tap," turned to a "thunk, thunk," along a five foot stretch on the south wall.

Catherine, standing farther back than the men, said, "If it's a door, one of the planks must be hiding the lock. To my eye, that plank looks different." She pointed to an especially weather-beaten board which reached neither to the ground nor to the eave. "See if it comes loose."

James inserted a pry bar under the side of the plank and applied even pressure. A sharp "SNAP" startled everyone as the board popped off and fell to the ground. It had been held in place by snap-clamps on its four corners. Behind the plank was a brass rectangle with a keyhole and a retractable hinged door handle.

Darcy had given the fourth key to Catherine. It fit the brass keyhole perfectly and released the deadbolt smooth as glass. James tugged on the door. It inched open. Over the enormous steel hinges was a plank mounted on an ingenious lever and roller-bar system that angled it back against the door upon opening. At this, a chorus of cheers and a frenzy of high-fives exploded.

"Go get the others," Catherine said. Jason retrieved Mariah and Darcy.

Behind the dilapidated exterior planks, the door itself was made of three-by-twelve oak timbers bolted together with steel straps. The inside walls of the building, behind the exterior planking, were solid concrete, six inches thick, crisscrossed with steel beams like the earthquake proofing in old brick warehouses in San Francisco. This was no simple shed. It was built to withstand earthquakes, typhoons, fires, and anything else that could destroy every other building on the property.

There was one big room with cabinets, shelves, work tables and laboratory-style stools lining the walls, interspersed with pieces of strange machinery. On the east end of the building were a toilet/shower, supply closet and office. At the northeast corner, stairs led to the "watchtower" above. It was empty. Its southern wall opened accordion-like onto an observation deck.

Darcy looked up from the middle of the main room. In the center of the ceiling was a five-by-five-foot square opening into the attic directly below the cupola. Running up the north wall from a maritime cleat, across the ceiling and into the opening was a thick rope guided on pulleys. As in the barn, the excess rope was coiled on the floor. "I'll bet Maxwell used this rope to open the lid on the cupola. Let's try it, James."

They unfastened the rope and gradually increased the strength of their downward pull. Mariah was watching from under the opening. "The trap door under the cupola's lowering down."

In a moment, the group heard the two latches release. The rope jerked with the release, then snapped taut again. The system of pulleys worked flawlessly to allow Darcy and James to hoist the cupola into its reclining position on the roof.

Sunshine smote the room, square on the floor, almost too bright for comfort. "The mirrors!" Darcy exclaimed.

The mirrors in the cupola were aligned so no matter where the sun was, at least in the middle hours of the day, direct sunlight was reflected straight down into the room. Mariah wagged her head. "Maxwell was obviously a mechanical genius."

Late in the afternoon, Ray returned from Flat River with Mariah's purchases, but no messages. Darcy received a sheaf of printouts, but her face clouded over at the absence of anything from Reinhold. She went outside on the deck to let the cold air restore her composure.

Ray and Paisley drove back to their farm to assemble a second load of contingency stores to bring up in the morning. Mariah invited James to dinner.

THE TUG CUT ITS ENGINE. The *Svetlana* shuddered as it stopped throbbing in resonance with the little vessel. The new winches of the Red Hook Container Terminal drew the ship snug against the fenders of Pier 9-A.

Reinhold's body turned hot with emotion as the *Svetlana* made contact with land. *Brooklyn. America at last.* Within forty-five minutes, backpack slung over his shoulder, he gave Captain Thorstaag a vigorous, farewell handshake and disembarked.

From the ship-to-shore communications center Reinhold had alerted Troy Blake to his day-late arrival. The reply instructed Reinhold that Blake International had a small branch office just a mile north of the container port, so he walked the all-but-deserted streets to Noble and Franklin and announced himself on the intercom beside a locked, steel door. The staff was expecting him, gave him a styrofoam cup full of overcooked coffee, and called Blake headquarters.

"Tie-line," the wrinkled clerk explained after hanging up. "Most phones are down, you know. Mr. Blake's assistant said a car'll be here for you in forty minutes. The men's room's down the hall to the left."

Reinhold riffled through the December issue of "Container Commerce" in the waiting room, his mind three thousand miles to the west, cycling over and over the limited possibilities for getting himself there.

Three magazines later, a uniformed man poked his head through the hall door. A two-inch scar curved under his right cheekbone on an otherwise seamless leather face.

"Malone?"

"That's me"

"I'm your driver." He jerked his head for Reinhold to follow. Out the back door, Reinhold slung his pack into the back seat of the waiting black limo and got in without comment.

They drove under the footing of the Brooklyn Bridge before circling back to the approach. A group of kids was playing baseball on a dirt lot sheltered by the bridge. Reinhold noted a few were of light European stock, but most were obviously from other continents. The pitcher hurled the ball toward the ten-year old at the plate. It was in midair when the limousine passed a warehouse, blocking Reinhold's view. He felt a twinge of disappointment. *I'll never know if it was a ball, a strike, or a hit. Maybe a passed ball or a home run.*

At each end of the Brooklyn Bridge, and again as they passed East Houston Street, the driver handed a paper to military guards, automatic weapons held ready. Each time Reinhold noticed a hundred-dollar bill clipped to the paper.

The city felt coiled, ready to strike. The press of people still animated the sidewalks of the Avenues, but only those in camouflage, with guns, looked anywhere other than down. Apparently, civilians dared not risk eye contact or facial expression. All body language, however, was taut as a lioness hiding day-old cubs. A still haze in the air seemed poised to rain fear and anger.

The limousine descended to an automatic garage door under the Blake Building. The driver punched buttons on a remote, and electronic security gave them entrance. To the right of three regular passenger elevators was a smaller one, its door stenciled with block letters, "BLAKE INTERNATIONAL—EXECUTIVE PERSONNEL ONLY." The driver nodded his head in its direction and said, "Push the button that says 'Headquarters.'" Reinhold did what he was told.

The numbered panel skipped from the first to the fortieth floor. When it lit up at forty-five, the elevator stopped and the door rolled open. Reinhold emerged into a dim, cherry-paneled foyer populated with Persian rugs, leather chairs and a single reception desk staffed by a short-skirted, silk-topped blond trying to look busy. Beneath the emergency light a wilted corporate bouquet scattered shadows over fallen petals and leaves.

The receptionist ushered Reinhold into a conference room. Troy Blake eyed the young woman and barked, "No interruptions, Susie. None." Then he raised both hands in a victory gesture.

"Reinhold Malone. You made it. Well done."

He walked around the ten-foot, circular walnut table and grabbed Reinhold by both shoulders, shook his hand and turned to his lieutenants. "Gentlemen. This is Reinhold Malone. Reinhold, this is Bebe Bassanti and Augustus Wilkinson, my two top men. I hope you slept on the ship last night, Reinhold, because I want to get right down to business while the four of us are here together. Are you on board?"

"I think you could say so." Reinhold rested his pack in a conference table chair and extricated a ragged brown envelope, laying it unopened on the table in front of him. He leaned back in his chair, sizing up Blake's men while they sized him up. Reinhold had heard about these two in Russia, but no one had been willing to offer many details. *Bebe the Bullet and Amazing Augie*—he remembered the nicknames.

Bebe would be the enforcer, Reinhold decided. His five-and-a-half foot frame was made of steel. Over it, Naugahide stretched tight as a drum. His eyes—steel, too. His soggy-ended cigar seemed more a compulsion than a habit.

Augie was reputed to have a photographic memory and a faculty for finance unequaled in the industry. He had the bearing of a gentleman, but a vacant stare, overslicked hair, and fingernails so exquisite they could be Faberge.

In comparison, Troy looked abnormally Middletown—silk turtleneck under a plaid wool shirt, cords, and L. L. Bean rubberized shoes. Perfectly ready for the country club, the yacht harbor or the grandchildren's soccer match, as required. Except for the gun riding comfortably under his left armpit.

Troy inclined his head toward his top men. "Now Bebe, Augie and I have been working on our plan for Russia. My people over there have given you their highest, unqualified assessment, Reinhold. They've never met anyone with better contacts, and they say your judgment's brilliant. So I'm going to trust them and be brutally frank with you. But first, as an aside, that little deal you've got in your envelope? Peanuts. Maybe we'll get to it and maybe we'll forget about it. That's not why you're here. Okay?"

Reinhold muted his surprise, and nodded assent.

"So, Reinhold, the disruption over this sea level situation's our opportunity. Especially in Moscow and St. Petersburg. I've got a third of a billion in liquid currency in various accounts over there. U.S. denominations, you understand. Reinhold, you are the key. The key, you hear? This one opportunity can set you up for life, Boy. As soon as we can get transportation, I want you back over there to capitalize on this. Augie and Bebe will follow separately, and meet you there. You with me?"

"How could I argue with that? What do you have in mind?" In a separate channel, Reinhold's mind was churning. *Hey, man, you think I'm going to argue with the Mafia, a gun and a genius? California. I've got to work California into it...*

They worked nonstop for three hours. Augie covered the table with maps, blueprints, spreadsheets. And the side-counters too. Bebe never said a word, but he took it all in. Never broke concentration. Susie interrupted once with a brown bag of ham and turkey sandwiches, cookies, soft drinks and beer. Reinhold took a Coke. The others, Coors.

Late in the session, Blake took Reinhold aside. He clamped a hand on Reinhold's arm. "My Boy. You need to take this man-to-man." He let silence add to his gravity . " I know about your wife, Darcy, and her background with the Brotherhood." He waited until Reinhold blinked. "This is hard, Reinhold, but apparently she panicked and took her mortuary's plane north. The FAA told us it crashed and burned in the far northeastern corner of California. They said there were no survivors."

Reinhold feigned shock. He had memorized Mariah's email to him on the ship. *Please God, let the FAA believe she's dead. And tell all the other bastards, too.* He reached out as if to steady himself against Blake, then rested his forehead on Blake's shoulder, as if he were a surrogate father. He counted off the time, then stood back, clenched his jaw, and shook his head without a word. A few more moments, and he muttered, "Okay, Man. Let's get on with it." He did not have to feign a struggle to concentrate for the rest of the session. His mind raced.

At dusk, Troy Blake's satellite radiotelephone beeped. "My wife," he said, rolling his eyes. He walked to the window. "Yes?" A two-minute silence ensued. He hung up, stared out the window. Five minutes. The others waited, eyeing each other, containing curiosity and alarm.

He punched speed dial and called her back. "Dotty, find Theo. I guarantee you he's in the poker bar over at the hunt club." Silence. "Find him, goddammit. Go with him to the field. Get in the Bell 427 with him and bring it in here. Have him land it on the veranda. He can do it." Another silence. "To hell with air traffic control. Do it, Baby, just do it." He listened. "Goddammit, forget the mascara and just go. A minute wasted could mean life or death." He punched the Off button, looked out the window again, then turned to the table.

Augie and Bebe's eyes were large. Riveted on Troy Blake. *I'll bet they haven't looked like that since the fourth grade teacher took their lizards*, Reinhold thought. Troy's face had the pallor of a cadaver. "Plan's changed." He took a long pull of beer. He stared at Reinhold a long time. He looked at Augie. Then Bebe. Reinhold winced. *What the hell is he doing? He's looking right through them.*

Troy spoke in a steady monotone. "Dotty said our office outside Buenos Aires called looking for me at home. She said tidal waves from Antarctica have destroyed Buenos Aires. They were hundreds of feet high, she said, and they're coming up the Atlantic toward the U.S. It's not on the government news channels. At least the ones she listens to. But her neighbor came over and said it was all over the underground radio. She said panic's spreading like wildfire. She and Theo are going to bring the helicopter in. If they're in time, we should be able to get away with our lives." Troy turned to Reinhold. "Theo's my son. He flew copters in the Air Force. When he got out I bought the Company a modified, long distance Bell 427."

Reinhold went out on the company's private rooftop veranda. The streets below were packed. Klieg lights cast garish shadows down every street. He could see all the way to Wall Street, and up to Central Park. Jammed people all the way as far as the eye could see. *Like pilgrims in Mecca for the Hajj.*

Troy opened the conference room door. "Susie, bring in the emergency radio." She set it on the table and turned it on. "Forget the government channels," Troy ordered. "They're nothing but autopilot propaganda. Find something else."

In a minute she said, "Here it is, sir. The underground broadcast I listen to at home. They broadcast from a different place every night to hide from the radio police."

The announcer's voice was shaking. *"All over the city people are trying to get from the streets onto rooftops. There appears to be no easy way out of the city. Traffic is gridlocked. The subways are down. We have reports of people leaping turnstiles and stampeding the platforms. The military must have orders not to shoot. Their visibility is low profile. The few security guards left are being overwhelmed by crowds. I have reports that people are stampeding up emergency stairways to the roofs."*

All five faces turned simultaneously to the foyer. The sound of fists pounding on the front doors was unmistakable. Screaming voices of a crowd in the public elevator space began swelling. The fists became feet and bodies slamming against the doors.

Bebe said, "Don't worry, we're impervious. They'll never get in." He motioned Reinhold to follow him. On the right side of the entrance alcove, Bebe unlocked a floor-to-ceiling panel. He and Reinhold threw their weight into the handles of a rolling, solid steel barrier. It slowly closed the gap and clanged against the other alcove wall. Bebe slid three steel bars into what appeared to be ventilation holes.

"This is double the thickness of tank armor. You'd have to tear the building down before you'd get around this security door. Some of the groups we deal with are capable of almost anything, you know. Especially those Middle East guys, and the ones from Bolivia."

The noise of the crowd halved.

Back in the conference room, Reinhold gestured out the window. "What's with the klieg lights out there?"

"Absenteeism got so bad we keep having power outages," Augie said. "To replace the street lights when the power's down, the mayor commandeered all the kliegs that weren't being used for night work on the sea walls."

Reinhold said, "I'd better email my brother." He borrowed Susie's desk, accessed the *Svetlana*'s account, which he had also memorized, and sent an email to Mariah's address.

> I've waited as long as I can to send you this. I may have to break off any minute. I made it to Troy Blake's place. A tsunami is headed our way from Antarctica. It destroyed Buenos Aires. Troy's son is supposed to get a helicopter here to rescue us. I don't know what's going to happen if he doesn't make it. I don't even know where we'll try to get to from here, if we get out. I'll communicate with you however I can, whenever I can. Pray for us. I've come so far, from Moscow. I'm only three thousand miles away, now. I feel very close. I love you, very very much.
>
> Reinhold

Several hours passed. Susie monitored the crackling radio. At intervals came ominous reports: "We've lost communication from London." "Miami's gone silent." "Atlanta's no longer transmitting."

"They say Atlantic City's broken off." The men stared at Susie, then at one another. The characteristic thump-pump-pump of a helicopter broke the spell. Its searchlight illuminated the veranda. Troy shouted, "Susie, fill the water bottles and bring 'em out." She ran out of the conference room to obey. "Augie,

Bebe, get your coats and let's go." They stepped to the closet. Reinhold threw on his backpack.

Troy yanked the veranda door open, grabbed Reinhold's left arm and nearly dislocated it catapulting him out the door. Reinhold stumbled, crashing to the veranda tarmac. Troy followed like a cat, grabbed a short two-by-four leaning against the veranda wall and jammed it through the vertical bars of the exit doors, trapping Bebe, Augie and Susie inside. He pulled his gun and screamed, "Get in the copter, Boy."

Reinhold scrambled to his feet, did as he was told. Troy clawed his way up the rope ladder as the helicopter lurched into a takeoff. He wrenched himself through the opening, pistol in hand, lost his balance, hit the doorjamb, managed to kick himself to the floor and stayed aboard. "Jesus Christ, Theo, you coulda killed me." A terror-stricken Dotty sat in the first passenger seat, clutching an air sickness bag.

Reinhold saw Bebe and Augie ram a file cabinet through the glass doors, afraid to shoot them out because of the bulletproof glass. Too late. The aircraft was over the streets.

He looked toward Wall Street, spotted what looked like a gray fog bank in the distance. But unnatural lightning was dancing along its crest, and it was moving with tremendous speed. He recognized the tsunami with certainty when the Statue of Liberty toppled like a plastic toy at its impact. In ten seconds it was at Battery Park. Klieg lights disappeared, skyscraper walls exploded as their structures swayed and fell like timber in the wave's savage onslaught. Even over the helicopter engine, the roar of destruction raged. The pilgrims simply disappeared.

The helicopter rose at max speed, searchlight skimming across the watery hell, an occasional human form surfacing, frantic for salvation. Troy knelt up, wrestled the door shut and collapsed against it. He caught his breath. "We can only handle the weight of three passengers and a pilot. I had this thing modified with double fuel capacity so we could get to my estate in Cincinnati without refueling, but we had to sacrifice seating. I need you more than them, Reinhold. I diversified my holdings worldwide so I could survive any disaster. You're my partner now, and we'll recover on the Russian play. You understand?"

Reinhold nodded in slow motion, eyes fixed on the dark waters below.

MARIAH FELT it must be about midnight. She slippered to the window. The snowtopped mountains were bathed in the ghostly light of the winter stars. The storm clouds had cleared. She wrapped herself in a blanket, sat by the window, dozed or slipped into a trance. Time drifted. Suddenly she leaped to her feet and grabbed the chair to defend herself. In a second, her mind caught up with her reflexes and she realized it was Darcy.

"I heard you get up, Mom. I couldn't sleep either. I had a nightmare."

Mariah leaned on the chair. "Me too, Honey. The pit of my stomach feels like a rack of eight-balls."

"It was about Reinhold," Darcy said

"He's on a skyscraper roof in New York. The streets below are jammed with people, like Times Square on New Year's Eve. Spotlights are crisscrossing, streaming across the crowds. Suddenly, there's lightning in the distance. A deafening roar sweeps over, louder than anything I've ever heard. Reinhold is terrified. All the lights go out. I see him rising up in a metal box on the top of some kind of a beam of light. Then suddenly, the air is filled with millions of ghosts—crying. Some look stupefied, searching for anything, anyone familiar—lost.

"I woke up, sick to my stomach, crying. I didn't know if Reinhold was dead or what. You know, he was supposed to dock in New York yesterday and email me. We've got to send Ray to town to check our email."

Mariah stared dry eyed and unblinking at the stars. "I think I had the same nightmare, Honey. But I didn't wake up. I had a second dream. An old man tried to help me. In the second dream, I mean."

"Mom, we've got to get out of here. We've got to get back to Oakland and get Dad."

In the dark, Mariah's eyes filled. Although she knew Elmer was dead, there was plenty of time to tell Darcy. She would not tell her now.

"Maybe there's a way to drive," Darcy said. "There's got to be a way through all the checkpoints. I've got to find out if Reinhold is okay. We've got to do something. We can't just sit here and play like we need a garden."

"My poor baby. Don't you think I want those things too? But we've got to stay calm, pick our time. We're in the middle of something beyond extraordinary, Darcy. I think the government knows the sea level threat is far bigger than the country imagines, even the media. Something has shifted—massively—for the country, for the whole world. These times are dark. Black, like the sky outside. But look, there are stars, the beautiful Twins. We have to bide our time. A mistake right now could be fatal. I think we're supposed to be here. I think we're supposed to wait, see what develops. In tai chi this would be a moment to yield. Let's go back to bed. We'll need our strength."

Darcy crawled into bed beside her mother and they slipped into slumber, spent but secure.

CHAPTER 72
Thursday, March 2

FROM THE KITCHEN WINDOW, Darcy saw James running up the road. After breakfast he had gone to the Royer property to work on a garden with Jason. His body language now telegraphed something far beyond mere urgency. Darcy yelled upstairs, "Come down here quick, Mom, I think something's gone wrong at the Royer cabin."

A minute later Darcy carried Tierney while Mariah held Finn, following James down the road. Between breaths he repeated his message: "There's been a big tidal wave on the East Coast. It's awful." He knew no details.

Mariah and Darcy exchanged looks from fear-filled eyes, their twin nightmares seeming prophetic. They rushed down the road alternating between a run and a jog.

In the Royers' living room the radio was the center of attention. Even Finn seemed to understand this was no time to cry or talk. A deep voice said there was no danger on the West Coast, that the levee projects were successful. "We'll bring you further details as soon as they become available," said the voice, and the program switched to a promotion for the Armed Services with a brass band in the background.

Peter tuned the radio down and summarized. A volcano had erupted in Antarctica, started a tidal wave which came north through the Atlantic hitting the East Coast in the night. Washington had evacuated top officials to Texas. "Rose just turned the radio on a few minutes ago, so I don't really know …"

He was interrupted by a motor and honking, and followed Jason out the door. Darcy heard Ray's voice, "My God, you can't believe what's happening. I don't know where to start." He came inside, Paisley trailing, ghostly pale.

Ray's words were a torrent, describing crowds on the streets of Flat River listening to reports from town authorities from the Hotel Niles balcony as short wave, police and military broadcasts came through

"They all kept talking about Mt. Jackson this, Mt. Jackson that. Seems Mt. Jackson's a big volcano down on Antarctica. They said it blew up last night. They said half the mountain fell into the ocean and started a tidal wave."

Darcy and Mariah stared at each other again, both remembering the articles Elmer had found just two weeks earlier about tsunami dangers from Hawaii and the Canary Islands. Their attention rebounded to hear Peter speak of the exact same research. He said, "I sent a message to the White House warning about just such a possibility. It is unbelievable."

Darcy mumbled, "Oh, God…"

Ray said there was little official news about the East Coast. The Internet was down.

"People were sort of hysterical," Paisley cut in. "I couldn't tell if it was one wave or a lot of waves. They were talking about waves hundreds of feet high."

Ray didn't break pace. "I heard they washed right over New York City, Miami, Atlantic City. Other people were pooh-poohing those stories."

Fresh nightmare images from the night filled Darcy's mind. She and her mother knew the worst. They heard Ray comment, "Of course, wouldn't you know. Texas. I'll bet they did know ahead of time."

A surge of simultaneous reactions swept the room, then subsided as Ray continued. He had been afraid the crowd would dissolve into a riot, but before leaving Flat River had paused to check Mariah's email. He handed Darcy a single sheet, then fixed his eyes on the rug.

"Reinhold," she said. Looking at James she added, "My husband." She read the message to herself. "He sent this from New York, apparently just before the wave hit."

She handed it to her mother and held the children tightly on her lap. "We need to pray for Daddy right now. I don't know what kind of trouble he may be in, but we need to pray for him." She shut her eyes. Tierney put one arm around Finn, the other around her mother's neck, and buried her eyes in her mother's shoulder.

Mariah read the printout silently. Then for a moment her gaze fell short of the paper. She whispered to her daughter, "He survived." Then she read it to the room, in a cold monotone to dam the tears.

Jason remained stoic while Catherine and Rose tried to offer him hope about his family in Maryland. "We just don't know, do we?" he said. "All we have is hope."

Peter broke the ensuing silence, adding scientific background and opinion to scanty fact. Occasional new government broadcasts reported "damage" from, or about, places like London, Rio de Janeiro, the Ivory Coast, Capetown. Peter translated "damage" as "probably total destruction they won't admit."

Conversations sprouted in hushed tones. After an hour, Mariah commanded attention. "I'm not sure this really changes much, here, for now. Maybe things will clarify in a day or two. It seems to me we should still just go about settling in here and assume we'll all be here for a few more weeks at least. If the West Coast is safe, well…" Her voice trailed off with an obvious lack of conviction.

Emotional overload retreated into action. Darcy said, "I'll take the kids back up to our house. They're going to need lunch."

Ray stood up. "I think we'll just unload and head back to the farm. We should be there to fend off anyone stupid enough to act on their bad ideas."

James walked back to the Maxwell compound with the women and children.

REINHOLD'S EYES snapped open to a momentary disorientation. The steady drone in his ears, the plush interior of the Blake helicopter, and the hint of dawn through the windows were dreamlike compared to the rigors of his trek from Moscow. Troy Blake had awakened him with a tap on the shoulder and was pointing out the window.

Reinhold saw a wide river, lined with marinas and industrial complexes. Troy motioned beyond, and Reinhold realized they were circling a horse paddock marked by a flashing red-and-white landing light. Up a slight rise from the paddock were hedged gardens. The knoll was crowned by a princely mansion.

Theo eased the helicopter down and cut the engine. Three men wearing overalls and Irish racetrack caps, and a woman in a white domestic uniform, ran from behind the nearest hedge to help. Troy tossed down the travel bag Dotty had packed, and the workmen helped her to the ground. Troy followed, then Theo. One of the men waited for Reinhold to climb down, pack on one shoulder. He closed the copter hatch and ran to catch up with the rest, now a good hundred feet ahead.

Between the first garden and the second was a double row of boxwood hedges with a five-foot wide passage in between. Reinhold side-stepped into the passage. He peered through the branches. No one noticed. He ran along the passage, stumbling over the lumpy turf in the half-darkness. His recollection, and prayer, was that this was the direction of the river.

Four hundred yards, and the passage fed into a gravel driveway lined with lawn. Reinhold cut his plunging run to a deliberate stride, down the drive to a paved street. With a confident air, he walked the streets for an hour, navigating always downhill, hoping to strike the river. He saw no pedestrians. Two cars drove by. The neighborhoods changed from estates to middle-class houses, then a sprinkling of smaller residences, duplexes and triplexes, and finally turned industrial.

Rounding a corner he confronted a small plaza focused on a crisp, white and black sign:

ST. PAUL OF THE SHIPWRECK CATHOLIC CHURCH
CINCINNATI, OHIO
Daily Masses: 7:30 A.M.—NOON—5:30 P.M.

His comprehension was numb. Somber knots of people clustered in the courtyard. Children clung to adults. He wandered through the crowd, into the entrance. The brick warehouse, long ago converted to a church, was cavernous. No pew was empty, but people were not closely packed. Reinhold slumped in a rear pew and closed his eyes.

Ireland, destroyed. Everyone I knew, probably dead. Mom, Dad, Grandfather, cousin Patrick. All the places of my childhood, gone in minutes. Please God. Why?

Three hundred mouths uttered the Mass responses in whispers, sobs, or not at all. The Father sermonized about the Great Plague, Holocaust and Red Man's decimation from the pox and swords of Europe. It sank in, but subconsciously, not at the listening. Today's loss was beyond comprehension, beyond precedent in anyone's experience.

Mass ended. Few moved. Some knelt again. Most just sat in the undercurrent of hushed conversation.

"Not from here?" A red-faced man extended his hand.

"No."

"Where?"

"I can't talk yet." Reinhold rubbed his eyes with thumb and forefinger.

The man moved beside Reinhold, put his arm around his shoulder. In a minute Reinhold blinked at his grizzled comforter. "I'm from Ireland. It's all gone."

The man shook his head. "My folks were in Atlanta. Must've died when it hit."

"I'm sorry."

"How'd you get here?"

"Look, I'm just lost. I've got to get to California. My wife and babies..." Reinhold's voice trailed off.

"I thought you said Ireland." Then he spotted Reinhold's ring.

Reinhold saw him staring at the Russo-Celt intaglio. "You know the Kirovniki?" he asked.

The man nodded. "My father was one. I have his ring. I will help you in any way. Our apartment is near here. You want to use our couch to get some rest?"

"Thanks. That would help. Reinhold's my name. Reinhold Malone."

"Adam Frankel's mine."

Adam knocked on the duplex door to signal he had a guest. "Honey. We have company again."

Inside, Reinhold lowered his pack beside an overstuffed, brown tweed chair in the cluttered living room. Adam's wife emerged from the kitchen, dishtowel in hand, every bit Adam's physical equal—about fifty, big boned, reddish-brown hair brushed back probably yesterday but not since, body type more of a pear to Adam's barrel look. Her ruddy complexion opened into a broad smile. She threw the dishtowel over the back of a chair and extended her right hand.

"Holly Frankel." Her smile flickered as she studied Reinhold's face. "You look familiar." Her eyes swung to Adam for information.

"Holly, this is Reinhold Malone. He was at Mass this morning. He seems to be Irish, Russian and Californian all wrapped up in one. Actually, all I'm sure about is, he's a Kirovnik."

Holly glanced at Reinhold's hand. He held it out to display the gold-inlaid sardonyx emblem. She turned to her husband. "Did you tell him?"

"You see, my father was born near Kiev, Ukraine," Adam said. "He became a barge man on the Volga. His mother was Irish and when his intelligence and integrity had stood the test of time, the Kirovniki inducted him. He moved us here in the fifties, so I never became eligible. But he taught me, 'Never fail a Kirovnik.'"

Reinhold explained his own membership. In Moscow real estate circles he had made many friends. In the international frenzy of the nineties, the Kirovniki inducted several Irish nationals.

The Kirovniki was a Russian Christian fellowship claiming Celtic roots in ancient times when Celt ancestors were scattered throughout Europe, from the British Isles to the Black Sea. Legend had it the fellowship started in Kirovograd, Ukraine. They followed many of the precepts of freemasonry, but were not secretive and had never crossed torches with either Rome or Constantinople. As a result, most brethren were Catholics, either Roman or Orthodox. Their relative openness had helped prevent corruption, and along with their loyalty to each other, their charity and integrity were beyond question. Reinhold had been the first non-Russian ever inducted.

Adam returned to his wife's first comment. "You do look…"

From the corner of his eye, Reinhold saw Holly shake her head, "No."

"…well, familiar, like Holly said."

Holly changed the subject. "What's your connection with California? I'm from California. Grew up south of Mount Shasta in a little railroad town called Dunsmuir."

Reinhold trusted them. "I moved from Russia to be near my brother in San Francisco when the ruble collapsed in 1999. Fell in love, married in a passion, had two kids. They're still in California." His throat choked. He sat down, looked at his feet, jaw clinched. Holly brought him a glass of water. He went on, "I'd just gone back to Moscow on a new real estate deal last month when the sea level panics began. I thought I might get stuck there. Things got bad in San Francisco, too, and my wife took the kids and her mother and wound up near a place called Flat River. Ever hear of it?"

"Of course. It's maybe a hundred miles east of where I grew up."

"I'm going to level with you. I've got to get there. I'll walk if I have to. Any help you can give me, great. It's all I have left, and nothing's going to stand in my way."

Adam exchanged glances with his wife. "I can help you lots. But you're exhausted. We both work, so you can sleep all day if you need to."

They ate breakfast, listening to the government radio. Reinhold had more information than the government gave out. Grief and incredulity were stark on all three faces as the two Cincinnatians left for work and Reinhold wrapped himself in a blanket on the couch.

By dinnertime, when the Frankels returned, Reinhold was up studying National Geographic maps he found in their bookcase. Holly popped open three cans of Christian Moerlein, the local brew, quartered a head of lettuce and set a casserole in the microwave.

Reinhold looked up from the maps. "There are lots of routes to California."

"Yes there are," Adam said. "Let me tell you what I might be able to do for you, Reiney. I'm a barge man. First mate, for the Ohio River Company. That means I run the show on my barges. The captain's officially in charge. He and the pilot steer, but I run the crew and make it work. I might just manage to get you on board as a deckhand grunt. If you work hard and everything clicks you could be in Little Rock in under two weeks. We're just at the end of my barge's twenty-day down-time, putting together our next run this week."

"Christ. That's great."

"Now here's what I heard today. They say sea level's going to rise—God only knows how fast. With the East Coast wiped out, the military's all over everything, retrenching in Texas. They've bumped the entire procurement of the barge fleet I'm supposed to take down the Ohio next week. They've got twenty thousand tons of sealed containers converging on us in trucks. They're going to have guards on board, and they'll be watching us like hawks."

Adam swigged his beer. "Think you can be a barge man?"

"You tell me how, I'll do it."

"This'll take me a few days, to set up a job for you. You'll have to occupy the time. Maybe you could help at the Church. Victims and refugees from the East Coast are already pouring in."

They all took a drink. Silence. Another swig.

"Reiney, you look like my brother." Adam blurted it out, then looked at Holly, whose eyes widened at the words. "Barney—he died two weeks ago."

It was Reinhold's turned to look stunned. "I'm sorry. What happened?"

"Well, it seems strange in these times for someone to die a natural death, but it happens even in the worst of times. We all knew Barney had a heart murmur. His wife threw him out about two months ago and he was living with us. Slept on that couch."

Reinhold shifted in his chair, leaned back.

"One morning I came out and he was… cold dead. I guess his heart just shut off. When I saw you in church, Reiney, I thought, 'Well I'll be damned, he sure looks like Barney.' That's why I sat by you."

CHAPTER 73
Saturday, March 4

"GOOD MORNING, Paisley. How were things at the farm last night?" Darcy was taking a break from seedling duty, and laboring mightily to contain the accelerating anxiety that was beginning to invade her every moment, distracting her from any task requiring extended concentration. "Could you use some help unloading?"

"Sure. You can put these two suitcases in the back bedroom. We divided our clothes in half last night, Ray got so worried."

"How bad is it?"

"Well, we stopped in Likely last night on our way through. The general store was closed, but the girl at the liquor store said three farms in the valley west of there were looted and burned yesterday, and one of the families shot dead in cold-blood. In Flat River it seems like every able-bodied man's an armed cop now, but some of the down-and-outers in the outlying trailer homes are running around stealing food and stuff. Or maybe it's outsiders passing through. I guess they burn places down to cover the evidence. It's pretty near impossible to keep order in the countryside when folks stop fearing arrest, you know, at least where it's so wide open, like up here in Modoc County."

"No worse than the cities, though," Darcy retorted, suddenly aware of the pain she had buried during the frantic escape from the Bay Area. "Sometimes I just don't get people. Where's Ray?"

"He drove the extra gasoline supply around to the back door of the barn."

They walked back to the truck. Paisley handed Darcy a metal box. "That's our tax records, the deeds, our wills—you know, the important papers." Darcy blinked at the solemnity of transporting this diminutive cache of the Over-croft's life. Paisley wrapped her own arms around a heavy, roped box, puffing under the strain as they walked.

"When we were in Flat River this morning, Ray got all kinds of rumors from Chet. He said the short wave kid heard sea level was up in San Francisco by another half foot. The Executive Committee called a town meeting, too. Chet said the County's on its own now, and they warned people they'd shoot on sight if they had to, to maintain law and order. They told everyone to con-serve food, medicine, everything else they could think of—you know, like gas, propane, ammunition. They're closing the schools. It's pretty bad, Darcy."

In the little kitchen, Darcy asked, as gently as she could, to herself almost as much as to her friend, "Do you think you're safe down there, Paisley?"

"Ray and I had a fight last night, Darcy." She swallowed hard. "Don't let him know I told. I'm afraid, down there. I told him that. He says no one'd tan-gle with him, because he's well known for his guns. But I know people up here don't like us much. We're still hippies to them. There's plenty of people who might take it out on us, now that they see others looting and burning and get-ting away with it. I finally gave Ray an ultimatum, and he said Okay, I should ask you if we can start sleeping up here. I brought some linens for the beds. Is it all right?" Paisley blinked tears off her lower eyelashes.

Darcy gave her a strong hug. "After the way you took us in, sight unseen, strangers in your home? Paisley. You'll always be welcome in my life. No mat-ter what. Ray can work the farm from here." Then she added, faltering, "Things'll get better eventually."

Paisley nodded, managing a brave smile through pencil thin lips, as they heard Ray's pickup start back down from the barn.

Night quiet had settled over the house. Mariah wrapped an extra blanket around her shoulders like a shawl and sat by the window. She invited the cold night air in through a two inch crack and imagined the nocturnal sounds that in the spring would replace the wintry silence. Lost in the grays and blacks of a landscape lit only by starlight, she indulged an imaginary dialogue with Elmer. It was her way of mining the richness of their love, while releasing his soul to its new journey, and hers to hers. Many new pieces had yet to fall in place, but this would be her home—and her community, precarious as it seemed. The old security of a home-centered routine, people in their proper places and the calendar predictable, had proved as illusory as a Tibetan yak-butter sculpture or a Navajo sand painting in a windy desert. And yet, Mariah mused, Could a new security be coalescing? Grounded in a growing knowledge of her own deeper patterns? In a new-found accuracy of intuitions, dreams and pictures? In a new freedom to shape reality by blessing rather than protecting, by encouraging people's spirits rather than their social roles, by openness to the unforeseen rather than adherence to the dogma of a plan? Her inner husband answered a resounding, Yes. Ahh, then to share? He answered, Not by persuasion, but by resonance alone, not as a leader but a bell, a lamp, a tone.

BOOK THREE

CHAPTER 74
Sunday, March 5

JASON LOWERY wore dark glasses. His eye had no pronounced swelling now, but a black half circle remained beneath it, a tangible reminder of their recent trouble. Although Catherine had no particular wish to relive the scene, she sensed it would be a mistake to bring it up in conversation as she and Jason hiked the trail beyond the Maxwell Acres compound after breakfast. Aunt Rose had sensed their need to be alone and suggested they "get some fresh air" before their meeting at the Maxwell Acres compound, and let her do the dishes. Their breath formed puffs of white as they trudged pensively, searching for the beginning of their conversation.

"What do you think of James Salas?" Catherine asked.

"What do you mean? He seems like a nice guy."

"He's keeping a lot under his hat, though. You know what I mean?"

Jason thrust his hands into his jacket pockets. "I think he's sincere. He's just a quiet guy. After all, he's been living in a monastery."

Catherine admired Jason and trusted his judgments, but her doubt lingered. "I'm just not certain he's leveling with us. His story's pretty sketchy, isn't it? Maybe it's just intuition, but I think we need to keep an eye on him."

"I feel responsible for him. If I'd been a little more careful we'd have passed him on the road and never interacted with him at all."

Catherine nodded. "Aunt Rose is feeling the same way, and her nursing instincts are fully activated too. I just hope he's not, you know, taking advantage of us."

"Give him a break, Cath. He's pretty well scraped up."

"Yeah, but he seems to be recovering pretty fast. Do you think he might have just been exaggerating?"

He stopped walking and faced her. "What's going on with you, Cath? You seem determined to find fault with the mysterious Mr. Salas. I can't think of anything to say against him though."

"Well, other than the fact that he's guarded, sort of, the only thing concrete I can offer is that when we unloaded the car a few nights ago, I felt something in the bottom of his pack when I carried it into the house. It felt like a gun."

Jason pursed his lips. "Right. That doesn't seem to fit, does it?" They resumed their pace.

"But think about it," he continued. "We're carrying a couple of guns too. This might not be a safe time to be traveling alone. I say we give him the benefit of the doubt. Catherine, if worse comes to worst, we've got to pull together here. We can't be casting suspicions on one another. What about that farmer and his wife? We've got to trust them too. Everybody's going to have a contribution to make to our safety and maybe our survival."

He was silent then, and the only sound was the scrape of their shoes on the ground and an occasional crunch of snow underfoot.

"What are you thinking now?" asked Catherine.

"I'm wondering about my family back East, how they're doing in all this."

Catherine held his arm against her side and pressed her ear to his shoulder. "Oh, Jason, I'm sorry. You must be sick with worry."

"I'll bet that's how they're feeling about me. I'm sure they want me home. I wonder if they went to our summer place in the Shenandoahs. They might be in a similar situation to ours."

"At least I have my family all here in one place, safe and together," said Catherine. She put an arm around Jason's waist, and he cradled her in his arm. Her hand reached behind his neck and pulled him down for a kiss. "I'm glad you're here" she whispered. *I'd probably be dead now if you weren't,* she thought. He held her close, sighing.

"We'd better get to that meeting at Mariah's," said Jason. "It'll help us get to know those folks—and we can keep an eye on James too, if you want."

Eli had shared dinner with Mariah and Darcy for two nights, beginning after their somber walk "home" pondering the shock of the tsunami. He felt a pattern being sown. As shadows crept from the western ridge Tierney would run out toward the barn, stop twenty feet short, lean over as if to bridge the remaining distance, and shout, "Ja-ames, come to din-ner." After washing dishes, Eli would roll a ball across the floor for Finn to push back toward him with a giggle, and when Tierney asked him to tell a story he remembered Jack and the Beanstalk. Although Eli had been awkward with the children at first, in the last two days he had reached out to them to gather their innocence, prizing the treasure he had squandered in his own life. Their easy acceptance of him gave hope for acceptance by others in "society." He had watched them playing in the dirt as the adults worked the soil gloomily, like drab Medieval peasants in war time, holding tight their fears. But the children held nothing back, Tierney squatting and stirring dirt with a trowel, talking to her work, Finn waving a stick and babbling in imitation. In the barn Eli wrote poetry by candlelight, including a haiku.

Early spring, morning,
    I sprout stiffly from the soil
       of children's blessing.

And now on the third morning Tierney led, tugging Eli by the finger, across the garden plot toward the main house. He had done his meditation and eaten a simple breakfast of bread and cheese. "Some more people are here," she told him. "Mommy wants you to come to a meeting." She looked up at him to gauge his attention. "It's a man and a woman, but he's her daddy." Eli saw charcoal clouds piling up in the southern sky.

For the second time Eli met Kim Royer and her father. "Rose tells me you're making a marvelous recovery, James," said Charles. Eli felt intimidated by the patrician, gray haired man in a black Air Force sweatshirt and the tall, self-assured young woman in fashionable jeans and Irish wool turtleneck. He nodded, wondering what impression they had of him.

The entire population of Greater Maxwell Acres seated themselves in a vague circle. Eli took a position on a floor cushion, across the circle from the bench occupied by the Royers, and to the left of Mariah, Catherine and Jason, in dining room chairs. Catherine would not be likely to scrutinize him, unless he spoke, and he was inclined to merely listen. His reserve made him feel again as an outsider, and his lower position emphasized his not belonging in this circle. Peter sat on the raised hearth, as if in the position of presider, across from the Overcrofts and Darcy, who held Finn on her lap in an easy chair. Tierney was swinging her legs from a kitchen chair, looking serious.

"Tea?" Mariah asked. Eli declined. He studied each face in the circle. Catherine and Peter, he concluded, are realizing they are essentially homeless, and are coming to grips with the fact that their lives, once so defined and scheduled, have now come to the edge of a precipice. Jason is facing the added possibility that his family is either dead or in unknown peril.

Mariah and Darcy face similar fears about their husbands. The Overcrofts have been thrown into emergency mode, their lives disrupted, but they are no worse off than other local citizens. As long as Modoc County has a semblance of calm, they're as well off as anyone else in California.

Eli himself was in a more secure position than he would have been anywhere else he could think of—as long as he remained James Salas. He also had the advantage now of living with the newcomers, sharing that distinction with them. How long could he continue as a vague stranger? Could he fall into his new identity and make it permanent? How permanent was this situation at Maxwell Acres, for any of them?

There was no evidence in their location of the calamity from the bottom of the globe, and news was inadequate to either increase or allay their anxiety. They were somewhat paralyzed by their lack of knowledge, the absence of something immediate to react to. Still, they were gloomy and numb, horrified, anxious.

"It appears that Mother Nature has pitched us a difficult state of affairs," Peter began, as if formally opening a meeting. "Charles and Kim, would you tell these folks where we stand, as far as you know?"

The Royers reiterated their news. Eli studied Kim, intrigued by her confident bearing. She was beautiful to him, as well as articulate and passionate. Everyone north of L.A. had been forsaken and apparently would have to fend for themselves or form alliances of neighbors or communities. "You should have seen him, this well-fed general sentencing millions of people to oblivion or death."

Eli listened, pursing his lips thoughtfully, aware of striking a pose for any who might be noticing him.

Darcy savagely gulped air. "Forsaken? What does that mean? A government, abandoning millions of citizens! That's not a government, that's…"

"But I can understand," Charles Royer interrupted. "Government has finally encountered a challenge it isn't up to." *Like the Roman Empire when the barbarians overran its borders*, Eli thought.

"Ironically, the highest officials have ensured their own safety and continuance," Kim added, "for the majority of people who will survive. What are the chances they'll put together something for the rest of us? The military will seek to ensure security and order. Humanitarian concerns will be secondary."

"Perhaps necessarily," reasoned the doctor.

Eli listened with intense interest, like a medieval peasant hearing a legend of Arthur and the Knights of the Round Table—these people lived in a world outside his experience. They were highly educated, and prosperous. The most affluent people he had known were drug dealers with two Cadillacs and diamond rings on each hand. The wife of an international businessman who could handle a Harley and fly a plane loomed like an Amazon queen of his imagination. Kim operated among those at the highest levels of government—he had lived at the bottom of the pile.

"It's pretty ominous," said Peter. "We might have to think in terms of staying here until the government can re-group and re-organize infrastructure, and that might be a long time, years, depending on how bad the damage is. We'll have to feed ourselves and not count on replenishing our supplies from outside our property."

"It's a good thing you advised us to stock up," Charles said. "We'd better take inventory and estimate how long we'll be able to keep going."

Finn had become squirmy on Darcy's lap. She lowered him to the floor. "We have quite a large supply of grains out in the barn," she said. "It ought to keep us going for a long while."

"We've brought a lot of our stuff here too," said Ray Overcroft. "Mariah offered to let us use her guest house. This morning I hauled in another load of supplies and equipment, and pulled in my trailer with the five hundred gallon tank of spare gasoline, too.

"Uncle Charles?" Catherine said. "Doesn't the government have huge stores of surplus grain? It seems we're always sending relief supplies to all sorts of Third World countries when they have famines or floods."

"Maybe," answered Charles. "I don't know how relief supplies will be allocated. It was always looked on as the country's destiny to go from coast to coast. Only now the coasts are apparently moving closer together. And without the Central Valley's agricultural output, the population might be too great to support. And infrastructure and transportation costs are going to be enormous."

Thunder growled in the distance, rumbled across the valley, and ended in a concussion just above them. Finn scrabbled back to his mother's lap. Tierney, sitting now at Mariah's feet, looked for any note of alarm her grandmother might show. There was none. Mariah stroked Tierney's hair.

"That's right," Kim said. "They'll have to have something more massive than the New Deal or the Marshall Plan, with very little in the way of treasure. I'm guessing something like the CCC, with labor for public works projects paid by food and shelter. I'm sure Thad Parker will try to generate some assistance for California, but who knows when?"

"I'm telling you," Mariah said, "those grain sacks out in the barn ought to keep us in food for months, if not years, presuming it's okay. And we've already got our garden going too, at least in the planning stages. You're welcome to use our land too."

Rain pelted the roof, a downpour that coursed down the window panes.

"It's funny," Rose said. "My maiden name is Farmer, and my grandparents had a farm in Iowa, but I never thought I'd become one. I'm afraid we don't have much experience."

Paisley broke in. "Don't worry, Rose. Ray and I will volunteer to expand the farming operation here. We'll just need willing laborers, like James here."

Eli flushed, with the eyes of the group on him. "I'm not a very experienced gardener. I've had only a little training in the monastery." He thought of Sister

Sharon's instruction in the monastery garden, and helping the Los Molinos monks in their orchards. The expertise he had learned was more a matter of respect for the land than practical knowledge. He glanced around the room, and was arrested by Kim's questioning look. He felt reckless joining the circle. He realized he was building up his prevarication, using elements of truth to promote a lie.

"Uncle Peter said you were on a mission for a priest," Kim said.

"Yes. It's confidential," he added, trying to sound matter-of-fact. He was afraid he sounded too guarded and curt. "Now I suppose it's been compromised by the turn of affairs…" He was trying to create a cushion of words to smother the curiosity he was enflaming. From the corner of his eye he saw Catherine lean toward him.

"Seems to me that's not enough in this situation." Catherine's voice was shrill. "It's a little too vague. We're in a position where we have to all trust each other and know where we're all coming from."

The note of hostility crackled, and the room fell silent. Eli returned Catherine's frowning stare, but kept his face a resolute blank. Instinctively he took a slow breath and strove for a centering point in his mind.

"It was for the abbot of Saint Mary's Abbey, Father Thomas…" he faltered, and looked from face to face around the room. And he decided to give it up. "I've enjoyed meeting all you folks," he began again. "Tomorrow I'll get to work on my bicycle and get back on the road."

An uncertain numbness hung in the room emphasizing the sound of the rain. Mariah broke into it. "Back on the road is a pretty risky proposition, isn't it, James? You've been dependable and hard working, and as far as I'm concerned you're welcome here. We need you."

"Catherine, you're right," said Peter. "We do need to trust each other, and there isn't room for challenging one another's integrity, is there?"

Catherine's lips were a tight line. She nodded meekly and stared at the floor.

Eli rescued her. "I admire your forthrightness," he said softly. "You said what's on your mind. I've been around a lot of people who keep their thoughts hidden, too much. It doesn't build trust. I'll try to be more open too." He was sincere, and it helped him to stay centered, relieved the burden of duplicity. He admired her gymnast's go-for-it attitude, her spirit and spunk in the face of the thugs who attacked her. He himself had been cowed by the likes of Dupree Ransom. If she knew the truth, she would understandably lump him in with Ransom and Perez, and to some extent, she would be right, he granted. *I hope I can follow your example, he thought. But not yet. I don't have the courage now.*

That night Eli and Mariah washed dishes together while Darcy read the children stories and got them ready for bed.

"Thanks again for going to bat for me," Eli said. "I'm afraid Catherine is right, you folks don't know a lot about me." He wondered if he was on the verge of another confession. His secret was a weight that had pressed on him for the remainder of the group's discussion.

"I know a lot by intuition," Mariah said. "It's surprising how much we perceive about people, sometimes more than they understand about themselves. I think I do know a lot about you, James. I just don't have details."

Like my name, Eli thought. He weighed the possibility of entrusting his identity to her, considered her strength and integrity. He shared a great deal with her spiritually, he knew. "What details do you need?"

"I'm sure they'll come with time," she said. "I sense that you seek healing, and that you have made a lot of progress."

"You're right." He placed a stack of plates in the cupboard, then leaned against the counter. "It's strange..." His voice faltered. He knew if he composed his utterance to protect himself, he would only create a barrier between himself and the person he trusted most since leaving the abbey. He plunged ahead. "Almost everybody here is oppressed by this terrible disaster. But for me, I'm maybe as content and free as I've ever been." He listened for his words echoing in his mind. "Does that sound strange to you?"

"Yes, frankly, it does."

"It's because of the healing. You know a lot about that don't you?"

"My husband and I have done a lot of studying about it, a lot of working with it." Mariah told Eli that Elmer had been a fine athlete in college, robust and strong, before his alcoholism took over. After he joined AA, he had contracted a neuromuscular disease that made his muscles deteriorate, sapped his strength. For a decade they traveled the world, sought seminars and teachers, poured through books, and he performed daily exercises. He had arrested his malady's progress, and more importantly had formed in himself a unique balance of body, mind and spirit—with the body as the weak member of the triad.

"I'd like to meet him. I hope I get the chance. Is he okay now?"

"He was always remarkably self-sufficient. I'm sure he could get along all right in normal times. But I had a dream about him a couple of weeks ago... This sounds strange to a lot of people, but I pay attention to dreams."

Eli felt there was something additional he was to understand, but it eluded him. "I know what you mean. I had a dream on the way here—before I met the Addisons. It left me with a sense that evil was lurking around, evil men. And then I met Peter and Catherine and Jason, and found out what happened to them. The evil men were the ones who attacked them… It's like the knowledge of them was in the air."

"In my dream," said Mariah, "my husband died."

Eli blinked. "Do you think it's true?"

"I cannot know, James. I keep it in my heart, but I have not burdened Darcy, or anyone else, with it. Whether his spirit is still in a body or not, doesn't affect us. But if we form a belief that he's gone, our nostalgia, grief and bitterness will take its toll. As long as it's speculative, I'll keep it inside."

"I understand." Eli pressed Mariah's hand between his own.

"What about Darcy's husband?"

"Our dreams of him are not as bad, but not reassuring either. That's why Darcy's so distracted and anxious."

Eli's eyes met Mariah's. "I'll pray for your family."

"ARE YOU ALL RIGHT, Reinhold? It's barely sun-up."

Reinhold had moved the couch cushions to the floor and was lying ramrod straight under his blanket with a wet towel plastered across his eyes. He heard Holly kneel beside him.

"Don't touch me," he said. "And don't talk loud. The pain in my forehead, my eye sockets—it's unbearable."

She dropped her voice to a murmur. "I heard you out here. Thought I'd check. You get migraines?"

"Never. Think this is one?"

Adam's sleep-husky voice blared out, "What's wrong?"

"Shhh," Holly whispered. "Migraine."

Reinhold eased the towel off but kept his eyes closed. He felt Holly slip her hand under his shoulder, "I don't think we have a prayer of getting medicine, or a doctor," she said. "But I know one thing that could help."

She helped him sit up, cross-legged, back to the couch. She knelt in front of him. "Keep your eyes shut, hands in your lap. This is simple biofeedback. If you had an itch in the palm of your hand, your attention would be focused right there. In that same way, now, Reinhold, I want you to put your attention into both of your hands. Imagine they're getting warm. They're in warm sunshine—lying on warm sand at the beach—in a sink filled with warm water and soft soapsuds—in the warm hands of your wife on a hot, moonlit summer evening."

She knelt patiently for three minutes. "Feel them getting warm?"

He felt a warm tingle in his hands. "Way warm. Even hot."

"Keep doing it. Your headache should go away. I'll be back in a while." Reinhold's breathing steadied, and the turnbuckle that twisted between his temples loosened. As the pain subsided he felt his neck relax.

He became aware of Adam and Holly nearby. "Better?" Holly asked softly.

Reinhold opened his eyes and nodded. "The biofeedback did the trick."

"They taught us at the Red Cross. I volunteered with them after our boys joined the army."

Reinhold ventured a diagnosis. "I think it was a combination of wanting to get out of here, on my way, and stress from the horrors I heard at the church."

Reinhold had volunteered at Adam's church. He had quit early the previous afternoon, however, staggered by stories from people flooding in from the East—thousands of bodies stuck in trees, hung up on telephone poles as the waters receded, pieces of houses, buildings, stuff from stores, mattresses, cars and trailers, trash, debris, sewage. The government presence on the edge of the disaster had been nil. People had stolen cars, given each other rides, killed for cars, walked out. The lucky few who had made it to Cincinnati were from the edge of the catastrophe, but they brought stories from further east that they heard along the way. Mixed in were descriptions of police trying to control the roads, even shooting and beating people when higher-ups weren't around. Reinhold lost control of his emotions when he imagined what might be happening in California. It doubled his desperate impulse to join the migration to the West.

"Just take it easy and get some food inside," Adam said.

As they ate, Adam laid out his progress. "I set things up with the Captain. He's a good man, willing to help you on my word. The barge has a crew of nine, and I pretty much trust most of them. We push off tomorrow. I brought some manuals for you. You're already a merchant marine, so you'll pick it up right off."

Reinhold took the manuals. "It seems the government doesn't want people moving around. Think they'll make trouble?"

Adam continued with the plan. "I'm going to give you Barney's papers." He stole a look at Holly. "They're still in my desk. I got him a job on the barge a month back. Ivan Barnabus Frankel. The crew knew him as Barney. We'll call you 'Ivan' and the papers will only be for the military. The Captain okayed it."

Reinhold rubbed his chin. Holly stared at Adam.

"You grow a small mustache," Adam went on, "chop your mop to a crew cut, and I swear you'll match his photo ID to a tee. Holly doesn't think it's such a great scheme, but it's up to you, Reiney. If you want to try it, you'll just have to risk it. Given what's happening—well, in my opinion you're in an all-or-nothing game anyway. But you call the shot."

Reinhold said, "Hell, I've come this far against rotten odds. Start calling me Ivan now, though. Okay?"

"Okay, Ivan," Adam grinned. Holly took her dishes to the kitchen without comment.

CHAPTER 75
Monday, March 6

KIM ROYER kept to the high side of the muddy rutted road from the Royer cabin to the Maxwell Acres compound, stepping as much as possible on patches of grass or gravel. She was on her way to offer assistance to Mariah and Darcy. Her parents and Uncle Peter didn't need her to take inventory of their supplies. Clouds were sweeping north, revealing an occasional slat of blue, but the southern sky was low and black. The storm would resume soon. She saw her young cousin approaching, picking her way among puddles with nimble grace.

"Did you get Jason moved in?" Kim called.

Catherine looked up. "Hi, Kim. Yeah, he's got a room next to James. They're making him a bed now. I'm surprised how comfortable looking that barn is."

Jason had had enough of sleeping on the living room couch at the Royer cabin, had asked Mariah if he could bunk in the barn. "She's really nice," said Catherine. "She said to tell you there's room in the main house for you, and me too if I want to stay there. I was just coming to tell you."

"I'd like to follow up on that. I'm afraid our cabin wasn't meant for our two families to stay for a long time."

Catherine fell into step alongside her cousin. "That sounds really depressing, 'a long time.' Are you pretty sure this isn't just temporary?"

"I wish I could be more positive. I thought it was a dream when I heard General Austin talking about shutting down the Western power grid and writing off millions of people. After Nine-Eleven people said it with heavy hearts: the world has changed."

Catherine squinted at the scudding clouds, as if estimating the speed of approaching calamity. "It's unbelievable, Kim. In fact, Ray and Paisley went to town to try to find some confirmation of what you and Uncle Charles are saying."

"Last time I saw you, you were about to compete against—Stanford was it? Now, for practical purposes, Stanford doesn't exist."

"That feels like ancient history. I'm terrified I might have to let go of practically everything in my life, except for Jason. Will there ever be a normal to return to?"

"Not to return to," said Kim. "We're going to adjust to a new reality, but who knows how long it will take for that to establish itself. I'm not sure what it will look like."

"Kim, you had a great career going, doing important things—and dating the richest man in California. Now what do you have to look forward to? Becoming a farmer?"

An image of Morgan Clark flashed in Kim's mind, his blue eyes earnestly trying to communicate his integrity. Accepting him might open the door to easy living in the worldly sense, but to no less challenging a life in its way than what faced her now. It could not have occurred to her then that Maxwell Acres was what her life had prepared her for.

They were near the end of the curving path near the main house, where Tierney sat on a porch bench, showing Finn pictures in a book. "It might come to that, becoming a farmer," said Kim.

"Kim, I'll go crazy if I have to stay here even two weeks. I won't do it. I can't."

Kim's expression was a painful smile. "I'm not sure I can either, or any of us. But suppose this is the crude beginning of some great important task—we'll have to look at it that way." She smiled, seeing Tierney entertaining her brother on the porch. "It appears that for now our world consists of about a dozen people. Luckily they seem to be good people." She noticed Catherine's sharp glance. "I'm including James."

HALFWAY TO FLAT RIVER, Ray and Paisley Overcroft drove through a clatter of hail, then rain. Lots of rain. They entered the town, windshield wiper valiantly slapping right and left. There was no movement on the puddled streets, but shops were lit, ready for business. Ray stopped first at the Downtown Barber Shop while Paisley tried to shop.

Tony the Barber was snipping around the edges of a talkative rancher. Ray took a seat and picked up a month-old *Newsweek* magazine. "Ice/Water" was the silvery-blue headline over a split photo layout showing Florida beach residents up to their knees in floodwater, and great white ice shards jammed together off the Antarctic coast.

"This'd be a perfect time for some terrorist to blow something up, like maybe the government, really deal us a death blow," said the rancher.

"Yeah, I s'pose," replied Tony. "But they're in the same fix as everybody else. Besides, far as we know, the government's back on its heels already. Why would terrorists do any more damage? They'd have to be really crazy."

"That's what they are," cried the rancher. "They're crazy. Probably think it's the end of the world and they've gotta help God out."

Ray stood and tossed the magazine on a nearby chair. "Hey, I'll see you later, Tony," he said. He would get better information visiting Chet at the feed store.

Chet Ragland had arrived at middle age with a small paunch and a pronounced limp, had sold his ranch north of Flat River, had taken over the Modoc County Cooperative, and enjoyed a modest degree of prosperity as proprietor of what most locals still called the Co-op. The old buildings, nearly in the center of town, had a worn, barn-like appearance, with corrugated metal roofs, but were still frequented by farmers and ranchers for feed and equipment. A solitary customer browsed the nail bins, apparently merely staying out of the rain.

"Chet, I've heard some really shocking news," Ray began.

"That's the only kind there is any more," answered Chet, carelessly loud.

Ray kept his voice low. "I've met an Air Force officer, and his daughter who works for a Congressman. They say the government's abandoning the West Coast."

Chet wrinkled his forehead, as if this would widen his droopy beagle eyes. "Now that's something I hadn't heard." He scratched his neck. "Let's check it out with Grady upstairs."

Grady Sumner swiveled in his chair when Chet and Ray entered his cubbyhole. Earphones and microphone were strapped over a backward baseball cap. "What's up, Chet? Hi, Ray," he said, peering through thick glasses. A gray sweatshirt with Duke University logo bagged on his light frame. His fingers still hovered near a dial on his radio. On the long table were scattered papers, notes scrawled haphazardly.

"You know Ray Overcroft," said Chet. "He has some inside news, from people close to the government. He says things are worse than the government radio lets on. Have you heard anything?"

"He's right," said Grady. A brief smirk appeared above his thin amber goatee. "I can listen in on all kinds of short wave broadcasts—police, military, government, and hams. It's like the original Internet, with chat rooms."

Sea level had risen to two and a half feet. Coastal port facilities were damaged world-wide. California's Highway 1 was closed, 80 and 101 cut in low-lying places.

"Diablo Canyon Power Plant's closed down and guarded," Grady added. "The coal burning plant in Watsonville is also down. All the large airports are secured for military use."

"The government says it's keeping things under control and setting up relief programs," said Ray. "That sound right to you?"

"Well, they talk about it." Grady frowned and canted his head. "But they seem more worried about keeping the water system intact. If the California Aqueduct goes, the state's done for." He pursed his lips. "Y'know, the sheriff and mayor asked me to tell them if I hear anything they need to know. It sounds to me like they need to know the government offices are pulling out."

Chet and Ray stared at each other, then back at Grady, who seemed amused at his impact on them. He shared freely, had them listen to conversations backed by a constant hiss punctuated by beeps and squawks. The medium was annoying, the content unsettling.

Ray splashed out to his truck to find his wife. They headed for the farm, Paisley upset by what she saw. Acquaintances had been more tight-lipped than she'd expected. The grocery store was nearly bare. People were apparently hoarding: toilet paper, batteries, bottled water.

Their conversation carried them through Likely, where they noticed an unusual number of cars and pickups parked at the store. People were congregating for gossip and support, they guessed.

The gate to the Overcroft farm hung twisted from its post. Ray eased through and proceeded at a deliberate pace, hit with a bitter sense of alarm upon seeing the barn's blackened, puckered roof and walls. The rain seemed to have extinguished the fire.

"Sunzabitches," Ray muttered.

Paisley reached out as if to brace herself against the dash. "Oh Ray, just look at the house." Several windows were shattered, the door gaped open.

"I don't suppose they've left anything worth taking," Ray said flatly. He felt more sad than angry. The wantonness of destruction was shocking, but the looting itself did not, after all, surprise him.

They toured the house for items of sentimental value. A few photo albums, along with trinkets from India, were strewn on the floor. "I'm not even sure I want to salvage anything," murmured Paisley.

Ray roamed outside. The greenhouse was intact, though empty. He began dismantling it and loading key pieces that fit into the pickup. He whistled sharply three times and their mutts, Coal and Good Dawg, came running. Paisley found a dozen chickens and stuffed them for transport into three old feed sacks. Three young goats grazed near the barn. Paisley tethered them in the back of the pickup.

Load full, hearts numb, they tracked the gravel driveway for the last time.

Paisley silently recalled the words to a folk song her mother had loved, *"Times Are Gettin' Hard,"* about bad luck and hard-hearted bankers forcing farmers off their land, the heart-wrenching farewells and the aching swell of faded promises and memories.

"It looks like Maxwell Acres is home now," Ray said. "It's certainly isolated. I think we can try to survive up there with folks we can trust and depend on. We don't have any choice anyway, do we?"

Paisley let silence be her response. Once through the broken gate, she did not look back.

"I'M NOT REALLY SURE I would've wanted to be there when the looters showed up," said Ray when the assembled community had learned the Overcrofts' news from Flat River and their farm. "It might have been a situation like you lived through." He nodded to Peter. "Even if we could have defended our place, it might have been just a matter of time before something like this happened anyway."

"Your absence made it easy for them," Peter said. "But like the bastards who attacked us, they would have held off unless—or until—they had an advantage."

"It's a lot less likely to happen here, isn't it?" Darcy asked. "We're pretty isolated, after all, and there are more of us."

"That's true," Ray said, "but I think we need a twenty-four hour armed watch."

Charles stood by the window, looking out toward his cabin. "I agree. From the front window at my place you can see all the way to the big oak at the bridge." He began deploying troops like a military commander, setting up a schedule for manning the watch station. "The women will have to do some of the sentry duty," he said, "and the dogs will be a big help at night. We have to be sure people experienced with weapons are on hand at all times." That included all the men, Catherine and, marginally, Rose. Eli stayed silent, not wanting to reveal his military service just yet.

"Darcy too," Ray said, "unless you mean only firearms." He recalled her in action on the highway with the pack of wild dogs.

Paisley let Ray do most of the talking. He and Charles and Peter dominated the discussion, while the rest remained glum and passive, weary with strategic details.

Mariah had a knack for choosing the right moment to speak. She shifted the discussion by pointing out that they were a community, that as a group they were blessed with talent and compatibility. "If I have to live through the greatest disaster since Noah, I'm glad to be here, with people I've come to admire." Eli returned her glance with a shy grin. "Given the circumstances, if Reinhold were here, I for one would be content."

Eli glanced at Darcy, noting that Mariah had not mentioned Elmer.

No one offered any counterweight to Mariah's observation. She suggested they firm up the living arrangements, recommending Catherine and Kim accept her invitation to live in the main house since the Royer cabin living room was now to be a watch station and not a suitable sleeping room. The Overcrofts occupied one of the two guest houses, the one not currently used for household storage, and Eli and Jason were content to bunk in the barn.

The meeting appeared at an end, until Darcy wondered about a need to organize the group, have a decision-making process. "Do we need to put someone in charge? Or can we make decisions by consensus? I suppose all of us are going to have to make sacrifices, and that can lead to resentment if we don't foresee it and make sure everyone is content with some kind of process."

"Aha!" Kim raised a conspiratorial eyebrow. "The specter of government rears its head. Do we need a dictator, or a council?"

"Judging by our process today," Mariah said, "it looks like Charles is our president, or mayor, or commanding officer."

Charles smiled at her. "Or you, Mariah. Listen, I'm open to suggestions for improving on my plan. Safety has to be our main concern right now. And then we'll have to pool our resources and talents to get us through this crisis, until the world stabilizes. Seems to me it could take years. If self-government needs to arise, it no doubt will."

REINHOLD SHIFTED from foot to foot on the front walk in the sunset while Holly held Adam in a lingering embrace. "Have a good trip, you big bear. Come back a day early and a dollar up."

Reinhold and Adam started for the river. Suddenly, Holly shouted, "Oh, wait a minute, Reinhold—I mean Ivan." She went inside, reappeared and handed Reinhold a small package.

"It's Barney's Bible. There's a lot of Bible Belt people where you're going. It's sort of—a credential. Just tell 'em Jesus guides your way and show 'em your Book. And if you get all the way, inside's a little envelope for my mother, if you ever could get it from Flat River to Dunsmuir. No promises, but I'll be hoping."

Reinhold tucked it into his backpack. In forty-five minutes he and Adam were aboard the fifty-six hundred horsepower towboat.

"*Wachabe*." Reinhold read the name. "Japanese?" he asked.

"Sioux. Means 'Black Bear,' guardian of long life, strength and courage. Captain Gunderson's mother was Sioux."

As the pistons whined and the eight-foot twin propellers churned the Ohio River into brown froth, the *Wachabe* nudged the fifteen-barge flotilla into the current under the watchful eyes of three Marines posted behind the wheel-house railing.

They couldn't be more than twenty-two, Reinhold speculated. *Might be trigger-happy.*

His musing splintered in the wake of First Mate Adam's booming voice. "Hey, you two. Curly, Ivan. Get out there and check the tow for water, make sure none of the rigging broke on launch. And give the navigation lights and sounders another check while you're at it."

The slip of the water beneath the catwalk was so close and fast it made Reinhold dizzy. "Mind if I walk on the inside, Curly?" he said.

"Get used to it, Ivan. Better get used to it."

CHAPTER 76

Tuesday, March 7

CHARLES SAT in an armchair looking out the window of his cabin in the cloudy mid-afternoon, along the road that disappeared around the old oak tree a half-mile distant. In his lap lay a pair of binoculars. Ray Overcroft's Remington hunting rifle with its scope sight stood in a rack to the side of the window, secured by an unlocked wooden bar. The window, the rifle, the binoculars were all to be manned round the clock, according to the plan Charles had devised to protect the cabin and Maxwell Acres from the kind of depredation the Overcrofts' property had suffered.

After the group meeting, Eli had said little except to make himself available for any assignment or position the group might give him, and to make his newly-repaired bicycle available for the group's use. When the topic of arms came up again, however, he joined Charles and Jason in owning his military training. Ray and Peter had done some hunting, and the plan called for one of the men to be near the watcher in case of a need for firepower. Rose had demurred: "I've even been here by myself and never yet felt the need to defend this property with a weapon." The Overcrofts' experience trumped her objection.

One-hour watches had been maintained during the night. Each watcher awoke a successor, with all of the Maxwell compound people standing their watches first. Charles had taken Rose's shift, passing over her so she might sleep through the night.

Jason called out, entering through the kitchen door, and Charles heaved himself out of the chair. "As usual, nothing to report," he told Jason. He was on the verge of voicing his doubts about the security plan. It seemed to be more disruptive than effective, a dull way to spend two hours a day, taking people from productive tasks. And yet, it was a factor in establishing a group cohesion as members of the team faithfully stood the watches. He noticed Jason was carrying a book. Was it a sign that alertness was about to diminish? He admitted to himself that he wished he had had something to occupy him.

"Hey, that's not Dr. Addison, out for a walk, is it?" Jason had automatically glanced out the window, and was pointing toward a figure approaching round the bend where the large oak stood sentinel. He fitted the binoculars to his eyes. "Whoever it is, he's walking slow and carrying something." He reached for the Remington.

"I'll go down and check him out," said Charles. "Just keep me covered. If more than one shows, maybe fire a warning shot."

Charles broke into a trot when he reached the road. He slowed to a brisk walk, searching the face shaded by an Oakland A's baseball cap. From sixty yards away he thought the intruder was somehow familiar. When the man waved to him, recognition snapped into place: Maurice Something... The man who had driven him here from the Flat River airport.

"Hey, Doc, how ya doin'?" said Maurice Beckwith.

"Maurice," Charles called, "What are you doing here?"

Under Beckwith's arm a towel was wrapped around something oblong which he held like a knight's lance. He cupped his free hand to his ear as Charles approached.

"Hey, Doc. I come up to see you, but my truck crapped out a half mile down the road," he said, jerking his head as if looking over his shoulder. He began to unwrap his bundle. There was a glint of metal. "I brought you one of those Lambert bar clamps you said you…"

The crack of a rifle shot cut him off. He pitched like a blindsided quarterback and scraped hard on the gravel. His baseball cap seemed to hang briefly in the air, as if it had been slapped from his head, and the bar clamp clattered on the road. Beckwith quivered violently.

Charles leapt to Beckwith's side, felt the wounded man's arm relax as he lost consciousness. He whirled and stood to wave a referee's time-out signal to Jason. A sickening reality dawned as he bent to examine the gash on the side of Beckwith's head.

By the time Charles made a pressure dressing from the towel Beckwith had brought, Jason had sprinted to join him. "I thought he was pulling out a gun!" he wailed. They carried the limp body to the cabin. Rose and Peter, responding to the rifle's report, had run out to help. The others were rushing down from the compound.

"Rose," Charles panted as they entered the cabin, "clear the table." His voice was a commander's again. "We'll have to clean and close this wound." She disappeared into the bedroom and emerged with a clean sheet, covered the table, ran hot water into a pot, and began washing her hands. After the men laid Beckwith on the table, Jason fell back against the wall and sank to the floor, gasping, holding his head like a cracked bowl.

THE VOLVO SEEMS happy enough, wedged against the granite outcrop where it came to rest as the waters receded. The vagrant pats its hood, praising it, "I always trusted that newspaper ad, where it said you were waterproof and could even float." He kicks two charging rats over the cliff. "Not today, you bastards. I worked too hard scavenging this food for myself." He studies the caved-in Lincoln Memorial across the reconfigured Potomac, and the stub of the Washington Monument, then yanks the Volvo door open and takes refuge from the evening onslaught of rodents too numerous to boot away.

"JAMES, I KNOW you understand healing. Will you join Darcy or Kim this evening? We're doing healing touch in shifts for Mr. Beckwith. His pulse and blood pressure dropped so low this afternoon that Charles said we were about to lose him, so Rose and I did a long session with him. Charles was amazed when he stabilized after a couple of hours."

Eli readily agreed, following intently Mariah's instruction.

Maurice Beckwith lay inert in Peter's bed, all but his face covered by a red and black Pendleton blanket. Mariah softened her eyelids, steadied her breathing, hovered both her open hands an inch above Maurice's colorless face, and eased them down along the contours of his body, maintaining the distance, never touching the blanket. When she reached his feet, she turned her hands toward the window and gave a sudden, violent sweep against the vacant air as if belting a volleyball sideways. Then she shook both hands by her side, fingers to the ground, and moved back to his head.

"Lay your hands over the crown of his head, James, the heels of your palms touching each other and the tips of your fingers on his temples. Pray for him and pass the energy right into his head, and will it to flow through him while I keep soothing the lines of his life force."

Eli eased into a meditative relaxation and focused on a task he trusted without understanding.

In a voice which could have been humming a lullaby, Mariah murmured, "Maurice, listen to me. Listen even though you may feel like you're far, far away. You're going to be fine. You don't have to go away. You can live with us here. You've been away from people who love you long enough, now. You can stay, and get strong. There's love here. More than we can use ourselves."

Mariah and James alternated roles for an hour. "We'll be back," Mariah said to Beckwith. "And others like us. Have a restful sleep, Maurice. Tell us your dreams, when you awaken, okay?"

"Would you teach the process to Kim?" Mariah asked Eli as they walked back to the Maxwell compound. "Without access to a hospital and little chance to restock medicine, we need to expand the number of us who can apply alternative medical techniques. Darcy's already adept, and she can teach Jason and Catherine. It'll be good to balance male and female energy, and I know Jason wants to help. He feels awful."

Eli's mind swam. The healing session had both exhausted and energized him. Now the prospect of sharing such intimacy with Kim Royer animated him. He was sure Mariah could read his reaction and strove to be casual. "I'll do my best."

CHAPTER 77
Wednesday, March 8

THE NEXT DAY the Maxwell Acres community logged two more visitors. Kim sounded the alarm with a triple burst on the Royer cabin's dinner triangle when a covered military vehicle, the equivalent of a civilian two-and-a-half ton pickup, chugged up the road. Two men emerged with their hands high when Ray met them with his shotgun. Eli waited inside the cabin door with a pistol, and Darcy with her martial arts weapons. Rose stayed with Beckwith, still sleeping in the bedroom.

Jason inspected the truck, loaded with weapons and supplies, while Ray and Charles questioned the two men. "We come in peace" said a lean bearded man in tattered clothes and a baseball cap. His partner, a tall, deep-chested Asian, wore U.S. Marine fatigues.

"We seek refuge," said the bearded one. "My name's Jacob Manikksen. My friend Nelson has defected from the Marines. I walked half-way up here from Berkeley after the apocalypse and he gave me a lift from down around Shingle-town. The lady down at Elmo's General Store told us you were here. We'd like to join you. But we're not freeloaders. Nelson has provisions and weapons in the back of the truck. And I have great technical skills." The two strangers stood below the porch. Eli and Darcy did not relax. Charles told the visitors to unload the truck onto a wooden platform beside the porch so he and Ray could evaluate the trade-off: refuge for goods.

The visitors explained that they trusted the store lady's advice that the people here were honest and fair. Besides, they admitted, they had little to lose. On the open road they each faced overwhelming odds against preserving their very existence let alone their supplies: the hostility they had observed in the countryside, Nelson's uniform identifying him as a defector, their exhaustion, unfamiliarity with the territory—all compounded to a likely death warrant.

Charles invited the two men to talk during lunch. The full community would come to a final decision afterwards.

Kim moved back out of sight with Rose and Maurice Beckwith. Mariah and Paisley had the children at the main house. The "interview committee"— Charles, Ray, Darcy and Eli—played it close to the vest. If the visitors had to leave, the less information they took with them the better.

Charles asked the two men to give an account of themselves. "Just one thing. You'd best be brutally honest. The most important thing we have here is trust in each other. If you lie about something, it's bound to catch up with you one way or another. Someone here'll figure it out and you'll be out of here faster than a rabbit escaping a foxhole."

Eli felt the unintended rebuke and set his lips in a tight line. Nelson Ichimura began.

His father, a Japanese immigrant, had died in 1984, when Nelson was four. His mother was from India and thirty-five years younger than her husband. She couldn't handle her unruly son, and used part of the insurance settlement to board him with a strict Catholic couple in Paramus, New Jersey. He went to a Catholic high school there that provided a sense of discipline, but he made few friends. At a summer camp he began studying martial arts, and even did a "fire walk."

"Think you could teach us?" Eli asked.

The young Marine didn't flinch. "It's been a long time, but... Yes. I think so."

"Go on," Charles said.

"I joined the Marines after graduation, and eventually I wound up in a small auxiliary unit at Travis Air Force Base."

Charles smiled. "I spent a lot of time there myself."

"We Marines were assigned to help protect the base. We were told civilians might mob it. We had trained for protesters, right-wing fanatics and terrorists. But general civilians? When they issued us live ammunition, I began to realize this was for real. And everyone's talk got so tough. It was worse than when we invaded Iraq. Most of the Marines were itching for 'action.'

"It was strange, but a couple of days before the tsunami, we were told, informally I think—maybe it was just rumors—that there were going to be major movements of troops and materiel to what was referred to as 'inland.' So when we got the orders that Travis was being closed, it wasn't exactly a surprise, but the reality still was beyond my imagination. We heard on the radio that the government had moved to Texas, that prisons were totally locked down, stuff like that."

Eli's imagination winced.

"A few elite military units were going to be left behind with major firepower to protect places like the Livermore Lab and the nukes at Diablo Canyon. Everyone else was being airlifted to other bases in the interior, with as much equipment, weapons and supplies as they could move. Then the rear guard ordinance teams were simply going to blow up everything else. Keep it out of the hands of anyone who could do mischief with it.

Charles shook his head in disbelief. "That's worse than I thought. Unbelievable."

"Three days ago I was assigned to a small unit: two five-ton weapons carriers and the two-and-a-half ton FMTV that's outside. We were ordered to load supplies and weapons for transport. We were loaded by late afternoon yesterday. A young Private First Class was assigned to me for protection. He was armed with a fully automatic M-16 A-2 and plenty of grenades. Each weapons carrier had a guard of six heavily armed Marines. The Sergeant in charge opened the travel papers—we were to deliver our materiel to the Sierra Army Depot in the mountains east of Susanville.

"The main highways were jammed solid with cars, so the officer in charge decided we should use the smaller roads. We stopped at a mall south of Chico. It was quiet when we drove in, but in three minutes about two hundred people from the neighborhood crowded around our little convoy. They were mostly Hispanics, blacks, some Asians. A lot of women. They were a little noisy, but not too unruly.

"Suddenly, someone in the crowd fired a gun. Or set off firecrackers. The boys who were guarding the weapons carriers panicked. They leaped out, deployed around their vehicles, and began firing their automatic weapons right into the crowd. People were going down. The people in back ran for their lives. Then it was all quiet, except for the screaming of the wounded people. Then the Marines went out into the parking lot and begin shooting the wounded people with their sidearms."

Nelson choked back emotion. "I can't even talk about it." He sipped some coffee.

"I had a flashback to something one of the older men at yoga camp gave me to read. He had photocopied the last chapter of a book called *People Of The Lie*. It was about the time in the Vietnam War when American GIs massacred women and children in a little village there. I was always impressed, even after I joined the Marines, by the officer who had radioed the report to the higher ups and then landed his helicopter to stop the massacre.

"I just started my engine and sped the hell out of there. I think someone shot after me, but I kept going. I radioed my commanding officer at Travis, like the guy did in Vietnam. I was surprised, although I don't know why, when he said pretty much what they told the helicopter pilot back then . He said, 'Look, kid, this is war. This is nothin' new. Fightin' men've been doing that shit for five thousand years.' I said, 'Roger.' Then I knew I was AWOL. I couldn't go back.

"I took the smallest roads I could find. I got lost, driving in circles. Twice I did risk stopping to siphon gas out of cars. When I stopped, I vomited from thinking about the parking lot. Finally, sunrise was coming. I was too tired to go on.

"I saw a little hollow between a railroad embankment and an irrigation canal. The hollow was filled with bushes and trees that would hide my truck. I parked and lay down on the seat for a nap. When I woke up it was about noon. I walked over by the railroad to... well, to go behind a bush. I was about to go back to my truck when I looked in the storm culvert under the embankment and saw Jacob there, just sitting, staring at me.

"We talked for an hour or so, looked at our maps, kicked around possibilities. He finally convinced me that where he was going in northwestern Nevada was probably the most remote place in America and I should take him there. We could work together to grow food and survive. So we drove north on the smallest back roads we could find. The further we got from I-5, the more normal the countryside seemed to be.

"About thirty miles west of Flat River, things seemed normal enough to stop at a store. Jacob went in. We thought his outfit would be less threatening than mine. Somehow he got the old lady talking and she told him about your place. She even knew where it was on the map. That's how we got here."

"That must have been Mrs. Whiting at Elmo's down at the Adin crossroads," said Ray.

"Thank you, Nelson," Charles said. "You've certainly been through some harrowing events. Anyone want to ask Nelson any questions?"

There were no takers. Charles said, "What about you, Jacob?"

Jacob Manikksen looked at each face. "This is going to be hard. Just hang with me if I need a break, okay? I'm at the end of my rope. In one week I lost everything in my life that was valuable to me, except what's in my head. If I can stay in my head, I'll be okay.

"My aunt was a nurse at the Berkeley Free Clinic. She practically raised me there, off and on. I mean, a lot of the time I stayed with other aunts, uncles, grandparents, you know, anyone in the family who would take a bad boy for a while. I don't even remember my parents. They died when I was little, in a rafting accident.

"I'm an inventor. An environmental radical, too, I guess. I protested the WTO for years. I got my undergrad degree at Berkeley, in math and physics. Then I got a job in China for a big consortium doing science there. After that, I came back to Berkeley, bought a dilapidated property, fixed it up, rented out rooms.

"I lived in a little shack at the back of the lot. Originally it must have been a greenhouse nursery. I insulated it so I wouldn't freeze. For heat I put passive thermal on the roof. It was like a studio apartment. I walled off one corner as a walk-in closet.

"I spent my time inventing stuff that was good for the environment. You know, windmills, bicycles. Stuff like that. Then four years ago I met Alanna Horowitz. Her mother was Irish, her father was Jewish. The opposite of me."

Jacob stared silent for a while, and bit his lip. "Alanna. You should see her. Flowing red hair. Peaches-and-rosebuds complexion, with a few Irish freckles. Took after her mother. She was tall as me, almost as strong. She could never decide what she wanted to 'do with her life.' So she bounced from cause to cause, like me. Plenty of commitment, nothing good enough to stick it to.

"I met Alanna at a place near here, called 'Burning Man.' It's not really a place, but a gathering. Sort of a convention of geeks that happens every September out at Black Rock Desert. That's just on the other side of the Sierras.

"Together, we were a great pair. We got a commune going in Berkeley. Not a location commune, but a spirit commune. Everybody lived in their own places. We combined food, grew our own in backyard plots, cooked and ate in groups, worked together on common ideals and goals, played together, sang, read plays, wrote stuff. Not a religious cult, though. But a lot of us did meditate, and things like that.

"We took care of a lot of people who couldn't care for themselves. Lots of us had jobs. We pooled our money and did things that had a real impact on the world. Good things. I mean, things that directly affected people. We converted my main building into a volunteer auxiliary of the Berkeley Free Clinic. It was really great. We all loved each other. Really. We knew it, and we expressed it. And the people in the community we helped—they loved us too, and showed it.

"I've been following the melting ice caps since grade school twenty years ago. In January, when things got dicey and the government started suppressing news, I kept up with my shortwave and the HAM bands. I also tapped into special government channels and hacked into some their servers. I listened to police, firemen, the local military. I know encryption and broke what I could. I couldn't decode it all, but it was clear the government was simply lying to us ever since the earthquakes and volcanic activity started.

"On Monday last week, the encrypted channels reported massive eruptions along three or four hundred miles of fissures under the ice on the land near the old Ronne Ice Shelf."

"That much. My God!" It was Peter's voice.

"They said the Ice Sheet on the land around the Weddell Sea couldn't survive with that much heat underneath. The real prediction, which they kept secret, was that enough ice would melt to raise sea level three feet, possibly ten.

"They realized all the frantic building of sea coast barriers was hopeless. They began stockpiling everything they could think of in the middle of the country—Texas, Kansas, around bases from the Appalachians to the Sierras. They knew civil control, even under martial law, was tenuous.

"They began to disseminate contingency plans for evacuating key people—military, government and corporate—from the coasts to inland government centers. All the while, of course, telling the public things were under control, stay calm, stay where you belong, keep going to work, report to the sea barrier projects.

"I kept my friends informed. Everyone knew it meant disaster, but we tried to keep our commune together, Alanna and me, so we could help the victims of the government's abandonment. Some people we knew tried to get out of the area. But to a soul every member of our commune stayed.

"We all knew things could come completely unglued. After all, they almost did before martial law. We talked about what we would do—I mean as individuals, not as a commune, if that happened. One by one, we put together emergency escape packs.

"Actually, we were more worried about the military turning ultra-conservative and going after us radicals and protesters than we were about a general collapse. We knew they'd already killed protest leaders, even though they blamed gangs."

Darcy startled the riveted group, "Did you know them? Their names?"

"Nathan Cathcart was arrested at U.C. Never seen again. I heard his wife Miriam was shot in a drive-by and a third, older fellow—Elmer Walters or something like that—was killed by a swat team ten days ago and his house burned."

Eli watched Darcy's face lose all expression, but neither spoke. Their eyes met as Jacob forged ahead.

"On Wednesday, early afternoon—just a week ago today, though it seems like a year—I was tuned into the military channel. They said the West Antarctic Ice Sheet was suddenly collapsing all along the Weddell Sea. Hundreds of cubic miles of ice were crashing into the water. Cubic miles! Not feet or yards—miles! About half an hour after that report, new, worse reports came in from the military at McMurdo Sound. The problem wasn't limited to the Ice Sheet. Volcanic eruption had occurred in Mount Jackson itself on the Antarctic Peninsula and the mountain's entire seaward flank collapsed into the ocean.

"I knew gigantic tsunami would be propagating directly up the Atlantic. I just sat there dumbfounded. I knew then that the east coasts of both North and South America would be completely destroyed. And the west coasts of Africa and Europe. Tsunami would destroy New York, Boston, D.C., London, practically the whole British Isles, everything in their way. We would be safe in California, from the tsunami, I mean, but not the rise in sea level. But, sea level wouldn't rise instantly. I calculated that would take a week or two.

"There was no public announcement anywhere. Unbelievable. No public announcement anywhere in the world, as far as I could tell. The only warning would be from people like me, with short wave radios. I figured, who'd listen to me? I only told my own people.

"The government, of course, over encrypted channels, was already coordinating a pre-tsunami evacuation to Texas from the whole East Coast. Following their contingency plan. They had GPS sensors on Mt. Jackson that had been warning for days of the flank collapse and tsunami."

"They also started ordering inconspicuous movements of some military personnel out of California. That, apparently, was according to a plan I hadn't heard yet, a higher level of classification than I could crack. Inconspicuous so as not to tip off the anesthetized masses, I presume.

"When the tsunami hit South America, word spread quickly. So government broadcasts finally had to report the destruction. But they also reported, unbelievably, that everything would be fine except the East Coast, that they had moved the government to Texas, that the construction operations on the West Coast would hold back the sea, and that everyone there should remain calm. At the same time they were secretly moving their people out of California!"

Heads wagged, foreheads wrinkled.

"I'm telling you the truth. That's what really happened. Among other things, when the tsunami hit Virginia, the Internet facility there called 'MAE East' went down. That's where half of all Internet transmissions from the whole world are routed. Major nodes in England and Europe, and Latin America, went down too. That's why the Internet collapsed Wednesday night. Some satellite links stayed up for a while. Local servers and lines hung on for a while longer. And of course short wave radio works as long as there's electricity. At least west of the Mississippi the electric power grid was still intact. So we still had power in Berkeley.

"Thursday in Berkeley things were unbelievably calm. Most everyone was either shell shocked or overflowing with compassion. And the rest, those tempted to act out of reason—the main military enforcers were still in place enforcing martial law, holding them back. Even though the government was already moving high-level people out, the rank and file were still in place, doing what the President ordered. Some people even went to work at the sea projects on Thursday. And of course, government broadcasts kept saying, 'stay calm.' It's very hard for most people to fundamentally disbelieve what their government tells them.

"It only takes eight hours for a tsunami to travel from Antarctica to North America. But because of the physics of fluid dynamics it takes forty hours for sea level to rise in North America after it starts rising in Antarctica. So all day Thursday, even though the Mt. Jackson 'echo tsunami' kept sweeping up the Atlantic, the Bay Area stayed physically unaffected all day. On the East Coast, it was another story. As block after block of the West Antarctic Ice Sheet, lubricated by volcanic heat and agitated by earthquakes, crashed into the Weddell Sea, their tsunami added to the Mt. Jackson waves. Together they destroyed everything for miles inland. Millions died. They said half the population, clear to the Appalachian Mountains. Fifty-five million. Same thing on the East Coast of Latin America—Rio, Buenos Aires—the West Coasts of Africa and Europe. The great libraries, the museums, the cultures—the central core of Western civilization, its critical mass. All gone.

"By Friday, there was too much ice in the Weddell Sea for further tsunami from the Ice Sheet. Sea level was another matter. I heard satellite photos showed the Ice Sheet crumbling along a three hundred fifty-mile front. The ice was being pushed into the ocean at eight to ten miles an hour. They predicted the collapse line would probably advance as far as three miles inland, maybe even more. Based on their guesses of the amount of volcanic heat and earthquake agitation, this could all happen within four, maybe even three, days. The government was laying plans on the assumption of at least a three-foot rise in sea level in under a week."

Peter Addison took in Jacob's statistics with a hand on his head, as if he were holding a wound. He shook his head in dismay. "I should have been there. I should have..."

Jacob went on. "The government's 'worst-case' plan had been designing the pull-out from both the East Coast and the West Coast for two fucking weeks. That's how far ahead they'd figured it out. They'd identified areas inland with the highest concentrations of oil and natural gas wells, reserves, military bases, refineries, power plants, industrial base, centralized infrastructure, stored farm surplus, high-yield farms—areas where they also thought long-term civil order could be imposed and maintained by force, and which could be defended from outside chaos. They identified corridors between some of these areas, and into other areas, like mines, where the military was to preserve highway and rail transportation, power lines, gas lines.

"By sometime Friday night, I heard, they had decided to fully abandon most of the West Coast, from California's central valley all the way north to Canada, and all the way from the sea to the Sierras. The rationale was simple.

"Fifty-five million people had died on the East Coast. There were another forty million in West Coast areas which were marked for abandonment. They said the rise in sea level would destroy the California Aqueduct, which would destroy all farming in the Central Valley. Without that food production, you couldn't feed those forty million people along with those in the center of the country. Nor did the military have enough soldiers or guns to maintain order west of the Sierras. They could, however, defend the mountain passes from anticipated warlord phenomena they expected to arise from the chaos. And from migrating survivors. So the plan was simply to abandon the area. Cut power, let the people die of thirst, starvation, or panic or disease or something, I guess, or survive as best they could."

In the cabin the mood was stunned numbness, jaws and lips grim and frozen.

"Alanna and I were resolved to ride it out, to follow our ideals, to be of service.

"By Saturday afternoon, reality was beginning to set in throughout the population. Big-time. People began to realize the awful truth of the news stories that had set off the famous Valentine's Eve Panic and crescendoed with the announcement of martial law in less than a week—the stories and theories that had been ridiculed by the President and his people. Panic was starting again, but now there were soldiers and police forces armed to the teeth everywhere, ready to shoot.

"But it was coming unraveled. There are an amazing number of military bases and stations around California. Anyone around any of those facilities saw the government pullout happening before their eyes. Since before sunrise on Saturday. There were helicopters everywhere. There were military truck convoys leaving every facility, all heading east. Wherever there were runways, cargo planes and aircraft of all descriptions were taking off in a steady stream. All towards the east. The message was unmistakable."

Charles nodded corroboration.

"When orders came through to a rear guard unit and they pulled out, panic and violence broke out immediately. Even early on Saturday morning, when some units failed to show, disorder developed within hours. Amazingly, local police still made a valiant effort at maintaining order. At least in any little pocket where they weren't overwhelmed. The pockets got fewer and fewer.

"Our clinic was swamped. Fires were breaking out. Drug gangs and organized crime were fighting for territory. Ordinary people who had guns were trying to stockpile food, water, medicine, whatever they could get. People along the shorelines were trying to take over homes higher up where they thought they would be safe from rising sea level and the storms and tides.

"People were dying. We were bandaging people with strips of sheets, and finally strips of dead people's clothing. Whatever we could get.

"Between stints at the clinic, I went back to my little shack and stayed glued to the short wave and police bands. By 2:30 that afternoon, they were reporting sea level had risen half a foot. And a big storm was coming Sunday. I changed my tennis shoes for my waterproofed backpacking boots.

"By 4:00 a.m.—it was Sunday morning now—I had passed the point of exhaustion, rebounded, and reached a new point of final exhaustion. Alanna and two friends had just gone on foot to the University first aid center to beg for morphine for our clients. I tried to re-energize myself by meditating, but you can't meditate when you're that tired. I just passed out on the yoga pad in my little walk-in closet.

"Next thing I knew it was mid-morning. I heard someone bump the door to my shack. I opened the door and there was Alanna, collapsed on the front step. I laid her on our bed. Her white clinic uniform was covered with blood from her chest down. She was dead." Jacob's voice shuddered and tears dripped from his eyes.

"I don't know how I kept going after that. I took all the dry wood stacked in the corner by the stove, and newspapers and fire starters, and I built a campfire-style pyramid in each corner of the room, one in the closet, and one by the front door. It was a sacred act. Our place would be her funeral pyre.

Jacob's head bobbed and a tear plopped in his lap. Darcy crossed to him and stroked his back. After a minute he took several long breaths. "I let go everything I was living for. It all went. I'm still letting go."

After a minute, he resumed. "Outside, there was chaos and violence everywhere. The air was heavy with smoke. As I walked toward the hills, every block had at least one building burning. It was worse in commercial areas. There was a lot of looting. You could hear gunfire here and there.

"Injured people called out to me. Other than that, no one noticed me. Or bothered me. I think partly because I'm not so tall, and I'm thin. But people have never noticed me. I became proud of that years ago. I read how primitive people moved and walked without drawing attention. I practiced. When I bought the rain gear at the flea market four weeks ago, I picked it for its non-descript greenish color."

Jacob described how he had hiked through the storm, slept in stables hidden by the hay, avoided checkpoints, authorities and marauders day and night. He had stowed away for much of the journey in a military equipment convoy until his path chanced to intersect with Nelson's. "So then we finally met the woman in the store, like Nelson told you."

"I'm sure that was Mrs. Whiting," said Darcy. "My mother met her and they became friends immediately."

"Yes. That was her name. There were no lights on in her store. She said the power had gone out a couple of hours earlier. I knew it was the government abandoning California. I didn't say anything about it, but I asked what she was going to do. She said she had a son who lived nearby. Susanville, I think. He wasn't a 'nice boy' like me, she said, but she'd probably have to make do and live with him.

"Then she told me about Maxwell Acres. She said she met the woman who had just moved into it. She knew there were a few other people up there, and they were good people. She said, 'You can't find better in this dangerous time, Jacob. You need people like that, and they need you.' She said, 'I'm warning you, Jacob, don't leave this area without going there. I'm sure it's the right thing to do.'"

Nelson and Jacob were unanimously accepted into the Maxwell Acres community. With the new arrivals soundly napping in the barn, the rest of the community made short work of distributing their cargo to storage locations around the property. Ray seized the moment, recognizing the opportunity that Nelson's truck represented. A work party caravanned to the Overcroft farm to salvage the remainder of the greenhouse. Many hands made light work and all essential elements of Paisley's system were in the truck and pickup in under an hour. They gathered up the remaining goats and chickens, and arrived back at the homestead in time for the evening meal.

CHAPTER 78

Thursday, March 9

ELI AND JASON helped Ray lay irrigation lines in the soggy upper garden.

Mid-afternoon, Mariah called out as she approached the sweaty crew. She was carrying Finn on her hip, while Tierney followed, studiously bearing a tray chest high, laden with a pitcher of water and three rattling glasses.

"Cutest Gunga Din I ever saw," Eli quipped. The three men were grateful for the refreshment, the attention and the distraction. The air was still, strangely sultry, after a brisk wind earlier in the afternoon.

Darcy appeared, striding around the corner of the barn. She was returning from the Royer cabin after her stint on the healing touch relay. "Good news," she hailed, "Mr. Beckwith is sitting up. He's taking nourishment, as Rose puts it."

"How wonderful," said Mariah. The men voiced their pleasure.

"Charles is just amazed. He said the recovery is miraculous. He was near death a couple of days ago, and now he can talk about it. Charles asked what magic we did to him."

"We'll keep doing it," Mariah whispered loudly with a smile. Eli winked at her.

Jason stepped forward. "Can he have visitors, I wonder? I'd like to talk to him."

"I suppose that would be all right," said Darcy. "Charles was eager to talk to him too, but decided he'd better wait until Mr. Beckwith gets more strength. Why don't you go down and ask?"

Jason handed his shovel to Eli and strode toward the compound. When he disappeared around the barn, Eli searched the sky. An eerie warm stillness hung in the air, like the expectant hush when theater lights dim.

A distant reverberation broke the spell. Their heads swiveled in unison toward the west, as the sound grew like an oncoming locomotive. Eli tentatively stepped toward the sound, now growing to a roar from up the valley. He raced, Jason's shovel still in his hand, toward the ravine that bordered the west edge of the property, the others following.

They halted at a rise above the gully, transfixed by the sight of a seven-foot high wall of mud-thickened water and ice crashing down the arroyo that formed the boundary of the homestead, logs and bushes pitching like toothpicks in its frothing head. *Flash flood!*

The group began to march downstream as if sucked along by a shock-line wake trailing from the gushing, tumbling torrent, all staring dumbly at the spectacle. Eli felt foolish holding the shovel, as if he could somehow use it to confront a sudden release of tons of water from an ice jam upstream.

The boiling head of the floodwaters dashed beyond the area of the Royer cabin, from which Peter, Charles, Kim and Catherine ran to join them. Moments later a thunderous crash reverberated above the roar of the rushing water as the flood's debris collided with the bridge. Simultaneously they saw half of the ancient oak collapse into the chaos when a heaving log rammed into the crux of its streamside root system and dragged it in with its inexorable momentum.

They hurried down the road toward the fallen oak. A small lake formed in minutes as logs and bushes and rubble jammed against the bridge. The road on either side of the bridge eroded in the muddy overflow, then gave way. The bridge clutched at its moorings for tormented seconds defying the water's weight and energy, then tumbled into the stream. It rolled over, pushed by the torrent, then fragmented into five chunks of useless concrete and torn aluminum. The lake drained and the flood moved on to the South Warner plain below.

Trotting from the barn, Jacob and Nelson straggled down the road to where the community was gathered, watching the spectacle. The assembled throng wagged their heads in respectful awe. No one spoke. They stared at the roiling brown stream, now receding.

Eli looked back over his shoulder. Ray Overcroft stood between Kim and Mariah, his arms around their shoulders as if comforting them. Kim bent to pick up a stick at her feet, and moved closer to the gully, next to Eli. He noticed Ray's hand slide down Mariah's back to her waist. Paisley stood glumly at a distance, staring at the ground, her lips forming a tight line. Mariah turned deliberately and took Paisley's arm as the group trudged back to the cabin.

Peter's explanation of the dynamics of flash floods highlighted the discussion. It gave them all time to assess their feelings and reflections. "Hmm. Well, we're really isolated now," said Charles, bringing people's practical thoughts to the surface. "It won't be easy to get out of here at all."

"Maybe that's not such a bad thing," suggested Jacob Manikksen. "It means it's harder for others to get in. Nelson and I can assure you it's pretty bad 'out there.'"

"Amen to that," offered Ray.

"Will we be able to get into town to replenish our supplies?" asked Rose.

"My FMTV up there's pretty rugged," said Nelson Ichimura. "I'm sure it'll get across the arroyo, no problem, once it's dry again."

"Or we can cut a crossing," said Jacob. "We don't necessarily need a bridge."

Charles capped the discussion. "Fortunately we're not desperate for anything right away. We have time to work it out."

Catherine and Kim stayed for an evening meal at the cabin. The others returned to the Maxwell compound for rest or meal preparation. Mariah nudged Eli and motioned toward Ray and Paisley, walking ahead in the dusk.

"The flood may be over, but there's still turbulence."

REINHOLD WAS on the front shift, up since 5:00 a.m., working the rigging and bumpers as the towboat backed off the headway to stop well short of the lock. They had to split the fleet to squeeze through the Smithland Lock just upriver from Paducah, Kentucky. It was one of four locks to be made today. Their military cargo gave them priority in the queues, so they should reach Cairo by tomorrow night and the Mississippi ahead of schedule.

"Hey, Mister."

Reinhold's head snapped up at the desperate half-whisper from the shadow between two packing crates. He tightened his grip on the cheater bar he carried for leverage on the ratchet winches. He peered into the dark. "Who the hell are you?"

"Look. I need a place to hide. Help me? Please."

"Come out where I can see you." A boy in jeans and a mottled maroon sweatshirt moved to the corner of a packing crate. "How old are you?" asked Reinhold.

"Twenty-one. I'm a long haul driver, but the Army took my truck. I've a wife and baby in New Orleans. I got to get back. This is my only way. Please, don't turn me in, Mister."

"How long have you been there?"

"Paddled over from the willows when you slowed down. Climbed up between two barges."

"You could have been killed."

"It don't matter. I'm trying to get home. Don't give a shit. I got to try."

Reinhold's eyes flicked to the Marine watching from the wheelhouse deck. He was not likely to think Reinhold was talking to a crate, and Reinhold couldn't risk his ticket for this kid. In an instant, self preservation overcame compassion. He backed away, shouting, "Stowaway. Stowaway. Get me some help."

"Fuck you, you sonnovabitch!" The boy vanished.

Two Marines ran to Reinhold, weapons poised. Reinhold motioned where the boy had disappeared. The soldiers were stymied. He could have turned in either direction and could zigzag between crates for hours.

They deployed to the inner corners of the barge—yelled for two deckmen to cover the outer corners so the intruder would at least be trapped on this barge. Then all hands could be assembled, once the fleet was anchored, for a crate-to-crate search to flush him into the open.

The Corporal was instructing the crew for the search when the pilot's voice blared through the power megaphone. "Fire. Fire." Smoke was rising from one of the packing crates. The pilot set off the alarm, which in ordinary times would bring the Lock and Dam fireboat.

The crew abandoned the Marines and scrambled for deck hoses which doubled as fire equipment. The Captain ordered them to stop. "Is there ammunition in these crates? Explosives?"

The Corporal said, "It's all equipment. There may be fuel in some, but no ordinance."

The Captain shouted, "Then get that fire out, Boys."

From the wheelhouse, the pilot's megaphone cracked again, "Another fire on Barge Five." A second cloud of smoke billowed up.

One Marine and three crewmen ran the catwalks to the stern.

Again the megaphone blared, "The fucker's overboard, swimming for shore."

A hail of bullets turned the river into a forest of water spouts. A Marine shouted, "I got him." A red slick began spreading on the water, swirling with the current toward the maw of the lock.

Reinhold vomited over the outside rail of the shoreward catwalk. Then he ran to help the nearest group put out the fire on his barge.

In the lounge, after the men had cleaned off the grime of firefighting, comments were cryptic and curt. The Corporal had debriefed each man behind the closed door of the computer room. Reinhold had been the last—forty minutes to the others' ten. Exiting the room, Reinhold stared at his interrogator with smoldering rage, and the Corporal returned the stare with equally intense suspicion.

"Captain Gunderson," the Corporal snapped. "I need to see you and Ivan. Alone. Now, everybody back to your duties." The crew stood still.

"Go ahead, men. It's okay," The Captain said.

The three went into the computer room.

"Captain, this man's a brand-new deckman, and now I find he speaks fluent Russian. What's going on here? You transporting Commies?"

"So what if he speaks Russian? Who knew? I sure as hell didn't."

Reinhold maintained a stony silence. *Stay cool. They've got nothing.*

A minute passed. Two. "I'll believe Ivan," the Captain broke the standoff. "For now. My first mate hired him and Adam's savvy, knows what he's doing.

I'm the Captain of this vessel and your only jurisdiction's the cargo. Now, we need to get it through the lock and keep pressing for Little Rock."

The Corporal whirled and stalked out.

CHAPTER 79
Friday, March 10

NOT A TREE REMAINS unsnapped or vertical anywhere in the Everglades. The tallest wave had rolled from Atlantic to Gulf Coast, crushing everything under a billion tons of water. The other waves had little to finish. Today, on a horizontal trunk, her nest precisely engineered against a vertical branch, a robin red breast lays her third turquoise egg.

IN THE MAXWELL ACRES COMPOUND they had decided group breakfasts would conserve fuel and food, and also get everyone going at the same time on the projects. There were no lists or rigorous schedules, and exceptions to the pattern were the rule, along with pandemic depression and head colds precipitated by the overload of horrifying events and personal losses. Paisley was missing from breakfast.

When kitchen duties were completed Eli picked up the covered pail of vegetable scraps to carry out to the compost bin behind the barn. Others headed off to their tasks, mostly to the garden. Eli set down the pail and was about to lift the lid of the bin when he saw Ray Overcroft striding with his gaze intent on the ground before him, a shovel slung over his shoulder, and Mariah alongside him. Their direction would take them to the wooded creek on the east side of the property, which Ray had planned to investigate for the purpose of diversion for irrigation. Mariah seemed to be studying Ray, but talking in the easy way women have. Her task was a social one, Eli decided, but he did not imagine that she was encouraging his forwardness at the flash flood scene. No, she had gone immediately to Paisley, as if to comfort her.

When Eli returned after a morning's labor to the house for lunch, he realized soon enough the effect of Mariah's confrontation. Ray was never subtle. At lunch, it was obvious he wanted to stay back that afternoon with Paisley. Ray must have been involved in two powerful conversations that day. At dusk, he and Paisley came from their house for supper holding hands, and she had a glow about her like a solstice sunset.

CHAPTER 80
Saturday, March 11

THE GARDENS in the meadows above the barn were beginning to take shape, and Eli felt a sense of pride or fulfillment in his regular schedule of labor—as a monk might do, he reflected. He was developing particular camaraderie with Jason, Nelson, Jacob and Ray, the men who were counted on for the heavy work.

Charles and Peter had decided to upgrade the rough trail between the Royer cabin and the Maxwell Acres buildings from its historical status as little more than a cow path. They commandeered the cabin's wheelbarrow to transport gravel Peter had located near the creek and were into their second day of the effort. Curiously, Peter managed to work wearing his shoulder holster carrying Celia's pistol. He had voiced his distress at the discontinuation of the night-time armed watch, and maintained this overt symbol of his dissent.

Mariah called it to Eli's attention, looking out the kitchen window after lunch. "Peter wishes he had stayed longer in Davis. He told me he's sure he would have been invited to join one of the scientific teams advising the government. What he really wants is to go to Antarctica. But that attack left a scar."

Peter and Charles leaned on their tools, apparently waiting for some burst of inspiration to energize them, and welcomed the appearance at their work site of Darcy and Finn. Eli felt a wave of compassion for the two men of science reduced to menial laborers, united in their love for a noble woman.

"It's a big loss to grieve," said Eli. "I'm sure it's like burying his wife again, and all the good times they had in their place."

"That's what Darcy's talking to them about, I'm sure. She told me an hour ago about an idea she had for a grieving ceremony, like one she experienced on a high school retreat. She said we all need to deal with our tremendous losses. And I agree. She's asking everyone how they'd feel about it."

"It's fine with me. I've had some retreat experience too, and I know how rituals can have a powerful effect." Eli spoke with earnest conviction, and let Mariah assume that his retreat experience was in the monastery. He was on his fourth life now. His second life began with Daddy Sisson and the fellowship of AA. The third began with the Retreat movement in San Quentin, and the deepening of his spirit. The fourth, ironically, was initiated by Dupree Ransom.

"I know I have very little to grieve, next to all of you folks," Eli said. "I admire how strong you have been, Mariah. I don't know what you said to Ray yesterday, but it made a big difference in him."

"We talked about forgiveness, how it's a rush when you truly forgive someone, and it fills you with love."

"That's true," said Eli. "That's a fact."

"I'm trying to be strong, James. But—" She sighed. "The Overcroft farm, invisible people looting and killing or turning into vigilantes armed like commandos. And here we sit, no connections to the outside world, our road cut by the flood, people getting sick, getting angry, bursting into tears, falling back into depression. Peter says sea level's up three feet. The world we knew is gone, all gone but these mountains. I'm trying to be strong, but sometimes it gets to me."

"I can't explain why, but—well, I'm not as discouraged as all of you might be. I can take most of this in stride, you see. And if you can't be strong all the time, maybe I can have a turn at it."

She smiled up at him, blinking with moist eyes. He wanted to hold her, comfort her. "What about your husband? You're being strong for him too, aren't you?"

"James, Elmer's dead." Her conviction was undeniable.

"How can you be sure?"

"A few days ago Jacob spoke of a protester in Berkeley who was killed, but he got the name wrong. He said Elmer Walters, but it was Wallace. Even before he said it, I knew. I told you I had a dream about Elmer... It was a powerful dream, the night he died—it's as if I was there with him."

"Mariah, I'm sorry." He reached toward her, and she stepped into his embrace. "He must have been a great man, to have the love of someone like you." Eli felt her head nodding against his shoulder.

"We all have our faults," she said softly, stepping back from Eli. "He did too. When our children were small—" She faltered. "Darcy had a little brother, who died when he was two. Elmer was supposed to be watching him, but left him with a man who was working on our house. The house burned down while Elmer was at a tavern."

"Oh, Mariah..."

"It nearly tore us all apart. I checked out for a couple of years, Elmer continued drinking for a while, and Darcy raised herself through high school. We all carried the scars of that, but time and a lot of effort and suffering have done good work with us. Elmer recovered through AA. I can say that now that he's

331

gone. After his disease and healing, Elmer devoted his life to others. He stood tall long after he was expected to die—until he did die."

"Does Darcy know?"

"Yes, she knows now. We had a good cry about it this morning. That's one of the reasons she's planning this ritual."

Peter and Charles had resumed their work. Darcy had moved on.

CHAPTER 81
Sunday, March 12

THE SUN DROPPED behind the western hill, initiating the final hour before sunset, to be followed by the gradual descent of day into darkness.

The previous afternoon, Darcy's conviction about the ritual's promise had built momentum as each individual agreed in turn to attend. The idea took hold, chatter dwindled, people turned inward, pensive, focusing on the profound feelings surging, often unacknowledged, through their blood.

In a nearly circular clearing in the woods not far from the eastern creek where Ray and Mariah had walked, Jason and Nelson laid the fire—a short, log cabin-style stack of firewood within a circle of small stones, with tinder and kindling in the center.

The clearing was peppered with boulders and held the unrotted cores of two ancient pine stumps. The absence of boulders in the central space made Eli wonder whether Native Americans might have held their own ceremonies here, before the White Man came. The place felt eerily sacred.

The shadow of the hill eclipsed the warmth of the sun, and dusk deepened into the velvet prelude of night. They donned their coats and eased toward the fire circle in ones and twos, overcoming an inescapable reticence to exposing their raw nerves from the recent tragedies to the scrutiny of the group. Eli supported Beckwith with a crooked elbow. Kim carried the wide-eyed Finn, who was fascinated by the rare, evening outing. Jason and Catherine came arm in arm, as did Paisley and her Ray.

Nelson set a match to the tinder. The blaze leapt skyward in seconds, illuminating faces. Darcy toned a somber but elevating invocation, ad lib. The crackle of the flames and the call of a loon gliding south to Blue Lake wrinkled the silence.

Peter stood, laden with emotion. "I've listed the things I've lost: my home, my profession, my library." He cast a wadded paper into the circle of rock and flame.

Everyone stood in respect and support. Separated by compassionate intervals of personal space and introspection, a litany of loss rose into the silent sky along with the smoke of the missives offered to the healing conflagration.

Eli read his short scribbled list to himself: Sharon, the Abbey of Our Lady of Peace, Los Molinos. He felt obliged to participate, again to maintain his current identity, and he wanted to advance the healing of his family, as he thought of this assemblage. He spoke only the last two items, and then listened to the others.

Old friends. Reunions. Home, Career.

My photos, gifts, souvenirs from Italy. Clothing, art. My orchids.

Leaders, bookstores, magazines. Seminars, lectures, travel.

My husband, My friend, My love, My secret.

My toys, The park, Goldfish Fred.

Winifred, the pub, all those children.

All the grandmothers and grandfathers.

The voices trailed off into mumbles and sighs. The paper casting ended. The fire died to embers. Some left, some stayed, arms on shoulders or hands in hands, staring upward into the star-speckled runways of Orion, Castor and Pollux, with their mythical Dogs in pursuit of the Stag.

CHAPTER 82
Monday, March 13

"I HAVE A FEW ANNOUNCEMENTS, men." Adam was addressing the assembled crew, the Corporal in attendance.

"We made it to Roseville in near record time, thanks to our federal friends. We're passing the lead coal hoppers off here for another towboat to take on down to Natchez—adding three more military loads to Little Rock. And three more Marines with 'em."

The crewmen stared at the floor.

"We'll overnight here so we can set the tow in daylight. It's traditional on my towboat to draw lots for shore privileges when we've got the chance."

The crew stirred.

"Especially here in Roseville." The men couldn't repress smiles and knowing looks. "I hear our new Marines've already made their mark with the ladies in town, waiting for us to get here. Probably wish we'd snagged on a sandbar for a day or two." He paused for chuckles. "I put ten checkers in the hat. The lucky six who pick the red ones get to go to town with the Corporal."

He passed the hat, conspicuously omitting Reinhold. Deckman Taylor passed. "I'll just rest up, thanks." He was a good Mormon. Everyone knew it.

In his eight days on board, Lobo Taylor had become Reinhold's best friend. After Reinhold had saved him from losing his left hand in a sudden barge buckle, he had shared his plan to quit in Little Rock and head for Salt Lake where his parents lived.

Adam motioned Reinhold to his office. "Reiney, I kept you here partly 'cause the guards demanded you stay, but mostly 'cause I've got a great plan. I asked Lobo to stay, too. I know he's trying to get west. Well, I learned some stuff from the Corporal. Most of the big crates, they're trucking 'em from Little Rock to Los Alamos, New Mexico. We're only a day from Little Rock, and it'll only take three, maybe four from there. Now the Corporal and I noticed some siding screws loose on one of those crates. He checked his manifest—it's got a generator inside, bolted to the floor. I said a couple of guys would screw gun it tight tomorrow."

Reinhold leaned forward.

"So here's the idea. Tonight you and Taylor get in there with some provisions. Ten gallons of water—should last over a week—five pounds of trail mix, a dozen empty Tupperware containers for your piss and shit. A flashlight. You'll both leave notes that you jumped ship because you were so bullshit about no shore leave. Then tomorrow, the boys'll screw gun the siding good and tight, not even suspecting. I'll give you tools to break out when you think you're safe, some rope, blankets. It'll save you a thousand miles and a couple of months. What do you think?"

Reinhold rolled it around in his head. "It could work. Risky, but... Lobo and I already talked about traveling together. He's a smart little tiger. A little nutty, but very good with his hands..."

Adam added, "I'll sidetrack the night guard before people start coming back from town. Let's say, 11:30. You'll have to move fast."

"I'm on."

"You want to tell Lobo, or you want me to?"

"Let me."

Except for the full moon, the plan was unfolding without a hitch. Earlier, they had sneaked the provisions behind the packing crate with a dolly under the pretense of setting up gear for making the new tows tomorrow. The loose siding was up-barge, out of view of the wheelhouse. Reinhold was inside, Lobo affixing a cleat on the inside of the siding so they could secure it from within until the crew screwed it from the outside.

Suddenly, emergency lights flooded the night. An alarm shrieked and the loudspeaker screamed, "Intruder. We've got an intruder. Barge Seven."

They heard the Marine clanging down the stairs, his boots scraping on the catwalk.

Lobo groaned. "I can't set this cleat. No way to hold the siding in." When Reinhold started out to help, Lobo punched him in the chest, sent him reeling back inside against the generator. "I'll take the next train. You've got kids out there. I've only got my Old Man and my Mamma in Utah. I'll get there on my own. Good luck, Buddy." He slammed the siding against the crate.

Before he could regain his balance in the dark, Reinhold heard two screws whir into place under Lobo's screw gun. The footsteps were close outside. Reinhold heard a small splash.

More footsteps. "Stop or I'll shoot."

Reinhold heard the boots run by. Then a large splash.

It was like being blindfolded in a movie. He thought, *Lobo must've thrown the screw gun over, then dived in himself.*

A burst of gunfire. Reinhold winced. Two more volleys. Silence. Another volley. More footsteps running to the edge.

Reinhold heard Adam. "What the hell? What's happening?"

The Marine's voice: "Another intruder. Threw something overboard and then jumped. I'm not sure I got him."

The pilot's voice: "Current's strong here. We'll never know."

CHAPTER 83

Tuesday, March 14

SERENE CLOUDS cover the Antarctic Peninsula. Rare, not to be a maelstrom driven by the devil's own vortices off Tierra del Fuego. From a cave in the vertical, seaward wall of the Vinson Massif, two gulls witness a gentle snowfall blanketing the mountain ledges—and the naked ground below, freshly out from under eons of ice.

ALONE with her mother in the livingroom, Darcy said, "Mom. I'd really like you to take me deeper into it."

"Do you think you're ready, Sweetheart?"

"Desperate, I think."

"That's a bad sign. That's the ego. Everyday ESP usually comes when your personal survival's at stake. At least survival of your ego. When you can self-regulate your ego, you can control your extrasensory faculty. Your self-esteem no longer blocks it, and remote knowing, both through time and geography, no longer threatens you."

"Give me some help here, okay, Mom?"

"Well, I sense you want it so much right now so you can look in on Rein-hold. Right?"

Darcy nodded her head, concurring with a little laugh.

"We have the ESP ability, you see—everyone does—for the good of the community, not the individual. If you just want to look in on Reinhold to re-lieve a personal anxiety—it doesn't work. On the other hand, you and I got those dreams to help this group survive."

Darcy looked unconvinced.

"When you first learn to turn your ESP on, when you want, it's still hard to channel. You're likely to see almost anything, not just what you're trying to see. To be able to use it regularly, on demand so to speak, you have to be prepared not to freak out no matter what you see. That's self-regulation of your ego. It changes the use of the talent from personal profit, in the broad sense, to the benefit of the group."

Darcy unfolded her arms, put her feet on the floor. Mariah knew she'd gotten enough.

"Okay, Baby. Let's do it. Get into that meditation space." Darcy shut her eyes, steadied her breathing. Mariah stood up to give her time, opened the windows on either end of the guesthouse. A cool breeze flowed through.

"Now you're going to feel your insides tighten at some of this. Your gut or your heart, maybe your lungs, are going to go hot, maybe cold, angry, fearful, sad... you know, any of that. When you feel it... immediately feel your feet on the ground, get that massive, steadying energy of gravity, the whole planet coming right up into your body. The minute you feel the up-charge, go to the top of your head and feel for something coming in from above—a ray of light, an energy, a hot flash, whatever. When you feel that one, let it flow down and meet the earthy one—they meet in the middle of your body. Pretend, or feel, that a spark ignites the mixture—a little spark, and a little mini-explosion— blows your ego-feeling, the anger-fear-sadness, into an expanding sphere of gas like a balloon that will get bigger forever. You don't change, however—just let it go, and you go on to whatever's next."

Darcy spoke in a monotone, indicating her deepening altered state. "Okay... Got it."

Mariah continued, "Now look at the screen on your eyelids. You see Reinhold making love to a woman." She waited for Darcy's emotion to rise. Then, in a slow, statacco cadence, "Go... Feet... Top of your head... Spark it... Now... Let it go." She waited. Then, "Reinhold's telling her embarrassing things about you." Mariah waited again, repeated the cadence. Then, "You see your father, blindfolded, tied to a chair, and a bearded man in a uniform, sweat soaked in patches, a beret on sideways at a rakish angle, about to beat him with a rubber hose. There's nothing you can do about it." Mariah waited again, repeated the cadence. "Are you okay?"

"It's hard, but I'm staying with it."

"It's not about you, Darcy. Not about you, personally. These are not your battles. Cannot be. Go into your heart. There's a place in there that's you, the way you were as the smallest child you can remember, the way you feel yourself in the middle of a dream, even a nightmare. That person you knew was You after they put you under with ether, that time they operated on you in Goa. That You is always the same. It's unchanged by those nasty pictures I made up. Stay with that You."

Eli entered the living room quietly and saw Darcy meditating. Mariah put her fingers to her lips in a silencing gesture, and went on, "Are you in that place of the central You?"

"Yes, I'm there."

"What color do you see?"

"Green. It's a little plant."

"What does it look like?"

"It's got a beautiful little orange flower blossom. It's like the Indian Paintbrush we see in Flagstaff."

"Go into the blossom. What do you see?"

The room was silent for a minute. Eli sat on the hearth, curious and respectful. "Two people," said Darcy. "A man and a woman, about my age... They're both quite lovely looking. Behind them there's a string of children, seven of them in descending order of height. The couple's too young for these to be their children..."

"Now, gently, Darcy, breathe deeply three times. Count your breaths. When you let the third one out, gently open your eyes and come back into the room." She waited until Darcy was alert.

Darcy didn't seem surprised or disturbed that Eli had been witness to the exercise. Her face looked calm and radiant, her voice was steady and clear. "How do you take that, Mom? What I saw?"

"It's not for me to interpret, Sweetheart. You have to make of it what you will. It seemed a little symbolic—seven's a traditional mystic number—but don't pre-judge it. I wouldn't try to draw a circle of restriction around it right away, by defining or interpreting prematurely. I'll be interested in what you come up with."

Darcy's energy seemed to drop a bit. "My ego needs a lot more work."

"How do you mean?"

"When I was counting myself back, I took a peek around for Reinhold. It seemed like he was fine, but all I could see was black and there was a vibration going on, like a diesel generator or something. I guess I wasn't really supposed to see."

Mariah chuckled. "The universe is full of cosmic humor, isn't it?"

"What are you doing?" Eli asked.

Mariah's eyes twinkled. "We were just practicing ESP. Taking a little break from the work. Would you like to try some?"

Eli grinned, embarrassed, wanting to take her seriously but a bit off-balance. He smiled, with a dawning sense of understanding what he had just seen.

CHAPTER 84
Wednesday, March 15

BY THE IDES OF MARCH, talk was widespread of Ray's decision to take his pickup across the gully on a mission to acquire necessities. Maybe even a few luxuries. As needs surfaced, items had been added daily to a growing shopping list thumbtacked on Mariah's kitchen wall.

Transiting the wash was easy for Nelson's rugged four-wheel truck. He drove over and back a half-dozen times to cut a primitive track for the pickup. But the rain-slickened red clay soil and the steepness of the gully walls conspired against Ray. Under the anxious watch of the other men who had volunteered to help with the crossing, Ray's pickup slid off the embankment, narrowly avoiding a rollover as it slalomed to the bottom. Forty-five minutes later they had chained it to the FMTV and towed it up the track to the town side of the little chasm. The "supply mission launch team" waved in unison as Ray chugged out of sight to play Santa Claus, or maybe Easter Bunny, for the tribe at Maxwell Acres.

The sunshine, and the catharsis of building toward the future of their hidden community, ultimately lifted their spirits as they regrouped in the compound and regaled the others with their morning's success, which was already assuming the proportions of legend.

CHAPTER 85

Thursday, March 16

OVER THE SIX DAYS following the most recent cluster of catastrophes— the Overcroft farm looting, Beckwith's injury, the flash flood—an embryonic sense of easy routine had begun to imbue Maxwell Acres as gently as a crocus heralds Spring.

Jacob Maniksen's unrelenting curiosity led him to a discovery of the system that had made the barn remarkably comfortable for those bunking in it. "I haven't traced the pipe work Mr. Maxwell put in, but I think he combined elements of twentieth-century passive heat pump technology with old Persian theories, along with insulation and airtight paneling in the living spaces."

"Unbelievable," Mariah said. "There's more to this place than meets the eye, Jacob."

"Jacob's a jack of many trades," Kim said. "His cryptology experience might help solve some of those riddles that Darcy says you found."

Mariah was newly inspired by the boy from Berkeley. She retrieved the list along with the keys from the desk in the office off the living room. The three of them sat around the kitchen table, Jacob reading the sheet aloud, studying the keys, turning them over and over in his hands with an extraordinary intensity. Mariah elaborated on the two puzzles she and Darcy had solved.

"I'll have to let this rattle around for a while," Jacob said. "I'm a big believer in the power of the unconscious mind, you know. Down in Berkeley, I used to work on math and physics problems and inventions on parallel tracks. When I was focused on one, I could almost feel my non-conscious brain running calculations under the radar, sorting out blind alleys from fruitful avenues on the projects I was ignoring. I've got these riddles in my memory bank now, and I'll let you know if anything pops out."

"Kim, why don't you two go to the storage shed and look around. I'm thinking we should move some of the grain supplies in there. See what you think. Anyway, Jacob, you'll love the collection of Victorian machinery Mr. Maxwell left in there."

"Mariah," Kim said, "I remember some of that machinery from when I was here in my school summers. That was before my brother died. He was really into machinery and Mr. Maxwell showed him all kinds of things. Mr. Maxwell said it was his 'museum.' He was very proud of his collection. I got to tag along, although what they talked about was mostly over my head. But Mr. Maxwell also had an amazing library in there."

"Well, it's gone now," Mariah said, "but do you remember the mirrors that reflect the sunshine inside?"

Kim looked vague. "Maybe it'll come back. I'm a little hazy on it all, it was so long ago."

"Maybe you and Jacob can figure it out together. The mirrors are up in the cupola, and you open it up by pulling the rope you'll find on the north wall."

As the heavy shed door swung open, Kim felt a wave of sadness that her brother wasn't with her. But it changed into anticipation as she saw the clever lock and hinge system she remembered from her youth, and then saw the beautiful antique machines around the main room.

Her elation shifted to a cloud of confusion. "This isn't the way I remember it at all," she said. "These machines look vaguely familiar, but Mr. Maxwell really did have an amazing library here, and this doesn't look anything like that. I do remember stairs, though…"

They went upstairs to the second-story watchtower on the east. It was empty, no shelves on the walls. Kim said, "This isn't it either."

They descended, Kim deferring her perplexity for the moment. "Let's see about the cupola," she suggested. They unhooked the rope from the marine cleat on the wall and opened the apparatus. Jacob was impressed.

A perfect, five-foot square of dazzling sunlight struck the floor beside them. Kim instinctively moved a step backward from the startle of its sudden appearance. Jacob simply froze in place with a whispered, "Wow."

"Oh my God. I think riddle No. 8 has something to do with this. It starts out 'Sun squared.' Right here, this is a square of sunshine." He sat down on the operator's seat of one of the machines and said, "Let me concentrate." Then, "Kim, go get the sheet of riddles. And bring key No. 8."

She left Jacob reciting over and over, trance-like from memory, the hypnotic rhythm of riddle No. 8:

Sun squared
Polar is cornered,
Slide the hickory d² ho.
Potlatch bared
Key is quartered
His story is hidden well below.

When Kim returned, Jacob began staring at the written poem. Kim stayed silent, aware that his brain did not operate on ordinary wavelengths. After a few moments he said, "This is one of those where they cut words apart, stretch some out, and throw in some code words too. This second line, here... I think it refers to the north corner of the room. See, he cut 'Polaris' in half—that's the North Star—and he added 'ed' to 'corner' to throw you off. The Polaris corner, over here."

He led Kim to the north corner, repeating, 'Slide the hickory d² ho, Slide the hickory d² ho...'"

"Hickory dickory dock, you think?"

"That's it, Kim. That's it. Look, here in the corner, in the floorboard trim. There's a little mouse hole. 'Ho' means hole, and 'hickory dickory dock' is the mouse reference. 'Slide the hickory d² ho.' Maybe this board slides."

He knelt on the floor, put his finger in the hole and pulled sideways, along the wall. It was only two feet from the corner to the first joint in the trim. The board slipped from the joint smoothly up over the next section of trim like a panel on a Chinese puzzle box, revealing a brass plaque with a circular cylinder lock and a hole for a circular key. Kim knelt beside him to inspect the discovery.

Jacob declared victory. "I was right. The 'latch' is 'bared.'" The key slid in perfectly, its grooves matching tiny teeth inside the lock. Jacob said, "It should operate with a simple quarter turn—the rhyme says 'Key is quartered.' And 'His story is hidden well below?' I think he buried the history of this place—'his story,' get it?—below this floor."

Kim turned the heavy brass key ninety degrees to the right. They heard an ominous whirring sound from underneath the floorboards—creaking, boards shifting, the sound of chains and pulleys, wheels and ropes. Behind them, a section of the floor began dropping away along the west wall of the room. The six-foot square section of the concrete floor on which the sunshine square was shining simultaneously began dropping away as well. When it had dropped about a foot, it began sliding to the north, under the floor of the room, like an interior hatch of a ship. The floor along the west wall was dropping at an angle, its left end hinged and its right end free, revealing a set of steps leading into a room below, which was brightly lit by the shaft of sunlight. Kim was exultant. "The library, Jacob. See all the books? Just the way I remembered."

Jacob was dazed by the brilliance of the mechanical system alone. "That guy, Maxwell. He set up counterweights and pulleys with tracks and sliders... the whole system's triggered by a simple turn of that tiny key. This guy was something else."

"We've got to get Mariah," Kim said. She ran to the main house, returning with Mariah, still wearing her kitchen apron. Jacob respectfully waited for their arrival, to let Mariah be the first to descend into the concealed chamber.

That night the evening meal conversation was dominated by two topics: the Underground Room, and Where is Ray? Mariah finally ended the bleak speculating about Ray, cautioning against attracting trouble by negative thought. "He must be hanging out with his friend Chet."

All had taken the opportunity to explore the mysterious cache in the underground room.

Around the dinner table, they now pooled what their separate observations had revealed, piecing together a comprehensive portrait of the information and mysterious unknowns Mr. Maxwell had so carefully hidden.

There was a small chemistry laboratory. There was a work table of tiny tools, vices and ocular magnifiers, not quite like a dentist's tool shop (although Charles did identify some specifically dental equipment), but bearing a greater resemblance to a jeweler's or clock maker's workplace. There was an apparatus that focused the mirrored sunlight horizontally to a single point generating intense heat on a small stand that held, interchangeably, either a small crucible or miniature kiln in which Jacob said one could melt any metal but the hardest tungsten. There was other machinery the function of which was not immediately obvious, even to the inventor/scientist, Jacob.

And then there was the library, every book well worn—volumes on intensive agriculture, natural and cultivated herbs, the geology, botany and other scientific explication of the South Warner Mountains and indeed all of Modoc County and contiguous environs; tomes covering the major religions, and many minor ones, Native American included, surveyed briefly by Mariah's knowledgeable eyes; a smatter of epic literature; texts on metallurgy and alchemy, astrophysics and astrology, philosophy and medicine; and notebooks filled with what appeared to be Mr. Maxwell's own work and writings.

The ebullient, sometimes cacophonous exchange, alternating between information gleaned and runaway speculation, crescendoed at the end to the Big Questions: What was Mr. Maxwell's intent? Why was it so well hidden? How did he die?

Sleep was fitful for all but the most exhausted workers that night.

THE BIG MACK DIESEL whined through its low gears. Air brakes squealed and the truck came to a halt. A mechanical overhead door clanked open and the truck drove through. Reinhold's eye holes gave him a view too dim to reveal details. While he waited for his eyes to adjust, he used up ten seconds of his flashlight battery to check his watch and write the tally on the plywood wall. He had been in the crate sixty-six hours.

After his crate had been forklifted onto the flatbed at the Little Rock barge dock and the caravan got underway, Reinhold had sawed two, one-inch square holes in the crate wall parallel to the highway, then duct taped the plywood squares back in their openings to reduce detectability when he wasn't watching the countryside roll by. He had cut a third hole by the forward, right corner of the crate so he could read highway signs along the way. He knew they were in Oklahoma, still six hundred miles shy of Los Alamos by the reckoning of his memory.

Reinhold heard a shrill voice. "Welcome to Oklahoma City, Sir." He assumed it was a guard.

"Give me a break, Mister." It was the truck officer's voice, now. "This ain't the city. It's so poor out here, I wouldn't even call it a suburb."

As Reinhold's eyes adjusted, he made out the interior of a gigantic military warehouse.

"Drive through that infrared screener gate, Sir, when those two vans have been checked."

The truck crawled forward twice in five minutes, cut its engine. Reinhold heard a high-pitched humming. The truck stayed still for another twenty minutes.

He couldn't distinguish any words, but he heard several men hold an animated conversation. From their inflections, he concluded it was a topic of surprise and grave concern. He heard his driver climb back to the cab.

The guard's voice ordered, "Take her over there to that Eurotech 9000 bay. Our new molecular signature scanner'll tell us what that warm spot in your generator crate's made of." The truck advanced again.

Reinhold's heart skipped a beat. His throat dried to a choke. He sat stock still on the generator's control case that had been his seat for the journey so far. Hardly breathing, he listened for any sign of his fate.

A new voice sounded, close enough to touch.

"It's definitely live, organic tissue. About the volume of a man. A lot of other materials that ain't part of no generator—water, titanium, traces of sulfur, some proteins the Eurotech 9000 doesn't have on its molecular map. Probably not plastics or other explosives, though—we've got all them profiled good."

Another voice took over. "Our protocol says to pump in stun gas in case it's espionage."

Reinhold heard several people climb onto the flatbed. An object like an aluminum ladder scraped against the crate. More scraping, then the sound of a drill against plywood. Reinhold flashed his light along the ceiling, saw the drill break through, then the black end of a hose poke in and a greenish gas begin to discharge from its filtered end. He braced the flashlight on the generator so its beam stayed on the expanding green cloud. Keeping careful watch on the gas, he jammed the keyhole saw through one peek-hole and frantically began saw-ing. As the gas neared his face, he sucked in a final gulp of good air and held it, praying he could cut through in time. His eyelids closed involuntarily against the searing sting of the gas, wouldn't reopen. By feel, he judged he'd sawed two feet down, made a small corner to the right, when the white hot pain of his bursting lungs took over. His exhale blasted out, his body inhaled despite his struggle against it. He lurched backward, braced against the generator and slammed his boots with all his strength against the plywood by the cut. He thought he heard wood splintering, then lost consciousness.

The walls and ceiling of the room were blinding white in the neon light. Reinhold was shivering, his hair, face and clothing drenched with cold water. He could feel it in his boots, too, and heard it squishing out the air holes as he moved his toes. His ankles were bound to a steel chair. His arms too, behind him. Two uniformed men, faces concealed by ski masks, were leaning back in black leather desk chairs.

"What's your name?" one of them demanded.

"Ivan Frankel." His vocal cords felt like knots on a cat-o-nine-tails.

"I don't think so, Malone." The other man stood and slammed his open hand against Reinhold's head, knocking him and the chair to the floor. The man grabbed the rope around Reinhold's chest and yanked him upright again.

"You'd best level with us, Pal."

Reinhold's lungs burned, his body ached. He kept quiet. The interrogator opened a manila file on his lap.

"Reinhold Malone. Irish immigrant. Fluent in Russian. Eight years in Moscow. Darcy, Tierney and Finn Malone last seen in San Francisco." He stared at Reinhold through the slits in his mask. "We know all we need to about you. Our database matched your fingerprints and DNA, both."

A third man entered the room. His military decorations revealed a high rank. "This is your only chance to stay alive, Malone. We've lost millions on the East Coast. One more life means nothing. But the catastrophe took down some of our best intelligence operations. If you cooperate, your Russian can be useful to us. And your knowledge of Russia. Would you like to live? Or shall we go ahead and fill this room with gas?"

Reinhold coughed out a barely audible, "Okay."

CHAPTER 86

Friday, March 17

A HALF-HOUR after sunrise Kim was on watch at the Royer cabin. A tiny movement by the old oak caught her eye. Through the binoculars, she saw Ray trudging up the road, laboring under an enormous backpack. She alerted the group, and Jason and Eli hurried down the road toward Ray.

As they approached him, he lowered the pack to the ground with simple deliberation, knelt slumping over one knee, and waited, panting and sighing, for their aid.

Discussion was not an option. Jason slung the backpack on his shoulders. Eli helped Ray up, gave his elbow as support, and the three men trudged up the valley, past the Royer cabin and on to the big house. They eased Ray into a chair. Mariah told the men, "I'll come get you when Ray can talk." An hour later, she gathered the community to hear Ray's story.

> *Ray's exhilaration at going to town eroded into uneasiness. He passed the first scattered houses and farms at the edge of town without identifying signs of any recent human activity. Horses and cattle in the pastures had a strange, untended look. Some of the houses or barns were burned. One corral by the road became an omen for Ray: Vultures were picking the carcasses of a milk cow and her calf. His foreboding swelled in the neighborhoods of Flat River, devoid of vehicular movement.*

Ray pulled into Chet's feed and tackle store. His boots in the gravel sounded thunderous. No town sounds met his ears. He opened the door.

From the unlit interior Chet shouted, "Who's there?"

"Hey, old buddy, its Ray Overcroft."

"What the hell you doin' here? I heard your truck. I thought you was the gestapo. Don't you know better? They're the only ones allowed to use gas."

"Nobody told me. What're you talking about, 'gestapo?' I just need some stuff, Chet. You still in business?"

"You caught me with an hour to go. It's no good for me to stay here."

"What are you talking about? Where's Harriet?"

Chet looked at him with wide eyes. "Where you been? No, don't tell me. I can tell you've been somewhere safe. Been ten days or more since I saw you."

"What's happening, Chet?"

"You know, when they cut the power a week ago Wednesday?"

Ray looked blank. He said, "A week ago Monday, the sixth it was, someone destroyed our farm. I took Paisley and..."

Chet held up his hand. "Look, we don't have much time. You never know what's gonna happen. Let me just tell you..." He looked around, then hissed, "After the power went out, we couldn't get Harriet's heart medicine. Without heat and hot food, she collapsed. I tried, Ray, but turned out I wasn't important enough around here for her to be admitted to the hospital. She died Friday, a week ago."

"I'm sorry, Chet," Ray started. Chet held his hand up again, shook his head, eyes rolled to the ceiling.

"People are dying all over. The mortuary was jammed. My neighbor and I finally just buried her body in the backyard. We said some prayers. I drug that heavy old spare shop door with my forklift over her grave. Somehow, I didn't want anyone to know where she was."

Ray was dumbfounded. Chet's jaw muscles were working hard, to hold tears back. "This is the end, Ray. This is a disaster. A fucking disaster. I've got to run to live. They abandoned that golf course community up north—you remember, Sunrise Village?"

Ray nodded. Chet continued, "I hear they have a spring-fed water supply and they can grow food on the golf course. I'm heading up there with some seed and tools. I hid a little gasoline when they came around, confiscating supplies. Late tonight, I'm going to try to sneak out of town without getting stopped. Make a run for it. I'm hoping they take me in up at Sunrise."

They heard two vehicles pull up out front. Chet nudged Ray's arm. "Get in the back room, Ray, quick. Hide in the closet in there, and keep quiet. They're probably here to confiscate your truck and take you in for questioning." Chet pushed Ray toward the door, then returned to the counter in the main store. Ray heard a thump followed by a grunt of pain from Chet's throat. Then he heard the store's front door open.

"Who's truck is that out there?" he heard a voice say. Then, "Hey Chet, man, what happened to you? Your head's all bloody."

Chet answered, "One of the farmers who used to do business with me just came in all desperate like. I think he meant to rob me. I started to fight him off, but he's bigger than me, so I grabbed my gun from under the cash register. Then he hit me with this ax handle, grabbed my gun and ran out that side door. You better be careful. You may need reinforcements. I'll be all right. It was just a glancing blow. But you better take care of that sonovabitch before he hurts someone else."

Two pairs of boots shuffled across the floor. The front door slammed. "Shoot his tires out," a voice growled. "We'll get his gas after we kill the bastard." Six pistol shots rang out. Ray's mind registered, *Sounds like a forty-five.* Then he heard the crackle of a two-way radio. The officer was calling for more cars with reinforcements for "another search and destroy game."

In a few seconds, Chet came through the back door, blood streaming down his forehead, face and neck, beginning to soak his blue denim shirt.

"Jesus Christ, Chet."

Chet waved his hand. "Here, climb the stepladder and get in the attic. Stay quiet until tonight. Then maybe you can get away when it's dark. You gotta get as far away as you can."

Ray reached out to touch his friend on the arm. "How about your head? What happened? Let me help you."

"I had to think fast to save both our lives. You're about the last friend I have. That ax handle was the closest thing I could find. I had to make it look real, or they would've taken me out and found you in a minute. They would've questioned you to find out if you have any supplies, then probably shot you. Everything's gone to hell, Ray. There's no power, little food, the Town Committee's gone completely berserk. The sheriff's office is in charge. All those gun-totin' young turks they deputized think they're a goddam private army or something. Things seem orderly around down-

town, but maybe that's because nobody goes there. But the further out you get the more fascist it is."

"Paisley and I left the farm and ... You know the old Maxwell place?"

But Chet interrupted, "Don't tell me another goddam thing, Ray. I don't want to have anything to tell them about you. Now do what I say and get in the attic. Now, man! If they come back, I'll probably have to help look for you. By the way, when you sneak out of here tonight, anything you want to carry with you, go ahead. Just take it. Everything that's not in my truck, I'm abandoning. And don't worry about me."

Ray climbed into the attic, laid three furniture moving pads on the floor by the hatch as a mattress, and kept a fourth to use as a blanket. Darkness enveloped him like a shroud when he replaced the hatch door. In the black he lay down and waited for his eyes to adjust. A slatted air vent materialized in the far end of the attic, through which Ray monitored daylight between periods of dozing.

When the air vent was no longer visible, Ray lifted the hatch door, listened, and dropped to the floor below. His ears picked up the scurry of mice. He had the sense a cat was creeping around inside, but as near as he could tell he was the only human present. His night eyes were at their sharpest and even without streetlights or automobile traffic he found the camping gear section of Chet's store. Mostly by feel in the dark silence, he loaded a backpack. Then he padded out the back door.

Ray scrambled for cover whenever he heard a vehicle. He decided to abandon Highway 395 and instead wind his way through the most isolated route he knew. He took the turnoff to Little Juniper Reservoir and followed the dirt road over the pass at Rock Spring before dropping down into the north end of Buckberry Valley.

By morning he was approaching the central part of the valley where Highway 54 turns right and drops back towards Likely. The south half of the valley was populated with new hobby-farms of recently retired city-folk. Apparently the population was either sufficiently armed, or sufficiently remote, that the looting and burning he had seen along Highway 395 was nonexistent here. Nonetheless, he concealed himself whenever he heard a motor.

Two hours after sunrise, he approached a small white house. To his surprise, in the backyard stood a young woman, tall with long black hair, setting out the wash on an old fashioned clothesline. She wore an orange blouse and a red and black ground-length skirt, and astonished Ray even more by waving hello. He walked to her fence and set down his load. There

was something about her—her carriage, the openness of her hand move-
ments, her steady gaze, the depth of her jet black eyes—that made Ray feel
utterly safe in her presence.

She introduced herself. Agnes Miniata was Native American, of the
Modoc tribe's matrilineal line. Ray remembered apprehensively the history
of her forebears, many of them murdered at Fandango Pass by Fremont in
1846, then by the rifles of the gold rush, and later by Federal Army cannon
in 1872 at Lost River and the lava beds south of Tule Lake. The latter, Ray
knew, is considered by some the Masada of the Native Americans. He
swallowed this knowledge with a dry gulp.

Ray described his odyssey.

Her voice was soft, musical. "You're not safe out here, either, my
friend. Come inside." It was not an invitation, but a command. Inside he
met three children, all eight or nine years old, all Caucasian.

Their parents had been killed, Agnes explained. They were from three
different families. She took them in when they came to her home school, the
only place they knew to come. None of them knew why the men with guns
had killed their parents, or why they weren't killed themselves, except
maybe that they hid and the men only wanted the food from their kitchens.
After Woody showed up, Agnes had gone back to his house to look for his
five-year-old sister and baby brother, but never found them. He had left
them to come for help.

"The tranquility you saw in the valley?" said Agnes. "It's like the
stillness of a full water pot in subzero weather—perfect and sound until,
without the slightest warning, the ice inside reaches critical pressure and
explodes the perfection into a thousand shards."

He was quiet. She scrutinized his face, then went on. "The valley's
armed to the teeth. Don't be deceived. Strangers die on sight to anonymous
gunfire. Sheriffs from Flat River come into the valley and take what they
want. Mostly food, and gas from peoples' cars, but I've heard of some los-
ing their medical supplies, and there are rumors that teenage girls have
been stolen from their families."

Ray nodded. It was too consistent with Chet's stories to doubt. He de-
scribed where he was going, and Agnes offered her map. She knew of the
Maxwell property. But Ray knew the way from Buckberry Valley and didn't
need the map. It was only twelve miles.

"That spring up at Maxwell's place," she said, "it was well-known to
my people before the White Man came. They called it Red Deer Spring.

Most of my grandfather's clan was gunned down there, trying to protect the sacred watering spot from desecration by gold-crazed men in 1849."

"I'm sorry."

She passed it by. "When I was ten, in the fall of 1987 during the harvest moon, my grandfather took me there. We walked all day on deer trails through the mountains. We slept there that night after roasting wild onions and acorns in the coals of a small fire.

"As the glow of the coals turned dark red under the ashes, we prayed for the souls of the massacred. My grandfather spoke at length to his spirit fathers and gave me messages from them as well. He told me, that night, I'm the pure, sixth generation descendent of the selfless Winema, Modoc peacemaker." Ray had heard the epic tale before, and nodded his admiration.

"The original homestead," she added, "had fallen in. This was five years before Maxwell showed up and rebuilt. By then, most of the land cleared by the original homesteaders had been reclaimed by the forest. But small patches of open grass could still be seen. My grandfather told me they were the same meadows our people used when they tended Indian rice grass long ago."

Agnes refused to let Ray go on during the daylight. He taught the children how to play checkers with thistle heads for pieces on a homemade grid he drew with chalk on the back of Agnes's breadboard. He spent the day running a grand tournament. Between rounds, he told them stories from his days in India. Agnes seemed enchanted as deeply as the children.

As dusk erased the brilliant sunset to reveal a star-studded night sky, Agnes fed Ray and the children a squash and potato stew. Afterwards, he stood on her front steps, poised to run the valley gauntlet protected only by the dark and his intuition. He was stooped slightly under the backpack full of the ordinary treasure he had risked his life to get.

He walked all night. He was sure he knew the way, but even so, in the darkness he had to backtrack more than once and use all his mental strength to calibrate his bearings. The waning moon, rising shortly before midnight, helped to a degree. At least it seemed to take the edge off the howls of roaming dogs rendered homeless by abandonment or death of their owners. Finally, in the blessing of the sun's early beams, he saw the fallen giant oak and the crumbled moorings of the bridge that once marked the entrance to Maxwell's Valley. He saw Jason and Eli hurrying to help.

Heads were shaking in disbelief that so much could go so wrong in so little time. How could the ligaments of civilized society become so torn and inflamed? In days, weeks? There were plenty of precedents: the Hutu/Tutsi con-flagrations, Guatemala, Watts, Sierra Leone, Afghanistan—the list was far too long—the fragility of order compressed by law, shattering like crystal in a train wreck when the trestle across the gorge is blown up. The calibration simply had to sink in—yet again. Chatter wouldn't help.

"The stark fact is we're here to stay," Ray said. "As a practical matter, there may be a few more rains coming before summer, and I think we should plant some fast-growing bushes in the roadway leading in here, maybe some grass too. Maybe the folks in Flat River think this place is abandoned and useless. Let's make the road look that way too. And we should erase that track we cut across the wash."

Darcy paced to the window. "I'm probably the last to come around to this. I've been denying the truth. I started out here thinking Reinhold would return, and we could get him and Dad up here for temporary safety. At first I thought in weeks. Then, maybe order would be restored in a couple of months, by fall maybe."

Charles and Peter averted their eyes from her uncalculated display of pain. Darcy continued, pushing the edge of her own coherency. "This is it, now. This community's all we have. The things we have in here—the food, supplies, skills and personalities. It's all we're going to get."

Jacob added momentum. "We're underway, at least. Nelson and I came here to stay anyway."

"Seems I did too," said Eli. "I like Ray's approach—let's be practical. I'd like to get some of us together and do some hunting."

"We'll have needs," said Paisley "some things can't be replenished. Things like candles, fuel. Things made out of cloth. We can grow our food, maintain our shelters and heat. But if we're going to be hermetically sealed, we have a lot to figure out."

Charles added, "Medicine."

Rose said, "Batteries."

The list grew as imaginations bored in on the new reality.

"Will I ever have friends to play with again?" Tierney asked her grand-mother.

Mariah took her on her lap and whispered in her ear, "Grown-ups think they know so much. But we don't always know. I feel sure you'll have some little friends. But don't wait around for it. You've got great friends here right now, even though they may be a little tall."

Tierney kissed her on the cheek and flashed her quick smile.

CHAPTER 87
Sunday, March 19

THE SOUTH ORKNEY ISLANDS' coastal lowlands are ruled by Emperors. This year, the slopes are more crowded, having yielded three vertical feet to the water at the command of the Mother Continent. But the Emperor Penguins' females have brought forth one precious egg apiece, as always. The Emperors have formed their circles, outer sentinels facing down the blizzards, inner replacements waiting their turn, eggs borne on feet and warmed by underbellies, females trusted to bring nourishment when they can. And tomorrow the sun disappears from the Antarctic Circle south. The dance will continue in the dark.

DARCY'S GRIEVING CEREMONY had made a profound impact on the Maxwell Acres community. Rose Royer suggested to Mariah and Darcy that their community meal at the main house be preceded by "a service of some kind, since it's Sunday."

Eli and Jason set up the dining room, Catherine and Kim and Paisley helped Mariah with the cooking. Ray slaughtered one of the chickens, and the cooks decided to make it go as far as possible by baking it into a casserole with rice and onions, dried mushrooms, a can of corn. Darcy baked two pumpkin pies. Rose baked biscuits at her place ahead of time. The meal was extravagant, but a boost for morale. Maurice Beckwith planned a sing-along for afterward. Ray tuned his guitar and clipped his fingernails.

Jason noted the need for more meat. "James we ought to take a day and go out hunting, like you said. Deer should be coming up from the lower elevations about now." Eli agreed.

With the casserole in the oven, Tierney was sent to call out, or tug on sleeves, to gather the community in the living room. Mariah had asked the assembly to bring any thoughts or readings they felt were appropriate.

"Let's start with a time of silence," she said. "You can meditate, or simply relax, have grateful rest. She lit a candle on a low table in the middle of the room. She nodded to Ray, who plucked a single note on the D string of his guitar. Eli recognized the Buddhist custom of beginning and ending sittings with the tone of a bell. He smiled and centered himself, concentrating on the diminishing of the string's reverberations. He felt a surge of gratitude and peace, and welcomed the images that came to him. He held each member of the community in a circle of light, feeling their energy, sensing their emotions. Catherine, he felt, had softened toward him, possibly because Kim seemed to accept him. The image of Kim excited him, and was followed immediately by the woman with the candle who beckoned him in his dream of his San Quentin cell.

Quiet inhaling and exhaling, an occasional whisper from the children. Eli noticed Tierney trying to imitate his cross-legged posture and his breathing. A Mona Lisa smile brightened her face, and Eli wondered if his own features were as serene and content.

A nod from Mariah, after patiently waiting for Ray to look up, brought the note that ended the silence. "I am grateful," she said, "for the sense of completion I feel from my husband, and I bless him."

Darcy echoed her mother, blessing Reinhold.

Rose opened her Bible. "I recognize the pain you must be feeling, Mariah and Darcy," she said, "and I am grateful for family togetherness. I feel even the presence here of our son Tom, Kim's brother, who was killed in action in the second Gulf War. He used to love spending time here at the cabin. I guess none of us would choose to be here now if we didn't have to be, but I love this passage, and it seems to say something about my feelings now:

> *Wherever you go, I will go,*
> *Wherever you live, I will live.*
> *Your people will be my people,*
> *And your God, my God.*
> *Wherever you die, I will die*
> *And there I will be buried.*
> *May Yahweh do this thing to me*
> *and more also,*
> *If even death should come between us!" ~ Ruth Ch. 1, V. 16-17.*

Charles squeezed her with a reassuring arm around her shoulders.

Maurice Beckwith cleared his throat. "I'm grateful to be alive. And let me be quick to say I hold nothing against Charles and young Jason for almost sending me to the next life. I don't hold any bitterness. I just wish Tess were here to get to know a fine bunch of people. For all I know you've extended my life. God works in mysterious ways."

Without comment, Eli recited from memory Robert Frost's exploration of the universal experience of choosing one's path in life, "The Road Not Taken".

In the brief silence that followed, he realized the questions his recitation must have raised in his listeners. What roads had he roamed that he had not revealed to them?

Mariah forestalled such questions. "This might seem frivolous to you," she said, "but I am serious. I like to praise our appliances, our equipment: the stove, Ray's pickup, our generator, and so forth. I affirm the sacredness of all things, animate and inanimate, and I determine to treat them with respect."

"I am grateful," said Jason, "in spite of the calamity that has happened, that I am still together with Catherine, the most precious thing in the world to me now, and that I have the friendship of James, whom I have come to respect." Catherine laid her head on Jason's shoulder, but did not speak. Eli bowed his head, ashamed that he was still unknown.

Nelson stood. "In the way of my ancestors I will bow to the earth, giving my respect. I feel we must cleanse ourselves from dominance and dedicate ourselves to fellowship with the land, the sea and the sky, whose beauty we share."

"I agree with Nelson," said Peter. "I have always taught my students that the earth is a living thing. I am awed by its power and majesty, and grieved by its vulnerability. The monumental event that has brought us together here, I'm afraid, is simply the working out of Nature's laws, for which we have shown too little respect."

"I am grateful to you all for taking me in," said Jacob.

"People in my profession," said Charles, "have been thought of as arrogant. I admit I felt I was wonderfully well educated and useful in society. Whatever validity there was in that view, I now feel that I am just beginning to learn. I thank God for a sense of humility which I hope never to lose."

Tierney whispered loudly to her mother, "Can I say something too?" Darcy smiled and nodded. Tierney swept a look around the circle. "I am grateful for Uncle James and Uncle Jason." Eli saw the unspoken need for her absent father.

Kim was last to speak. She held a creased scrap of paper. "I am grateful for the majesty of the wilderness, even though Nature threatens us now. Like James, I have a poem that speaks to me and for me. I have carried Rilke's poem "*The Man Watching*" with me since college. Part of it addresses the necessity of living through this challenge of ours with grace, maybe with courage."

She recited from memory the lines that urged them to wrestle with angels, in spite of the inevitable defeat, because the struggle strengthens and the opponent is benevolent.

Eli nodded appreciatively, and her smile delighted him.

When Mariah thanked everyone for their participation, and announced dinner would be ready soon, the silence prolonged itself. No one moved. Maurice Beckwith began humming "Amazing Grace." Several others joined in, adding harmony to the melody. When the tune faded to a close, conversation began and rose steadily to a high volume which continued during the meal.

Charles brought out a bottle of wine from his cellar. Eli declined the wine and again felt conjecture swirl around him, but he had determined to keep his abstinence. He felt his secret was waning and must soon die.

Maurice Beckwith's sing-along began the cleanup period with "I Been Workin' on the Railroad," as Ray stood strumming his guitar near the kitchen. The job was done practically without effort, and the singing continued for an hour, with everyone required to suggest a group song, or perform a solo. Tierney sang, with accompanying gestures, a child's song about a little man in the woods who saved a rabbit from hunters. Finn basked in the applause when he performed a lopsided somersault. "He didn't stick the landing," Catherine quipped.

Late in the afternoon the celebration wound down, and the residents of Maxwell Acres took advantage of remaining daylight to work on personal or group projects. Jason and Catherine walked hand in hand toward the woods as the Royers took the opposite direction, hand in hand, toward their cabin.

Eli remained in the main house, helping Darcy and Mariah finish tidying up. "You folks are great," he told them. "You've really made a strong sense of community here. This was a remarkable event."

"Thank you," said Mariah, and Eli admired the simplicity with which she accepted his compliment. She did not deflect or minimize it, making it an exchange of gifts. She lifted the compost pail, but Eli took it from her.

"Let me take care of that," he said.

"Let's do it together." On the way to the compost pile she took a shovel from the tool shed. "I liked your recitation of the poem," she said. "Can you recite others from memory?"

"I guess about a dozen. When you love a poem, you return to it often, and after a while it becomes part of you. Sometimes when I'm walking by myself I recite poems, the way Maurice hums tunes."

"You're a man of many parts, James. I've sensed a melancholy about you, like the stereotype of an artist or poet. You've had sadness and struggle in your life. But you seem more... at peace here than any of us, and you've made wonderful contributions to what you called our sense of community."

"Thank you." He emulated her grace in accepting praise, but it was a struggle. He could not look at her. Anguish droned like a swarm of bees in his mind. Her acceptance of him seemed unconditional. She had confirmed him as part of the finest society he had ever known. Was it because he had kept himself a stranger? The weight of shame pressed a long sigh from his lips. They had reached the compost pile. He set the pail on the ground and felt the solid base of the earth under it.

"My name is not James," he said, removing the lid from the compost bin. The words escaped him before he could censor them. Tiny flies composed a subtle cloud over the compost. Scraps of decomposing organic material lay among thin layers of dirt, with worms burrowing through the heap, digesting the waste, transforming it into soil.

His words echoed in his mind: "My name is not James." They were both a bridge and a barrier. He felt Mariah's effort to comprehend, felt his world turning. Mariah regarded him with a mild, searching gaze, waiting. Eli dumped the pail of kitchen scraps onto the compost pile.

"I'm Eli Barnes. I'm a convict, number D15078, escaped from San Quentin State Prison—a month or two ago. God, it seems like years." He looked her in the eye now, open to contempt or compassion.

"I was in prison sixteen years. You're absolutely right about a life of struggle and sadness. And you can guess why I'm at peace here—this life might be hard for most of you, but not for me. I've told you I'm a refugee from a monastery, but I'm a man convicted of murder, a recovering alcoholic—not someone welcome in many places."

Mariah registered curiosity rather than surprise. "What you're saying fits with what I've sensed about you. But there is no doubt about your monastic training, I can see that."

"Well, that part's true, a little. I've been meditating in prison for years, and I spent a few weeks in two monasteries recently. But basically I've been lying to you folks."

Mariah jabbed the shovel into a mound of dirt, then swung it over to sprinkle on the scraps Eli had dumped. "I'm sure there's an intriguing story in you."

Eli accepted her invitation and delivered a capsule of his years in prison, his escape from San Quentin. Of his time before prison, he said simply, "I was a wild, out-of-control kid, a drunk, a reckless, aimless rebel." He spoke of Daddy Sisson, "who made a man of me," and the Retreat volunteers whose constancy made love a prospect in his life.

Mariah listened, leaning on the shovel. "Remember a couple of weeks ago I told you I knew a lot about you, just not the details? Now that I've heard some of them, I don't think it will make a difference with our little community. When they know this about you, I don't think they'll accept you any less. You don't have to remain a prisoner of your past, and you're not that wild, aimless kid any more."

Eli drank in her compassion, then closed his eyes. Mariah touched his arm. "You'll still be James to me," she said, "until you choose to name yourself to the rest. I think that should be soon."

"Thanks," he breathed, trying to imagine himself announcing his identity to the community, picturing their reactions. Would it diminish or increase Catherine's enmity? Would Kim turn away?

Mariah read his thoughts. "Catherine has been frightened. I think she's mellowing," she said. "And Kim I'm sure feels quite warmly toward you. It won't be as hard as you imagine."

Eli replaced the cover of the compost bin and smiled, in spite of himself. "How do you do that?" he said. "A guy can't even think around you, can he?"

Eli returned the shovel to the tool shed and rinsed the compost pail. When he replaced it in the kitchen, Tierney and Finn had nearly settled down from the exhilaration of "the party." Tierney had not napped all day, and they were now accustomed to living according to the rhythms of daylight and darkness, so a residual solo chorus of "Oh Susanna" was interrupted by a yawn as the sunset glow deepened to rust.

Eli said goodnight to the little family, but Tierney begged him for a story. "Jack and the Beanstalk," she insisted. Finn was asleep in his mother's lap before the giant hurtled from the clouds to his demise. "Thank you, Uncle James," said Tierney, and she hugged him.

Kim was a charmed witness to the scene, entering discreetly. She wore the Irish wool sweater and jeans Eli recalled from their first meeting. "Mom reminded me tomorrow's washday," she said when Darcy escorted the children to their bedroom. "I told her I'd gather it all together and take it down to the cabin first thing in the morning."

Eli had three sets of clothes: James Salas' pants, shirt and sweater that he wore departing San Quentin, a change supplied by Father Terrence, and supplemental clothing provided by the monks at Los Molinos. He had borrowed a shirt from Jason for the Sunday celebration. Rose Royer had offered her electric washer and set up a schedule for doing the community's laundry. If electricity was unavailable, they would use a tub and hand-wringer in the barn, where Eli and Jason rigged a clothesline. Mariah ducked out to fetch a small laundry bag, and Eli volunteered to gather it from the "men's dorm" in the barn.

"I'll go with you," said Kim, and the heart thump in Eli's chest echoed in his head. He had spoken with Kim many times while working or at meals, but never since their hour with Maurice had they been alone. Now Mariah's words resounded in his mind: *Kim feels warmly toward you.*

The brightest stars made a faint appearance as the rust drained, leaving a violet band blending from the western ridge into dark blue and charcoal.

"So you're a storyteller as well as a poet," Kim said.

Eli studied the dark ground as if a stumble were imminent. The word storyteller stung him.

"I liked your poem today," he said. "I'd like to hear the rest of it."

She closed her eyes a moment, then began. After several lines she faltered. "I still have it here." She drew the paper from her hip pocket and held it for him to squint at in the failing light. Eli barely breathed, so close to her, and the words on the paper were indistinct to him. She resumed, her voice soft and intoxicating.

"That's a great poem," Eli said when she finished. He sighed, not daring to raise his eyes to hers. "That's what a poet wants to do, make you reach out, and discern truth."

She smiled up at him. "I liked the Frost poem too," she said. "Have you memorized others?"

Eli took a long breath. His voice was a murmur, but distinct and steady, as he recited Stephen Spender's *"I Think Continually of Those Who Are Truly Great,"* with its rhythmic catalog of images in praise of the literary lights of his day—of those, Eli thought, exalted in any endeavor. He forced himself to keep his cadence steady, and a part of his mind was reading her, absorbing the mystery of her and reaching out to embrace her.

"That's wonderful," she said. "Do you think of specific people when you say it?"

"A few," he said, aware of his evasion. He would have mentioned Daddy Sisson, several of the Retreat volunteers, Sister Arlene, Mariah. He swallowed. "From now on I guess it will remind me of you."

"That's sweet," She took his arm as they continued ambling, past the barn. All of his attention focused on the contact of her hand, the communication of her body against him at each step. The twinkling Sirius rose above the eastern ridge like a beacon, outshining all other stars around it.

"The children really love you," she said. Before he could respond, she added, "I'm glad you're here too."

Eli stopped abruptly, turned to face her. He petitioned her moonlit face, urgently, unable to speak. When his voice arrived, it was breathy. "I'm... happy too. I'm very happy."

Her chin dropped and her lips parted as if to speak, but she did not. She made an almost indiscernible movement toward him, and their hands clasped as she turned her face up to him for a kiss. They held each other lightly with hands and lips until her arms encircled his neck. And when they parted, he examined her eyes, her faint smile, to imprint the moment on his memory.

"James..." she whispered, but said no more, as if she were simply declaring him, fixing him in time and space.

In this new reality his fears reemerged. He felt he could reveal himself now, but the event was too precious and delicate to risk, or to encumber with the clumsiness of confession. They stood relaxed in the darkness, his arm encircling her as she pressed her forehead into his neck.

Footsteps. Eli turned and placed himself protectively between Kim and the sound. Two figures slowed their pace as they approached, recognizing Eli and Kim in the moonlight.

"Catherine," called Kim. "It's Kim and James." Catherine and Jason were returning from their after-dinner stroll to Eastside Creek. It was easy to imagine how they had spent the hour, but the names "Kim and James" were not so readily associated at Maxwell Acres. The walk back to the house and barn was chatty, but did not touch on the feelings and questions of the four. Eli remembered to fetch the laundry.

A mist of starlight
    descending as honeyed wine
        will not astound me.

He lay awake for an hour, examining the day's events. And when he slept, the dream came again of the woman with the candle, and she had Kim's face.

CHAPTER 88

Monday, March 20

REINHOLD SAT on his cot reading Barney's Bible. His captors had taken away only his tools, his razor and his ID papers. From the moment he had agreed to translation duty, his treatment had been mysteriously benign. He surmised the military government felt in desperate need of Russian intelligence, with their key think tanks lost when the tsunami hit Washington, Boston, New York and other East Coast centers. And what wasn't wiped out instantly would have been decimated in the chaos and disease that reigned immediately after.

His attention was broken by a rap on the door. "Come in." In came the only person he knew so far. "Morning, Omaha." He closed the Bible and laid it on the taut blanket.

Upon his arrival at the intelligence facility he had been released into the custody of Sergeant Omaha Chang. He couldn't decide whether she looked more Mongolian, Chinese or Native American. After two meetings with her in the austere rec room of his locked corridor, he had learned her mother was half Chickasaw and half Jamaican and her father was born nationalist Chinese from Taiwan. They had reared her where her dad had grown up—in Mobile, Alabama, which explained a curious hint of Southern twang in her speaking. Her Russian, learned at Duke, was excellent. She was about Reinhold's age, two-thirds his height and weight, and wore her jet black hair in a tight bun that matched the impeccability of her Air Force uniform.

She sat in the plastic chair by the door, the only seating other than the one-piece toilet in the far corner by the sink.

"Tomorrow, Reinhold, I'll take you to the translation center and we will see how you do."

"Okay." He looked her in the eye. "Where am I, Omaha?"

"Classified."

"This place feels heavy. Very heavy. The air smells like split peas. It reminds me of a tour I once took into Hoover Dam. I think we're underground, or in a mountain maybe."

He scrutinized her face for a reaction, thought he caught a flicker of astonishment, admiration even.

"Do you believe in the Bible?" she countered, eyeing his reading material.

Reinhold took a risk. "Of course. It's the word of God. It says we can only come to the Father through Jesus." He picked up the Bible again and held it in his lap. He took a quick breath and shot, "Don't you?"

Omaha's eyes swept back and forth, then around the room. She pushed her rear into the back of the chair, which shifted and bumped the wall. "Why... Yes. I do."

"Good." Reinhold decided on the full shock treatment, to press his advantage, "How do you know I'm not Satan?"

Her eyes widened. He stared, deadpan, waiting. He let time flow, burying her under the weight of silence. His risk and method paid off.

"From your heart. 'By their fruits shall ye know them.'" She answered correctly, he judged, based on his experience with a dozen fundamentalists with whom he had engaged throughout his travels.

He balanced the Bible on his thigh and reached both hands toward hers. Hesitantly, she clasped his hands. He had heated them nearly to a boil, it seemed to him, with the technique Holly Frankel had taught him, and which he had practiced for hours during the entombment in the packing crate.

She tightened her eyes, almost imperceptibly, and recited, "Lord, Jesus. Bless this man. Let me trust him, and let neither of us deceive."

"Amen, Sister."

She stood to leave. "We should work well together. I'll come for you after breakfast in the morning."

IT WAS FORTUNATE that Nelson Ichimura had hunting experience. Eli and Jason admitted they would not have known how to gut and field-dress the deer. Their hunting foray had been facilitated by Kim's knowledge of the terrain. She and her brother Tom had accompanied Mr. Maxwell on hikes in the forest, beyond what he had called "the promontory"—the steep horseshoe-shaped slope north of his property with a talus formation near the top that made it virtually impossible to approach or even see Maxwell Acres from that direction.

They had crossed Eastside Creek and wended their way up along switchbacks to a place Kim remembered as a likely site for deer. Catherine had insisted on accompanying Jason. "I'm strong, I can help carry the deer back." It was Jason's shot that felled the buck, after Catherine had spoiled his first chance by startling a group of deer into flight, underestimating their sense of hearing. Eli had intervened when Jason felt obliged to reprimand Catherine for her carelessness. A sullen pout showed her resentment at being thus rescued. Eli shrugged inwardly. But now, with the venison hanging from an improvised pole, the group trudged merrily along a vague trail.

But Eli could not shake a weight of apprehension, aware it made him seem aloof from Catherine and Kim, who led the march homeward chatting like sorority girls. He felt edgy, reminiscent of his depression at Hat Creek. He searched his mind for a cause as he shouldered the back end of the pole from which the deer hung, the head swinging near the ground. Perhaps it was that the report of Jason's rifle had cracked the stillness of a bright midday, sending out a message of their presence. He glanced at Nelson, who was walking beside him with a distracted air, like a hound sniffing the wind.

"What's up?" Eli asked.

361

"I heard something," Nelson said blankly. "Something's behind us."

Eli craned his head. "Could it be a bear coming out of hibernation?"

"Not likely. Bears aren't subtle or sneaky."

"I'll drop back and check it out," Eli said. "Hey, Kim, it's your turn to be porter."

Catherine and Jason were happy to walk ahead, holding hands, as Kim and Nelson hoisted the carcass. Eli took advantage of a cluster of piñon pines to break off from the group and make a wide uphill circle. If someone were trailing them, Eli would soon be following him.

The sounds of his companions receded. He squinted through the brush. The scrape of footsteps directed his gaze to a crouching form visible through a screen of shrubbery below him. He fell in behind, his rifle ready, acutely aware now of patches of gravel and the sound of his own shoes. He was afraid he might lose track of his mark. At the top of a rise he saw him clearly, a broad-backed man in a long leather jacket. A shudder of recognition seized him. He knew the cocky rolling gait, even on the slanted and uneven surface.

Eli froze, then hurried ahead with all the stealth he could muster, debating whether to call out. Dupree Ransom vaulted over a fallen log, stiff-arming it with his left hand. In his right hand, flung out for balance, he held a black revolver.

As Eli arrived at the same log a twig snapped under his foot. He dropped to a knee and drew a bead on Ransom. Lithe as a puma Ransom whirled, pointing his pistol. "Drop it, Ransom, or you're dead," Eli shouted.

Ransom lowered the pistol, pointing it at the ground. "Is that you, Barnes? Damn, I wondered what the fuck happened to you. Newspaper said you was with me and Erik on the lam. How the hell did you get away?" His voice was hoarse, but upbeat, boisterous. His manner sharpened Eli's alarm. He must not drop his guard. He wondered if Perez was nearby, but dared not take his eye off Ransom. The man looked weathered and weary. The edge was off his hardiness. What had survival in the wilderness reduced him to? He might be starving, trying to hunt with a pistol.

"Where's Erik?"

"He's right behind you, man." Eli's senses were piqued. He heard nothing but the breeze fanning tree limbs and the chirp of a bird, the silence of the forest.

A squirrel skittered along a limb. It was enough distraction for Eli to turn his head involuntarily at the prospect of the specter of Erik Perez.

A shot rang out and the bullet whizzed past Eli. Reflexively he ducked behind the log. There were two clicks of Ransom's pistol. Eli raised himself and fired at Ransom, who was already running. Eli sprinted down the trail.

"James! Are you all right?" It was Kim's voice.

Then Nelson: "James, talk to me!"

They had dropped their cargo when they heard voices, and came running toward the sound of gunfire.

"The guy shot at me," called Eli, showing himself. "He went down the hill."

Jason and Catherine were right behind. They all followed Eli at a trot, but they neither saw nor heard the fugitive. His footprints were plain enough in the moist earth, until they were lost among rocks or fallen tree trunks. Nelson read the trail, Eli and Jason peering off into the trees, their rifles ready.

"What did he want?" asked Kim. "Why did he shoot at you?"

"Stay behind me," Eli whispered, signaling quiet with an upraised finger.

Nelson tracked Ransom past a grove of ponderosa pines. And then to the edge of a steep drop-off. "It's the promontory—above the property," whispered Kim. Maxwell Acres lay a mile or so below, but not visible from here, an important factor in its isolation. The tracks became disordered, heading in several directions, along both sides of the precipice and back toward the ponderosa grove, with skid marks, as if there had been indecision, panic. Did he go over the cliff?

Nelson veered off the west edge of the promontory, while Catherine accompanied Jason toward the east, looking down the slope. Eli felt a peripheral awareness of Kim staying close to him.

There was a sudden rustling above them. A black form loomed and dropped out of the ponderosa pine, knocking Kim and Eli to the ground. Eli was stunned, his wind knocked out. Vaguely he heard Ransom snarl: "Don't you even move, Bitch." He perceived that Ransom had grabbed the rifle and held its barrel to Kim's head, his fingers entwined in her hair. Eli willed his paralyzed diaphragm to expand, but he could only rasp and suck a thin stream of air.

The others scrambled back, but froze at the sight of Kim in Ransom's grasp. "It's him!" shrieked Catherine. Ransom shielded himself behind Kim, backing toward the edge of the precipice where he could not be flanked. He jerked her hair down so that she assumed a seated position. He crouched behind her, the point of the rifle still jammed into her skull.

Eli raised himself to all fours and felt a feeble flow of air. He gasped. "Don't hurt her, Dupree... Let her go... I'll kill you."

"I won't be the first one you've killed, will I?" Ransom had guessed the essential deceit in Eli's relationship with this group. His snide smile showed his relish of revealing Eli's secret. He was wild drunk with a renewed sense of domination.

"Toss them rifles in the bushes and step away." Kim gave a little cry as Ransom jabbed the rifle against her skull. It had the effect he wanted. Nelson and Jason reluctantly lay their rifles down. Kim's eyes were wide with fear.

"Never thought I'd see you again, Barnes. What you doin' huntin' with these nice people? You tell 'em you was a choirboy?"

Eli's jaw was clenched. He felt his pulse throbbing in his neck and temples. His mind was churning, taking in every detail of the situation. He knew all their minds were racing too, knew they were forced now to link him with Ransom. He saw the sneer turning Ransom's lip down. The loathing and dread on Kim's face. He forced down the rage urging him to leap suicidally to ram the heel of his hand through the bridge of Ransom's nose, forced himself to seek a calm, clear space where a hundred alternatives presented themselves and were evaluated in a second.

"Let them go, Dupree," he said evenly. "You can have all we got. There's meat here, and the rifles. Take everything." He swung his pack off his back. Ransom reflexively crabbed backward, dragging Kim with him. She gagged with his forearm around her neck, closing her airway.

"You damn right I can have 'em," shouted Ransom. "I can have anything I want here, including these bitches." He guffawed, a long musical sigh gulping air, like a swimmer, between notes of laughter. "I sure am glad the pigs didn't get you that night we got out of the house, man. I should have known you'd go right to the fine folks with your sweet pious talk. I shoulda just followed you. Did you tell 'em you was saved? You sure as hell didn't tell 'em you was a fuckin' lifer."

Eli sensed the silent comprehension in his companions, saw it mirrored in the dismay that blended into Kim's terror.

"Where's Perez?" Eli temporized. His mind was laboring furiously, like a crazed mouse in a maze, seeking the path anew after each dead end.

"We was livin' off the land up here, gettin' by. 'Fraid we sent some folks to heaven. But now Erik's dead. He was strong. Lasted more than a week after that bitch's old man shot him when we came by lookin' for some help." He nodded toward Catherine, who returned his malevolent sneer with utter contempt of her own. "Erik suffered at the end, got real crazy. Don't you worry, little girl, I'll get to you soon enough, and I'll show your man there how to treat a woman right." He jerked his arm up under Kim's chin, eliciting a yelp that froze his audience. He raised her and himself to a standing position. "Now you dudes get over here." He tilted his head toward the precipice.

"Wait!" said Eli. "There's something else in here, Dupree." He held his backpack up before him. "I know you want it. You have to see it now, or it won't do any good."

There was a second of indecision. Ransom was on his guard, uncertain, his confidence disordered.

"Here, I'll show you," said Eli. He dipped unhurriedly into the bag, like a magician gauging his audience's suspense, and gripped the useless pistol Erik Perez had given with a derisive taunt on the night of their escape. He raised the pistol deliberately until the barrel appeared to Ransom over the top of the bag, like a knight's lance over his shield.

"You always overplay your hand, Dupree. You've got only one cartridge in that rifle. If you shoot her I'll have three bullets in you before you know what's happening, and then I'll empty the damn clip! Or you can shoot me and you'll be defenseless. And right now I'm the only one here who doesn't care if he lives or dies."

Ransom saw it was true. His tongue moistened his lower lip, like a tired spaniel. Kim felt the barrel of the rifle begin to swing away from her head, and made her own motion simultaneously. She spun toward Ransom flinging her left arm upward. The rifle exploded.

Eli sprang at him, tossing the useless pistol aside. As Eli slammed into Ransom's rib cage like a linebacker, the rifle flew from his hands and clattered down the slope, coming to rest on a rock as Eli and Ransom grunted and grappled above. Ransom's exposure to cold and hunger had taken a toll, but his strength was still enormous. Eli's ferocious determination surged up from a pit of righteousness and despair.

Nelson and Jason retrieved their rifles, but could not get a clear shot. "Get clear of him!" shouted Nelson. He advanced to beat Ransom with his rifle butt.

Bellowing curses, Ransom clenched Eli's throat in both his hands, yanking him, shielding himself from Nelson, as Eli flailed, rasping for air to sustain his struggle. Ransom clutched Eli in a death grip, as if determined to drag him to hell.

Ransom's contorted face was a blur. Eli crouched and lunged upward, his doubled fists aimed between Ransom's massive arms at his nose. The vise on Eli's throat loosened, and Ransom was propelled backward, but as he toppled, he grabbed Eli's wrist and pulled him over the escarpment, snarling in rage. A mighty squealing grunt rolled down the slope as Eli landed on top of Ransom, then tumbled and slammed against a boulder.

Blackness engulfed him.

Light from a single eight-hour candle in a red glass cup played in a blurry circle on the ceiling. Two of the shadows on the wall were those of Kim Royer and Mariah Wallace, as they sat near the bed in which Eli Barnes lay unmoving, a circle of gauze around his head. The candle was at Mariah's back. Kim's face was not serene. Her lips were set in a determined line, her eyes downcast, focusing on her task of healing touch. Her right hand rested on Eli's shoulder.

"Mariah," whispered Kim, as if to awaken her vigil partner. "What if he's in a coma?"

"We won't dwell on any bad consequences," whispered Mariah, leaning in close to Kim. "We envision only that James will completely recover. He's not in a coma. Your father says he's sleeping." Charles Royer had told them it was a good sign that Eli had regained consciousness less than an hour after his injury and had been awake several times before nightfall.

Eli lay in Peter Addison's bed, with two sutures in his scalp several inches above the eye. His breathing was slow and even. Peter was sleeping on the living room couch.

Kim resumed her determined meditative posture. After a moment she blinked, and stared inquiringly at the older woman. "Mariah, you know, don't you? His name is not James. He knew that man, they are both escaped convicts."

Mariah nodded, aware that Kim could not see, in the shadow, her smile of amusement or her look of reassuring tenderness. "Yes, he confided it to me. It's quite a story. I told him that he would be James to me until he chose to reveal his secret to the community. When I saw you walking out together on Sunday evening, I was sure he was going to tell you. As for being a convict, I wouldn't put too much weight on the label. We all can see what a good man he is. He told me he'd been in prison sixteen years, most of his adult nearly half his life, I suppose. I think he must have repaid his debt to society."

"I don't care if he's James or Eli, he is the least self-centered man I've ever known. Before the disaster I dated the proverbial man who has everything. And I suppose that now he still has a lion's share of whatever's out there to have. But I'd say James has—I mean Eli—has the greater wealth."

Mariah took Kim's free hand. "I should say he has. He has you, doesn't he?"

CHAPTER 89

Tuesday, March 21

DAYLIGHT in the room was faint, but it hurt Eli's eyes when he first awakened. Then he became aware of two pleasant sensations. A foot away was the face of Kim Royer, and the warm pressure on his hand was from both of hers.

"Don't move, just relax," she said. She released his hand and left the room.

Eli became aware of Maurice Beckwith grinning at him from a nearby chair. "Now you just relax like she said, the doctor'll be in directly," said Beckwith, his voice soothing as a lullaby. "I knew you'd come around. That woman wants it too much for it not to happen."

Eli opened his mouth to speak, but found he didn't know what to ask. He squinted around the room and discovered he was in the same bed where he had spent his first night at the Royer cabin. Beckwith stood and stepped toward him. "I'd like to take this opportunity to say thank you for your part in my recovery, when I was the patient in this bed. Kim told me you were the first one of the men to sit in vigil with me."

Eli blinked. He understood Beckwith's words, but still did not comprehend his situation. A hollow throb pressed resolutely outward from his skull, and there was a sensation like a hot knife slicing his forehead. When he attempted a deep breath to clear his head, a steel band seemed to clamp around his rib cage, and he grimaced with pain.

"Just relax, like Kim said," repeated Beckwith.

As if he had conjured her, Kim appeared at the door, leading her father and mother.

"Let's see how you're doing," Charles said cheerfully. He shined a penlight in Eli's eyes and grunted, while Rose checked his pulse. "Squeeze my hand," said Charles. "How do you feel?"

"I have a headache." Eli wondered at the hoarseness of his voice. It grated in his head. Rose put a blood pressure cuff on his arm.

"Can you touch it where it hurts?" asked Charles. Eli reached up to touch the side of his forehead, found it covered with a bandage. "That's good," said Charles. "You banged your head on a rock, luckily enough in a place where your cranium is solid. You seem to be doing pretty well now. You'll have a goose egg for a while, and some bruising to match your neck and ribs and arms, but it looks like you're out of the woods. I'd be surprised if you're not stiff and sore when I let you get out of bed, but nothing's broken. You just have to stay quiet and rest for at least a day or two, I would think."

Most of the doctor's words registered. The scene on the mountain returned to his memory. The last he recalled was tumbling down the slope toward the talus rock with Dupree Ransom.

During the day a stream of visitors accounted for Eli's last eighteen hours: Catherine had run down the mountain to Maxwell Acres to fetch her Uncle Charles, the rest of the men, and supplies to retrieve him from his precarious ledge twenty feet down the precipice, where both he and Ransom lay inert. Nelson kept his rifle ready in case Ransom regained consciousness, "although for all I know he's dead." Jason and Nelson would not allow Kim to attempt reaching Eli. Jason found a way of traversing the face of the escarpment. He examined Eli and reported that he was still breathing, but unconscious. "I'm not going to try to move him until Dr. Royer gets here," he said. When the men from the compound arrived, Charles was lowered on a rope, and he and Jason immobilized Eli on an Army cot to be hauled up and stretchered back to the compound.

None of the visitors mentioned Eli's identity, but none of them called him James. They did not tell him what became of Ransom. Eli assumed Ransom died in the fall. In the afternoon he began telling people to call him Eli instead of James, and volunteered details of his life in prison. But they had been cautioned by Dr. Royer not to let Eli talk too much. They told him to breathe evenly and focus on the healing of his tissues. He slept much of the afternoon, and through another night accompanied by his healers. Kim kissed him goodnight, and later took a shift in the room before daylight.

Next morning Eli was eager to get out of bed, but Rose firmly forbade it, until her husband gave the okay. Then she prepared Eli's brunch. Eli moved in jerks and shuffles, since Charles' prophecy of pain had been fulfilled. He napped again in the afternoon, then received another round of visitors, in groups of two and three. Kim and Catherine were dinner guests at the Royer cabin. Eli apologized to Peter and Catherine for his deceit when he first encountered them. Catherine followed her father in assuring him of forgiveness. "You've earned the respect of everyone here," she said. "I'm sorry I was the last to accept you."

"You know," Peter said, "if we had known the truth about you that night, with what we'd been through, I'm sure we'd have left you there."

Eli nodded solemnly. "When you told me your story, I pictured Ransom and Perez. They were the two guys that made me escape from San Quentin with them..." He winced. "I thought I'd never see them again."

He wondered why everyone turned to Charles. "Eli," said the doctor, "when we climbed up there to fetch you, your former associate was still breathing too."

Eli stared. "What... what happened?"

"He was covered with dirt," said Peter. "One of his legs stuck out at an impossible angle, and only his eyes moved. He asked why we didn't kill him. Jacob reminded us we couldn't do that."

"He suffered a spinal cord injury," said Charles. "I suspect it's lower cervical spine, or upper thoracic. It's difficult to tell without an x-ray, and difficult to treat in any circumstances, so it's a wonder he's still alive."

"Still alive?" gasped Eli.

"It's doubtful he'll ever walk again," said Charles. "I'm not sure about the use of his arms. Jacob devised a special cot for him. He's in the barn."

CHAPTER 90
Wednesday, March 22

HIGH ON AN IRISH mountainside, the father and his eldest son return from seeking others below. Return empty. "We saw fires across the valley, but the destruction was too thick to cross. This summer, please God, we'll find others who survived. But now, we must plant the seeds we have and find what food we can." The family of seven makes the sign of the cross in unison, and sits to a stew of potatoes and game.

DARCY LEANED on her shovel, wiped her forehead. Nelson was spading the row next to her. The temperature was only in the seventies, but the direct sunshine was heating up the meadow workers. "Hey, Nelson. You want to walk up to the spring for a drink?"

"Good idea."

At the lower end of the spring's exposed water flow, a tin cup had been secured by a length of twine to a root protruding from the arroyo bank. They each had a sip of the cool, sweet water from the cup.

Nelson drank in a draft of air as well. "Do you think everyone in the world who has a spring has a tin drinking cup there too? Not just in this country. I've probably drunk from half a dozen springs, including in Europe and Asia, and every time, the little tin cup."

"I don't know," Darcy replied. "It just seemed like a good idea at the time. Maybe it's just my imagination, but it seems to make the water taste better. Different anyway."

"Ions," Nelson said. "Someone told me it was ions from the tin."

"Ions! Hey, you've picked up more education than you led us to believe." Then she injected a serious note in her voice. "Nelson, I'm trying to, well, deepen my intuition. To do that, you need someone who really understands you, who'll give you a nudge when your egotism gets in the way. Would you be my friend?"

Nelson voiced surprise. "I hardly know you, Darcy. And I'm sure not a psychologist."

Darcy gave not an inch. "Over time, I'd like you to understand me and... Well, become a real friend. A friend is one who will always be honest with you and tell you objectively when you're not being your own best friend, when you're not living up to your potential, or swerving from your purpose. I'd just like to have a handshake on it and see where it goes."

Nelson pondered the thought. "We're going to be here a long time, aren't we Darcy? I'm just a kid, but I'm, you know, flattered. I mean, honored that you'd pick me." He shook her hand.

At the touch, a familiar theme sprang into Darcy's mind, uninvited like a will-o'-the-wisp out of a swamp fog. *Japan.* The phantom of her past which still visited in the dark and was still secreted from her lifetime's confidant, Mariah. Nelson was from Japan, at least descended from that land. Would she have to...

Darcy suddenly held her finger to her lips. "Shh." She was looking up the hill behind Nelson, scanning the forest. In an instant her eye motion froze, her body tensed on high alert. She whispered, "Don't move." She watched for another minute.

Nelson sat calmly—a trained, superficial calm that masked the taut readiness of his nerves and musculature. "What do you see?"

"I think someone's up there. Turn around now and see if you can see anything."

Nelson's eye had been trained to spot people in camouflage on military exercises. With only the slightest movement he gestured with his forehead. "Up there, maybe. Between those two madrones. It's a person, a woman."

The woman in the forest sat stock still, but a subtle shift in her presence was proof she knew eye contact had been made. She, too, waited and watched. A breeze rustled through the trees. Then she rose and, with confidence and dignity, strode directly toward Nelson and Darcy, down a barely discernible animal track between low brush and tufts of springtime grass and wildflowers

She stopped ten feet from Darcy, who had advanced a few steps up the hill past Nelson. Darcy's heart was beating fast, and her body was on fire with electricity. It was the woman she had seen in the vision.

"I am Agnes Miniata, Modoc tribe," the woman said in perfect English. She held up her left hand, palm open in the universal gesture of peace. She motioned Darcy to a cedar log at the side of the trail, moved to it and sat.

"Are you occupying this land?"

Darcy nodded. "Where did you come from?" she asked.

"I fled anarchy in the Buckberry Valley. A posse of men was headed there from Flat River to take the farming land away from those of us who were still living there. Many places had already been burned, and many people killed, at random, but this was an organized assault. My partner walked and ran yesterday all the way from Flat River to warn me. He worked for the old police force down there and overheard their plans to take the Valley today. We left last night under cover of darkness, with two mules from an abandoned farm and seven children orphaned by the violence in the past week."

The woman's dark eyes flashed. "Can we live with you here?"

Darcy's heart hammered, her breath suspended. *I thought it was symbolic...*

"They're hungry." Agnes motioned back up the trail. "If you turn us away, I wouldn't blame you. There'll be somewhere else we can get to. I know these mountains well. And if not... We are ready to accept what the Providence dictates. Even death in the Warner Mountains, if that's our fate, just not death at the hands of the posse from the town."

Darcy turned to Nelson. "Go back with Agnes and help them down here. Bring them to the compound. I'll go back and tell everyone. We'll get blankets and warm food ready. Don't waste a minute."

Agnes touched Darcy's forearm with warmth and gratitude, then led Nelson up the trail.

Suppertime would never be the same. Every night, a party for twenty-five. And now, on average, there would be two birthdays a month. Culinary preparation would henceforth involve a master chef and two sous-chefs—and larger cleanup crews, for which fortunately there were many new candidates. Eli, Jason, Ray and Nelson had set up two temporary plank-and-sawhorse tables reaching into the foyer perpendicularly from the original dining room table in the big house. For seating they brought chairs and benches, and two empty wooden crates, from the other buildings.

The community had galvanized around the arrival of new members, once again. Because of the children involved—"The promise of the future," Rose had pronounced—this reorganization was vastly different than those occasioned by the arrivals of Beckwith, Jacob and Nelson.

First, of course, there were all the new names. Agnes' partner was Shaz. Remembering him was easy compared to the names of the children, now being busily memorized around the grown-up community, generally in order of age: Jenna was 16—Godfrey, 12—Lydia, 11—Val had just turned 9—Melissa and Woody were both 8—and scrawny Lawrence was a scrappy 7.

It was decided, smoothly and without dissent, that Agnes and Shaz would live in the west guest house and function as guardian parents for the four youngest children, Val, Melissa, Woody and Lawrence. Jenna, Godfrey and Lydia would live with Ray and Paisley, at least to begin with. Jenna hedged her bet and quickly befriended Catherine, confiding that she would prefer to live with the "women" in the big house, if and when allowed.

In the kaleidoscope of discussions that led to the immediate configuration, Darcy had one moment when the buzz receded and she received with an uncontainable smile a thought, clear as a bell, from Paisley—*God has just provided the family I always wanted.* Darcy knew, too, from the smirk Ray wore all afternoon, that he had tuned in the thought himself.

A furniture fabrication assembly line in the barn was devised by the increasingly proficient cadre of carpenters. Plans were formulated not only for bed frames, but for tables and chairs for the dining room, bureaus, and extra seating for various living spaces. A second assembly line began to coalesce in Ray and Paisley's place, to pattern, cut and sew changes of clothing for the threadbare orphans out of fabric Paisley had brought from the farm before its destruction. For the moment, that violence was forgotten, along with the new implicit threat—the expansion of Flat River's hegemony into Buckberry Valley only twelve miles away.

CHAPTER 91

Thursday, March 23

THE CHIRPING of birds, rustling of leaves in the occasional breeze, gentle rush of the snowmelt tracking down Eastside Creek, were balm to Mariah's spirit. A startled rabbit scurried into the underbrush as she passed the fire circle. Just below the waterfall, she came upon Darcy, teary-eyed, drawing circles in the dirt and scratching them out with a twig.

"Want to talk about it?"

Darcy snapped the twig and threw it into the creek. "Mom, I had friends. A job and a wonderful husband. I had a career. In a beautiful city. I'm a city, career woman, not a pioneer farmer. When I ask Am I happy, I want the answer to be Yes, yes, yes, and twirl around the room—not sit on a log. Isn't that what life's about?"

Mariah looked at the pines swaying in the breeze on the ridge, and said, "I don't think life's about happiness. That's something Madison Avenue and Detroit sold us, and the Joneses next door. We have moments of happiness, then sadness, happiness, then anger, and on and on."

"Well, what do you think it is about, then?"

"Peacefulness, Darcy. Peace amidst the experience. You can be peaceful even when you're sad or angry. You can be happy and not peaceful. Peacefulness is a state, not an emotion. When you say, Yes, I'm happy, you're averaging out a bunch of emotions over a frame of time. I read a study once which said you have to be complimented ten times for every insult before you'll check the I'm happy box on a questionnaire. But peacefulness is different.

"Peacefulness can be found. And cultivated. Across all the emotions. In fact, once you've felt real peacefulness, deep down in your core, you learn to spot an emotion and immediately link it to that peacefulness. When your emotion is happiness, the peacefulness magnifies it, sometimes into ecstasy. When your emotion's anger, the peacefulness converts it into Emperor energy, it becomes your friend and helps you change the cause, or at least cope skillfully without damaging someone else. And peaceful isn't passive, either. Action can be peaceful, will be, once you know."

Her daughter smiled again. "Mom. All you have to do is adjust the mirror by the tiniest degree and everything suddenly looks so different, so understandable. I'm sure glad I brought you along when I decided to spend the rest of my life here." She felt the cold shadow clinging to her exuberance once again, however, cast as always by the one, unshared secret from her years with Mahmoud, the weight of which still kept her from soaring as her mother's equal. She rationalized that it was now irrelevant, here in this farthest corner of the land. But she knew this excuse, too, was a temporary blanket.

Darcy squeezed her mother's hand. Mariah didn't let it go, but pulled her upright and led her on up the creek, past the waterfall to the mirrored stillness of the pond above. They skipped some flat stones to the other side before returning to the energetic tumult of the ever more populous Maxwell Acres.

CHAPTER 92
Friday, March 24

"I SEE you found the place where my tribe held their ceremonials long ago."

Agnes approached the fire circle, with Darcy, Eli, Nelson and Shaz. They were gathering firewood and tinder into bundles.

"I was a little embarrassed to say so," Nelson said. "But when I first came over here, it sure seemed like a holy place."

They told Agnes how intense the grieving fire ceremony had been, as if some outside spiritual force had amplified their home-grown ritual.

"I should have known you wouldn't just be roasting marshmallows around a campfire here. The place probably would have hidden itself from you, if that had been your plan." They sat. She went on to paint a vignette of what her people's legends said occurred here in the old time.

"Are all your ancestors Modoc?" Darcy asked.

"Only half. My mother was a full Modoc. But she fell in love with a Hopi smokejumper who had come over from Arizona to fight a forest fire one summer. He stayed, and they planned to get married. But they couldn't agree on a last name. He wouldn't take her Modoc name, and she wouldn't take his Hopi one. So they both changed their last names, legally in court, to 'Miniata' and then had the judge marry them on the spot. They had gone to the library and took the word from the species name for the Scarlet Paintbrush, *Castilleja miniata*. I've always loved that story."

Darcy felt a tingle up her spine as she realized that even this detail had come through in her ESP session with Mariah in the vivid image of the flowering Indian Paintbrush. *Wait until Mom hears this*, she thought. She saw Eli grinning at her.

"How about you, Shaz?" she asked.

"I'm originally from Turkey. My folks brought me to San Francisco in the sixties. My real name's Yeter Gersel, but the friends I ran with at Lowell High School nicknamed me Shaz."

"Are you really a Sufi?" Eli asked.

"My mother was. We just say a person 'is' Sufi. Not is 'a' Sufi. It's not supposed to be a group thing, something you're part of, or join. The word sort of means that you're permeated with the Sufi way of thinking or being, you're integrated in the Universe, not a loyalist in some splinter group. That's the theory, anyway. Like organized religion, however, you can get caught up in structure and hierarchy. The Sufi way's not immune from that malady either. But basically, it's the most pacifist, purely mystical branch of Islam."

Agnes patted his arm. "I'm grateful he kept the peacefulness and gentleness, even if he did scrap the doctrine and the dogma."

He looked tenderly back at her. "I prefer Hopi prophecy, which Agnes carries in her soul." She looked at the toe of her moccasin. Shaz went on, "Maybe someday she'll tell you some of it. But she lets me tell people the nutshell version, that their prophecy predicts a collapse of civilization, wherein 'two-hearted' people, the ones who split materiality from spirituality, die out and the 'one-hearted' ones succeed to the earth."

A deeper quiet settled on the group. Darcy noticed Nelson's vacant stare, looking at her but seeing something else. She felt her own two-heartedness and an increasing drive to heal the rift, to share the burden she alone still bore.

The explosive caw of a crow gliding low overhead startled them, and as it receded into the distance they became aware of approaching voices. It was Ray and Jacob returning from the waterfall up Eastside Creek, where Ray was planning a diversion dam and ditch for irrigation, and Jacob was now investigating whether he could engineer a waterwheel in the same project to power an electric generator.

The Lunch Bell sounded.

Returning to the compound Ray nudged Shaz. "I hear you worked for the Flat River Police Department. I understood after the power went out they got into a turf battle with the Sheriff's Office and lost out."

"Lost a couple of officers, too. Everyone disputed what happened, but one thing was indisputable. There was a shootout. It's fair to say the Police Department 'is no more.' But because I'm one of only three people who can maintain their newest communications equipment, the Sheriffs weren't too subtle in threatening me if I quit. I made my decision Monday night, though, because I overheard their plans to take a posse to Buckberry Valley. Knowing specifically who was signing up, I knew they'd wind up just shooting indiscriminately, Agnes and all the families, women and children included. They were the crazy ones, who'd take the mission to clear the Valley as carte blanche to rape, kill and destroy. I slipped out during a beer break at midnight and ran on foot all the way to Agnes's house."

"You think they'll come up here eventually?" Ray asked.

Shaz looked at him sharply. "Nope. That's why we came."

"Why are you so sure?"

"Three reasons. First, one hunter guy started talking about the old homesteads. He named the Maxwell Place along with two or three others. The officers at the top ridiculed him. The police chief, Dick Jones, said the lawyers sold the Maxwell homestead a year ago to some old guy who died and left it to relatives in the Bay Area. He wasn't even sure the relatives ever showed up, and if they did, they probably took one look and left, because—these are his exact words. He said, 'They ain't nothin' there but a couple ol' ramshackle shacks anyway, nothin' worth the time o' day.'"

Ray snickered.

"Second reason is, the cops have burned up so much of their gasoline since the railroad and gas tankers quit running that their appetite for taking equipment anywhere outside the city is way below zero. Buckberry Valley was a prize worth gas, but not this little place. And third, even if they did decide to extend their turf or go on raiding parties, they'd go up 299, or over to Surprise Valley. I think Hell will freeze over before you see any of them up here."

At lunch, much of the talk was about Shaz's intelligence from inside the Sheriff's Office. Darcy's awareness was continually drawn to Mariah, who remained reticent and simply studied the assembled faces.

She found herself saying, "I've been thinking about how hard it was for Agnes and her band to come in over the ridge, how Dupree Ransom and his friend were wandering around the mountains but completely missed our place, and now how Shaz describes the improbability of the town militia coming up here. And I've been thinking about the enormous task we're setting out on here. We've got to grow our food, make our clothes, make this place work, teach these kids, keep learning ourselves. I'm thinking the huge effort to maintain an armed watch down at the Royer's Cabin just isn't the way we want to live. We already gave up the night watch."

Darcy stood. "We may actually attract what we fear." For an instant the fear from her own past nudged forward—she deflected an inner voice saying Heed your own wisdom. She returned to the discussion. "I say, let's not put that energy out there. We need every hand to move our little lifeboat forward in the most positive possible direction. Peter and Maurice could be running a full-time school in the Underground Room."

Nelson voiced what Peter was thinking. "What if they do come up the road, guns blazing?"

"Or over the ridge? Or from the promontory?" Charles added.

Mariah stepped in, "One, we'd feel it coming. Two, practically everyone here can help defend us, if it's ever needed. And three, I agree, we shouldn't spend one iota of energy being defensive any more. This is an experiment, or could be, which has seldom, if ever before, been seen in history. Every fiber of everyone's being should be poured into it. And what if the forces of darkness snuff it out, despite any defense we might raise at the moment? The legend would live on. This way of life cannot be stopped. The light would not go out. Our advance would propagate down through history, like Masada, and Tule Lake, the Maya from Puerto Vallarta, the Exodus from Egypt, the Pioneer Spacecraft heading for Alpha Centauri. In fact, I think Charles should be writing this history as we go, instead of maintaining a gun watch over the fallen oak."

"If you don't mind my saying so," said Peter, "I think it'd be flat out naïve to abandon our watch. It's already deteriorated dangerously. I for one don't ever intend to go through an experience again like we did in McCloud. I aim to be ready when the time comes." He patted the holster against his ribs. "The founding fathers of our country recognized that we have to 'provide for the common defense.'"

"But it's easy to go too far with that," said Kim. "Working in government I saw up close the billions spent on defense, saw that much of it was wasted and misdirected. For one thing, 'defense' often became a disguise for swaggering around the world imposing economic policy and enforcing the will of corporate power. Thad Parker was constantly trying to rein in a military machine that had to find a use for its might. We would have been better off spending most of those billions building the foundations of prosperity and peace."

Agnes' voice was quiet and wavering at first but rose with a passion echoing Darcy and Mariah. "You know, it was hard for Darcy to see me, sitting on the trail by the spring. I can testify, it takes no effort whatsoever to avoid drawing attention to yourself. It's like being invisible. Everyone can learn. Everyone has done it at one time or another. It only takes being truly centered in your peacefulness. Not as a control system but simply your personal peacefulness with your life and death at every moment. You know, death's not the worst thing. We all live on. The worst is to not grow in consciousness, to fail to add to the collective experience of all things through this mysterious enterprise of incarnation. For thousands of years, humankind has linked survival with power, with defense, with police and armies. It's time to join the forces who have unlinked that in the past and add our weight to the evolutionary advance."

In turn, Jacob retold his experience of invisibility as he trudged through the open streets of Berkeley to his safety. Eli brought in anecdotes from his days in prison and experiences on his trek to freedom. Kim and Nelson added parallel principles from their martial arts. Paisley and Ray brought up legends from their learning in India, and Rose began to correlate the surging movement with fragments of prayer and Scripture quotes. "The leaders wanted to arrest Jesus, but he passed from their midst."

Peter was the lone objector, and lapsed into silence as the idea encompassed the group, like ripples on a pond, and when the last ripple came to rest upon the shore and the reflective mirror of still water was restored, Charles spoke. "Where's that history book with the unwritten pages? Up in Maxwell's workshop? I think I'll take a look at it."

CHAPTER 93
April

IN THEIR TWENTY DAYS of collaboration, Reinhold and Omaha Chang had formed a partnership of equals. Their skills of spoken Russian and written Cyrillic were indistinguishable. Reinhold's lifelong outdoorsmanship and his ordeal since leaving Moscow matched Omaha's Air Force survival training and special assignment in Kazakhstan.

And they had finally reached rapprochement on the subject of religion. Omaha twice had maneuvered Reinhold into admitting weakness in citations of Chapter and Verse, while Reinhold had niggled ruthlessly at her inability to keep the sequence of Jesus's ministry straight.

She finally admitted, "Look, I knew from the start you used biofeedback to heat your hands that day. I can do it, too. I played along because I'd already assessed your skills in Russian. Your guess about being at NORAD inside Cheyenne Mountain, the recklessness of that prayer and hot-hands ploy... Let's just say the excitement of the challenge outweighed the risks of holding you in high esteem."

On April Fools' Day, Omaha had shared a rare joint with Reinhold. In the euphoria Reinhold told her about Darcy and the children, then indulged his curiosity.

"How'd you get this past the Eurotech molecular signature screens?"

She laughed and said, "Inside job. I'm friends with the entrance guards. They let me hike for exercise on the slopes below the mouth of the Tunnel at the South Portal, as long as I stay within the perimeter. Actually, it's more like rock climbing. My longest hike was six hours—last summer. Anyway, a guy I know in Colorado Springs flew a radio controlled model airplane inside the perimeter and dumped a bunch of marijuana seeds. Guess what? They grew.

378

Naturally. So now I just go harvest a hit when I'm feeling lucky, after I've come inside through security. You can pick a lot of weed in six hours. Simple, huh? It doesn't hurt that I pass a little to the security boys, too. They can't figure out how I do it either. But then, why would they care?"

Reinhold never underestimated Omaha's ingenuity again.

A few days later, with brass jazz on the rec room speakers masking their words from Big Brother's snoopy mikes, Reinhold unleashed a rare diatribe. "Your boss, the Military. You've got to admit, Omaha, they're no better than the Nazis. Or Stalin. No one has any rights any more. They have the license to kill at a whim. Or worse. You saw the bruises on my face. They don't even have to be careful, like they used to. Remember? They used to beat people where it didn't show."

Her face clouded over. "I hate them, too. I hate it all—now. I used to be proud, after I got out of the Academy. Even though I had to favor my way through a couple of sticky spots. But since the Joint Chiefs okayed Code Byrdland and the Mt. Jackson event struck, I lost it... I hate myself, too."

The next day she shared another joint with Reinhold. Her inhibitions eroded further, freeing her to reveal what, days before, would have been anathema. "I've reached a turning point in my life, Reinhold. For the first time ever, I've come to trust someone. You. This morning a weight was added to that, which makes it unbearable. My superior officer added two items to your dossier. They're bringing some men from Santa Fe who think you have useful information about an art theft ring—they think your wife told you where the art is, and they can use it to get to the petroleum powerbrokers in the Middle East. I don't quite get it, but on Tuesday you'll be moved to the Maximum Security Interrogation level. Secondly, the computers turned up your involvement with Troy Blake and they're bringing him here to negotiate your release into his custody. If you survive interrogation, that is."

Reinhold's mind cleared instantly. "That was my wife's involvement. I don't know anything."

"They're not likely to believe that. Your life's in the balance again, Mister."

He hissed, "Why'd you tell me?"

Omaha glanced around the rec room. They were still alone. She said, "Don't look at the cameras." She breathed deeply and spoke almost without moving her lips. "I think together we could get out of here and survive."

Reinhold held his expression, for the security cameras. Except for his eyes. They felt like lasers.

379

She elaborated. "On one of my hikes I discovered an eighteen inch wide crack in a rock under the perimeter fence. I wriggled through it as a test. I know these mountains. You game?"

Reinhold answered, "If I got started again, I'd go straight to Espanola."

"I know Espanola. Its due east of Los Alamos."

Reinhold's mind reeled. *She needs me more than I need her. She's lost her tolerance for the war machine. She's panicked, and her days are numbered, too. Nonbelievers can't survive this system.* He threw out the bait. "There's a guy there who'd fly me west. You too. Think you could spring us?"

"Watch me."

The following morning was Palm Sunday. For days, Omaha had been touting Reinhold's biblical enthusiasm to one of her entrance guard friends who prayed with the charismatics. He now considered Reinhold one of the flock and no longer a security risk. This morning, Omaha convinced him to let Reinhold go with her on a "hike."

"It's okay, Brother," she said. "To Praise the Lord for His Wondrous Creation. Besides, I'll have my sidearm if he needs any gentle persuasion." She patted her weapon. Reinhold saw the guard slip Sergeant Chang a knowing wink. She did look downright arresting in her camouflage, with a lethal thirty-eight strapped to her hip.

Omaha and Reinhold had calculated they could look natural and still wear enough warm clothing on the "hike" to survive over the western pass if there were no storms. In addition, Omaha had sequestered in her day pack three mylar heat-retentive blankets from the triage supplies. She knew enough about edible forage to last for weeks. And she had three topo maps that covered the territory from Cheyenne Mountain to Alamosa. There they would hit the Rio Grande, which ran square between Los Alamos and Espanola.

The getaway was simple, as Omaha had predicted. They just walked down the fern-covered slope under the Douglas firs, slithered under the perimeter through the crack and headed west into the mountains.

The red and orange sunset was brilliant. It was a welcome relief from the blinding glare of the afternoon sun on the snowfields they had been unable to avoid. They had sheltered in a small cave. Over the whistle of the breeze they heard the helicopters.

"They can't see us," Omaha said. "I'm surprised they're wasting fuel even looking."

"We only made three miles, by the crow," Reinhold said.

"Yeah, I know. With a six-hour lead they could still track us if they went all out. But I'm betting we're not important enough, in the scheme of things. They just have to file a report for the muckety-mucks. It'll say 'We tried.' And that'll be the end of it."

"My. Aren't we humble?" Reinhold was now admiring Omaha's escape skills. Under her command they had crossed and double-crossed streams, walked up and then back downstream on rocks more than once, leaving scent on both sides at random spots. Eventually she took off their boots and saturated the bottoms of their bare feet with mountain wintergreen for a half-mile. She knew dogs couldn't tolerate its sting in their nostrils.

Reinhold breathed deeply, felt strangely safe again. They supped on Alpine onion bulbs and Rocky Mountain wheatgrass that was only digestible in the spring, and wrapped themselves in separate mylars. Then they spooned together on their makeshift fir-branch mattress and draped the third mylar over their survival huddle.

Omaha muttered, "Goodnight, Johnboy. Tomorrow we climb to Cripple Creek."

For three days, ridge after mountain ridge had punished the fugitives. They had faced down a thousand granite boulders and a dozen slushy snowfields, remaining alert for helicopter patrols and taking instant cover from their high-tech sensors.

Now in a quiet valley, Omaha said, "Sit down and rest a while. I'm going to get some game." She motioned to a stand of brush in the shade of a cliff.

"I don't need a rest," Reinhold protested. "I'll help."

"You've sounded like a herd of elephants behind me all day. You don't have a clue how to do this."

"Oh. You do?"

"You bet your butt, I do. My Grandmammy used to take me out in the Bayou and let me track with her. She was the last Chickasaw huntress—her name translated, 'Hunts-Like-A-Cat.' We'd practice, as she put it, 'Walkin' like a feather, movin' like a shadow, visible as a cobweb.' You stay put, white boy. I'll bring something back."

She did. They cooked the cottontail over the coals of a smokeless mesquite fire, ate, then moved on.

As their third day crept to a close, Reinhold heard Omaha's warning, thirty yards ahead. "Hold up. There's a structure. Better watch a minute."

There were no signs of habitation. They eased their way around in a wide circle, staying out of sight. Pine needles covered the window sills. An undisturbed remnant of snow glistened in the shadow of the southerly door post.

She pierced the silence. "Hello, the house." Not a sound came back.

She sat down in the shadow of a tree, dug her heels into the ground and braced her pistol on both knees. "I don't think anyone's in there. Go see. I'll cover you."

Reinhold obeyed, strode to the front door, attempting a nonchalant demeanor. He knocked. Again. Nothing. Tried the doorknob. The door swung open. He eased a look inside, then turned and shouted, "No one here. Looks like a rancher's summer line shack."

Omaha came down. "Let's sleep here, tonight."

"Good. My left foot's killing me."

They opened the windows to air out the winter dampness and sat on a stump in the sunshine.

"Let's see your foot," Omaha demanded. When it was naked, Reinhold lifted it for her inspection.

"You goddam fool. You've got a blister the size of a half-dollar right on your fucking heel. You're going to have to rest it now, or it actually could kill us both. Why didn't you stop when we could have minimized it?"

Reinhold felt his face redden and didn't answer. His soldier-turned-nurse had him limp to the cabin, where she rubbed first-aid iodine on the heel until it worked through and stung under the blister cap. "We'll have to stay here a couple of days. The iodine'll harden your skin faster than it would on its own. Keep it elevated, and stay off it. With luck we'll be on the trail again Saturday."

"That's Good Saturday."

"Go to hell."

Outside the cabin, the rancher had built a cement cook grill. On another hunting foray, Omaha had brought a second rabbit down with her throwing knife. Now, in the dwindling daylight, with Reinhold languishing on his bunk, she tended a fire to a bed of coals while she dressed out the carcass. Grilled rabbit thus was added to their feast of onions and wheat grass that night.

"Tomorrow and Friday—Good Friday, Bozo—I want you to pour your Jesus heat into that heel all day. I don't believe in miracles, but biofeedback can concentrate lymph and white blood cells wherever you focus. It should help. I'm going to hike down to Westcliffe and see if I can befriend anyone. If I get lucky, they might give us some provisions."

Thursday, Reinhold meditated all day. That is, in between irrepressible anxieties. *What if she gets killed? Or captured? Or just keeps going? How long'll I wait? How'll I eat? And drink?*

He felt California was a million miles away. This was harder than being in the crate. At least there, he had been all on his own.

Just before dusk, he heard footsteps. He got up, hid behind the door, both hands on a two-by-four he'd found. The door swung open, slowly. Then he heard, "Reinhold? Reinhold, it's me."

"Thank God." He stepped out of the shadow. Omaha holstered her thirty-eight and grabbed him with both arms.

Not even trying to suppress a smirk from her lips and a rise from her eyebrows, she said, "Yup. Got lucky. Usually do. Country boys can't resist camouflage fatigues on a woman."

She pulled her loot from a ragged old backpack, item by tantalizing item. Jerky, candy bars, peanut butter, raisins, soda crackers, milk powder, more jerky. A cowboy's rope and two blue bandannas. Finally, four hard-boiled eggs, two oranges and a pair of apples. "For tonight and tomorrow," she said, fondling the fruit. "Let's eat."

Easter Sunday brought more sun.

On Friday, Omaha found a creek, took a swim, soaked up some sun, made a woodwind from a hollow reed, and flavored the wind with random melodies—some tinkling of China, some swelling with the rhythms of Jamaica, some haunting like ghosts of her ancestor's plains. By Saturday, Reinhold's heel was trail worthy and they had descended out of the San Isabels, cut south of Rosita, and turned due west up the eastern slope of the Sangre de Cristo. It had been easy going, on a relative scale.

Today it was Reinhold's turn to wake first. "Happy Easter," he said.

Omaha sat up, rubbed her eyes and beamed. Reinhold admired her perennial capacity to rocket from a deep slumber to full alert instantaneously. She reached in her pack and Presto, out came an Easter egg.

"Where'd you get that?"

"I saved it from Westcliffe. I reddened it with wildflowers while I watched you swim the other day."

Reinhold blushed. *That stealthy little wildcat,* he thought. He hadn't even sensed her presence.

He felt attracted to Omaha right now. It was not the first time, but it was the strongest yet. His inner turbulence boiled up, on cue. He felt his love for Darcy, longing for reunion and unreached depths he now knew were possible.

He felt the recurring guilt at leading Omaha along, using her as his ticket to California. He weighed these feelings against the physical magnetism of the moment.

He ate the egg. They broke camp and pushed on.

Coming down off the Rio Grande Ridge, their way was blocked by a steep-sided wash running high water from the melting snow. They turned back, retracing their steps to find a fording opportunity. Finally, after passing up two questionable routes, Omaha made a decision.

She eased down the crumbly bank on her rump, bracing where she could against rounded, basketball-sized rocks embedded in the sediment ages before. There was no shore or beach—the torrential waters came right to the bank. A series of flat-topped, desk-sized boulders presented the path to cross, if one were willing to leap over the rapids in between. Omaha balanced on the bank, waiting to rope herself to Reinhold before her first attempt. Reinhold slung the daypack over his right shoulder and began sliding down Omaha's track.

Without warning, a foothold broke loose. Reinhold dropped six feet. His right hand grabbed a manzanita bush clinging to the bank. It held, but he could feel a tear in his shoulder muscle as the extra weight of the pack whipsawed. He cried out from the pain and let go. The backpack continued its trajectory and Reinhold plummeted with a small avalanche of stone and gravel toward the rapids. At the last second, he lashed out with his left-hand, but the tuft of grass he grabbed was no help, and he plunged into the roaring ice water.

The shock of the icy cold forced an exhale, and he choked on the water that came in with his truncated inhale. Desperate for air, he tumbled head over heels, then wrenched to his side and rolled. He kicked against the bottom of the wash, arm limp, trying to propel himself to safety as he saw a dry-topped boulder looming in his path. He nearly made it, but hit the side and scraped back to the waterline. His useless right arm slammed between the boulder and a second rock protruding from the torrent. The arm wedged tight, his body weight swung with full force downstream. His leg crashed against stone. He felt his shoulder joint separate from his upper arm. But the muscle and ligaments held, and his body drifted in the wake of the boulder, his face in the air where he could cough the water from his windpipe and gasp a life-giving gulp of air back in.

Tethered by his dislocated arm, he washed side to side with the waters until Omaha could inch her way down the bank to him. A broken pine stump became the anchor for her rope, the other end tied around her waist, with a free length to secure Reinhold's body if she could. She plunged in, wading and stroking her way to her companion. She hooked her arm under his left armpit from the back, curved her elbow and secured a grip against the nape of his neck. She managed to lunge with him upstream to dislodge his right arm, tied the loose end of the rope around his chest, and worked her way back to the bank with him in tow. She tied him to the pine stump, climbed to the top of the bank and hoisted him foot-by foot until he lay on the grassy edge of the embankment.

He sat up, his right arm dangling by his side like a cheesecloth sac full of inert muscle tissue. The knob of his upper arm bone made a horrifying bulge in front of its socket. As he struggled to maintain a coherent consciousness, however, Reinhold became aware of another center of pain. He examined his lower left leg. An oval of black and blue, with jagged red webs radiating out from it, and a strange, protruding lump underneath, convinced him he had also broken his tibia.

Omaha's decisiveness was paralyzed. Reinhold's eyes met hers. His jaw worked furiously to hold back the moans his injuries demanded. His mind was racing through a hundred action choices, none of which seemed realistic. Gradually, through the haze, a memory surfaced: an old friend's story of dislocating his shoulder on a solo kayak run down a wild river. His friend would have died from immobilization had he not devised a do-it-yourself solution, which later made its way into survival manuals. The memory snapped into place and Reinhold acted.

He put a stick between his teeth to take the pressure of his bite at the pain he was about to induce. With his left-hand, he seized his right wrist, brought his right knee to his chest and curved his right wrist around his foot. He grunted, "Onaha, add your grif to strengfen my han so my wris doesn' slif out."

Then he jammed his right foot suddenly forward. He heard a sickening snap, and the pain shot far above his threshold. He lost consciousness.

When he regained an aching awareness and looked to his right shoulder, he saw the bony knob had slipped back into its socket.

Omaha looked as pale as Reinhold had ever seen her. He said through the fog of continuing pain, "Okay, Omaha, let's bind it in place and figure out how we can get some treatment."

"It's about noon. Due east of here is Crestone. I can get there and back by dark. First let's dry you off. Then I'll bind your shoulder and wrap you up so you don't go into shock. If your leg is broken, I'll have to convince someone to come and carry you out."

She took off all Reinhold's clothes, wrung them as dry as possible and laid them in the sun on warm, black lava boulders. Using the bandannas to fend off rope burns, she bound his forearm between his chest and his belly, elbow at a right angle, and created a triangular brace around his shoulder to keep the whole assemblage in place. At the end, it was a picture-perfect first-aid triumph, lacking only a photographer and publisher.

Together, the two decided to leave Reinhold's leg alone, lest they make the injury worse. If she failed to get help, they could probably fashion a splint and some kind of crutch to get out of the mountains to a place where folks might take pity on him.

The pack had fallen free and caught on a bush at the water's edge. After Omaha bound Reinhold's shoulder, she found a suitable spot for him to sit, and laid their scant remaining cloths over him so he wouldn't burn in the sun. She arranged the best cushion she could for his leg, using grass and soft dirt.

Every ten minutes she moved the steaming clothes to new boulders. In an hour they were nearly dry again, somewhat stiff.

She got him dressed, wrapped him in the mylar blankets so the remaining dampness wouldn't chill him, left the water and food within reach, and headed toward the west once more. Alone, this time.

On the edge of Crestone, Omaha felt a strange quiet. The scattered buildings looked like any other Colorado farming crossroads, except for several well-constructed complexes interlaced with luxuriant shade trees. And there was a large field with well-cropped Bermuda grass and several dozen house-sized tents with multicolored triangular banners flying from their tent poles.

A woman in a yellow and orange dress was walking down a road that led away from the tents and would intersect with Omaha's. Omaha slowed so they would meet. The woman's countenance, under stringy blond hair, red dot on her forehead, was peaceful and direct.

"We saw you walking down from the hills," the woman said. "I came to meet you. My name is Katja."

Omaha stifled the emotion welling up from her gratefulness, put her palms together in front of her breast bone, and said, "My partner's injured in the hills. Can you help?"

Within half an hour, four young men carrying a bamboo litter from the Yeshe Khorlo, a Bhutanese Tibetan retreat center, set out jogging and walking, with Omaha in the lead. They reached the clearing where Reinhold was waiting and returned with him to the Crestone Sanctuary by sundown.

A Sanctuary doctor confirmed Reinhold's broken tibia, administered a partial anesthetic of aromatic herbs and traditional painkillers, and set the bone. As to Reinhold's shoulder, the doctor concluded that, as best he could tell without an x-ray, the socket setting was as good as he could have done himself. "Barring complications," he said, "your body will be healed in eight to ten weeks."

They curtained off a corner of one of the tents, and with the help of a tofu and bean sprout broth, more aromatic herbs, and bitter herbs as well, Reinhold slipped into a long sleep. They set up a cot for Omaha, too, then took her to the other side of the complex for dinner.

In the bustling eating tent, from Katja and her friends Omaha heard an overview of the Crestone story. A pair of philanthropists named Strong had consolidated part of an old Spanish land grant known as the Baca Ranch in the 1970s. They gave pieces to a broad collection of religious, educational and intellectual groups, including Roman Catholic Carmelites, a variety of Buddhist groups encompassing Zen, Tibetan and other traditions, organizations from India, Bhutan, Native American Nations, the Sri Aurobindo worldwide community, and more.

In the chaos that surrounded the collapse of ice in Antarctica, general restrictions on movement and civil liberties followed by military law and the aftermath of the tsunami made Crestone hard to reach. But its reputation was universal, and people had been trickling in regardless of the difficulties. So all of the spiritual centers in the valley had pooled their resources and created the Sanctuary. There was pervasive optimism that the intensive agricultural methods already well founded within the community, and abundant water from the snowy heights, could sustain practically any population that could manage to arrive.

Omaha returned to her cot at midnight. A brilliant half-moon was rising over the Sangre de Cristo. With that as her only light, Omaha changed into the flannel nightshirt Katja had given her. She knelt beside Reinhold's head. She whispered, "I don't know why we are together, and I don't know how long it will be. Though you are unconscious, your heart hears me. I pray you will be able to return to your family, who I have grown to love through you. You have brought me thus far for a reason, which may take my lifetime to find. I am grateful, my friend. Sleep well. I will."

LATE IN THE AFTERNOON, Easter Sunday, Agnes Miniata stole a private moment with Rose. She had shown intense interest in the Royers' health care teamwork as they examined each child in turn for immediate needs on

387

their day of arrival. She confided, "I too am an herbalist, Rose. I was taught Native American healing practices by my grandmothers."

Then she made a different connection. "Rose, having you and your husband here is a miracle for me. You see, the week we got here, I missed my period. Three days ago, when the moon was full, I tested myself with herbs in the way of my ancestors. I am with child."

CHAPTER 94
Sunday, May 7

DARCY TRIED to sound noncommittal to mask the intensity she felt her face might reveal. "Nelson, would you take me and Mom on a hike? It's such a gorgeous day. You go on hunting trips, so you must know some great spots."

Without hesitation, Nelson said, "Sunflower Knob. It has a spectacular view. I'll get the binoculars."

Mariah volunteered to carry the canteen, and Darcy a lunch. They climbed to the promontory, then zigzagged across half a dozen saddles and ridgelines to the towering outcrop overlooking Buckberry Valley five miles below. The view was breathtaking, although the sight of tiny, burned-out houses through the binoculars betrayed the recent violence made nearly invisible by the distance.

Their meal consumed, Darcy revealed her ulterior purpose. "Mom, I want to come clean to you with the final truth about my involvement with Mahmoud. Nelson's here because he agreed to be my ego brake."

Early on in her unfoldment to Nelson, Darcy had told him what her mother already knew. But the unspoken shadows had gnawed at her conscience with increasing ferocity in the light of the trust-based community growing at the homestead.

As an apologia she started, "I wanted to protect you, Mom, from this. At least that's what I told myself all those years. But I've come to realize it was really to shore up my façade, and unless I share the burden, I'm afraid I'll lose my way again."

Nelson tossed a pebble over the precipice, and Mariah simply nodded encouragement with a softened countenance.

"Not long before they killed Mahmoud, I had come into our apartment through the laundry room off the kitchen one evening. You almost never heard that door, and this night was no different. Mahmoud had two associates in the kitchen. They were shouting, and no one knew I was there. I stopped and listened to see if it was safe. In a scant few minutes I knew I'd heard too much, and I sneaked back out, walked the streets until midnight. When I got back, they were gone and Mahmoud was asleep in front of the TV."

"What did you hear?" Asked Mariah.

"The most recent shipment of their stolen art I had arranged under the gallery's export license had gone to an address in Japan, a place called Tokugawa Island."

Nelson twisted toward Darcy, his eyes wide. "That's just off the coast toward Korea, west of where my grandfather spent his final days—at the Eheiji zen temple in the western prefectures. The only thing on that island was the stone foundation of a castle destroyed in the great Shogunate wars of the eighteenth century. Then in the 1980s one of Japan's wealthiest industrialists rebuilt it for himself. His grandfather was one of the Shinto generals who took Japan into World War II."

"Well, that fits," Darcy said. "I'd heard about the billionaire, but I didn't know what Mahmoud's ring was shipping to him. Sealed under the backing of lesser paintings, I learned that night, were the two Rembrandts stolen from the Gardner Museum in Boston in 1990. Mahmoud was trying to negotiate a higher fee to ship the next installment, the Vermeer from that same heist. The industrialist was striving to amass the world's greatest collection of stolen art in the secret gallery in his castle. He even owned the legendary Amber Room that Peter the Great commissioned, which disappeared in the Nazi takeover of St. Petersburg and has never been seen since."

Nelson flicked a crust off his knee. It caught in a tenacious cliff rose clinging to the rocks.

Darcy stared vacantly into the distance. "That's when I quit. I refused to launder any more of Mahmoud's art. They were desperate, and they murdered him as a threat to me. But I had already removed Mahmoud's records in those boxes I stored in Oakland, Mom. I told you they were schoolbooks. Since I no longer controlled the ex-im license, and they were afraid to kill me for fear of a runaway investigation, they left me alone after that. But I've always borne the guilt for those Rembrandts, and for protecting Mahmoud's clients' locations. Not just Tokugawa Island, but some of the other places in the Middle East where we shipped. And you and Dad could have been in danger if anyone figured out you were storing Mahmoud's records. Every time I brought Tierney and Finn over to your house I thought of those boxes in the attic and how they should be destroyed. And my lies all those years. It's been gnawing at me. It's ironic, isn't it, that the records burned in February when they killed Dad?"

Mariah stayed still. Darcy read compassion in her eyes but was mystified by the laughter in her voice. "That's not the highest irony, Baby. Some of the world's greatest masterpieces survived the tsunami only because of you. The museums in England, Boston, New York, Washington—they were all destroyed with everything inside. At least the art you people dispersed still exists."

Nelson was shaking his head.

"You didn't exactly bargain for this, did you?" Mariah asked. "Well, it doesn't have to go any further. No one we should ever have to deal with would care much, would they?"

The conversation was cut short. Nelson held up his hand. "Voices." They all listened. He stood, peered over the cliff, surveyed their surroundings in an instant. If the visitors were unfriendly, they were trapped. "Quick. Follow me. We can't take any chances." He scrambled around the left side of the outcrop and down a series of ledges jutting out like steps to a final ledge large enough for the three of them to sit on. One slip of the foot, or a loose stone, would catapult a climber into a hundred feet of thin air, but they were out of view from atop the rock.

The voices got closer. They stopped directly above. "I woulda swore I saw people here," sounded a phlegmatic growl. A boot thumped, and a fist-sized rock bounced twice and hurtled downward.

"We hoofed all the way over here for nothin', didn't we? Asshole."

"I saw them, I say, or my name ain't Able Martin."

"You've taken me wild goose chasin' before. Jerk."

"You fuckin' fool. You know someone's been poachin' our game. We heard them shots. I keep smellin' smoke, too, goddammit. In these crazy mountains, the wind just blows every which way so you can't tell where it's coming from. But you keep that Bowie knife sharp, McCoy, and I'll take you where you can use it soon enough."

Nelson made them stay motionless for fifteen minutes. Then he stole slowly upward, knife unsheathed. After a couple of minutes, which seemed interminable below, he said, "I can't spot them with the binoculars. Let's try to get back."

The return trip was about silence and vigilance. Nelson alone spoke, and only once: "We'd better start hunting with Mr. Maxwell's crossbows—they can't be heard. And check the wind direction when we have fires." To Darcy, the Rembrandts seemed diminished in significance by the time they reached the compound.

CHAPTER 95
Summer

BY EARLY SUMMER there was an education experiment underway at Greater Maxwell Acres. Actually, every person on the place was a teacher, and to some degree every person on the place was also a matriculant. Only the Internet could have made it more intense, and Jacob said he was working on that. Every activity a teacher might have labeled "educational" fit like the joints of a finely dovetailed hardwood cabinet into the profusion of activities swirling within the community.

Jacob had started the experiment the day after Darcy, Agnes and the rest had made the case for no more armed security watches. Part of the rhetoric that night had been the necessity to educate the newly arrived children. The next day at breakfast, Jacob unfolded a passionate tale from his experiences in Berkeley.

"One of my lifetime favorite people," he said, "was a man about sixty years old who had fathered two spectacular children late in life. He himself was the product of an Eastern boarding school, an Ivy League college and a Midwestern law school, after which he had joined a commune and was a poorly-paid carpenter/philosopher in Berkeley the rest of his life. His children attended a school in the Berkeley area modeled on the Sudbury Valley School in Massachusetts.

"The founder of Sudbury Valley had concluded that children were natural, unlimited learning machines, and wondered why in America, with food and technology aplenty, and a surplus of almost everything, children were learning so poorly—not only that, but the successful ones often lacked initiative, enthusiasm, spunk.

"He found that our lockstep, kindergarten through twelfth-grade system had been created several centuries back by the Prussians to standardize the knowledge and pliability of young men being groomed for the army. That was almost all the boys in Prussia in that war-torn era.

"He found that the industrial revolution perpetuated the system for economic convenience—a rigorous, grade based, advance-at-the-end-of-the-year-or-else, conformity-rewarding system—killing spirit, spawning ciphers who would come to work on time, need little stimulation, accept outside agendas, do what they were told.

"So he started over. Kids came and followed their own interests. Literally. There was no curriculum. Adults didn't teach. They created the space. And they did their own work right there—bicycle building, wood working, computer operations, art, cooking. There was, strictly speaking, not even an administration.

"The sole purpose of the adults was to let the kids' work with them if they were interested, learn all they knew by interaction, and facilitate anything else any child wanted to learn about. Animals? Take them to the park. Bacteria? Scrounge for microscopes, or head to the Museum of Science in Boston, or beg entry to a lab at Harvard, MIT or some biotech company—whatever it took, but free if possible. Some of the kids didn't learn to read until they were ten and wanted to read a bicycle magazine. Then they learned in a few weeks."

Jacob made the case that the eight children at the homestead, including Finn, and even the four next-oldest people going right up through Jenna, Catherine, Jason and even Nelson who hadn't gone to college, made up a critical mass that was ideal for the Sudbury model. He argued that, with self-imposed isolation from outside civilization, the focus on agriculture and a sustainable livelihood, and the incredible depth of materials and objects Maxwell had concentrated in the Underground Room, you couldn't ask for a better world of resources for a few adult facilitators to manage. The budget issue was simple, too—there wasn't one.

Jacob was heavily occupied with his project of creating a waterwheel powerplant at the eastside waterfall to bring enough electricity for minimum conveniences and a satellite Internet connection. So he turned the idea over to Kim, Eli, Darcy, Agnes and Shaz.

Within a week they had so enthused Peter and Charles that the two senior statesmen of the community all but bowed out of significant agricultural duty. They began working almost full-time in what became known as the Sudbury Shed. A good deal of time was needed from the other five progenitors for projects essential to everyone's livelihood, but they spent as much time as could be spared at Sudbury Shed themselves. Everyone else did too, by summer's end.

Everyone shared their newly learned knowledge whenever a listener asked. They all discovered there is nothing like being a teacher to turn you into a manic student of the subject being taught.

Darcy, Kim and Nelson taught all comers, including each other, their variations of martial art disciplines. Old and young alike grew steadily in strength, agility and wisdom. The community's unstructured self-dominion steadied its keel.

As for Mariah? Between managing the big house industry of nourishment and participating in the daily labor of agriculture, she garnered Maxwell's selected volumes of eclectic mysticism and other spiritual exploration to deepen her own experience of what she called the "hidden universe." At least when she was not being called upon to take other members of the community deeper down their own next steps into intuition, extrasensory perception or other faculties of the body/mind/spirit triad.

CHAPTER 96
Tuesday, July 4

"HOW DO I LOOK?" Reinhold asked. He had painted a red, white and blue Tao symbol on a T-shirt and was headed to tiny downtown Crestone for the parade.

"Crestone's used to a schizophrenic fourth," Katja laughed. "For twenty, maybe twenty-five years. On the one hand, downtown they have the red, white and blue marching bands, firecrackers and military stuff. Meanwhile, out here in the Baca 'burbs we have the counterculture celebrating with beige tofu and our many-colored Eastern banners. And we're not talking East Coast, either."

Omaha was wrapped in a white sari. She said, "I think I'll stay away from downtown. Someone might recognize me, even without my camouflage. Have fun, Reinhold. I'll see you at the fire tonight." He smiled and nodded. But the smile seemed vague, and the nod tentative.

For Reinhold, the evening fire was the perfect blend of East and West. It was quiet and meditative. Those who weren't living out a vow of silence—whether temporary or lifelong, and both were represented at Crestone—often sang twentieth-century folk songs and cowboy ballads to gut-stringed guitars.

The half-moon floated in the blue velvet between sunset and black night as the singing began. "Just like University days," Reinhold commented. Omaha nodded and moved closer to his side. He flinched ever so slightly.

"Tomorrow I'm leaving for Espanola." He sounded abstract to himself. "Probably just in time. I think some of the fellows downtown today might have been from Cheyenne Mountain. One of them looked me over pretty hard. I'll feel better fishing my way down the Rio Grande. I think I'm a lot more competent on my own now."

He was silent for a long time. "I was stone lucky to have you with me thus far, Omaha. If I ever get home, I'll probably never be back. I'll think of you, out here on your way to Nirvana or the Bardo."

Omaha smiled. "Maybe we'll sing these songs there. With all our loved ones. Who knows? Even the gurus say, 'Who know?'"

Omaha had committed, after forty days, to the Yeshe Khorlo way of Tibet and had renounced her worldly claim to possessions, a husband or children. She had told Reinhold she was free now, happier than she ever imagined, more peaceful than she ever expected.

He, on the other hand, was committed to the West. He had sampled all the practices around the valley, as he gathered strength for his single-minded mission. "I've probably learned more than I can talk about," he joked with Omaha. "Maybe I'll find out what I learned here, someday. When I find Darcy. And the kids." He threw a twig into the fire, embodying into it the conflicted emotions swirling through his mind, watched quick flames lick around it, mercifully consuming it in seconds.

Omaha bantered back, brow wrinkled, "Those who know, do not say, and those who say, do not know."

Reinhold left before sunrise.

CHAPTER 97
Early August

"I WOULDN'T eat that fish," a voice volunteered from the shadows.

Reinhold cautiously turned his head from his tiny, smokeless fire, letting his eyes adjust. "Why?"

"Catch it in that pool up there?"

Reinhold nodded.

"Probably radioactive. Of course, whose living very long anyway?" A thin man with thin hair stepped toward him. He wore a denim jacket and pants.

Reinhold asked, "From around here?"

"Los Alamos." The man jerked his head to the west.

Reinhold offered him some water. "Got it up-river from that pool. Would it be okay to drink?"

The man nodded. He drank large gulps, looking sidewise at Reinhold. A few drops trickled down his stubbly neck.

"I used to work at the Weapons Lab at Los Alamos. Ten years. I kept track of radioactivity counts."

"Used to?" Reinhold retrieved his canteen. He did not ask or offer a name.

A few weeks before, the man explained, the government had installed a team of armed monitors to control every move of the director and his staff. The top monitor had unlimited discretion. He brought in a team of experts to dismantle most ecological controls and safety systems to boost efficiency. "Experts, hah!" he snorted. "Not on atomic weapons or particle research. They all believe in Armageddon."

"What will you do?"

"I have no idea. You?"

Reinhold hesitated. "You die out here if you travel with anyone, if you tell anyone much. You may die anyway, but you stand a better chance on your own."

"I have a map." The man offered it to Reinhold, his gesture one of pathos and desperation.

Reinhold was unmoved. "I wouldn't trust anyone, if I were you. If you're going cross-country, I'd circle down past Santa Fe, then east. I hear they have food once you're on the Great Plains, and the communities are kinder. If you can offer useful work, they sometimes even take you in, I hear."

He threw the fish in the bushes. "The coyotes and raccoons probably don't live long enough for radioactivity to hurt them anyway." He kicked dirt over the fire and said, "Do you want a head start or do you want me to go first?"

The man's face fell with disbelief. "I... Well, I guess I'll just stay here an hour or two. Think things out, you know?"

"Okay. Good luck to you."

Reinhold picked his way south through the rocks and tamarack thickets. From his topo he had calculated he needed two more miles and then could cut east and find Sylvester's house. It had been five years, but he was confident he could find his way if no authorities noticed.

He took the right fork at the "Y" and approached Sylvester's place through the rear, recognizing the home-pruned fruit trees and the unrefurbished irrigation ditches from the 1930s. The absence of dogs seemed ominous.

Suddenly, a short, fat woman with unkempt salt-and-pepper hair and a faded red serape appeared. She screamed, dropped her bucket and ran. In seconds, a tall, brown-faced man wearing a flat-brimmed black hat stepped into view pointing a rifle at Reinhold's stomach. Reinhold threw his hands up and spoke quietly.

"I am a friend. A friend of Sylvester's." The man did not move. "Sylvester Isham. Is Sylvester Isham here?"

The man yielded no expression. He motioned Reinhold toward the main house with his rifle. Hands high, Reinhold walked to the rambling adobe. Two others opened the gate for them. Once in the patio, a fourth man, old and wizened, stepped out of the house.

"Who are you?" he asked.

Reinhold explained, by demonstrating a knowledge of the house's contents, among other things.

The old man, Chaco, spoke perfect English. He had served in the U.S. Army in Korea. "Five months ago, at the time of martial law, Sylvester took his plane to Mexico. He gave this place to us for safekeeping. My tribe owns the airstrip a half-mile up the road. Sylvester can return and claim possession anytime during his life. Until then, we use it for a community center. He didn't expect to come back."

Reinhold was devastated. The prospect of crossing the great American desert in the heat of the summer overwhelmed him. But he had to reach the Sierra passes before snowfall. He wavered under the unbearable weight of the moment. He considered returning to Crestone, settling there. Or maybe these folks would let him stay here. They seemed to trust him.

A tortured cry echoed from the bedroom hallway, followed by the crash of overturning furniture. The younger men ran into the hallway at an urgent hand signal from a tribeswoman about Reinhold's age.

Chaco put his hand on Reinhold's. "My grandson, Kingsley. He is not in his right head. I am afraid he will die. He was to be our chief—chief of all Pueblos—was to unify the nations. My powers as medicine man have become weak. Emory and Hubert came from Hopi, our brothers to the West. They have learned the oldest ways, Hopi medicine, and have shown much power, but they, too, have had no effect."

"What's the matter with him?"

"High fever. Hallucinating. He becomes a madman. Then like a baby, crying and moaning for his mother." Chaco withdrew to a chair, thoughtful. "He is our smartest youth. He went to Harvard, learned the science and the thinking of the Europeans, the Americans, the Asians and others. He came back a year ago. Before the disasters, he acted strangely. Ten days ago, when the moon was full, he fell into this spell."

Reinhold had witnessed many healings during his weeks in Crestone. He had made mental note of the rituals from the variety of traditions. He had little to lose and much to gain if he could help here.

"Let me see him."

Chaco stared at Reinhold, unspeaking, studied his travel-worn clothing, torn and dirty, his hands and face weathered brown, his full red beard, washed that morning in the Rio Grande. Chaco stood, and with a slight motion of his head signaled Reinhold to follow.

In the bedroom where Reinhold and Darcy had slept five years earlier, the young man lay pinioned to the bed by Emory and Hubert. The woman bathed his forehead with a cold towel. Reinhold motioned her back, pulled a chair beside Kingsley's pillow.

"Kingsley, listen to me." The youth's head thrashed from side to side.

"The wisdom of your fathers, Kingsley, and their brethren here on the plateau, is present in this room. I carry the wisdom of others. Lao Tzu, Buddha, Gilgamesh and Confucius, Jesus and his many saints, Mohammed, and other wise ones of Africa, Australia and South America. Their words, what they passed down from mouth to mouth through each new generation, can help you now."

Reinhold heated his hands. He laid them on Kingsley's chest, cupped them over his heart. "Breathe slowly, Kingsley. Feel the energy."

The youth's head became still, his eyelids relaxed. His body unwound to a comfortable repose.

Reinhold nodded to the three men. He turned to Chaco and said, "Tell them to put their hands on mine. And you, too."

Chaco smiled. "They know English."

The weight of the ten hands fell and rose with Kingsley's breathing. Reinhold turned to the woman and said, "Take his hands. Put them on his temples and hold them there with yours." She looked willing, but made no move. Chaco translated, and she did as Reinhold had instructed.

Reinhold lowered his voice to a whisper. "Kingsley, you feel heat on your chest. Focus on it. That heat is not from us. It is not from outside. Your nerves can only feel heat when that heat is in the cells of your own body. It is *your* heat. You own it. Inside. Understand me. The heat of our hands helps your *own* heat build up inside your *own* cells. That is what you feel. It is inside. All of the healing is inside you, Kingsley. Know this. Never from the outside world, always from within. That is the wisdom of all who have taught the truth."

The men slowly withdrew their hands. The woman placed the cold towel over Kingsley's forehead and eyes. The men followed Reinhold out. The woman sat in the rocking chair by the door and began knitting.

For two days they repeated the ritual at sunrise, noon and sundown. Kingsley regained consciousness, and control. His fever dropped and his strength returned.

On the night of the full moon, August 9, Chaco lit a fire in the front court-yard. Thirty-four men, women and children sat on blankets in a circle. Chaco sprinkled cornmeal over Reinhold. Emory recited a Hopi monologue. Hubert chanted and danced to the North, the West, the South, and finally the East, including the moon and the stars and the world under the People's feet in his prayers.

Kingsley stood. He announced, "Our brother, Reinhold, has saved my life. He brought the fire of life to the cold knowledge I learned in the White Man's University. He showed me how to self-heal. Emory and Hubert return to their people tomorrow. Reinhold is destined to journey onward to his own people in California. Emory and Hubert will take him as far as they can."

Before sunrise, Reinhold, Emory and Hubert squared their faces to the set-ting moon and headed west-north-west into the vast desert of what the White Man had named the Navajo Reservation. Reinhold's boots were in his pack—on his feet were moccasins. They made no sound and left little imprint.

Within three weeks, they made their last camp at Blue Spring on the Little Colorado River near the Hopi salt mines of antiquity. They had passed famous cities of the ancients and had rested with Emory and Hubert's clan south of First Mesa. Reinhold was more apprehensive than ever about the remaining demands and obstacles of his journey.

He and Darcy had visited the Hopi villages on their way to Espanola five years before. But now the towns were empty. Dust blew through the houses and plazas where families had been vibrant and kachina dances had filled their hearts. Members of the Hopi nation had been forced to a binary choice. Some had left, and a few joined the new powers, but the bulk of the nation had re-turned to the ways of their ancestors, eating from tiny plots of corn and squash, except that now they lived not in pueblos but in invisible houses bur-rowed into disparate sandstone shelves and the sides of canyons and arroyos.

When the government had consolidated to Texas, many economic func-tions had been given over to the unfettered control of corporate institutions already in place. These corporations before had been required to pay at least the appearance of obeisance to a rule of law. But now, as at Los Alamos, the managers of the giant coal and power company that dominated the resources of Northern Arizona had been imbued with the cover of martial law, with hastily granted military commissions or reliable squadrons available to enforce their decisions.

Rather than mine the coal without safeguards for ecology or human life, brave Navaho and Hopi men had dispersed their families into homes too far apart and too well hidden to permit search and arrest by over-burdened security forces. Then they had dynamited the slurry pipelines and high tension powerlines.

After that, for Hopi, or Navajo, to be seen was to forfeit one's life. Initially, the corporations arrested those they saw, but the secret ways of the clans had soon been taught to all men, women and children, and when a person was seized, they now knew how to summon the help of an ancestor, exhale one final time and gently return to the spirit world voluntarily, leaving their bodies limp and inert in the mystified custody of their would-be executioners. The feds soon recognized futility and left them alone.

Reinhold had no interest in returning to his spirit state, even if the instruction had been offered. So his apprehension mounted as he bid farewell to his guardians and climbed out of the Little Colorado for the final trek into Flagstaff to seek Darcy's family and his next way forward.

CHAPTER 98

Saturday, August 19

NEW LAGOONS dot the uninhabited coast of Australia's Northwestern Territory. The barren rocks of the shoreline are submerged, and even though it is winter, the gentle pools among the sandy hillocks are teaming with new life—new marsh grass, insects, birds and furry creatures, forging a new balance all their own.

"I'VE ALMOST GOT IT, KIM."

Because of his near obsession with Mr. Maxwell's collection of antique gadgetry, and his daily work of calculating and drawing improvements for the homestead's operations, not the least of which was the waterwheel generator up Eastside Creek, Jacob had been allocated a medium-sized workbench all his own in the *premiere etage*, as the basement room of Sudbury Shed was called by Godfrey and Lydia, who were studying French under Kim's tutelage. He had copied the longest unsolved riddle from the chamois bag in large letters, and had tacked it on the wall over his workspace. He was now reciting it, over and over, as he had done to solve previous riddles, letting ideas bubble up serendipitously from his unconscious.

The riddle was a dozen lines long—six childishly rhymed couplets with a bizarre mix of non-English words and phrases, and nonsensical, not very profound, mythic allusions:

> *mirror mirror crucible square*
> > *press the grain that shineth there*
> *beyond the oak is only air*
> > *the mother yields the load to bear*
> *septem novem pure and rare*
> > *curse o' the bull au yonder glare*
> *travel deep in the centaur lair*
> > *caveat emptor greed beware*
> *raison d'etre tout les guerres*
> > *the touch that killed the king is there*
> *but be ye balanced, wise and fair*
> > *transit septem mater mare*

In another few seconds, Jacob snapped his head backward and whirled around to face Kim directly, his face glowing in a childish smile. He was waving a piece of paper, not one square inch undecorated with an every-which-way hodgepodge of words, doodles and indecipherable scrawls. "The final clue just fell into place. What do you think?"

He pointed to the north wall. The stand on which the sun-furnace crucible was mounted rested there in its usual spot. It was mounted on tracks embedded in the floor so, when rolled into place in the center of the room, it would snap into exact alignment with the solar mirrors in the cupola. Once there, the vertical shaft of sunlight was captured by a parabolic mirror mounted on the stand. This mirror focused all the sun's rays, much like a giant magnifying glass would do, onto a single point occupied by the crucible. The intense heat at the focal point would raise the crucible's temperatures to industrial-level which could melt almost any metal placed in it. Debate continued in the community about Maxwell's use for this device. Many believed he was conducting alchemy here. There were half a dozen texts on alchemy in his library.

Jacob revealed his mind's newest hypothesis. "Until now, I believed the 'crucible square' was the little, cube shaped pedestal on which the crucible sits. And I was stuck, thinking that 'the grain that shineth there' referred to different kinds of grain he would use in alchemical experiments, the 'shining' being the light when they burned. But I always foundered on the 'oak' and the 'mother.'"

"But today, Kim. Today…" He stood, grabbed her hand and pulled her to the wall by the stand. "Help me roll the stand into the room." That done, he turned and pointed to a square shape on the wall discolored from the other wood because the stand protected it from the light, air and dampness that gradually fades or shades natural wood paneling. "It's just like the discoloration you get behind pictures on wood walls."

He bent down and put his face near the wood, inspecting it minutely. "I knew it. Kim. This is oak. This wood panel's oak. See the grain of the wood? It's still shiny, because the crucible stand protected its original finish. This has got to be 'the grain that shineth there.' And there's a square, hairline seam around this shiny square. What also came up when I was meditating on the riddle just now is that the 'mother' is the Mother Earth behind this wall. That's why he cut this north wall into the hillside. I think behind this oak panel there's a passage. That's the 'air' in the riddle."

"Here," he took Kim's hands. "Press evenly on this panel with me and see if it opens."

It did. Like the secret panel in the desk in the barn, it was held in place by pressure-release latches, so when pressed, they disengaged and it fell forward, into the room.

A cold draft flowed out against Jacob and Kim. The back of the panel had been well sealed, but they could now smell the signature dankness of a subterranean earthen chamber. Jacob grabbed the battery-powered high-intensity LED headband light he often used at his work desk to read at night. He clicked it on and aimed it into the darkness. A crawl-space sized passage sloped down at a steep, thirty-degree angle. His light penetrated only about thirty feet.

He ran to the storage closet and retrieved a spare rope.

"Shouldn't we get the others?" asked Kim.

Jacob shook his head. "I'm not sure what we'll want to do with the knowledge of what I might find. The clues leading to this passage only took up three and a half lines of the twelve-line riddle. There are a lot of warnings after that." He recited, "'Curse o' the bull—the centaur lair—caveat emptor greed beware—raison d'etre tout les guerres—the touch that killed the king is there.' It's seriously bad stuff. This is one of those moments Mariah talked about, Kim. I have a very strong sense I should investigate first, before we expose the community to risks we can't evaluate. Are you with me?"

"Yes. Just be careful, okay Jacob? What do you want me to do?"

He wrapped the lead end of the rope two times around a galvanized pipe embedded in the cement floor—the standpipe served to anchor one of the storage cabinets in the room. Then he tied the lead end around his waist with a rescuer's bowline bight knot. He laid the remaining coil of the rope on the floor beside the pipe, handed the slack to Kim and said, "Feed this from the coil as I go in. I'll tug it as I go to signal you for more. If the ground gives way and the rope starts to surge through your hands, just rotate immediately and pull the rope back against your hip. Your weight's more than enough to create friction around the stand pipe that'll hold me in place. Then you can tie the rope and go get help. Put these work gloves on."

He fastened the LED lamp around his head and crawled into the passage. His silhouette against the light in front of him dimmed rapidly. In two minutes, she couldn't see him at all.

Kim shouted into the passage, "How're you doing?"

"Fine. Just fine. So far. It's opened up." His voice echoed weirdly up the dark passage. "There's a natural cavern big enough for me to walk in, up-right. There's a three-foot wide stream flowing on the bottom, down through the cavern. It's coming from the north. I think the spring that surfaces up at the end of the property is probably an offshoot of this larger water flow."

She waited. Jacob was silent. She listened, leaning toward the passage. Silence.

"Are you okay in there?"

Nothing. She shouted again. Then she heard, "I'm coming out." His voice was strained, charged with emotion, peculiarly distant. She swallowed hard and put a lid on the racing of her mind, which was forming images of worse and worse disasters by the second. She heard his voice again, grunting with physical effort, "The slope of the drop off's... stable enough for me to climb up... I'm doing fine... we'll pull the rope out after I get back out."

He emerged, his hands, knees, lower pant legs and boots caked with the damp earth over which he had crawled.

"What is it, Jacob?"

In answer he reached in his shirt pocket and pulled out his red bandanna, folded into a little package. He walked over to the crucible stand, rope still around his waist trailing from the open passage, and unfolded the handkerchief. There was a rattling as if gravel was falling out onto the surface of the stand.

"Gold, Kim. There's gold all over the bottom of that stream bed. It must be a natural sluice box from millions of years of runoff that's been eroding a vein of gold somewhere deep in the mountains where this subterranean river

402

comes from. There were documented cases of incredible placer deposits like this which were found by the first wave of Forty-Niners in the gold rush. One was called The Blue River because the nuggets were all embedded in blue quartz. It was legendary in its richness."

Then his words came tumbling out, like the nuggets from the bandanna. "As I crawled out, the whole rest of the riddle suddenly made sense. The 'mother' lode—it's a pun. 'Septem novem'—that's 7 and 9 in Latin—the atomic number for gold is 79. 'Pure and rare'—that's gold too. 'Bull au yon'—AU is the symbol for gold. Bullion—another pun. 'Travel deep in the centaur lair'—that's a cave, I went deep into a cave. 'Caveat emptor greed beware'—greed for gold, it's the ultimate greed. 'Raison d'etre tout les guerres'—this is the reason for all the wars: economics, money, greed. The warning from history? Midas touch—'the touch that killed the king is there.' And the ending. I found the reference in Maxwell's old book of heraldry, but I never understood it. The book said the motto, 'transit septem mater mare' was a poorly bastardized Latin crest of a clan in Scotland famous for traveling, but massacred to extinction for their gold and silver mines in the sixteenth century. They translated it to mean 'Travel the Seven Mother Oceans' As I was crawling out that passage, a picture—like, you know, a vision—came into my mind, clear as a bell. I don't know how Maxwell found the opening, but when he did, he wormed his way in and found the gold. He had the shed built into the hill over the spot, and then invented the mirrors and the crucible to melt the gold and make small, refined ingots that financed his travels and purchases the world over, over all the 'seven seas.' His final warning was that you have to be 'balanced, wise and fair' to quell the greed and use the resource for good purposes."

"This changes everything, doesn't it Jacob?"

Jacob nodded his assent. "It could. It could. It'll be an ultimate test, kind of. Somebody might get greedy. It would only take one person. If the world finds out about this, we'll all die, like the Scottish clan, and they'll rip the Earth open and mine the gold until it's gone, which wouldn't take very long. It would be very ugly, wouldn't it?"

Kim turned practical. "Let's put the panel back, Jacob. Wrap up the gold, put it back in your pocket. Clean yourself up. Then let's get Mariah and Darcy aside and let them help us decide how to bring this information into the community in a safe and positive way. I feel like the fate of our little world's in our hands now, Jacob."

"I know what you mean," he answered, still terrified by the dimensions of the future this discovery could create. "It already *was* when we pushed on that oak panel."

Mariah and Darcy sat side-by-side on the largest log bench at the fire circle. Darcy welcomed them with a smile. "We both sensed a spike of energy hit the homestead about an hour ago. We came over here to sit with it. We each picked up your names or faces, so seeing you is no surprise."

Mariah reacted to the sequence of events Jacob related. "This clears up something I was wondering about from the Journals." She had brought Maxwell's personal journals from Sudbury Shed to her bedroom in the big house for personal examination. "He wrote about going into the mountain and finding gold, which he then traded for currency on his travels, to pay for the antique machines and other things he bought and shipped back from abroad. I wondered why he didn't say 'mountains' plural. I imagined he was hiking into the wilderness and had a special creek where he panned for gold dust and nuggets. I guess he didn't want to spoil the riddle, so he was ambiguous, but literally, he went into, inside of, the mountain right here."

She collected her next thoughts for a moment. "His journals answered a bigger question for me too. From the day we moved in, I'd been pondering why this place was so put together when he died, the storage shed and upper room in the barn both perfectly arranged and locked, the desk all cleaned and empty save the machinery files and the hidden panel, the underground room so well hidden, and supplies, blankets, even rooms for a dozen people or more. And the painstaking riddles, so clearly designed for the right people to discover and decipher.

"Well, in Virginia Beach, after Gertrude disappeared taking their unborn child with her, Robb Maxwell finished his engineering degree and then became involved with the psychic research that's thrived in that city for a hundred years. He didn't claim to have foreseen the disaster in Antarctica, but for years he believed a catastrophe was coming. When he finally found out where Gertrude was, he left his granddaughters the mansion and enough money to live on, and moved to Modoc County with the intention of establishing a center where a community could experience what he called the Unseen Mysteries.

"He kept hoping Gertrude would join with him. She wouldn't trust him with her heart again, but allowed their son to visit twice. And while Maxwell waited for her, with his remaining fortune he built what we've found. He wanted her to be involved in finding the right people for what he envisioned as their community. Not his, but theirs.

"He had nearly completed the physical facility when he began having premonitions of his own death. He didn't make predictions in his journals, but he clearly believed that all his work and intentionality had created something like a force field, like a beacon, to attract a community, whether he died or lived to complete the job.

"His last entry appeared to be the day he died—maybe the day before. His son was, he wrote, socially dysfunctional, although talented. Mr. Maxwell was profoundly saddened by what he refers to as his son's 'failure to understand.' Though he was accepting and philosophical, the burden of this grief was one of the last things he wrote about. There's no clue from his words how Mr. Maxwell might have died, but he did write in a shaky scrawl at the end, 'When I lie down after this, I feel it will be for the last time.'"

Mariah's eyes were moist while she told the tale, but her voice never wavered. She ended, "We are fulfilling the destiny he dreamed. Whether he drew us here or we all, one by one, perceived the energy and ourselves made the choices that led us here, doesn't matter. It doesn't need to be known. And we would carry on just the same, whether we knew his story or not. It's the ultimate mystery of this strange and lovely place."

Knowledge of the gold spread slowly through the community. Mariah and Darcy had undertaken a one-on-one spreading of the news, knowing that a group meeting would have an undue multiplier effect on the significance of the discovery.

Jacob left it up to Mariah, Darcy and Kim. His sporadic moodiness became deeper than usual. His quirks were tolerated out of a very specific context. He had brought a battery-powered shortwave radio in his backpack when he escaped Berkeley. Unlike Rose's AM radio, which brought in government propaganda from Las Vegas, Salt Lake and occasionally Phoenix, Jacob received broadcasts vastly more disturbing, and had the task of sorting out deliberate misinformation sent by nefariously motivated broadcasters, including those trying to disrupt the government's functioning, from accurate information being conveyed by the legitimate, well-intentioned underground. He heard of terrible deprivation, oppression by loosely regulated power groups, both governmental and private, and personal anecdotes from shortwave radio owners desperate to tell anyone their tragic misfortunes or connect with pockets of resistance or survival. So Jacob bore a heavy burden, having constantly to judge what was true and false, and how to paint an accurate picture of the outside world for the well-being of his community. His moodiness was warranted. Everyone could tell when information was weighing heavily on his psyche.

The difference this time was the information had to do with forces that lay directly underfoot at Maxwell Acres. Echoing from memory into his daily rhythm came the frequent chorus, *the touch that killed the king is there.*

Kim, of course, first shared the weight of the gold discovery with Eli. He kept it to himself. He grasped the wisdom of letting it circulate solely within his personal thought, to sort his own spirit-judgments from the flailing of his ego.

The next person Kim told was her Uncle Peter. An hour later he and Jacob had crawled back into the cavern. Peter verified Jacob's theory of a millions-of-years old natural placer sluice in the underground limestone cavern. Later, when Eli asked if it was a lava tube, Peter described how at this elevation there was a limestone strata in which underground water would dissolve limestone caverns which then became channels for underground streams, even rivers.

Peter also clarified that Maxwell must have found a classic blowhole. "Blowholes are openings of vast underground caves and cracks in the earth, in which the volume of air is big enough that changes in atmospheric pressure makes them act like bellows, pushing air in or out depending on whether high or low pressure is over the blowhole." Mariah remarked that blowholes existed all over northern Arizona in her childhood and were often considered sacred by the Native Americans.

The geology was only of passing interest, however, and discussion gravitated toward whether the gold was a resource for the community or not. It took only a few evening's discussions to conclude that parlaying the gold into commercial value for the benefit of the community would require conditions that probably would not exist for years, perhaps decades.

The easiest conclusion, based on the experiences of Ray Overcroft, Agnes and Shaz, was the foolhardiness of risking passage of the knowledge of a gold lode to Flat River or any other nearby area of the abandoned territory, which now was essentially a patchwork of warlord turfdoms.

Secondly, according to Jacob's shortwave information, the military government was imposing heavy penalties for aberrations from edicted currency and precious metal controls. Even to be exposed to that risk, however, would require members of the community to travel into the military enclaves east of the Sierras or south of the "Grapevine" in old Los Angeles/Orange County. A consensus soon formed on the undesirability of anyone undertaking the arduous expeditions trade would require, and the lack of a need for it in any event, given the success of the subsistence efforts of the community.

The final result was that Peter and Jacob returned to the cavern's streambed the small sample of gold Jacob had brought out in his handkerchief. Knowledge of the homestead's rivulet of the yellow metal, which throughout history had been such a curse to individuals and nations alike, was not forgotten, but seemed to sink gracefully, like the gold in the stream, to the bottom of people's priority lists.

CHAPTER 99

Late August

DUPREE RANSOM had been avoided by all but four people after he was carried down the mountain to Maxwell Acres. The universal concern was for "James," as Eli continued to be called by some for a week or so. Mariah Wallace was one moved to pity for the twisted, broken man left on Eli's bed—because it was the only space immediately available. Charles and Rose Royer came when they had seen to Eli's diagnosis and treatment. By then Mariah had bathed Ransom as best she could, given Charles' preliminary injunction against moving him. Nelson Ichimura remained with her for security.

Ransom was not an easy patient. Keeping himself still, as Charles warned him to do, clashed with his nature. Anger and fear dominated him, grimacing growls alternated with wretched whining, and blasphemy with despair. Charles and Rose kept their steely professional demeanor in the face of his scorn and curses. Their Vietnam War experience had been boot camp for this event. "Why don't you just kill me?" Ransom repeated. Charles had only a few doses of a mild sedative, which calmed Ransom for a period of sleep that first night, and the next day. Later on, Agnes and Rose prepared herbal teas to soothe him.

From a picture in a Sudbury Shed library book, Jacob and Ray constructed in a single day a crude version of a Stryker frame, on which Ransom was strapped. On it he could be turned upright, prone or supine, depending on his need or preference, or doctor's orders.

"You have a damaged spinal cord," Charles told him, "but it's hard to tell the extent of the damage yet. You have a little feeling and motion in your arms, but it's too soon to tell how much of that you'll retain. It's doubtful that you will ever walk." Ransom responded with grunted obscenity.

Mariah kept the patient fed and hydrated. Rose cleaned him and tended the catheter that dripped his urine into a bottle under the Stryker frame. It was a month before Ransom could sit up without restraints on his head.

No one was inclined to move him to better medical facilities. Especially Ransom himself. He knew he would be executed on sight in Flat River, in whose vicinity he had committed many crimes in his short residence in Modoc County. And of course, there was no possibility that community members could safely transport him without exposing themselves to danger. They were his jailers now in a society that had no capital punishment. He was, as he had long been, society's burden.

He remained angry and depressed into the summer months, but Mariah maintained regular contact. She made a gift of routine, so that Ransom came to expect her punctual ministrations, and they never flagged. She began to administer healing touch, although she held little hope for restoring his body— it was his spirit that needed healing. She guessed that caring touch had long been absent for him, and from the first day made a point of punctuating her communications with a pat on his arm or shoulder.

"Dupree, you're probably as well physically as you're going to get," Charles told Ransom in July. "You probably won't recover any more movement in your arms and legs. The danger is going to be in your lungs. With your immobility, we always have to be aware of the possibility of pneumonia." Rose administered regular treatments to clear Ransom's lungs, checking him with her stethoscope.

His surliness wore off gradually, and more Maxwell Acres folks began interacting with him. Beginning with Melissa and Woody, the children began taking turns feeding him.

Several of the community members had obvious reasons for turning away from Ransom. Mariah pointed out that their hatred had its most pronounced effect on themselves. Eli concurred. It was a central point, he told her, of the forgiveness ritual that was part of the Retreats he had worked on with Bud August, James Salas—"the real one"—and others in San Quentin.

A small red pepper
    clings to a twisted stalk
       trampled in the spring.

CHAPTER 100

Friday, September 1

PETER ADDISON rolled his head shoulder to shoulder. He heard static in his neck and a sound like rocks tumbling over each other in a brook. He moaned. Charles and he were doing maintenance on the upgraded pathway between the Royer cabin and the Maxwell compound.

"You've overdone it, Peter," Charles said. "You'd better rest." He gave Peter exercises to relieve the pinch in his neck and the snag in his lower back.

"We'll call you for lunch," Mariah told him.

"Never mind, I'll get my own. Somebody should be down at the cabin anyway, wouldn't you say?"

"That's not clear to me," said Mariah, "but I suppose it wouldn't hurt."

"They're your dreams."

Peter eased himself into the watcher's chair near the cabin window and poked the power button on the radio. The news on what the group derided as "public radio"—the government band—was not exactly useless, Peter decided. He felt he could glean valid information by comparing the official line to the ham broadcasts he devoured with Jacob, desperate to glean information about "the greatest natural history event of our time." He pictured world coastlines re-carved by inundation, pillars of ice torn from glaciers as if by an immense Samson and hurtling to colossal plumes of ocean spray. He yearned to see the catastrophe face-to-face, as an astronomer might harbor a stubborn longing for a suicidal flight to view a supernova or red dwarf or pulsar at close range.

"It's important not to slouch," Charles had told him. Peter sat straight in the chair until he tired of it, then groaned down to the floor for Charles' stretching exercises. He enjoyed his solitary rest, relished any privacy he could seize. He found it impossible to conform completely to the ethic of Maxwell Acres. It was a mystery to him how Jacob or even Jason could accept Mariah's unorthodox views. Give up the defense watch in favor of "sensing" the approach of strangers? He shifted his shoulder holster to accommodate his position. Now Eli and Mariah were reporting fresh "dreams" of caution. The braided wool rug beneath him was not uncomfortable enough to prevent drifting off to his own brief dream.

His eyes blinked open. Something demanded he look outside. Had he heard a sound, or only dreamed it? He rolled stiffly to his knees and peered over the edge of the windowsill. Not fifty yards away, a lanky figure leaning forward under a bulging backpack ambled toward the cabin. Peter felt for his Colt thirty-eight as he labored to his feet and lurched toward the door.

He stepped off the porch, pistol raised to shoulder height, pointed to the sky. The stranger did not break stride and showed neither surprise nor alarm. Beneath a straw plantation hat an expectant smile spread across a face Peter noted as handsome.

"Dr. Royer?" He continued his confident pace. "Remember me?" He doffed his hat as if to seal recognition.

"Stop right there." Peter's voice cracked, and he cleared his throat. He leveled the pistol, and the stranger strode three more steps before halting.

"It's been a long time, Dr. Royer. I'm Malcolm Whiting, Robb Maxwell's son."

"I'm not Dr. Royer. What's your business here?"

"Ah, then, Mr. uh, Wallace?" The casual smile flashed again.

"You didn't answer my question. What's your business?"

"Just paying a neighborly call, Sir. I own the eight acres adjacent to Dr. Royer's property. Well, I've never lived here, but I thought someday I would build a cabin. Maybe the time has come. Know what I mean?"

He had unbreakable affability, like a car salesman; the smile never faded.

"You alone? D'you have a weapon?"

"Yes and no." The grin widened, and Malcolm Whiting bobbed his head in appreciation of his answer's humor. "I'm an innocent puppy. You've got nothing to fear from me, Mr. ..."

"I'm Dr. Peter Addison. Charles Royer's my brother-in-law." Peter decided Mr. Whiting was likely as innocent as he claimed. He slid the Colt into its holster and extended his hand. In the few seconds of their handshake, the notion flashed into Peter's mind that this was a moment of truth. If the young man intended harm, he might have taken advantage of Peter's holstered vulnerability. He did not, and the conviction established itself that Whiting would be a sound addition to the community.

"They'll be ringing the lunch bell in about an hour," said Peter. "I'll take you up to meet the rest of our little community."

They spent the hour exchanging stories of their experience of the catastrophe, their arrival at Maxwell Acres. Whiting had prospered in the real estate business in Susanville. He had an interest in ski lodge concessions at Mt. Lassen. "It turned out when the crisis came my set of friends in Susanville were the wrong ones. And besides, I was afraid there'd be a jailbreak at High Desert State Prison before they got a chance to bus the cons to prison farms down south. Anyway, I got out of there and went to Mother's place in Adin. She told me about Mrs. Wallace coming here to my father's old place." A friend of his mother's had taken her to safety near Lake Shasta but had no room for him, so he got a ride to Likely and hiked in.

Whiting showed great interest in Peter's account of the community's self-governance and farming operation, described in mostly positive terms. But Peter couldn't disguise a certain frustration and restiveness. "If I hadn't come here I would probably be in Antarctica by now. I would have made it happen somehow, in spite of the mess that's out there..."

"Well, it's not so bad *out there*," Whiting said, "if you know how to take care of yourself and if you can be on your own." Peter stared at him, wondering what experiences had led to this observation. "But it looks like you've got a sweet setup here, if you don't mind my saying so. I could add my acreage too, if it would help."

"You'll have to tell your story again, sort of around the campfire," Peter said. "Then they'll teach you the secret handshake and chant the magic words. We always seem to make room for one more. Up in the barn, I suppose." On his own, Peter had accepted Malcolm Whiting into the Maxwell Acres community.

"JUST PUT THE SACK in the hutch, Godfrey. The rabbits'll find their way out after you close the door." Eli had taken the twelve-year-old on an excursion to check the traps they had constructed and set in likely places to snare game. Three hefty captives were their reward, but at the cost of missing the community lunch.

Eli washed up in the barn, where he found Melissa and Woody feeding the paralyzed Dupree Ransom.

"How you doin', man? These kids aren't mistreating you are they?"

Ransom pursed his lips, as much of a smile as anyone had got from him. "These kids is all right."

Eli's progress toward the main house was arrested by a disquieting sight. Kim stood next to a tall, sandy-haired man, along with her father. She laughed and reached to touch the man's arm, as if for balance. Eli wondered what unsettled him, other than what he recognized as a stab of jealousy. Perhaps it was that the man was clean-shaven, in contrast to the men of Maxwell Acres, none of whom had shaved for months, except Peter. And Eli had recently dreamed of the green jeep that appeared at the monastery in Los Molinos, a symbol of danger from "the outside." Yet the guy seemed perfectly at ease, as if he possessed the place and the time.

Kim welcomed Eli by clasping his arm to her side, as if she claimed him. "Malcolm Whiting, this is Eli Barnes, one of the original members of the community." The man's firm handshake moved sideways as well as vertically, a gesture of overconfidence, and Eli detected a chink in the self-assured grin, a flicker of facial muscle quick as a serpent's tongue. Could Malcolm have recognized his name?

Kim continued the introduction. "... Malcolm was telling us about his memories of this place. He said his father told him how he looked forward to our visits as kids. Now it looks like he'll be adding to our population and—ten acres is it?—to the property."

Malcolm put a hand on Charles' and Kim's shoulders. "I'm glad I found you all here. It looks like there's security here and a great sense of togetherness." He looked up at Eli. "The world needs more of that."

"Oh, Eli," Kim said, "you must be hungry. I'll get some stew ready for you and Godfrey." She nodded to Malcolm and strode into the house.

Charles took Malcolm by the elbow. "We'll have to get started making you a bed. Eli, would you mind if Malcolm bunks with you for now?"

"Sure. I'll help with the bed right after I eat." Eli watched them go, wondering, among other things, why Malcolm had a last name different from his father's.

He asked Kim about it a few moments later. "Apparently Malcolm and his father didn't really get along and saw each other infrequently. His parents weren't married, so he took his mother's name."

"He seem all right to you?"

"He's easy enough to get along with. He and Uncle Peter hit it off right away. He seems to have become one of us without any debate. Not that there's much choice, since he owns the adjacent property. What do you think of him?"

Eli took her hand. "When I saw him standing there with you, I got a little jealous. So maybe my opinion is off kilter. I knew a lot of social misfits and con men in prison, Kim—I imagine he's meeting Dupree about now. He's smooth and subtle where Dupree's easier to read. I'm sorry. I don't know where this is coming from, just a feeling."

"Mariah would say you have to pay attention to that."

"Yes, and I will. But I remember when Catherine doubted me at our first group meeting, and Peter said we shouldn't question each other's motives if we're to survive together. You all gave me a chance, and I'm willing to let Malcolm prove himself."

She squeezed his hand and kissed his cheek. "At least you'll be able to keep an eye on him."

CHAPTER 101
Saturday, September 2

REINHOLD paralleled the road, staying a hundred yards inside the ponderosa pine forest. He remembered visiting Mariah's sister-in-law, Delphine, on Schultz Pass Road, north of Flagstaff.

A single rifle shot broke the air. The sound told Reinhold the owner was well within range. He crouched behind a log, made no sound for a half-hour, motionless except to periodically flick black carpenter ants off his moccasins. Finally, he heard a truck start up in the direction of the gunfire, watched a glint of blue creep through the dense forest.

In another half-hour, Reinhold approached Delphine Wallace's driveway. The sign hanging from the crossbar of the gate was crisply lettered in Old English script: "*Welcome To The Wallace Spread.*" Wired to the gate was a warning: "*No Trespassing.*" Two hundred feet up the drive nestled the little stone house in the pines, just as Reinhold remembered.

"Delphine," he shouted. The front door opened. He recognized the stately figure of Darcy's aunt. "Delphine, it's Reinhold Malone."

"Well, I'll be… Ignore that sign and you come on in here."

She held out her arms. "My, my, I never expected this." She looked him over—buckskin shirt, brown jeans and moccasins, weather-beaten face and dusty beard. "You better come in and tell me what's going on."

As they entered the kitchen, a man with blood-covered hands and forearms came through the outside door carrying a bucket. He looked ten years Reinhold's senior, ten or fifteen younger than Delphine. He announced, "I've got the heart and liver here. Never did like buck kidneys."

Delphine introduced her partner, Winston O'Leary. "Winston shot a buck an hour ago just up the road. He's dressing out the carcass in the barn."

When they had cleaned up, Delphine poured three shots of Bourbon, neat. She laughed, "No ice, what with the power quotas and all."

After Reinhold recounted the events that had brought him to Flagstaff, the conversation turned to California. Delphine asked, "What do you know about Mariah and Darcy? And the children? Our last phone call was in mid-February, when Darcy said they were going to fly over here. They never arrived."

Reinhold was curious that she omitted Elmer's name, but told her of Darcy's email before the tsunami. He observed Delphine exchange glances with Winston. Winston nodded encouragement.

"I don't know whether it was reliable, Reinhold," Delphine said, "but around that same time one of my friends told me about a newscast she heard. They reported civil disorder was rampant in Berkeley. Fomented by local radicals, like during the Vietnam War. She said it all died down after the key leaders were killed by gangs." Delphine's eyes filled with tears, and her voice trailed off.

Winston finished for her. "They said one of the leader's names was Elmer Wallace. We assume it was Delphine's brother."

"I'm sorry, Delphine. I hope it wasn't. If I get there, please God, I'll try to find out and get word to you."

Delphine nodded, and forced a smile.

Later, over roast venison and a breaded squash casserole, Delphine and Winston assessed the massive changes that had occurred in Flagstaff, and the nation, since the catastrophes. It was Reinhold's first chance since leaving the barge five months before to hear a reliable account, albeit from the limited vantage of the specific locale. In Crestone, as people had arrived from disparate and sometimes nefarious circumstances, an ethos had arisen in which the past was neither questioned nor described and all talk had focused on moving forward.

Flagstaff's primary employer in recent years had been the government, and under martial law, naturally the local bureaucracies remained fully employed. The government's primary tasks were first to maintain civil order and second to regulate and allocate all resources. "Emphasis on 'all,'" Winston noted, "which includes currency and credit as well as food, water, power, fuel, education, communications, travel, and industry—you name it, they run it."

The town's second economic mainstay, tourism, was dead of course, given the petroleum shortage after international shipping stopped when sea level rendered deep-water ports worldwide unusable—for up to ten years, word had it. Logging, the lumber industry and ranching, however, were deemed essential to national recovery. Before the crisis, these had become nonexistent in Flagstaff, blamed locally on environmentalism, recreational lobbies and an eight-year drought. But the drought had ended, and the federal government had shipped in cattle and sheep by rail. There was a similar frenzy of reconstituting lumber mills and logging operations, freed in the national interest from prior restrictions.

The federal government had also mandated that education continue, so the schools and University were operating under a semblance of normalcy.

Much of the city's light manufacturing had been commandeered for the military and the oil and gas industries, but the fabrication of Gore-Tex continued, the Ralston Purina dog food factory was converted to human consumables, and the printing industry shifted gears to produce forms by the billion to operate the government-directed economy.

The government had relocated, under force where necessary, those who had serviced tourism. But others whose jobs had disappeared were prohibited from moving and faced interminable dole lines for food, clothing, retail items in short supply, and minimal bank scrip in lieu of currency. Circulation of money had ground to a halt from hoarding after the mint was lost in Philadelphia and East Coast bank reserves of legal tender bills were destroyed by the sea.

Delphine's older son, Nicholas, thrown out of work when civil engineering shrank under the oil shortage, started his own enterprise fixing, maintaining and even building bicycles, which had become the transportation of choice for all who couldn't afford gasoline or obtain fuel vouchers—in other words, nearly everyone. Her younger son, Julian was in high demand as a carpenter and tradesman, rebuilding the lumber mills.

Delphine had closed her real estate office because property transfers were now only by military permission and commissions were outlawed. Winston had worked in her office, and when his parents were forced to relocate to Nogales she had taken him in at The Wallace Spread.

Delphine had the good fortune of a small but reliable spring. It had never dried up during the drought, and she was able to channel it into drip irrigation to raise squash, beans, quinoa and fresh vegetables over the summer. When authorities had diverted public water supplies to industry and military facilities, Julian had salvaged a mile of garden hoses for his mother.

All summer, Delphine and Winston had lived on homegrown produce while secretly building a winter stockpile of cereal, flour and other staples they were allocated in the dole lines. Winston brought in all the game he could kill—deer, rabbits, squirrels and, Delphine suspected, dogs and cats as well. Pets had been declared illegal due to food shortages and their owners had been forced to put them down or abandon them. In the early months, dog packs had been a menace, but they had been hunted into scarcity by fall. Winston and Delphine turned the meat into jerky for the winter months ahead.

At the end of the meal, Delphine offered another shot of Bourbon, with the apology, "The powers-that-be make sure booze stays in the stores, but sugar's something else, I guess. No more desserts, unless we start collecting wild honey."

Reinhold declined the whiskey. "What do you actually know about the fate of California? I've heard snatches of guesswork, but I really couldn't believe what people were saying."

"What did you hear?" Delphine asked.

"The general claim was that misguided liberal factions had succeeded in an armed revolution of sorts, and had thrown the federal government out. I figured that story had been put out by government propagandists."

Again, Delphine and Winston exchanged anxious glances. "You know, Nicholas was in the Army back in the 1980s. He swore me to secrecy about where he heard this, but things in California are worse than you can imagine, Reinhold. I'm sorry to have to tell you this, but if you don't know already, you need to."

"Just tell me."

"Well, a friend of Nicholas's was in the Army, in intelligence. He was serving in California. He was so appalled, he went AWOL in May from a convoy moving his unit to Oklahoma. I won't say where he crossed paths with Nicholas, but Nicholas vouched for his honesty. The young man said the federal government first diverted all electric power inland after sea level rose, abandoned California north of L.A. because of food shortages, and stationed troops in mountain passes to keep the population from migrating to the interior. Oregon and Washington too. Most of the population died from anarchy, starvation, disease and deprivation, and where people did survive they fell under the thumb of organized crime, armed survivalists and military defectors, or occasionally a power group of Bible-wielding Christians."

Reinhold stayed impassive. He said, "I think Darcy and Mariah are all right. I got an email after they left Oakland. They didn't have enough gas to get here and went north to where I'm headed. I'm going to rest tomorrow and be going the next morning." He outlined his plan to ride the rails across the Colorado River at Needles and on into the Sierras, where he would trek north to Flat River.

Winston banged his shot glass down on the table. "That'd be a fatal mistake. I've heard a dozen reports of hobos shot by railroad security. Their tight as a drum about people without papers. Especially on railroads and cross-country trucks."

They debated other routes. Most possibilities seemed equally dangerous, or too difficult to achieve by mid-October snowfall at the California/Oregon border. Hubert and Emory had offered to take Reinhold clear to the Sierras on their clan's horses if he needed, so Reinhold charted a route up through the Hopi lands, around the north end of the Grand Canyon crossing the Colorado

River at Lees Ferry, then connecting the dots through St. George, Ruby Lake, Emigrant Pass, Winnemucca, Rye Patch Reservoir, and finally to the Sierras and across into Modoc County.

The following morning, well provisioned out of the generosity of his wife's in-laws, Reinhold backtracked to Blue Spring. There he camped overnight. As the first vestige of light in the east signaled the end of night, he headed north into the barren Painted Desert and followed the landmarks Emory and Hubert had instructed.

Three hundred steps west from the tree-that-looks-like-an-eagle, high on the bank of a waterless arroyo as promised, Reinhold found the gentle outline of a trap door marking Hubert's family home. He uttered the coyote call he had been taught. Hubert's blind father opened the hatch and Reinhold touched him on both shoulders.

"They shot Hubert," the old man said.

IN THE BEAM OF LIGHT penetrating the limpid flow of water beneath Sudbury Shed, a grain of sand faltered and slid into blackness. Billions of such particles and beads had washed down this stream in the million years of its coursing through its limestone tunnel. If they tumbled into streambed fissures they were swept out, unless they were heavier, like the nuggets and grains of gold now illuminated by the beam from the miner's lamp affixed to Peter Addison's head.

He fitted a narrow plastic spoon to the downstream end of a crack and coaxed it forward, ushering gleaming bits of the precious metal from their seats. Then he tilted the spoon to a precise angle to preserve his find through a slow journey to the water's surface, and thence to a pouch hanging from a cord around his neck. He smiled appreciation for the size of these gleaming bits of gold.

It was 2:00 a.m. For two weeks Peter had added to his store of gold, weeks of nocturnal bending, wearing rubber farm boots and squinting along the stream bottom, the true cause of the back strain for which Charles had prescribed rest and stretching. Peter estimated the value of his cache was nearing six thousand dollars—according to the pre-tsunami price. Now it would be more, since U.S. currency was a chancier medium of exchange in the Abandoned Territories.

In his two weeks of secret mining, Peter had drawn Rose's attention. "This insomnia of yours is a concern, Peter. You're obsessed with this security issue." That was fine. She was accustomed to his late night walks with Cappy to "check the perimeter," and did not investigate if she heard him stirring in the middle of the night.

Peter scooped another streak of tiny nuggets. He had acquiesced in the consensus to keep the gold a secret. But the knowledge of wealth underfoot had gnawed at him, as did his swelling ambition to be at the site of the greatest scientific event of the age. He was atrophying in a dull western corner of North America while lesser men might be on the leading edge of research and discovery. He regretted his haste to leave Davis at early signs of instability. Malcolm Whiting's words had echoed daily since their first meeting: he could survive on the outside "if you know how to take care of yourself and if you can be on your own." Determination was not an issue. And gold was the key.

He would make his way to San Diego, still under government control, to the Scripps Institute. He was confident of his welcome there, the recognition of his value as a leading earth scientist. He would be of service to the government—to the world. He would leave a legacy of discovery for future generations. He might even include a chapter on enlightened governance for the preservation of the natural world, highlighting principles developed at Maxwell Acres.

Water dripped from Peter's fingers as he straightened. He nudged a spoonful of gold crumbs into his pouch. The gold would serve the community as well. He would acquire needed goods not available at Maxwell Acres, and provide for their safe transport. Medical equipment and supplies for Charles and Rose, electronics for Jacob, winter coats for everyone. He solidified his plan in a lengthy note which he would leave for Charles and Rose to find, kept for now at the top of his pack, waiting in his closet for the moment he would choose for slipping away.

He had considered taking Malcolm into his confidence, inviting him along on the adventure. Whiting was rugged and experienced. But something stayed the impulse. Malcolm was still resolutely affable, but he had moments of distraction, aloof pensiveness, interspersing his light-hearted banter or sincere engagement. Peter decided he did not know him well enough, and his plan must be all-or-nothing.

With wrinkled fingers he drew the string tight on his pouch. Enough for tonight. He sloshed to the passage leading up to Sudbury Shed. He crept back to the cabin for sleep.

Time was Dupree Ransom's only possession. In prison he would have used it to augment his body, to plan and implement strategies for enrichment, domination or escape. In prison, time was a treasure to spend. In the barn at

Maxwell Acres, it weighed him down like a treasure chest he was forced to carry across a wasteland with no destination. In the spring he survived, dozing twelve hours a day. Then as his body diminished he became a volcano, dormant for long periods, erupting with rage and invective, smoldering. He was suicidal but impotent. By the end of summer his fury was spent and he settled into routine and resignation. But still he suffered most under his burden of time when night neglected to furnish him sleep.

He had heard the final clatter of building a bed for the newcomer, Malcolm, during the day. He had borne the silence of the evening meal time, until young Godfrey brought him his portion. Then there was a murmur of conversation in Eli's room, no doubt an explanation of this invalid to whom he had nodded when introduced. Then the day disappeared, candles and lanterns snuffed, and blackness enclosed him, the dread of sensory deprivation unallayed by slumber. For hours, all that assured Dupree Ransom of life's endurance outside himself was the distant chirp of crickets, and when they stopped, only the faint current of wind.

CHAPTER 102
September 9

A CREAK. Ransom blinked. A thump and a rustle. He turned his head toward the sound from the next room. Indistinct words, grunting, a thump on a wall. Then silence, save, Ransom thought, for heavy breathing that diminished to stillness again. What had the sequence of sounds amounted to? In prison a hundred men would perceive, a hundred heads nod in grim silence. He pictured a man lying stifled, another standing over him. Then there were slow footsteps not meant to be heard, but Ransom heard them. Under his door a flutter of light as someone crept along the passage with a flashlight.

Ransom opened his mouth to call out, but his breath locked. The former Dupree Ransom had had enormous strength and cunning, and raw mettle for confronting peril, when his grit could rise above his fear. But now dread suffocated him, when he might be snuffed as easily as a baby. He heard only the noiseless squeal of constricted breath seizing his throat as the footsteps stole past his room.

Peter yawned. Surely he had enough now. Not just for tonight, but for his journey.

He trudged several steps upstream and turned his head to shine the miner's lamp toward the passage fifteen yards behind him that led up to Sudbury Shed. When he turned his lamp and attention back to the streambed, he immediately noticed a small gleaming pocket a foot below the surface. One last dip into the treasure.

A scraping sound froze him. He turned back to see a wobble of light playing on the cavern wall opposite the passage. Someone was sliding down the incline. Peter snapped off his light, pocketed his mining spoon, and waited in darkness. Someone else had made a nocturnal visit to Sudbury Shed, had descended to the lower room and found the open entrance to the passage. There was no way to close it from inside.

Peter felt for a place of concealment against the cavern wall in case the newcomer turned his light toward him. Could he stay undetected? He pushed himself flat against the cold rock wall, struggling against a sneeze. Who was it? Jacob? Eli?

The intruder's flashlight made a jerky, inquiring circle of the cavern, playing on the uneven walls. Water slipped past Peter's feet. His muscles tensed as he breathed into his belly, not allowing the slightest friction of air in his nostrils.

"I know you're here. It's obvious, you know. The entrance to this cave was left wide open." It was Malcolm's voice, with a menacing tinge. "You'd better show yourself to me."

Peter remained motionless.

"You know what?" Malcolm let his words echo. "I can make this cave your tomb." The echo prolonged a harsh chuckle. "It won't be hard to close off the entrance so you can't get out."

Peter weighed the threat, felt a convincing tone of malice—and madness. He drew his gun and sloshed a step forward, and immediately Malcolm's beam assaulted his eyes.

"Dr. Addison, I presume!" Then the light snapped off. Malcolm had seen Peter's gun. "Just stay where you are, Peter. I have a gun too."

Peter wondered if Malcolm was bluffing. They stood in darkness dense as a grave.

"What are you doing here, Dr. Addison?"

"The same as you, I suppose." Their words echoed along the cavern, making a slow-motion conversation as each waited for the falling reverberations.

"Same as me? Impossible. You didn't come to kill, did you? My guess is you're here for gold. There's gold down here, isn't there?"

"What's that about killing?" Peter did not want to speak, in case the gun was not a bluff and his voice revealed his position too precisely. He shifted a step to his right.

"I'm going to kill my father, once and for all." Malcolm's voice had a toneless, machine-generated quality, except that the last two words were shouted, and repeated themselves in dying sequence.

"Your father died years ago." Peter temporized, desperate to understand and to escape. He shifted to his right until he leaned against the cavern wall.

"Stand still!" Now Peter was convinced—Malcolm did have a weapon. "I smothered my father with chloroform. But, you know, he didn't completely die. He was so stubborn, he wouldn't even die." Malcolm's voice quavered, screeched, and finally whispered. "He follows me around, he brings this shed with him. I half-killed him right up that passageway, in that room where he made his gold bars. Now he follows me and closes it in around me. He'll make it kill me back... I'll have to burn it down."

"Why did you kill him?" Peter murmured, but his voice rang clear in the natural echo chamber. He crouched, soundlessly.

"I'm his only son, for God's sake. He wouldn't give me a goddam thing, with all his money, all his gold. He was ashamed of me. I wasn't good enough for him." Malcolm whimpered now, his voice distorted and blubbery, weeping.

"You people were good enough for him!" He snorted, disgusted. "He didn't even know you, but he left the secret of his fucking gold for you to find. And I wasn't worthy." The last word was elongated and guttural. "I'm glad I snuffed him. I snuffed his contempt, and his judgment, and his savior of the goddam world attitude!"

Malcolm wailed, until his passion was spent. When he spoke again, his voice was calm—and menacing. "You people are so fucking good. You deserve this place, and not me. And I'm not good enough for you either, am I? Well, this place is going down. Good old Robb Maxwell is going to burn this time and stay dead. You'll have to go with him, I'm afraid."

"Malcolm, you can have the gold. It'll take care of you, and we'll never go after you."

"Oh, I'll get the gold. It's my birthright, you know. It's a bonus to have the gold finally. And the fire's going to put an end to... good... old... Robb... Maxwell."

End of bargaining. Peter took a slow breath, drew the miner's light off his head and held it at arm's length to the side, above the middle of the stream. He extended his gun hand straight ahead. He flicked the light on, only an instant of light flashed in the tunnel, illuminating for a half-second the figure of Malcolm Whiting. An answering flash exploded from the muzzle of Malcolm's gun, and Peter fired three times toward the burst.

He saw nothing then, heard nothing. Even the gurgle of the water was gone, as if Peter's ears were packed with tree sap. He crouched against the wall, waiting. He was afraid to turn on his lamp again, but the blackness had deepened—he sensed that his visual apparatus had shut down, protecting itself from the assault of the muzzle flash. Only the tactile sense remained, and he felt a pounding in his chest, a heat expanding from his face. He felt for the wall with the heel of his hand, rested on it with his elbow.

After a length of time which he could not determine, a painful tone signaled the return of his hearing. As the ringing began to subside it was accompanied by a series of whining grunts, splashing—Malcolm writhing and gasping in the water. Peter eased himself along the wall, struggling for balance as slick stones in the current deceived his feet. Though he assumed Malcolm was also blinded, he had to continue in stealth and darkness for fear of revealing himself to the madman, who might still be armed. He guided himself by the sound of Malcolm's thrashing and moaning. When Malcolm was no more than arm's length from him, Peter cowered against the slanting approach to the entrance passage, hearing Malcolm raise himself against the wall of the cave with a hideous wail, then pitch into the stream, splashing Peter.

Peter had to try the lamp. His vision had returned, he discovered, enough to discern Malcolm's sodden form creeping forward, both hands in the stream. Peter holstered his gun and scurried up the passage to Sudbury Shed, Malcolm's heaving grunts and his own fear propelling him.

He lay back against the wall of the lower room. He realized he was sobbing in frustration and fear. He stared at his soaked pants, tucked into rubber boots, toes pointing up. They were real, he decided. Was anything else real in the grotto below? He stilled himself to listen for sounds—nothing. He struggled to his feet and leaned into the draft from the passageway. A noise of faint labored breathing rose on the gust of cool air. He couldn't leave. He searched the room, found the coil of rope, secured one end to the crucible stand, and descended once again into the cavern.

Malcolm had strength enough only to hold his head out of the water. Peter lashed the rope around him twice under his armpits. He heaved, pushed and dragged the quivering body until it lay on the smooth incline. Malcolm's tortured breaths came at rasping intervals, Peter's in ragged puffs, as he crawled up to the lower room. Then he heaved on the rope. Dragging Malcolm into the room consumed a quarter of an hour, and when he tumbled to the floor, both men lay motionless.

When he had rested, Peter rolled to his knees, stood, turned off the miner's lamp and dropped it on the floor, then staggered up the stairway and out into the eerie first light. A figure appeared in the doorway of the barn, a shadow in backlight. Peter recognized the figure of Eli Barnes, leaning on the door frame. Eli called out to him, but Peter threw his arm in urgent signal toward Sudbury Shed and continued stumbling toward the cabin.

CHAPTER 103

Sunday, September 10

PETER HAD at least a four-hour start. Debate, indecision and planning had increased it. But by midmorning Jason set out with Eli's bicycle to track him down. His first thought had been to take Ray's pickup or Nelson's military vehicle. But he had no vehicle pass from the authorities and could be stopped. Even tire tracks on the dirt and gravel road might lead outsiders to discover Maxwell Acres. Besides, the bicycle would be sufficient to catch Peter, and would be the better choice if the journey needed to go cross-country, rather than on roads. He took no weapon, only the martial arts skill he had learned from Darcy in Sudbury Shed, and Jacob's instruction about "being invisible." Rose had provisioned a backpack.

Long downhill stretches of the ride to Likely convinced Jason he was making up much of the lost time. Peter on foot could make no more than three or four miles per hour, and the bicycle was exceeding thirty at times with the aid of gravity.

The story of Peter's departure was pieced together from the note Rose had found on his bed, supplemented by the rantings of Malcolm Whiting before he died.

"He's got a lot of gold. It'll be the end of this place," Jacob had said.

Catherine's eyes were red. "It'll be the end of him first." She had pleaded to go with Jason.

"If I can find a short-wave operator, I'll send a message. Listen at seven o'clock every night," Jason told Jacob. "Hopefully I'll be back tonight or tomorrow, though."

"I'll bring him back, Catherine." Jason kissed her teary face and hurried away.

423

CHAPTER 104
Mid-September

THE HARVEST was in full swing by mid-September. Vegetables, of course, had been picked and eaten regularly since mid-summer, but the simultaneous maturation of crops that required the full growing season was threatening to overwhelm the homestead labor force. All activities at Sudbury Shed had ceased, with the sole exception of Charles making entries in the history he was writing and the after-dinner candlelight regimen of Jacob monitoring the shortwave. Construction of Jacob's waterwheel at the Eastside Creek Waterfall had been completed, but not in time to transfer the generator from the barn or string the transmission lines before the harvest.

Earlier in the summer, thanks to the speedy harness training of Agnes and Shaz's two mules, the irrigation diversion dam and ditch had been completed just in time, before the crops began consuming more water than Maxwell's storage tank could replenish from the spring each night.

Each life threat to the meadow gardens had been met within one or two days after discovery of the enemy, not entirely eliminating but at least minimizing the loss of plants. Insects had been defeated by controlled use of the chickens and goats as emergency vacuums. Rabbits, porcupines, deer and, late in the summer, elk had ceased their trespassing when confronted by the combined one-two punch of chicken wire fencing and the three dogs. Cappy, Coal and Good Dawg had been trained to relish barking at night prowling animals.

Several species of birds had been fended off at various points of the summer by an assortment of devices created by Jacob and Eli, all operated by the younger set—amazingly accurate gravel-scattering catapults, noisemakers, and kites with all manner of art-covered tails descending from bright box, diamond-shaped and glider-wing-style kites depending upon the sophistication of their young operators.

During harvest, breakfast was served as soon as the slightest hint of daylight glimmered over the eastern ridge, and by the time the sun itself popped up, every man, woman and child was in one meadow or another bringing in the largess of the land. Corn aplenty. Beans and peas whose vines had climbed the corn stocks, shaded by their broad leaves from the summer heat. Wild rice. The heavy clumps of quinoa seeds. Carrots, turnips, beets and parsnips. A dazzling variety of herbs.

424

Those who were not in the fields were in the barn laying in the produce according to storage procedures instructed by Ray and Paisley, or outlined by Darcy, Mariah and others from notebooks left behind by Maxwell himself, keyed to the sacks of grain and bags of seed he had locked in the "Upper Room." Corn for drying was shucked. The bitter resin of the quinoa was rinsed into vats for later use as soap, and next year as an organic insect repellant for other crops. Preserves and pickles were processed in the kitchens.

CHAPTER 105

Sunday, September 17

EVEN DURING the rigors of harvest, The Maxwell Acres community honored the need for rest and renewal, and resumed the ancient tradition of Sabbath. The adults relished a day of play or relaxation no less than the children. It was a day for picnics, reading, games, storytelling, creative expression, usually spontaneous. The work week had its share of planning and structure; no one pursued it on Sunday, except for those involved in meal preparation and cleanup. Several of the adults noticed with amusement that the children often used the day to charge back into their studies in Sudbury Shed.

"Hey..." A voice rang in the trees across Eastside Creek. It was not loud, not a shout or yell, but in the silence Ray, Paisley and Mariah were enjoying on their Sunday rest it could have been the blast of a diesel locomotive.

The voice again rang out. "Hey, Ray. Is that you? It's Chet, old buddy. Chet Ragland."

"Holy smoke, Chet." Ray leapt to his feet. "I never thought I'd see you alive again, man. Get over here and meet Mariah. Don't slip on those mossy rocks, though."

"I've got someone with me. Okay?"

Ray hesitated, remembering the violent men Chet had been with at the store when they were together last.

"She's my partner. You know... We're lovers."

Ray tried not to bellow, but his voice boomed with exuberance, "Get over here, you son of a gun. I gotta give you a big bear hug."

A diminutive young woman, pale in the face but sunburned from foot travel, strawish blond hair swirled in a rough bun, walked discreetly around the two dancing men and held her hand out to Paisley.

425

"I'm Vivienne Knecht. Ray and I aren't married, but we're together. Nobody's officially marrying these days in our community. Everyone calls me 'Viv.'"

Agnes rang the Lunch Bell. Because she was now "showing" in her last trimester, she had been relieved from harvest labor and was managing meals instead. On the way to the big house, Mariah mischievously continued her silence, other than a whispered aside to her daughter, leaving the full surprise for Ray to convey and enjoy at the midday meal.

> Chet had succeeded in the plan he told Ray at their last meeting. Under cover of darkness, he outran the one sheriff's vehicle that tried to intercept him on his race north, out of town. Chet's superior knowledge of back roads and shortcuts left the officer to explain his embarrassing failure to his comrades, and Chet wound up at the abandoned golf course community, Sunrise Village, thirty miles north of Flat River. "About halfway between Goose Lake and Crowder Flat, not too far from the State line."
>
> Forty people had coalesced there during the disastrous federal abandonment of California and the cutting of the power grid that followed. Chet speculated that Sunrise Village was ignored by the authorities in Flat River as a result of their own massive problems, coupled with severe conservation of gasoline, as the nature of the predicament dawned on the Emergency Committee.
>
> According to information that later came to him, the population of Flat River was decimated by starvation, violence and disease, declining from three thousand to about three hundred over the next month. There were no supplies from the railroad or commercial trucking. No mail. No air connections. Without power, not only was there no heat, but the city water supply lost its pressure because the pumps were electric. When people used up their food, and their supplies of bottled water and soft drinks, and then the water from hot water tanks and toilet tanks, gunfights broke out as those without tried to take from those who still had supplies. All the stores and warehouses were looted by armed groups in the first week or ten days.
>
> As people died, sickness from the rotting corpses spread other diseases in the town. It turned out that three hundred was the maximum supportable population. The limiting factor was finally the amount of water that could be raised manually from the Pit River. With water, there was enough canned and dry food to sustain that small critical mass until it

426

could regroup into some kind of community. The power structure was so heavily based in guns and weaponry that it was little better than a warlord fiefdom set up with Sheriff Norregaard as lord.

Over the summer, the Sunrise Village community was able to engineer the golf course water supply system into agricultural irrigation. People scrounged seeds from various sources and planted community gardens. Until the first vegetables could be eaten, they survived on food foraged in the forest, wild game, and domestic animals they could either poach from outlying farms and houses or find running wild after they escaped from other looting incidents. The Village had plenty of guns itself, elected its own committee to govern and vacillated between a town hall 'democracy' dominated by a strong-man mayor and a gangland hideout ruled by the three toughest gunfighters in the house.

About the first of September, the crowd in Flat River began to believe that the Villagers were laying up a surplus of food from their golf-course harvest. In fact, the rigid structure of the Village government fostered little passion for cooperation or creative problem solving, and the harvest was headed for dismal failure. Nevertheless, Sheriff Norregaard led a posse of twenty armed men through the hills to the west of the Village. But when they attacked, they were outgunned by two ex-Special Forces vets with one semi-automatic weapon apiece—not a massive armory, but weapons they were trained to employ with maximum impact. So the Sheriff, who survived in the rear ranks and called the retreat, went back to Flat River vowing revenge.

The women, who outnumbered the men almost two to one, made a stab at turning the oppressive Village government around, but Chet concluded the effort would come to nothing, so he and Vivienne packed their backpacks and quietly left two days after the full moon. He picked that night because the first two hours after sunset would be moonless and they could get a good distance away unseen. Thereafter the moon would light their way.

They headed south, then angled east around Goose Lake and climbed to the highest trail in the Warner Mountains, traveling at night. This because there were a number of known pockets of extreme and violent folk trying to survive on fish, game and natural foods there. It was said they stayed put and were intensely territorial, and would shoot anyone on sight in what they considered their "territory." Chet remembered Ray uttering the words "Maxwell Place" just before he climbed into the attic at the

Feed Store in March, and he knew approximately where the old Maxwell homestead was. "Right near Sunflower Knob."

Chet brought his story to a close. "We were praying it was you down here, Ray, this morning on the ridge watching everyone go up to those meadows. You could just as well have been one of those packs armed to the teeth who would kill us on sight. You can't imagine how I felt when we snuck down to the creek over there and it turned out to be you sitting on that stump."

Chet and Viv joined the homestead group with the intention of staying permanently. The first three nights the newcomers spent in Jason's vacant room. Despite the harvest activity, which Viv joined, Chet, Ray and Nelson took leave from it. They worked furiously to stitch together the sizable pile of animal hides that had been accumulated and cured over the summer from regular hunting trips led by Eli. By the third day, they had created a double-insulated deerskin yurt, which then became Chet and Viv's home, on a patch of flat ground behind Ray and Paisley's cabin.

The new arrivals soon absorbed the patterns of functioning that had become woven into the fabric of the homestead community. Viv was not only young but open. She had graduated from the University of Oregon six years earlier and came to Flat River as the wife of a U.S. Forest Service anthropologist whose only job offer had taken him to the Modoc County Ranger Station.

They had not yet had children, by the time of the calamity. Her husband had been killed defending their home the second day after the power was cut. No one bothered her as she ran hysterically from the town. She happened to be sitting in despair on the corner post of a small stone bridge, nearly dead from hypothermia, when Chet started to drive across it without headlights. Her dress was light yellow. Only stars and the Milky Way provided light from the sky, but Chet's eyes picked her out, and he drove her to Sunrise Village on that night of his own despair. At the University, Vivienne had been on the fringes of several self-styled and not very deep student meditation groups, but it was enough to have left her well receptive to the process that had coalesced at the homestead.

For himself, Chet was a Flat River High grad and had attended the Flat River Community Church all his life. It was a hybrid of Congregational and Unitarian, but Chet never spent any intellectual capital on their mix of doctrines and dogmas, or even the theories or the sermons. What he liked was the singing and the feeling of quiet peacefulness for that simple hour of the week. So although he had no abstract grounding, or experience either, that prepared him for the spirit he was suddenly exposed to at the homestead, neither had he any resistance or barrier in his heart. He became an apt and instant practitioner, resonating well with Eli, Shaz and, of course, his old but now re-engineered friend, Ray.

Chet, however, was a pragmatist, too. It took him a while to accommodate the group's belief that arms and guards were inappropriate. Reciprocally, the freshness of his and Viv's witnessing of the desperation "outside," the wanton self-interest of those in charge and those with guns, the general oppression of fear as the new world without law had collapsed around the populace, reverberated within the homestead community. They realized again how precarious their existence was, so near to a territory of both primitive and sophisticated brigands, killers and militia. But a sense of self-directed destiny continued to outweigh a sense of pending doom.

CHAPTER 106
Tuesday, September 19

IN THE HOUR before first light Cappy lay on the braided wool rug in the Royer cabin. He raised his head, ears forward, thumped his tail on the floor, and issued a single sharp bark. He heaved himself up and trotted to the window, whimpering out toward the darkness with his paws on the sill. He barked again.

Charles Royer shuffled out of the bedroom in untied shoes, buttoning his pants. He found the flashlight in the kitchen and opened the door. Cappy shot past him into the night, toward the road.

"Cappy! Are you glad to see me? I'm glad to see you.!" Charles knew the voice. Jason had returned.

Cappy laid his chin and one paw on Jason's foot while Rose prepared soup and listened to his weary story. He had made his way on foot by night following the highway nearly all the way from the Sierra Army Depot. "I had to keep my senses open for approaching vehicles. I had to assume they were all hostile, but there were only a few, so I made good time. I slept during the day."

Charles sliced bread for him, interjecting, "We got more and more worried. Then last night Jacob received a radio message from Peter, from Scripps. He found a colleague with a ham radio. So we knew you were at an army installation. He had to be careful, apparently, and spoke vaguely. He said something about you maybe finding a back door."

Jason resumed, "He probably didn't tell you about the two guys that picked him up hitch-hiking down the highway. They rolled him and took the gold. I found him on the side of the road, down by a crossroads called Ravendale, scraped up a little, but not seriously hurt. He wouldn't listen to any talk of coming back to Maxwell Acres, and I refused to leave him. So we rode double on the bike until we were picked up by an Army jeep.

"They took us to a refugee camp they called SAD City—because it's at the Sierra Army Depot. After a few days, Peter was able to get an interview with an intelligence officer. He convinced the guy to call Scripps, where some scientist apparently vouched for him. So the Army flew him down on the next cargo shipment.

"If you have some skill they can use, they reassign you somewhere. Otherwise you're pretty much stuck there for the duration, unless you escape."

"And how did you?" Rose asked.

"It's really not hard to get past the razor wire perimeter," said Jason. "The MPs just let you go, I guess, unless you're headed south—the Nevada border's like a steel curtain, I hear. They know you have about one percent chance of making it if you head any other direction."

"Peter said he hated to leave you," Charles said. "Once again he mentioned the North Atlantic Current. He said Scripps has backups of the research lost when the tsunami hit Woods Hole on Cape Cod. Their most recent data showed the current might even stop this winter or next spring, and Peter said we should plan for shorter growing seasons and a ten to twenty degree drop in average temperatures. But around his own work, he's enthusiastic and rejuvenated. He's at meetings all day, and even at night he has dinner meetings with these guys who don't seem to sleep, there's so much data and theory flying around. They're already planning on him as part of the research team on an icebreaker to Antarctica."

"That's great," Jason smiled. "Oh, and he told me that the guys who robbed him don't know where the gold came from. He told them he was from McCloud."

"Sleep a little," Rose said. "We'll wake you when it's time for breakfast at the main house. They're going to be delighted to see you."

They were more than delighted. Catherine ran to him and threw her arms around his neck, as the others gathered around in welcome. "I dreamed about you last night," Catherine said. "I knew you'd come home. But I dream about you every night!" She leaned back from him. "I'm going to trim your beard and give you a haircut and then a bath up in the creek!"

No one ventured near the creek until they had returned.

CHAPTER 107
Saturday, September 30

COOLING in the shade, Reinhold and Emory rested on the old wooden bench, backs against the stone wall of the long abandoned truck stop. The chill of the night lingered in the rocks, providing a blessing for the travelers in the late morning heat.

Emory pointed to a low, frame building a quarter-mile ahead. Its sheet-metal roof shimmered like a mirage in the unrelenting sun.

"Piute," he said.

"How do you know?"

"Eyes of an eagle. Besides, I knew we were close." Emory smiled at his little joke. The door was covered by a hanging tapestry, a Native American rug, and the Piute were the only tribe anywhere near Imlay, Nevada. "I'll make contact. You stay here."

In under an hour, he returned. "They'll take you to Vya through the Black Rock Desert and High Rock Canyon, and from there to the Sierra summit."

"I can trust them?"

"Hopi and Piute are allies. I told them what you did for the Plateau people in Espanola, and they will help us repay our debt to you, my Brother. Go alone to them. I will return from here."

Reinhold clasped his guardian, guide and friend in a long embrace. "I hope we shall meet again."

Emory reminded him, "It is inevitable, in the Spirit World."

Reinhold strode toward the Piute house, not looking back.

As he approached, he noticed the back-end of a camouflage-painted, military vehicle extending past the far corner of the house. The pit of his stomach tightened, but he trusted Emory's judgment and knocked on the door post. A young Piute man moved the tapestry aside.

"They call me Chipper." He touched palms lightly with Reinhold and motioned him inside.

Around a kitchen table sat four Caucasian youths, their tin Sierra cups arrayed on the red-checked oilcloth cover. Three boys and a girl, all barely out of their teens, Reinhold judged. The girl stood, offered her hand, "I'm Victoria. This is Fred, Kip and Indiana."

431

"Coffee?" Chipper said, to which Reinhold nodded. He went on, "These folks came to Burning Man the last couple of years. Heard of Burning Man?"

Reinhold shook his head.

Kip explained. "It was a festival on the Playa where thousands of us celebrated ecological innovations for a spectacular week every year in September. No spectators, only participants. Geodesic domes, closed-cycle waterworks, anything anyone wanted to invent, bring, and then take home again. There was art, performance, music, love, exuberance. We never left anything behind. No trash, garbage or anything. It was a celebration of the unlimited future."

"What do you expect this year?" Reinhold asked.

Indiana spoke up. "If there's four of us trying, there's others. We've spread the word in coded, ham radio lingo. Instead of the Playa, we're gathering further north, at Soldier Meadows Ranch. The theme's 'continuous community' this year. You know, how to stay good in these bad times."

Victoria took her turn. Her father was in the Army in Salt Lake City. "But he's a pushover. A subversive, in his own way." She giggled at the thought. "He requisitioned our truck and got us travel papers." She grinned again. "Chipper's coming with us because he's our safety in case of trouble. Like, you know, local legitimacy or something."

The gnawing in Reinhold's abdomen did not abate. This didn't feel good, but he was stuck. It was the best he had.

Soldier Meadows Ranch was a ghost camp when they arrived at sundown. Not a breath of life. A sheet of plywood had instructions, painted in axle grease:

SITE MOVED TO HIGH ROCK LAKE.

They camped. Reinhold smelled marijuana smoke coming from the tent of the four youths late into the night. He and Chipper folded their tribal blankets into sleeping cocoons and laid their heads on their packs under the dazzling Milky Way.

Next morning, a quarter-mile from High Rock Lake, they slowed to a halt as a lone figure stumbled into sight, arms waving frantically. As he approached, they saw his shirt and pants were red with patches of blood. He collapsed in Chipper's arms.

Victoria gave him canteen water. Wild eyed, he coughed out, "Go back. Go back. Army up there—killing everyone. I pretended like I was dead, and they left, around the east side of the lake. They're storing nuclear stuff here—from power plants and weapons labs in California."

Reinhold heard a motor, saw dust rising on the road behind them. He touched Chipper's arm. Chipper guided the wounded man toward the truck. "Get him in. Everyone get in. That's the military."

They raced for the lake, turned west, away from where their wounded passenger said the soldiers had headed. The injured man lost consciousness just as Indiana jammed on the brakes. A military troop-carrier was blocking the road ahead, a half-dozen soldiers deploying in formation at its side.

There could be no escape up the steep slope away from the Lake. They abandoned the bleeding victim and scattered toward the lake, hardly more than a marsh. Just short of the water, Reinhold shed his backpack and splashed with the others into the warm shallows through marsh grass and last year's stubbly reeds. They were in calf-deep when gunfire erupted.

Fred was four feet ahead of Reinhold and slightly to his right. Reinhold heard a dull "thump" and saw Fred spin violently to his left as a cone of red spray erupted from his lower chest. Reinhold lurched toward the water, praying to avoid the lethal bullets. He slipped, grabbing a handful of reeds for support. They broke, and he rolled as he hit the water with his back. Fred's body slammed on top of his hips, pinning him underwater.

Reinhold held his breath. His mind was crystal clear. He had to stay invisible. He separated a single reed from the clump in his grip, brought it to his mouth and poked it into the air. He blew, to clear the passage. It was hollow, unjointed, and its walls intact. *Thank you, God.*

Over the sounds of air in his windpipe, Reinhold heard three more muffled bursts of gunfire. Then silence.

Reinhold thought of nothing but his breath. He steadied it, let it breathe him rather than the other way around, in the manner taught by the Tibetans in Crestone. His body calmed. In five minutes, his mind was calm. He realized he could stay there indefinitely, prevented from floating by the weight of Fred's lifeless body. He began to count breaths to measure time, knowing every minute would seem like an eternity if he allowed his thoughts to roam free.

He lay in the sun-splashed water for what he hoped was well over an hour. When he had passed the forty-five minute mark by breath count, he thought he heard the vibration of engines start up and then recede into the distance. After perhaps another half-hour, he committed. Slowly, trying to avoid the smallest ripple, breath by breath, he raised his nose and forehead above the surface. He rolled his head to the left so the water would run out of his eye socket. He waited. Finally, he opened his right eye, blinked it clear. He craned his neck toward the shore. The only vehicle was Victoria's. He raised more, braced on his elbows, surveyed everything within his vision. Eventually he spotted three other bodies in the grass. He alone had lived.

Reinhold heard gunfire in the distance intermittently all afternoon. He stayed in the water, taking advantage of Fred's dead weight. Part of the time he re-submerged, finding the reed perfectly adequate for air. He pictured both entrances to the lake blocked, and more unwitting kids taken by surprise. He tried to quell his imagination.

As dusk shaded into darkness, he kept track of the military vehicles by their headlights. Before it was completely dark, he crawled out of the lake. His backpack looked like a soldier had rifled through it, but Reinhold was able to reassemble his things. He opened the door of Victoria's vehicle. The injured boy lay across the back seat, dead, one arm folded across his middle, the other flopped to the side, as if he were playing guitar.

Under the ceiling light Reinhold scanned the interior for anything useful. He filled his water containers, took the trail mix from the glove compartment, removed a cache of topo maps and a pair of light binoculars from the door pocket.

In the dwindling light, he searched the landscape with the field glasses for signs of soldiers or other threats. Nothing. At least, nothing he could see.

Reinhold invoked a benediction on his dead companions and headed west by due reckoning, climbing into the Sierra to put as much distance between himself and the killers below as possible. In the morning he could locate his position on a map and chart his way toward Flat River. For now, every sense was operating at peak alertness, not only to warn of the known dangers behind, but unknown ones in the night ahead.

CHAPTER 108

Sunday, October 1

BY THE TIME the crescent moon adorned the evening sky in the final days of September, the Maxwell Acres harvest frenzy had abated to allow resumption of more normal activities. Sudbury Shed resumed its buzz of learning, the student body energized anew by the "working vacation."

Jacob finished jerry-rigging the power transformers needed for transmission of electricity from the Eastside Pond waterwheel to the homestead. The power lines were strung, using up about half the electrical wiring supply Mr. Maxwell had left coiled on pegs in the barn wall.

Early one morning, the Maxwell Acres generator was gingerly transported from the barn to a shed newly constructed off the end of the waterwheel axle. The entire community, save three, was gathered at the site. Catherine and Jason alone had volunteered to stay at the big house with the napping Finn and were primed to signal an accolade from the triangle at the first sign of electricity.

Bearings oiled, pulleys checked, failsafe devices triple tested, and alignments surveyed multiple times, the activator lever was ceremonially thrown by Powermeister Jacob. The waterwheel rotated its first real-time revolution, the generator powered up on cue, and electricity flowed effortlessly to waiting light bulbs at the big house, followed within seconds by celebratory clanging from the compound. Cheers arose, hugs circulated, Mariah wiped a tear from Jacob's eyelash, and life changed dramatically once again on the little homestead in the hidden valley of the South Warner nook of the Sierra Mountain Range.

Self-discipline was challenged with new tests presented by options of nighttime activities under electric lighting. Then, too, consensus had to coalesce around what appliances to operate. And when. Maintaining the waterwheel bearings, let alone prolonging the ultimately limited life of generator parts that could not be replaced, provided high motivation to generate electricity as infrequently as possible. The process settled down soon enough and major improvements were integrated into daily life.

The battery for the Royers' laptop could now be regularly charged, and its use immediately became the prized resource of most learners at the Sudbury Shed. Jacob had prepared for the arrival of electricity by erecting a transmitter antenna on the roof of the watchtower-room, so he could transmit ham radio signals as well as receive them. And the generator's success now gave the green light to his wintertime project, building a satellite receiver/transmitter dish to attempt the ultimate dream of an Internet connection.

Other projects proceeded, beyond those based on electricity. There was the conversion of the septic tank systems, both at the compound and at the Royer cabin, into human night soil boxes. There was the construction of insulated containers to allow decomposition of regular compost to continue throughout the winter—without them, the compost would be frozen for nearly six months a year. There was the completion of the beer-making apparatus, and the tiny winery, and Jacob's chemistry-set distillery to eke real spirits from the anticipated homemade wine and beer, or even old fashioned corn mash whiskey, for toasts at major banquets should the occasion arise.

Chet and Viv threw all their being into full participation in the broad spectrum of activities. More importantly, however, they became sponges for the wide variety of "quietude practices," finding that every member of the homestead community had modified the simple templates originally launched by those who had arrived with prior experience—Mariah first, followed by an explosion of revelations from the others—Darcy and Kim from their martial arts, Eli and his Zen from prison amplified by his monastic gleanings, Nelson with his fire walk, Rose from a lifetime of Episcopalian prayer, Paisley and Ray from their years in India, Agnes from her Native American people, and Shaz from his Sufi upbringing.

Before the moon was full again in October, Chet and Viv were fully integrated into life at the humming old homestead.

Permeating it all was the overall preparation of the place for winter, with greater earnestness than ever in light of Dr. Addison's warning of additional climatic threats ahead—the greenhouses, seedling trays in the barn, stalls and pens for the mules and goats, nesting boxes for the chickens, firewood stacks for cooking and heating, and repairing or newly fabricating winter clothing, including moccasins for everyone.

CHAPTER 109

Saturday, October 7

TIERNEY was the first one downstairs at Saturday sunrise, just as the full moon set in the west. Close behind, Darcy heard her footsteps cross the living room floor, stop, then race back to the stairs. She had one hand on her chest, the other on her forehead, and her eyes and mouth were as wide with emotion as Darcy had ever seen. She motioned her mother to bend down, cupping her upper hand to the side of her lips in whisper-in-your-ear mode. Darcy hunkered down, sitting on one boot heel.

"There's a man sitting on the porch and I think it's Daddy."

Darcy cocked her head. She didn't want to exacerbate whatever might be going on inside her little girl—delusions, fantasies—but her face automatically reflected her wonder.

Tierney dragged her reluctant mother to the door, jabbing her finger vigorously at the porch, miming urgently, *Go out. Go out and see.*

Darcy kept her eye on the little worried face as she opened the door. She turned her head to the porch as her foot crossed the threshold and then suddenly drew back.

She leaned weakly on the door post. A red-bearded man sat, his knees drawn up, his head nodding forward under a ratty, leather out-back hat. "Reinhold? Reinhold? Is it really you?"

His eyes leapt to life within their dark and sunken sockets. He beamed a drawn, weather-beaten smile.

Tierney squealed. "Daddy, Daddy. I knew it was you. I knew you'd get here someday." She ran into his open arms, nearly knocking him off the steps.

It took Reinhold days to piece together the hideous journey he had now completed. Trauma after trauma bubbled into the telling, layer after layer of tragedy and horror, escapes from death too numerous to count, cruelties and oppression in an amped-up, nailed-down, schizoid world kept under a semblance of control, here and there, by a military dictatorship employing sophisticated technology, raw brutality and haphazard discipline.

To questions at that first breakfast he answered only, "I got here. I got here." But his mind was clear, evidenced by his insatiable questioning of everyone about life on the homestead and how it came to be.

Eventually, Reinhold would recount his odyssey to Charles for a separate history, place by place, mile by mile, day by day, person by person. In the meantime, for everyone else, in anecdotal mode, not narrative, he gradually described the events of his trip, his thoughts and observations, and his emotional and spiritual reactions, tailored to the interests of each person or small group with whom he worked and played, integrating into the community as quickly as had Chet and Viv just weeks before. Conversations between the traveler and each member of the community, including the children, were shared and compared by all participants, including rehashes by Reinhold himself, until his unique knowledge was embedded firmly in the worldview of all who lived there.

The awesome power of the tsunamis hitting New York City had no less force than religious myths of destruction throughout the ages. The difference was, Reinhold had the eyewitness truth engraved into his personal memory. The chaos, death and destruction of civilization in the aftermath was likewise an epic unequaled in the annals of history and literature.

The day after his arrival, Reinhold was helping Darcy with the breakfast cleanup. He stopped stock still in front of the leaded glass window-hanging, which was spewing sparkles and rainbows throughout the room as usual. He stammered, "Where... Where did you get that?"

"It was a gift. Why?"

"I saw its exact twin in an abandoned shop in the little town of Questa, New Mexico, on my way down from Crestone. I wonder what story they could tell."

Darcy laughed, "Maybe someday we should go get it."

CHAPTER 110
Early November

WITH WINTER PREPARATIONS accelerating, casual talk turned to holidays. There grew a movement against Thanksgiving. Not against giving thanks, but against the overload of that specific tradition.

First there was a general acknowledgment that, although Thanksgiving was "The" family holiday of the year, it stimulated inevitable comparisons between the way governments were now sacrificing whole peoples at a stroke and the way European conquerors destroyed the Native American nations they found.

Then, too, it was broadly felt that, although the highest civil ideals of the American Republic were values whose preservation was essential, the flagrant nationalism inherent in the link between Americanism and the Thanksgiving holiday was a phenomenon almost no one wanted to honor any longer. The destruction of the U.N. in 2005, and the ensuing wars, genocide and enmities that then proliferated under the emblazoned banner of preemptive self-defense, were now all too tragically visible as anachronistic nationalism run amok. Had the Antarctic disaster not occurred, it seemed as if the world was headed anyway for a collapse of civilized structure from military conflict alone. No one wanted to host that discussion around a celebration of thanks for the abundant harvest and openhearted community now burgeoning at the homestead.

And yet, Halloween and All Saints Day traditions drew deep loyalty from everyone, reflecting roots traced beyond Medieval Christianity to the depths of Celtic festivity and even more ancient prehistory. To allow time for adequate preparation, Darcy and Agnes prevailed with a plan to celebrate the Mid-Quarter on November 7th, exactly halfway between the Fall equinox and the Winter solstice. Probably the origin of universal Fall fertility rites anyway in the northern hemisphere, some people rationalized, much as Groundhog Day originally marked the halfway point from the Winter solstice to the Vernal equinox.

Not only did the Sudbury Shed bunch throw itself into creating fantastical infrastructure for the Festival—decor, banners, skits and tricks—but to a person the entire population of the homestead joined the mood. Ray and Maurice became the Simon and Garfunkel of the compound. In the barn woodwork shop, Eli, Jason, Reinhold and Charles crafted drums and rattles, and never-before-seen percussion instruments of their own invention. On quiet evenings, Shaz and Agnes could be heard on the western ridge practicing duets, he with his reed flute and she with her treasured ocarina.

Catherine and Paisley choreographed graceful dances, not only as individual performances—for Catherine had studied ballet, and Paisley had been taught belly dancing by Hindu experts in her Peace Corps days—but with parts for Lydia, Val, Melissa and others. They finally ensnared not only Tierney but Rose, Viv, Darcy and Mariah in the end. All men, of course, were banned during rehearsals. Even Finn, who was handed over to his father during the secret preparations.

The day arrived. Charles again raided his wine cellar, and Mariah produced a bottle of old brandy Mr. Maxwell had tucked away in a crate of Victorian gadgets. Pageantry, storytelling, music making, dancing and oratory filled the gaps between multiple courses of a paced-out meal that lasted from mid-afternoon to well past midnight.

A lengthy break was taken midway. Although more than one couple was absent, there remained a critical mass to view a spectacular sunset in whispered amazement. The peaceful adulation of the divine palette grew to a crescendo of praise to the full moon for rising suddenly over the eastern ridge after the purple twilight faded into black velvet and the starry constellations gradually appeared. Two by two, missing lovers returned and the revelry proceeded, settling finally into yet another of Ray and Maurice's now fabled sing-alongs around the generous fireplace of Maxwell Acres.

Breakfast was poorly attended the next morning, the bulk of the population sleeping in on the groggy Sunday morning. But everyone came to lunch. The Sunday mid-day meal had by now become an eagerly anticipated opportunity for group sharing of its individuals' spiritual yearnings. This Mid-Quarter Sunday was no different, but was marked as well by an overtly evolutionary announcement. Chet, Viv and Maurice were planning to leave. Their destination? Sunrise Village.

As Chet and Maurice had spoken over the weeks, Maurice discovered he knew at least nine of the people at the golf course-turned-farm. Additionally, Viv had convinced Chet that many innovations of the homestead could be applied at the Village, and the tangible example of Maurice's healing could open the minds and hearts of people there. The idea grew, that an intuitive, trust-based mode of living might germinate in the aftermath of the summer's failure at the hands of the more traditional governance.

Mariah had offered a supply of seeds and cuttings that could grow in the greenhouse atmosphere of the golf course community's converted swimming pool/exercise facility, supplementing their hunting and foraging to enhance their survival the coming winter. If the Village could make the shift to the co-operative, growth-oriented process so vividly demonstrated at the homestead, perhaps they all could survive. Chet and Maurice agreed it was worth the potential sacrifice.

The next day all members of the homestead joined in preparing for the trio's departure. Jacob worked out a series of communication protocols for Chet to use on the Village's ham radio, which would not attract attention from threatening governmental agencies who might happen to listen, but which would reveal to Jacob and his cadre of ham radio monitors how things progressed at the Village.

Missing details of passive heating systems, greenhouse techniques and other operations around the homestead were added to the repertoires of the departing members.

A final salon, impromptu as always, arose the night before they left.

"How do we get it all started, once we get there?" Viv asked nervously.

Rose replied, "Well, here it picked up speed when Maurice was dying from Jason's rifle shot and Mariah got the healing touch relay going."

Charles backed her up. "In my opinion, it saved his life and triggered a healing response in his body that I couldn't kick-start with traditional medicine."

"People will believe Maurice's story, to some degree," Rose went on, "but you should spread the healing touch as fast as you can, and maybe a healing will occur in your community when the need arises. But any transforming event could pop out of the universe and help get people's attention. Just wait. You'll see."

Later, Chet wondered, "Why aren't people energized over there like we all are here?"

Eli attempted a response. "We needed to survive, but no one got their ego in the way, or grabbed for power. Pretty quick, Mariah and Darcy, and then others, showed by their lives what turns everyone on—consistently, you know, day to day. That secret is deepening contact with your own soul. Look deep enough, you find your community's more important than your own life, but you have to see your own truth first. When you look to the bottom stone in the foundation here, that's what you find. And then, the kids. No one stands in their way, either. If you ask me, that's the key."

Jacob took a different tack. "Once I heard a tape by the man who named the Human Potential Movement. He questioned why we couldn't make peace as enthralling as war. War is so enthralling, he said, because of the astounding bonding between soldiers in battle, because you never know when you awake in the morning if you'll be alive that night, and because of the 'lust of the eyes,' meaning that in war people see things they never see in other times. He suggested we needed to make living peacefully as vivid as war, on those three levels. I think that's what's going on here. I've never seen people bond like this before—and we've learned how to live one day at a time, thanking the past and planning ahead but living lightly as if this day were the last. And third, everyone sees things deeply, behind the veil of ordinary reality. I think we have vivid peace going on right here. And when you live that way, Chet, all your energy goes into what you're doing. Maybe that's part of the secret, too."

Jason offered his agreement. "Catherine and I found, if people can just stay with peacefulness, the quietness, the answer comes and the thing moves forward. It's not magic. It's just human. I like the line that says, 'When magic becomes scientific fact we refer to it as medicine or astronomy.' Around here it's, well, like when the magic becomes the way we live, we call it the homestead way. Well, no one else does, but I do."

"Me too," said Catherine.

Ray spoke up, too. "The part that impresses me is the self-correcting part. If the group stays open, stays with it, it's not a vote or even as formal as a consensus, but each move gets us closer to what's best."

"Way leads on to way...," Eli quoted Robert Frost, and everyone laughed and nodded with gusto.

Reinhold bit his lip uncomfortably and took a different tack. "I'm the newcomer. It's only been four weeks, and I'm coming on strong to all these things you're talking about. But, my friends, make sure you keep your eye on the eastward direction."

"What do you mean by that?" Chet asked.

"We're perched here on the edge of the Sierras. Don't forget the kind of military might I came through for over two thousand miles. They'll rebuild the seaports eventually, squeeze every drop of oil out of anything they can. And they'll be back. Back to California, the fabled West Coast. It's the destiny of the continent, at least in the minds and hearts, such as they are, of every military patriot in charge of anything east of here. There's oil in California. And fertile soil, once they have the resources to rebuild the water systems. With the population down by thirty million, from what I hear, it's simply turf for the taking. Modoc County may be remote, but it's like a tiny rabbit sandwiched smack between two hungry, snarling bears, warlords to the west and dictators to the east."

The room was silent. Mariah stood up from her bench, stretched, and leaned against the foyer door-jamb. "Reinhold carries wisdom none of us have had access to. He's a great blessing, to keep us aware. Carry his message with you, too. Of course we may be swiped clean by the paw of a bear, or be dinner for them both. And we may not. The forces we've put into motion here should serve you well no matter what. Take them out there, live them, propagate them, and I say, let come what may. And to season what Reinhold just said, I have a final point."

A pin drop could be heard, in the tension of the moment.

"A few years back I was powerfully moved by an essay written by a Tibetan monk named Tenzin Gyatso. It was April 26, 2003—my Mother's birthday. I never forgot it. He said destructive emotions like anger, fear and hatred give rise to dangerous impulses. He called on individuals and leaders alike to learn to curb these impulses, impulses that in his view collectively can lead to war and mass violence. Mindfulness meditation—that's what he called it—strengthens neurological circuits that calm a part of the brain which triggers fear and anger. That was his way to create a kind of buffer between the brain's violent impulses and our actions. I memorized his words: 'If humanity is to survive, happiness and inner balance are crucial… We need to be guided by more healthy states of mind, not just to avoid feeding the flames of hatred, but to respond skillfully… The war against hatred and terror can be waged on this, the internal front.'"

Nelson asked, "Who was that? I don't recognize his name."

Mariah looked at Jenna and smiled. Jenna looked into the fireplace, then into Nelson's eyes. "Tenzin Gyatso is the fourteenth Dalai Lama."

CHAPTER 111
December

CHRISTMAS CAME. Almost too soon.

No sooner had Maurice, Chet and Viv stuffed their backpacks and headed over the western ridge than Agnes had gone into extended labor, giving birth finally on December 1st to healthy twins, first a girl and five minutes later a boy. Catherine, who was two months pregnant, reflected, "Nine months to the day since the tsunamis."

The twins remained nameless for over a week while a good-natured debate raged through the homestead. The names finally emerged—Robb and Gertrude, in honor of Mr. Maxwell and his lady love.

Eli was back regularly hunting meat and hides. He and Kim were wildly and visibly in love. Likewise Nelson and the young but very grown-up and beautiful Jenna were committed as a pair. The winter darkness brought flowers to the refurbished romances of Ray and Paisley, Charles and his Rose, and in a different way added luster to the new responsibilities of Agnes and Shaz, and the expectant Catherine and Jason. Darcy was in heaven with the reincarnated Reinhold.

Love permeated the air, and spilled over to the tribe of children who were beginning to consider every adult as yet another facet of a multi-parent cornucopia. Tierney, who was spending more and more overnights in both the east and west guesthouses, to the delight of their adult and youthful occupants alike, thrived in the everyone's-a-parent atmosphere, but she had the added ecstasy of her own real parents being reunited at last. And Finn—as usual, Finn just took it all in stride, including the new infant twins, which represented an altogether unique chapter in his tiny repertoire of experience.

Jacob claimed early winter angst to explain his regular depressions, but everyone knew it was because of setbacks on the Internet connection satellite-dish project. His moods never persisted, however, because Sudbury Shed was now aflame with a new craze, not to the exclusion of the still rampant learning juggernaut, but in addition to it.

Christmas presents were being churned out with phenomenal ingenuity both in the Shed and, under the watchful eye of wood masters Jason and Ray, over at the barn as well. Decorative wood boxes for personal things. New musical instruments, including a whole family of percussion devices cascading from the inspiration of those created for the Mid-Quarter festival by Eli, Jason and Charles. Even small items of convenient but non-essential furniture. Art to enliven people's walls. Puzzles and toys of ingenious design.

And jewelry for everyone—necklaces, bracelets, rings and earrings assembled with loving care from wooden beads, porcupine quills, nuts and seeds, garnets culled from an old prospector's shaft discovered on a field trip into the mountains, sparkling quartz crystals and jet black obsidian chips, and much else from the bounty of the earth.

Even more exciting to the young craftspersons, Jacob had made a foray into the depths of the cavern, returning with a supply of nuggets and gold dust, which he then melted and shaped in the solar crucible and kiln. He produced an array of sheets, rods and wire from the precious substance. He then ran several seminars, improvising from a goldsmithing article in one of Maxwell's alchemical texts.

For weeks thereafter, the incessant chatter of secretive hammering, hammering, hammering when no adults were present, emanated from the *premiere etage*. With days to go, fabrication drew to a close. Golden adornments of every style and fashion emerged from the creative labors of the eager young hands, wrapped lovingly in scraps of anything or encased in handmade receptacles of bark, wood, even cornhusk, for opening on Christmas Day.

The final preparation was a meeting with Dr. Charles Royer, "Himself," filled with begging and cajoling until he agreed to pierce anyone's ears upon request on Christmas Afternoon. He held his ground at ears, against all grievance, rejecting any possibility of lips, nostrils, navels and other spots of fashionable repute.

Decor from every tradition represented in the community was invented for the occasion and appeared in every house and room—and on selected exteriors, too. Special holiday food was planned and prepared. Performance arts were not neglected, and once again songs and skits and dances were charted and practiced.

So, Christmas came. The homestead halls resounded with the joy. Prayer mingled with the mistletoe. Nostalgia and occasional sadness for times long past provided leavening for the exuberance of the community's flowing current of lives and loves. Music was all pervasive. The receiving and giving of gifts, both public and private, was scattered through the day. No eyes stayed dry too long, not from grieving but from the joy of the spirit running unfettered through the hearts and souls of this little band of refugees who had not even met a mere twelve months before.

Revelry was punctuated by Eli reciting haiku:

Gifts of gold and song
　　Crafted from our souls' delight
　　　Tell us who we are.

　And Kim overcame his objection, and read the poem he had written for her.

You held my arm while we walked—
We might have floated in soft
musical darkness of space
with all the stars so distant
the only vista is an aimless
sprinkle of white on black.
Those motes of light astonish
in their perfect silent harmony—
so far apart they cannot know
the harsh tumult of another, yet
they circle close drifting in the void
and hold each other in balance.
Each is a vault of the riches
of the universe, each could spawn
a million worlds to walk in.
I'm content to walk in every one;
tonight a treasure spun and flung
from a golden star treasures me!

　In addition to the stories that tumbled out ad hoc throughout the day, from every tradition that could be recounted by the grown-ups to any available youths with time to listen, after the yam, nut and gooseberry sugar pudding had been consumed, Kim solemnized the occasion for the children gathered cross-legged in front of the fireplace by a rendition of the festival's deepest origins.

　She dramatized the sun's slow journey ever southward from the peak of summer with dwindling daylight and the gradual increase of winter's biting cold. She portrayed the fears of earliest humankind, that sunlight would die altogether and famine envelope the land, carrying them all into the final darkness of perpetuity—how they prayed and prayed as the days grew shorter—how the sun's downward journey then slowed, perhaps, they thought, because their gods had heard their fervor—how their early astronomers, from ancient observatories in places like Egypt, Stonehenge, Babylon and Chaco Canyon, noted the sun's descent come to a halt on what we now call December 22nd—and how on the third day after that, they could first measure the sun's slight movement back toward the north, toward fuller days and warmer times when

445

food could grow and birds and animals of the forest could prosper once again—how religions later grew to celebrate this return of light, Divine Light in their rhetoric, into the world—and how the early Christian Church, not knowing the true date of the Christ Child's birth, adopted the same symbolism on the same holiday for a holy Mass commemorating His own coming into the world, God Incarnate, and thus the festival came to be called Christ-Mass.

The quiet warmth and Kim's mesmerizing presence weighed heavily on the eyelids of her young audience. One by one, they picked their favorite grown-up to snuggle with on chairs and pillows around the room, dozing off while the grown-ups continued the celebration at their own level.

Thoughts turned to Viv and Chet and Maurice. And Peter. Before he left, Ray and others had scrivenered Maurice's prodigious storehouse of sing-along songs, and Rose, Catherine and Jason had filled out a fine quartet with Ray to all but fill his shoes. Jacob's ham radio had brought consistent news from Sunrise Village, first that they had arrived safely, and periodically thereafter that the way of quiet wisdom was seeping through their ailing community.

The next thought may have been inspired by Kim's rendering, or the general spirit of the season, or fervent prayers for success at the Village. To be sure, there had also been talk among the Sudbury Shed facilitators that someday the older children would have to pilgrimage to the outside world for a reality check—like Native American initiations, vision quests. Whatever the source, nostalgia for time past transformed into fantasies and visions of a better future.

Jason and Catherine brought forth a pipe dream of their own. "Maybe, when our baby's out of diapers," said Jason, "we could take a mule, go south along the Sierras, and settle in the community Jacob heard about not too far north of the Grapevine, where the group is farming with snow melt from the Sierras, providing food for the Los Angeles basin. Perhaps in some small way, we could lighten their interactions with the military government, which still operates the lands, cities and ports in the south. The way of quiet wisdom we've found here, might one day reduce their dependence on organized government to the point of benign irrelevance."

Nelson and Jenna followed the lead and described their fantasy travels too—ideas of heading deep into the Southwest, carrying the process forth for maturation and innovation in the vast variety of cultures they had heard of or could imagine.

Reinhold's exposure to hundreds of pockets of goodwill in his long journey homeward fueled the zest for releasing into the withered, hardhearted rubble of the old civilization spores and seeds from what they now conceived as a new incubator for human evolution.

Kim voiced her optimism that they might contact and inspire Thad Parker, and men and women like him, who might still have positions of authority and influence in what remained of the USA. Morgan Clark would be a more difficult project, but the last time she had seen him he said he was changing. Perhaps the corporate chieftains would be the last to give consideration to the new way, unless or until the weight of suffering caused by greed enveloped them too. She would not put them finally beyond hope of embracing it.

Mariah predicted that, as emissaries left, new people would be guided to this sacred place in a continuing renewal of the community. She set forth her belief that this was indeed her final home, and that its grace would always consist of the goodwill fostered by its grounded love.

But she revealed the peppering of her dreams with dire images, and this suggestion touched off recognition among the rest—images of cold and scarcity, and of hard-hearted strangers driven by desperation or lust for power. The melancholy Jacob reminded them of Dr. Addison's warnings of the stoppage of the North Atlantic Current and the climatic catastrophe it could produce for in northern latitudes. They might never again have the ideal conditions they had enjoyed this first year at Maxwell Acres.

Mariah softened their dark foreboding. "We've survived the darkest time in modern history," she said. " There's no reason we can't continue the good will that brought us through it." She then revealed yet another of Robb Maxwell's seemingly inexhaustible store of surprises. She went to the fireplace and took the silver box in her hands. "Last week, the eighth riddle finally made sense to me," she said. "In Mr. Maxwell's journals, I found sketches of a monogram, which he attributed to early Maxwell artifacts he had seen in a Scottish museum. It was on the chamois bag. And late in his last diary he referred to a gift he'd made for Gertrude after he rebuilt this homestead, as a wedding present should she deign to marry him. He eventually gave it to her despite her steadfast independence, though for years he had kept it on the mantel. That tipped me off.

"I thought, 'the monogram on the bottom of the box.' Sure enough, it was the same—an 'M' for Maxwell. I guess I just knew it had to return the mantel. I can only imagine with what sentiment she gave it to me. After I discovered the monogram and put it together with his wedding present reference, I thought of the eighth riddle, a couplet which went,

> *In the one-way golden light from high,*
> *which shineth through the dome,*

Two treasures wait to right the wrong,
from whence amour had flown.

"He hoped this gift would undo the wrong he had done to Gertrude in their youth. The dome would be this amber piece." Mariah pointed to the amber dome on top of the lid.

"When I was alone one morning after that, I held it in the sunlight and looked through the amber—the sunshine was the golden light. I could see two objects embedded in this little, silver setting below the amber. I noticed for the first time that there was a seam, unwelded, around the bottom of the setting. I pried at it with my fingernail, and it opened."

Mariah demonstrated. The little trap door on the underside of the box's lid popped open and two pea-sized spheres fell out into her hand.

"This pair of matched diamonds were the objects I saw. Mr. Maxwell had hoped, I believe, that Gertrude would forgive him for his youthful folly and he would have these stones set in wedding rings for the marriage he dreamed of."

The box and gems passed from hand to hand, around the room.

Mariah continued, "I think these diamonds now belong to the twins Robb and Gertrude, in memory of the tragic figures for whom they're named. Maybe one of you young goldsmiths could create settings someday, so when the twins grow up they'll remember how they symbolized the promise of our future."

CHAPTER 112

January

JACOB AND RAY had devised a wheelchair so that Dupree Ransom could enjoy being outdoors, and by midsummer he was eating some of his meals at the community table. He had lost his chagrin about being fed "in public." He confided to Mariah one day that he admired the workings and cooperation of the Maxwell Acres community—and its compassion. "Even Eli and his woman, they talk to me and feel sorry for me."

By the end of September, Ransom's muscles had atrophied. He lost bulk as he had lost swagger, and by Christmas he might have echoed Ebenezer Scrooge: "I am not the man I was." In addition to reading to him daily, Eli taught him rudiments of meditation and sat with him each morning. After the community's Mid-Quarter Celebration, Dupree told Mariah and Eli: "I want to find some way I can be of service around here. But I don't have no skills. I can't even teach the kids, 'cause what I know ain't nobody wants 'em to learn."

Mariah counseled that he could be of service by being authentically himself, perhaps by the inspiration of accepting his limitations, if nothing else. Specific service might sprout from this seed.

The next day Ransom asked Eli to teach him a story he might tell to the children. Eli taught him "Jack and the Beanstalk," Dupree's version of which Tierney delighted in correcting. Charles and Rose added to his repertoire, and then Agnes and Shaz. By Christmas, Dupree's storytelling skill was well established through meticulous rehearsal, and he began augmenting with his own innovations. At the community's Christmas celebration, he told the story—long forgotten in the turmoil of his life—of his favorite Christmas in childhood.

On a frosty January morning after their meditation, Dupree surprised Eli with a request. "I remember that Retreat in San Quentin," he said. "Do you think we could have one of them forgiveness rituals here? I didn't really pay attention then."

Eli and Mariah arranged it for an afternoon at the circle of stones, and all of the community chose to attend. After a period of silence, all were asked to write on a piece of paper the names of people they would like to ask forgiveness of. Tierney wrote for Dupree, just initials, which she was able to form with care if not precision. Mariah gave a short homily on the value of letting go of hurt. "If when you bang your shin on a stool in the dark, you relax and let energy flow in your body, rather than holding yourself tense, the pain subsides quite soon. The same is true in relationship with others. If you hold on to an injury, you continue to be injured. We all want to be forgiven. Let us offer pardon to each other on behalf of those we have offended."

Eli lit a small fire, and then held his paper in the flames. Everyone followed, Tierney acting for Dupree. They saw puffs of their breath in the still air, and listened to the fire popping. Silence was broken by a weak cough from Dupree. "I don't know how long I'll be around," he wheezed, "but I'm glad I had the opportunity to settle down, even if it's like this. I want you all to believe me. I'm really sorry for the trouble I caused you."

The community surrounded Dupree's wheelchair and one by one they touched him and spoke gently to him. He was unable to speak, but he bobbed his head vigorously, and though his lips turned downward, his brimming eyes smiled.

His health deteriorated steadily while days grew ever colder, as Dr. Royer's warning about compromised lungs was realized. The community continued ministering to him. Agnes and Paisley created herb teas to ease his symptoms,

Rose or Jacob bathed him, and there was always someone near him for conversation if he desired.

By the end of January the bitterness of winter gripped the homestead. Dupree could no longer leave his room for the shock of the cold air. On the morning of their last conversation, Eli brought in a simple meal. He dipped a spoon deliberately into a dish of oatmeal and scraped the underside of it on the bowl's edge, then arced it over to Dupree's waiting mouth. He waited to see if Ransom would swallow or cough.

"How about some of this tea Agnes made for you?"

Speech for Dupree was a great effort, so he chose his words. "You're a good man," he hissed.

"Johnny Diaz told me to stay out of your way," Eli said carefully. "Lord knows I tried, Dupree." Ransom tried to return Eli's wide grin. "We're both lucky," Eli said.

Eagles fold their wings,

  twisted clouds slump to the hills—

    Leave windows open.

Johnny Diaz died alone, thought Eli, while Dupree Ransom was surrounded by caring folks. Johnny faced death with a meager dignity, a melancholy resignation. Ransom died grasping the treasure of Dismas, the "Good Thief." He was prepared for it—one might say he died in peace. Yes.

ART

FRONT COVER

THE RISING, NEW YORK CITY. Crayon, Pencil and Oil, created for *The Rising* by Tim Holmes, the first American artist ever honored with a solo exhibition in the Hermitage museum in Saint Petersburg, Russia, where three of his works remain in the permanent collection. He is recognized for many international human rights projects and peace awards such as the U.N. Peace Prize for Women. Among his collectors are Archbishop Tutu, President Jimmy Carter, President Vaclav Havel, and Coretta Scott King. Holmes has lectured and taught workshops around the country and believes that art is medicine that will help heal the world. Holmes' art can be viewed at http://www.blueuniverse.com/thsculptures/.

BACK COVER

"ANTARCTIC ICE SHELF VISTA." Photograph by Helmut Rott. The original inspiration for *The Rising*, the image bore the comment "It's all gone but the mountains." The image, along with the explanation set forth at p. iii, was the *Astronomy Picture of the Day*, May 27, 2002 (http://antwrp. gsfc.nasa.gov/ apod/ap020527.html). Photo Credit & Copyright: Helmut Rott (Helmut.Rott@uibk.ac.at) (U. Innsbruck-http://dude.uibk.ac.at/)(http://www .esa.int/export/esaSA/ESAPEIF18ZC_earth_1.html)

DIVIDER PAGES

BOOK ONE

SAN QUENTIN STATE PRISON, CALIFORNIA. Monotype, created for *The Rising* by Tim Holmes (see above).

BOOK TWO

DARK NIGHT TSUNAMI, NEW YORK CITY. Monotype, created for *The Rising* by Tim Holmes (see above).

BOOK THREE

MODOC COUNTY CALIFORNIA HOMESTEAD. Monotype, created for *The Rising* by Tim Holmes (see above).

ILLUSTRATION, PAGE 248

"LAWYER'S MAP." Ink rendering for *The Rising* by Robert L. Lustig. Lustig was born in Oakland, California and is a World War II veteran (U.S. Army Corps of Engineers in the South Pacific Campaign, with honorable discharge and a bronze star medal). A University of California, Berkeley graduate, and a self-employed architect in Oakland since 1958, he is a Member of the American Institute of Architects and the California Watercolor Association.

ABOUT THE AUTHORS

TOM POLLOCK was born in Flagstaff, Arizona. Home educated to grade eight on a local cattle ranch, he graduated from Andover, Harvard and Boalt Hall (University of California). He rowed for the USA in Tokyo's 1964 Olympics. An attorney for thirty-five years, spanning Wall Street, a windpower corporation and private practice, his interests include science and modern humanities.

JACK SEYBOLD grew up in California's Central Valley, played varsity basketball at Saint Mary's College, served in the Peace Corps in Brazil, and earned an M.A. in linguistics at San Francisco State. A teacher for thirty-five years, he wrote poems, short stories and magazine articles, edited several newsletters and participated in prison ministry. Active interests include music, acting and golf.

EACH AUTHOR has been married for thirty-eight years. Each has two children. This is their first novel.

BACK COVER

"Explanation: It's all gone but the mountains. Most of the sprawling landscape of ice that lies between the mountains visible above has now disintegrated. The above picture was taken in Antarctica from the top of Grey Nunatak, one of three Seal Nunatak mountains that border the Larsen B Ice Shelf. The other two Nunataks are visible in the picture taken in 1994. Over the past several years large chunks of the 200 meter thick Larsen B Ice Shelf have been breaking off and disintegrating. The cause is thought to be related to the local high temperatures of recent years and, possibly, global warming. Over the past few years, the area that has disintegrated is roughly the size of Luxembourg. As ice shelves break up, they unblock other ice sheets that fall onto the ocean, raising sea levels everywhere."

The above text accompanied the image on the Back Cover when both appeared as the Astronomy Picture of the Day for 2002 May 27, titled "Antarctic Ice Shelf Vista" (see photographic credit and copyright information above).